T   8/2019

HOMELAND

HOMELAND

HOMELAND

Fernando Aramburu

TRANSLATED FROM THE SPANISH BY

Alfred MacAdam

Pantheon Books, New York

Translation copyright © 2019 by Alfred MacAdam

All rights reserved. Published in the United States by Pantheon Books,
a division of Penguin Random House LLC, New York, and distributed in
Canada by Random House of Canada, a division of Penguin Random House
Canada Limited, Toronto. Originally published in Spain as *Patria* by Tusquets
Editores, S.A., Barcelona, in 2016. Copyright © 2016 by Fernando Aramburu.

Pantheon Books and colophon are registered trademarks of
Penguin Random House LLC.

Library of Congress Cataloging-in-Publication Data
Name: Aramburu, Fernando, [date] author.
MacAdam, Alfred J., [date] translator.
Title: Homeland / Fernando Aramburu ; translated from
the Spanish by Alfred MacAdam.
Other titles: Patria. English
Description: First American edition. New York : Pantheon Books, 2019
Identifiers: LCCN 2018031975. ISBN 9781524747121 (hardcover : alk. paper).
ISBN 9781524747138 (ebook).
Classification: LCC PQ6651.R26 P3813 2019 | DDC 863/.64--dc23 |
LC record available at lccn.loc.gov/2018031975

www.pantheonbooks.com

Jacket photograph © Metin Demiralay/Trevillion Images
Jacket design by Adalis Martinez

Printed in the United States of America
First American Edition

2 4 6 8 9 7 5 3 1

CONTENTS

HOMELAND

HOMELAND

High Heels on Parquet

Poor thing, there she goes: about to crash into him the way a wave crashes into rocks. A little foam and goodbye. Doesn't she realize he doesn't even bother to open the door for her? His slave and more than his slave.

And those heels, those red lips when she's already forty-five years old: what for? With your standing, girl, with your position and education, what would make you carry on like a teenager? If *aita* were here to see . . .

Getting into the car, Nerea glanced up at the window where she assumed her mother would, as usual, be spying on her through the curtain. Even if she couldn't see her from the street, she knew Bittori was staring at her, whispering to herself, there goes the poor thing, a trophy for that egoist who never thought for a second about making someone happy. Doesn't she realize that a woman must be really desperate if she has to seduce her husband after twelve years of marriage? It's a good thing they never had children.

Nerea waved goodbye before getting into the taxi. Her mother, on the fourth floor, hidden behind the curtain, looked away. Beyond the tiled roofs was a wide strip of ocean, the lighthouse on Santa Clara Island, tenuous clouds in the distance. The weather lady predicted sunshine. And her mother looked again toward the street and the taxi, which was now out of sight.

She stared beyond the roof tiles, beyond the island and the blue horizon line, beyond the remote clouds, and even beyond that into the past forever lost, searching for scenes from her daughter's wedding. And she saw Nerea once again in the Good Shepherd

Cathedral, dressed in white, with her bouquet and her excessive happiness. Watching her daughter leave—so slim, such a smile, so pretty—Bittori felt a premonition come over her. At night, when she went back to her house alone, she was on the verge of confessing her fears to her photograph of Txato. But she had a headache, and besides, when it came to family matters, especially his daughter, Txato was sentimental. Tears came easily to his eyes, and even though photos don't cry, I know what I'm talking about.

The high heels were supposed to make Quique voracious. *Click, click, click*—she'd dented the parquet. Let's see if she punches holes in it. To keep peace in the house, she didn't scold her. They were only going to be there for a minute. They'd come to say goodbye. And him, it was nine o'clock in the morning and his breath stank of whiskey or of one of those drinks he sold.

"*Ama*, are you sure you're going to be okay by yourself?"

"Why don't you take the bus to the airport? The taxi from here to Bilbao is going to cost a fortune."

He: "Don't worry about that."

He pointed out they had baggage, that the bus would be uncomfortable, slow.

"Right, but you have enough time, don't you?"

"*Ama*, don't make a big deal out of it. We decided to take a taxi. It's the easiest way to get there."

Quique was beginning to lose patience. "It's the only comfortable way to get there."

He added that he was going to step outside to smoke a cigarette—"while you two talk." That man reeked of perfume. But his mouth stank of liquor, and it was only nine in the morning. He said goodbye checking his face in the living-room mirror. Conceited ass. And then—was he being authoritarian, cordial but curt?—to Nerea: "Don't take too long."

Five minutes, she promised. Which turned into fifteen. Alone, she said to her mother that this trip to London meant a lot to her.

"I just don't see what you have to do with your husband's clients. Or is it that you've started working in his business without telling me?"

"In London I'm going to make a serious attempt to save our marriage."

"Another?"

"The last one."

"So what's the plan this time? Going to stay close to him so he doesn't take off with the first woman he sees?"

"*Ama*, please. Don't make it harder for me."

"You look great. Going to a new hairdresser?"

"I still go to the same one."

Nerea suddenly lowered her voice. As soon as she started whispering, her mother turned to look toward the front door, as if she were afraid some stranger was spying on her. No, nothing. They'd given up on the idea of adopting a baby. How they had talked about it! Maybe a Chinese baby, a Russian, a little black one. Boy or girl. Nerea still held on to her illusion, but Quique had given up. He wants his own child, flesh of his flesh.

Bittori: "So he's quoting the Bible now?"

"He thinks he's up-to-date, but he's more traditional than rice pudding."

On her own, Nerea had investigated all the legal formalities involved in adoption and, yes, they satisfied all of them. The money involved was no problem. She was willing to travel to the other end of the world to be a mother. But Quique had cut off the conversation. No, no, and more no.

"That boy's a bit lacking in sensitivity, don't you think?"

"He wants a little boy of his own, who looks like him, who will play for La Real some day. He's obsessed, *ama*. And he'll get what he wants. Wow! When he digs in on something! I don't know with what woman. Some volunteer. Don't ask me. I don't have the slightest idea. He'll rent out some womb, pay whatever you have to pay. As far as I'm concerned, I'd help him find a healthy woman who'd make his wish come true."

"You're nuts."

"I haven't told him yet, but I imagine I might get a chance in London. I've thought it through. I don't have any right to make him be unhappy."

They touched cheeks by the front door.

Bittori: okay, she'd be fine on her own, have a great trip. Nerea, out in the hall as she waited for the elevator, said something about bad luck but that we should never give up happiness. Then she suggested her mother change the doormat.

MILD OCTOBER

Before what happened with Txato, Bittori had been a believer. When she was young, she'd nearly become a nun. She and that friend of hers from the village. Better off not remembering her. Both of them abandoned the plan at the last moment, when they had one foot in a novitiate. Now all that stuff about the resurrection of the dead and eternal life and the Creator and the Holy Spirit seems like fairy tales.

She was annoyed by something the bishop said, but she didn't dare refuse to shake hands with such an important gentleman. Instead, she looked him in the eye, silently communicating that she was no longer a believer. Seeing Txato in his coffin undermined her faith in God.

Still, from time to time she'd go to mass out of habit. She sits on a bench in the back of the church, looks at the shoulders and necks of the priest's attendants, talks to herself. It's that she's so alone at home. She's not the kind to hang around in bars or cafés. Shopping? Only for necessities. And only because Nerea makes a point of it, because if she didn't she'd be wearing the same clothes day after day. After Txato's death, her coquettishness vanished.

Instead of wandering the shops she prefers sitting in church and practicing her silent atheism. The faithful gathered there were forbidden blasphemy and contempt. She looks at the statues and says/thinks: no. Sometimes she says/thinks it shaking her head as a sign of rejection.

If there's a mass in progress, she stays longer. Then she methodically denies everything the priest says. Let us pray. No. This is the body of Christ. No. Again and again. Sometimes, with all due discretion, she takes a little nap.

When the sky was dark, she left the Capuchin church on Andía Street. It was Thursday. The temperature was pleasant. At mid-afternoon, she'd seen a neon sign in the drugstore that read 68 degrees. Traffic, pedestrians, pigeons. She spied a familiar face. Without hesitating she crossed the street and entered Guipúzcoa Plaza. She followed the path around the pond, amusing herself watching the ducks. She hadn't strolled around there for such a long time. If memory served her, not since Nerea was a little girl. She remembered black swans that were no longer to be seen. *Ding dong ding.* The carillon in the provincial government office jolted her out of her daydream.

Eight o'clock. A temperate time, a mild October. Suddenly, she was reminded of the words Nerea had said to her that morning. That she should change the doormat? No, that there's no reason to give up happiness. Bah, just nonsense you say to old people to cheer them up. It wasn't hard for Bittori to accept that it was a stupendous afternoon, but that wasn't enough to make her happy. She needed more. For instance? Who knows? That they'd brought my husband back from the dead. She wondered if after so many years she shouldn't think about forgetting. Forgetting? What's that?

A smell like algae and ocean moisture was floating in the air. It wasn't even the tiniest bit chilly, no wind blowing, and the sky was clear. A good reason, she said to herself, to walk home and save the bus fare. At Urbieta Street, she heard her name. She heard it clearly, but she didn't want to look around. She even sped up, but it was no use. Hasty footsteps caught up to her.

"Bittori, Bittori."

That voice was too close to go on pretending she didn't hear it.

"Did you hear? They say they're giving up, that they're not going to attack anymore."

Bittori could only remember the days when this very neighbor avoided running into her on the stairs or waited at the corner, getting soaked in the rain, standing there with her shopping bag between her feet, so the two of them wouldn't meet at the door.

She lied: "That's right. I heard that a while ago."

"What good news, no? We're finally going to have peace. It sure is time."

"Well, let's see, let's see."

"I'm happy especially for people like you who've had such a rough time. I hope all this is over once and for all and that they leave you in peace."

"You hope what's all over?"

"That they stop making people suffer and that they defend themselves without killing."

And since Bittori, silent, showed she had no intention of continuing, the neighbor said goodbye as if suddenly in a hurry.

"I'm off. I promised my son red mullet for dinner. He loves them. If you're going home, we can walk together."

"No, I'm meeting someone right over here."

So she wouldn't have to see her neighbor, she crossed the street and strolled around awhile in no particular direction. Because, of course, that jerk, while she's cleaning the mullet for her son, who's always seemed dumb to me, aside from being an idiot, if she hears me come home a little after she gets there, will think: how about that, Bittori didn't want to be with me! What? You're slipping into rage, and I've told you time and again. Okay, leave me in peace.

Later, on her way home, she rested her hand on the rough trunk of a tree and said to herself: thank you for your humanity. She rested it later on the wall of a building and repeated the phrase. And she did the same thing, without stopping, at a stationery store, a public bench, a traffic light, and other objects she found along the way.

The entryway was dark. She was tempted to use the elevator. Careful. The noise could give me away. She decided to take off her shoes and walk up the three flights. She still had time to whisper a final word of thanks: banister, thank you for your humanity. She inserted the key in the lock as stealthily as she could. What does Nerea see in this doormat that makes it so bad? I just don't understand that girl anymore, and think maybe I never understood her.

A short while later, the telephone rang. Ikatza was napping on the sofa, a ball of black fur. Without changing position, eyes half open, she watched her mistress step toward the phone. Bittori let it stop ringing, before redialing the number that had disappeared from the screen.

Xabier, excited, *Ama, ama*. Turn on the television.

"I already heard all about it. Who? The upstairs neighbor."

"Oh, I thought maybe you hadn't heard."

And he sent her a kiss, and she did the same, and they spoke no more, and said goodbye. She told herself: I'm not turning on the TV. But soon enough her curiosity got the better of her. On the screen, she saw the three hooded men wearing berets, seated at a table, Ku Klux Klan aesthetic, a white tablecloth, patriotic banners, a microphone, and she thought: the mother of the one who spoke, would she recognize his voice? Repulsed, she turned off the television.

"Tomorrow I'll come up to tell you. I don't think you'll be happy, but, well, it's the news of the day, and you've got a right to hear it."

With the lights out, she tried to force herself to cry. Nothing. They were dry. And Nerea hadn't called. She hadn't even bothered to tell her if they'd reached London. Of course she was probably very busy trying to save her marriage.

3

WITH TXATO IN POLLOE

It's been a few years since Bittori last walked up to Polloe. She could still do it, but she gets tired. And it isn't that getting tired matters to her, but why bother, come on, why bother? Besides, depending on the day, she gets stitches in her stomach. Then she takes the number 9, which leaves her a few steps from the entrance to the cemetery. When the visit is over she walks down to the city. Walking downhill is a different thing.

She got out behind a lady, the two of them the only passengers. Friday, calm, fine weather. And she read the inscription on the arch over the entrance: SOON IT WILL BE SAID OF YOU WHAT IS NOW SAID OF US: THEY DIED!! I'm not impressed by these funereal phrases. Sidereal dust (that one she'd heard on TV) is what we are, the same stuff you breathe when you grow mallows. And even though she, too, detested the repugnant inscription, she was unable to enter the cemetery without stopping to read it.

Girl, you could have left that coat at home. It was too much. She'd put it on only so she could wear black. She was in mourning for the first year; then her children insisted she lead a normal life. A normal life? Those naive kids had no idea what they were talking about. Wanting to be left in peace, she followed their advice. Which doesn't take away from the fact that it seems to her a lack of respect to walk among the dead wearing bright colors. Anyway, she opened the closet early in the morning, looking for something black that would cover her other clothes, which were of various shades of blue, saw the coat, and put it on, knowing she'd be hot.

Txato shares a grave with his maternal grandparents and an

aunt. The grave, on the side of a road that rises gently, is one in a row of other, similar graves. On the headstone, the first and last names of the deceased, his date of birth, and the day he was killed. But not "Txato," his nickname.

During the days before the burial, some family members from Azpeitia advised Bittori not to include on the headstone any allusions, emblems, or signs that would identify Txato as a victim of ETA. That way she'd avoid problems.

She protested: "They already killed him once. I don't think they'll kill him again."

And it isn't that Bittori had wanted an explanation of how her husband died inscribed on the stone. But all anyone had to do was try to dissuade her from doing something and she would insist on going ahead with it.

Xabier said the relatives were right. And all that was engraved on the stone was the name and the dates. Nerea, over the telephone from Zaragoza, had the nerve to suggest they falsify the date of death. Shock: why?

"I thought it would be better to have the day before or the day after the attack on the stone."

Xabier shrugged. Bittori simply refused.

A few years later, when they painted graffiti all over Gregorio Ordóñez's stone—he rests about three hundred feet from Txato—Nerea, so out of line, brought up that old matter, which all of them had forgotten. Looking at the newspaper photo, she said to her mother: "See how it was better to have *aita* a little protected. Look what we didn't have to go through."

Then Bittori slammed her fork down on the table and said she was leaving.

"Where are you going?"

"I've suddenly lost my appetite."

She walked out of her daughter's apartment frowning, striding angrily, and Quique, as he lit a cigarette, rolled his eyes.

The row of graves stretches out one after another at the side of the road. The good thing for Bittori is that since the grave site is a few inches higher than the ground, she can sit down without difficulty on the stone. Unless it rains. Since the stone is usually cold (and covered with lichen and the inevitable filth of the years), she always carries in her bag a square of plastic cut from a shopping bag along with a kerchief, which she uses as a cushion. She sits down on it and tells Txato what she has to tell him. If there are people nearby, she speaks to him with her thoughts. Usually, there is no one around.

"Our daughter is in London by now. At least I suppose she is, because she hasn't bothered to call me. Did she call you? Me she didn't. Since there was nothing on TV about a plane crash, I figure the two of them have reached London and are fighting it out to see if they save the marriage."

The first year, Bittori put four flowerpots on the stone. She took regular care of it. It looked pretty. Then she went a while without going up to the cemetery. The plants died. The next batch lasted until the first frost. She bought a large flowerpot. Xabier brought it up on a hand truck. The two of them planted a box tree in it. One morning, they found it tipped over, the pot broken, part of the dirt spilled onto the stone. From then on, no decorations on Txato's grave.

"I'm talking the way I want to talk, and no one will stop me, especially you. And if I make jokes? I'm not the way I was when you were alive. I've become bad. Well, not bad. Cold, distant. If you come back to life, you won't recognize me. And don't think your darling daughter, your favorite, has nothing to do with this change in me. She drives me crazy. The same as when she was a girl. With your blessing, of course. Because you always defended her. You left me with no authority, so she never learned to respect me."

There was a sandy space three or four graves up, next to the asphalt road. And Bittori sat staring at a pair of sparrows that had just landed there. The little birds spread their wings and took a sand bath.

"The other thing I wanted to tell you is that the gang has decided to stop killing. We still don't know if the announcement is for real or if it's only a trick to gain time and rearm. Whether they kill or not will matter little to you. And don't think it matters much more to me. I need to know. I always have. And they aren't going to stop me. No one will stop me. Not even the children. If they ever find out. Because I'm not going to say a word to them. You're the only one who knows it. Don't interrupt. The only one who knows that I'm going to return. No, I can't go to the jail. I don't even know which jail the criminal is in. But they do, and I'm sure they're still in the town. And besides, I need to see what condition our house is in. You, stay still, Txato, Txatito, because Nerea is out of the country, and Xabier, as always, lives for his work. They won't find out."

The sparrows disappeared.

"I swear I'm not exaggerating. I've got this very great need to finally be okay with myself, to be able to sit down and say: It's over. What's over? Well, look, Txato, I have to figure that all out. And the answer, if there is an answer, can only be in the town, and that's why I'm going there, today, this afternoon."

She stood up. She carefully folded the kerchief and the square of plastic and put them back in the bag.

"So now I've told you. You're staying right here."

4

WHERE *THEY* LIVE

Nine p.m. In the kitchen, the window was open and the smell of fried fish wafted out to the street. The newscast began with a story Miren had heard on the radio yesterday afternoon: the definitive cessation of the armed struggle. Not the cessation of what some people call "terrorism," because my son is no terrorist. She turned toward her daughter: "Did you hear that? They're going to stop again. Let's just see how long it lasts."

Arantxa seems not to understand, but she gets everything. She made a slight movement with her face half turned away—or is it because her neck is twisted?—as if to express an opinion. With her you could never be sure, but Miren knew that her daughter had understood.

Using her fork, she sliced the two pieces of breaded hake. The pieces are not very big, so she can swallow them without difficulty. That's what the physical therapist, a very attractive girl, recommends. She's not Basque, but still . . . Arantxa has to make an effort. If she doesn't, there will be no progress. As the edge of the fork hits the plate it makes a noise, and, just when the breading split, for an instant a tiny cloud of steam rose from the white flesh of the fish. "Let's see what excuse they come up with now not to let Joxe Mari go free."

She sits down at the table near her daughter, never taking her eye off her. She just couldn't be sure. Arantxa had choked more than once. The last time, during the summer. They had to call the ambulance. The howl of the siren all over the neighborhood. My

God, what a shock it was. By the time the emergency medics got there, she'd pulled a chunk of steak this big out of her throat.

Forty-four years old. The oldest of the three. Then came Joxe Mari, in the Puerto de Santa María Penitentiary. They make us go all the way to Andalucía, the bastards. And finally, the kid. That one goes his own way. That one we never see.

Arantxa grabbed the glass of white wine her mother poured her. She lifts it, trembling, to her mouth with the only usable hand she has. The left is a dead fist. As always, she held it tightly against her side, near her waist, unusable because of a spastic contraction. And she gulped down a good mouthful of wine, which, according to Joxian, should make us all happy, especially if we think that until a little while back, Arantxa ate through a catheter.

A trickle of liquid ran down her chin, but it doesn't matter. Miren quickly wiped it clean with her napkin. Such a pretty girl, so healthy, with such a future before her, the mother of two small children, and now this.

"So, you like it?"

Arantxa shook her head.

"Listen here now, it's not cheap. You're getting spoiled."

The television commentaries followed one after another. Bah, politicians. An important step for peace. We demand the dissolution of the terrorist gang. A process is beginning to take place. The way to hope. The end of a nightmare. They should turn over their weapons.

"Give up the struggle? In exchange for what? Have these people forgotten about the liberation of Euskal Herria? And what about the prisoners rotting in jail? What was begun must be finished. Do you recognize the voice that read the communiqué?"

Arantxa slowly chewed a piece of hake. She again shook her head. She had more to say, and stretching out her good arm, she asked her mother to pass her the iPad. Miren stretched her neck to read what was on the screen: "It needs salt."

Joxian walked in just after eleven p.m. with a bundle of leeks. He'd spent the afternoon in the garden; his hobby now that he was retired. The garden is right next to the river. When it overflows—the last time was at the start of the year—goodbye, garden. There are

worse things, says Joxian. Sooner or later, the water recedes. He dries
the tools, sweeps out the shed, buys new baby rabbits, replaces the
ruined vegetables. The apple tree, the fig tree, and the hazelnut tree
survive the flood, and that's all. All? Since the river carries industrial
waste, the silt gives off a strong smell. He says it's a factory smell.
Miren snaps back: "It smells of poison. Someday we're all going to
die with horrible stomach cramps."

Another of Joxian's daily amusements is to play an afternoon
game of cards. Four friends play *mus* over a pitcher of wine in the
Pagoeta bar. As far as the four of them drinking only one pitcher,
well, that remains to be seen.

Judging by the way he was carrying the leeks, Miren assumed
he was drunk. She told him his nose was going to get as red as his
dead father's. She knows he's been drinking when he starts scratching his right side, where his liver is. Then there's no doubt about
it. He scratches the way other men make the sign of the cross or
knock on wood.

He just doesn't know how to say no. That's the problem. He
drinks in the bar because the other men drink, too. And if one of
them were to say "Okay, let's dive into the river," Joxian would go
right along with them like a little lamb.

In any case, he came home with his beret all twisted, his eyes
glazed, scratching his shirt right over his liver, and he got sentimental.

In the dining room, he gave Arantxa a slow, tender kiss on the
forehead, almost slobbering. He practically fell on top of her. Miren,
on the other hand, pushed him off. "Get out of here, you smell like
a tavern."

"Come on, sweetheart, don't be so hard."

She stretched out her arms with her hands open to keep him at
a distance. "You'll find some fish in the kitchen. Probably cold by
now. But you can heat it up."

Half an hour later, Miren called him in to help her get Arantxa
into bed. They picked her up out of her wheelchair, he holding up
one arm, she the other. "Have you got her?"

"What?"

"I asked if you've got her. Tell me if you've got a good grip before
we both fall over."

An immobilized foot makes it hard for Arantxa to walk. Sometimes she takes a few uncertain steps, using a cane or helped by another person. To be able to walk around the house, to eat on her own, to be able to speak again: those are the family's principal hopes for the short term. As for the long term, we'll just wait and see. The physical therapist encourages her. She's a beauty. She speaks very little Basque, almost nothing, but that doesn't matter.

Father and mother together stand her up next to the bed. They've done it many times. They've had lots of practice. And besides, how much could Arantxa weigh in those days? About ninety pounds. Not more. And to think how strong she'd been in her time.

Her father held her up while Miren pushed the wheelchair toward the wall.

"Don't you let her fall, now."

"How could I ever let my daughter fall?"

"You're capable of anything."

"You're talking nonsense."

They glared at each other, he with his teeth clenched as if to keep some obscenity inside his mouth. Miren pulled back the covers and then the two of them, carefully, slowly, have you got her?, placed Arantxa on the bed.

"You can leave now. I'm going to undress her."

Then Joxian bent over to kiss his daughter on the forehead. And to say good night. "See you tomorrow, *polita*," as he caressed her cheek with his knuckle. And then he made for the door, scratching his side. He'd almost left the room when he turned around and said: "On the way back from the Pagoeta, I saw light in the house that belongs to *those people*."

Miren was taking off her daughter's shoes. "Maybe someone was in cleaning up?"

"Cleaning up at eleven at night?"

"I have no interest in those people."

"Fine, I'm just telling you what I saw. It wouldn't matter if they came back to the town."

"It wouldn't matter. Now that there's no armed struggle, they can strut around."

Moving by Night

Some weeks after becoming a widow, Bittori spent a few days in San Sebastián. More than anything else, so she could stop seeing the sidewalk where her husband was killed and so she wouldn't have to go on suffering the menacing stares of the neighbors— friendly for so many years and then, suddenly, just the opposite. She could also stop seeing the graffiti on the walls, especially the one on the kiosk in the plaza, one of the last ones, the one with the bull's-eye above the dead man's name. It appeared, and in a few days, goodbye.

In reality, her children tricked her into going to San Sebastián. Jesus, Mary, and Joseph: a fourth-floor! When she was used to living on the second.

"Of course, *ama*, but there is an elevator."

Nerea and Xabier agreed they had to get her out of the village at all costs, out of her hometown, where she'd been born, where she was baptized, married, and then make it hard for her to return, even subtly keeping her from doing so.

So they set Bittori up in an apartment with a balcony from which she could see the ocean. The family had spent a long while trying to sell it. They'd placed an advertisement in the paper. They'd even called several interested parties. Txato had bought it months before being murdered. He'd wanted somewhere outside the village to hide.

There were lamps and some furniture in the flat. Her children told Bittori to move in provisionally. You talked to her, and she understood nothing. It was as if she'd gone mad. She was apathetic, she, who was always such a talker. But now she was like a statue. It actually seemed she was forgetting to blink.

Xabier and a friend from the hospital brought over some essentials. They would drive to the town in the van late in the afternoon, when it was getting dark, so they wouldn't call attention to themselves. They made perhaps ten trips, always after sunset. One day they'd bring this; the next, something else. There wasn't much room in the vehicle.

They left the double bed in the house in the village because Bittori refused to sleep in it without her husband. But, finally, they managed to remove lots of things: dishes, the dining-room carpet, the washing machine. One day during the week, while they were going about their business loading some boxes, they were insulted by a gang of Xabier's old acquaintances; some of them high-school friends. One, angrily chewing his words, said that he'd memorized their license-plate number.

On the way back to San Sebastián, Xabier realized his friend was having an anxiety attack and that if he kept driving in that state, they were going to have an accident. So he convinced him to pull over to the side of the highway.

The friend: "I can't do this tomorrow. I'm sorry."

"Calm down."

"I'm really sorry. Really sorry."

"There's no need to go back. The move is over. My mother has enough with what we've brought already."

"But do you understand me, Xabier?"

"Of course. Don't worry."

A year went by, then another, then more. Meanwhile, Bittori secretly had a key made for the village house because she's no fool. And what about it? First Nerea; then, a few days later, Xabier. *Ama*, the key? You have one. No, it's that. They were united against her. She told each of them that she had no idea where she'd left the key, how scatterbrained I am!, that she'd look for it, and finally, after a few days, she pretended she'd found it after a lot of searching. But of course by then she'd had a copy made at the hardware store. She lent the key to Nerea, who from time to time (once or twice a year?) went to check on the place and do some dusting. Her daughter did not return the key, and Bittori never expected her to.

On one occasion, Nerea brought up the possibility of selling the house in the village. A few days later, Xabier suggested the same thing. Bittori suspected the two of them had come to an agreement behind her back. So when the three of them were together, she confronted them: "As long as I am alive, I'm not selling my house. When I'm dead, you can do whatever you like with it."

The children exchanged a quick glance. They did not contradict her. The subject was never broached again.

She took it upon herself to go to the village in the most discreet way imaginable, on bleak days of wind and rain, when the streets would be empty, or when her children were busy or traveling. Then, she would let seven or eight months pass without going back. She got out of the bus on the outskirts of the town. So she wouldn't have to speak to anyone. So no one would see her. She used backstreets to get to her old house, where she would spend an hour or two, sometimes more, looking at photos, waiting for the church bell to ring out, and then, after making sure there were no people around the entrance, she would return by the same route she'd used to arrive.

She never went to the cemetery. What for? Txato was buried in San Sebastián, not in the village, despite the fact that his paternal grandparents were resting there in a family mausoleum. But it was impossible. She was strongly advised against it. If you bury him in the village, the grave will be attacked, it wouldn't be the first time something like that happened.

During the ceremony in the Polloe cemetery, Bittori whispered to Xabier something he'd never forgotten. What? That rather than burying Txato it seemed as if they were hiding him.

TXATO, *ENTZUN*

How slow the bus is. Too many stops. Hmm, another one. The two women, with the usual physical traits, were sitting next to each other. They were returning to the village just at sunset. They both spoke at once without listening to each other. Each one involved in her own thoughts, but they understood each other. And as they sat there, the one sitting next to the aisle gave the other, sitting next to the window, a light nudge with her elbow. With a rapid nod of her head she called her now-attentive partner's attention to the forward part of the bus.

In whispers:

"The one in the dark overcoat."

"Who is it?"

"Don't tell me you don't recognize her."

"All I can see is her back."

"It's Txato's wife."

"The one who was killed? How old she looks!"

"The years go by, or hadn't you noticed?"

They kept quiet. The bus went its way. Passengers got on and off, and the two women kept silent, staring at nothing. Then one of them, in a low voice, said that poor woman.

"Why poor?"

"How she must have suffered."

"We all suffer."

"But she must have had a really rough time."

"The conflict, Pili, the conflict."

"No, it's not that."

And after a while, the one whose name wasn't Pili:

"How much would you like to bet she gets off at the industrial park?"

They looked away as soon as Bittori stood up. She was the only person to get off.

"What did I tell you?"

"How did you figure that out?"

"She gets off there so no one will see her, and then she tiptoes to her house."

The bus drove off, and Bittori, do they really think I didn't see them?, set out in the same direction through the zone of factories and workshops. Her expression, not haughty, never that, but serious, her lips pressed tightly together, her face raised because I don't have to hide from anyone.

The town, her town. Almost nighttime. The windows glowing, the vegetal scent of the surrounding fields, few passersby on the street. She crossed the bridge with the lapels of her coat raised and saw the calm river with its gardens on the bank. No sooner had she gotten among the houses when she began to have difficulty breathing. Asphyxia? Not exactly. It's an invisible hand that squeezes her throat whenever she returns to the town. She walked along the sidewalk, neither hurrying nor slow, recognizing details: in that doorway, a boy told me he loved me for the very first time in my life; taken aback by the changes: those street lamps do nothing for me.

It wasn't long before a whispering reached her. Like a fly that had buzzed in through a window or from the darkness of an entryway. Barely a slight noise that ended in *ato*, which was enough for her to figure out the whole sentence. Perhaps she should have come later, when people were indoors, on the last bus. Well, here you are. What about the return? I'm spending the night. I've got a house and a bed.

Outside the door of the Pagoeta a group of smokers clustered together. Bittori was tempted to avoid them. How? By turning back and sneaking behind the church. She stopped for an instant, ashamed she'd stopped. So she went on walking in the center of the street with forced naturalness. Her heart was beating so hard that for a moment she was afraid the men could hear its pounding.

She passed closely by without looking at them. Four or five with a glass in one hand and a cigarette in the other. They must have recognized her when she was close because there was a sudden silence. One, two, three seconds. They started talking again once Bittori reached the end of the street.

Her house with lowered blinds. On the lower part of the facade, there were two posters. One, which looked recent, announced a concert in San Sebastián; the other, faded, shredded, announced the Grand Worldwide Circus, exactly in the place where one morning there appeared one of myriad graffiti: TXATO ENTZUN BOOM BOOM BOOM.

Bittori passed through the entryway, and it was like entering the past. The lamp she'd had all her life, the old creaking stairs, the line of collapsing mailboxes with hers removed. In his day, Xabier had taken it down. He said to avoid problems. When he removed it, a square appeared the color the walls were painted long ago, when Nerea had yet to be born, nor had Miren's son, that criminal. And it's the only thing for which I wish there to be a hell—so the murderers will go on living their eternal sentence.

She breathed in the scent of old wood, the cool, enclosed air. And finally, she noted that the invisible hand had released her throat. Key, lock: she entered. Again, she ran into Xabier, much younger, in the hallway, saying with tearful eyes all that about *ama*, let's not allow hatred to embitter our lives, make us small, or something like that, she couldn't remember exactly. And her spite in that same spot, so many years ago:

"Sure, right away, let's sing and dance."

"Please, *ama*, don't make the wound bigger. We have to make an effort so that all of this which has happened—"

She interrupted him:

"Excuse me. All this that they did to us."

"—doesn't turn us into bad people."

Words. There's no way to get them off your back.

They never let you really be alone. A plague of annoying bugs. She should open the windows wide so the laments, the old, sad conversations trapped in the walls of the uninhabited house, could flow out to the street.

"Txato, Txatito, what do you want for dinner?"

In the photo on the wall, Txato half smiled with his murder-able man's face. All you had to do was look at him to realize that someday he'd be killed. And what ears. Bittori kissed the tips of her joined ring and index fingers and then deposited it on the black-and-white face in the portrait.

"Fried eggs and ham. I know you as if you were alive."

She turned the tap in the bathroom. Just look, water came out, and not as rusty as she'd imagined. She opened drawers, blew away the dust on some of the furniture and other objects, did this, did that, walked over there, walked over here, and, at about ten thirty, raised the blind in the master bedroom just enough so the light inside would filter out to the street. She did the same with the next room, but without turning on the light. Then she brought a chair in from the kitchen and sat down to peer through the open spaces, completely in the dark so her silhouette wouldn't be outlined in the light.

Some kids passed by. People just walking along. A boy and a girl who argued as they strolled; he tried to kiss her and she fought him off. An old man and a dog. She was sure that sooner or later she would see one of them outside her house. And how do you know that? I can't explain it to you, Txato. Female intuition.

And what if the prediction were to come true? Well, yes it did, even if Bittori had to wait a long time. The bells in the church tower rang out eleven. She recognized him instantly. His beret pulled to one side, his sweater over his shoulders with the sleeves knotted over his chest, and some leeks held tightly under his arm. So he still tends his garden? And since he'd stopped in the circle of light from the street lamp, she could see his grimace, between disbelief and shock. Only a second, not more. Then he started walking again as if someone had stuck a needle in his backside.

"What did I tell you? Now he'll tell his wife he saw light here. She'll tell him: you've been drinking. But her curiosity will be piqued and she'll come to resolve her doubts. Txato: want to bet?"

It was eleven. Don't get impatient. You'll see that she'll come. And she did come, of course she came, almost at twelve thirty. She stopped barely an instant in the light of the street lamp, staring at the window with neither incredulity nor surprise but rather with angry eyebrows, and immediately returned to her own house, stamping the pavement and fading into the darkness.

"You've got to admit she's kept her looks."

7

Rocks in the Knapsack

He rolled the bike into the kitchen. It's light, a racing bike. Just another day, Miren, standing before a pile of dirty dishes: "For luxury baubles you've got money, eh?"

Joxian retorts: "Actually, I do have money, so what? I've also been working my whole life like a mule. We've been screwed."

He brings the bike up from the basement with no difficulty, without touching the walls. A good thing we live on the first floor. He rests it on his shoulder as he did as a young man, when he'd taken part in cyclo-cross competitions. It was seven a.m. and it was Sunday. He would have sworn he made no noise. Even so, there was Miren sitting at the table, in her nightgown, waiting for him with a face full of reproach.

"Would you mind telling me what you're dong with the bike in the house? What do you want to do, get the floor dirty?"

"I'm going to adjust the brakes and wipe it down before I go out."

"So why can't you clean it outside?"

"For shit's sake, because you can't see anything out there and it's colder than hell. And by the way, why are you up so early?"

Two sleepless nights in a row. He could tell by the shadows under her eyes. The reason? The light that came through the blinds from the house that belonged to *those people*. Not only Friday, yesterday too, and, if you push me a little, from now on, every day. So people can say oh the poor victims and oh let's stroll along with them with smiles on our faces. The light, the blind, the people who'd seen Bittori on the street and had nothing better to do than to come here and tell all, it had brought up old thoughts, bad thoughts, but when I say bad I mean bad.

"This son of ours has made our lives difficult."

"Right, and if people in town hear you, we'll have a better life."

"I'm just saying it to you. If I don't talk to you, who will I talk to?"

"Since you've become so *abertzale*, such a Basque patriot. Always the first, the one who screams loudest, the revolutionary woman with balls. And when tears came to my eyes in the visitors' room at the prison, boy, did you get mad. 'Don't be soft'—he imitated her voice—'don't cry in front of the kid, you'll get him depressed on me.'"

Many years back, how many?, more than twenty, they began to suspect, discover, understand. Arantxa, one day in the kitchen: "Come on now. All those posters on the walls in your room. And the wooden statue you had on the night table, the one with the serpent wrapped around the hatchet, what about that?"

One afternoon, Miren had come home upset. In San Sebastián, she'd seen Joxe Mari involved in a street fight. Who saw him?

"Who do you think? Bittori and I. Or do you think I've got a boyfriend?"

"Okay, calm down. He's young, he's got hot blood. He'll get over it."

Miren, taking sips from a cup of linden tea, invoked Saint Ignatius, begging protection and counsel. And while she peeled garlic to encrust in the flesh of a sea bream, she made the sign of the cross with the knife. During dinner, she never stopped making a speech at the silent family circle, predicting serious trouble, attributing Joxe Mari's tricks to the influence of bad company. She blamed Manoli's son, the butcher's son, the whole gang.

"He's become a thug, what with the way he dresses and that earring it gets me all nervous. He had his face masked with a hanky."

At that time, Bittori and she were friends? More, sisters. You can't know how close they were. They almost became nuns together, but Joxian came along, Txato came along, *mus* partners in the bar, dining pals, usually on Saturday, members of the Sunday gastronomic and cyclo-tourism societies. And the two women got married in white dresses in the village church, with *aurresku* as they left, one in June and the other in July of the same year, 1963. Two blue-skied

Sundays, as if ordered for the occasion. And they invited each other. Miren and Joxian held their banquet in a cider bar that wasn't bad at all, truth be told, on the outskirts of town. But, after all, cheap and with a country odor of mown hay and manure. Bittori and Txato held theirs in a fancy restaurant with uniformed waiters, because Txato, who as a boy had walked in worn-out sandals, had founded a thriving shipping company.

Miren and Joxian spent their honeymoon in Madrid (four days, a cheap rooming house a short distance from the Plaza Mayor); Bittori and Txato, after an initial visit to Rome and witnessing the new pope greeting the multitude, visited several Italian cities. Miren, as she listened to her friend tell the tale of the trip: "Anyone can see you married a rich man."

"Girl, I never thought about it. Since I married him randomly . . ."

The two friends were returning from a churro shop in the Parte Vieja of San Sebastián that afternoon of disturbances. They stopped at an intersection that led to the Bulevar. A city bus was burning in the street. The black smoke plumed against the facade of a building, obscuring the windows. The driver had been beaten. The man, fifty-five years old, was still there, sitting on the curb, his face bloody, his mouth open as if he couldn't breathe, and next to him two passersby taking care of him, consoling him, and an *ertzaina* who, judging by his gestures, was telling them they couldn't stay there.

Bittori: "There's trouble."

She: "Better go up Oquendo Street, and we'll take the long way around to the bus stop."

Before turning the corner, they looked back. In the distance, they could see a row of trucks from the *Ertzaintza* parked alongside the City Hall. The officers, wearing red helmets, their faces covered with ski masks, had taken up positions. They were firing rubber bullets at the crowd of young men gathered in front of them, shouting out a chorus of the usual insults: sellouts, murderers, sons of bitches, sometimes in Basque, other times in Spanish.

And the bus kept stoically burning amid the street battle. And the thick, black smoke. And the smell of burned tires that spread through the nearby streets poisoned pituitary glands, made eyes burn. Miren and Bittori heard a few passersby complain in low voices: we all pay for those buses, that if this is what you call defending the rights of the people, let's cut it short here and now. A wife shushed her husband: "Quiet, someone might hear you."

Suddenly they spotted him, one more among the hooded men, his mouth covered with a handkerchief. Hey, Joxe Mari. What's he doing here? Miren almost called him by name. The kid had left the Parte Vieja using the same street the two women had used a few minutes before. Six or seven of them stopped, the butcher's son and the son of Manoli, from the corner where the seafood shop was. And Joxe Mari was one of those who ran to distribute backpacks along the sidewalk. Some others gathered around, stretched out their hands to get Miren didn't know what out of the packs. Bittori had good eyes and told her: stones. And so it was: stones. They hurled them at the *ertzainas*.

8

A Distant Episode

The small concentration of morning light glinting off Joxian's bicycle spoke was enough to evoke in Miren a distant episode. The scenario? That same kitchen. The memory brought on a tremor in her hands as she prepared dinner. Merely remembering it gave her a touch of the asphyxia she attributed to the heat and smoke rising from the frying pan. Not even with the window open was she able to get a good breath of air.

Nine thirty, ten, and finally she felt him arrive. The unmistakable noise of his footfalls on the building's stairway. That mania of his for running up the stairs. He's about to enter.

He did enter, huge, nineteen years old, hair hanging down to his shoulders and that damn earring. Joxe Mari, a healthy, robust boy hungry as a bear: he'd grown until he became a tall, wide-shouldered young man. He was eight inches taller than anyone else in the family, except the youngest, who was also getting tall, though he was a different kind of boy. I don't know. Gorka was slim, fragile; according to Joxian, with a better brain.

Her eyebrows broadcasting her annoyance, she wouldn't let him come over and give her a kiss. "Where have you been?"

As if she didn't know. As if she hadn't seen him that afternoon on the Bulevar de San Sebastián. Ever since, she was imagining him with burned clothes, a cut on his forehead, lying in some hospital.

At first, he answered with evasions; he'd become very much his own person. Mmm, you'd have to use a corkscrew to get anything out of him. And since he wouldn't explain himself, she did. The time, the place, the backpack full of rocks.

"You wouldn't by any chance be one of the men who set fire to the bus? Don't you be bringing us troubles."

Not troubles, not a damn thing, he shouted. And Miren? Well, first she quickly shut the window. The whole town will hear. Occupation forces, freedom for Euskal Herria. And she snatched the handle of the frying pan, ready to defend herself, because if I have to smack him I will. But then she noticed the hot oil and, of course, forgot about it. Joxian still not home, Joxian in the Pagoeta, and she there alone with her wild son who was shouting at the top of his lungs about liberation, struggle, independence, so aggressive that Miren could only think: this guy's going to hit me. And he was her son, her Joxe Mari: she'd given birth to him, nursed him, and now what a way to scream at a mother.

She took off her apron, rolled it into a ball, and threw it to the floor in a fury—or out of fear?—right where Joxian stood his bicycle now, where does he get off with this stuff, bringing that thing into the house? And she didn't want her son to see her cry. So she dashed out of the kitchen, her eyes squeezed shut, her lips puffed out, her features disfigured by grief when she burst into Gorka's room and told him go find *aita*. And Gorka, bent over his books and notebooks, asked what was going on. His mother made him hurry and the kid, sixteen years old, ran out at full speed toward the Pagoeta.

A short time later, Joxian walked in, scowling: "What did you do to your mother?"

He had to look up to speak to him because of the height difference. In the flash of light off the spoke, Miren saw the whole scene without straining her memory. There, in small scale, were the tiles covering half the wall, the fluorescent bulbs that flooded the formica cabinets in a humble, working-class light, the stink of fried food and the stuffy kitchen.

He was on the verge of punching him. Who? The powerful son against the stocky father. Joxe Mari had never gone up against him that way. There were no old debts to settle, because Joxian was never an abusive father. That guy a child beater? No, he would curse in a low voice and take off for the bar the minute he sniffed discord. He always left everything to me, bringing up the boys, their sicknesses, peace in the house.

With the first jolt, Joxian's beret flew off his head and landed, not on the floor, but on a chair, as if ordered to sit down. Joxian stepped back astonished, fearful, his thin gray hair in defeated disorder, his status as alpha male in the family lost forever but not fully accepted, no, not at all, at least until that instant.

Arantxa once said to her mother: "*Ama*, know what this family's problem is? That we've spoken to one another very little."

"Bah."

"I think we don't know one another."

"Well, I know all of you. I know you too well."

And that conversation, too, remained in the bicycle tire, held in the glint between two spokes, along with the old scene, oh dear, that I'll never forget as long as I live. There she could see Joxian, poor thing, leaving the kitchen with his head hanging down. And he went to bed before his usual time, without saying good night, and she did not hear him snore. That man hasn't slept all night.

He didn't speak for several days. He spoke little. But now, less. Joxe Mari the same, silent, silent for all the four or five days he was still living in the house. He only opened his mouth to eat. Then, one Saturday, he packed up his things and left. At the time, we didn't imagine that he'd left for good. Maybe he hadn't imagined it, either. On the kitchen table, he left us a sheet of paper: *Barkatu*. He didn't even sign it. There it was, *Barkatu*, on a sheet of paper ripped out of one of his brother's notebooks, and nothing more. Neither *muxus* nor where he'd gone, not even goodbye.

He came back maybe ten days later with a bagful of dirty clothes and a sack to hold another load of the belongings he'd left in the room, and he gave his mother a bouquet of calla lilies:

"For me?"

"If not for you, then for who?"

"Where did you get these flowers?"

"From the flower shop. Where else would I get them?"

She stood there staring at him. Her son. When he was small, she'd washed him, dressed him, spoon-fed him porridge. No matter what he does, I said to myself, he'll always be my Joxe Mari, and I have to love him.

While the drum in the washing machine went around and around, he sat down to eat. By himself, he almost finished the loaf of bread. What a tiger. And just then his father came back from the garden.

"*Kaixo.*"

"*Kaixo.*"

That was their entire conversation. When the spin cycle was over, Joxe Mari put the wet clothes in the bag. He'd set them out to dry at his flat. Flat?

Now I share a flat with some friends, depending on who's going out on the highway to Goizueta.

Joxe Mari said goodbye, first kissing his mother and then patting his father on the back affectionately. Carrying the sack and the bag of laundry, he went off to his world of friends and God knows what, that even if he was nearby, in the same town, his parents had no idea of. Miren remembered that she'd looked out the window to watch him walk off down the street, but this time she had no chance to finish off the memory, since Joxian suddenly moved the bicycle, and the glint from the spoke disappeared.

9

RED

Ikatza came home to bring her a dead bird. A sparrow. The second in three days. Sometimes she brings mice. People know the cat has this way of contributing to the family economy or to show her thankfulness for the treatment she gets from her owner. Without the slightest difficulty, she climbs up the horse chestnut tree until she reaches a branch that enables her to leap onto one of the balconies on the fourth floor. From there, she moves on to Bittori's, where she usually leaves her gifts on the floor or on the dirt in one of the flowerpots. If she finds the door open, it's not unheard of for her to leave it on the living-room rug.

"How many times do I have to tell you not to bring me dead animals?"

Did they make her sick to her stomach? A little, but she's not in the mood to complain. The bad thing is that Ikatza's gifts remind her of violent death. At first she would sweep them off the balcony onto the street, but some fell on cars parked in front of the entryway. To avoid quarrels with the neighbors, she brings the dead animals to the rear of the house. There she uses a stick to push them into the dustpan and then, with all discretion, tosses them into the brambles.

Wearing rubber gloves, she was doing exactly that when the doorbell rang. To keep from upsetting his mother, Xabier usually announces his arrival before opening the door.

Seeing the gloves: "Have I caught you in the act of cleaning?"

"I wasn't expecting you."

Tall son, short mother, and a brushing of cheeks in the foyer.

"I had an appointment with the lawyer. A trivial matter that kept me there for only a few minutes. Since I was in the neighborhood, I thought I could drop in and at the same time draw some blood. That way you won't have to go to the hospital tomorrow."

"Okay, but try to bruise me less than you did last time."

Quiet by nature, Xabier was talking about whatever came into his head to distract his mother. About Ikatza's sleepy eyes, as the cat licked her paws sitting on the armchair. About the weather forecast. About how expensive chestnuts are this year.

"What do chestnuts matter to you with the salary you pull in?"

Bittori, her sleeve rolled up, leaning on her elbow over the dining-room table, wanted to talk, not to be talked to. She was dying to talk about one particular subject: Nerea.

Nerea this, Nerea that. Complaints. A furrowed brow, reproaches.

"I can tell you all this because you're my son, and I trust you. I can't deal with her. I never could. They always say the first time you give birth is the worst, that it clears the way for the ones that follow. Well, the fact is that giving birth to her hurt me more than giving birth to you. And I mean a lot more. And then, what a difficult child. And as an adolescent, don't get me started. And now it's even worse. I thought that after all that with *aita*, she'd start to focus. Mourning embittered me."

"Don't say that. In her way she's suffered as much as you and me."

"I know she's my daughter and that I shouldn't talk this way, but why should I hold in what I'm feeling when, even if I do, I'm not going to stop feeling it? Each time it gets harder and harder not to get furious. I'm too old to put up with certain kinds of behavior, understand? Four days ago she went to London with that playboy husband of hers."

"Let me remind you that my brother-in-law has a name."

"I can't stand him."

"And it's Enrique, if you don't mind."

"As far as I'm concerned his name is Cantstandhim."

The needle easily penetrated the vein. The slim tube rapidly turned red.

Red. Xabier, Xabier, you have to go home, something's happened to your father. That the something was bad was understood. And those words, something's happened to him, continued to resonate in him in a lasting moment outside the flow of time. He was given no more details, and he didn't dare ask. But he immediately realized from the expression on the face of the woman who reported the news, and from the expressions on all those he walked by in the hall, that something very serious must have happened to his father, something red, the worst. At no time did he consider the possibility of an accident. As he made his way to the hospital exit, he saw sorry faces filled with compassion, and one old friend who immediately turned away in order not to join him in the elevator. So it was ETA. While he crossed the wide expanse of the parking lot, he imagined three possibilities: restricted mobility, the rest of his life in a wheelchair, a coffin.

Red. His hand was trembling so hard he couldn't get the key into the ignition. It fell to the floor of the car, so he had to get out and look under the seat. Maybe it would have been wiser to take a taxi. Do I turn on the radio or not? In his haste, he'd forgotten to take off his lab coat. He talked to himself, cursed red lights, cursed. Finally, as the first houses in the village were coming into sight, he decided to turn on the radio. Music. Nervous, he twisted the dial. Music, ads, trivialities, jokes.

Red. The *Ertzaintza* forced him to detour. He parked in a no-parking zone behind the church. If they want to give me a ticket, let them. It was pouring rain, and he ran home as quickly as he could. By then he'd heard the news on the radio, although the reporter had no information about the physical condition of the victim. Besides that, he'd mispronounced Txato's last name. Between the garage and his parents' house Xabier saw blood mix with the rainwater slowly washing to the curb. He was running so quickly, so nervously that he almost ran by the entry. To the *Ertzaintza* agents, he identified himself as the son. Whose son? No one asked. His lab coat opened the way for him, even if he clearly looked like a member of the murdered man's family, not a single *ertzaina* even considered asking him where he was going.

"She still hasn't called."

"Maybe she did and you'd gone out. I called you yesterday and the day before. You didn't answer. That's one of the reasons I came to see you. I wanted to make sure you were okay."

"And if you were so concerned, why didn't you come sooner?"

"Because I knew where you've spent the last few nights. The whole village knows."

"What does anyone know about me?"

"They know you get off the bus at the industrial park and that you make your way to the house trying not to run into anyone. Someone in the hospital who saw you told me. Which is why I wasn't alarmed. And it may be that Nerea's made more than one attempt to talk to you. I'm not going to ask you about your intentions. It's your village, your house. But if you decide to revive stories from the past, I'd be grateful if you'd keep me informed."

"It's my business."

Xabier put his instruments and his mother's blood sample in his attaché case.

"I'm part of that story."

He went over to the cat, who let herself be petted. He said he wouldn't stay for dinner. He said other things. He kissed his mother before leaving, and since he knew she would appear at the window, he looked up before getting into his car and, supposing she was behind the curtain, waved goodbye.

10

TELEPHONE CALLS

The phone rang. It must be Nerea. Bittori didn't answer, even though all she had to do was stretch out her hand. Let her call, let her call. She imagined her daughter on the other end of the line saying, with growing impatience: *ama*, answer; *ama*, answer. She didn't answer. Ten minutes later, the phone rang again. *Ama*, answer. Upset by all the noise, Ikatza took advantage of the open balcony door and made for the street.

Bittori made her way over to Txato's photo, practicing a few dance steps.

"Like to dance, Txatito?"

Seconds later, the phone stopped ringing.

"It was her, your favorite. What do you mean, how do I know? My dear husband, you knew about trucks and I know about my things."

Nerea did not come to her father's funeral or to his burial.

"I may get Alzheimer's, I may forget you were murdered, I may forget my own name, but I swear that as long as I have my memory, I'll remember she denied us her company when we most needed her."

The previous year the girl had moved to Zaragoza to study law. The student apartment she shared with two girlfriends on López Allué Street had no phone. Once when she visited her, Bittori wrote down the telephone number of the bar on the street floor in case of emergency. Cell phones? As far as she could remember, few people used them back then. Until that moment, Bittori had never been in a situation where she had to call her daughter urgently. Now there was no choice.

Because of the tranquilizers, the shock, and the grief, she was in no condition to string together two phrases, so Xabier, at her request, called the bar, explained who he was, said with sorrowful calm what he had to say, and told the bartender where he could find his sister. The extremely considerate man: "I'll send someone over right away."

Xabier added to please tell his sister to call home as soon as possible, repeating that it was extremely urgent. He did not tell him the reason for the call, because his mother asked him not to. By then, television and innumerable radio stations had spread the news. Xabier and Bittori supposed Nerea had already learned what happened on her own.

But she didn't call. The hours passed. The first official statements: a brutal attack, a cowardly murder, a good man, we condemn, we unconditionally reject, et cetera. Night fell. Xabier again called the bar. The bartender promised to send his son again with the note. Nothing. Nerea didn't call until the next morning. She waited in silence while her mother finished crying, and wailing, and cursing, and telling her in a broken voice the details of what happened. Then, decisively, she said she wasn't leaving Zaragoza.

"What?" Bittori's sobs suddenly stopped.

"You're to be on the first bus home. Be serious. Your father's been murdered, and you're happy."

"I'm not happy, *ama*. I'm very sad. I don't want to see *aita* dead. I couldn't stand it. I don't want my picture in the papers. I don't want to put up with the stares of the people in town. You know how they hate us. I'm begging you to try to understand me."

She spoke quickly so her mother couldn't interrupt and so the grief that was rising from the center of her chest didn't cut her off. She went on talking with her eyes blurred with tears:

"No one in Zaragoza can connect me with *aita*. Not even my professors. That will let me live here in peace. I don't want anyone at the law school whispering about me: look, that's the daughter of the guy they killed. And if I come back to town now and they show me on TV, every dumbbell at the university will know who I am. So I'm going to stay here, and do me the favor of not judging my feelings. I'm as broken up as you. I'm begging you: let me choose my own way to grieve."

Nerea hung up before Bittori could get a word in. She didn't come back to town until a week later.

She thought it through. People in Zaragoza (from the law school, the neighborhood, friends) who might know that she was the daughter of the last, soon the next-to-last, victim of ETA: her roommates. Her last name is fairly common in Euskadi and turns up frequently in other places. In case someone asks her if she's a relative of the businessman from Guipúzcoa murdered by ETA or if she knows him, she'll deny it all.

Before her roommates found out, that boy José Carlos came to pick her up to go to a neighborhood bar where they were supposed to meet up with other students. They all intended to go, later that afternoon, in several cars, to a party at the veterinary school. While they joked and laughed, the news hit Nerea. Taking José Carlos aside, she asked him to say nothing to anyone and to go back to her place. They locked themselves in. The boy failed to find words of consolation. For a long time he was ranting on about the terrorists and against the current government, which does nothing, and because his desolate friend wanted him to, he stayed to sleep with her.

"Are you really in the mood?"

"I need it."

And he excused himself beforehand in case he couldn't get an erection. He never stopped talking:

"They killed your father, fuck, they killed him."

Unable to focus on the erotic games, he cursed while she tried to close his mouth with kisses. At around midnight, she got on top of him and they consummated a rapid coitus. José Carlos went on muttering exclamations, obscenities, categorical rejections, until finally, overcome by fatigue, he turned over and stopped talking. Next to him, with the light out, Nerea spent a sleepless night. Leaning against the headboard, she smoked, reviewing memories of her father.

The telephone rang again. This time, Bittori answered.

"*Ama*, at last. I've been calling you for three hours."

"How was London?"

"Fantastic. No matter how much I tell you, I still won't say enough. Have you changed the doormat?"

Flood

Three days of biblical rain. At night in bed, Joxian nervously listened to the drumming against the roof tiles and the streets. During the workday at the foundry, whenever he looked outdoors he shook his head with growing disquiet looking at the continuous flood that blurred the nearby mountains and made the river rise dangerously. The garden, damn it to hell. And it never stopped pouring. It's been three days already and probably more to come.

The vegetables themselves were the least of his problems. I can just replace them. The trees? They can take it. Even the hazelnut bushes, the hell with it. He was more concerned about losing his tools or that the flood had washed away the wall separating the garden from the river along with the shed where he kept rabbits. He talked about it with a workmate.

"The wall, if you'd used cement, you'd have no problems."

Joxian: "The wall or the wall's mother doesn't really matter. But with the wall gone, the river probably washed away a ton of dirt. I'll have a huge hole there. More like a ravine. The rabbits most likely drowned. And the grapevine, well, I don't have to tell you."

"That's what you get for putting the garden on the *erribera*."

"We're screwed, because that's where you get the best crops."

At the end of the workday, Joxian went directly from the factory to the garden. Was it still raining? Pouring. As he came down the hill, umbrella, beret pulled over one ear, he saw that the *Ertzaintza* had stopped traffic on the bridge. The rapidly flowing, filthy water was inches from lapping over the guardrail. Nice picture! If the water is almost jumping over the bridge, what damage will it have done in the garden, which is on lower ground? He detoured around a block of houses. Because, of course, it's one thing if the river overflows and quite another if, along with flooding, it pulls things up, drags them away, and destroys everything. He pushed a doorbell button, explained his intention with his mouth next to the intercom, and they let him in. And in a friend's house, from the balcony that overlooked the river:

"Holy mother! Where's my garden?"

Tree trunks were like foundering canoes, branches poking up, sinking into the light-brown water. An oil drum passed by, rusty, bouncing along like a puppet. Rising from the river's rage was a strong smell like mold, moss, and stirred-up putrefaction. The friend, perhaps to rein in Joxian's laments, pointing his finger at the opposite bank:

"Just look over there at the Arrizabalaga brothers' workshop. They're ruined."

"My rabbits, son of a bitch."

"This is going to cost them a fortune."

"After all the work I put into that. I even made the cages myself. Damn!"

A few days went by. The rain stopped. The river receded. Joxian's rubber boots sank calf-deep in the water-soaked soil of the garden. The muddy trees survived; as did the hazelnut bushes and, miracle or good roots, the grapevine. The rest, enough to make you weep. The wall that bordered the river disappeared, simply yanked right out. Not a single tomato plant or leek left, nothing. On the lower part, next to the shore, the current had washed away a vast swath of dirt along with everything that was there: raspberry bushes, gooseberry bushes, the *txoko* for the calla lilies and roses. The shed lost the boards on one side and the roofing. The rabbits were in their cages, caked with mud, swollen, dead. The tools—God knows where they were.

During those days, Joxian, in his free time, just sat on the sofa in the dining room, his elbows resting on his thighs, his head in his hands. A statue of sorrow. People asked him questions, he didn't answer.

"Want the newspaper?"

No acknowledgment. Until finally Miren lost patience.

"For God's sake, if losing the garden hurts you so much, go down and fix it up."

Docile, he got up. It wasn't as if he'd been waiting for orders.

The next day he seemed more animated. He went back to playing cards with his friends in the Pagoeta. He returned home from the bar almost euphoric because his friends had given him the idea of building a reinforced concrete wall between the garden and the river.

"After all, how much can it cost you? Pennies."

He told Miren over dinner, conger eel in sauce, wine laced with soda water, scratching his right side, that Txato had offered to deliver a truckload of dirt to replace what had been washed away.

"It must be good dirt, right? From Navarra. Taking advantage of a shipment. He'll bring it free of charge."

But first he had to construct his wall. And before that a cleanup. Too much work for one man. When would he do it? After work?

Miren: "You figure it out."

She told him to ask their sons to help. So Joxian waited up for Gorka to come home and said to him: Gorka, on Sunday, lend a hand, you and your brother. And the kid said nothing. That boy's got no get-up-and-go. To put some life in him, his father: "When we three finish we'll head for the cider bar and have a steak. What do you think of that?"

"Okay."

He said nothing more and Sunday came. Sun, good temperature, and the river once again between its banks. Joxian abandoned taking part in the current phase of the bicycle tour because while the bike is important, the garden is more so. The garden is his religion. He said it in those words once in the Pagoeta, as a retort to some jokes his friends were making about him. That when he died, God shouldn't bother him with paradise or other such nonsense; let him give me a garden like the one he has now. And they all laughed.

Out in the street:

"Did you tell Joxe Mari to be here at nine?"

"I didn't tell him."

"What? Why?"

Then he told his father, he had to tell him, there was no way out of it.

"For two weeks now, my brother hasn't been living in town."

Joxian stopped dead in his tracks, an expression of surprise on his face.

"Well, he never said a word to us. At least not to me. To *ama* maybe, I don't know. Or did all of you know and me not? Where is he living now?"

"We don't know, *aita*. I imagine he's gone to France. I was assured that as soon as he can he'll tell us."

"Who assured you?"

"Friends in town."

They said nothing more as they made their way to the garden. As soon as they got there, Joxian asked:

"If he's in France, how the hell does he get to work?"

"He quit."

"But he hasn't finished his apprenticeship yet."

"Even so."

"And handball?"

"He gave that up, too."

The two of them alone did the work, at opposite ends of the garden. At about eleven, Gorka told his father he had to go. He gave him, how odd, a farewell hug. They never hugged, and now, why?

All alone in the garden, Joxian went on shoveling filth until dinner. He used the hose to clean here and there, set the tools rescued from the mud out to dry in the sun. "France? What the hell has that fool got to do with France? And if he's not working, how is he living?"

12

The Garden Wall

They constructed the garden wall. Who? Joxian, Gorka, who promised to bring a friend that never turned up, and Guillermo (Guillermo!), in those days still a pleasant and cooperative son-in-law.

Years before, Arantxa, in the kitchen:

"*Ama*, I've got a boyfriend."

"Really? Someone from our town?"

"He lives in Rentería."

"What's his name?"

"Guillermo."

"Guillermo! Isn't he in the Guardia Civil?"

Anyway, without Txato's help they'd never have managed. How the hell could they manage? It's that Txato, aside from lending them the formwork, arranged for a cement truck—Joxian never found out how much it cost or even if the man who operated it had charged or not charged. Txato said to him: take it easy, the construction company owes me favors. So Joxian only had to pay for the cement. He still hadn't finished fixing up the garden or repairing the shed, but he was pleased by the sight of a shiny new garden wall that would stand up against floods, at least, according to Txato, floods like the one of the previous month.

A problem: opposite the garden wall was a hollow big enough for a fish pool. Fish this size, said Joxian, holding up an imaginary fish the size of a tuna. Txato simply said: forget it, we can fix that. He fulfilled the promise he made in the Pagoeta. He was slow to fulfill it. How long did it take? About two weeks. Until there was a shipment for Andosilla in Navarra. On the return trip, Txato ordered the driver to bring a load of garden soil. Apparently he was owed favors in Navarra, too. Many people owed Txato favors. And Joxian, of course, was thankful. And if it's necessary to pay, we'll pay.

Another problem: they unloaded the dirt; Txato at the wheel, the dirt of a more reddish color than the original soil, which, apparently, was good for grapevines. Moreover, they discovered that the amount they'd transported did not fill in the hollow.

Joxian: "We'd need at least three truckloads."

Solution: "We'll put in terraces."

"You can divide the garden into two levels, connected by steps or by a ramp for the wheelbarrow. Then, if the river floods again, the water will settle in the lower part of the garden. With a little luck you'll only be screwed out of half the garden and not all of it like this time."

Txato was quick, always thinking, he had ideas. In that, everyone agreed. To him the old praise applied: cleverer than hunger itself. Joxian, on the other hand, lacked mental agility. Things as they are. If he'd been brighter, he'd have been able to be a partner in the trucking business. But he hesitated, lacked spirit. Miren talked him out of it. Txato was the businessman and the brave man. In town, all the neighbors said it until from one day to another, TXATO ENTZUN BOOM BOOM BOOM, they stopped mentioning him in their conversations, as if he'd never existed.

Yes indeed, he had ideas, but he also had a problem. What was that? This one:

"They've sent me another letter."

ETA, armed organization for the Basque revolution, writes to you to demand the delivery of twenty-five million pesetas as your donation for the maintenance of the armed structure necessary for the Basque revolutionary process toward independence and socialism. In accordance with the information services of the organization, etc.

He lost sleep.

Joxian: Of course, who wouldn't lose sleep?

"What about your family?"

"They don't know."

"All the better."

To protect them from nightmares and because at first, how naive, but how naive! He thought the problem had a quick solution, as if it were a simple business transaction. I pay and I'm left in peace. The letters, signed with the serpent wrapped around the ax and the symbols of ETA, had been sent to the business. The first 1,600,000 pesetas. Without saying a word to anyone, he got into his car and drove to the meeting in France with Father Oxia, ETA's money collector, of the moment. He came back to town relieved, listening to music as he drove along the highway. A dirty trick, but what could you do about it? A few days later, there was an attack with one dead, a desolate widow, orphans, and declarations of condemnation and rejection, and Txato felt a twinge of guilt, damn it to hell, thinking that his money might have been used to buy explosives and pistols, and Joxian said he agreed, that he understood. But after all he did pay and he thought that for a time, perhaps a few years, they'd leave him in peace. Right, right. Not even four months had passed when the next letter came.

"Now they're demanding twenty-five million pesetas. That's a lot of money, a hell of a lot."

Joxian, in solidarity: "These things shouldn't go on among Basques."

"Tell me the truth: do I look like someone who exploits others? My whole life, all I've ever done is work like a mule and create jobs. Right now I've got fourteen employees on the payroll. What should I do? Move the business to Logroño and leave them stranded without salaries, insurance, or any other damn thing?"

"They must have made a mistake and sent you a letter meant for someone else."

"I'm not poor, no. But between the expenses, these taxes, those taxes, and other things I won't mention so I won't sound like a broken record, but you can just imagine: repairs, gasoline, outstanding debts, and other stuff like that, don't think I'm swimming in liquid gold. Swimming? Bullshit! I don't know what people think. I'm still driving the same car I did ten years ago. Some of my trucks are really old, but where am I supposed to get money to buy new ones?

I took out a loan to buy two new trucks. And what really hurts is that some of the men I've given jobs to are probably the ones who told the terrorists all about it: listen, this guy's rolling in cash."

He nervously shook his head, bags under his eyes from sleeping badly.

"But it's not just about me. Listen. That gang of murderers doesn't scare me. They can shoot me, then I'll have some peace. I'll be dead, but at peace. In the letter they talk about Nerea. They know where she studies."

"Are you serious?"

"That's what gets me down. What would you do?"

Joxian scratched his neck before answering: "I'm clueless."

They were in the shadow of the fig tree, smoking. The weather was fine, and on a rock a lizard was sunning itself. The truck in the middle of the garden with its wheels half sunk into the soft earth. From the other side of the river came the constant *clack-clack-clack* of some machine or other in the Arrizabalaga brothers' workshop.

"Think they pay too?"

"Who?"

"The Arrizabalagas."

Joxian shrugged his shoulders.

"I've only got three options. Pay, move the company, or take my chances. What I can't wrap my mind around is why they've got it in for me after I paid them what they demanded and didn't make them wait."

"I don't understand these things, but it still seems to me there's been a mistake."

"I already told you they talk about Nerea."

"Maybe they sent you the letter they'd send you next year without realizing it."

Clack, clack. Txato, after tossing his cigarette butt to the ground and stepping on it: "Could I ask you to do me a favor?"

"Of course, name it."

"Look, I've been thinking. I have to talk to them, with one of the chiefs or with the person responsible for finances, and explain my situation. The priest I met with is just an intermediary. Maybe they'd take less or let me pay them in installments, get me?"

"Sounds like a good idea to me."

Clack, clack. They could hear birds and the noise of cars and trucks crossing the nearby bridge.

"I need to talk to Joxe Mari. That's the favor I'm asking from you."

Joxian, an expression of surprise on his face: "Joxe Mari's not in ETA! Can't be! Besides, he's gone away. Where? We just don't know. Joxe Mari is a dope and a lazy dope at that. He left his job, and Miren says he's taken off to see the world with his friends. He might be in America now for all we know."

Clack, clack, clack.

13

The Ramp, the Bathroom, the Caregiver

From the start, Miren saw it all clearly. If they hadn't been living on a low floor they'd have had to move. Why? Damn, because we couldn't be getting Arantxa up and down the stairs every day on our own. Can you imagine that? There were only three steps separating the entryway from their landing and front door. Not a great distance, but even so, over the long term it's going to be impossible.

"You're out of the house, I don't have the strength or—just suppose—I get sick on the street. What am I supposed to do? Ask for help? Leave Arantxa all alone in the entryway?"

She told him he had to figure out some solution, and Joxian didn't hesitate for a second. He clapped on his beret, went to the Pagoeta, and there the advice of his pals sent him to a carpenter's shop, where he ordered a ramp. The carpenter, after taking the measurements, built it, tested it, and set it up. One morning the neighbors discovered that three-fourths of the small stairway was taken up by that wooden structure, which also extended about one and a half feet beyond the lowest stair onto the entryway's tile floor, the idea being to make the incline less steep. Joxian and Miren tested rolling the wheelchair up and down, first without Arantxa, then with her in it, and no doubt about it, from that day on, the three steps would no longer be an obstacle to getting their daughter out to take the air.

For the neighbors, on the other hand, there barely remained eight inches of stair from the entryway up unless, like the children, they went up and down on the ramp, which is exactly what Miren suggested to one neighbor who complained because the whole project was carried out without consulting the neighbors.

"Listen, just go up the ramp. What's the problem?"

A double problem. For them: if someone slips and breaks something. For us: every time someone walks up or down the ramp you can hear their footsteps in the house, which means we'll never get a night's sleep. In the bar, Joxian picked up the idea of covering the wooden surface with carpeting. Miren, delighted. Carpeting—why didn't we think of that before? It will simultaneously silence the footsteps and keep people from slipping. So they had it installed. Someone they knew did the work; carpenter's glue, reinforced with nails.

Joxian, reading the future: "People will use the carpet as a doormat. I don't even want to think about how it will look when it rains."

The neighbors, indifferent or resigned, perhaps wanting to avoid arguments with the family of an ETA member, swallowed their protests. All but one: Arrondo, on the third floor, right side. Actually, his wife sent him to demand they take the whole thing away immediately. The stairs belong to everyone. His mother, eighty-eight years old, can't cross over it, et cetera, et cetera. She and Miren had had a nasty encounter coming out of mass, trading tigerish, disdainful glares. And one Saturday, Arrondo, a man of few but strong words, came downstairs with an ultimatum: either they take down the ramp or he would, God damn it!

It was Miren who opened the door, while Joxian hid in the kitchen.

"You're not taking anything down."

"Is that right?"

Arrondo is big and imprudent. He didn't think, never calculated the consequences, his wife had pushed him into it. Anyway, he took up the ramp and threw it into the corner where the mailboxes were. Man oh man, Arrondo. You're in a nice mess now. Miren, without taking off her apron and still in her slippers, went over to the Arrano Taberna. It was early, there were few. Didn't matter. Two were enough. Twenty minutes later, Arrondo had put the ramp back in its place. There were no more complaints, and it remains there: ugly but useful.

Joxian: this could have been taken care of in another way. How? In another way, he didn't know how, nicely, by talking.

"And so why didn't you come out and talk, since you've got so much to say?"

The ramp wasn't the only change they introduced to adapt the flat to Arantxa's needs. They completely redid the bathroom. By the time they were done it looked nothing like its original self. To carry out the reworking they followed the instructions in a prospectus sent them by Rehabilitation Services. Guillermo paid for part. Miren: of course, he wanted to get her out of his sight as soon as he could. Here, here's the paralytic, I return her to you, I've already found another woman to warm up my bed. And he kept the children, and Miren in church to the saint of Loyola: Ignatius, I beg you to punish him, you choose any way you like. And then give me my grandchildren and get Joxe Mari out of jail. If you just give me all that, I'll never ask you for another thing. I swear.

Net result: when Arantxa moved in with them, the bathroom looked like it belonged in a hospital, with an unenclosed shower and no step, easy access. What else? With grab bars, mats to prevent slips, lever-style faucets; what the director of Rehabilitation Services in the hospital recommended and had put into the prospectus.

But to wash her properly it takes two people. Miren on her own can't manage, because Arantxa, so thin at first, gained weight and is now back to normal. She has to be undressed, she has to be placed on the special chair for the shower, soaped up, dried, and dressed.

"Okay, okay, don't explain what I already know."

And Joxian, who wanted to take off as soon as possible to play cards in the Pagoeta, was happy to contract the services of an assistant. Because what Miren won't accept under any condition is that Joxian look at or touch Arantxa naked, even if he's her father. Never.

The next day Joxian walks into the house and what does he see? A small woman with the eyes of an Indian and long, straight black hair who receives him with a curtsy, with two rows of smiling teeth, who calls him sir, sir!, and says: "Good afternoon, sir. My name is Celeste, at your service."

From Ecuador. Cute, no? And modest.

Joxian, that night in bed: "Where'd you find her?"

"By asking. Did you notice how clean and proper she is?"

"Yeah, but where did you find her?"

"In the butcher shop, talking. Juani says: listen, I know some people from Ecuador, and the woman cleans houses for very little money. They live in a van. And yesterday I was pushing Arantxa around and I asked for her and here she is. A treasure. I told her that one of my sons lives in Andalucía and that I visit him once a month. Celeste says I shouldn't worry, that she'll take care of Arantxa.

"And how much do you expect to pay her?"

"Ten euros whenever she comes."

"Very little."

"They're poor. She'll be thankful."

14

Last Snacks

Bittori prefers toast and marmalade and decaf coffee from a machine; Miren likes hot chocolate and churros. Even if they make you fat! Who cares? Did they get along? Very well. They were intimate. One Saturday the two of them were going to a café on the Avenida, the next Saturday to a *churrería* in the Parte Vieja. Always to San Sebastián. They called it both San Sebastián and Donostia, its Basque name. They weren't strict. San Sebastián? Okay, San Sebastián. Donostia? Okay, Donostia. They would start speaking in Basque, switch to Spanish, go back to Basque, that way all afternoon.

"Can you imagine if we had become nuns?"

They laughed. Sister Bittori, Sister Miren. They had their hair done, they rehashed the village gossip, they understood each other without listening, since they usually spoke both at the same time. They criticized the priest, that skirt chaser; they flayed the neighbor ladies; about house and bed they told everything. Joxian's hairy back, Txato's lascivious mischief. They told it all.

This too:

"We know he's in France but not in which town. Finally that bandit wrote us. Poor Joxian's so mortified he can't sleep. He wonders what we could have done to deserve this."

That afternoon of toast, rain, and wind. The coffee shop full. They had a corner where they could talk without being bothered.

"I couldn't bring you the letter. Joxe Mari won't let us. He said we should destroy it. So, even though it hurt me to do it, believe me, I tore it to pieces. Joxian was hysterical. I don't see how I can put it all back together. My dear man, just eat it. He took matches and burned the shreds in the sink.

His girlfriend or whatever she is, because these days you just can't know, brought the letter to us. Miren's thesis: they couple like rabbits. Of course, since they have ways of not ending up pregnant. That she affirmed often, and Bittori agreed. They were convinced they'd been born thirty years before their time. Franco, the priests, your precious reputation, how naive they were. That's how they thought, snacking, one eye on the nearby tables in case some local was listening in.

The letter: by mail? No, dear. They use their own channels. No return address. So we're left not knowing where he's gone to live. Visits are not allowed. Just a few years ago you could cross over to see them, bring them clothes and anything else they might need. Now they have to be careful because the fascists are hunting them down.

"Aren't you afraid something terrible will happen to him?"

"Joxian is. Sometimes he doesn't go to the bar because Joxe Mari's picture might be on the newscast. I'm calm. I know my son. He's clever and strong. He'll know how to protect himself."

Between bites of toast and sips of café con leche, Miren quoted passages from memory. That they weren't to take rumors seriously. People talk without knowing. And much less the lies in the newspapers. That he understood militancy as a sacrifice for the liberation of our nation and that if anyone came to *aita* or *ama* with the tale that he'd joined up with a band of criminals they shouldn't believe it, that the only thing he was doing was giving his all for Euskal Herria and also for the rights of those who complained and did nothing. There were many *gudaris*, he affirmed. More and more. The best of Basque youth. He concluded: "I love you both. I'm not forgetting my brothers. A big *muxu*, and I hope you're both proud."

Ikatza came over warily and leapt into her lap, patiently waiting to be petted. Bittori's fingers make sure her collar isn't too tight, they play with her ears, rub eyelids that stay shut for the sheer pleasure of contact. Bittori rubs her hand over her back and as Ikatza purrs, says to the cat that I'm really sorry, Ikatza my darling. Can you imagine? I'm sorry about my best friend's son, who quit his job, quit the handball team, quit his girlfriend or semigirlfriend, to become a gunman in an organization dedicated to serial murder.

And Miren? Well, let's see, Ikatza, now that you ask, I'll tell you what I think. Deep down, and may Txato forgive me, I understand her. I understand her transformation, even if I don't approve. Between that snack in the café on the Avenida and the next one in the *churrería* in the Parte Vieja, my friend Miren changed. Suddenly she was another person. In a word, she'd sided with her son. I haven't the slightest doubt that she became a fanatic out of maternal instinct. In her place, I might have behaved the same way. How can you turn your back on your own child even when you know he's doing bad things? Until then, Miren hadn't taken the slightest interest in politics. I wasn't interested then or now, and as for Txato, even less. Txato was only concerned with his family, his bicycle on Sunday, and his trucks the rest of the week.

Were those people nationalists? Not even remotely. Or much like election day with that "vote for people from here" stuff. Me, Ikatza *maitia*, I never heard them express any political opinions. And of course, Arantxa, as an *abertzale*, just the right amount and perhaps not even that. The younger one, nope, he was a blessing. Really, I don't think they brought up their children to hate. Friends, their cliques, bad company, they're the ones who slipped the poisonous doctrine to that rascal, a doctrine that led him to destroy the lives of God knows how many families. And he even thinks he's a hero. He's one of the hard men, they say. Hard men or savages. He doesn't even know how to open a book.

It was the following Saturday when for the first time she noticed Miren had changed. After churros and chocolate, they walked as usual toward the bus stop, and what do they see? A demonstration, the usual kind, on the Bulevar. The same old song: banners, independence, amnesty, *gora ETA*. Lots of people. Two or three from the village, rain and umbrellas. And instead of avoiding the crowd, Miren said: come on, girl, let's go. She took her by the arm, pulled her along, and the two of them walked right into the heart of the mob, not out front but not bringing up the rear, either. Suddenly, Miren starts in and begins to shout at the top of her lungs the slogans the demonstrators were calling out. *It's you fascists who are the terrorists*. Bittori was at her side, a bit astonished, but, well, along for the ride.

She knew nothing. Txato never said a word. That's the way it was, Ikatza. The pigheaded fool kept it all a secret. To protect us, he said later. Great protection! They could have blown us all to bits with a bomb.

She found out from Miren, who learned it from Joxian, who heard it straight from the lips of Txato himself when they were in the garden the afternoon he'd brought in the truckload of dirt from Andosilla. Miren couldn't imagine her friend didn't know.

"There's no way to see him. Because if we could go we'd have said, listen, talk to your bosses, they should do something to leave Txato in peace."

Bittori, suddenly suspicious:

"Leave my husband in peace?"

"Because of the letters."

"Letters? What letters?"

"Oh dear, the two of you haven't talked about it?"

15

Meetings

Two gobs of white shit, already dry, on the tombstone, and one still bigger dripping down the names on the stone. In denial, she attributed the vandalism to the damned pigeons. A bird: how could it release such a quantity of excrement? Hundreds, thousands, a sea of graves, and the sluts had to come and release their mess on Txato's headstone.

"My dear husband, they did a great job on you. Maybe this will bring you luck."

Always with her jokes. What was she going to do? Open up the wound again every day? She cleaned off as much as she could with dry leaves and handfuls of grass. What was left she consigned to the next rainfall. She whispered just that as she contemplated the horizon beyond the city, where a solitary cloud was visible in the distance. As usual, she spread out the plastic square and the kerchief.

"Every day now I go to the village. Sometimes I bring along food I heat up there. Know what? I put a geranium on the balcony. You heard me right. A good big one, red, so they know I've come back."

She told him she no longer got off the bus at the industrial park. And the day before yesterday—this you won't believe—she worked up enough courage to go into the Pagoeta. It was eleven a.m. There were few people there. At first sight, no one I knew. The bartender's son was working behind the bar. Bittori spent several days mortified by the temptation to set foot in that place after so many years. She was neither thirsty nor hungry, and, if pressured, not curious, either, but some more intense craving boiled deep down in her thoughts.

"Fine. I can understand myself by now."

Flowing out to the street, the usual noise of voices punctuated by the odd snort of laughter. Should I go in or not? She went in and silence fell. There were maybe a dozen patrons. She didn't count them. Silent, they averted their eyes, but to where? Well, to anywhere she wasn't. And the boy passing a dishcloth between the plates for brochettes didn't look at her, either. A silence: aggressive? Hostile? No, rather more questioning, of surprise. Wondering if she was sure.

"Txato, you just notice things like that."

The bar is L-shaped. Bittori took a place at the shortest side, her back to the entrance. Failing to get the bartender's attention, she looked around. The floor with its two-colored tiles, the fan hanging from the ceiling, the shelves with rows of bottles. Except for a couple of details, the bar looked the same as it always had. It was the same as it was when Bittori would come in to buy her children popsicles. The unforgettable lemon and orange popsicles from the Pagoeta, which were nothing more than fruit drinks frozen in molds with a stick in them.

"Barely anything's changed, I swear. The tables where you men played cards are right where they were up against the wall moldings. There is no foosball, no pinball machine like the one that made so much noise, but there is a slot machine. One of the few new things I saw. Oh, and the struggle for the prisoners over the bar. Soccer posters and pictures of fishing boats instead of the old bullfighting posters. It seems the business is in the hands of the son.

Finally he came over to her: "What'll it be?"

She vainly tried to meet his gaze. The kid, thirty-three, but for her a kid, earring in one ear, a tuft of hair hanging down the back of his neck, was still busy with the rag, but not as far off, six or eight feet, as he was before but right in front of Bittori. To force him to speak, she asked if they had machine-dispensed decaf. They did. The others picked up their conversations again. Bittori did not identify their faces. But that man with the white hair, could he by any chance be . . . ?

"I don't doubt for a second that all of them were thinking the same thing. That's Txato's wife. When I left, I really wanted to turn my face toward them and calmly announce from the door: I'm Bittori, is there some problem? Can't I be in my own hometown?"

Do not show bitterness. Do not cry in public. Look everyone in the eye, look straight into cameras. She promised herself that in the funeral parlor, with Txato in the box.

"What do I owe you?"

Without raising his eyes, the barman named a sum. Not wanting to dig around in her purse, Bittori paid him with a ten-peseta note. As she waited for her change, she shifted toward the angle in the L. There it was. What? The coin bank. On the front part, a sticker: *Dispersiorik ez.* Burning inside her was an irresistible desire that ran down her arm to the elbow, then to the hand, then to her pinky. Don't let them see me, don't let them see me. On the sly, she extended her finger until her nail was grazing the lower part of the bank. Nothing, not even half a second, because she instantly pulled back her finger as if she'd touched fire.

"Don't ask me to explain it because I don't understand it myself. I got carried away."

She walked out to the street. Blue sky, cars. Before she reached the corner, she saw her.

"At first I didn't recognize her."

And when she finally realized who it was, Jesus, Mary, and Joseph! She stood there transfixed by the sight and also by a kind of sorrow. I mean paralyzed, totally paralyzed. They went their way, and Bittori was unable to move. Nailed to the ground. But it's . . .

"Let me tell you."

Bittori walked up the sunny side of the street, across from which walked a tiny little lady with features like those of the Andes Indians. From Peru or someplace like that. That's it, that lady was pushing a wheelchair, and in it was seated a woman with her head slightly falling over one shoulder and one hand clenched like those people who can't open them. The other hand, though, she could move it.

"Then I realized she was waving to me. In any case, she was shaking her hand near her chest, as if saying hello to me. And she was looking at me, but not directly. Let me see if I can explain it to you. With her head over to one side and a big smile, a violent smile, with a bit of saliva in one corner of her lips and her eyes squinting.

At first sight unrecognizable, I swear. It looked as if she were suffering a convulsion, understand? Okay then, it was Arantxa. She's paralyzed. Don't ask me what happened to her. I didn't have the nerve to cross the street and ask."

She wasn't sure if Arantxa was waving hello or if she was signaling her to come close. Her caretaker was too busy pushing to notice. So she wheeled her down the street in no particular hurry, and Bittori, feeling it all deeply, was unable to move until they disappeared.

"So, Txato, now I've told you. And what do you want me to say? I felt sorry. Arantxa for me was always the best person in that family. When she was a little girl, I liked her. The most sensible and normal of all of them, and the only one, as I told you before, who took pity on me and our children."

Having picked up the square of plastic and the handkerchief, Bittori made her way to the cemetery's exit. She strolled around, now this way, now that, always on the lookout so she wouldn't run into anyone. Near the end of the path, in the hollow between two graves, she saw a female pigeon and a male pigeon all puffed up to court her. Hey! She scared off the birds, stamping hard on the ground.

16

Sunday Mass

It's the same old church bell, but on Sundays, at first light, it doesn't sound the way it usually does. The peals follow on one another calmly, lazily, as if announcing: neighbors, *clang*, it's eight a.m., *clang*; as far as I'm concerned, *clang*, you can stay in bed, *clang*.

By then Joxian's been pedaling for three-quarters of an hour along country roads. Where did he say he was going? What difference does it make? For sure it's to a bar in the heart of Guipúzcoa where they serve fried eggs with ham. All the circuits of the cyclotourism club end with a plate of fried eggs and ham and then back home.

So it's eight a.m. The sound of the alarm coincided with one of the last peals of the bell, and Miren, without combing her hair, in her nightie, opened the door for Celeste, who had the courtesy to bring her (and it wasn't the first time) half a loaf of fresh bread for breakfast.

"Sweetie, you shouldn't have bothered."

If there are two of them, it's easier to get Arantxa out of bed. Miren takes charge of the head and the trunk. First, of course, when she raises the shade, she bestows on her daughter a few morning words of tenderness in Basque: *egun on, polita,* and things like that. Celeste repeats *egun on* in an Andean accent and takes hold of the legs.

The instant they begin to move her, Miren starts giving orders: hold on, pull, lift, raise, lower, not to exercise power or to be authoritarian. Why, then? Because she's afraid Arantxa will fall, and even though it's never happened, she worries. Her eyes widen, she gets nervous, and often Celeste has no choice but to calm her down.

"Take it easy, Miren. Now we can raise her up."

As usual, they seat her in the wheelchair. Then Celeste went before the mother and daughter, opening doors. Supported by the two women, Arantxa stands up. She's not lacking strength in her legs. What is the problem? She has a stiffened foot. Dr. Ulacia predicted that within two or three years, Arantxa, either using a cane or supported by another person, would be able to take a few steps. She emphatically refuses to reject the hope of seeing her walk someday inside the house.

They sat her on the toilet seat; immediately after, on her special chair, under the shower. And Celeste took charge of soaping and rinsing her, because she's better at it and because she's more patient, and because she's, how to say it?, gentler, something Miren wasn't completely aware of until Arantxa, one day, told her, using her iPad: "I want Celeste to shower me from now on."

"Why?"

She typed again: "Because you're too rough."

She has no voice. Sometimes you can guess from the quivering of her lips that she's trying, pushing but always in the end frustrated when her attempts at language fail. There is an unbridgeable gap between the strain of her facial muscles and actually emitting comprehensible sounds. Even so, it's essential to lavish praise to stimulate Arantxa. That's what the physiotherapist advises, that's what the neurologist, the director of Rehabilitation Services, and the speech therapist advise:

"Miren, praise her. Praise her constantly. Praise any attempt Arantxa makes to speak or move on her own."

Between Miren (hold her tight, move over there, careful now) and Celeste they dried and dressed her, and Celeste combed her hair while Miren set about preparing breakfast. It's easy to comb her hair because it's short. They cut it off without her consent in the hospital. What resistance was she going to put up in those days when the only part of her body she could move was her eyelids?

Celeste left, the bell rang out ten, then eleven.

"Okay, let's go to mass."

Arantxa quickly pulls out her iPad. Her mother: "No, I already know what you're going to tell me."

And sure enough she puts it in writing: "I'm an atheist."

"Let's not get started with that again. If you don't want to, you don't have to pray. But don't think that you're going to stay here alone or that I'm going to miss Sunday mass because of one of your whims. You can go to perdition as well in church as at home."

She snatched away the iPad, because it's getting late, she said, and wheeled her rapidly down the street, the mother in a bad mood, the daughter in a bad mood, but Miren has a reason. If she doesn't get to the church early she may find her place, at the end of a pew, next to a column, taken. She puts Arantxa in front of the column, at her side; that way, the wheelchair gets in no one's way, she's got her daughter protected from drafts, and she can converse perfectly well, without craning her neck, with the statue of Ignatius of Loyola which is close by. Where? Halfway along the wall, resting on a corbel. To tell the truth, as a general rule, what the priest says matters very little to Miren, and besides, she knows the mass by heart. But speaking with Ignatius, making him promises, proposing deals, begging him, reproaching him (there are days when she tears him to shreds), is very important to her. She's got twice as much confidence in him as she does in Joxian.

In sum, what she will not under any circumstance do is to sit with Arantxa in the first rows of pews. Never, never, never. She still blushes thinking about that Sunday, how embarrassing. The first time she had no idea where to place the wheelchair. In the center aisle? Bad idea. So she moved farther to the front than anyone else, thinking that since no one would be walking there, the chair would get in no one's way. God, did she learn the hard way! Arantxa just out of the hospital, Miren harboring the illusion of a miracle. But Jesus took the daughter of Jairus by the hand and said, "Little girl, I say to you, get up." Something like that, but this girl was a paralytic, not dead. Not the least of the problems was that Don Serapio took it upon himself to speak into the microphone to greet Arantxa before mass. And then, during the sermon, he made her an example of our Lord God's infinite goodness. To Miren, those words did not seem improper. The church was fairly crowded, all people they knew, and a bit of consolation and encouragement and being singled out didn't hurt, right?, and by the way, maybe the unbelieving daughter might recover her faith.

Then came the moment for Holy Communion, and what does Don Serapio do? The man is a meddler. Well, with all solemnity he comes down the three steps that separate the altar from the pews and comes over to Arantxa full of benevolence, seriously, even he was carried away with emotion, and has her take communion. Jesus, Mary, and Joseph! But she hadn't made her confession. But she doesn't believe in God. Let's just see if, stubborn as she is, she spits out the host. And what if she chokes? Anyway, after mass, on the way home, Arantxa opened her mouth and there, stuck to her tongue, was the softened host. Okay. What to do then with the Body of Christ? Nothing. Miren carefully took the moist wafer and put it in her own mouth. She closed her eyes right there on the sidewalk, muttered a short prayer, and that was her second communion of the day. What else could she do?

She found her usual place unoccupied. Ignatius this, Ignatius that. Joxe Mari, the poor boy, so far away, and all he did was fight for Euskal Herria and you know it. The girl, well, you see the fix I'm in here. And the youngest doesn't visit or call. At her side, Arantxa either slept or pretended to sleep as a form of protest. I swear! Since she can't shout . . . And if people see her, so what? May the blessing of God Almighty, Father, Son, and Holy Spirit, descend upon you. The mass had gone by in a flash. She waited for people to leave the church. How slow some of them are, damn it. With the church empty, she got to the sacristy. And Arantxa? Well, it's no tragedy if she's alone for five minutes.

She got right to the point: "My nerves are shot, Father. I can't sleep a wink at night. I sense that she's come to make trouble, that's for sure, to destroy us. We're victims of the state and now we're victims of the victims. We're getting it from all sides."

Finally, she told him her request. That he speak with her, that he please find out what her intentions were in coming to the town every day, that he convince her not to leave San Sebastián.

The priest, a bit too familiar, put a hand on her shoulder and simultaneously gave her a blast of halitosis: "Don't worry, Miren. I'll take care of it."

17

A Little Walk

It's nice to have a son who, despite all his many and important concerns, sets aside for his mother the morning of a workday. Here he comes, handsome, even if his shoes don't match his outfit. Taste, I mean good taste in clothes, he just doesn't have it. Some people's sons become terrorists. Mine became a doctor. Why not say it when it's the truth? Forty-eight years old, good position, owns his own house, but still no wife or children. Alone, always alone. He doesn't even go in for travel like his sister. I wonder if he's happy, if he enjoys life.

Mother and son exchange a kiss standing next to the clocks in La Concha, where they agreed to meet. He suggested taking a seat in the coffee shop of the London Hotel. She wouldn't hear of it. Lock myself away in a restaurant with the fine weather we're having? Not a chance. Xabier looked around him as if to make sure his mother was right. And yes, the clear sky, the light breeze, and the agreeable autumn temperature were an invitation to take a little walk.

"What would you like to do?"

"Let's go over there."

Bittori jabbed her chin toward the Paseo de Miraconcha. She didn't wait for her son to agree but instead set out in that direction and Xabier immediately took his place at her side.

"How is it possible you still haven't found a woman? I can't figure it out. You're good-looking, you're in a prestige profession. What's missing? You don't need money. Women have to be flocking after you!"

"I don't turn my head to check."

"Listen here, and don't think I'm going to hit the ceiling. But might it be that you prefer men?"

"What I prefer is my work. Helping patients, curing the sick. things like that."

"You brush me off by being evasive."

"I'm no good for matrimony, *ama*. That's all there is to it. I'm no good for sculpture or rugby, either, but you don't bother to ask me anything about my relationship with activities like those."

She grabbed him by the arm. A mother showing off her son along Miraconcha. On the left, intense traffic, bicyclists going in both directions, people walking and people wearing sports gear out jogging. On the right, the bay, the sea, the familiar aquatic festival of blue and green tones that cheers the eye, with modest surf, waves, small boats, and the marine horizon in the distance.

The previous evening they'd talked by telephone, so Bittori knew that Xabier had carried out an investigation and was bringing her the results, though she didn't know what they were. Well, let him talk; she couldn't stand the suspense.

"I have to tell you before anything that this is the last time I'll be doing this. Giving out confidential information about patients could cost me my job. This time I could count on a woman I trust who was the one who gave me the report. But even so, you've got to tread lightly when you do things like this."

His mother: get to the point and tell me what I asked you to find out. They continued walking (the sea, the white railing, Mount Igueldo in the background), and he begins his story, saying:

"Two years ago, Arantxa had a stroke. Don't ask me what the circumstances were because I couldn't find out anything about them. In the report it states that she was initially admitted to the ICU in a hospital in Palma de Mallorca, so we can assume she was on vacation there when she had the attack. And the problem, I can say with real certainty, was extremely serious. Arantxa suffered what we call locked-in syndrome because of the occlusion of the basilar artery."

"I see you're a doctor."

"Okay, calm down, I'll explain it all. All the blood that goes to the nervous system flows through that artery. You could say that it controls the zone where all the paths that lead to the spinal medulla converge. Damage in that area can deprive the body of all movement.

That's what happened to her, see? Her mind becomes the prisoner of a paralyzed body. And though she can hear and understand, she cannot react. She can only move her eyes and her eyelids."

She's the last person in that family Bittori would wish to suffer anything bad. One day she was walking along the street. Was she already married to the Rentería boy? Yes, but she still had no children. Txato wasn't taking part any longer in the cyclotourism stages and had stopped playing cards with his friends in the Pagoeta, which really pained the poor guy, even if he would say "Bah, there are worse things."

Graffiti had appeared on the walls. One of the many: TXATO TXI-BATO, Txato the snitch. Though it rhymed, the intent was to defame and cause fear. Somebody does one thing, someone else does something else, and when the catastrophe that they've all caused hits, none of them feels responsible because, after all, I just painted, I just revealed where he lived, I just said a few words to him, sure, offensive words, but only words, fleeting sounds. From one day to the next, many people in the town began to ignore him. And it wasn't only that they didn't say hello. That was nothing. They refused even to look at him. Lifelong friends, neighbors, even some children. What could innocent kids know? But of course they listen to the conversations of their parents. She ran into Arantxa on the street. And she didn't bother to whisper. Good and loud she said it. Anyone nearby would have heard her: "What's being done to you is a dirty trick, and I don't go along with it."

She said only that. She didn't wait for an answer. She didn't kiss her on the cheek as she did in the past. But she gave her a pat of solidarity on her shoulder before going on her way. More or less that's what she said. Maybe a few words were different, because memory slips sometimes. But in any case she made that gracious gesture Bittori won't forget. Me forget? Dead first.

"She was in serious condition when she went into the Palma hospital, and they had to do a tracheotomy, put her on a respirator, and carry out other procedures I don't have to describe because I don't think you'd be interested in knowing them. What you do have to know is that in those instants, Arantxa couldn't breathe or speak or, of course, feed herself. In sum, her life depends completely on external aid."

They killed Txato one rainy afternoon, a few yards from the entryway to his house. And the priest, that smartass, insisted to Bittori that the funeral take place in San Sebastián. Why? It's that if we do it there, more people will come. And she: "No way, we're from this town, we were baptized in this town, we were married in this town, and it was in this town my husband was murdered."

The priest gave in. He officiated at the funeral. The bells pealed the death knell. There were few people from the neighborhood in the church, a couple of politicians of the constitutionalist splinter, some relatives who came deliberately, and little more. Company employees? Not a one. In the homily, not a word about the attack. A tragic event that moves all of us. She didn't see Arantxa, but Xabier says she was in the rear pews with her husband. They did not come to her to express their sympathy, but they were there, unlike certain others. And Bittori will not forget that, either.

Meanwhile, mother and son reached the Antiguo tunnel—and what should we do now? They decided to go back. Xabier in an explicative mood, though he simplified his medical jargon. Bittori, pensive, stared fixedly beyond the city, the mountains, and the far, scattered clouds, images she'd never seen that she was seeing now for the first time: Arantxa covered in tubes, Arantxa saying yes or no exclusively through her eyelids. They deserved it. Well, not that, not her, definitely not her.

"*Ama*, I don't think you're listening."

"Will you be having dinner at home?"

"I can't."

"Got a date? What's the name of the lucky girl?"

"Her name is medicine."

The best-case scenario according to Xabier: Arantxa could someday walk around in the house, either using a cane or helped by other people. She can eat on her own, but not without supervision as she ingests liquids or solids, and it's not impossible that in the future she may phonate.

"May what?"

"Speak."

Aside from those objectives, and no matter how much effort she puts into her rehabilitation (and according to what I've been told she works really hard at it), Xabier did not believe she would ever have what we would call a normal life.

And just when they were about to separate at the clocks in La Concha:

"Weren't you going to give me the results of my blood tests?"

"Oh, good thing you reminded me. I almost forgot. There are some figures I don't like, so I've asked Arruabarrena to check the tests. No hurry, okay? A routine thing. Just to be sure, you know. Besides, you're as solid as an oak tree."

They kissed and said goodbye. Bicycles, prams, urban sparrows all passed by.

"And this Arruabarrena, who's he?"

"A friend, and one of the best specialists we have."

She watched him walk away. She knew, intuited, that after taking a few steps he'd turn around. Out of curiosity, out of habit, to check on her? And he did. Bittori, who hadn't moved, in a soft voice: "He's an oncologist, right?"

Xabier nodded yes. He waved his hand as if to brush off any dramatics in the situation. He went off between the rows of tamarisk trees, a bit stooped in the shoulders, perhaps because he's tall and used to looking down when he talks to people. It seems a lie that a man of his caliber could be a bachelor. Could it be because he dresses in such poor taste?

18

An Island Vacation

No, these things happen because they have to happen or, as her mother would say, because God or Saint Ignatius, representing God, wanted it that way. What bad luck, why me? Et cetera. She repeated again and again and again the litany of complaints recited by all those singled out for adversity (ha, ha, ha, don't be such a cynic, girl). And she once wrote on her iPad to Gorka, her sad—or simply shocked?—little brother, that since he was a writer maybe he'd like to write her story. An expression of alarm came into Gorka's eyes, and he hastily responded no, that he only wrote books for children. Arantxa again turned the screen toward him: "Someday I'll write it, telling everything." That wasn't the first time she announced—was it a threat?—that intention.

Whenever she did, Miren would get furious.

"What are you going to write when you can't even brush your teeth on your own? And what for? To tell the entire town the disasters that have fallen on our house?"

She stared at them (in the kitchen, Sunday, roast chicken) from her wheelchair, more lucid (don't be so smug, girl) than all of them put together. What a gullible family! Her father very aged, wrinkled with sorrow, an oil stain on his shirtfront, not understanding for twenty years now anything of what was going on around him. Her brother Gorka, who lives—hidden?— in Bilbao and for long periods of time gives no sign of life. The other absent brother who isn't there but comes up constantly in conversation: the strongman of the family rotting away in jail, for how many years now?, I can't even remember. And *ama*, who possesses, approximately, the same sensibility and empathy as an exhaust pipe; but she cooks well, truth be told. And she looked at her father and mother busy chewing, silent, their faces bent over their respective plates and a flood of bitterness, or was it rancor?, began rising within her, from her chest to her throat (control yourself, girl) and she closed her eyes and was once again driving the rented car along the service road among the pines a few miles outside of Palma.

They vacationed at Cala Millor. Who? The mother and the daughter. Two weeks in August in a cheap hotel with no view of the sea, but not at all far from the beach. Endika, seventeen then, did not want to go with them. No, no, no. The girl had no real desire, either, but Arantxa convinced her with the promise of fun, a bit of sentimental blackmail, and the purchase of a camera even though her grades were terrible. The important thing for Arantxa was to lose sight of Guillermo. If it were up to her alone, she would have gone anywhere, but the idea of leaving the children to the tender mercies of their father was unconscionable. Their marriage? Bah, you really couldn't call that a marriage. One fight led to the next. Day after day of not speaking to each other, exchanging looks of contempt, hatred, disgust, when there was no way out of looking at each other. But the children. But the economic ties. But the flat they'd bought together. And their relatives, what would they say? Arantxa decided she would never give in, but deep down I felt tremendous insecurity, seriously, and he was going out with some woman without bothering to hide it.

"You refuse to screw. Well, I've got to do something with my dick."

That was his style. Right in front of the kids. And if not right in front, close enough so that they could hear the curses, the reproaches, the shouts.

Ainhoa, fifteen years old:

"Me, *ama*, I'd rather stay here with my friends."

"I'm asking you, please."

The two women went alone. Guillermo drove them to the airport. Ainhoa asked him to put on some music, which he did at full volume. So he wouldn't have to talk, I suppose. He just left the bags on the ground, quickly kissed his daughter, said have a nice flight, whether to them or to the clouds it wasn't clear, because he spoke staring into space like a saint in a holy picture, and immediately drove back. He didn't even bother to help them carry their suitcases to the check-in.

Me, I'm taking care of myself, heading for the dirty trick awaiting me among some Mallorca pines, exactly at the moment when I was enjoying a few days of relaxation without tears, rage, fights; in the company of my daughter, the sun, the salt water, and some erotic adventures with a foreigner staying at the same hotel. More than anything, to feel those old tickles again and recover from the humiliations of Guillermo, who played the Casanova, the stallion, when really he was nothing more than a barely vibrating pig in bed.

They passed Manacor, left other towns behind. Symptoms? Not a one. She could imagine the car they'd rented in her memory as, without much appetite, she chewed the chicken her mother had cut into small pieces for her; a moment of happiness. She, driving. Ainhoa wearing sunglasses in the passenger seat exchanging text messages in her bad English (if you'd only listen to me and study) with a German boy she'd met on the beach and fallen madly in love with. How beautiful love is at that age. And the pines in the distance, the blue morning sky, all prepared to burst the bubble.

She can't feel her legs. And she manages, not knowing how, to stop the car in the middle of the highway, unless it was the car that stopped on its own, because at that point there was a bit of a hill, and Arantxa, as soon as she could, put on the hand brake, since she could still move her hands, as well as think and speak and see and breathe and, in reality, nothing hurt.

"*Ama*, what are you doing? Why are you stopping?"

"Get out and ask for help. Something's happening to me."

Friday. What bad luck, my children, why did this have to happen to me? She said that to herself in the ambulance. One of the emergency staff was asking her questions. To keep her conscious? She answered distractedly. Almost all the space in her mind was taken up by her children, her job as a saleswoman, her future, but above all her children, still so young, what would become of them without me? Saturday, Sunday, Arantxa calmer and calmer, convinced that this is nothing more than a scare. Ainhoa, hysterical, behaving badly. How? First, she did not want to take a room in a hotel in Palma or go back to the hotel in Cala Millor; second, that the island now seemed like a prison to her and she wanted to go home on the first plane. They let her sleep in the hospital on a chair next to her mother. Guillermo in part or parts unknown. Endika, who knew where he was? Not at home, of course. I hope he's not getting into trouble. And finally, on Monday, the doctor talked about releasing her the next day, in a self-confident voice he suggested that Arantxa have an exhaustive battery of tests in her hometown. So she spoke by telephone with her mother and then with Guillermo, that there was no need for them to come to Mallorca to get her, that she'd return with Ainhoa as planned. She even decided to spend the five days she had left of her vacation in Cala Millor. Ainhoa:

"I'm bored here."

"What about the German boy? Aren't you going to say goodbye to him?"

The German boy, suddenly, annoyed the hell out of her.

"Don't talk like that, people can hear you."

An hour and a half later, at nightfall, Arantxa was covered with tubes in the ICU. The second stroke had just hit her, the strong one, accompanied by unbearable pains. She heard everything. The doctor, the nurses. And she couldn't answer and suffered a great deal of anguish, my God, what a moment, she was horrified to think they might put her in a coffin and bury her alive.

"Listen, honey, you're not eating, why?"

She opened her eyes. She seemed surprised, even astonished to see her mother opposite her, her father to the left with greasy lips, tearing into a chicken thigh.

19
DISCREPANCY

But how hot it is in this land. Miren thought the sea cooled the islands.

"No, *amona*."

"It's the same heat as when I visit *osaba* Joxe Mari."

The flight? A disaster. She landed in Palma five and a half hours late after an interminable wait in the Bilbao airport. She withstood the thirst, withstood it for a long time, she went on withstanding it the best she could, but finally she had to give in and make an unforeseen purchase. She drank a small bottle of still mineral water because even though the budget didn't allow for luxuries, she didn't feel like drinking from the faucet in the bathroom. I'd get sick for sure. She deluded herself thinking she could satisfy her thirst with what they'd serve on the plane, but time went by (one hour, another . . .) and she felt as if a handful of sand was blocking her throat. So there was no way out: she went to the bar and brusquely asked for her modest drink.

What was going on? Well, all planes except hers were taking off. Between the loudspeakers' flight announcements (to Munich, Paris, Málaga, boarding at gate . . .) came emissions every two seconds about keeping your possessions in sight at all times.

So she asked travelers here and there who, like her, were waiting near the boarding gate. Listen, excuse me. And some were foreigners who were as in the dark as she was, so she couldn't figure out how to find out why, come on now, because if the plane is parked at the loading gate with our baggage in it, why they won't let us board.

And what with my daughter so far away in the hospital. Now she wasn't looking at her watch with the nervousness of before but with the start of resignation and slow rage, and she decided (heat, sweat) to go upstairs to slake her thirst. Which she did, first removing the slice of lemon, which she enjoyed, and finally she chewed up the white part because she was also feeling hunger pangs.

Leaving the bar, she saw two members of the Guardia Civil coming toward her. She stared at their uniforms, not their faces. And a brusque qualm along with an invincible repugnance impelled her to stop next to the balustrade. Near to them, she discovered they were two young officers, a man and a woman. And since they were amused in their conversation, she took a good look at them. What should I do? These *txakurras* know for sure. Close now, she was upset by the woman's natural smile and the blond ponytail poking out underneath her cap. She looked around. Let's see if there's anyone here from the town, in which case I'm in trouble. And she dared: excuse me. She asked the woman. She doesn't look like a torturer. And the officer, in a cordial tone that also disconcerted Miren, said that the airport at Palma de Mallorca was closed.

"What do you mean, closed?"

The man answered:

"Yes, ma'am. It's because two of our comrades were attacked. But don't worry. It's probably just a provisional measure and you'll be able to travel."

"Oh, okay, okay."

And she did get to Palma. The city below, transformed into luminous dots, the sea how black it is, and in the distance, a final remnant of the purplish glow of the sunset. Too late to visit Arantxa in the hospital. Ainhoa was waiting for her at the airport as they'd agreed.

"Okay, tell me."

"*Ama* is in serious condition, with tubes all over her."

"Your *aita* could have come in my place. This little joke is going to cost me a fortune."

"He said he'll come on Monday and that he'll take me home the next day."

"Oh, so he doesn't intend to stay? What nerve. All the work and all the expense for me."

"*Amona*, I don't like it when you say bad things about my *aita*."

A nurse, Carme, very sweet, helped Ainhoa during the first days, until Miren arrived. Consoling her, being kind to her, she said she wasn't to worry, that she would help her. And she drove her to get the luggage from the hotel in Cala Millor. Along the way, explanations about her mother's condition and words of encouragement.

"You'll have to love her a lot."

She invited her into her home in Palmanova, where she lived with her two small children and a husband who's so fat, he must have weighed at least three hundred pounds. Once upon a time he must have been handsome with his blue eyes. He was from Germany, his face was a little red (okay, really red), and when he spoke to me you could hear his accent. When they spoke to their children, he spoke German and she spoke that Basque they speak in Mallorca.

Once Miren confirmed the date of her arrival at Palma, Carme reserved a room for her and Ainhoa with two beds in a boardinghouse, far from the tourist zones, far from the hospital as well, but what can you do? She followed the instructions Miren gave her over the telephone.

"Listen, it can't cost too much, because we aren't rich."

"I'll do what I can."

Did she? Above and beyond. Room without breakfast, without views of the sea, next to a noisy highway, far from the center of town, but cheap, which is what Miren wanted, since she thought she was in for a long stay. She nervously calculated the expense. And how are we going to get Arantxa home with an ocean to cross? Ignatius, get me out of this predicament, please, I beg you. What about Guillermo? Why didn't he take care of things, he's her husband after all. No, he's got to work. No, it's that his boss. No, it's that in a few days, I can't . . . Excuses.

Ainhoa told Miren about the terrorist attack that took place right near Carme's apartment and how the whole building shook. In the living room, a picture had fallen off the wall. The glass broke, along with a lamp below the picture, and Carme's fat husband started ranting and raving in his own language, and the children were crying, frightened by the blast and, Ainhoa thought, by their father's shouting. Carme and Ainhoa had just returned from the hospital when the explosion went off a few blocks away. Where? The radio told them it blew up right outside the Guardia Civil barracks. Immediately, the sirens began to howl and there was a strange smell in the air.

"Know what, *amona*? Yesterday, at exactly that time, I passed by that street with Carme in her car. The bomb could have blown the two of us up."

"Don't shout, there are people here."

Ainhoa, her eyes wide, got carried away by her enthusiasm.

"And a neighbor lady told us that the firemen had to pull body parts down from a tree."

"Enough, enough, we're eating."

The two had walked into a bar not far from the boardinghouse to eat some snacks.

"Try to understand that this mess with your mother is going to cost me a ton of money. So I've got to be very careful about how much I spend. Tomorrow we'll buy food in some supermarket and we'll eat it in the room even if it's cold. So we won't die of hunger, okay?"

Ainhoa, still immersed in her own thoughts: "I don't like the fact that they kill people. We're far away from Euskal Herria. Why are the people here guilty for what happens there?"

"Listen, did we come here to eat or what?"

"The bomb could have blown Carme and me up."

"That doesn't happen, because they're really careful when they set off an explosion. What do you think, that they just blow anyone up? Did you ever hear of an explosion at a school or a soccer field full of people? The bombs are to defend the rights of our people, and they use them against the enemy. The same ones who tortured *osaba* Joxe Mari and are still torturing him in jail. If you don't understand that, then I don't see what you can understand."

Miren stared directly at her granddaughter. Ainhoa looked carefully to the right and carefully to the left, but not at the eyes of her grandmother. They were sitting at the table in a corner, and the girl, fifteen years old, was grudgingly nibbling at her snack.

"My *aita,* too, doesn't like the killing."

"It's your *aita* who's put these ideas in your head."

"I don't know anything about ideas, *amona.* The only thing I'm saying is that I don't like all the killing."

"They kill and they are killed. That's how wars work. I don't like wars, either, but what do you want? That they should go on pound-ing the Basque people until eternity?"

"Good people don't kill."

"Sure, that's something else Guillermo told you."

"That's something I say on my own."

"When you're grown up, you'll understand. Come on, finish up and let's go, I've had a busy enough day without having to put up with your nonsense."

Then Ainhoa, as if talking to herself, said/whispered, her voice cut off by an attack of tears, that she wasn't hungry anymore and left the rest of her snack, more than half, on her plate. Miren, her face stern, also didn't finish off her own.

20

PREMATURE MOURNING

Saturday morning. Ainhoa suffered a big letdown. Big? No: enormous. But it wasn't the first: it began when her grandmother, with whom she didn't get along, arrived. Guillermo: "Who can get along with a woman made of marble?"

The Saturday letdown hurt Ainhoa more than a slap in the face. Before they left for the hospital, she asked her *amona* to buy her a phone card for her cell. Miren made a sullen face when she heard the word "buy." Later: it's getting late, where do you buy things like that, how much does it cost? And no sooner had the girl, in her sweetest voice, mentioned the price than Miren said no, no, and no, and she went on to enumerate all her expenses.

"If it's just to pass the time chatting with your girlfriends, you can wait, because you're going on Tuesday. How lucky you are! I'll be stuck here taking care of your mother."

"*Ama* for sure would have bought me the card."

"But I'm not your *ama*."

Miren went on talking and complaining and never stopped complaining, while Ainhoa, resentful, looked any which way, at the other passengers in the bus, the houses, the pedestrians, at anything but her grandmother's face, ostentatiously refusing to speak to her.

Talking from the hospital, alone, she told her father, *aita*, this is what's going on, I won't be able to call you, et cetera. He: "Hang on until Monday."

And they agreed to meet that day at a certain hour in the reception area of the hotel where Guillermo had reserved a room. Long in advance, Ainhoa was there waiting for him, very put together, with all her belongings in a suitcase, since the last thing on earth she wanted was to go back to the boardinghouse.

And Miren, what did she say? What could she say? Well, that the father and the daughter had pulled off a good deal. When she got back to the boardinghouse at about eight and discovered that her granddaughter's things weren't in the closet, she understood what had happened. Well, then, so much the better. More room for me and less expense.

Guillermo got out of his taxi at the hotel entrance. The happy girl ran out to hug him. Questions, answers, rapid words, and at the end another hug, as if he were saying: stay calm, I'm here with you now, everything will be okay now; she: it's been horrible, thank God you're here. They barely spoke about Arantxa. Every single day, Guillermo called to get information about her condition, which contradicted Miren's belief that he was heartless; that his wife was of no interest to him. The only question he asked the girl was whether there had been any changes, and Ainhoa said no, that *ama* was still covered with tubes, but: "I think she'll never move again."

They went up to the room, Guillermo showered, and then father and daughter strolled through the center of Palma. They went into one of the large stores, and Ainhoa bought the card for her cell, and before turning in, they had dinner on the terrace of a restaurant with views of the port.

"I'm fed up with bananas and snacks."

In the sunset, the masts of the boats became silhouettes. There was a light breeze, which made it exceedingly pleasant to be there. Smiling suntanned faces everywhere, elegant ladies, and sparrows on the ground hoping for some edible charity. Ainhoa asked the waiter for a second and soon a third Coca-Cola in order, as she put it, to make up for those her grandmother had refused her on the previous days.

"*Aita*, I'd rather not go to the hospital tomorrow. I just don't want to see *amona*. You go, and I'll wait for you in the hotel, and then, in peace, we can take the afternoon plane. After all, *ama* won't know anything about it."

But there was no such flight. What? A change of plans. The girl didn't understand. Guillermo was visiting Mallorca for the first time, and, of course, wanted to get something out of it. His boss had let him take off until Thursday.

"Wow, *aita*."

Gestures that were requests for calm.

"Tomorrow I'll go to the hospital by myself. I'm sure one of the doctors will explain to me what kind of future your *ama* faces. It doesn't matter to me if I run into *amona*. But if I do see her and if it's possible, which I doubt, to have a rational conversation with her, I'll explain to her the future that awaits me and which you and Endika already know about. When the visit's over, I'll come back to pick you up, and then we'll have two days to do whatever we like. We can explore the island, go for a sail. Whatever you like. Only fun, I promise. But let's keep *amona* in the dark because I don't want her spoiling our lives."

Tubes, respirator, probes, machines, and, in the bed, the immobile body, her eyes open. Guillermo, wearing a surgical gown, plastic booties, craned his neck to get his face into Arantxa's visual field. Her reaction? Nothing. No reaction again when he kissed her cheek. Only a slight blinking. Her eyelids didn't manage to close completely. In a low voice (he'd been given instructions as to how he should speak), he told her he'd come to take care of Ainhoa, but it was as if he were speaking to a statue. He also said he was very sorry about what had happened to her. Because you just never know, and the walls have ears, and of course she was awake.

"Do you hear me?"

Nothing. To experiment, he slowly pulled his face back and, yes, she followed him a little, not very much, with her eyes. Then, not discounting the possibility Arantxa could hear him, he thanked her for their years together, for the children they shared and the good times; he asked forgiveness for the bad times and began to shower her with whispered and heartfelt expressions of affection when his mother-in-law burst in, brows furrowed in anger. This despite the fact that hospital regulations stated that visitors were only allowed in the room one at a time during visiting hours, but the nurses obviously hadn't seen her.

Miren started up with the reproaches. The first because of his black shirt. He was in premature mourning. The fact is that he, gray slacks, black loafers, decided to wear dark clothing after his daughter informed him over the telephone days before that a priest had administered last rites to *ama*. And he, frankly, thought Arantxa could die at any moment. So with no bad faith, he packed dark clothing in his suitcase. Besides, what did he know, since he always let Arantxa dress him—she always bought his clothes and told him, every day, what he should wear.

The issue mattered so little to Guillermo that he didn't even bother to defend himself from his mother-in-law's verbal assault. God, what a harpy. He wouldn't even look at her. But the old girl kept on swinging, breaking the rule about speaking in a low voice. And the moment came when the accusations turned to money. At that point, Guillermo, enough is enough, decided to stand up to her. And he said this, and he said that, calmly, without shouting, without obscenities. And also to put a finish to it all:

"My definitive separation from Arantxa has nothing to do with what's happened. We settled all that long ago. Our children know all about it and accept it. So there's no need to take it out on me or say only you carry the load. And how about some respect, if not for me, at least for your daughter, a person I'd never call a load. Unlike you."

He tossed her two fifty-euro notes. "Take this to cover any expenses my daughter may have cost you."

And he walked out.

21

The Best of All of Them

He remembered his promise that if he found out any new information he would tell her immediately. So, during a break at work, he closed the door to his office and called her.

On the desk: a computer, papers, this, that, and the other, and a photograph in a silver frame. His father. The dead man's gaze was direct, clean, good-natured, with some slight evidence of menace in the brows: I forbid you to be unjust. The face of a hardworking and efficient man, of few but well-defined ideas and an infallible business sense.

His mother didn't answer. Might she be in the village? He let the phone ring a good while. Fourteen, fifteen rings. If necessary, he would let the phone ring all day, until his mother understood that this was no wrong number and no survey being carried out by the telephone company, that this wasn't the con man of the day trying to sell her paradise in the form of an advantageous (for whom?) contract, but him, come on now, I know you're there. Sixteen rings. He went along counting them at the same time he made a tiny check on the pile of notes, and then his mother answered.

A suspicious whisper:

"Yes?"

"It's me."

"Something wrong?"

He wondered if she recalled Ramón.

"Which Ramón?"

"Ramón Lasa."

"The guy who drove the ambulance?"

"He's still driving it."

So this Ramón Lasa is a peace-loving man, nationalistic, but not mixed up in terrorist activities, though he no longer lives in the village he still goes there a lot to visit his family and because he's still a member of the local gastronomic society. Xabier ran into him in the hospital cafeteria. For sure he knows something. And even if he doesn't, no big deal. To sound him out, he went over to him and asked out of the blue, as if when he spotted him standing at the counter stirring his coffee, his curiosity suddenly got the better of him.

"Do you remember Arantxa?"

"Of course, the poor thing. She comes in for therapy during the afternoon. I've driven her myself more than once."

To his mother:

"So he wouldn't suspect I'm investigating, I told him that I'd just learned that Arantxa had a stroke and I included some details: that it was in Mallorca, that it happened in the summer of 2009, you see what I mean. Nothing he didn't already know. How awful, right? Which is true, because frankly I'm sorry about it, because of all the members of that family she was the best."

"The best? The only good one."

"What I wanted to do was to squeeze some information out of Ramón without arousing suspicion."

"Okay, get to the point. What did you get out of him?"

Well, a few details that in the village were secrets for no one. First of all: the minute she ended up the way she ended up, her husband took off. The village verdict expressed by Ramón Lasa: he's a hopeless bastard.

"The bit about 'hopeless' he didn't say. You can believe me that it was easy to guess from the emphasis he put on the word 'bastard.' He told me—you won't believe this—that the guy has custody of the children. Just the daughter, because the son's about twenty now."

"Does she live with her father?"

"That I didn't ask."

"Silly boy."

Alberto (it's really Guillermo, but I didn't say anything so I wouldn't reveal that I know more than I'm showing) lives with another woman. Married or not, Ramón couldn't be sure, because he has no idea if he divorced Arantxa. In any case, he's never in the village. The children turn up to visit their mother.

And he added:

"Are you really interested in finding out if they were divorced? My mother will know for sure. If you want I can call her. She's awake by now."

"No, don't bother. It's just that I found out a while ago what happened to poor Arantxa, and I was just stunned."

There was more. This Alberto (I know, I know, Guillermo for God's sake) sold his apartment in Rentería and gave Arantxa her share. Also that a collection was taken up in the town with little banks in bars and shops, and with a raffle, and a benefit soccer match and Ramón doesn't know what else, but the fact is that lots of people contributed to pay the bill for transporting Arantxa from the hospital in Mallorca and for her being admitted to a specialty clinic in Cataluña.

Xabier looked straight into his father's eyes. Be fair, be honorable, be upright no matter what happens and no matter what people say. His mother fell silent.

"Are you listening to me?"

"Go on."

"Ramón didn't tell me the name of the clinic and I didn't ask him so I wouldn't reveal my true intentions. And I didn't have to. It wasn't hard to find out that Arantxa received treatment for eight months in the Institut Guttmann. Let me explain. It's a center in Badalona dedicated to the treatment and rehabilitation of patients with spinal-cord injuries and brain damage. The best money can buy. Of course, that involves expenses way above that family's economic level."

"As long as I've known them they've had money problems. And your father helped them out secretly, never expecting to be paid back. You see how they thanked us."

"The fact is that Arantxa received treatment in the Guttmann until she could finally return to the village, and now she gets rehabilitation with us."

"Anything else?"

"That's it. Did you go to Arruabarrena's office yesterday? What did he tell you?"

"Oh dear, I forgot. I'm so scatterbrained."

"It's important you be examined."

"Important or urgent?"

"Important."

They said goodbye, souls in pain, with cold affection, with affectionate coldness. And Xabier, wearing a white gown, stared at the dots scattered over the top sheet of the sheaf of notes. Then he looked into his father's eyes, don't be unjust, take care of *ama* for me, and beyond the desk, the white door that one afternoon, many years earlier, how many?, twelve or thirteen, opened suddenly and there she was, with a mournful look on her face, standing on the threshold.

"I've come to tell you that I'm the sister of a murderer."

He invited her to come in and sit down, but Arantxa declined his offer and just stood there.

"I imagine you're all having a hard time of it. I'm really sorry, Xabier. *Barkatu*."

On her lower lip a hint of sobbing. Perhaps that was why she spoke so quickly, so her tears wouldn't break her voice.

Arantxa, visibly nervous, spoke about solidarity, sorrow, shame, and at the same time brusquely placed on the desk a green-and-gold object that at first Xabier didn't recognize. Speechless, uncertain, he became suspicious. He even shifted his weight back in his chair, fearing that her act involved violence. It was a simple costume-jewelry bracelet, a child's toy.

"Your father bought it for me when I was a little girl, during a fair in the village. We were all walking in the street, you won't remember, and Txato bought one like it for Nerea. I was jealous. I wanted one, too. My mother said no. Then Txato, without saying a word to anyone, brought me to where this black guy was selling cheap jewelry and bought me this little bracelet. I came to give it back to you. I found it in the house and don't feel worthy of keeping it. I would give it to Bittori, but I don't have the nerve to look her in the eye."

Xabier, a distant man, within the fortress of his composure, made a gesture of approval and that was all. Not one word. Only that gesture, as if saying, fine. Or perhaps, I understand, it's okay, I don't have anything against you.

Days earlier, the National Criminal Court had sentenced Joxe Mari to 126 years in prison. Xabier found out from Nerea, who'd heard it on the radio. They weren't sure they should tell their mother. Xabier thought it rotten to keep it from her and called her, but Bittori already knew everything.

Later, the years passed. Xabier just doesn't feel like counting them and here he stays, in his office. He spoke a bit with his mother, he looked at the door, he opened one of the side drawers on his desk, where he keeps, he has no idea why, Arantxa's plastic bracelet along with an already-opened bottle of cognac.

22

MEMORIES IN A SPIDERWEB

Nobody knows this but me. What about her? Well, maybe she does remember the kiss, unless the damage to her brain has wiped her memory. Unless in those days she'd kissed so many boys that she'd lost count, or maybe she'd been so drunk that night that she wouldn't remember what she'd done and with whom.

And it's that these girls, forty-year-old frumps now, when they lost their heads with a guy, they just wouldn't stop, while the boys were naive when it came to erotic-love matters, at least I was. What Arantxa certainly doesn't know is that she was the first girl to kiss Xabier on the lips.

At the end of the workday, he'd gone into his office as usual, closing the door. On the desk, the photo of his father, the bottle of cognac. And with melancholy calmness, he made an inventory of the furniture, the ceiling, and the walls in search of memories.

He could have left by then, but at home, on a workday, there's horror. Even if he turns on all the lights, he's pursued by a kind of half-light that coats the room in a tenacious filth, weighing down his eyelids. Every blink, clang, a persecution, whose onslaught he can only escape with sleeping pills. He often fought his loneliness among strangers, frequenting social networks under a false identity. He exchanged salacious items. With whom? No idea. With Paula, for example, or Palomita, pseudonyms behind which might be hiding a dirty old man from the province of Soria or a teenage girl from Madrid still up this late at night. He got into forums to argue, to defend political positions that disgusted him, making sure to include as many spelling errors as possible. And he also sent sarcastic notes to comment on articles in the digital columns of this or that newspaper, just for the fun of offending, of playing behind the mask of a false identity in order to overcome his incurable timidity and to feel himself to be other than the solitary forty-eight-year-old man he actually was.

So quite often after work, Xabier preferred to stay in his office for an hour or two in case someone from the cleaning service or some member of the office staff walking down the hall saw light under his door and came in to chat with him for a while; but he also harbored the superstition that within that room his memories were more agreeable than all those he might dredge up at home. At the same time, he read journals related to his specialization, gave reports a quick look, or thought about old and, if possible, pleasant adventures from his past, until, under the influence of the cognac, he began to lose control of his thoughts. Having reached the threshold of drunkenness, he left the hospital until the next day.

But he still hasn't reached that moment and he's drinking slowly, savoring the cognac and staring calmly at the wall in search of some sequence or other from his past. In the corner where the walls meet the ceiling, there is a tiny spiderweb the cleaning people haven't noticed, a cobweb only perceptible to the attentive eye. Barely a shred of gray gauze abandoned by the inhabitant who wove it. And his memory is caught there, the memory of Arantxa's kiss. How old could I have been? Twenty, twenty-one? And she? Two years younger.

Things of no importance that happen in village festivals. People dance, drink, sweat, and everyone knows everyone else, and if you're young and a breast comes within reach, you grab it, and if some lips come too close, you kiss them. Nothing, crumbs devoured by oblivion, which does not keep Xabier's memory from suddenly recovering them as his gaze becomes ensnared in the spiderweb.

It's before he goes into the army, and he's studying medicine in Pamplona. He's got a reputation for being a drip, being formal, locked within himself; in sum, for being what he is, a serious guy, why not be frank? Friends? His usual gang, before successive marriages disbanded them. Not a drinker, doesn't smoke, is not a glutton, not a sportsman or rock climber, but despite all that well thought of because he's part of the human landscape in town, he went to high school with the other boys, he's Xabier, as much a part of the village as the balcony on the town hall or the linden trees in the square. You might say that the future is waiting for him with open arms. He's tall, good-looking, but even so has no sex life. Too rational, too timid? According to his friends, at least some of that must be the case.

He takes a sip of cognac without taking his eyes off the small spiderweb. Why is he smiling? It's just that it amuses him to evoke the episode. On one side of the plaza the Saint John's Day bonfire is blazing. The streets are packed with people. Children are running around, happy faces are shining, tongues are licking ice cream, uninhibited neighbors are shouting to one another from one side of the street to the other. Heat. But isn't he living in Pamplona? He is, but he came to spend a few days with his family (and to have his mother wash his clothes), to enjoy the old village and have a few drinks with his buddies. It's just at sunset when they're coming down the street and run into Arantxa and her girlfriends. Laughter, more bars, and she's talking to him, about what? He can barely understand her in all that revelry. And she goes on talking to him, he realizes that for sure, with her face very close to his. Her face, and despite mascara and lipstick he only sees the oldest daughter of his parents' best friends, almost a cousin he's seen as a little girl playing with Nerea a thousand times.

Which is why when, in the red half-light of the pub, she suddenly puts her hand on his fly, Xabier doesn't understand the meaning of the move. He thinks it's a joke, some mysterious mischief. And he stares as in a dream at the tiny remnant of the spiderweb and sees himself kissed, and powerfully, by someone he considers practically a member of his own family. Arantxa's anxious tongue seeks his own. It's as if he's paralyzed by shock, also by a growing terror, when he understands that this fusion of lips lasts longer than it should and seems to be getting serious, and some family member, some acquaintance, his own friends, Nerea, who's in the back of the bar, might at any given moment turn their eyes toward them. Arantxa, sweat and perfume, presses her body against Xabier's side. She growls into his ear, I'm soaking wet, and asks him if he wouldn't like to slip out with her and go somewhere where no one can see them. For Xabier, even now, an incestuous proposition.

Now, in his office, he starts laughing. How could you pass up an opportunity like that? The girl offering herself, the girl filled with desire, and desiring and willing. But no, because of Pamplona, the career. He felt embarrassed, wouldn't dare, was guided in the secrecy of his student room by masturbatory laws that led just as directly to pollution but without the complications of having a girlfriend. And he looks at the spiderweb and laughs. And he looks at his father's tranquil brow and laughs. And he takes another swig from the cognac bottle and laughs. He laughs without knowing why, because in reality he feels dirty, slimy, moldy with sadness. Be just, be upright. Yes, *aita*. He notes that he's reached the point where if he drinks one more drop he'll have to leave the car in the lot and take a taxi. So he puts the bottle back in the drawer, damn the whore, why didn't I screw her? Answer: because you are an asshole. His father, from the photo, and Xabier gets insolent: you shut up. It would definitively be better to call a cab.

23

Invisible Rope

He thought: it's only five minutes. I'll go down and come back. He'd previously found out when she'd be arriving and when he was just about to enter the corridor that led to the physiotherapy room, Itziar Ulacia called to him from behind. Dr. Ulacia was alarmed, waving her arms, as if to stop him. They know each other, and spoke familiarly.

"Let me warn you that her caregiver isn't with her today. Her mother is. You'll see."

Xabier thanked her and retraced his steps.

The next day, at about the same time, Dr. Ulacia called him on his cell. That if he wanted to see Arantxa he could go downstairs perfectly well, because this time she'd come with Celeste.

"Who's that?"

"The Ecuadorian woman who takes care of her."

This time, Xabier wasn't as determined as he was the day before. Do I go or not? On the one hand, his mother traveled to the village every day, got off the bus at a downtown street, walked into the shops; in a word, she showed herself. And now I take advantage of these physical-therapy sessions to approach the daughter. She'll tell about it on the iPad at home. What would her parents think? They're always going to suspect we've elaborated a plan to get some kind of revenge on them.

Compassion, an invisible rope tied around his neck, pulled hard on Xabier. Don't deny it. You feel sorry for her because she's an intimate part of your past. But aren't you indirectly feeling sorry for yourself? He was talking to himself without realizing people were starting to notice. Two white robes that crossed his path interrupted him in surprise. Was something the matter? No, nothing. And he sought the solitude of his office even though he had a case that needed immediate attention.

Heat. He unbuttoned the top buttons of his shirt, tried to loosen the noose, but it was hopeless. The rope constricted, so finally he could do nothing but allow himself to be led.

You wouldn't believe it: all day surrounded by broken bodies, often dying, hopeless bodies; bodies with only hours left to them, mothers of two or three children who would never live to see the next Christmas, boys (most of them bikers) chosen for death in the prime of their youth, all that flesh with first and last names that would soon appear in the obituary columns, and he there, immune to compassion, keeping calm, austerely, professionally consoling desolate relatives, doing his job (be just, be honorable, be upright) with all the diligence you can muster. And nevertheless, now he was experiencing a different feeling, even though he had no medical responsibility at all for Arantxa. Or was it for that very reason that the case made such a deep impression on him: because he had no chance to establish with her the kind of connection he would have with any patient? The question remained floating in the air, in the dull light of the fluorescent bulbs. There was no time to find an answer, because he'd already left the elevator and entered the rehabilitation floor, walking quickly because of the incessant pull of the rope.

At the end of the hall he spotted, sitting on a bench against the wall, the Ecuadorian. The diminutive woman with Andean features was guarding the wheelchair. When the doctor approached her, she quickly stood up and greeted him with a slight bow. Xabier, inexpressive, ceremonious, responded, without looking her in the eye.

And he entered. Two physical therapists were joking with a ten- or twelve-year-old boy. They'd tied him to a gurney and stood him upright. With a clinical eye, Xabier conjectured: cytomegalovirus. He said hello, they said hello, the boy stared at him through his magnifying lenses, and a bit beyond Xabier saw Arantxa stretched out on a gurney before she saw him. The young woman who attended her signaled that she knew about his visit. She was going through a soft stretching and contracting knee exercise with the patient. As he approached, Xabier noted hypertonia and obesity. Looking at her in profile, with her short hair, he wouldn't have recognized her at first sight. Then he did when he stopped next to the gurney, where he could see her features at close range. Perhaps to mitigate the effect of the surprise, the physical therapist had prudently informed Arantxa in a relaxed way that he'd arrived:

"You've got an important visitor."

Xabier waited for Arantxa to react before offering her his hand. The first second was all surprise, perhaps fear. Then she offered him a smile, the result of a sudden tightening of her face. The right side of her body was paralyzed. She squeezed his hand in her right hand. Then she made a face Xabier couldn't interpret.

"How are you doing?"

Awkward, inhibited, with no gift for speeches: he said he was very sorry for what happened, that Dr. Ulacia had told him all about it. Arantxa listened joyfully, with an expression of undeniable fascination, as if she couldn't believe that the well-mannered gentleman in the white robe standing before her was really Xabier.

"Are they treating you well?"

She nodded.

Xabier managed to concoct a circumstantial question to the physical therapist about the exercise she was going through with the patient, and while she gave the obvious explanations, Arantxa tried to say something and shook her good hand. At first, they didn't understand her; but one of the physical therapists taking care of the boy a few feet away understood that Arantxa was asking for her iPad. She went out into the hall and asked the Ecuadorian woman to bring it in. Which she did. Arantxa took off the cover and wrote with an agile finger: "I've always liked you, you bastard."

With all the strength in her facial muscles, she smiled. A bit of saliva collected at the corner of her mouth. She looked so happy, with such a joyful expression on her face. So now or never: Xabier took the bracelet out of the pocket of his robe, grabbed Arantxa's right hand as if he were going to take her pulse, and slid it onto her wrist.

"I've been saving it for you all these years. Please, never give it back to me."

She stared up at him for a while, serious, before writing: "What are you waiting for? Give me a kiss." He kissed her on the cheek. Then he said he had to go, that he wished her the best, and muttered other polite things. Arantxa signaled him to wait a moment. She wrote, using one finger on the keyboard, and then showed him the screen: "If you have a stroke, we can get married."

24

A Toy Bracelet

A simple geranium put her in a bad mood and now this. This is worse than the geranium, but the fact is (what did they think, that I was just going to give in?) it's part of the same maneuver. If she'd discovered the pot on her own, she'd have remained perfectly calm. So, a flower pot, who cares? But no, this one and that one had to come with the gossip:

First Juani:

"Did you see? She's put a geranium on her balcony."

And Miren kept silent and did not take a look. After a while, walking down the street, another woman:

"Hey, did you see?"

This time, too, she had no desire to see, even if there were only a few steps separating her house from the one belonging to those people.

The geranium drove her crazy that night, because Joxian came home from the Pagoeta telling the same story, that someone had said what will Miren think when she sees it. So the next day she went to see the famous pot, and there it was. A common geranium plant with two red flowers, as if saying I'm back, I'm planting my flag here, and now you're all just going to have to get used to it.

To Joxian she said:

"A crappy geranium, and when the cold comes, unless she puts it in the house, goodbye."

"It's her house. She can do what she likes with it."

And just when she'd convinced herself that the best thing to do was forget about it and go on with her life, which gave her more than enough headaches by the way, and besides, what's she going to do to me when I've got the whole town on my side, the doorbell rang. She opened the door and before Celeste had crossed the threshold with the wheelchair, Miren recognized the bracelet. That's all I need. First the geranium and now this. She took advantage of the greeting kiss to examine the bracelet closely. There wasn't the slightest doubt. Images of a distant summer flooded into her mind, a hot afternoon with a village festival. Franco had died the year before; that, too, she remembers. The two couples strolling along with all their kids. They'd all laughed at the *bertsolaris'* songs. Miren less than the others because Joxe Mari was ruining her afternoon. A restless boy, a difficult boy, a damn nuisance. Always hanging from the side of the bandstand and a *bertsolari* chewed him out. He tried to jump off the merry-go-round while it was still moving, somewhere along the way he'd gotten a grease stain on his shirt and Joxian was proud of the fact that he had a son who behaved like a mountain goat.

"He's not a mountain goat, my dear. He's a healthy boy."

And then he split a seam on one side of his trousers, and I felt like giving him a good smack right there on the street. All the work involved in washing and sewing was for her. She muttered: "Just you wait and see when we get home."

Joxian bought each child an éclair. And that pig Joxe Mari finished his in two bites. He then took a bite of Nerea's and of course she didn't want to eat it after that. And Joxian bought her another—what, are we rich or what? Then Joxe Mari tried to steal Gorka's; the poor little guy couldn't have been more than five, but still he defended himself, and his brother got mad and smashed the éclair in his face and we had to clean him up with a napkin from the bar. He also stained his T-shirt. More work for me.

Txato and Bittori were about to go on vacation with their kids to Lanzarote, where they would buy us an ugly statue of a camel. Out of respect, we put it on top of the television set, because they might come by the next day and ask about it. And Bittori going on about Lanzarote, the hotel, showing off, laughing because neither Joxian nor Miren knew where Lanzarote is. So, it got a bit late and the two families decided to go home to give the children dinner and put them to bed. That way they could go out later without their kids and enjoy the night, and Miren, well, all she really wanted to do was to get into bed and rest.

On the way to their respective homes, they passed a row of street vendors. There was something for everyone: handmade ceramics, sandals, pocket books—anything and everything. And Txato, who was like a gunslinger from the old West when it came to pulling out his wallet, stopped at the stand of a black man selling costume jewelry and bought Nerea a bracelet, which was a dirty trick because of course Arantxa wanted one and we have three children, not two like them, and Joxian made a crap salary at the foundry and they had enough to go to Lanzarote and for many other luxuries. So it was no to Arantxa. And she, on the verge of tears, made a scene. She put up such a fuss that Txato grabbed her by the hand and without asking Joxian or me, brought her over to the black vendor. And now she turns up in my house more than thirty years later with the same one, because it is that bracelet with green beads and sort of goldish, no doubt about it. What did it cost Txato? A few cents. Miren was enraged, but she swallowed her anger, where does he get off giving a lesson to her and Joxian about how to make our children happy?

Or am I wrong? Miren couldn't stop looking at the bracelet. An amused Arantxa was watching television; Celeste said goodbye using those sweet and affable courtesies that no one here uses anymore but which are really nice. And Arantxa said goodbye in her jolly way, waving her good hand, and Miren did the same in her style, a bit dry, as she accompanied her to the door, but instead of simply letting her out, she stepped onto the landing with Celeste.

"Listen, where did my daughter get that bracelet she's wearing?"

"A doctor gave it to her. It's pretty, isn't it?"

"Right, very pretty. But you mean a male nurse gave it to her?"

"No, no. A doctor came by. I don't know what his name is. I never saw him before. And I thought the doctor might be a family friend because he only came to see Arantxa and after a few minutes he gave her a sweet kiss on the cheek and she seemed happy, blissful the whole time. They chatted. I mean, the doctor chatted and Arantxa answered with her iPad, and at the end he gave her the little bracelet."

"You didn't by any chance catch the doctor's name, did you?"

"Oh dear, no, unfortunately, Mrs. Miren, it was just that the physical therapists called him 'doctor' a few times. But if you like, I can find out tomorrow. He's a tall doctor, gray around the temples, and wears glasses. I never saw him before. Is it serious?"

"No. I just wanted to know."

Joxian came home at the usual time with the usual glassiness in his drunken eyes, scratching his shirt where his liver was. The breaded anchovies were crackling away in the frying pan, the window wide open so the smoke would drift out to the street. Arantxa was hypnotized by the steam coming off her bowl of soup. Joxian kissed her on the forehead. Then, sitting at the table, he sighed with fatigue.

"I'm not hungry at all."

Miren, with a severe look on her face:

"What? Don't you even wash your hands?"

He rubbed them together as if he had them under the faucet.

"They're clean."

"What a pig."

And off he went to the bathroom to wash them, grumbling but docile. Back in the kitchen, Miren, behind Arantxa's back, made signs to him he didn't understand.

"What?"

She pursed her lips and shot him a furious look so he'd pretend nothing had happened. And she shook her head as if saying: God, the patience you need with this man.

Finally, Joxian noticed the bracelet. He's hopeless at pretending and Miren would have happily cracked him over the head with the frying pan.

"How cute!" To his daughter. "Did you buy it?"

Arantxa shook her head vehemently and tapping the tip of her index finger again and again against her chest sounded out with her lips two words: it's mine. Joxian sought an explanation in his wife's sullen face. In vain. And so it went, until dinner was over. He kept his mouth shut so he wouldn't make a fool of himself.

Later on, in bed, in the dark, the couple whispered.

"Come on, it isn't possible."

"I bet my life on it. Txato bought her that bracelet on a festival day years and years ago, when the kids were small and we were all still friends."

"Well, what's the difference? Arantxa must have found it in a drawer and put it on."

"What a fool you are. She didn't find it. A doctor gave it to her."

"You're driving me nuts. Txato bought it for her . . ."

"Quiet down."

In whispers:

"Txato bought Arantxa a bracelet when she was a little girl. I'm with you that far. Then the years go by and a doctor gives the bracelet to our daughter. I don't understand a thing."

"The only thing I see clearly is that there is only one doctor who could have done something like that, aside from kissing Arantxa on the cheek."

"Who?"

"The older son, who for some reason I don't get kept the bracelet."

"You watch too many soaps."

"They're planning something. Don't you see that? They've intruded into our lives and now we've got them right here with us, in our bedroom, even in our bed, they've managed to get us talking about them all the time. Why do you think that woman has come back, that she lets herself be seen, that she put a geranium on her balcony, and goes into the village shops? They're coming after us. Something has to be done, Joxian."

"Right, go to sleep."

"I'm serious."

"Me, too."

A little later, he began to snore. For Miren, turned on her side, wide awake, the darkness was filled with faces, lights, sounds. Immediately the geranium appeared, then the bracelet. And Arantxa eleven years old, making a fuss because she wanted a bracelet like Nerea's. And she saw Joxe Mari smashing the éclair in Gorka's face. And Txato, who had a way of pulling out his wallet like the cowboys in pictures when they draw their pistols. And she saw that woman, whose name she will not speak because it burns her mouth. That woman, who has returned with bad intentions, and if she thinks I'm just going to sit here and take it, she's made a big mistake. She couldn't sleep. Another sleepless night. Her head filled with thoughts, the darkness filled with ghosts. She went to the kitchen, it was after midnight, and wrote *"Alde hemendik"* on a sheet of paper. I'll slip it under her door and then we'll see who scares who more. She got ready to go out, but what if she recognizes my handwriting? She took another sheet. She repeated the words, changing her writing and using only capital letters. She went out to the landing with her shoes in her hand so those who were sleeping wouldn't hear her, slipped them on as she stood on the mat, went down to the entryway, and opened the door. Did she go out? Just one step? Well? It was raining. Rain and wind. It was raining furiously. The drops were falling sideways. What a horrible night. She said to herself:

"Humph."

She immediately tore up the paper, put the pieces in a pocket, and went back to bed.

25

DON'T COME

The doorbell rang. The short, dry sound surprised Bittori, who was sitting in the living-room armchair, leafing through the jackets of her old collection of vinyl. This was the first time she'd heard that strident ring, so familiar to her in another era, since she had come back to the village house.

She wasn't alarmed. Was she expecting a visitor? Yes and no, because I always supposed that sooner or later someone, more accurately some woman, would come to poke her nose in, to question me, to find out my intentions.

She didn't have to wait long, a few days, before she ran into a woman she knew on the street. The meeting was so badly staged that she hadn't the slightest doubt it wasn't accidental.

"Jesus, Bittori, how many years it's been since I saw you last. This is great! You're as pretty as ever."

Some acidic words rose to her mouth: really, you know what it is? They do you a favor when they kill your husband and leave you a widow. But she swallowed those words. She'd seen her at a distance, posted on the corner. She's waiting for me, she's going to ask me the questions people have told her to put to me. She did ask them, pretending that they were just then occurring to her. One of the women who didn't go to the funeral, who never expressed her sympathy, who cut us off when the graffiti started. Don't hate, Bittori, don't hate. She answered the woman evasively, vaguely, giving her a fake smile that left a gelatinous, cold sensation like a dead jellyfish in her mouth.

She opened the door. Don Serapio. What an unctuous look in his eyes, what sweetness in the arch of his brows. Those pale, delicate hands that spread apart, that join together, the clerical collar, the aftershave lotion. And meanwhile, she, her face like quartz, never blinked. Shock? Not even a smidge. The same as if she'd opened the door and found no one standing there.

The priest walked in expecting a hug. This man was always looking for skin contact. Bittori brusquely recoiled, keeping her distance. He said in Basque that he'd come to pay a visit. She scrutinized him, one hand on the edge of the door as if contemplating the possibility of slamming it in his face. She answered familiarly, in Spanish, that he should come in.

He may rule in the house of God, but in my house, I give the orders. And Don Serapio, over seventy now, walked in making note of floors and walls, furniture and adornments, which made it seem he used his eyes as if they were cameras. According to his nose, it was about two p.m., because he could smell the beans and sausage Bittori was heating up in the kitchen.

"Are you living here now?"

"Of course, it's my house."

Bittori let him have the armchair where she'd been looking over her record collection so that every time he looked up his eyes would meet the photo of Txato hanging on the wall. She brought in a chair from the kitchen for herself. The priest initiated a casual conversation, praising Bittori, making gestures of bland amiability, his words pregnant with humble intonations, always trying to control the narrative; but she, in the few instances she spoke up, was defiantly resolved to pull away from Basque and toward Spanish, which she did so well that Don Serapio acquiesced and stopped speaking Basque.

He leapt from one trivial theme to another, from the weather to health and family, until Bittori, who as yet had not eaten and had little patience left, cut him off:

"Why don't you talk about what you came to talk about?"

Now unable to avoid it, Don Serapio shot an instinctive glance over the head of his stern interlocutor, at the framed photograph of Txato.

"Fine, Bittori. I don't know if you've noticed that your presence in the village is causing some nervousness . . . Maybe 'nervousness' is not the right word."

" 'Alarm'?"

"I've expressed myself badly. I'm sorry. Let's say that people see you come to town every day; they feel strange and ask questions."

"And how do you know they ask questions? Do they visit the church to tell you?"

"In a small town like this news travels fast. The fact is that ever since you started coming people have been talking. You're in your own town, no one argues that point. And as far as I'm concerned, you're welcome here. But, things are more complicated than they might seem, and the fact that you have a legitimate right to return to your house doesn't negate the fact that other neighbors also have their rights."

"For example?"

"For example, that they be allowed to rebuild their lives and have some chance for peace. The armed struggle hit our town hard, but we must not forget some of the actions perpetrated by the state security forces. We had people killed, your husband, may he rest in peace, and those two members of the Guardia Civil who died in the attack on the industrial park. Without trying to minimize those terrible tragedies, which caused so much pain, we shouldn't lose sight of the suffering of other people. There was repression here, there were house searches carried out for no good reason, innocent people jailed and mistreated or, to be more precise, tortured in their cells. At this very moment, we have nine sons of the town living out long jail sentences. I'm not going to go into whether they deserve punishment or not. I'm not a jurist, certainly not a politician, but just a simple priest who would like to help the townspeople live in peace."

"Are you insinuating that this peace is endangered because the widow of a man who was murdered comes to spend a few hours in her own house?"

"Not in the slightest. I've only come to ask a favor in the name of the townspeople. If you do me this favor I'll be profoundly grateful. If you don't I'll simply have to accept your decision. I know you've suffered, Bittori. The last thing I want to do here is call your feelings into question or reproach you in any way. I've always had you and your children in my prayers. And believe me, if your husband is not at this very moment in the presence of the Lord, it isn't because I haven't begged for it a hundred or a thousand times. But just as God deals with the souls of the departed, I have to deal with the souls of the living in my parish. Do I do it well, do I do it badly? I'm sure I make mistakes. I'm sure I don't use the right words for the occasion and more than once I've said things I didn't mean to say. Or I spoke when I should have kept my mouth shut. I'm not perfect, because no one is. Even so, I have to carry out the mission entrusted to me until my time on earth is done. Without being cowardly, without giving up. Do you understand that I can't go to the house of one of those families, who are also broken up, and tell them, no, I'm sorry, your son fought in ETA, you're on your own. Would you do that if you were in my place?"

"If I were in your place, I'd make myself clear. What do you want from me?"

This time, the priest, instead of raising his eyes to the photo of Txato, kept them focused on the floor, between Bittori's feet and his own.

"I want you to stop coming here."

"To stop coming to my own house?"

"Just for a while, until things settle down and there is peace. God is merciful. For what you've suffered here, you will be rewarded in the next world. Don't let rancor take possession of your soul."

The next morning, still short of breath, Bittori went up to Polloe to tell Txato. She spoke standing, because it had rained hard and she preferred not to sit on the moist stone.

"That's just what he said. That I shouldn't go to the village so I don't get in the way of the peace process. So you see, victims get in the way. They want to sweep us under the rug. We shouldn't be seen and if we disappear from public life and they get their prisoners out of jail, well, that's what they call peace and everyone's happy. Nothing ever happened here. He said it's time we all pardoned one another. And when I asked to whom I should beg pardon, he answered no one, but that unfortunately I was part of a conflict in which all of society was implicated, not just a group of citizens, and that he can't write off the fact that if they should ask my pardon, they in their turn should expect others ask pardon from them. And since this is very difficult, the priest thinks that the best thing is that now when there are no more attacks, that the situation should cool down and that anger should cease and that with the help of time the pain and grievances will lessen. What do you think, Txato? I didn't lose control, but I also didn't keep quiet. I said:

"Listen, Serapio. Anyone who doesn't want to see me in the village can put four bullets into me the way they did with Txato, because I intend to come here whenever I feel like it. After all, the only thing I can lose, my life, they broke apart many years ago. I don't expect anyone to ask forgiveness from me, although, come to think of it, it does seem to me it would be a humane thing to do. And that's enough, because my dinnertime is passing by here. Tell the person who sent you to see me that I won't stop until I know all the details about the murder of my husband."

"Bittori, for the love of God, why dig around in that wound?"

And then I answered him:

"To drain out all the pus that's still inside. If I don't it will never heal. We have nothing more to say to each other." He left the house looking down in the mouth and with an expression that said he was leaving offended. Who cares? As soon as I saw through a space in the curtain that he'd left the street, I ran to the kitchen to eat a good plate of beans because I was dying of hunger. What do you think, Txato? Was I right? You know I've never lacked character."

26

With Them or with Us

The cool, misty rain, smacking against the graves, made an autumnal noise: Bittori liked it. Yes, because aside from cleaning all this up a little, it gives me the impression that life actually reaches the dead, no? I understand myself.

Thinking these thoughts, she dodged puddles, protecting her plain hairdo with her umbrella. She was tempted (and not for the first time) to carry snails from the paving stones off for the pot. It wouldn't stop raining, and as she left the cemetery it so happened that the city bus was just arriving, so she took it. What am I going to do? She reviewed circumstances and conditions. I still have beans left over from yesterday, I filled Ikatza's bowl with food, no one's waiting for me at home. It really annoyed her that Don Serapio would even think she would agree to his request that she not allow herself to be seen in the village for a while. So she got off at Bulevar, bought two rolls in a nearby bakery—he's got a lot of nerve, that man—and went off to the village on the first bus.

She heated up yesterday's leftovers and ate them. She did this, she did that. The afternoon passed as she plugged in wires, reestablished connections, chores that Txato usually took care of. Finally, she managed to get the record player working. And in the silence between two old songs, the sounds of a pealing bell reached her. It was Saturday and she grabbed her umbrella and left. To go where? Where else? To seven o'clock mass. And when she walked into the church, she felt the urge to sit in the first pew as she did that afternoon of the funeral; but she thought it too serious a provocation. So she went to the other extreme, the last pew in the group to the right, from which she could keep an eye on the entire expanse of the church.

By the time mass began, the church was acceptably filled, though not to the extent it was in old times. No one sat near Bittori, from which she inferred that her presence hadn't gone unnoticed; but it's all the same to me, I didn't expect to be greeted with applause in this temple of the Lord where supposedly love of one's fellow man is preached.

The empty seats around her made her all the more visible, so as soon as the priest, in a green chasuble, entered the church from the sacristy through the door opposite the altar, she discreetly moved to the group of pews on the left, finding refuge behind some strangers. And when she casually turned her head to one side, she discovered the wheelchair parked in front of the column.

Without having seen her, Miren found out Bittori was in the church. She'd entered with her daughter just before seven. Someone kindly held the door open so they could get in. Who? Doesn't matter, anyone. And she made herself comfortable in her usual place, Arantxa at her side, the statue of Saint Ignatius of Loyola a bit farther off, in the half-light of the lateral wall. Just then, a mouth whispered in her ear. Miren nodded discreetly, acknowledging that she knew, and did not turn her face to the right, neither then nor at any time during the mass.

She just keeps on daring to do more and more. Through the space between the column and Arantxa's neck, she cast a glance of furious reproach to Ignatius. Whose side are you on, with them or with us? The mass had barely begun when she felt the temptation to leave. Coming here is a lowdown, dirty trick! All the peace they ask for in their demonstrations and in their newspapers, and when there finally is peace they don't even wait two days to screw it all up. She was just on the verge of leaving when it came to her. Me, leave? She's the one who should be going. And to Ignatius: if you like her more, you can both leave.

The sermon. One on one end of the pew, the other on the other end with three or four parishioners between them, Don Serapio spotted the two of them from the dais with a railing he used as a pulpit. He made no mention of them, no chance of that, but he suddenly abandoned the bland subject he'd prepared and set about improvising, with, truth be told, a little disorder at the out-set, phrases about peace and reconciliation, forgiveness and living together in harmony, all directed, nobody can tell me otherwise, principally, if not exclusively, at the two women.

He told a story, an event, a parable, who knows what to call it, about two people who shared strong bonds of friendship, and how both were happy for it; then they became enemies and were unhappy, but God wanted them to reconcile and, though it wasn't easy, after a time they did reconcile and in that way they recovered their former happiness. Because, as Jesus Christ said, thou shalt love et cetera. And the priest warmed to his subject, and on and on and may peace come. And he delivered—a rarity for him since he tended to be stark and leaden—a fiery sermon that went on for twenty minutes.

In the face of all that, Miren no longer spoke with Ignatius of Loyola. You never give me anything I ask for. From that point on, grim-faced, she stopped talking to him. Immersed in grief and worry, she did not at first notice that Arantxa was waving her hand at that woman. Horror. Even her head was shaking under the weight of her smile. Her eyes were smiling, her lips, her forehead, her ears were all smiling. A scandalous smile. Was she having some kind of attack? Although, thinking it through, perhaps she wasn't waving but showing her the cheap bracelet, which she'd refused to take off at home. Come on, girl, it's only a toy. Discreetly, she released the wheelchair's brake, and using her foot, she managed to turn the chair so that Arantxa was facing the altar, but since the idiot—God grant me patience—fought to turn her face, her mother pushed the chair a bit more and another bit more toward the wall, which made it impossible for Arantxa to communicate with that woman.

Every so often, Bittori would notice that Arantxa was waving to her, and looked toward the left. By sticking her neck out, she managed to distinguish, beyond the three or four profiles between them, a bit of the mother and all of the daughter. Until, at a given moment, how strange, she noticed that the wheelchair was no lon-ger in the same position and that there was no possibility for her to return Arantxa's smile.

With her palms pressed together, Miren stood up to take com-munion. She's probably looking at me. I can feel her piercing stare.

And yes, she was staring fixedly at her, how much sanctity, she actually thinks she's going straight to heaven. Let's just see when she gets there with her robes stained with my husband's blood. A small line formed before the priest. Bittori felt a desire to join the communicants. What does it matter that she neither believes nor practices. And when the other woman, with the sacred body on her tongue, returned to her seat by walking up the central aisle, perhaps, who knows, their eyes met for an instant. Bittori imagined the scene. Instantly, a wave of euphoria came over her. But when she began to stand up, a sharp pain in her stomach, the third or fourth in the past days, kept her down. She endured five agonizing minutes, so dizzy she thought she might fall over. She closed her eyes, breathed slowly, recovered, and now, with mass over, people began filing toward the door. When she finally managed to stand up, she noticed that the wheelchair had disappeared.

She was one of the last to exit the church. When she walked out into the darkness of the plaza it was raining, and most certainly because of the rain, people quickly scattered. She hadn't walked five steps when two shadowy figures approached her.

"Remember us?"

She couldn't identify the voice, couldn't see their faces clearly, so it took her a few seconds to recognize them; but then, close up, yes So-and-So and Mrs. So-and-So, an older married couple, people from the village. They whispered:

"We saw you in church and it makes us both very happy. And then I said to this guy here: let's wait for her. We think a great deal of you. We've always thought a great deal of you."

Then the man spoke in such a low voice that the patter of raindrops on her umbrella forced her to listen closely:

"We've never been nationalists. But of course it's better that no one around here know that."

Bittori thanked them. Then she begged them to excuse her because she was in a hurry.

"Of course. We won't hold you back."

In a hurry? Not a chance of that. She disappeared in the darkness, turned into an entryway, and stood there awhile leaning against the wall waiting for the pain to pass.

27

Family Dinner

Sunday, paella. Nerea arrived first, without high heels but wearing lipstick and without her husband. Mother and daughter pressed cheeks together at the door.

"So how was London?"

Nerea brought a doormat as a gift she'd bought somewhere or other. She pronounced the name with a certain mouthy overacting, perhaps out of the inertia acquired in the two weeks she'd been practicing the language.

"Pretty, don't you think?"

A doormat with the picture of a double-decker London bus on it. Bittori agreed with phony enthusiasm that it was pretty, but why spend all this money, child? Nerea stepped onto the landing to exchange the new mat for the old one. She leaned the old mat against the wall so she could bring it down to the garbage later.

"And Quique? Doesn't he like paella?"

"No more Quique. I'll tell you later."

Ikatza was napping on the sofa. She let herself be petted, barely opening her eyes. Outside, a gray day. The buzzer rang. Xabier kissed and hugged his mother, kissed and hugged Nerea. He paid no attention to the cat and didn't even notice the new doormat where he'd just finished wiping clean the soles of his shoes. He brought a bottle of wine and flowers. He really shouldn't have. The three only ate together on odd occasions. Christmas, Bittori's birthday, and today? No special reason, simply because Nerea had come back from London or it had been a while since the three of them had gathered around a table. Xabier told about the sad case of a patient in his hospital, then he told about a quite funny case, but after the first how were they supposed to laugh? They attacked the appetizers. Nerea expounded on her touristic adventures (we went here, we went there, we passed through this) and her brother, as he opened the bottle, noticed the absence of a certain narrative element. He called it out:

"What's Quique up to?"

"I imagine he's still in London."

Curiosity and bewilderment stopped him midway in the act of removing the cork. Bittori quickly intervened:

"They've broken up again."

"We haven't broken up."

"You've separated."

"It's not the same thing."

"But the fact is that the two of you have always lived in your own flats. Or am I mistaken?"

"You're not mistaken."

Since they were going to find out sooner or later, Nerea recounted, revealed, provided details.

"So now you know. It was a separation by mutual agreement. Whether it's permanent or not, time will tell. Quique offered to send me a monthly allotment. I turned him down, of course."

Her mother's eyebrows raised.

"Why not?"

"Because I'd rather not be thankful for anything."

Xabier offered his mother wine, which she refused; Nerea, too, wanted none. He was about to pour himself a glass but he decided not to and placed the bottle, still full, on the far side of the table. Bittori got up to go to the kitchen for the paella. Nerea: did she need any help. And Bittori, no.

With their mother out of the room, brother and sister exchanged whispers.

"I'm begging you not to bring up that matter."

Back from the kitchen, Bittori caught the last word.

"Which matter?"

The straw trivet, with black burn marks on it, was one the family used back in the village, when the children were small, when their father was alive; and also the paella pan, which had lost some enamel around the edges. Years ago, Nerea would wear herself out telling her mother to throw that Paleolithic junk out and buy new things. And with the same museum-piece napkins or used-clothing-shop napkins, Txato had wiped the grease off his fingers more than twenty years earlier.

The last wisps of steam were rising from the rice. Bittori serves Xabier. Her favorite child? Favorite because he was useless for practical matters? Nerea is another kettle of fish. She decisively snatches up the skimmer and serves herself while she enumerates breakfasts, lunches, dinners of dubious quality in London. And when all of them are in the process of raising forkfuls of paella from their plates to their mouths, she launches into an exposition of her short- and medium-term plans. In short:

"I finally decided to do it, that as soon as possible I'll attend a healing meeting at the prison."

Silence. That's the theme. Since no voices of disagreement arise, she goes on:

"I've spoken by telephone with the mediator. A really nice woman. She inspires confidence. Not so much at first, but after I got to know her better. I told her I was back from London, and that I'm ready to take up the preparatory interviews again. What else? I'm telling you all this because I don't like doing things behind your backs. I suppose you're against the idea."

Mother and brother, serious, actually inexpressive, the two of them, stared at her and then, simultaneously, stopped staring. Did they take her seriously or not? The working of jaws was audible. Their eyes remained fixed on their plates, which little by little emptied. Then Bittori slowly sipped some water, passed the worn napkin over her lips, and asked in a neutral, machine-like voice:

"What do you hope to achieve?"

"No idea. I still have no idea who I'd meet with. I only know one thing. I want one of them to know what they did to us and what we've gone through."

"You mean what *you've* gone through."

"Right."

"And afterward?"

"I'll listen to what they have to say."

"Are you expecting them to beg forgiveness?"

"Well, to tell the truth, I haven't thought about that. According to the mediator, until now all those who have taken part in the meetings have felt good about it. It's not clear to her that any of them regret what they did. There are some victims who at the end consider themselves better people. Feeling some relief doesn't seem insignificant to me. And starting from that point, I say welcome to anything positive that comes. For instance, that the wound stop oozing pus and heal. There will always be a scar. But a scar is a kind of cure. I don't know about you, but I'd like to see the day when I look in the mirror and see something more than the face of a person reduced to the status of victim. They've promised me maximum discretion. The newspapers won't find out."

Xabier, his brow furrowed, said nothing. On several occasions during the previous days, he'd urged Nerea to keep their mother out of this issue. Why? So she wouldn't worry. But as it turned out Bittori reacted calmly.

"Look here, my girl, do what you think makes sense. I'm not against it. A person speaking for the Directory of Attention to Victims informed me a while back about these meetings so I'm more or less aware of how they work. I'm just not convinced by the idea of talking with just any murderer. I think it's a waste of time. They've damaged me so much that nothing can close any wound. My entire body is a wound. I don't think I have to explain it to you. And if I were left with a scar after all this it would be like the scar of someone whose body was burned from head to toe. Maybe I would go to look the man who killed *aita* in the eye. I'd have a few words for that guy." To Xabier: "What do you think? Or has the cat got your tongue?"

Xabier sat there downcast.

"This is a personal thing. I'm not getting involved."

"I'm asking if you're going to one of those meetings, too."

"No."

It sounded definitive. It also sounded aggressive. And Nerea, pushing her not-completely-empty plate toward the center of the table, to signal she'd finished eating, said:

"After the meeting, I think I might move to a different city. I don't know which. I'm not excluding the possibility of leaving the country."

They accepted what she said without judging, without asking questions. Then they moved on to talk, succinctly, seriously, about ordinary matters, and the first to go without coffee or dessert, because it was a Sunday and a game day, was Xabier, who had been a member of the Real Sociedad soccer club since he was a boy, though he goes infrequently to the stadium. Nerea helps clear the table. Now that the two women are alone, Nerea asks her mother what she thinks of her projects for the future.

"You're old enough to know what you're doing."

"Would you rather I end up like my brother?"

"What's wrong with your brother?"

"He's the saddest man I know."

"And what the hell do you know about sadness or anything else?"

"Well, I've got more than enough reasons to be a wreck. But look, in London, the same night when I agreed with Quique to separate for a while, I took a walk along the river. I asked myself: what do I do? Jump into the river and goodbye, baby, or do I look for a way out of the labyrinth where I've spent so much, too much, time? And I saw the dirty water flowing and the reflections of the city in the water, and then I saw people and heard music coming from someplace nearby, the breeze blew into my face, and I came to a conclusion: screw this, Nerea, lift up your head, don't give in, live, that's the idea, girl, you may be fucked, but get moving, fight, look for something. By the way, I found out you're going to the village every day and I think it's a great idea. I imagine you're looking for something, too."

"Looking for something? I'm not looking for anything. I go to my house. Can't I go to my house? Does that bother you?"

There was rage in her eyes, in her pursed lips. They didn't say another word. And a short while later, leaving the flat, Nerea noticed that the old doormat was not on the landing.

28

Between Brother and Sister

November gray. It was drizzling when Nerea walked through the entryway. At the bottom of the hill, directly in her path, a black umbrella hid the face of a lurking man. Nerea's heart leapt. Why, when there's no more terrorism? The presence of a solitary man posed that way and looking like that made her suspicious. To play it safe she crossed the street. Then he turned. It was Xabier.

"Didn't you say you were in a hurry to get to the soccer match?"

"I changed my mind."

Why? Because he thought it more important to speak with her alone. Nerea: he shouldn't scare her like that. He: she should relax. It was simply that since they saw each other so little they had few chances to talk in private. They agreed to walk down to San Martín Street. Along the way she told him to close his umbrella because the rain had stopped and he closed it, and in a bit they sat down in the café of the Europa Hotel.

"I didn't know you liked cognac."

"Well, someone has to drink something. We can't just sit here without ordering something, right?"

She ordered chamomile tea. The paella had left an oily aftertaste in her mouth and a heaviness in her stomach.

Xabier paid no attention to his sister's complaints. Without preliminaries, he went straight to the point:

"You and I should have met before going to *ama*'s house. Believe me when I say I was really uncomfortable. We should have agreed on a series of points to protect her from more suffering. You were in the wrong, but I realize that I'm partially to blame for not having stepped in."

"You mean for not telling me to shut up."

"I mean that all you had to do was tell your plans for the future little by little. Simple prudence or something you may never have heard of before: subtlety."

"You mean the kind you're practicing right now?"

"The story of your umpteenth separation would have been enough. It would have been better to hold off on the rest for another time. Anyway, to you it probably looked as if *ama* reacted calmly. Let me tell you, her calm is all appearance. It's the mask she's been wearing since she became a widow. She pretends to be strong. But if you took a good look, which I did while you went on and on, sometimes in a kind of euphoria, which I have to say caught my eye and not in a positive way, you'd have seen in *ama*'s forehead, in her eyes, that each word you spoke was like a stone hitting her."

"Is that so? Well, it's odd that you saw that because I never saw her raise her eyes from the plate."

"Some things you see without having to look at them. Listen, Nerea. Maybe your separation from Quique has affected you more than you're showing. Only you could know that. While we were eating, the impression I had of you was of a woman who suddenly wants to do a lot of things, no matter what happens, without taking into account the repercussions of your acts for the people around you. Really, you didn't seem to be yourself."

"And what if I'm not myself? You think I have to adopt your way of being?"

"Before your trip to London, you promised us you'd given up the idea of the healing encounter. And now we find you want to go on with the program. Why? So you can achieve some psychological well-being before you leave? Every man for himself, right? Could you really feel well-being seeing how *ama* is doing? I couldn't. Maybe I could feel it for a minute with a repentant murderer standing in front of me. But then I'd go back to San Sebastián and realize that the relief I'm feeling does nothing for those I love, but just the opposite, and then I'd go back to feeling the way I did before, or worse."

"Are you accusing me of egoism?"

"Let's just call it naïveté."

"Xabier, I'm not your little eight-year-old sister. It's been a long time since we were kids. I don't need a mentor. I can handle myself on my own."

"I'm not denying it. That's why I'm here talking with you, because you're a person who's supposedly able to make decisions, which doesn't free you from making mistakes. Mistakes that can hurt others, which is the case now."

"You're exaggerating."

"You're taking what happened to *aita* and making up your own personal version of it. You're looking for a way out that works for you or for your plans or whatever you want to call them. Ultimately you stand like God himself, you begin a new life in Shangri-la, with palm trees lining the beach, but you don't bother to think that maybe if you really do that you make the pain of those who remain here even greater."

"The two of you are emotionally blocked. *Ama* and you are in a pit of sorrow and anger and melancholy you can't get out of and I'm not even sure you want to get out. I've touched bottom. Enough is enough. Something inside me has to change. That's why, after analyzing myself, I thought about going up to one of those murderers and telling him: you did this to me, these are the consequences, you take them, they're my gift to you, and then I'd move far away with or without his asking forgiveness, move to a place where no one recognizes me or whispers behind my back. A place where I can dedicate myself to doing something for others, I don't know, for abused women, orphans. So forget the egoism. Actually, it seems more egoistic to stay in this city licking my wounds to the end of my days. Stop staring into that damn glass of cognac. Look at me. I'm separated from my husband, I have no children and am menopausal. You're hurting me and making me want to throw this tea in your face."

He didn't change expression. Didn't look at her. Didn't move his eyes away from the glass, not even when he said to his sister:

"There's something you don't know. I'm sorry I couldn't tell you sooner. It's another reason why we should have met before. I think *ama* is sick. I don't know what's wrong with her. The results of her last tests don't promise anything good. While you were in London, I managed to get her an appointment with one of the best oncologists around. But when the day came, *ama* didn't show up at his office. She says she forgot. I doubt it. I'm trying not to alarm her. I said it was a routine examination. Of course she isn't dumb. She knows more or less what her symptoms mean. I'm asking you please to put off your plans. In my opinion it would be better to forget about them as long as our mother is still alive. It would be an act of generosity on your part if you didn't commit yourself to actions that could worsen her problem."

"Cancer?"

"Most likely."

Xabier, two cognacs and what his sister had, went over to the register and asked for the check. He also asked the man who won the match. Zero–zero in the first half. He didn't sit down again when he went back to his sister.

"Think about it, and when you reach a decision, please tell me."

"No need to think. Tomorrow I'll call the mediator and tell her to forget about it. The good doctor has once again won the day. But I assure you that one day, I don't know when, I'm going to leave this damn place."

Xabier leaned over to give her a fraternal kiss on the cheek.

"Tough times."

"You're telling me."

They parted company cordially with no show of emotion, without smiling. He walked out, and it wasn't raining. She stayed in her corner seat, staring through the window as if hypnotized by the grayness in the street.

29

A Two-Colored Leaf

To justify how long she'd been sitting in the café, she ordered mineral water. Outside the afternoon was turning dark. Cars passed with their lights on. Were there people in the café? Just a few. Nerea changed tables. Now she was sitting in a place closer to the glass door, where she could better observe the passing cars. She felt enveloped in a pleasing sensation of seclusion. Alone, sleepy, she had no idea where she should go.

The cars did not form a continuous, unbroken line but ran in clusters controlled by the stoplights at the start of San Martín Street. This circumstance generated a soft pleasure for Nerea and made her sadness, her aftertaste of oily paella more bearable.

And suddenly, growling away, a bus passed by, but not a city bus. And she was inside it. Here we go, my youth and I heading to Zaragoza, to take the fourth-year law course following the desire, the imploring demands of *aita*, who wanted to protect his daughter at all costs, so many years ago.

To Pamplona on a Roncalesa bus, early in the morning, what a weep session. My girlfriends, Thursday dinners, motorbike excursions, the discotheque. She abandoned all of it in that distant month of October. And Zaragoza meant nothing to her. A city without a beach, without a bay, without mountains, what a nightmare. How can you live so far from the sea? But *aita* insisted: there's no way out, believe me. The sooner she left Basque country, the better. To Barcelona, to Madrid, wherever she chose. And she shouldn't worry about expenses. The point was to get somewhere safe. Get her degree in peace and quiet. Since she was accepted at the University of Zaragoza, she went to Zaragoza, weeping until Pamplona, where she had to change buses, in a better mood during the second part of the trip. Why? In Pamplona, in the café attached to the bus station, she had a café con leche and a slice of potato-and-egg tortilla and, son of a bitch, it seems that with your stomach satisfied life starts showing a more beneficent aspect. A boy traveling to Logroño—or was it someplace else? she can't remember—came over to her, flirting, flattering, full of illusions. And she, to pass the time but without ever losing sight of the clock on the wall, let him build up his hopes and gave him a phony telephone number and a kiss on the lips. The tortilla and the boy combined to make it a happy morning. She slept until Tudela and reached Zaragoza dying of hunger, but fine.

She'd only been to the city once before. Two days of hellish heat; two nights in the nocturnal oven of a boardinghouse. She matriculated and looked for a student apartment. In a kiosk in Plaza San Francisco, she bought a copy of *El Heraldo de Aragón*. She tossed it out shortly after, keeping only the rentals section. One in Delicias, one in Las Fuentes, apartments here, there. The names of the neighborhoods meant nothing to her. And the heat. At two in the afternoon not a soul on the street. Not a bird, not a fly. She stepped into a phone booth. The telephone was so hot she had to use a tissue to pick it up. She dialed one of the many numbers. She was quoted a rent so low that she grew suspicious, to the point of asking if the place was in Zaragoza itself. What? In the middle of town and not in a village in the province. She noted a reaction of concern on the other end of the line. It's in the middle of town, of course. Then she thought: damn, what am I getting into? Anyway, she caught a taxi with the idea of taking a look at the place because she wanted to get home as soon as possible and to do that she had to resolve the housing issue immediately. She thought it a good sign that the driver recognized the address right away. She concluded that the street was known and would therefore have those things no civilized street should lack. What things? Streetlights, sidewalks, shops. For a moment she was tempted to ask the driver if the place was far away, but she bit her tongue. First out of shame, because of course any person of minimum intelligence would have bought a map of the city, and second because if the guy realizes I don't know where things are he'll take the long way around to jack up the fare. They went up to Torrero. Beyond the canal, almost within sight of the cemetery, the driver announced: here we are, and she paid and got out. The flat? Fine. Clean, the opposite of dark, simply furnished. The views very ugly; but wait a minute, you're not here on vacation. To tell the truth, Nerea had already accepted the place before the door opened, as she walked up the stairs to the entry. It's that she recalled her mother's advice to her. That the important thing, my girl, is that you have a roof over your head when classes begin; then when things calm down you can find a way to make yourself more comfortable. She also told her that when she entered the building she should check the condition of the mailboxes. Because, damn it, poverty tends to take poor care of them, while people doing okay try to keep them clean and neat, and as she said, all she had to do was see the mailboxes to get an idea of what kind of neighbors live in a building. The mailboxes made an excellent impression on Nerea, as did the cleanliness of the stairs and walls, and when the door opened and she shook hands with her future roommate, she was more than convinced she'd found a place in Zaragoza.

During the months she lived there, she barely saw her roommate, a girl from Huesca. Actually, she never knew for sure what she did. She was not, of course, a student. The downside of the apartment: the school was really far away, as were the bars and other places to have fun. Then the *cierzo*, the icy Zaragoza wind, and fog. Winter came and was it cold, Jesus! She bought a space heater. It barely helped. If she moved a few yards from it, the piercing cold was unbearable. Net result: at the start of the next year she moved to the flat on López Allué, better heating and better location, although more expensive as well. She shared it with two girls from Teruel. One, younger than she, was also a law student; the other in humanities. They got along well together right from the start.

Zaragoza. If her brother only knew, if her mother only knew. Except for the beginning, when she shivered with cold in the Torrero flat and felt alone, as if wrapped in a membrane of nostalgia, she was close to happiness. She didn't realize it at the time. She limited herself to exhausting the pleasing possibilities of youth. She soon made friends. People so open, so healthy in spirit, and so pleasant in character, she never found anywhere else. And she, without scanting her studies (she didn't fail a single examination), frequented the night, physical love, alcohol, and, but less often, cocaine and marijuana. And she learned to get along without the sea, and she forgot the worrying and dramatic things which, perhaps, she should not have forgotten. The fact is she didn't forget them. Or they came to her muted by distance or simply didn't reach her because her family, especially *aita*, always so protective, did not in any way, shape, or form want them to reach her.

That gray Sunday in the café of the Europa Hotel with her glass and her bottle of mineral water on her table, she watched the cars pass and remembered faces and places in Zaragoza, anecdotes and parties, and so many adventures typical of student life, and again she experienced the sensations of her past, and all the good memories suddenly seemed to her like the leaves of trees. Which trees? Who cares? Like those leaves that are one color on one side and another color on the other, one side shiny green, pleasant to see, the other a paler shade of green which was the green of guilt and remorse. She stared at her hands and was sorry she'd been young; even worse, she was sorry she'd been happy.

Her mother, by telephone, reproached her for not visiting. They felt abandoned now that so many people in the village had stopped speaking to them. Barely a minute later, her father came to the phone and, lowering his voice, told her, "Don't come, girl, don't even think of it, we'll visit you, and if you need anything, tell me." Damn, how much he loved her. My *aita*, my old man. In Zaragoza, she thought he'd sent her to study far away to free her from the persecution he was being subjected to. Because she did know about the threats and the graffiti and that they'd begun the preparations and administrative shifts to move the business to a more peaceful region. Nevertheless, she did not know what her mother told her when they'd already buried *aita*. In an extortion letter they'd enumerated a series of details about Nerea. All of them accurate: the place where she was studying at the time, her dinners on Thursdays with her girlfriends in San Sebastián's Parte Vieja. They even knew what color her motorbike was and where she usually parked it.

30

To Empty Memory

She'd finished the water by then. Seven fifteen p.m.: she decided to pay up and leave, but . . . But what? An interior voice said to her: Nerea, don't be an idiot, don't even think of locking yourself away in the solitude of your house with your head filled with memories; pour them out here and now; empty your mind. Think: the night is long and November is humid, dark, a bastard of a month.

At this point, she felt a sad-sad weight that kept her from getting out of the chair. She waved the bottle of mineral water at the waiter to signal she wanted another even though she wasn't thirsty. She was ashamed of sitting there like that without buying something.

She, her mother, her brother, all three had become satellites of a murdered man. Whether they wanted to or not, their respective lives for long years now had been rotating around that crime, that perpetual focal point of, of what?, of sorrow, of pain. It has to end but I don't know how to end it. Whenever I come up with an idea, someone comes along to knock it down.

The waiter brought the mineral water and a glass with ice in it and a slice of lemon. And she, tired of staring at the traffic, withdrawn into her tedium and nostalgia, forgot to thank him. She, within herself, as if she were in a meeting room at the prison sitting opposite a repentant ETA member: my family doesn't know where or when I found out. They always thought that the news had come to her from her roommates, informed by the son of the bar owner. On the other hand, what difference does it make? She told her mother she'd been with some girlfriends and had come back to the apartment late, very late at night, and knew nothing about what had happened.

A lie. At around five in the afternoon, as she was leaving the library, she heard: there's been an attack. Someone, behind her, asked: where? But Nerea, in a hurry to get back to her apartment, dump her things, and get ready for the party the students in the Veterinary School were throwing, paid no attention to the dialogue. An attack: so what? It simply did not arouse her curiosity. Tomorrow, maybe, I'll read about it in the paper. And in the apartment, the lights out, there was no one. She showered without wetting her hair, because outside it was cold and rainy. And then one of her roommates turned up. Hi, hi. But not a word about attacks. We know that Xabier had yet to call the bar owner, unless his boy had rung their bell when none of the three girls was at home. Before six, Nerea was ready. In point of fact, she didn't do much primping. In those days, she wasn't as fond of makeup as she is now. She sprinkled on some perfume and that was that. A boy she knew, what was his name?, José Carlos, came by and picked her up.

They formed a group of ten or twelve students, boys and girls, some Nerea didn't know. And off they went, gathering in a bar on Maestro Tomás Bretón Street with the idea of warming up with a few drinks and at the appropriate time, she did not know when exactly, they would climb into several cars since, according to what she'd heard, of course, the Veterinary School was all the way to hell and gone. She had not the slightest idea where it was. She asked if it was too far to walk to and people laughed. She became serious. More, she tensed up. Thinking she was angry, one of the boys said he was sorry. And a girl: what's wrong with you? She did answer the girl but evasively: nothing, just that. Another girl asked if she was feeling okay and she again said she was fine. What was she going to say?

Just by chance, she saw her father's picture on the screen of a television set up on a high shelf against the wall and she knew. Did she just suspect? No, she knew with absolute certainty from the first instant. Immediately in the running commentary at the bottom of the screen her certainty was confirmed: BUSINESSMAN MURDERED IN GUIPÚZCOA. Nerea, surrounded by laughter, by trivial, happy conversations, hid her emotions. Her heart was pounding so violently that it caused a sharp pain in her chest. As soon as people stopped talking to her, she turned her eyes to the television again. On the screen she saw people she couldn't hear because of the racket in the bar. People speaking into microphones. A gentleman with a white robe, *lehendakari* Ardanza with a serious face. And finally she saw a street and a facade she easily recognized.

She couldn't hold in her urine. Thank heaven she was wearing black jeans. She feigned naturalness. She whispered to the imaginary terrorist standing before her in this improvised and illusory healing encounter in the Europa's café: I still sat at that table another five minutes. She even attempted to smile at the joke a boy made and drank down her beer with fake calm. All these details after all these years felt like burning coals inside her. She had no one to whom she could unburden herself. To her family? Impossible. Even though they'd suffered the same disaster they wouldn't understand her. To Quique? That guy was always too wrapped up in his business to take any interest in stories about my life before we met.

She made a covert sign to that boy, José Carlos, who wasn't a boyfriend; but, well, she couldn't talk to any of the other men in the bar with the same sense of security. And the guy understood that she wanted to talk with him alone or who knows what he understood if in fact he understood anything. He just followed Nerea out to the street and then farther, almost all the way to the corner. Night had fallen. She, her thighs covered with pee, waited at a certain distance from the bar before turning around. Then she hugged José Carlos and exploded. God, what sobs. The boy was dumbfounded. What's the matter, what's wrong? Did those guys insult you? She: my *aita*. That was all she could manage to articulate: my *aita*. And the astonished kid: what are you saying, what's happening? Until, finally, Nerea managed to take a deep breath and tell her story. She asked her friend to get her back to her apartment.

She also asked him not to leave her alone, but to stay with her all night. Yes, whatever you want, whatever you want. They went up to the flat. And Nerea, before anything else, washed up in the bathroom. Immediately after, one of her roommates came to tell her that the boy from the bar downstairs said she was to call home and that it was urgent. Nerea: yes, the ETA has murdered my father.

The girl, who knew nothing until that instant, clasped her hands to her head and burst into tears. And the other roommate—horrified, what's going on, what's going on—burst into the corridor. She said something naive: is your father in the Guardia Civil? And she, too, burst into tears. Nerea begged José Carlos to go to her room with her. But aren't you going to call? She: would he please stay with her and not leave her alone. They went to bed and he, they killed your father, fuck, they killed him, and he had a hard time making love. He cursed, swore, fell asleep. And Nerea, in bed, in the dark, smoked one cigarette after another until she finished her pack and his. She would have smoked every cigarette in the universe.

Finally, the sun came up. The spaces between the blinds lit up with the clarity of the new day. Nerea felt a comfortable sensation, as if she'd found refuge in a date different from yesterday, which she knew she could never forget. As when an earthquake is over, or a fire, some devastating event, and you realize standing in the ruins that you've survived. My things. What time could it be, seven, eight in the morning? The room reeking of smoke, with no consideration whatsoever she shook José Carlos who was sleeping like a baby at her side. He could leave now, she told him. And the boy, thin, downy legs, dressed as quickly as he could and ran out, so eager to obey that he forgot to recite me any pretty words and to give me a farewell kiss.

And then alone, something very strange took place: everything was normal. As on every other morning, the traffic noises resounded, it rained as it always rains, along the sidewalks paraded pedestrians with umbrellas. What else? People went about their business as if there had been no attack the previous evening. Naked, Nerea peered out the window convinced there was a plot against her. She hated the morning and the rain and the house across the street and a lady walking her dog. Every object seemed to say to her: well, yes, you father's been murdered, so what? Beetles and chickens die, too. That thought cut her to the core. Suddenly she felt as if she had awakened from a bad dream to a worse one. She took a compact out of her bag and for the first time took a look at her eyes, her nose, her forehead, all victims of terrorism. The morning coolness that came through the window began to enter her body and she instantly understood that what happened the previous evening was true and that not even it was the worst thing, that the worst was yet to come and that she wouldn't be able to postpone it much longer. She experienced a violent chill thinking that she had to call her mother.

No one knows, no one can know. Without breakfast, without washing, she walked to a street phone on Avenida Goya. It must have been 8:30 a.m. Okay, she didn't call until after ten. She walked up the street and down the street or absently along Fernando el Católico and Gran Vía and back and each time she came to the telephone she went around it, getting soaked with rain and trembling because she was afraid to tell her mother she didn't want to travel to the village even though she had no pending examinations or urgent schoolwork. So? It's that I don't want to see the body or the coffin or the grave, that's horrible to me, and I also don't want to be connected with the murder or for reporters to come to interview me or take pictures so that all of Zaragoza knows who I am. She never stopped rehearsing the possible conversation she would have with her mother. I'll say this, I'll say something else. And at a magazine stand on Gran Vía, her father's face on the front page of a newspaper and she came within a heartbeat of buying it but she didn't dare. Why? She was so very ashamed.

She traveled to the village seven days later, when her father had already been buried and was no longer the most recent person killed by ETA. *Ama* never forgave her. I know it. I don't need her to tell me. Nerea's seen it over the course of all these years in myriad gestures, in the tone of certain words, in reproaches about secondary matters. Nerea would have wanted to tell all this to a repentant terrorist in jail and get it all out of her system the way you might vomit old, burning coals. It can't be because the good doctor says that she shouldn't. She doesn't want problems with the family; let's let sleeping dogs lie.

"Check, please."

31

DIALOGUE IN DARKNESS

In the kitchen as afternoon came on, she let him have it. She didn't even give him a chance to kick off his shoes. How could he not tell her that ETA was sending him letters?

"I thought that being married meant we told each other everything, or at least the important things."

Sitting in his chair, Txato, not at all perturbed, untied his shoelaces without looking up at Bittori who, standing in front of him, her face red with anger, would not stop talking. On and on. After a long day's work, he sighed toward the floor as if to say: when will this storm pass?

"How did you find out?"

"Talking with Miren."

"I wanted to take care of it on my own so you wouldn't get upset."

And Bittori went back to her tirade. After a while he interrupted her. What were they having for dinner?

"Monkfish in sauce. Why do you ask?"

"Because I have no appetite whatsoever."

They spoke little during dinner, each one immersed in their own anxious thoughts. Txato said only three things: that she, with her scolding and complaining, was not making things easier for him; that you only talk about things like this in secret; and that someone ought to cut Joxian's tongue out for revealing it to his wife and God only knows who else.

From the kitchen, he went directly to bed. To the sack, as he put it. Bittori stayed behind washing the dishes. It was useless for Nerea to remind her from time to time that the family had enough money

for a dishwasher. But Bittori was having none of that—as long as
I have my own two hands I'm fine, and that a contraption like that
is nothing but a useless expense, that they use a lot of water and
electricity, and when you get married, do what you think best in
your house but leave me in peace in mine.

Txato usually stayed out of these domestic squabbles. Dishwasher, no dishwasher, it was all the same to him. An early riser,
he also went to bed early. On workdays, at six a.m. he was already
taking care of business in the office. And on weekends, since he
was taking part in the Sunday phases of the cyclotourism program,
he was also up and about before sunrise. It might happen that on
some occasion or other, caught up in a hard-fought game of *mus*,
he could forget to check his watch, but with few exceptions, the day
normally ended for him at ten p.m.

The only thing that would have kept him up at that hour was
the rebroadcast of soccer matches on Basque television. He would
watch the matches until it came time to clear out, because Bittori
controlled the TV, and Bittori liked to watch her programs alone.

Once dinner was over, Txato got into bed, as always, on Bittori's
side. From the earliest days of their marriage, he warmed the bed for
her. Even in summer. A habit not born from any agreement between
them and one he never stopped practicing even on days when there
was some matrimonial argument in progress. Later, Bittori would
join him, at eleven or twelve, and he, without waking up, would
slide over to his side.

And Bittori did come. Often she would leaf through some ladies'
magazine; but this time she immediately turned off the lamp on
the night table. She remained sitting up in the darkness, her arms
crossed, her back against the headboard. And he, who snored, was
breathing quietly, so Bittori knew he wasn't sleeping.

"How long are you going to wait before telling me everything?"

Txato didn't answer; but she knew that he was wide awake and
didn't bother to repeat the question. After a few seconds he clicked
his tongue as a sign of annoyance and, clearly unwilling, brought
Bittori up to date on his persecution, skipping no details, without
omitting his visit to France. On the other hand, he said not a word
about the references to Nerea in the last letter.

"What do you intend to do?"

"Wait."

"Wait for what?"

Bittori felt him roll over toward her in the darkness.

"I paid them already for this year and they're not going to get any more out of me. The bastards have demanded a huge sum, right at the moment when I've taken on debt and made purchases, and when a few of my slow clients just aren't paying. Remember that we still owe part of the money for the San Sebastián apartment. Who knows, there might have been a mistake. Some jackass who does the books didn't write down my payment or wrote it in the wrong place. How would I know if the guy I handed the envelope to didn't just keep it to pay for his fun? Or maybe Joxian's right and the second demand was really meant for someone else. That's why I think that for the moment it's better to do nothing and wait for time to clear matters up. And if it's me who's mistaken, they'll be making their demands soon enough."

"To tell you the truth, I'm a little afraid."

"What good does being afraid do?"

"Those people are bad and they've got a lot of friends in the village."

"The people around here know me. I'm from here, I speak Basque, I don't get involved in politics, I create jobs. Besides. Whenever they take up a collection for festivals, for the soccer team, or for whatever, Txato gives as much as anyone. If someone from outside comes around to hurt me, I'm sure they'd stop him. Watch out, he's one of us. Besides, they can always talk to me, you know that."

"I think you're too sure of yourself on this."

"Don't think I'm a dumbbell. I've taken precautions. As far as the business is concerned, I'm safe and sound. I've got a way to defend myself."

"Is that right? What have you got, a pistol hidden in a drawer?"

"Whatever I've got hidden in the drawer is my business, but let me tell you again that I'm okay on all that. Could all this get complicated? If it does, I'll just take the trucks somewhere else. To La Rioja or somewhere near there. I started out with less when I was young and did I get ahead or didn't I?"

"Well, even though you're from here, I wouldn't be surprised if one of your workers has given information about you to ETA."

"Could be."

"Have you talked with any of the other businessmen from around here?"

"Why bother? I'm sure they all pay. I suggested that much to the older Arrizabalaga. I saw he was beating around the bush, not wanting to say anything. These matters, as I said, have to be resolved individually."

Bittori slid down under the sheet and the blanket until she was flat on her back. The noises of the neighborhood, though muted, could be heard, a couple of voices in the street, the garbage truck. And the couple was shoulder to shoulder, backside to backside, and it was then that Txato, his face turned to the wall on his side of the bed, let it out, he had to let it out, we know it weighed too heavily on his tongue:

"I want Nerea to study far away. Wherever, but away from here, after this summer."

"Wait a minute, where's this coming from?"

"It comes from the fact that I want my daughter to study far away."

"Did you talk to her?"

"No. But when you see her, you can bring it up so she'll know where I'm coming from."

They fell silent. Below the balcony, a pack of partiers passed by. Then there was a silence broken by the church bell marking the hour. Txato, breaking with custom, did not snore all night.

32

Papers and Objects

As they covered him with the slab, Bittori thought—her eyes dry, because from now on I'm not going to cry even if they rub onions in them—that the next time light shines into that hole it'll be when they bury me. She clung to the conviction that this man took a basket of secrets with him to his grave.

She often reproached him about it—you criminal—especially during her first visits to the cemetery.

"You kept me in limbo. I don't think you told me even half of what was happening to you and what they were doing to you. Txatito, the day they set me down next to you you're going to have a lot to tell me."

But before she went home she forgave him. Fourteen farewells. How many times Bittori and Nerea heard Xabier say all that stuff about "that's the way the terrorists defend the interests of the working class." Having no choice, Xabier closed down the business, not without first asking his mother if she wanted to take over. Me? He asked Nerea the same question when the girl finally found it in her heart to come to the village. Me? And he couldn't do it, either. So, with the help of a financial consultant they sold whatever they could sell and the rest they just abandoned.

Xabier hung a sign on the gate: CLOSED BECAUSE OF DEATH. For a few instants, his mother came out of her languor to whisper that he should put CLOSED BECAUSE OF MURDER. He didn't do it. And the employees? Not a single one attended the funeral. Two did come to the burial in San Sebastián.

Days after, an employee representing the entire staff came to the owner's son to ask him when they should return to work. Even then, the employee forgot to give his condolences. Xabier stared at him with pity and repugnance. Do these people actually believe the owner can be murdered and nothing changes? Xabier gave him a song and dance with professorial calm and high-flown language. And since the employee, deaf to explanations, insisted on knowing when they should begin to work again, Xabier, at the limits of his patience, told him he was just a simple doctor and that he lacked the competence to run a shipping company.

He had a lot of trouble going through the papers in the office, the negotiations with banks, the cancellation of orders (some international), the sale of property, the dismantling of the business, and a million bureaucratic glitches he finally turned over to specialists, following the recommendation of a colleague at the hospital.

That same colleague had a suggestion, which he passed on to his mother: a possible solution intended to preserve jobs. What was it? Turn over the business under favorable economic terms to the employees.

Not a chance in the world. Bittori suddenly forgot she was in mourning. How could he possibly think to suggest such a hideous idea? Those employees went out on strike any number of times, on some occasions accompanied by broken windows, picket lines at the entrance, and threats to *aita*. Among them there was a leader, a very aggressive guy, something or other Andoni, with the emblem of the Basque trades union, the Langile Abertzaleen Batzordeak, on his overalls, who took the leading role and who had, on his own, robbed Txato of innumerable hours of sleep. Txato had fired him, but he turned up hours later with two killers from the union and forced his way back in. What about the other workers? Some, true enough, were decent people, but did they make any gestures of solidarity, of compassion, after the murder? They could have sent a sympathy card. But not even that. Only two of them turned up at the Polloe cemetery and they never said a word.

"I'd rather throw it all away."

Xabier loaded his car with boxes of note cards, bills, shipping notes, and all kinds of other documents, some perfectly ordered in ring binders, others loose. We wouldn't want. What? Well, we wouldn't want someone to take advantage of the fact that the owner was not there and that the place was closed down. Someone could rob the place. People who owed money trying to erase any record of their debt. Followers of the cause who wouldn't be satisfied with the murder.

Nerea:

"We're getting paranoid."

"Could be."

Those piles of papers didn't rouse Bittori from indifference. They should tell her where to sign and that was that. She wanted to know nothing about the business. The business, she said, was part of Txato, like his protruding ears and his fondness for bicycling. Xabier studied his mother carefully to see if she was joking, but she wasn't. Darkly, she predicted that if her children took control of the business they would have the same fate as their father.

On the other hand, she took a great interest in preserving the personal objects the dead man kept in his office. One afternoon, Xabier brought them to the San Sebastián apartment in several cardboard boxes. Some time later, she and Xabier brought them to Nerea, who still keeps them in her house.

And Bittori told Xabier he could leave because she wanted to look over Txato's belongings by herself.

"Would you allow me a small commentary on the contents?"

"No."

"Did you know that *aita*—?"

"I said no."

And she meant it. She walked him to the door. A kiss and *agur*. Alone in the flat, Bittori, scat, chased Ikatza off the sofa, sat down, and opened the boxes. Txato never told her he kept a pistol in the office. A surprise? No. I always thought he did. Didn't he always say he felt safe there? She felt the heft of the black weapon. Could it be loaded? The cold metal, her fingers far away from the trigger. But the temptation was great. She aimed at the ceiling light. What does the person who fires feel when his victim falls, when blood begins to pour out of the holes the bullets make in the body?

She took out half a dozen small boxes, twenty cartridges of 9 x 19 mm bullets, all unopened except one. Txatito, my gangster, my gunman, how were you going to shoot someone when you were a saint? Why weren't you armed the day when? Maybe, I'm thinking, you could have defended yourself.

She put those mortal artifacts on the floor and took out the framed photographs her husband had displayed on a shelf in the office: one of the two of them young, smiling, in front of the Tower of Pisa; one of each child, Xabier at the age of twelve or thirteen, Nerea, really pretty in her first-communion dress; another of the four of them together, all dressed up at the door of the Azpeitia church, at a relative's wedding, and two others of Txato, each with one of his children.

Bittori took out other objects that interested her less. Ballpoint pens, a fountain pen, trophies from the cyclotourism club and from various *mus* tournaments, and a candle in the shape of a cactus given to him on some occasion by Nerea, his princess, his favorite, the one who didn't come to the burial. In sum, sentimental trivia, decorations, souvenirs. And the extortion letters? Not a one. Maybe Txato destroyed them. Maybe Xabier filed them among the other papers.

33

GRAFFITI

The office was in a loft. It was a simple platform on iron columns, with a glass partition that allowed the boss to take in the interior of the warehouse with a glance, and a window that overlooked the esplanade. Txato had set it up that way so he could, as he said, keep an eye on the operation. Txato was a very controlling person. He would have wanted to do everything in the business: administration, close deals, supervise loading and unloading, oiling motors, check tire pressure, wash the trucks and drive them. He noted departures and arrivals, equally attentive to the arrival of a client or some unexpected visitor. As soon as he heard the sound of a motor, he was looking out the window.

The lot was surrounded by a six-foot concrete wall, which supported an even higher wire fence. A sliding gate sealed the entrance at night. During the workday, it was usually open. The village boys would ask Nerea when she was a little girl if her *aita* had built a prison. And she, to follow the joke, answered that yes he had and that the employees were the prisoners.

One day, at the first hour of the workday, Txato was at his window watching the coupling of a truck and a trailer. He didn't trust the men. He never trusted them. Not even his most veteran drivers. When they'd finished, the truck moved out. Then a part of the wall until then hidden by the truck came into view. And from his office Txato read the large, twisted letters inscribed in spray paint: OPPRESSOR SHORTY.

That was the first graffiti directed at him. At first, he believed it was just hooliganism. More than the accusation, which did annoy him, and more than the dirtying and ugly act itself, which annoyed him even more, and more than the translation into Spanish of his Basque nickname, which drove him wild, he was disturbed by the fact that the words were on the interior side of the wall. Which meant that an intruder had entered, at night, into his space. Bittori, who was drying her hands on her apron, did not discount the possibility that it might be an employee. Txato came down from the office using the narrow, steep metal stairs, where one of these days, in Bittori's opinion, "you're going to kill yourself," and was more concerned to cover up his rage than to watch where he put his feet. He walked to the area set aside as a repair shop. There he asked for a can of spray paint. He could have ordered an employee to cover up that stupidity, but Txato was a man of passion, of let's-get-going, of rapid decisions, and also a man who took on the greatest possible number of jobs, manual or bureaucratic. So, that was that, he went to the wall and wiped out the offense.

At home, during dinner, he told Bittori. Together they went over the names of the employees (she called them "workers") trying to figure out the possible culprit. Someone full of resentment, someone who thought he'd been treated badly by the boss. But as usual, without witnesses or proof there was nothing to be done. It didn't occur to either of them to connect the vandalism with the extortion letters. Weeks passed, they forgot the incident, and followed their daily routines.

After a Saturday in mid-March, the lives of Txato and his family were never the same. What time did it happen? Joxian and Txato came up the street disputing some point or other because they were as fond of arguing as they were of each other. They were partners at *mus* and quite good at it; but sometimes, as we all know, the cards favor our rivals. Then, on the way home, it wasn't strange that they'd be walking along each one blaming the defeat on the other.

They'd eaten at the gastronomic society—each one with his own dish, whatever his wife had prepared at home—and since they'd planned to be out early the next morning, they played cards before dinner and not after as they did on other evenings. The next day a rather long route in the cyclotourism program awaited them, one that would end in a bar in the center of Zumaya.

They were on the way home, between sober and drunk, enmeshed in one of their usual disputes, obscenities flying back and forth, with no limits because their friendship was in no danger. With the heat of their conversation and the weak light of the street lamps they didn't notice some fresh graffiti covering the older tags along with many posters covering the lower part of the facades. At first, they didn't notice one that was still wet next to the entryway to Txato's house. The two friends had stopped to finish off their argument. They were saying good night, one said let's hope it doesn't rain tomorrow, and the other: okay, you pain in the ass, seven thirty in the square, when Joxian's attention was struck by his friend's name written on the wall.

"Holy shit."

"What?"

TXATO TXIBATO. Son of a bitch. And Joxian: cover that up before you go to bed, you can't play around with that. They said goodbye and Txato, grumbling, the assholes, instead of going up to his house went to the garage where he stored some old cans of paint. Me, an informer? They wrote that so they could get a good rhyme. I've never talked to a cop in my life. Another problem: he had no brush. Or maybe he did, but with his nerves on edge and the anger he was feeling he couldn't find it. Finally, he did find a small brush, paint, and some newspaper. For better or for worse, he managed to make both words illegible, staining his trousers in the process. Bittori would make a racket. Let her make a racket. Informer. In a village like his, the worst calumny. It was the same slogan that was written on the wall surrounding his business a few weeks back.

He fully intended to buy fresh paint the next day, as soon as he got back from his bicycle excursion. He told Bittori all about it in bed. And she:

"So, you think they may paint more graffiti."

"I'm starting to think it's not just a simple prank. We have to be prepared."

"In that case, why bother painting over them? That's a losing strategy. And tell me, did you see if there was more graffiti along the street?"

"I was walking with Joxian and we didn't see any others."

"Are you sure?"

"Absolutely sure? No. But it's late now and I'm in my pajamas."

Informer, oppressor, traitor. They'd written all of that, in Basque and in Spanish, on his street, on the surrounding streets, in the square. A classic persecution campaign. At least twenty tags in the old part of town. So many all at once can't be the work of a single vandal. And God knows what there could be on the houses in the outskirts. Here we see careful planning and many hands. He left his house early wearing his bicycling outfit and couldn't believe his eyes. Txato this, Txato that. *Herriak ez du barkatuko.* That was the program in play. And when he got to the square and joined the other bicyclists, he noted what? He noted something, lukewarm greetings. Eyes that avoided meeting his. He missed the jokes from other days, although it could be that he'd suddenly become susceptible and a victim of his own imagination and suspicion.

They started off. Fourteen or fifteen, the usual men. Other members of the club had already left or would leave later. And the only one who pedaled near him was Joxian, who was also more silent than usual. Before they left the last house in the village behind, the shout of a boy from a window insulted him:

"Txato, son of a bitch!"

Not a one of his group did a thing to defend him. No one made a comment, a reproach, a reply to the insult. The group began to disperse. It was the usual thing. Some were faster than others. And Txato was left alone with Joxian, who the whole time stayed two or three yards behind him without saying a word. And going up the Orio mountain, he lagged even farther back even though he was a better hill climber than Txato.

They finally caught sight of Zumaya. They knew the bar from other years. Inside, someone would stamp the card where the various stages of the tour that season were listed. And then, the reward for all their effort, fried eggs and ham. They could hear voices and laughter from the street. Txato walked in. There was a sudden silence. And that was just too much for him. He couldn't stand any more. He didn't have his card stamped. Without saying goodbye to anyone, not even Joxian, he got on his bike and set out for home on his own.

34

MENTAL PAGES

When he was arrested, Joxe Mari's hair hung down to his shoulders. What became of those curls, of the tickle of hair on his forehead and also here at the nape of his neck? Better not to think about it. When he looks at himself in the mirror, he says: that's not me.

And one year passed, two, four, six years passed, each one with its Christmas, with the village festivals celebrated without him. Actually, everything happens now without him. He doesn't see the river flow, doesn't hear the church bell ring, and right at this moment he'd pay millions (which he doesn't have) to eat a few figs in his father's garden. To keep from putting himself in a foul mood, he chooses not to count the years of jail time he still has to endure; although there in the depth of his vague hopes, he doesn't discount the possibility that maybe the organization, maybe the national government, maybe international pressure, et cetera. Some nights, in the dark, he tries to re-create in his mouth the taste of *chacolí*, the sharp wine of the Basque Country, or of cider, it's all the same. And sometimes it seems to him that he almost tastes them.

In his sixth year, he began to lose his hair. Okay, that's the least of his problems. Once he leaned the crown of his head against one of the bars on his bed and, damn, he felt a chill on fuzzy skin he'd never felt before. Now he's bald. Completely bald. If he ever gets out, no one in the village will recognize him. He's shaved his head down to the zero point so no one will notice, so it looks as if he's got no hair because that's the way he wants it.

His mother does not like his shaved head. Truth be told, she didn't like his long hair in the old days, you look like a beggar, nor did she like his earring or his militancy, although with regard to that she changed overnight. For his sake? Certainly. *Ama* is strong. God, what courage she has. The old man is another story, like Gorka. Peace-loving, soft. I take after *ama* and that's how I am and that's why I'm here and why I'm going to be here a long time. Where? In my cell. In the fucking cell in the fucking jail until the next transfer or until they let me out.

Today he's *txapeo*, but because he's pissed off, see? Nothing to do with the struggle or the protest. Just to be alone and not to go out into the patio and the corridors and see the same faces I see every day. As he does so often, he stretches out in bed, picking over memories like someone leafing through a photo album. Sometimes he's there for two or three hours mentally reviewing pages of old stories, and although on the one hand nostalgia eats away at him, on the other he manages to get the hours to pass without tedium. Come on, what more do you want; they're just a few hours taken away from the mountain of years left on his sentence. In such instances, the surprises are what he likes most. Because he's calm, sunk in his memories, staring at the ceiling, and suddenly such and such a memory comes to him or yet another from such a long time ago, from when he was free and had hair and played handball and drank all the *chacolí* or cider or beer he wanted.

They must have been how old, ten or twelve years? Something like that. The two of them together, he and Jokin, inseparable, going up into the neighboring hills with slingshots to hunt birds. They made them out of forked hazelwood branches, strips of rubber cut from inner tubes, and a piece of leather. One Sunday, he remembers, taking advantage of the fact that it was a festival day and there was no one at Txato's business, they climbed over the entry gate to get to where they stored old wheels and there, using a knife, cut the strips from an inner tube. The ones they made that time were the best slingshots they ever had. Seriously. They could send a projectile all the way across the river and it would fall far beyond. Using ball bearings or stones, they tried to bring down birds, but as far as he can remember they never managed to get a single one. However, they were good at breaking bottles or hitting the traffic sign at the far end of the industrial park, until finally with all the stones they fired at it they chipped the paint to the point that not even God could have read the sign. One afternoon, Jokin got the idea of taking shots at windows. Crash, the broken glass collapsed. They started running, and someone came out and shouted at them—son of a bitch. Well, if you want to catch us, start running. And they broke up laughing. Eleven, twelve years old. Snot-nosed kids. About that time, the armed struggle began. We carried it in our genes. He smiles staring at the ceiling. What am I doing here, laughing while I'm racking my brains? He becomes serious. He turns another mental page.

When they were older they went out hunting with a decoy. He and Jokin, and sometimes Koldo as well. He tells the ceiling that using a decoy works better with smart guys than with jerks. Koldo was neither the one nor the other, but he had a goldfinch that could sing its head off. I never saw anything like it in my life. Koldo would hang the cage in the bushes. The damn goldfinch, *peep peep*, off and running with singing. The three friends would wait silently about twenty yards away, smoking. Not a word, not a sound. Then all of a sudden there would be a signal and we'd jump like hell out of our hiding place. And the birds, scared out of their wits, would get stuck to the branches covered with birdlime. And even without scaring them, don't tell me. They would try to get away but it was useless, and the more they flapped their wings the more they got stuck to the branches. There were afternoons when we'd catch, no exaggeration, seven or eight goldfinches, always watching out that the Guardia Civil didn't catch us. At night, our *amatxos* would fry them up for dinner. What a great life, how awful that you grow up. Later on, Koldo became a goldfinch. Meaning he sang. But why hold it against him? They beat the crap out of him in the barracks over in Intxaurrondo. They dunked his head in water. The damned tub. And of course he gave them names. He and Jokin: he shouldn't worry when, after all, sooner or later they would be coming for us. They ran away to France, and after a few months they found Koldo by chance in a bar in Brittany.

"Listen, you have to forgive me. I didn't think I'd get out of there alive."

"Relax. We're going to give them a dose of their own medicine."

When they used Jokin's pellet gun they got fewer than they did using the decoy. But the pellet gun was a marvelous toy, they shared it and had one hell of a time. Later, when they were in the organization, when they did the weapons course, the instructor was left with his mouth hanging open. Shit, boy, where did you learn how to shoot like that? Better than some veterans, who were all talk but were blind when it came time to hit the target. Jokin, in village festivals at the shooting stand, *bam bam, bam bam,* never missed, that despite the fact that they'd deliberately twisted the sights out of alignment. The old guy at the stand said enough is enough and with a really mean face grabbed the rifle. He played dumb so he wouldn't have to give Jokin the prize. But then a lot of us gathered around the stand. The old man had no choice but to give up the prize, some crappy stuffed animal.

It was about then that Joxe Mari had his first thoughts about what it was like to shoot another person. Sometimes they'd shoot a cat. But a human being is something else. And he whispered to Jokin: can you imagine? A thought like that never passed through Jokin's head. The pellet gun was for having fun, he said. He would dream about getting older and hunting with a more powerful weapon, not to shoot at little birds or cats but wild pigs and deer. He dreamed about going on a safari in Africa.

As he talked about all that, the two of them hidden behind some bushes, Joxe Mari aimed at the house owner who was cutting the grass on the hill in front of them with a sack over his head to protect him from the rain. Joxe Mari pressed his finger against the trigger and imagined the house owner suddenly falling forward badly wounded and rolling down the hill. Jokin said in a low voice that weapons aren't toys. How old could they be then, sixteen? Not older. At night he dreamed that a patrol car with sirens blasting came looking for him because he killed a policeman, and many years later, his eyes fixed on the ceiling of his cell, he remembered the scene with the homeowner.

35

A Box of Flames

On the counter: one row of different-colored piggy banks and another with photos of jailed militants, the pad with tickets for the raffle with a *mariskada* as a prize, and to one side, along the wall, the display of key holders, lighters, flags, scarves, and other things. The two friends waited in a tavern on Juan de Bilbao Street, sitting in the back, almost in the dark, abstaining from alcohol. Jokin asked the barmaid with short, straight bangs who was nodding her head to the music for a glass of tap water and she gave it to him.

Every few seconds Joxe Mari glanced at his watch. And Koldo, where the hell was he? Jokin amused himself turning the pages of *Egin*. The tavern was half empty. All the *abertzale* boys shouted slogans at the demonstration about the recent capture of a cell. Also, the village cohort, which had moved to San Sebastián as if on the way to war, because no matter how you look at it this is a war. Or a conflict or whatever you'd like to call it. And with the cohort went Koldo, who'd been ordered to join his two friends as soon as the first demonstrators reached the Bulevar, where the usual ritual would be carried out. A member of the Herri Batasuna National Committee would stand in the music kiosk and read a communiqué and at a given moment two men wearing hoods would step up to burn a Spanish flag. Meanwhile, the six members from the village would carry out their action in another part of the city, not far from there. That's what they'd been getting ready for since yesterday evening.

They were nervously waiting for Koldo, not drinking a drop of alcohol. Others drink to get courage, but they have conviction and discipline. Botching the job was improper for Basques (Joxe Mari). Fear, for anyone who needs it (Jokin).

Koldo, Koldito, come a-running if you have to, but don't let us down. Why all the hurry? Because they didn't want the *jarraitxus* from Rentería to beat them to the punch. It happened once before that those guys were quicker on the draw than they were and they got all the praise. So what? Well, they just set fire to a new launch worth more than twenty million pesetas, a Mercedes, and that will really put a dent in the municipal treasury. And they had to settle for an old, broken-down Pegaso, which burns much worse and doesn't cost the Town Council even half what the Mercedes costs. On top of that we saved them the costs of having the thing junked.

Koldo comes in, checked shirt, prominent jaw. He orders a short beer. No one says a word.

"For fuck's sake, guys, my mouth is dried out from shouting."

This is not the time for arguments. They leave him standing at the bar. The barmaid, what a cutie she is, cheers them on.

"Come on, champs, kick some ass."

To avoid having the bottles rattle, Joxe Mari carries his knapsack close to his body. They dash along Narrica Street. Koldo catches up, running at full speed.

"Wait for me, you bastards."

At the far end of town, at the Bulevar, you can hear the crowd chanting slogans. And Koldo, one step behind his friends, makes his report breathing hard: a shitload of people, the buses rerouted. The other two neither look at him nor answer. Then Joxe Mari does stop for an instant next to the display window of a hat shop.

"Are there many *txakurras*?"

"No. A few *beltzas*."

The passersby not involved in the demonstration, prudent and fearful, leave the area. Blue sky, a pleasant afternoon, baby carriages here and there. But you sense a tension in the air, a strange transparency, the prelude to the fight.

Jokin wants to know if Koldo saw the Rentería guys.

"No."

"Okay then, let's go."

And the three of them make their way, in Indian file. Joxe Mari, the tallest, the most powerfully built, in the middle with his knapsack filled with Molotov cocktails. Walking neither slowly nor quickly, they make their way through the mob of young people who are shouting *Presoak kalera, amnistia osoa.* They say nothing. The demonstrators get out of their way, because they see something in them, notice something about them that says it would be better to let them through.

Following their plan, they join the rest of the group at a public bench in Guipúzcoa Plaza. Opposite them, a charming scene of pigeons and sparrows, grandchildren with grandparents, ladies with dogs, boyfriends with girlfriends, and passersby coming and going along the gravel paths under the trees.

Tons of greetings. The six boys head for Avenida, three on one side of the street, three on the other. Just before they get there, they gather together next to some scaffolding that rises to the top of the facade. There they cover their mouths with handkerchiefs and pull up their hoods. Jokin prefers the balaclava. Koldo ties on Joxe Mari's handkerchief so he doesn't have to put down the knapsack.

Now they know they're being watched; now how their appearance, look, look, attracts a lot of attention. Some people, when they see them, cross the street and stand there whispering; but no one tries to stop them. No one rebukes them or calls the police. And everyone realizes these boys are going to raise a ruckus.

In a few minutes they catch sight of a city bus. Coming from Echaide Street, it has just entered Avenida and is heading toward them. In its normal route, the bus would have continued straight on to the Bulevar, which is now occupied by the demonstrators. The boys see it's a number 5, with passengers, though not many. Bad luck: it wasn't one of the new ones. But, once they'd covered their faces, they had no choice but to act. With no hesitation Jokin said: that one.

They let a few cars pass, but they stopped the one right in front of the bus. One slapped his hand down hard on the hood, another opened the driver's side door, ordered the driver, a woman about thirty years old, to get out, and quickly, four of them slid the vehicle around so it blocked the street.

"My daughter, my daughter!"

Koldo pushed her back with a harsh shove.

"Get the fuck out of here."

He almost knocks her down. The woman, who's lost a shoe, fought to get back to the car. And from the other side of the street, a gentleman shouted:

"Leave her in peace, you thug."

The bus, now that the street was blocked, had to stop. And since the boys abandoned the car, the woman seized the chance to pull a two- or three-year-old girl out of the backseat.

The bus driver, how did he react? Did he fight back? Was he paralyzed by fear? Jokin ordered him to open the doors, but the guy doesn't understand. They used a slingshot to send a ball bearing into the windshield. It leaves a crack in the glass without piercing it. If it hits the driver in the face . . . Finally, we see he understood what the man with the balaclava was ordering him to do and he opened the doors. A dozen terrified passengers rushed to get off. Right then, the first incendiary bottle exploded inside. Joxe Mari gave instructions:

"Aim for the seats, the seats."

The driver jumped out. It took him a few seconds to notice one of his shoes was burning. He kicked it off as fast as he could. Not wasting a second, he crossed the street slapping his hand against his smoking trouser cuffs. By then, the bus was an enormous box of flames. A dense cloud rose, grazing the facade closest to it. The curious massed at a prudent distance. One of the aggressors took several pictures with a pocket camera.

Once the action was over, Joxe Mari, his fist raised, shouted with his eyes fixed on the bus enveloped in flames.

"Gora Euskadi askatuta!"

"Gora!"

"Gora ETA!"

"Gora!"

The six boys started running, some along one street, others along the parallel street, heading for the Bulevar. They had planned to regroup in the Guipúzcoa Plaza. The rest of the way they ran along with their faces uncovered, calmly conversing.

"Mission accomplished. Time for a drink."

At that very moment, the carillon in the city hall tower was chiming in the purple afternoon light.

From A to B

Congratulatory hands patted Joxe Mari's back from time to time. A wide, hard back, a muscular wall covered by a striped sweatshirt. As soon as they walked into the bar: this guy, that guy, the sister of the cousin of, there you go, pats on the back. Joxe Mari, just nineteen, was sitting at the table right opposite the entrance to the Arrano Taberna. The gang chatted, over the loud rock music. A bad place for conspiracy, according to Jokin.

"They can hear us from out on the street."

Anyone who entered or left had no choice but to pass behind Joxe Mari's back. And he responded to the congratulations with a gesture of dignified pride, since in reality he'd done nothing, as he said half apologizing, but his duty. That morning the village handball team had beaten the Elgóibar squad, 25 to 24. Joxe Mari had scored seven goals. Everyone praised him:

"They're going to make a professional out of you."

"Well, we'll see about that."

At the other end of the table, Jokin was painting a halcyon picture of socialism and independence, with the seven territories of Euskal Herria united and purged of social classes, where even the grass, want to bet, will speak Basque. And then, in his opinion, get along with the Spaniards and the French, see?, but they in their house and we in our house. He laid out the strategic steps following the path established by the Alternative Basque Liberation Movement (KAS). The boys were drinking their heads off, some wine-and-Coke calimocho, some beer, all with a unanimous expression of approval on their faces.

The only one who from time to time became distracted, who looked in other directions or raised his eyes toward the television set, was Joxe Mari, to whom every two seconds someone who'd just walked in or was just leaving said a few words.

Jokin slammed his fist on the table.

"Anyone who gets in the way, blocking the achievement of our objective as a people, must be eliminated. Even if it was my own *aita*, God damn it. It's like going from A to B. We're in A"—he put the tip of his index finger on the table—"and B is there, where that glass sits. Well, we're going to B no matter what it costs."

The circle of friends seconded him in gestures and words. One:

"Day by day, each one in his village or his city, we're moving this thing forward."

Another:

"But it's going to cost a lot, you know? The state is tough."

"The state is a motherfucker."

And Jokin, gesturing as if to demand proprietary rights over the conversation:

"Greater empires have fallen. Look at Napoleon. Today you kill one soldier, tomorrow another, and at the end you wipe out the army."

They made toasts, joking, all of one opinion, for the postulates of the KAS. And Joxe Mari neither toasted nor realized what was happening because he was chatting with a guy standing next to him who worked in the same place. The boys asked him for his opinion.

"You all know I don't like politics. It doesn't matter to me who gives the orders. I'm only fighting so Euskal Herria will be a lib-erated nation. The rest you can figure out on your own. This guy here"—meaning Jokin—"has said it all: we're going from A to B and when we get to B leave me in peace. I'm heading for the hills, I'll plant some apple trees, set up a chicken coop, and you can all go fuck yourselves."

Voices of disagreement instantly rose:

"We have to think of the working class as well."

"And besides, we'll have to expel the Spanish occupying forces. Not as easy as you say."

Joxe Mari swallowed some calimocho and staring with utter calm at everyone sitting at the table said:

"You complicate everything. Look, if we have independence, the rest we can arrange among ourselves. Improve the lives of workers? Perfect. We'll do it. Who's going to stop us if no one from outside is governing us? The question of the Basque language: the same thing. Every son of a bitch will learn Basque and that's that. The Spanish police and army? Well, if we're independent, we will already have given them the boot. We'll have our own police and our own army, and me my chickens and apple trees."

"What about Navarra?"

He snorted before answering:

"If we don't have Navarra then we haven't reached B and there is no Euskal Herria. And the same goes for the Iparralde territories. Don't you see how you're complicating things?"

He said nothing more because someone was waving to him from the street. Josune: short bangs, hair going down her back, leather bracelets on her bare arm. Joxe Mari runs to kiss her. She steps back flashing stern eyes. She doesn't want him to kiss her out on the street, how many times does she have to tell him?

"What's wrong?"

"I saw your sister in the plaza with some guy who seems to be her boyfriend. I mean I guess because they were dancing so close. Arantxa lets herself be kissed in public. I don't like that stuff."

"So you're here to tell me gossip?"

"I deliberately went over to them so she'd introduce me. He isn't from the village."

"Look, *neska*, my sister is older than I am. She goes out with anyone she likes. I don't get involved."

"Don't you even want to know what his name is?"

He didn't care.

"Guillermo."

Joxe Mari didn't think the name was either bad or good. The last name would be something else.

"What's his last name?"

"I didn't ask."

"If he joins the family we'll give him a nickname. Don't worry."

And the fact that Arantxa was going out with a boy and that she'd brought him to the village to show him off to her friends and maybe even the family also mattered to Joxe Mari not a bit.

"He's an outsider. You can tell just looking at him. And he doesn't speak Basque."

"How do you know?"

"For Christ's sake, when Arantxa introduced him I spoke to him and the guy didn't understand and we had to go on in Spanish. It would be hell if a Spaniard were to worm his way into the family. Maybe he's even from the police and using the pretext that he's going out with your sister he's busy spying on all of us, beginning with you."

Joxe Mari furrowed his brow.

"The fact that he doesn't speak Basque doesn't mean that . . ."

"Doesn't mean what?"

Laughter, blaring voices, and the music flooded the Arrano Taberna. And Joxe Mari scratched his head and looked: right over there, his gang busy drinking, happy, and standing in front of him, Josune, with a stern expression on her face.

"Okay, when I see her I'll ask about it. Are you going into the tavern?"

"They're waiting for me at home."

"And when can someone give you a kiss?"

"Not here."

"Well, let's go into that entryway."

They did and they embraced in the half-light between the door and the row of mailboxes, until they heard the footsteps of someone coming down the stairs.

37

THE CAKE OF DISCORD

There's an explanation for Gorka's crushed nose and the chip in one of his incisors. When he was nine, he was run over by a van. It could have killed him. And he wouldn't have been the first in the village. Convalescing, he asked his parents, using that sweet, singsong tone he's lost now but which from time to time is audible in his adult voice, if he had died, if they'd have placed a cross at the side of the road the way they did for Isidoro Otamendi, who got killed one morning going to work on his motorbike.

Now that the shock had passed, Joxian was making jokes:

"Of course. But we'd have set up an even bigger one. Made out of iron so it would last for years and years."

Miren didn't think the conversation was funny.

"Shut up, all of you. Wait and see if God doesn't punish us."

A thin, fragile boy. Then, with the onset of puberty, he sprouted and walked hunched over as if he were ashamed of his height or perhaps of the acne dotting his cheeks. People would say to his mother on the street that if he kept on that way he'd be a hunchback. Miren felt that as if it were a shot.

"What do you want me to do? Punish him so he stops growing?"

By the time he turned sixteen he was the tallest in the family. Another more robust, more solid, and less elastic boy wouldn't have survived the accident, they said. Who said? His mother, his father, all of them. Gorka learned to smile without showing the cracked tooth, but there was no way to hide his smashed nose. A little smashed, don't exaggerate, in his mother's opinion.

"Would you rather be dead?"

For him, very smashed, totally smashed, *ama*. Also for Joxe Mari, who ramped up his brother's complexes calling him boxer and challenging him to fight. As a joke, he would stand in front of him and pretend to be intimidated:

"Don't hit me, don't hit me."

During the first weeks after the accident, the boy had some rough nights. The images of being run down would appear in his mind again and again, whether in dreams or in his agitated half-sleep. Always the same images. The vehicle came at him and struck him. The vehicle came at him and struck him. The vehicle came at him and the only protection he had was his pillow. Joxe Mari, who shared a room with Gorka, complained in the kitchen.

"He screams at night and doesn't let me sleep."

He imitated his brother, exaggerating his miserable cries. He pitilessly mocked him. Joxian would intervene, conciliatory and paternal, okay now, let's calm down, looking sorrowfully at his younger son.

Miren on the other hand didn't beat around the bush.

"How about not bothering your brother at night."

In his nightmares, tires squealed; he turned his head; that gave him time to see the headlights of the metal beast. How quickly and how directly they came at him. They were already on him: ten feet, five feet, one foot. It was impossible to avoid them. The dream contained details that had not been in his memory before: the roadway wet with rain, the faint light of the gray afternoon, the bumper that looked to him like a mouth with rings of rust about to devour him.

Then legs that come running to him. Someone, the driver?, blurts out an obscenity in Spanish. Which obscenity? He doesn't remember. The only thing he knows is that the obscenity wasn't directed at him. Maybe it meant annoyance. Maybe stupefaction. The smell of gasoline, of wet asphalt, and he was conscious when they pulled him out from under the van, which was like pulling him out of a dark drawer. He doesn't know who pulled him out. Must have been the driver. And he was bleeding from his mouth and nose; but nothing hurt. Nothing? He shook his head no. Not even his broken arm hurt, at least at the beginning. It felt as if it were asleep. Gorka fell facedown on the ground. Could have been killed. He felt so ashamed he didn't cry. Joxe Mari, at home days later, pestered him.

"Of course you cried."

"I didn't cry."

"Liar. The whole town heard you!"

And on and on that way until he made him cry. But that happened at home, when Gorka was recuperating with his face all deformed from a huge hematoma and with his arm in a cast. Out on the road, next to the van, he didn't cry a single tear. He was too embarrassed. There were gawkers gathered on the sidewalk and people looking out of windows.

"Isn't that Joxian's younger son?"

He'd dirtied his clothing with blood and the filth from the asphalt. Oh boy, when *ama* finds out. He'd lost a shoe. The driver himself brought him to the hospital in the van.

They treated his arm. Not his nose. When he was still a boy the imperfection didn't show. But later, when he reached puberty, as his face changed it was obvious his nose wasn't properly shaped. He had a deviated septum, smashed or twisted, no one knew for sure. On the other hand, anyone could see his broken tooth. Without tenderness, his mother consoled him.

"Can you breathe?"

"Yes."

"Can you bite?"

"Yes."

"Well then, that does it. What more do you want?"

The man who ran Gorka over was a fifty-year-old gentleman from Andoáin, who worked as a distributor for a commercial cake business. Two weeks after the accident he went to see the boy at home. An affable man, he'd called several times to see if Gorka was getting better, if he was okay, if he could lead a normal life. You could see he was concerned. Anyway, one morning he rang the buzzer. Miren opened the door and it happens that Gorka was in the *ikastola* with his arm in a cast. The man left a cake as a present for the boy.

"Actually for the whole family."

A cake with a sponge base and a thick layer of chocolate and cream decorated with marzipan cherries.

The discord began just before dinner. The family member most outraged was Miren. She remembered that the previous night, before she went to bed, the cake was still whole in the refrigerator. When she got up in the morning a bit more than a quarter of it was missing. Her first, not to say her only, suspicion: Joxe Mari, the family glutton. Because I don't think his father would. Or maybe he did? One of them was with his handball team in some town in the province, the other was riding his bicycle. When they get back, one or the other, I don't know which, but we're going to find out. Arantxa noticed that her mother was talking to herself, grumbling.

"What's wrong with you, *ama?*"

"Nothing."

They said nothing more. The father arrived, the son arrived, separately, a few minutes apart. What time could it be? One p.m.? About then. Hungry, tired, Joxian wearing bicycling clothes, they asked what was for dinner. Reproaches, accusations, arguments, that's what there was for dinner.

Joxe Mari had no problems with confessing. But wait, the cake had already been cut when he took a slice for breakfast. That's why he thought it was there for everyone.

"What do you mean, already cut?"

"A slice larger than the one I took was gone. I swear to God, *ama.*"

Miren, with angry eyes, clenched her teeth, turned toward her husband, and began to shout without giving him time to explain himself. And Joxian, shaking his head, said he didn't do it. And she, well then, who if not you. He confessed that before leaving the house he couldn't resist the temptation to eat three marzipan cherries, but that was all. He hadn't touched the rest. Joxe Mari didn't believe him:

"Come on, *aita*, it can't be."

"What can't be?"

"When I got up a big piece of the tart was gone and you left the house before I did."

"May God strike me dead. How many times do I have to tell you I only ate three pieces of marzipan? A slice was missing when I opened the fridge."

They all looked at Gorka.

"No, I didn't do it."

Miren sprang to the boy's defense.

"Leave the kid in peace. It's his cake. As if he'd eat it all by himself."

And Gorka, please don't argue, the cake is for all of us. The little boy's sweet, conciliatory words only enraged the family more; to the point that Miren, in a fit of anger, tore off her apron and said:

"You can eat without me."

She walked out of the kitchen stamping her feet in spite and came back a minute later walking slowly and with a calm expression on her face, since in the meanwhile, Arantxa, whom she met in the dining room, what's going on, *ama*, what are you all shouting about?, stated in a matter-of-fact voice that:

"Last night I was hungry so I cut myself a slice."

"You took the first piece?"

"You mean I wasn't supposed to?"

The five of them ate in silence. It was Joxe Mari, once the dishes had been removed, who placed the cake on the table and got the big knife out of the drawer.

"Come on, let's stop this silliness. Who wants some?"

Arantxa shook her head no. Miren didn't bother to answer. She started washing the dishes. Joxian:

"Share it with your brother."

Gorka only wanted a little piece. Joxian thought it was too little.

"Give him a little more."

But Gorka claimed he wasn't hungry. Joxe Mari pulled the cake over to himself, clearly intending to wolf down the rest. His father stared at him in astonishment. After the appetizers, the chickpea soup, the roast chicken with potatoes, of which he'd eaten by himself as much as all the other members of the family together, how is it possible there would be room in his stomach for such a huge quantity of dessert? Under the table, he kicked Joxe Mari's leg. Once he caught his attention, he signaled that he wanted a piece. Joxe Mari surreptitiously gave him a piece behind his mother's back. Joxian wolfed it down. Then it was Arantxa, holding in her laughter, who also asked Joxe Mari for a slice.

38

Books

After his septum was crushed, Gorka opted for solitude. His brother and sister weren't around the house much. He only went out to go to the *ikastola*. Why? Books, or as his father, with concerned wrinkles in his brow, put it, the goddamned books. The boy had caught reading fever.

His parents became increasingly disturbed. Not exactly because of the books. What then? Because he spent so many hours locked away in his room, Saturdays and Sundays, too, often until Joxe Mari came home and ordered him to turn out the light. A strange son. And Joxian:

"A shame he doesn't have a window in his head so we could look inside."

At night, in bed, the parents talked in low voices.

"Did he go out?"

"Are you kidding? He spent the whole afternoon reading."

"He's probably studying for an exam."

"No, I asked him and he says no."

"The goddamned books."

One morning, standing in front of him in the kitchen, his mother amused herself watching while the boy ate. Hunched over, his bony hands around the coffee cup, his hair greasy, acne. Miren bit her tongue, but she finally had to let it out.

"Listen here, could it be you have psychological problems?"

Fourteen years old. His friends would pass by to pick him up and he didn't even come out to say hello. What the hell was wrong with him? Was he sick? Or was he angry with them? After a while, they stopped coming. And Joxian became desperate.

"Damn it to hell. What a kid."

Joxian went over to him. He put a friendly hand on his shoulder. He offered him two hundred, three hundred pesetas.

"Go on, have a good time."

"*Aita*, I can't."

"Who's stopping you?"

"Don't you see that I'm reading."

"Come on, I'll give you permission to smoke."

"No, no, *aita*. Lay off, please."

Sometimes, Joxian, somewhere between being supportive and just plain curious, would ask him:

"What are you reading?"

"A Russian writer. It's about a student who kills two women with a hatchet."

Joxian left the room confused, concerned. Fourteen years old, all day stuck at home like a monk. Is that normal? Thinking about it, he stopped in the hall, he scrutinized an object, it didn't matter which object: the picture of Ignatius of Loyola, the built-in cabinet, a doorknob, anything that seemed to him visibly comprehensible, and for a few seconds he searched the object for something, even if he didn't know what—an order, an answer, an explanation for what he wasn't able to understand. Until he got to the Pagoeta, the image of Gorka hunched over the book, the goddamned book, wouldn't fade from his thoughts.

At night, in bed, he said to Miren:

"Either he's very intelligent or he's dumb. I can't figure out who he takes after."

"If he's dumb, he takes after you."

"I'm being serious here."

"Me, too."

And the fact is he gets mediocre grades in school. Naturally not as bad as Joxe Mari's were. Joxe Mari and sports, yes; Joxe Mari and manual labor, that, too: but Joxe Mari and studies (the same thing happened later on with the theoretical courses in the metallurgic company where he was an apprentice) were like oil and water, which didn't keep him from mocking Gorka.

"Come on, who are you trying to kid? All those books just to pass those shitty math and English courses?"

It was Arantxa who passed on to her younger brother a love of reading. How so? It happens that every so often, on his birthday, his saint's day, Christmas, or for no particular reason, she would give him comic books; as years passed, the odd book. The same thing, in point of fact, she did with Joxe Mari, but with no result. In this case, as Arantxa would put it, the famous parable of the seed in fertile land or in the desert was apt. Joxe Mari is an intellectual wasteland. But in Gorka, favorable soil, the passion for reading germinated.

There's more. Arantxa, when Gorka was a toddler and she barely nine or ten, liked to read aloud to her brother, the two of them sitting on the floor or he in bed and she at his side, traditional stories, Bible stories from a picture book for children.

While he was recovering from the car accident, Arantxa got in the habit of going to the municipal library to find books for him. Gorka by then was reading on his own, sounding out the words, and he began to acquire taste: Jules Verne, Salgari, soon Sven Hassel's war novels, and others about spies and detectives, all in cheap pocket editions.

Later on, without telling her parents, why bother?, Arantxa started lending him her own books, about thirty of which she kept in a cardboard box on her dresser. Love novels mostly, along with an abridged edition of *War and Peace*, Pérez Galdós's *Fortunata and Jacinta*, and six or seven by Álvaro de Laiglesia which Gorka didn't like as much as she did, but in any case he happily read all of them.

And when his parents started to criticize him for staying home instead of going out on the street to have fun with friends, Arantxa told him, when they were all alone, in a voice filled with mystery, that he wasn't to pay them any attention.

"Read as much as you can. Get culture. As much as you can, the more, the better. So you don't fall into the hole so many in this country are falling into."

Hole or no hole, Gorka dedicated himself to reading with passion and Joxe Mari, whenever he saw him with a book in his hand, joked:

"Listen, since you're such a reader, could you read the lines on my hand?"

One night, each boy in his bed, Joxe Mari spoke to him bitterly:

"You'd be better off dropping those novels and joining the struggle for the liberation of Euskal Herria. Tomorrow there's going to be a demonstration at seven. I expect you to be there. Some friends of mine have been asking me where you've been keeping yourself. The boys from your group are front and center, but no one ever sees you. What am I supposed to tell them? Well, you see, he's become quite delicate and spends his days reading. Tomorrow at seven I want to see you in the square."

And Gorka went, what else could he do? To be seen. He said hello to this guy, to that other guy, and Joxe Mari, who was one of the those carrying the banner at the head of the demonstration, gave him a wink. Gorka, mixed in with the mass of young people, shouted slogans with moderate enthusiasm. In the same way, his fist held high like the others', he sang the "Eusko Gudariak." By eight, he was back at home reading.

39

I the Hatchet, You the Serpent

And they grew, Gorka taller, Joxe Mari wider. Their only resemblance was their last name. Joxian's friends teased him. Did he feed the one but not the other? At home, he carefully omitted any reference to jokes about his sons. They drove Miren nuts. What a brawl she had with a neighbor who insinuated Gorka had a tapeworm.

While Joxe Mari was still living with the family, one brother slept on the left, the other on the right, their respective beds in opposite corners of the room with a space between them covered by a carpet.

And since Joxe Mari's bed was on the window side of the room, there wasn't enough space for his sports and patriotic posters. So, today a poster, tomorrow a picture, he invaded Gorka's space. Gorka's night table stood right below a poster showing the hatchet and the serpent and the motto *Bietan jarrai*.

Gorka's only poster was a large-scale reproduction of the famous photo of Antonio Machado in the Café de las Salesas.

"Who the hell is that guy?"

"Come on, you know who he is."

"No, seriously. Tarzan's grandfather?"

"A poet."

This was an ideal line for Joxe Mari's sense of humor: exactly the answer he was hoping for so he could show off his wit:

> *Oh, poet,*
> *Your verses fill the halls*

Please unzip my fly
And just massage my balls.

One day when Gorka was out, Joxe Mari used a felt marker to draw a beard and the kind of sunglasses blind people wear on Antonio Machado's picture, and near the poet's mouth he put a comic-book-style balloon inscribed: *Gora ETA*. And he joked, assuring his brother with a sarcastic expression on his face that the old man with the hat knew what he was talking about. Gorka, resigned, even apathetic, let himself be humiliated. Which disgusted Arantxa, who often scolded him for being that way:

"Why don't you defend yourself? Why don't you just contradict him?"

"I don't want to get him mad."

"Are you afraid of him?"

"A little."

When it came to intellectual matters, Gorka was vastly superior to his brother. In bed, in the dark, Joxe Mari often continued arguments he'd just had in the Arrano Taberna with his gang. His face toward the ceiling as he took nervous drags on the last cigarette of the day, he would advocate the armed struggle and independence, and no one could change his mind about that. The theoretical fussing of some friends annoyed him no end. He would only discuss objectives: the incorporation of Navarra, the expulsion of the Guardia Civil, those things, damn it, things you can understand without the need of philosophic blather. And when the dialectical annoyance had subsided, he would turn to Gorka and, friendly, fraternal, calm, are you asleep?, would make requests like this:

"All right then, explain this Marxist-Leninist stuff to me, but in words easy to understand, and do it fast because tomorrow I have to get up early."

The younger brother also outmatched Joxe Mari in his use of Basque. He regularly read literary works by *euskaldun* writers and since the age of sixteen wrote poems in Basque he showed only to Arantxa. And, well, without exaggerating, he could run rings around Joxe Mari and his friends, who spoke only what they spoke, which was kitchen Basque and street Basque slightly improved in the *ikastola*. The boys would meet in their homes to make posters written by hand that they would then paste up on the town walls. It often happened that Joxe Mari brought them all to his room and there Gorka showed them the grammatical and spelling mistakes they would have committed, some of them whoppers.

His brother, annoyed but impotent, was suspicious.

"Are you sure?"

"Of course."

"Okay, I'll figure it out."

Ultimately, they would listen to Gorka and correct their mistakes, and it wasn't unusual for them to ask him directly, even before they began, how to write this or that. It was about then, *poliki*, that Joxe Mari began to recognize his brother's merits and to respect him. Which is to say that one night, right after he came home from the Arrano, he announced from bed to bed for no good reason whatsoever:

"You study that Basque, because that's part of the struggle too."

In other words, *bietan jarrai*. It was obvious, wasn't it? His argumentation was simple, brusque, elemental: he would be the hatchet and Gorka the serpent. A fine pair. Somebody in the gang must have opened Joxe Mari's eyes. How so? Well, from one day to the next he stopped making fun of his brother, of his love of books and his solitude.

And he begged for (not like before when he demanded) favors. Such as? Three days later, Saturday, they were going to celebrate at the town handball court a welcome-home homage to Karburo.

"Didn't you say he was a jerkoff?"

"Who? Karburo? A total jerkoff. It would be impossible to be a bigger jerkoff. But he survived seven years in jail for defending the cause and he deserves an *ongi etorri*. One thing doesn't exclude the other. We've got it all set up."

"So what do I have to do?"

"Photos."

"Of Karburo?"

"Of Karburo and everybody else. You take your camera, go to the ball court, and start taking photos right and left as if you were the photographer at a wedding. As many as you can, okay? From the ones that turn out okay, we can make posters for three hundred pesetas each. It's Jokin's idea. I told him you've got a fucking great camera. The rest of the photos I can put in an album. I've already got a name for it: the *gudari* album. We'll pay the costs, okay? You've got nothing to worry about there."

And Saturday came and its afternoon and Gorka, not visibly enthusiastic, headed for the ball court with his camera hanging around his neck. As he was getting ready to leave the house, in the hall, Arantxa, with reproach in her eyes, asked him why are you going when even I can see you're not in the mood.

From the kitchen, Miren butted in:

"Come on girl, let him go. He should get out once and for all!"

Toward the center of the ball court, hugging the lateral wall, was the dais. Behind it hung a banner: KARBURO ONGI ETORRI. To one side of that salute, a black-and-white photo of the honoree when he was younger, had more hair, less of a potbelly, and a smaller double chin; on the other side, above a red star, the motto *Zure borroka gure eredu*. Police? Not a sign of them, which was not to say that there might not be some agent disguised as an ordinary citizen in the crowd, at no small risk to his health, because everyone knew everyone else. A crowd of *ikurriñas*, a large turnout of local youth. Nor was there any lack of forty-year-old berets or the odd grandfather. And *bing, bong, bing, bong,* a boy and a girl near the dais were beating the sticks of a *txalaparta*. The public sat in the stands as they do when there's a handball match. Someone greeted Gorka:

"Hey there, photographer."

A means, as good as any other, to take attendance, to tell him we've seen you, we know what your job is, good that you're here. Gorka never stopped taking photos. Of the *txalaparta*, of the audience, of the still-empty dais. He had several rolls of film in the pocket of his windbreaker. Nerea, *abertzale* at the time, smiled at him as she passed. Gorka pointed the camera at her; she stood still, posing as if she were sending him a kiss until he took the shot. He should make a copy for her, okay? Gorka nodded his head. Every few seconds, someone else would ask for a copy.

A few steps farther on he ran into Josune. He asked about Joxe Mari.

"I just left him in the Arrano."

A minute later, applause. Karburo entered the ball court making the sign of victory with his fingers. He was flanked by two leaders of Herri Batasuna and several councilors of the same ideological persuasion. Gorka preceded them, taking photos. In fact, he was the first to go up on the dais. Camera in hand, he went up, came down, went this way, that way, without anyone's taking note of him, the invisible man. He photographed everyone who spoke at the microphone, along with the mayor, who didn't speak but who was present, and the *aurresku* dancer and the *chistulari* who played the music, while accompanied by a small drum. He photographed Karburo, who was moved, thankful, fat, wearing a plaid shirt, his fist in the air, tears in his eyes as he called to mind the comrades still imprisoned, he said, in the extermination jails of the state. More applause, *gora ETA* and flowers, given to him by a little girl in peasant costume.

Everyone stood up to sing the "Eusko Gudariak" with their fists held high. When the song was over, someone runs in. Who? Two boys wearing hoods leap up onto the dais. One unfolds a Spanish flag. Jeering whistles all around, great fun. The other uses a lighter to set fire to a gasoline-soaked cloth. Gorka, at a few meters distance, took photos.

Escorted by a hundred or so boys, Karburo was led to the Arrano Taberna. Amid applause and *goras* to ETA, he took down the photo of himself as a prisoner hanging on the wall. From there he passed into the dining room, where he was presented with an homage of traditional snail stew. Gorka used his last roll of film in the dining room and went home.

"Aren't you going to stay to eat?"

"My folks are waiting for me at home."

He was reading until late. When the bells struck twelve, he turned out the light. After a bit, Joxe Mari walked in.

"Well, did you see me?"

"I don't understand why you guys cover your faces when everybody there knows you."

"Did you get photos of us?"

"One when you got there, but it must have come out badly because you were running super fast. Ten or twelve as you were setting the flag on fire and a few more as you left."

"They have to be developed as soon as possible."

"I hope the man from the photo shop doesn't tell the cops."

Joxe Mari fell silent for a few seconds. In the darkness, the burning tip of his cigarette glowed.

"I'll kill him."

40

Two Years Without a Face

She didn't remember the last time she'd looked at her face in the mirror. It must have been in the Cala Millor hotel. Where else? She tried to reconstruct the room from memory. Twin beds, the functional furniture, the wallpaper. Exactly what you'd expect in a cheap hotel. A place to sleep and little more. It didn't even have a view of the sea. What it did have was a small bathroom with a shower and above the washbowl a frameless mirror. Did she admire herself before setting out on the road toward Palma with Ainhoa? Of course, you can't imagine she wouldn't. From the time she was a little girl, Arantxa was in the habit of fixing herself up nicely. Not because her mother made her, which she did, but for the pleasure of feeling attractive. Arantxa was a really pretty girl—according to her mother, the prettiest in town. With that face and those eyes and that mane of hair she was destined for flirtation.

Guillermo, twenty or so years back, right after he started going out with her:

"How pretty you are! How can anyone have such a pretty face?"

"This face and other things I won't mention are for the man who loves me."

"In that case it must all be for me, because the way I love you I don't think anyone else can love you."

"We'll see about that."

Not even in the Palma de Mallorca hospital, where they shaved her head, not during the months of treatment in the Institut Gutt- mann did Arantxa look at herself in the mirror. At the time, no one knew that, not the doctors, not the attendants, only me. And when, sitting in her wheelchair, she would pass by a glass door, she would quickly close her eyes. She did not want to have any idea of how she looked. Why? Because she'd decided to put all her energy into getting better and she was convinced that if she saw her reflection in a mirror she would simply fall apart.

At first she could only move her eyelids. She could hear and understand everything and she remembered everything and wanted to talk, to answer, to protest, to request, but couldn't. She couldn't even open her lips. She was fed through a tube into her stomach. Arantxa, Arantxa, look: you've become a mind trapped in a useless body. That's what she was. In her dreams she imagined herself locked inside a suit of medieval armor that kept her from expressing herself or moving, but with the visor raised so she could see. Horror. Her vision was good, but she did not want to see herself. I'm sure I'm very ugly, drooling, my features all twisted, in which case, she often thought it, I'd rather be dead.

"Why do you close your eyes?"

At the time they renovated the house, Miren bought a full-length bathroom mirror. Ironically, she bought it so her daughter could see herself. Then she realized.

"For Christ's sake. What you don't want to do is see yourself."

She immediately shouted to Joxian to come and cover over the mirror with newspaper.

"Until you change your mind. Because, obviously, it cost us a fortune, so you can understand why we aren't going to throw it out."

Joxian, regretful:

"Don't worry, girl. We'll cover it up and it'll be fine."

The other mirrors in the house were either—like the one in the vestibule or the decorative one in the dining room—too high, or beyond her reach—like the one in her parents' closet or the odd hand mirror in some drawer. She tried not to look at herself in shop windows, when she was taken out for a stroll. But there were two unavoidable occasions: when she was photographed and when she was surrounded by physiotherapy machines, but I don't care because I never saw the photos.

The townspeople continually flattered her. The priest, too. The priest more than anyone else. How pretty you look. Ciao, pretty girl. In sum, that sort of insincere and pious stuff from which the word "pretty" was rarely missing. Arantxa found it detestable. She wrote her mother on her iPad: "Tell them that 'pretty' isn't my name."

"Come, come, leave them alone. If they call you pretty they must have good reason."

After managing to stand up with the help of two physiotherapists for the first time since the fateful morning of her stroke, Arantxa made it clear she wanted to see herself in the bathroom mirror. By then she was eating and drinking on her own, though never alone, no way, out of fear she might gag. More: she'd recovered the use of her right hand (the left was still stiff, though not as tight as it was at the start) and little by little, very little by little, she was making small progress with speaking.

She clung to the hope that she'd be able to walk, at least around the house, that one day she'd be able to go to the window on her own, to reach objects for now beyond her grasp: ordinary actions for others; for me, glory. And what joy the day she came home from therapy with the good news that she'd stood up for a moment. Celeste, who'd seen it all, confirmed it for Miren, weeping.

"Come, come, why are you crying?"

"Excuse me, Mrs. Miren. It's that I've prayed so hard for this moment to come. I can't help being overcome by happiness."

The two of them as usual bathed her the next day. Careful, hold on to her, don't let her go. The usual. Drying her was much easier now than it had been because with her mother's strong arms holding her up, it was possible to stand Arantxa on her own two feet.

"Miren, are you crying?"

"Me? Water must have gotten into my eyes."

And she turned her face away under the pretext of concentrating on the task of drying her daughter. Meanwhile, Arantxa emitted a chain of yelps. She wanted to talk, wanted to say things. Her yelps formed a barely sonorous ribbon, the agonizing attempt to enunciate a phrase. Celeste understood.

"The mirror?"

Arantxa nodded. Her mother:

"Do you want to see yourself?"

The same answer. Then Miren asked Celeste to rip off the sheets of newspaper and Celeste quickly pulled down those held in place by adhesive tape and finally, after two years of not seeing her own body, held up by her mother, naked, Arantxa gathered up the courage to look at herself in the mirror.

She scrutinized herself with a serious expression on her face, resting on one foot and on the toes of the other. She'd put on weight. Yes, yes, quite a bit. Those thighs. And the rest, breasts, hips, stomach, all of it seemed to have dropped a few inches down. And such pale skin. Her left hand, clenched, she held against her ribs. I don't like my shoulders, either. I've never had shoulders like these, all rounded.

She liked her face even less. That's me, but that's not me. Eyes without the vitality they had once upon a time, stupid. One side of her lips slightly lower than the other and a general lack of expression in the features. Gray hairs, so many gray hairs. Furrows in the brow. There's a lot of worry and lots of sorrow and many nights of insomnia accumulated in those furrows, problems and disappointments from before the stroke, but only I know that.

Miren, right behind her, asked if she was happy. She answered, without taking her eyes off herself in the mirror, that she wasn't. So you're sad? Not that, either.

"For heaven's sake then, what?"

Out of Arantxa's mouth came another discordant, incomprehensible ribbon of screeches.

41

Her Life in the Mirror

It was raining. What should we do? On Sundays Celeste did not usually take care of Arantxa unless Miren went to Andalucía to visit Joxe Mari.

"So we can't go anywhere."

Four in the afternoon. During the morning they didn't go out for their usual stroll because of the terrible weather. It wasn't simply raining; there was a demonic gale blowing. There is always the possibility of covering Arantxa and her chair with a special raincoat bought for that purpose, a kind of sleeping bag with a hole for her head and a hood, and then going out even if only for a short while to get some air, but what we've got today is practically a hurricane.

Miren:

"Good thing we went to mass yesterday."

Sitting in her wheelchair opposite the balcony door, Arantxa was looking out onto the street. Blasts of raindrops crashed furiously against the windowpanes. A gray afternoon, howling wind. Arantxa bored and irritated. She wrote on her iPad, "Take me to the bathroom." And in the bathroom, as soon as she was opposite the mirror, she signaled to her mother to leave.

"Before you refused to look at yourself; now you stare at yourself all the time."

Arantxa typed the letters with an angry finger: "I don't owe you any explanations."

Offended, her mother left.

"Listen, I never asked you for any."

The door slammed. And Arantxa locked away. It was all the same to her. What a disgusting mother. She's mistaken if she thinks that she's punishing me like that. What Arantxa wanted was solitude. Her greatest desire, finally to be alone, out of the visual field of advice givers, wheelchair pushers, feeders, protectors, and people usually helpful who at all hours exhibited for her benefit their prodigious (I die laughing) capacities for patience in all its different dimensions: patience-tenderness, patience-compassion, patience–badly dissimulated anger, patience-rage because she didn't do them the favor of dying. They could all go to hell. Since the afternoon of her disaster, she hasn't been the owner of her life. And she wanted to be alone, damn it, alone. To look at herself in the mirror? Well, so what?

Tense, defiant she looked into her own eyes, expecting the movie of memories to begin, the tale of her broken life. That's right, broken, broken into shards of glass like a bottle that's fallen to the floor. And each shard a memory, an episode, the dispersed shadows and figures of yesterday.

Mirror, mirror, tell me when, tell me where, tell me who. Arantxa evoked a Saturday in 1985. It had come to her before. The boy was neither handsome nor ugly, neither tall nor short. He went a lot to the KU discotheque, and even if you don't do it intentionally, you end up making eye contact. He usually went there with his male friends and she with her girlfriends. But really the guy didn't interest her. Maybe because of his clothes, I don't know, maybe because of the way he danced. A bit like a gorilla, no charm, no waist. Not a speck of elegance. And the way he moved his head, please! He looked as if he were driving nails in with his forehead. So, just one more in that dancing, young crowd.

During one of who knows how many evenings she noticed he was staring at her. Other guys were looking at her, too, and from time to time she even danced close with one or another. Whenever that happened, it bothered her that they'd try to make her laugh. The thing was that all of them, at least at the beginning, would try to be funny. And yes, in his eyes there was a powerful determination, a predator's fixity that she liked, and no sooner had they changed the lighting, turning on the purple bulbs, and slow music began than he dashed over to her and she, standing next to the bar, turned him down.

The boy (twenty-three years old; Arantxa nineteen) did not try
to convince her. Nor did he reveal that the rejection annoyed him.
He revealed nothing, but he smelled good. He went on studying
her in the violet half-light with those quiet and confident eyes, as
if waiting for Arantxa to change her mind. She turned her back
on him. A second later, as she turned her head, she saw him make
his way around the edge of the dance floor, calm and stiff, heading
toward the sofa where his friends were sitting. In the air an agreeable aroma was still floating. She noticed it again an hour later
while she waited on line with her friends at the coat check. She
turned around to locate the origin of the fragrance, and there he
was, right behind her.

"Maybe you'll be nicer some other time."

She felt a sudden rush of anger. Where did he get off? And on top
of that, right there in front of everyone, including her girlfriends.
She refused to look at him, much less answer. He went on talking
to her nape. Both flattering and brazen, pretending they'd known
each other all their lives. Finally, Arantxa retrieved her coat. Then,
full of rage, she turned to the boy and said, disdainfully, that he
should stop bothering her, that she had a boyfriend.

"That's not true."

"And what do you know about it?"

"It isn't true because Nerea told me."

That was disturbing.

"Are you spying on me?"

He answered with provocative composure that he was and added
that he was certain she'd be difficult but that in any case he was not
going to give up just like that. So now you're lecturing me? Who
does this jackass think he is? Arantxa felt an enormous desire to
slap him.

Now she smiles, so many years later, looking into the mirror
remembering the scene. The girls gathered at the waiting area of
the parking lot. Are we all here? As usual, Nerea was missing, still
standing at the entrance to the discotheque making out with who
knows who. Once they were all present, they made their way, happy
and chatty, to the bus stop. Arantxa sat next to Nerea. She asked her
friend, who said:

"His name is Guillermo. He lives in Rentería. He's a bit serious but very good-looking. And he's got a touch of the poet. When he dances close he says very pretty things that seem taken from books. And yes, he asked me what your name is and if you have a boyfriend. Maybe he's fallen for you."

"Well now, if he's such a catch, why didn't you keep him?"

"He's not my type. His family is from a town near Salamanca."

"So what?"

"Nothing, but as I said, he's good for a dance. For more than that, no."

She indeed had her points, not any touch of the poet exactly, but she certainly was racist and *abertzale*. Then things don't go the way we'd like and sometimes go exactly where they should least go, isn't that true?

The next Saturday came. The purple lights, the slow music: she saw him coming. I have no idea why he bothers when I'm just going to brush him off again. And she was intending to do just that, darling mirror, Saturday after Saturday, whenever he came over to ask her to dance. She imagined the question, the expectation reflected in his eyes, perhaps a reproach or an expression of disillusion as the denouement to the scene and finally his back, the back of a failed lady's man, as he drifted away. What Arantxa did not foresee was that his cologne preceded him.

"Well, care to dance?"

Seven months later, she introduced him to her parents.

42

The London Incident

Looking into the bathroom mirror, speaking without a voice: I remember; boy, do I remember. Those things you just can't forget. After the London incident, the two of them agreed that, let's see, first she would meet his parents—he was an only child—and later on he would meet her family. Guillermo had his suspicions, but did not fully grasp Arantxa's strategic design.

"I wash and shave every day, I respect you, I've got a job. Why do you think they won't like me?"

"My town is smaller than Rentería. In my town, everybody knows everybody. You have to introduce new people little by little."

"What does this have to do with your family? Don't you all get along?"

"We get along."

"I still don't get it."

"You'd understand if you went into my brothers' room and looked at the walls."

Hold on a minute. It really wasn't necessary for both of them to meet the respective fathers and mothers, brothers, uncles, and whatever else. So? It was Arantxa's idea to establish a formal basis to their relationship after the London incident.

As far as we know, he behaved properly. Which did not diminish the fact that Arantxa was hurt he didn't go with her. Yes, it hurt me, but he had to work. Except for that one thing, he was decent in everything else. If he'd been a bastard, she would have ditched him and saved twenty years of married life. The final years were awful, true, but Endika and Ainhoa wouldn't have been born. It's too late now to fix things, anyway.

Seeing that Arantxa was terrified, Guillermo offered to find someone reliable who could make the trip with her.

"Well, it would have to be more someone I would find reliable and not you. And above all, who's going to pay for all of it? This is already going to cost us an arm and a leg."

He had a heart-to-heart with Nerea. Look, this is what's happening. Arantxa's friend got excited about the idea of a trip. Wow, a weekend in London. *My name is, I come from.* And of course she didn't have the slightest problem in hitting up her adorable *aita*, who after all is a businessman, for the money to pay the airfare, the hotel, and various expenses. She was euphoric, impatient to board the plane. Arantxa, worried, had to ask Nerea to calm down, and said to her:

"Look, this isn't a vacation."

"I understand, I get it. No need to worry. I'll be at your side the whole time."

She put her hands, one on top of the other, on her chest as if she were a saint on a postcard.

"*Hello*, London. I always dreamed about visiting you."

"There won't be any time for being tourists."

"So what? The important thing is to be able to brag about being in England."

Oh dear, Nerea was frivolous. Even so, Arantxa thought it unfair to get angry with her, since after all she was doing her an immense favor in coming with her, paying out of her own pocket (or Txato's pocket, may he rest in peace) for the trip and the hotel.

Guillermo paid Arantxa's expenses. All of them? Down to the last cent. Giving praise where praise is due: she didn't have to convince him. He did not hesitate to part with a good slice of his savings. Because manias and defects, as you well know, mirror mirror, that man's got them by the dozen, but he was never a cheapskate, never, neither with me nor with our children. Truth be told.

At that time, he was working as a junior administrator in Papelera Española. He earned a modest salary, but what do you want? He was young, not tied down with family obligations, and could save since he lived with his parents, who went on feeding him as they did when he was a boy, if in fact he ever stopped being one.

His father, who retired that year, had been working as an unskilled laborer in the paper company since the fifties. He remembered when Franco—a tiny little man in a suit and hat—came to inaugurate the new factory in 1965. The man arrived already married from a village in the province of Salamanca. They hired him at the paper factory and there he stayed, tied to a machine until he retired. With a good record, we may add, which facilitated the company's subsequent hiring of his son.

A third person, aside from Guillermo and Nerea, knew about the London incident. Arantxa's mother? No. Joxian? Are you kidding? Nobody tells him anything. Who, then? Nerea's brother. Arantxa went to him, dying of fear, urgently asking for help. This is what's happening. And she asked him to keep it a secret and Xabier of course did exactly that. In 1985, Xabier was still studying medicine in Pamplona. It was he who made the contacts, pulled strings, and found someone to organize everything connected with the London clinic for the pregnant friend of his sister.

No one else ever found out. Not Guillermo's family and not Arantxa's other girlfriends. Not even, later on, her own children. She never wanted to tell them. Why do it? Tell her mother? She'd have to be insane. That was all she needed. Considering how religious she was.

Nerea flew the afternoon before on a regular plane. She had a few hours to stroll around London, see tourist sights, go shopping, take photos, and take advantage of having money and free time. Arantxa, a day later, took a charter with thirty or forty women from all over Spain who were going to London for the same purpose she was. Some not as young (thirtyish, she calculated) and others just entering puberty. Among them, a girl of about fifteen accompanied by a serious-faced gentleman who might well be her father.

Arantxa had a scary moment in the luggage-pickup area. The suitcases came out one after the other but hers didn't. Oh, *ama.* The people who'd traveled with her on the plane were leaving, the conveyor belt carrying the luggage moved with a noise she thought increasingly sinister, and her suitcase did not show up. Could they have lost it? Could another passenger have taken it without real-izing? When finally it appeared, she let out a sigh of relief. Arantxa found herself all alone. Then she had problems figuring out where she was. It took her a long while to find the exit. Again she felt all alone. Even worse, lost. What should she do? She decided, breath-ing anxiously, to take a taxi. Her hands shook when she showed the driver a page of her notebook where she'd written the name and address of the hotel. Along the way the man spoke to her several times; she said nothing because she knew not a word of English. It took so long to get to the hotel that Arantxa thought: damn it, I bet this black guy's kidnapped me. And a voice inside her was say-ing that the driver was probably taking the long way to run up the meter. Finally, they reached the hotel. Standing outside the entrance, a bus from which emerged some girls who'd traveled on the same plane. Son of a . . . If only she'd been a little wiser, she could have saved the taxi fare.

At the reception desk, there was Nerea, who promptly made her head pound telling about her adventures on the streets and in the shops of the city.

"Nere, don't leave me alone."

They agreed they'd sleep in the same bed that night.

"Are you afraid?"

Jesus, what a question. Afraid? No sooner had she gotten into bed than she began to toss and turn. She got up because she felt nauseated. Her bare feet on the old, worn-out carpet. Her mutter-ing, laments?, in the bathroom. Panic had seized her right down to her bones. And it wasn't only about the operation, though there was that, but not so much, because Xabier, over the telephone, had given her a series of calming explanations and she more or less knew what to expect. The problem was made more serious by her complete ignorance of English. She did not think herself capable of traveling alone through London, finding the places she was sup-posed to find, asking for help if she had to. An unbearable sensation of abandonment gripped her. And sitting in her wheelchair before the mirror she remembers that she thought: look here, if I get lost, if a car runs me down, if I pick up an infection in the clinic because of a lack of hygiene or who knows what, if I twist my knee going down some stairs, and if I can't get home on time and, finally, if for some reason or another my parents find out, if Don Serapio finds out, if the whole town finds out, what a nightmare.

As it happened, this she found out the next day, her mother and Nerea's mother, who in those days were intimate friends, went, as they usually did, to San Sebastián to have a snack and they spoke about their daughters, both coincidentally traveling, no kidding, using words Arantxa could easily imagine.

"Nerea took off on Thursday for London with a university friend."

"Really? My Arantxa is in Bilbao. She went yesterday to go to a concert by some singers but don't ask me who they are because I know nothing about modern music."

The girls got up early. Nerea went downstairs to have breakfast. Arantxa, who could swallow no food, made do with a few sips of water. How nervous! At the agreed time they left the hotel— one confident and chatty, the other with her heart in a knot—for the street where the office of the organization that managed these affairs was located. There were recently remodeled buildings next to others that looked old; some, actually, with a lot of filth on their facades. The one that housed the organization was one of those. Nerea was the first to spot it from the opposite sidewalk.

"There it is, the one with the blue door."

As soon as they entered they were making disapproving faces, then came pure, hard horror. Seriously. Why? Well the narrow stair-case that led to the second floor was covered with trash. Even a toilet bowl tipped on its side. What the hell was a toilet bowl doing on a stairway? And the same question applied to the plastic bags, papers, a bottle, spilled milk. How disgusting.

"I'm going back, Nere. I'd rather have the baby."

"Calm down. Since we've come this far, let's take a look, then you can make a decision."

Nerea caressed her hair, kissed her cheek, consoling, tender; in sum, she convinced her. And, hand in hand, they went up and waited their turn in a room holding several chairs and a leather sofa with split cushions and posters on the partitions. Arantxa recognized a girl who had traveled with her the previous afternoon on the plane. Shortly after, the girl, who was about fifteen, arrived accompanied by the serious man who might have been her father. There were more people. Also a man, half asleep and filthy, who looked like a drug addict. And the girl from the plane heard them talking and asked if they were Spaniards. Nerea said they were Basques and then the girl, without being asked, told her story.

Finally, they were seen. Nerea translated as best she could. Arantxa signed where she was told to sign. Then she was given a document for the doctor who one hour later examined her in a clinic in the heart of London. They walked down the garbage-strewn stairs. Arantxa in a low voice:

"Would you mind telling me why you and the lady in the office were laughing?"

"It was nothing. She thought I was the one who . . . You get me."

Out on the street a vehicle from the organization, filled with young women and those accompanying them, was waiting. First it went to the clinic and from there, once the necessary tests were done, to a large house outside the city center. It was a residential neighborhood with low houses decorated with widow's walks, chimneys, and gardens. Trees lined the sidewalk and the streets were clean; nothing at all like some filthy slum. Hmm, that's better.

What else? Mirror, how curious you are. A jolly nurse who spoke broken Spanish received them. Arantxa waited in a room decorated with modern furniture and houseplants. She remembers a girl with Asiatic features, another who might have been from India, and several Spanish women who had been on her plane.

And that was it. After a forty-five-minute wait, she was given a plastic bracelet with her name on it and a paper hospital gown, and she was asked to remove her clothing. The doctor arrived, a man with pleasant features, a graying beard, and nice manners, a man who exuded serenity. Dr. Finks, that was his name. A. Finks. He did his job, did it well, and that was all, mirror. Only one thing: when I woke up from the anesthesia, I gagged as if I were going to die, but since I had nothing in my stomach, I didn't vomit. And Sunday, early in the afternoon, that I remember as well, it was easy to sense a different feeling on the plane. All those women looked more relaxed and of course were chattier than they were on the flight out.

43

A FORMAL COUPLE

The London incident united them. From then on, they were a real couple, the kind who like to walk down the street hand in hand. Some time later, they were married. He came to meet her at the airport with a bouquet. He was consoling and tender; caressing, but courteous. He used unusual expressions in melodic phrases. His care was sincere and she pressed her forehead against his chest to show she forgave him the untimely, unexpected pregnancy.

She gave Guillermo a bottle opener she bought at the last moment in a souvenir shop at Heathrow. The handle was a miniature red telephone booth. Years later the bottle opener reappeared in the apartment they shared. Arantxa did not hesitate to toss it into the trash. The gadget brought back bad memories for her and perhaps also for Guillermo, who never missed it (or perhaps he did and just never mentioned it).

Accomplices in the secret, the two of them made a tacit agreement that they would never mention the matter of the abortion. But the subject was there, always there, in their conversations, in their exchanged glances and, which was worse, at least for Arantxa, like a stain following their children.

During the two decades of their marriage, Arantxa and Guillermo made several trips abroad. To Paris with the children, twice to Venice, to Morocco, to Portugal. Never to London. Neither one ever suggested it. And at times, not always, but at times, when speaking with an old girlfriend she happened to run into in the street or as she was taking care of some administrative arrangement, if she was asked how many children she had, Arantxa would stop and think. Not for long, half a minute, just long enough not to miscount. Three? Two.

Over the years, the London incident (what would that child who was never born be like today?) withdrew to the edges of her mind, never falling completely into oblivion. Suddenly, because of the stroke, it was present again in her memories. God's punishment? Assuming God exists. Masochistic whims of a brain trapped in an inert body amusing itself with the torture of episodes from the past? And it happened right in the Palma hospital ICU. Immobile, tubes everywhere, a night she cannot forget, that painful adventure which even now, with her in her wheelchair in front of the mirror, in her parents' house, unavoidably returns to her memory.

The episode united them. Now they saw each other every day in San Sebastián. During afternoons of fine weather they would sit on a bench; they shared a bag of roasted chestnuts or peanuts or some pastries or bonbons, and kiss. On rainy days, the only thing they could do was kiss in some café or movie. Guillermo, who was a smooth talker, would say pretty things in Arantxa's ear. When nine o'clock came, each one would take a different bus and so, kisses and sweet words, one afternoon after another.

"Sweetheart, we should start thinking about me meeting your family and you meeting mine."

"Let's begin with yours."

"You talk as if there might be problems for me in your house."

"Nothing like that. It's only that there are fewer of you and it will be easier. Meanwhile I can get mine ready."

On Saturday, Guillermo (or Guille) brought her to dinner at the house in Rentería. Fourth floor. The door opened. Angelita: short, wide, plump, sixty years old. By way of welcome, she planted two kisses like two cream pies smack on Arantxa's cheeks: rotund, creamy, effusive. My mother never kissed me like that. As a result, as soon as she entered the flat her fear vanished.

The father, more distant, but even so open in his cordiality. Rafael Hernández, a simple, timid man wearing checkered slippers and a wool jacket. Arantxa, being cautious, spoke to him formally. By no means! Kind, humble, they spoke to her informally. And Angelita, trying to treat their guest kindly, showed her the house.

"And this is where my husband and I sleep."

Arantxa visited them several times before introducing Guillermo to her family. As far as she's concerned, she would have happily slept over. So why didn't she? Well, Guillermo's parents were terrific; but, depending on which issue you touched, a bit (quite) old-fashioned. And she answered: Guille dearest, but if you and I . . . but what about London? And he: yes, yes, but she should please understand him. So every once in a while, at nightfall, they would climb up Mount Urgull to carry out, using a condom, hastily, fearful of being seen, a silent coitus behind the bushes, briefly pleasant for him, accepted resignedly by her, the one whose backside always had to suffer the thorns, the sharp stones, the moisture of the grass.

The bathroom mirror asks if she loved him. The way I love my children, no. Impossible. But in a certain way she did love him, mostly at the beginning. If she hadn't she wouldn't have gone through all the trouble to introduce him to her family. She'd never brought a boy home. Guillermo was the first. And the last. She began one day by mentioning him to her mother in the kitchen. And when she immediately added that he lived in Rentería and that his name was Guillermo, Miren, listening in a sleepy way, not especially interested, suddenly developed furrows of suspicion on her brow and had to ask, filled with misgivings, if the boy wasn't a member of the Guardia Civil. No, he was a junior manager in a paper factory. She asked if he was making a good salary and that was that. Not a word about I'm happy to hear you have a boyfriend, nothing about when are we going to meet him, nothing about anything.

A few hours later, she made the same revelation to her father. Perhaps she chose a bad moment. Joxian was getting ready to leave the house for the Pagoeta. Her father did not cover up the fact that he was in a hurry. It's possible he wanted to leave before Miren got back from shopping. These matters of boys and girls, love and courtship simply didn't matter to him. Even so, he did dedicate a minute to his daughter. Filled in a bit about Guillermo, he said he was happy for her. Then:

"Does *ama* know about it?"

"Of course."

"Why don't you bring him around someday and I'll bring him to the gastronomic society to eat. Does he like bicycling?"

"No he doesn't, *aita*."

Joxian, apparently displeased, didn't know what else to say. He patted his daughter on the back, as if to show his approval, clapped on his beret, and left the house.

Arantxa confided more in her younger brother. Fifteen at that time. Very tender. She needed an ally and Gorka was the only member of the family to whom she opened the doors of her intimate life from time to time. He seemed quicker than her parents.

Gorka asked, first of all, what the boy's name was.

"Guillermo."

"Guillermo what?"

"Guillermo Hernández Carrizo."

"Is he *abertzale*?"

"He's not interested in politics."

"Well at least he speaks Basque, right?"

"Not a word."

"That means Joxe Mari's not going to like him."

Arantxa glanced at the walls covered with posters: amnesty, *independentzia*, ETA, photos of jailed militants from town, Herri Batasuna electoral posters.

"Why do you think he won't like him?"

"You know perfectly well why."

And it was Gorka, fifteen years of age, thank you, who gave his sister the idea of strolling with Guillermo through the village. She should appear with him, they should dance on Sunday in the plaza, and then we'll see what happens.

And that's what they did. They went into a bar, then into another. *Kaixo* here, *kaixo* over there. They covered the entire center of town holding hands. And in the plaza, under the dense foliage of the linden trees, they danced to the rhythm of the songs played by a musical group in the kiosk. It was there Arantxa spotted Josune, who was observing them at a distance and pretending not to, and she whispered into Guillermo's ear:

"Right over there is a girl who goes out with my brother. Don't look at her. You'll soon see how she manages to find out who you are and if you speak Basque."

At home, during dinner, Joxe Mari talked about his handball match. Neither he nor his parents and much less Gorka made the slightest allusion to Arantxa's boyfriend, whose presence that afternoon at the dancing in the plaza was in all likelihood the talk of the town at that moment.

Two days had to pass before Joxe Mari stuck his shaggy head through the door of his sister's room and said:

"A little bird told me you've got a boyfriend."

There was a jolly expression on his face. Arantxa looked him in the eye as if trying to discover some sign of hostility, but there was none. He added in the same festive tone:

"Let's see if someday you can make me into an uncle."

Weeks later, Joxe Mari moved into an apartment in the village with some friends. Only then did Arantxa dare to bring Guillermo to her parents' house.

44

PRECAUTIONS

Txato was the way he was: turned within himself, a hard worker, stubborn. And that stubbornness which, hmm, made him a bit difficult to live with (argue with him? Jesus, Mary, and Joseph!) also enabled him to start a business from nothing, with more illusion than capital, next to the river, on a lot filled with brambles which he got on loan, and eventually to not only keep the business going but make it prosper. But that stubbornness was also, as Bittori said, his perdition.

She often chewed him out for it in the cemetery.

"You'd be alive today if you weren't so hardheaded. You could have paid. And if you didn't, you could have moved the damn trucks somewhere else as you yourself said so many times but you never did it, and to boot you knew I'd have followed you."

He'd come home and tell nothing about work. If Bittori asked him how the day had gone he'd answer invariably in a dry, evasive way that it had been fine. And she was never sure if "fine" meant badly or just okay or if "fine" really meant fine. To take the measure of his mood, she would search his face. Txato would get annoyed:

"What are you looking at?"

And according to his expression, the shine in his eyes, the wrinkles on his forehead, Bittori would try to figure out if her husband was calm, if he had worries.

"Has it been a long time since they threatened you?"

"A good while."

"Think they've forgotten about you?"

"I don't know and I don't care."

Now that Nerea was in Zaragoza, Txato thinks the fear doesn't weigh down on him as much. We'll never know. That man, Bittori said, was buried in a shroud of secrets. It's true that he looked less anguished after his daughter left to study far away. And Xabier? Well, since he wasn't living in the village, Txato thought he was out of danger.

At home, he stopped talking about the letters. But if Bittori reminded him of them, it caused him boundless irritation.

"God damn it, if I haven't told you anything it's because there's nothing new."

Txato, Txatito. Bittori would repeat it to herself even if it was irrelevant to the situation at hand, more with sorrow than with tenderness. This is the truth: he was left more isolated than the numeral 1 on the clock face. Friends? He didn't go to see them, they didn't come to see him. They isolated him at the same time he isolated himself. He stopped playing cards at the Pagoeta, stopped having Saturday dinners at the gastronomic society. Once he accidentally ran into Joxian on the street. They looked at each other, Joxian fleetingly, he fixedly, with expectation, waiting for he didn't know what, a sign, a gesture. And Joxian raised his eyebrows as he passed as a kind of greeting, as if to say no, I'd stop to talk to you, but . . .

Txato hung up his bicycle. Hung it up forever. He brought it down to the garage and there it hangs, held up on the roof with two hooks and two chains. He stopped paying his dues to the cyclotourism club. No one wrote to remind him. And at the end of the season, no one sent him the invitation all members received with the announcement about the date and the plan for the annual assembly. The certificate, diploma, or whatever it was where the stages the rider finished and the points he won was folded in half and stuffed into his mailbox. Whoever brought it didn't bother to ring the doorbell. It didn't matter at all that Txato had been president of the club for five years. They could go to hell. And on Sundays, Bittori, who before would complain that on the one day of the week when they could be together he was always with his bicycling friends, now had to put up from morning to night with her husband's foul mood.

All his life Txato had liked walking to work, rain or shine. It wasn't more than fifteen minutes away. By bicycle even less. Ever since the Sunday when the graffiti appeared he'd only gone out in his old Renault 21. As he put it, it was so no one would have to avert their eyes or cross the street. On Saturday afternoons, and this was new for him, he would go with Bittori to San Sebastián. They would go to mass and have a snack together in the same café on Avenida de la Libertad that Bittori frequented with Miren when they were still friends. And both Txato and Bittori noticed that a few acquaintances who cut them cold in the village said hello and even stopped to talk with them for a while, what a nice day, no?, here in San Sebastián.

Txato took his precautions. He wasn't a fool. To begin, he never parked his car on the street. Bittori:

"Don't even think of it."

He had his own garage. But even so, he crouched down to look at the undercarriage before he got in. Later he got the idea of placing boards around the car, all connected in such a way by string that if someone, after getting into the garage, itself difficult, would move them, even a few inches, he would notice. At his business, he reserved a space for himself in the parking area for trucks, a place he could observe from the office window.

There was one problem with the garage. It was located around the corner in the house next to his. That forced him to walk the forty or fifty steps between the garage and his entryway. It was in that short passage he was killed one rainy afternoon; but, as Bittori, sitting on the edge of his grave, said to him:

"They killed you there, sure, but they could just as well have killed you somewhere else. Because those people, when they're out to get you, never stop."

At first, he painted over the graffiti painted on the metal garage door. He'd picked up a can of white paint expressly for that purpose; but it was useless. The next day the graffiti was there again. Txato *faxista*, oppressor, kill him, ETA. Things of that sort. He got used to not looking at the graffiti. They started urinating on the door, which took on a vaporous odor.

He read in a newspaper that potential victims with fixed routines were the most exposed. That is, easy targets. For a few months, he wouldn't leave the house at the same time two days in a row. He also changed his route. He would come home at one or one

thirty or even two to eat or he would eat at the office whatever Bittori prepared for him. And in the evening, he did the same thing
whether the workday ended at eight or nine, at nine thirty or ten.
The irregular schedule drove him crazy, after all he was the guy who
bragged that he worked with the consistency of a watch. And when
he had his daughter at a safe distance in Zaragoza and also because
the criminals—who tried to make his life impossible—had reduced
their persecution, he ended up going back to his old routine and his
usual habits, except when ETA committed a murder and, at Bittori's
urging, he stepped up his precautions for a while.

One thing he often did was open the kitchen window or the
curtain on the balcony door a little so he could keep an eye on the
street. He took care not to let Bittori see him. She would get mad.
Why? It seemed to her that he was dirtying the curtain and the
window frame.

Years later, in the cemetery:

"Those people didn't stop outside the entryway. Didn't it occur
to you to think that the person watching you was a neighbor who
also pushed aside his curtain so he could take note of your com-
ings and goings and then report them to the terrorists? I wouldn't
be surprised if it wasn't a certain slob who never washed his hands
before sitting down at the dinner table. Neither before nor after.
And of course someone you knew, and if you pressure me a bit,
someone who owed us favors."

45

Strike Day

The elected deputy for Herri Batasuna, Josu Muguruza, thirty-one years old, was assassinated in a Madrid hotel during dinner. Net result: general strike. Moderately supported in big cities. In towns, support is obligatory. A complete shutdown (stores, bars, workshops) or you know what the consequences will be. From the top of the hill, Txato could see some of his employees standing at the gate, from which hung a banner used on other occasions. There were three: Andoni, wearing an earring, and two others. The rest of them had stayed home. One telephoned the previous night and Txato—fed up with people calling to threaten him and curse him out, fascist exploiter, son of a bitch, time to make your will—hesitated before picking up the receiver. Finally, on the outside chance it was Nerea calling from Zaragoza, he did. But it wasn't. An employee wanted to inform him politely that he would prefer to work.

"If you want to work, why don't you?"

"Well, it's like this, the other guys . . ."

Early in the morning when he got out of his car outside the gate, those three were standing guard there. Cold, frost on the grass, and the morning mist rising from the river that remains floating for hours in the low spots. He looked them over carefully:

"What's all this?"

Andoni, his face grim, chin stuck out defiantly:

"No work today."

"No work, no pay."

"We'll see who loses."

"We all lose out on this."

Txato tried to fire that smartass once before. He was a mediocre mechanic, and lazy. Right before his boss's eyes he tore up the letter of dismissal without bothering to read it. Hours later he turned up accompanied by two individuals who identified themselves as members of the LAB union, linked to the Basque liberation movement. The threats reached such magnitude that Txato had no choice but to reinstate that swine whose mere presence made his blood boil.

The three strikers kept warm by making a fire in a metal barrel. They were burning boards, branches, sticks. Txato pointed out in no uncertain terms that they'd appropriated a barrel that didn't belong to them. To say nothing about the boards. In the weak morning light, the sun still behind the mountain, the fire turned their faces red. Txato: the faces of animals, of people with social resentments who bite the hand that feeds them.

Bittori:

"Right, but without them who's going to drive the trucks, who's going to fix them?"

He ordered them to move aside the barrel because he wanted to open the gate. Andoni, sullen, definitive, repeated that today no one worked. The other two kept quiet. Inhibited? It's that stopping the boss from entering is a serious thing. And, eyes averted, behind Andoni, their leader, they pushed the barrel aside.

Andoni threw a fit:

"What are you doing?" Didn't he see what they were doing? And he added, furiously, with hatred, biting out the words: "Okay, but *not one truck leaves the yard.*"

Txato hid in his office. Through the window, if he stretched his neck, he could see the three-man picket line. They fought off the cold by jumping up and down, blowing on their hands. They gave off steam, they chatted, they smoked. Jerks. Their heads have been filled with slogans. Easily manipulated monkeys, eager to obey. And how thankful they were when he hired them! Bittori:

"Hire people from around here so the salaries don't leave."

Why he gave Andoni, the guy with the big balls, a job was, more than anything else, because some people she knew came to Bittori begging and wheedling and if only please and so on. If he only knew then what he knows now!

He wasted no time and called several clients to inform them of the situation. That he was very sorry and that they please understand. Later, his mood improved but still annoyed, he made more calls, modified the schedule, arranged changes of date, had to cancel an important job, gave instructions by telephone to his drivers that they should be back on the job that same day so they could park their trucks in a free space in the industrial park. And when Txato saw that another two strikers had joined the original three, including the polite guy who'd called the previous evening, he reached the conclusion that things just could not go on this way, I have to do something, these jerks aren't going to make me acquiesce.

By telephone again he confirmed that buses weren't running because of the strike. At around nine thirty in the morning he called for a taxi. He put on his sheepskin jacket and, without turning off the light so the strikers would think he was still in the office, he left the building by a back door that led to the river. A bit farther on, before getting to the bridge, a path opened to the highway. He didn't have to wait five minutes. Before ten, he got out in the Amara neighborhood of San Sebastián.

A surprise: the woman Bittori never liked opened the door. She said the woman was a simple (she separated the syllables: simple) auxiliary nurse. Whenever she recalled the profession of her son's girlfriend, she wrinkled her nose, slightly curled the corner of her lip.

"Male doctors with female doctors, male nurses with female nurses."

And then she'd start making negative judgments, she has no taste in clothes, she's pretentious, she uses too much perfume. It was hard for her to conceal the aversion she took to Aránzazu from the first instant. And her loathing grew to abhorrence when she found out the woman was divorced and older than Xabier.

"What does this innocent need, then, a second mother? Doesn't he see that this con artist is trying to take advantage of his position and his salary?"

It didn't matter to Txato. If she was the woman his son chose, she was fine with him.

He wasn't expecting to find her in Xabier's flat.

"I hope I'm not interrupting."

"Not at all. Come right in."

He asked to see his son. He'd be out in a jiffy, he was taking a shower. And Aránzazu, barefoot and wearing little by way of clothing. Were they living together? It didn't matter to Txato. His theory: his children, as long as they're happy, the rest is secondary. But Bittori:

"What you want is for them to be happy so they leave you in peace."

"Well, suppose that's true, what of it?"

There was the noise of a hair dryer, the woman wore dark red polish on her toenails, and on the wall there was an oil painting of San Sebastián by someone named Ábalos. More than once Xabier had suggested to his father that he invest in art, but I don't understand anything about that stuff, son.

Txato asked if the strike had spread to the hospital.

"Strike? No, not that I know of." And when Xabier, white bathrobe, walked into the living room: "Have you heard anything about a strike?"

"No."

"Well, your father's employees didn't come to work today."

Txato confirmed what she said. Father and son hugged, and Xabier smelled of cologne and said sarcastically:

"I've got to operate this afternoon. Let's hope for the sake of the patient's health that a picket line of strikers doesn't burst into the operating room while I'm at it."

His father didn't laugh at the joke. To the contrary, he frowned, put on a hard expression, and fell into a severe silence.

"What's going on, *aita*?"

"Nothing."

Aránzazu, women's intuition, told them she was leaving so they could speak in private. They should please allow her five minutes, she needed no more time, to get dressed. Xabier let a silly "but" slip through his lips like a drip of saliva.

"But . . ."

Txato suggested to Xabier that the two of them should sit down in the corner bar, where he would be waiting. In the bar, there was a lack of intimacy; too many ears. Besides, Xabier wasn't in the mood to drink anything. So they walked along these and those streets. Looking for trees and quiet, they reached the Paseo del Árbol de Gernika and, talking and talking, they walked to the María Cristina Bridge and back.

"It would be better that *ama* didn't know I came to see you. Mind you, she knows the basic information. I've held back some details. I don't want her to worry about problems that may be solved already and that's why I wanted to talk to you. You're a man with a brain. For sure you can advise me."

"Of course, *aita*. What's it all about?"

"The whole town's up in arms against me."

"Don't tell me they started insulting you again with graffiti."

"For the time being, they're leaving me alone. Maybe they realize that I'm not the businessman wrapped in millions they thought I was. Or maybe some recent negotiations have slowed their greed."

"What negotiations? You never mentioned anything."

"What do you want me to do, publish it in the newspaper? I used a middleman to request a meeting in France. The idea was to explain my financial situation, that they see I've gotten myself involved in investments, and that I ask them for an extension or that they let me pay in installments. I've heard about others who do it that way and that those bastards are sympathetic if you show you want to pay."

"Before you were against paying."

"I'm still against paying, it's screwed us completely, but what do you want, for them to kidnap me?"

"What did they say?"

"I went to the meeting. I arrived right on time, you know how I am. I don't like making anyone wait. The one who waited was me. More than two and a half hours. No one came. You know that ever since that thing about the Liberation Group they've been super suspicious. God knows if some cop in an unmarked car followed me without my noticing but maybe they did. I asked for another meeting. They turned me down. Sons of bitches! But I do think they see good intentions in me and for that reason they're leaving me in peace while they're busy making someone else's life hell. But I have to do something, Xabier. In our town, I'm way too exposed.

Just this morning three idiots closed down my business. They've got big balls. My own employees decide whether to work or not. I don't have the slightest doubt that at least one of them is telling the organization everything I do. Remember Andoni, Sotero's nephew? He's the worst. He's a really bad person."

"What are you waiting for? Fire him."

"Someday, when things calm down."

"Look, *aita*, if you're the owner of a business, you can't mix with the working class. I'm not a classist, but what can I say? Any guy who just doesn't like you or who envies you is going to try to hurt you somehow. He doesn't even have to make an effort because you're standing right there. Probably he walks right by your door every single day. You and *ama* should live somewhere else and go to the town only to visit or to work. What does graffiti really accomplish? Let them paint all they want. If you're not there to see them . . . But when you start with graffiti, where do you stop?"

"I'd move, but your mother . . ."

"*Ama* would move, too. She's dropped hints about it more than once. I've heard her. The thing is, the two of you don't communicate."

"Well, since I gave up bicycling and playing cards in the bar we've been spending more time together than ever. We almost never go out in town. I go from home to work and from work to home, and she's stopped shopping in town."

"That's no kind of life."

"That's the life we have. It could be worse. My father fought in the war against Franco. They smashed one of his legs and he was in jail for three years."

"And you, are you sure you're taking precautions?"

"Rest assured that I am. If they want to hurt me it will have to be outside the village. When I'm there I walk around as if I had a hundred eyes."

"So where do we stand? Do things look good or bad?"

"Bad. I'd really like to move the business to a quieter place. To La Rioja, to Zaragoza, but it's complicated. Almost all my clients are from this area. A week doesn't go by without someone needing urgent service. And I mean *urgent* urgent. And if you're far away, how can you react quickly? They'd just call another trucking firm and that would be that."

"Another possibility would be for you set up a branch office and move the business little by little."

"I'd need a partner, someone I could rely on who could hire employees there or who would take care of the business here. I can't be in two places at once. What would be best for me would be a simple solution that wouldn't eat up too much time."

"Close down the business, sell it, live off your savings."

"Are you nuts? The business is my life."

"In that case, I only see one solution. If you agree, I'll help the two of you find an apartment and you'll come to live in San Sebastián. In the city, you'd both be more protected. Anyway, what difference would it make to you to drive to work?"

"An apartment means a big expense. I think your mother wouldn't . . ."

"Yes or no? Should I try to find one?"

"Okay, take a look. Then we'll see."

46

A Rainy Day

It rained the day Txato was murdered; a gray workday, the kind that stretches out indefinitely, when everything is slow, wet, when there's no difference between morning and afternoon; a normal day, with the peaks of the mountains surrounding the village lost in the clouds.

Txato got to the office early. Early? Yes, just after six, it was still dark. He ripped off the old page from the calendar on his desk and read what was underneath. On a page in his agenda, he immediately wrote the number of days he'd gone without smoking: 114. He was proud to connect his perseverance with a long column of numbers and Bittori was happy he wasn't filling the house with smoke that yellowed the curtains and left a disgusting smell on the walls, the furniture, in the very air they were breathing.

Txato didn't know, how could he possibly know?, that he was seeing the world, taking care of chores, having thoughts for the last time. For him the sun had come up for the last time. He picked things up, touched them, looked them over on the last morning of his life.

From home to work, he took the usual precautions. The boards and the ropes around his car, anyone could see that, were just as he usually placed them. He drove along these streets instead of those, glancing every so often into the rearview mirror. And without knowing it, he was on the verge of frustrating the attack being prepared for him. He scheduled a working lunch with a client in Beasáin; but at ten in the morning, the client called to reschedule. An unforeseen problem had arisen.

"Of course, no problem."

Deep down, Txato was happy because he had no appetite for driving in such bad weather on highways in such bad condition. Then, a fatal decision, he went back to his usual routine, the one known by those ordered to execute him. He telephoned Bittori to tell her he'd be eating at home, and that's what he did, and he ate and never ate again.

Inside the garage, with the motor turned off, Txato remained at the wheel for a minute or two so he could listen to a song he liked on the radio. When it was over, he got out, put the boards and ropes in place. He looked at everything around him without suspecting that he'd never see it again: the pails of paint lined up on a shelf, the bicycle hung from the ceiling, the barrels of wine, the spare wheels for the car, tools and junk—not a lot—piled close to the walls to leave room for the car in the middle. He walked out to the street humming the song he'd just been listening to in a low voice. He pulled down the metal gate. It was raining hard and he had no umbrella, but it was only forty or fifty steps to the entryway.

It was then he saw him, powerful, wide, standing on the corner. How could he not see him when, in this bad weather there wasn't another soul on the street? Even with his hood over his head, Txato recognized him. By his general appearance, by his huge body, by whatever it was. He walked over to him, crossing to the other sidewalk, and spoke to him.

"Well, well, Joxe Mari. You're back? I'm happy to see you."

Those eyes, those tightly closed lips, those tense features. Their eyes met briefly, and in Joxe Mari's there was a mix of hardness and discomfiture. It was raining on the two men and the gray tiles on the sidewalk. Some were missing. In the holes the filthy water was accumulating. Some wires ran up the facade of the house.

The church bell struck. For a second they stood there one in front of the other, calm, silent, Txato expecting Joxe Mari to say something, Joxe Mari paralyzed, his hands in his jacket pockets. Suddenly he averted his eyes; suddenly he was about to speak, but he didn't speak; suddenly he turned around and took off, almost running down the street, leaving Txato alone on the corner, wanting to speak, wanting to ask him.

In the kitchen, as he took off his shoes, to Bittori:

"Why don't you turn on the light?"

"Why, when you can see clearly?"

"You can't guess who I ran into in the street. You could try for a whole month and not figure it out."

Steam was coming out of a casserole, a steak was sizzling in the frying pan. The only light in the kitchen was the faded gray that came in through the window covered with raindrops.

Bittori, wearing an apron, busy at the stove, deaf to Txato's words:

"Should I fry you some peppers?"

"I saw Joxe Mari."

She spun around as if someone had stuck a needle in her back, her eyes popping out of her head.

"The son of those people?"

"Who else?"

"Did the two of you talk?"

"I did. He walked away without saying a word to me, though he was this close—he gestured with his thumb and index finger—to saying hello. I think it took him a moment to remember that his family isn't speaking to us. He's just as massive as he always was and has the same dumb face."

Sitting opposite each other, they ate and drank. Txato chewed noisily. He said he was happy he hadn't gone to Beasáin in this weather. Bittori wasn't so happy.

"Well, if you had gone you'd have saved me some work. Because when I'm by myself I don't cook. Good thing I had meat in the freezer."

"If it comes to that, my dear, we could have gone to a restaurant in town."

"And waste money?"

After a while, Bittori went back to the subject of their previous conversation. Between her eyes there were two suspicious wrinkles.

"But he's in ETA, isn't he?"

"Who?"

"Who do you think? Doesn't it seem odd to you that a man from ETA is just strolling through the town when under normal circumstances he wouldn't want the police to spot him? Tell me something. Did he have an umbrella?"

"An umbrella? Let me think. No. He had his hood over his head.

But I already told you that I spoke with him. I mean, he wasn't hiding or anything. He probably came to see his family."

"Are you sure he wasn't spying on you?"

"Why the hell would he be spying on me? Didn't I tell you I was right in front of him the way I'm in front of you? What kind of spying is that? And if he wanted to hurt me, why did he just leave when I was standing right there?"

"I don't know, but I don't like this."

"Come on. You're paranoid. The number of ice creams I bought for that kid in the Pagoeta when he was little! The sad thing is that he went away, because if he really belongs to ETA, damn it, I would have had someone who could put me in touch with his bosses and then I could explain how my finances are going."

They finished eating the last meal of Txato's life. Bittori immediately began to wash the dishes. He said he was going to have a siesta. He stretched out on the bed with his clothes on, on top of the bedspread. That was the last time he slept.

47

What Became of Them?

He was the weakest of the three. Miren, sullen:
  "Not the weakest. No. The one weak one."
Koldo, a secondary player since he was a boy, the kind who goes through life in the shadow of others. He informed on them in the Intxaurrondo barracks.
"If he didn't, your son and Jokin would still be here with us, I swear, setting fire once in a while to a garbage can, sure, but without getting into the armed struggle. They gave him a beating? They beat up a lot of guys, you know, guys who put up with the punches and the tub and said as little as possible."
Miren had a grudge against that boy like nothing you've ever seen. Her breathing hastened if you mentioned his name.
Joxian, on the other hand, couldn't stand the boy's father, one of his workmates at the foundry. They'd shared a shift at the mouth of the furnace for many long years and hundreds of times poured molten metal into molds with their own hands. Herminio, an assimilated Spaniard, and immigrant from Andalucía, came to the village as a young man to put food in his mouth; he courted Manoli, a Basque from a tiny hamlet, naive and huge, so now he thought himself more Basque than God Himself. Did he speak Basque? Sure, *kaixo, egun on*, and that was that. Men like that, there were thousands of them, and thanks to his son, a softy, my son was God knows where, risking his life, with no profession, without a future, without a family, and what can I say about poor Jokin?
A worker retired. Management replaced him with Herminio to polish pieces, file the burrs off castings, and stuff like that. From

then on, he and Joxian didn't often see each other. And Herminio wasn't the kind to play cards in the bar with his friends (friends, that guy?) or to bicycle. He was either in the foundry covered with dust or binding books at home to pick up extra money. In truth, with the distaste Joxian had for him it was better he stayed out of sight.

Occasionally during breaks one of them would go out behind the foundry to smoke a cigarette and he'd run into the other.

"Know anything?"

"Nothing."

Always the same question, always the identical answer. They were always secretive if there were other workers around. They chatted about soccer, jai alai, any subject except politics and their missing sons. They stood silently one next to the other, smoking, their eyes fixed on the mountains in front of them.

There was a time when Herminio went in for offering up toasts with cheap boxed wine whenever ETA killed someone. One afternoon, with other workmates present, Joxian called him out:

"Come on, Herminio, stop fucking around, this is no game."

At home, Miren:

"He's a wholesale jerk."

"He tries to be clever and it just doesn't work."

One day during a cigarette break, the two of them met alone at the entrance. Filthy overalls, rust-colored faces, blackened boots.

"Know anything?"

"Nothing."

"Well, we do."

Joxian saw the joy in his eyes and the violent urge to tell; his yellow teeth, one molar sleeved in gold. Whispering, confidential:

"He's in Mexico, a refugee."

"How did you find out?"

"He wrote a letter to my sister who lives in Córdoba, and that's how we found out."

"Does he say anything about Joxe Mari?"

"He doesn't mention him by name. If you want, Manoli can ask him directly. She's going there this summer."

Disappointed, Joxian shrugged his shoulders. Summer wouldn't come for another five months. What would Koldo know by then about his son?

"The trip costs an arm and a leg," Herminio started, back to his own story, "For now, we think she'll be the one to go, to bring him clothes and whatever else he needs. He's far away from us, but at least he's out of danger. Finally we'll be able to sleep well."

He was practically doing one of his Andalusian folk dances. Joxian went directly from the foundry to his house to bring the news to his wife. God, why didn't he just keep his mouth shut! He hadn't seen Miren cry with such bitterness in a long time. And she threw her apron against the wall calendar as hard as she could. Lamentations, sobs, rage, sorrow, pain. Why did this have to happen to them? Where can he be? Who's going to take care of him if he gets sick? And Joxian: she should stop screaming, people on the street will hear her.

"Let them hear. Very clever, that dear little Koldo, the one who named names and who's now safe and sound. I only hope one of those snakes they have in Mexico bites him."

"Okay, okay, that's enough of that."

And at night, Miren in bed in the darkness:

"What I want is for the police to catch Joxe Mari and end all this once and for all. I never stop praying to Saint Ignatius. Please, let the French police catch him. Not the Spanish police, no. Let him be in jail for a while with no problems and then they can give him back to me. What do you think?"

"The same thing. But whenever I said it you threw a fit."

"What can you know about how a mother feels?"

"And what about what a father feels, what about that?"

The next day, both calmed down, they agreed that exile was preferable to Jokin's fate. What happened to him? Well, he went nuts. In '87 he went out to the hills and shot himself. Weeks went by before a shepherd accidentally found him in a gulch in the province of Burgos. He was unrecognizable, in an advanced state of decomposition, and half eaten by animals. He was carrying a false identity card. From the photo, the Guardia Civil managed to identify him. ETA repudiated the official statement in a communiqué. A mob crowded the town square to receive the coffin wrapped in an *iku-rriña* and it was raining. It always rains on such occasions. Miren:

"Silliness."

But Joxian does think it always rains whenever they hold a celebration of that kind. The church, overflowing, with people standing. Many faces from elsewhere and politicians. Don Serapio, during the homily, visibly having difficulty controlling his emotions, talked about "the tragic death of our beloved Jokin, the circumstances of which we hope one day will be revealed." And then a long line of umbrellas made its way up to the cemetery. The "Eusko Gudariak" was sung at the grave site, there were plenty of long-live-ETA cheers and promises of revenge, and at the end, everyone filed toward the exit, leaving the funeral wreaths and the silence of the crosses behind in the rain.

Josetxo closed the butcher shop for several days. A few months later he was diagnosed with cancer. He lasted a year. He never got over the loss of his son.

Joxian:

"As far as I'm concerned, it was the death of Jokin that caused the sickness. A man as strong and healthy as he was. Otherwise I can't figure it out."

A week after the funeral, pushed by Miren, he went to see him for the first time in the butcher shop. A hug, tears, sobs. What a huge body Josetxo had. When the butcher calmed down, they talked in the back room, and Joxian asked what happened.

"They all lie. The police lie, the *abertzale* left lies. Everybody lies, Joxian, I'll tell you that. No one has any use for the truth."

He was destroyed. And the same went for Juani, his wife, though she consoled herself with prayer. What Josetxo told him that afternoon in the butcher shop, Joxe Mari would confirm to Joxian a few years later in a face-to-face they had in the Picassent prison. The French police captured Potros hiding under a bed in a house in Anglet. They found a valise and in the valise more than thirty pounds of documents, among them a list with hundreds of names and vital information about militants on active service. How's that for a leader! They even caught Santi. The authorities released the information a few hours later in the news reports on the SER channel. And of course there was a general stampede and arrests by the dozens. Jokin became paranoid. Josetxo expressed it in his own way:

"He thought they would be coming for him, in those minutes he was in the safe house alone, and he panicked. His comrades from the *talde* lost track of him and he turned up after a while. He'd killed himself."

And Joxe Mari, on visiting day in the jail, whispering in Basque, confirmed the story.

"What they told me was that he'd been odd for a while. He thought there were microphones hidden everywhere, even in the shower. They told me he went so far as to turn his clothes inside out. He trusted no one. Now, that he'd end up the way he ended up, none of us ever imagined that. It was a blow, *aita*. It just destroyed me. And if you want me to tell you the truth, after that I became a little disillusioned about the struggle."

48

Late Shift

The whole damn day rain and he had to work the late shift. Before leaving for the foundry, he looked out the window: overcast sky, the street wet, few people around, and a single, all-encompassing cloud, hanging so low that it got tangled up on the church lightning rod.

Joxian never had a driver's license. He either walked or biked to work. Not on his good bicycle, of course. During the work week he used an old one with a basket and a fender that he didn't have to dry carefully. A farewell kiss? Not part of their regular routine. In the vestibule, he stopped at the built-in chest. Dilemma: a poncho or an umbrella? The poncho meant using the bike; the umbrella a twenty-minute walk downhill to the foundry. He chose the umbrella.

And off he went, passing a few people on the street. He clocked in and, as he did every day, put on his overalls, boots, gloves, helmet, and entered the dark heat of the workspace. Those were not prosperous days for his foundry or for the metallurgic industry in general. Even without being fully aware of the specific caprices of the business, he could sense it. Before, they produced more, there were more orders, the staff was larger. Well, that was someone else's problem. He had only a few years left before retirement. His long experience operating the furnace made him practically irreplaceable. At least, that's what he thought. A worse future was in store for the young men if, as people said, the owners decided to close down the business. After all was said and done, his kids were grown up and he had a guaranteed pension.

Midway through the shift, a truck driver brought the news. More

exactly a shred of news he'd just heard on the radio while driving. What happened, what time it happened, where it happened.
Details? Few and vague. The only certainty: that at around four in
the afternoon a person was shot on a street right in the center of
town. It wasn't clear whether the victim was dead.

Joxian heard the news when he stepped outside to smoke. He
asked:

"Was it a cop?"

"No idea."

"We'll soon find out."

When his shift was over, Joxian went home. Every day I get more
tired. The years, well, they don't pass in vain. He went along as he
had before along the deserted streets. The morning shifts were less
tiring for him. You leave work with the illusion of having free hours
ahead, the incentive of a hand of *mus*, friends, some soccer match on
TV before you go to bed. On the other hand, now he had no other
choice but to eat, unwillingly, the daily fish, because this woman
has fish mania, then go to bed early and the next day take it easy
during the morning.

Night had fallen. It was still raining, and he couldn't focus on
anything that didn't seem all too familiar: the usual facades with
lights on behind the windows, the trees in the plaza illuminated
by a few streetlights, that hissing sound of tires on wet asphalt. No
police, no sirens, no blue lights. On his way home, he found no
evidence of the attack. Here the houses are neither burning nor in
ruins. He saw habitual things: dark doorways, streetlights, open bar
doors from which came the noise of conversation and the odd guffaw. Temptation to walk in, drink a small glass or two of wine and
nibble a couple of salt peppers while he smoked a cigarette, a kind
of reward for having finished off the day, but that was out: look
what time it is, how tired I am, and then that ill-tempered woman,
no, better not stop.

Miren didn't give him even the time to carry his umbrella to the
bathroom. She blurted out:

"Txato is dead."

It had been a long time since anyone spoke the nickname of his
old friend in that house.

"Stop fucking around."

For a moment, Joxian stood stock still, immobile. Like a post. He didn't even blink. And without looking directly at his wife, he asked how it happened.

"The way these things happen. It couldn't have caught him by surprise. The graffiti announced it."

"Was he the one killed this afternoon? Don't screw around, now."

"Well, I'll screw around if I like. Txato's dead. That's what war is all about. People get killed."

Fucking shit, fuck all. He didn't stop shouting obscenities, shaking his head with disgust. He tried to eat. He couldn't. His hand shook so much that he couldn't hold the spoon, and that annoyed Miren.

"What? You're going to get all sad now?"

Fucking shit, et cetera.

"A Basque, from our town like you and me. Shit, if you said it had been a cop, but Txato? I never thought he was a bad person."

"It has nothing to do with good or bad persons. The life of the nation is at stake. Are we *abertzales* or not? And don't forget you have a son in the struggle."

She got up from the table angry. She washed the dishes in silence, and Joxian didn't move from his place. After a while, she came to the kitchen to tell him they were talking on television about what happened, but he still didn't move. Did he want to watch? He shook his head no.

"Well, I'm going to bed."

Joxian didn't leave the kitchen. He poured a glass of wine from the big bottle he stored under the sink and then another and then another. When he was finished drinking, he went to bed. With the lights out, Miren said:

"If you cry for that guy, I'll sleep in another room."

"I'll cry for whoever I fucking care to cry about."

The final black moments of the night passed. Joxian, in bed fully dressed, did he sleep? Not even half a minute. As soon as light came through the blinds, he got up. Where was he going? No answer. A long stream of urine flowing in the bathroom broke the silence. And instead of going back to bed, Joxian went out to the street without breakfast. At that time, when he was on the late shift? He rode his bicycle without a poncho even though it was raining. He rode along this highway, that other highway. Where he was going didn't matter. Halfway up the Orio hill was the little pass where in the old days he would have little races with Txato, races Txato always lost because no matter how much heart he put into the pedals, he didn't have the cyclist's legs that Joxian did. On the side of the road, with no witnesses, he stopped to let out all his feelings.

A little before one, he got home soaking wet. He washed and put on clean clothes. On the table, a plate of lentils and a steak with fried garlic. He took a banana to the foundry and decided, frowning, not to speak with anyone all day. He was keeping his promise until late in the day. Then Herminio came over to him during cigarette break, that idiot Herminio, who comes over and says:

"I'd swear I saw Joxe Mari in town yesterday."

"You swear lots of things."

"No, seriously, when I was on my way to work. He was in a car."

"Buy some glasses and stop fucking with me. My son is far away. Not as far as yours, but let's just say far enough."

"It's just that, in profile, it seemed to me . . ."

"You were mistaken."

Joxian tossed the cigarette onto the ground even though he hadn't smoked even half. As he stamped his foot on it, he whispered an incomprehensible word. Then he went back into the shop.

49

FACE THE MUSIC

One afternoon, as he did every year halfway through autumn, he sold Juani his rabbits. Seventeen in all, beauties. He sold them cheap—a friend's price—but felt he wanted to settle things quickly. Why? Because often, at the butcher shop, Juani would slip Miren a couple veal cutlets, a couple of links of pork sausage, or some blood sausage, whatever she could pilfer.

Joxian was cleaning the empty cages, intending to fill them with baby rabbits. It was ten a.m. Sun, serenity, chirping birds, and at times the *clack-clack* of some machine in the Arrizabalaga brothers' shop on the other side of the river. He had replaced an old rusty screen and was carrying the cages out of the shed, when he saw her, standing with her bag and her gloomy face at the entrance to the garden.

He looked at her and instantly there were sparks. Surprised? Not really. Joxian expected to run into her sooner or later on the street, now that she spends so much time in the village. What he did not foresee was that she'd come looking for him. Let's see if Miren is right: this nut is taking advantage of the fact that the armed struggle is over to persecute us.

He turned his back on her and went on fixing up the cages. She'll leave soon. He felt her cold gaze on the back of his neck, pure venom. He no longer experienced the placidity his small garden paradise usually afforded him. Even the birds had stopped singing. And the Arrizabalagas' machine was silent. To look busy, Joxian moved the cages, angry with himself for not finding a way to end the situation.

After so many years, how many? at least twenty, she spoke to him.

"Joxian, I've come to talk."

"So talk."

That was brutal, Joxian, that was brusque, and since he noticed it himself a sudden flush of shame flowed over every inch of his face. God, how peaceful things had been until that moment! There was nothing he could do but turn his head. She:

"Won't you invite me in?"

"Come in."

Bittori came in along the gently descending path, between the rows of leeks on one side and the rows of escarole and lettuce on the other. Impassive, she looked everything over. Did she remember, recognize? She stopped two steps away from Joxian; praised the garden. How pretty, how perfectly tended. Pointing toward the seed-bed, she asked if that was the dirt from Navarra that her husband had given him. And Joxian, his head down, nodded.

Were they hostile? No. Rather, they were curious, each one study-ing the other. Joxian, intimidated, defensive:

"Why have you come?"

"To talk."

"To talk about what? I've got nothing to say."

"Yesterday I was in Polloe. I go a lot, see? I sit on the edge of the grave and speak with him. He asked me to send you regards."

What's she trying to do? Provoke me? He didn't answer. His hands filthy from garden work, his beret covered with dust, which he took off so he could mop the sweat off his head with a handker-chief; his boots the ones he wore at the foundry. Joxian had gotten old. He was gray around the temples and bald above. The years had taken their toll on Bittori as well.

"I haven't come to argue. You never did anything to me, and I don't think I ever did anything bad to you. And if I did I'd have no problem asking your forgiveness."

"You don't have to ask me for anything. What happened, hap-pened. Neither of us can change that."

"What did happen? I only know one part. I thought maybe Joxian can finish the story. It was that hope which brought me to your garden. I only want to know, and then I'll leave. I promise."

"So, you come to the village every day so people can tell you things about the past."

"The village is as much mine as it is yours."

"I don't deny that."

"But it's obvious you take me for an outsider, for someone who just visits. You're wrong. I'm living in the house I've always lived in. You know it well. You visited us often enough."

"I don't care where you live."

For the first time since she arrived, a hint of a smile appeared on Bittori's lips, the slightest arch of a smile. Her eyebrows became less sad. And on the tip of one of her shoes there was a speck of mud. There they were: she on one side and he on the other, separated by a small section of the path. And Bittori made a show of making sure she didn't trample any lettuce.

"You were my husband's best friend. I'm still seeing the two of you on your bikes, at the jai alai court, or playing cards in the bar. And I remember Miren saying to me, Bittori, my husband is married to your husband. We couldn't separate them with a hatchet."

"She said that?"

"Ask her and you'll see."

Careful, Joxian. This woman wants to catch you in her web. Why did you allow her to enter your garden? He saw himself, he couldn't stop it, younger, leaving Txato behind at the Orio pass; he saw himself with him betting two hundred pesetas at the town ball court; in the gastronomic society kitchen heating up dinner; in the Pagoeta, arguing, but how can you be such a jerk!, to go all in with those shitty cards you're holding.

Nostalgic, his eyes softened in hers.

"I was always his friend."

"But you cut him and stopped coming to our house."

"What does one thing have to do with the other?"

"You didn't even go to the funeral. The funeral of your murdered friend."

"You're throwing all that in my face? Even if I didn't speak to him he was my friend. And I didn't speak to him because I couldn't speak to him. You two did a bad thing. The two of you should have left the village. One year, two, whatever it took. He'd be alive now, you could have come back. And besides, being outside, many of us would have lent you a hand."

"About the others I can't say, but you still have time to help me."

"I don't know how I can do that. You can't make time go back-wards."

"You're right. We're not going to bring Txato back from the dead. But you could do me a favor. It's very easy. All you have to do is to ask your son one thing for me."

"Don't stir up those waters, Bittori. We've suffered, too, and we're still suffering. Get on with your life, let us get on with ours. Each in his own house. Now we have peace. The best thing would be for us to forget."

"If you're suffering, how are you going to forget?"

"I don't think Miren would be happy to hear all of what you're saying to me."

"She doesn't have to find out."

Joxian, after a brief moment of vacillation, scuttled into the shed, announcing with his obstinate silence that he considered their con-versation finished. Bittori, out of sight:

"Aren't you even curious to know what it is I'd like to ask Joxe Mari?" She waited in vain for an answer. Then she continued. "Someone saw him in the village the same afternoon Txato was killed."

From inside the shed:

"Tittle tattle."

"Come out of there. Face the music."

He came out. His lower lip was trembling slightly. That glitter in his eyes, is that a tear?

"At the trial they didn't bring that up."

"Ask him for me, Joxian. Ask him the next time you see him if he was the one who shot. I have to know quickly because I don't have long to live. Believe me, I'm free of rage. I'm not going to turn him in. The only thing I don't want is to be buried without knowing all the details of the attack. And tell him that if he asks me for forgive-ness I'll forgive him, but he'd have to ask me first."

"Bittori, do me a favor. Don't stir up these waters."

A useless request, you've already stirred them up. Bittori took a look around. The seedbed, the cement wall, the fig tree.

Holding his beret in his hands, Joxian watched her walk along the sloping path.

50

A Cop's Leg

Before even giving him his welcoming kiss, she asked him if he'd seen the news. Upset, limp, Gorka nodded yes. And he said he felt ashamed, very ashamed.

"I'm not surprised. Who wants to have a murderer in the family?"

A plea began to form in Gorka's expression, as if he were saying, your words are very strong, please don't speak that way. The crimes attributed to Joxe Mari's cell made him shiver.

Arantxa patted him approvingly on his long, bowed shoulders for not having followed the same path as our brother. And she added, imitating the voice of the TV reporter: the dangerous terrorist. Three militants were being sought. Their photos on the screen. Young Joxe Mari's with his long hair and earring was the one in the middle.

He's certainly become famous. Someone called Arantxa from the town. Who? A friend from old times. To congratulate her.

"I felt like telling her to go to hell. I didn't have the nerve. What would I get for my trouble? Hostility, criticism, and being shut out by everyone."

Her prediction about Joxe Mari's future now that he's being hunted: blown up by a bomb he's carrying, and we have a funeral with the coffin wrapped in the *ikurriña*, with traditional dances and the rest of the folklore program, or the security forces capture him at some time or other. The second option would be the best for everyone: for his potential victims, for his relatives, because we know that wherever they lock him up he will cause no damage and run no risks, and for himself, because that way he'll experience solitude, which helps men become serene and reflective.

Gloomy and sorrowful, Gorka nodded again. He'd kindly visited his sister on the occasion of her birthday and because his parents phoned to say she was pregnant. Gifts? Two. A little book for children, in Basque, *Piraten itsasontzi urdina*, the blue pirate ship, his first published work, how pretty, really, very pretty, and flowers.

Gorka and Arantxa agreed they wouldn't say anything more about Joxe Mari. Enough is enough. Or weren't there other important matters in their lives? Arantxa left the living room to get a vase. Married to Guillermo, she lived in Rentería, in an apartment in the Capuchinos neighborhood. And the photo of Joxe Mari, who, of course, is a hero now for the boys in the village . . . So there was no way to avoid it; with the flowers in the glass vase, and having rapidly dispatched some other trifles, they went back to talking about their brother.

Arantxa:

"I called the *aitas* immediately."

"What did they tell you?"

"*Ama* is very combative. She understands nothing about politics, has never read a book in her life, but she shouts slogans the way others set off firecrackers. I get the idea that she walks through town memorizing what she sees on posters. Above all else she defends her son. I don't know"—she put her hands over her stomach—"what I would do in her place. *Aita*, as always, remains silent. One thing, though, he takes advantage of the fact that Joxe Mari isn't in the house to buy *El Diario Vasco*."

"I remember the tantrum our brother threw, saying that he was buying a pro-Spanish newspaper. When the only thing that interests *aita* in the paper is the sports pages."

"And the obituaries."

"Okay, right, and the crossword puzzle."

"As if he had any interest in politics, come on! Why can't he read what he likes?"

"Well, he changed over to *Egin* because of Joxe Mari. Then he'd head for the Pagoeta to read the *Diario Vasco* he's been reading his whole life."

"And what about *ama*? Every time she visits she brings *HOLA!*

and all the movie magazines I've already read. Everybody in this family is nuts, don't tell me otherwise. In 1975, you were very little, so you won't remember, she cried when Franco died. Really, at home sitting in front of a black-and-white TV, she wept the tears of a grieving Spanish lady. But you're better off not remembering. The last time she came she asked if we'd given any thought to a name for the baby. Before I answered I noticed that her brow was wrinkled. So as a joke I said his name would be Juan Carlos, like the king. She almost fainted."

Brother and sister shared coffee and pastries. Good chemistry between them. Arantxa and Gorka always understood each other. When they were small, later, and now. Through the window a commuting neighborhood, the facade of an apartment building. Clothing hung up to dry on a clothesline. On one of the balconies across the way, a butane cylinder. A man wearing a T-shirt leaning on a windowsill smoking. Guillermo said that a while back it was possible to see a part of Mount Jaizquíbel from here, but then they built that ugly apartment house and no more view.

Arantxa asked her brother about the time when he shared a bedroom with Joxe Mari:

"Didn't he try to convince you to throw some rocks in the demonstrations?"

"All the time. What saved me was that I was still a kid then. He would tell me that in three or four years he was counting on me to be right out front. Then he would contradict himself. Once we turned up at some anti-police riot and he got pissed off. He shouted to me: get behind, don't you see that you might get hit with a rubber bullet?"

"But why did you go to the riot?"

"What the hell, everyone was going."

And in his opinion, it was the same thing for Joxe Mari, at least at the beginning. A game with his friends, a sport. You go, you see some danger, once in a while you take a hit, and you go on living. Later in the tavern, you drink, you eat, you talk with the gang, and you notice with an agreeable tickle that you've picked up the fever heating everyone else up, the fever that unites them in a cause. At night, in bed, Joxe Mari would brag. That he'd crack a *beltza* on the helmet with a rock. That he'd set fire to a bank machine, the fifth that month. He would turn toward his brother to drink in the admiration pouring from him: the same pride he showed when he talked about his victories with the handball team. Just what I said, a sport, fun, until suddenly the abyss.

Now that he thinks about it, Gorka thinks Joxe Mari entered the territory of pure, hard hatred and aggressive fanaticism when they found the handcuffed body of that bus driver from Donostia in the Bidasoa River.

"Zabalaza?"

"That's the one."

Gorka remembered that his brother came home in a frenzy. He didn't have the slightest doubt—and neither did his friends—that the bus driver died in the Intxaurrondo barracks where they tortured him. They killed him, he died by accident, whatever it was, and then they set up a story about an escape that not even a baby would believe. Gorka, shocked, watched his brother walk from one side of the room to the other. And inside Joxe Mari boiled with rage, more intense and fervent than usual, and Gorka noticed in his words and obscenities a furious desire to destroy, to take revenge, to cause damage, a lot of damage. Against whom? Doesn't matter, to cause damage no matter what or where.

"He taught me how to make Molotov cocktails. One Saturday I had to go with him out to the quarry. I was to leave the books. I made half a dozen bombs following his instructions and we threw them, *bam, bam,* against a boulder."

Some time later, he hit a cop with a Molotov cocktail on the Bulevar in Donostia. It didn't matter if they were cops or the Guardia Civil. One of the guys' legs caught fire for long enough to have burned. Luckily, his buddies managed to avoid a tragedy.

"Joxe Mari couldn't see that inside the uniform there was a person who earns a living, who may well have a wife and kids. I didn't have the courage to say it to him, but as far as I'm concerned, I swear, anyone who denies that a person is human because they're wearing a uniform seems terrible. Anyway, the next day he was mad because the newspapers didn't mention the cop's leg."

His friends in the gang treated him to dinner—the prize for anyone who set fire to a policeman.

51

IN THE QUARRY

L ike the movies. Seriously. Gorka left his house at midmorning on a Saturday to go to the library. How calm everything was: blue sky, few clouds, nice temperature. He saw her, big, thick, on the opposite side of the street. Josune, who instead of responding to his greeting, *iepa*, put her finger on her thin lips demanding silence.

She was walking one step behind him.

"Don't turn around. Keep moving, keep moving."

He didn't turn around and he did keep moving. When they turned the corner, she ordered him in a low voice to wait for her in the church. They separated.

Gorka sat in the last pew. The church was empty. The only light was coming though the stained-glass windows high above. If the priest turns up, what do I say to him? That I'm having an attack of devotion? Josune made him wait more than twenty minutes. Highly suspicious, he guessed something serious had taken place. He leafed through the late library books he'd already read. He stared at his watch, stared at the altarpiece, at the statues, at the columns; he again stared at the books. Finally, he noted, because of squeaking hinges and because of the sudden brightness streaming in behind his back, that the girl had opened the door. Josune waved to him to meet with her under the stairs that led up to the choir loft.

"If someone comes in, even someone you know, we go our separate ways. I warn you, they're following me."

"Who's following you?"

"Who else? The *txakurrada*. I'm not sure, see? But who knows if they're using me to catch more of us. Joxe Mari is looking for you."

They whispered to each other in the dark enclave. Gorka, worried, bent his body forward so he wouldn't smack his head against the lower part of the stairway. Josune never took her eye off the center of the church and the pews just in case someone appeared suddenly.

"Your brother and Jokin are waiting for you at the quarry. They'll fill you in. I don't want problems. I put a lot at risk just bringing you the message."

"Wait a minute, will I be in danger?"

"Just make sure no one's following you. Then those two will tell you what they have to say."

They agreed that she would leave the church first. Gorka would wait another twenty minutes inside. The longer he waited, the better.

"Remember to ask your brother if he's got anything to say to me."

Gorka decided to go to the library first. Why? Because the books he was carrying would slow him down and also not to arouse suspicion. It may be that having seen him with Josune, the authorities might be keeping an eye on him as well.

Josune:

"They know that the ones who escape will still try to talk with their families and their friends to ask for help, money, whatever. So, *kontuz*. That's all I have to say to you."

And off she went, corpulent, her mouth without lips. What can my brother see in that girl? I can't figure it out. But now he too was caught up in the fear. Fear of what? Fear of whom? No idea. In any case, he stayed inside the church for half an hour. He tried to read, but no luck there.

He went out into the plaza. He stopped to look around. To the left, to the right, far off, at windows. The butane truck, familiar faces, pigeons looking for crumbs. He felt a wild disquiet. Son of a bitch. And just when I was feeling fine. He passed by Josetxo's butcher shop. Could he know his son and my brother are in trouble? And leaving the library without the book he was going to check out, he entered an alley. He looked both ways. No one. And from now until Monday, what will I have to read?

Taking a roundabout route, he walked up to the quarry. Down below, over the village rooftops the church bells pealed out noon.

Scent of the countryside. Scattered, tranquil cows. Gorka looked back every so often. No one. A strategy: he left the road to cross a piece of the mountainside that was devoid of trees, still moist from morning dew. Behind him stretched a wide area covered with grass where the people following him, if there were any, would have no place to hide.

He found his brother and the other guy in a ruined house. On seeing him, one whistled loudly. And I took such care so he could whistle? They asked him if he'd been followed. He thought not.

"What are you two doing here?"

"Nothing, the *txakurras* caught Koldo yesterday and came for us at dinner time. Luckily, we got away."

They escaped in the clothes they were wearing. They spent the night huddled in a corner of that storage space or shed without doors or windows which had also lost a part of its roof. Jokin: at least it's not winter. In their minds, there was room for only one idea: get across into France as soon as possible. But under these conditions, it would be impossible. Jokin was wearing bedroom slippers. Joxe Mari, in shirtsleeves, complained of fatigue and hunger. Jokin had no cigarettes.

"You don't smoke, right?"

Joxe Mari cut off his brother's answer:

"The only thing this guy does is read."

Between them the two friends had only a little cash. A little, sure, but how little? In truth, very little. Some change in their pockets, some of which Joxe Mari used to call Josune from a pay phone.

An error by the Guardia Civil enabled them to escape.

"The dumbasses went to the wrong flat."

Did they make a mistake? Up to a certain point. Prior history: days before, from the second floor where they and Koldo were living, the young men noticed that a pipe was broken on the third. There was an enormous wet stain and black rings (mold?) on the ceiling. The breakage did not seem recent. Until now no one had noticed it. There was no alternative: repairs had to be made. The owner suggested they move into the flat on the right side of the ground floor as long as the repairs went on. Meanwhile, to compensate for their trouble, they wouldn't have to pay rent. Money saved. They accepted.

In sum, the Guardia Civil knocked down the door of the first apartment because they were moving on the information they'd pried out of Koldo. As the friends found out months later, the cops practically drowned him in the tub and beat him until he was unconscious. In the afternoon, they'd arrested him on the street and brought him to the Intxaurrondo barracks. There were no coincidences or accidents: they were looking for all of them but only grabbed one. Koldo talked because, of course, in situations like that how are you not going to talk? But he kept to himself (or fainted before he could reveal it?) that one detail about the temporary change in apartments.

When Koldo's pals came back to the apartment, at around nine, they were surprised not to find him there. Where's that asshole gone? It was his turn to make dinner. There wasn't even any bread in the house. Just then they hear the racket of running boots. Where? Outside on the stairway. Did you hear that? Jokin peered carefully out of the ventilation window in the bathroom. He saw the Guardia Civil vehicles.

"They're coming for us."

They jumped out of the kitchen window into the backyard. Joxe Mari didn't even have time to turn off the TV. Agile, they slipped away in the darkness and ran toward the mountain. The moon illuminated their path. They arrived out of breath, slept badly, that is if you can call that sleeping. With no bed, no blankets, without the consolation of cigarettes. A fucking mess, but shh, silence. That was the nature of the struggle.

"Brother, this is the moment when you can't let us down."

"What do I have to do?"

"First, you go to the Arrano and you speak with Patxi. If he's not there, don't talk to anyone. Understand? To no one. He should give you instructions for us about how we get to Iparralde along with some sandwiches and something to drink. But watch out. Don't carry the food on a tray balanced on your head because in the village there will be *txakurras* posing as peasants. I imagine Patxi will give you some money for us. You pack it all up nicely and you bring it to us."

Gorka nodded.

"Don't even think of going home to tell all this to the *aitas*. I'll write them as soon as I can."

"And don't go to the butcher shop. And if you run into any member of my family on the street, you keep your mouth shut, okay?"

Gorka said yes to everything. His brother:

"Now comes the part where you need finesse. Behind the house you'll find our bicycles, lined up against the wall under a little roof. You open the lock"—they handed him two keys—"and you bring one bike and whatever Patxi gives you for us. You'll know which bike is Koldo's because you don't have the key to his lock. While we're eating, you get the other bike. We'd like to get going at the latest by four. If it can be earlier, even better. Everything depends on you."

Gorka returned to the village, carried out the instructions he'd been given, came back on a bicycle carrying an envelope Patxi gave him in the Arrano, but without sandwiches or drinks. In the envelope, cash for Jokin and Joxi Mari.

When Gorka reached the quarry he found them having an argument.

"You can hear the two of you from far away."

Jokin demanded that Gorka go to the apartment and bring him some shoes. He did not want to go to France wearing slippers. Besides, a guy bicycling in slippers is going to catch someone's eye. Joxe Mari changed his mind. To his brother:

"Take the key. If you see there's no one around, go in. If you get in, bring shoes for Jokin and for me a jacket you'll find hanging behind the door."

"And cigarettes."

"But only if you see you're in no danger. I don't want them to grab you because of us."

Gorka came back shortly with the second bicycle. He said he didn't enter the apartment because he saw odd-looking people around the entry. A rotten lie. What he didn't want to do was put himself in more danger than necessary.

Joxe Mari:

"Okay, it doesn't matter."

And Jokin:

"What size shoe do you wear?"

And he exchanged his slippers for Gorka's shoes, offering this argument:

"Hey, you only have to go from here to home."

They said goodbye with hugs and pats on the back. Joxe Mari planted a resounding fraternal kiss on Gorka's cheek:

"You're great, you've always been great, God damn it."

Just when they were about to separate, Gorka remembered Josune's message.

"If you've got something to tell her."

"Tell her to get on with her life."

The two friends left, and Gorka, sixteen years old then, watched them disappear on their bicycles, heading for the highway, Joxe Mari wearing the wool jacket he'd borrowed, the other one wearing his shoes. Suddenly Gorka felt a foreboding sensation.

52

A GREAT DREAM

"So why didn't you tell me all that back then? I thought we could confide in each other."

"I was sixteen. I was scared. Look, when the Guardia Civil came a few days later to search the *aitas'* house, I was sure they were coming after me, that it had nothing to do with Joxe Mari, who after all was long gone. How many nights I didn't sleep because of that!"

"And you didn't tell the *aitas,* either?"

"I told no one."

Arantxa scolded him severely. Didn't he understand that when he went to get the bicycles he became the accomplice of those apprentice terrorists? Her judgment (as she made it her features tensed, her lips pursed, her eyes became tigerlike): it was an abuse that Joxe Mari had used him as a go-between with the Arrano Taberna knowing how that compromised him. Even if he was just a kid, if the Guardia Civil caught him:

"They would have beaten the shit out of you."

She softens her eyes. Naive, more than naive. But okay, it's been a long time since all that happened. Now jolly, she offered him another cup of coffee.

"The two of them rode down to the highway and I asked myself, why are they so happy? I had the feeling I wouldn't see them again for a long time."

"You can visit Jokin in the cemetery. As for our brother, we saw him today thanks to his photo on the TV news. Or have you seen him during the past few years?"

"Me? I have no idea where he went."

Gorka understands that as long as he lived in the village it would be hard for him to stay out of the *abertzale* business. In a small town, he says, you can't be invisible. When there were demonstrations, homages, fights, and there was something like that going on all the time, it wasn't that someone called the roll. But there were always eyes dedicated to checking who was there and who wasn't there.

He tells his sister that from time to time he would go into the Arrano. He would order a short beer, let himself be seen for a quarter of an hour, and then goodbye. He didn't like the place, not even its smell. He was never a smoker or a drinker, and sports, frankly, as he says, don't rock his world. Everybody knew about his love of reading. Everybody knew that he was not fond of partying or going out at night. Usually he stayed at home or in the municipal library. *Kartujo,* they called him in mockery. But deep down they respected him for his knowledge of Basque.

And for another reason. Because of something, he admits, that protected him.

"Being Joxe Mari's brother gave me prestige. Having a brother in ETA, a great claim to fame! I could seem an odd, introverted guy to them, not sociable, but no one had any suspicions about my politics."

"What? You have political thoughts?"

Gorka could not repress a smile.

"Every five months I get a political idea. But it passes quickly."

At that point, he remembered an incident. With whom?

"With *ama*. One afternoon she comes into my room to call me out for being at home amusing myself with books while my brother is sacrificing himself for Euskal Herria and the townspeople had demonstrated to protest something I can't remember. And she insinuated that if Joxe Mari found out, he would be really angry."

"And what did you do?"

"What could I do? I grabbed my umbrella and went down to the demonstration to shout a few times."

Even though he'd not yet turned seventeen, he made his plans. The only thing that could get me out of this passivity would be a change of air (Donostia, Bilbao, even out of Euskadi) and study. To embark on university studies, his great dream. Basque philology, psychology, in that direction. To study anything in a university in Paris, London—can you imagine doing that? He never mentioned a word of his intentions to his friends.

"You did talk to me about them."

"I began the round of consultations with *aita*."

Sunday afternoon. He supposed he'd find him in the garden. So, he walked down and there he was, collecting leaves and branches to make a bonfire. He wasn't ignorant of the fact that this man, an amateur gardener in his leisure hours with his dust-covered beret and his hands hardened by decades of work in the foundry, did not have the last word on the subject that mattered to Gorka, even if he was the one who brought in the salary that supported the family. Even so, Gorka tried to sound him out for his opinion.

To study? Joxian thought it was a stupendous idea. Another man dreaming while still awake: a doctor son like Txato's, a man with a mind who runs a business, a gentleman with a dresser filled with ties. Gorka reminded him that studies (tuition, books, perhaps travel, and a student room in a city) would imply expenses. Until then, his father had forgotten that detail.

"Oh, shit. Well, you'll have to ask *ama*."

Miren didn't hesitate. Not a chance.

"Unless you work to cover your expenses yourself. With the shitty salary your father brings in we live day to day, where are we going to get that kind of money? If we really tighten our belts we could help you a little: but it wouldn't be enough for the whole program of studies."

Immediately, she started in with complaints, lamentations one after another. What with Joxe Mari in France, that we just make it to the end of the month.

"And if I ask for a loan?"

"From who?"

"Txato. Before, you were good friends."

"Are you crazy? We don't speak to him!"

And from complaints and lamentations she moved on to criticism and accusations, to contempt and condemnation, and she worked herself up to such an extreme of rage that Gorka never again mentioned the subject of studies in his parents' house.

"It was then you talked to me, wasn't it? But that was impossible.

I swear. As a saleswoman in a shoe store I earned a modest living. Guille and I had decided to get married and we needed every red cent."

"I understand perfectly. I'm not bitter about it. In fact, two or three years from now I'd be able to pay my own way, but I think that train has already passed by for me. Things are going well for me in Bilbao. I earn a little in the radio station, not a lot, but that's in exchange for being able to dedicate myself to what I like most, which is writing. As you see I already have one book. Maybe next year I'll publish another. I've been invited to a round of readings in different *ikastolas*. They pay well, actually very well. I contribute to the spread of Basque. I'm moving forward. What about you?"

Arantxa clutched her belly with her hands.

"I'm going to move forward too. In four months unless something goes wrong."

"Have you picked out a name for my nephew?"

"Of course. Restitution."

"Seriously, now."

"Endika or Aitor. Those we're considering. Which do you like better?"

"Endika's the one I like better."

53

THE ENEMY IN THE HOUSE

Nerea loved that motto on everyone's lips, the one you could read on so many walls: *Happy, Combative Youth*. And, happy, combative, young, she voted for the Herri Batasuna party. She couldn't imagine doing anything else. Certainly, she liked the idea of joy more than the idea of combat. Throwing stones, setting fires, crashing cars? That was for the boys. That's what she and her girlfriends thought. So as soon as the rough stuff began, let's get out of here, we're in the way, they abandoned the scene. But they did go to mass meetings and demonstrations, because the fact is that in the village, more or less all the young people took part in them. Even the children of those who immigrated to the Basque Country from other parts of Spain participated, along, of course, with the children of the mayor, a member of the Basque Nationalist Party. One of them studied with Nerea and together, working with other students, they unfolded banners, put up posters, distributed pamphlets, or painted graffiti on the walls of the school.

Nerea traveled to Arrasate (Bittori called it Mondragón) in March of 1987. She learned the news in the Arrano Taberna.

"What do those people say?"

"That Txomin Iturbe is dead."

"How?"

"In a traffic accident in Algiers."

"For sure?"

"There's nothing for sure in this business."

God knows if secret agents of the Spanish state or assassins from the Antiterrorist Liberation Groups had fiddled with the brakes.

Several faces seconded that supposition with their expression. Patxi took down the framed photo of the dead man. After wiping it clean, he placed it on the bar where anyone who entered the tavern could see it.

The newspapers over the next few days confirmed the official version. An Algerian policeman who was with him in the car died as well. And to dispel all doubts, a female ETA militant implicated in the accident had her arm in a cast. All lies, but as Arantxa said in a low voice when she was alone, sad and with a brother in France learning to kill, unless he'd already gone into action: in this land of ours the truth died a long time ago.

"Are you going to go?"

Arantxa, not at all happy about the idea, replied:

"Of course, *ama*. All the young people in town are going."

All? Arantxa didn't go. The evening before, Saturday, she said she didn't feel well. Fever, shivers, a cold. The four girlfriends agreed that the best thing would be for her to go to bed as soon as possible. Hot milk and honey, that's the trick, and sweat under the covers. That way she might be able to get up the next day sufficiently recovered to attend the funeral in Arrasate. So Arantxa quickly left. And the rest of her group, on their way to the discotheque, planned the next day's travels.

They'd been told that at midmorning two buses would leave the town plaza (expenses paid by the Town Council); but no, the girls preferred to travel on their own in Nerea's car. Txato's car actually, which Nerea would ask to borrow, certain that her father would let her use it because, first, he doesn't need it on Sundays and because, second, he never denies her anything.

"I don't think what you're doing is right."

"Just a freaking minute, *ama*. All my girlfriends are going. What would they think of me if after planning all this I call them to say I'm standing them up? Even Arantxa, who felt crappy, ran home to rest so she can get up tomorrow healthy."

"You know that man was a chief in ETA and had lots of people killed."

Nerea, rolling her eyes, was losing patience.

"Try to understand that for years Txomin was the leader of the struggle of our people. He gave up everything, his home, his job, his family, all for Euskal Herria. And attempts on his life have been made more than once. He's an idol for Basque youth. A hero. What am I saying, a hero? He's God. So, do me a favor. When you're walking around town or in the shops, bite your tongue before you criticize him, because you could find yourself in trouble and, incidentally, get *me* into trouble. Besides, what do you know about politics? Go to mass, *ama*. Pray and take communion, and let the rest of us do our thing."

Ten p.m. Txato still hadn't returned from the gastronomic society, where right about now he'd be finishing supper. It's true he wouldn't come home too late because tomorrow, the Sunday phase of the cyclotourism program, he'd be getting up early. When he did get home, Nerea had already gone to bed. At that time, Txato had no graffiti on his walls, he still went down to the bar every day and had supper on Saturdays with his friends, but he'd already received more than one letter from the organization. Nerea didn't know. Xabier, either. And Txato and Bittori spent a good while whispering in bed.

"Try to understand her, dear. She's young."

"She's old enough to know that what she's doing isn't right."

"Well, considering it objectively, I think it's better she go to Mondragón."

"To support a gang of mafiosi who are extorting money out of her father?"

"Nerea knows nothing about it. I'd rather she didn't. That way she won't be afraid. Let her go with her girlfriends and have some fun."

"So she can shout *goras* to ETA. Have you been drinking?"

"Very little. As long as my daughter is with *abertzales*, they'll leave her in peace."

"The way I see it is that we've got the enemy right here in our house."

"All the same, my problem will get solved, and we won't have to worry our children."

"The thing is, you let that girl do anything she likes. I mean really, like going to the funeral of an ETA chief in a car belonging to someone they've threatened. My God! Have you ever seen anything that absurd?"

She should try to understand; Nerea's young. They went on arguing and muttering for another twenty minutes until, backs turned to each other, each one fell asleep.

As he did on so many other Sundays, Txato got up early. Pulling aside the window curtain a bit, he checked, using the streetlight, to see if it was raining. In the kitchen, dressed in bicycle gear, he had a cup of black coffee without sugar as his only breakfast. He took along a pear and an apple for the road, filled his canteen with water, and walked out into the dawn to get his bicycle out of the garage.

Later in the morning, Bittori, sweet, affectionate, tried to dissuade Nerea, who was already prepared to leave.

"And if I ask you as a favor?"

"I can't, *ama.*"

"Do it for me, for your mother."

"Do you want me to look bad with my girlfriends?"

Bittori clenched her teeth. Because she was angry? No, to stop an involuntary flood of words. If they'd gone on arguing one minute more, she'd tell her daughter about the blackmail letters. Jesus, Mary, and Joseph! What would Txato say?

They parted coldly, not saying a word, without a farewell kiss. And Bittori looked out the window to watch her daughter get her father's car. Nerea, willowy, hopped around, more like a little girl than a full-grown woman.

Behind the curtain, Bittori shook her head in disgust.

"What an idiot you are!"

54

THE LIE ABOUT FEVER

It was after eleven. How much after? Fifteen minutes, maybe a bit more. Detail: on the balcony of the town hall, the *ikurriña* was waving at half staff. Toward the mountains, you could see clouds (there had been flashes of lightning in the early hours of the morning); there, toward the river and the highway to San Sebastián, as well, but with bursts of sunlight. The buses filled with travelers, mostly young people, had just departed.

Nerea drove into the plaza with a flurry of jolly honks of her horn. Under the portico, her two girlfriends were waiting, both carrying *ikurriñas* wrapped around poles. What about Arantxa? Even before she got out of the car, she asked about her. The other girls thought Nerea must have gone to pick her up. Could she still be sick? She lives on a street close by, just behind the church. Nerea: she'd be right back. And while her friends warmed up inside the car, because while it might not be cold out, damn, the air is quite cool, she trotted to her friend's house. The house she'd visited so many times, where as a little girl she'd slept on innumerable occasions. The house that, in those moments Nerea couldn't imagine, she'd never visit again.

The familiar door, the brass plaque with the last name, the door-bell pushed for the last time in her life.

Miren opened the door.

"She's in there. I don't know what's wrong with her."

And she invited her in. Nerea went straight to her friend's room. She found her in bed fully dressed. Had she jumped back into bed when she heard her arrive?

"You're not well?"

She answered that she wasn't completely well; although, frankly, the way she looks, the power of her voice, her decisive gaze, are not what you expect from a sick person. At first, she used the same arguments as Bittori. The only difference was vocabulary. A tough man, leader of executioners, a man who decided about the life or death of others. And with her back resting against the pillow, she imitated him:

"Kill that guy, kill the other guy."

Unlike Bittori, Arantxa didn't speak with a pained grimace on her face or with frightened eyes. On her youthful face, there is dejection. Dejection? More: bitterness. Transparent bitterness that allows a glimpse of what's behind it: indignation. Her words confirmed it:

"Go without me. I no longer have the stomach for joining in that carnival of death. In other times, I would have gone along. Now it's impossible."

"Because of Joxe Mari?"

"When he joined the organization, the scales fell from my eyes. It isn't that I suddenly see things differently. It's that I finally see them."

"Come on, don't be a wet blanket. We don't have to be in the first row."

"Nor the fifth or the last row."

"It's just for a short time. Then we'll take the car and the four of us will see what's doing over there. I was thinking about Zarauz, but I don't really care. If you like, we can go somewhere else. Just imagine we're going out to have some fun."

Nerea's joviality clashed with Arantxa's frigidity. A sudden silence between the two friends. Two, three seconds without blinking: a frozen scene. They looked each other over carefully. One surprised and bewildered; the other hard and distant—accusing? The other:

"What should I do? They're waiting for me."

"If you have to go, just go."

Something silently breaks between them in that instant. What? A line of affection and confidence, an old, tacit pact between two girlfriends. For some trivial reason, the bouncer at the KU discotheque wouldn't allow one of them to enter one Saturday. That was a long time ago. Then the rest of the group refused to go in. Either all or none. And right in front of the corpulent bouncer they tore up the tickets they'd just bought. Screw you.

"May I ask a favor?"

"Of course."

"Don't tell any of this to the others. Tell them I have a fever, that I'm not well."

Pensive, disappointed, Nerea left that room to which she would never again return. She passed through the dining room, through which she never passed again, and spoke for the last time with Miren, who asked her, with the house door already open:

"What's wrong with her?"

"A slight fever."

"What's wrong with that girl is that ever since she's been going out with that guy from Rentería she's been odd."

Minutes later, Nerea repeated the lie about the fever inside the car. The three friends set out. The highway dry, thank heaven, with a good bit of traffic until Beasáin, then no more. We'll be the last ones there. One of them said that without Arantxa it wasn't the same, that they wouldn't have such a good time. A good time?

"We're going to a funeral, remember?"

The usual thing in that time: they ran into a Guardia Civil checkpoint. Where? About five or six miles before Arrasate. They got on the end of what first looked like a traffic jam. Then they saw it wasn't, that up ahead were the police checking the cars one by one, asking to see the identification cards of one and all. Parked on the side of the highway were half a dozen Guardia Civil vehicles, and stretched across the road were two spiked chains, one at the start and one at the end of the checkpoint. Up on the embankment bordering the highway were several Guardia Civiles, each with his finger on the trigger of his submachine gun. Hidden lower down in the bushes was another with his weapon at the ready. And a third stationed behind a tree. All of them prepared to fire.

An imperious hand ordered them to stop. Nerea rolled down her window. Officers of the Directory of National Intelligence. No good afternoon or please. The cop took their identity cards to a van where they were given the usual examination. They had no prior crimes, no charges against them. When the officer returned with the cards, he came lethargically, to steal their time, to make them understand who was in control on this stretch of the highway, between this mountain and the next: where were they going? As if he didn't know. And why did they have to answer? Better to stay out of trouble. So Nerea, the involuntary spokeswoman, the driver, used the Spanish name for the town:

"We're going to Mondragón."

They were ordered to get out of the car. But not in a friendly way: get out of the car. With an oral blow of the hatchet:

"All three of you out of the car."

A wave of the cop who spoke to them summoned another two. Masculine hands searched them. One girl: how humiliating. Another: how disgusting. They would shudder recounting the incident in the Arrano Taberna a day later. And Nerea, with tears in her eyes, had to open the trunk: her father's raincoat, a bicycle pump, her father's umbrella, and the rolled-up *ikurriñas*.

"What's this garbage?"

"Two flags."

"Unroll them."

Nerea unrolled them, already biting her lower lip in an incipient pout. There they were, two flags recognized by the Spanish Constitution. And suddenly the sarcastic familiarity:

"What's this, going to the mass for the ETA guy? Do you really think God will receive him in His glory?"

Nerea maintained a dignified silence. Certain she'd overcome the urge to cry, she dared to look the cop right in the eye. Black eyes in which she saw her own reflection. Lord, her mother again delivering last night's and this morning's sermon and also Arantxa fully dressed and in bed. No doubt it would have been better to travel with the large group in one of the buses. And as she thought that, she felt a spark of courage in her chest.

"I'm waiting for an answer."

"We are not going to a mass."

The Guardia Civil launched into a tirade against Txomin the murderer, the terrorist, and may all of those bastards die like that, et cetera. With an authoritarian snap of his chin, he ordered the three girls to get out of his sight immediately. Pulling away, Nerea saw in her rearview mirror that the Guardia Civil had ordered the car behind theirs to stop.

55

LIKE THEIR MOTHERS

One asked the other. Well? Wasn't this the café their mothers came to on Saturday to have a snack? Arantxa thinks maybe they went to a churro bakery, but she's not certain. What she does know without any doubt is that her mother still likes churros and that sometimes, when she comes to San Sebastián, she buys half a dozen and then eats them cold at home. Nerea would swear that when they were still friends Miren and her mother usually had toast and jam in this café.

And what were those two doing there? For a long while neither had news of the other. They met by chance a short time back. They almost collided at the corner of Churruca Street and the Avenida. It was impossible to just keep going. In Nerea's case, the surprise contained a drop of concern. Nothing really, a passing suspicion, unnecessary, because there before her, overflowing with affection, was Arantxa's smile. With no hesitation, she swerved to kiss her. They looked each other up and down and each interrupted the other to express admiration.

They agreed, do you have the time? to bring each other up to date on their private lives. Where? Not in the street, of course. It was beginning to get dark and a disagreeable wind was blowing. Nerea pointed to the nearby café. And there they went, arm in arm.

"How long has it been since we've seen each other?"

Umm, ever since Arantxa moved in with Guillermo in Rentería, about a year and a half.

"I was suffocating in the town. I know it isn't right for me to say it, after all I was born there, grew up there, and had all my friends there. But I couldn't stand it anymore. Lots of people living there have their lives ruined because of politics. People who give you a hug today and tomorrow for whatever someone's said to them will shun you. I was insulted because I was going out with a man who wasn't Basque. What do you think of that? They'd say, what would Joxe Mari say if he found out?"

"Quit kidding. Who said that to you?"

"Josune. What hurt me most was that when she spoke to me we weren't alone. She held a kind of people's trial, understand? I kept my mouth shut. In a country like this, the best thing you can do is keep quiet. But the next time I saw her on the street I stopped her, I told her I'll fall in love with whoever the hell I want, and I told her to go to hell."

"Good work."

"She wasn't the only one who had a bad opinion of my boy-friend. My mother, to go no further, had the same prejudices. Little by little she's accepted things. From time to time she even visits us in Rentería. Poor Guille. He's such a nice guy. He's started taking Basque lessons, but I don't think it's going to work out. I don't think he's got any talent for languages."

A waiter came over to their table. What would they like to drink? Arantxa, hesitating for an instant, asked for this; Nerea, not hesitat-ing at all, asked for something else and at the same time asked the waiter if was possible to lower the volume on the music.

"As I was saying, I stopped going into the bars in town. Well, I stopped going into the Arrano a long time ago so I wouldn't have to see my brother's picture on the wall. My life was elsewhere, with my Guille and my job in San Sebastián. It's a crap job but you've got to eat. I felt an enormous desire to abandon the town. 'Desire' isn't the right word: obsession. I finally got it through my thick skull that I had no future there. I felt very uncomfortable. Even now, remembering all that, the names of places, the faces of certain individuals, I feel a clot of repugnance in my mouth. Forgive me for getting overexcited. I didn't like certain stares. I imagine Josune campaigned against me. But not only Josune. As soon as I could, I moved into an apartment with Guille. There we are, married by a judge. We're not doing badly, working and saving to have as decent a life as we can."

"How did your parents react?"

"My mother wasn't exactly pleased that I moved in with my boyfriend. Because of what people would say—my daughter's shacked up with a guy—she would let me have it. As if we were still living in Franco's days. She and lots of others think they're very revolutionary and they go to demonstrations and shout slogans, but in reality they're stuck to tradition like barnacles and they're as ignorant as rocks. Look, *ama*, I said to her, we'll fix that up in a second. And I got married. A Tuesday in January, with no white dress, no guests, no bullshit. Mortal sin gone: isn't that what you wanted? For my mother, who dreams that Don Serapio will marry her children and that she'll toss sugared almonds to the kids on the church stairs and show off in a fancy dress, that was a complete drama. That, she wasn't going to forgive, you just don't do things like that to your mother. A month later we celebrated the wedding in a restaurant with Gorka, who absolutely refused to wear a tie, my parents, and Guille's parents. My old man got sentimental. I don't know if it was because of the champagne—it never sat well with him. Right then and there he starts remembering Joxe Mari. It occurs to him that we're not all present and he starts crying like a baby. Now, in his favor I have to say he gets along fine with Guille. Even before the wedding they understood each other. I think it was after Guille helped him in the garden. One day, I said to him: *aita*, how happy I am you like my boyfriend, or at least you like him more than *ama* does. And he says to me: it's that your mother, she's got a bad nature!"

The waiter came back with the order and put the bill on its little saucer down near Nerea. To punish her for asking to have the music volume lowered? She repeated the request. The only response: they did lower the volume, but they couldn't lower it any more. The waiter said nothing more. He tended to another table, and the music was as loud as it was at the start.

"Damn, but this tea is hot."

"Do you have any children?"

Busy with her tea bag, Arantxa shook her head to say no. Nerea was shocked that her friend would answer like that, without looking her in the eye. So, she pressed her:

"No children in the family plan?"

Then Arantxa looked up.

"There's something I haven't talked about to Guille or anyone else. I can tell you because you went with me to London. I'm starting to believe that in the clinic they maybe didn't do everything properly. Even though my gynecologist says there's nothing wrong, something isn't working right, and that I can tell you breaks up my happiness a little."

"So, you are planning to have children."

"We've been trying now for a while. The idea that they may have left me sterile frightens me a lot, let me tell you. Anyway, tell me about yourself, your life, your plans. I've told you my part, which is not a great deal, as you can see. Are you still studying?"

Nerea was licking the teaspoon. Why is she holding back? For a moment, she gave the impression she was trying to see herself in Arantxa's chestnut eyes. Sincerity in exchange for sincerity, she said:

"I was on the verge of giving it up. But after all is said and done I'm going to listen to my father and, when summer's over, I'm going to continue the program in Zaragoza."

"You don't seem too happy about it."

"I had problems at home. I let drop a few words I shouldn't have. I admit it and I'm sorry. Anyway, my father forgives me no matter what I do. That's not the problem. At the same time—and this gets me off the hook—my parents didn't want to tell me what's going on. To protect me. I found out after. At first, I just didn't understand them. But, okay, *aita*, why the hell do I have to study far away? I'm doing well here, in my hometown, with my friends. And he, hemming and hawing, that I should think about finding another university because it had already been decided that I was not going to stay in Basque Country. My mother agreed with him. And Xabier, who they'd already told everything before telling me, also agreed. I went against them, thinking they were working like a team so they could treat me like a little girl. And I didn't only oppose them. I got furious! It was then I said words that now burn me in memory."

"I know your father has been threatened. Is that the problem?"

Nerea nodded yes.

"I don't know the details. At home, they said nasty things about your family. And it's that my mother has gone nuts ever since Joxe Mari ran away to France. I've heard her say really ugly things about

Txato. And don't think anyone can argue against her. When you think of the friendship between our two families! A friendship I still believe in, by the way. Look, here I am talking with you, and liking it a lot. If I walk out of here and see Bittori across the street I'll run over to give her a kiss. Okay, so if you want me to tell you the truth, I understand why your father wants to get you far away from town."

"What my father doesn't know and doesn't have to know is that it wasn't he who convinced me."

"It wasn't?"

"Something happened in the Arrano Taberna. No one told you about it?"

"I know nothing. Probably because I hardly ever go there."

"For certain, negative waves about my father got to the tavern. And I had no idea. One afternoon, any old afternoon, I walk in and ask Patxi for a drink. I thought that since he was busy cleaning glasses he didn't hear me. So, I asked again. He didn't look at me. How strange. The third time, he comes over with a bad look on his face and says to me, literally, just as I'm telling you, that there's no reason for me to be there and that I should never come back. I froze. I didn't dare ask why."

"Those things you understand without explanations."

"I went straight home. My father came home from work. I hugged him, soaking his shirt with tears, and I told him that yes, I was going to study far away. So that's it, in a little while I'll look for a place in Zaragoza, a city I know nothing about. We try to give meaning, a form, an order to life, and at the end life does with us whatever it wants."

"You're telling me!"

56

PLUMS

You ask yourself, was it worthwhile? And the only answer is the silence of these walls, your face older and older in the mirror, the window with its bit of sky that reminds you there is life and birds and colors outside—for other people. And if you ask yourself what bad thing did you do, the answer comes back: nothing. You sacrificed yourself for Euskal Herria. Very well, dear boy. And if you ask again, the answer comes: I wasn't smart, I was manipulated. Are you sorry? He has days of depression. It pains him that he did certain things.

This is his life for one year and another and another until he loses count. He thinks, he rethinks. You have to fill in the loneliness somehow, don't you? The truth is that with every day that passes it's harder for him to stand the presence of his comrades in jail. Should he pray? No, that's not for him. For his mother, yes. She comes to see him once a month and says:

"My boy, every day I ask Saint Ignatius to get you out of jail or at least to put an end to your being so far away and bring you closer to home."

At first, he looked for company. In the patio, he would chat about sports with the regular prisoners. Within the ETA prisoners group, he was known to be a hard man, loyal, orthodox. The years, the silent walls, his mother's eyes in the meeting room ate away at him, forming an internal hollow as if he were just the bark of an old tree. More recently he would use any pretext to be by himself, and precisely in this instant, when he hadn't foreseen he would be remembering, he sees himself in the telephone booth just outside of town, a finger in his ear to block out the sounds of passing trucks. Josune, nervous, doesn't want problems. In the town, everyone knows they took Koldo away and that the Guardia Civil tried to capture them. They agreed that Josune would tell Gorka to come up to the quarry. And so many years later, in his cell, Joxe Mari realizes that if Josune's line had been tapped by the police he would have put the girl in serious difficulties, and let's not even talk about Gorka.

Jokin:

"What does Chubby have to say?"

"That she'll look for my brother and that we shouldn't get her into trouble."

"Did you tell her she should ask Gorka for some size 42 shoes?"

"I forgot."

"Your brother, what size does he wear?"

"How the fuck would I know?"

Patxi's envelope also reappears in his memory. Its content wasn't at all bad: six thousand pesetas. This is beginning well. And a note that ended with words of encouragement and a *Gora Euskadi askatuta*. In the note, an address in Oyarzun and the nickname of the person who would meet them there. They should ask for Txapas. There's no signature, no letterhead, nothing that might lead the police to the Arrano in case the letter was intercepted. A smart guy that Patxi, not like me or poor Jokin. They robbed him of his life, they robbed me of my youth.

It was a good distance to Oyarzun and Joxe Mari hadn't eaten. On top of that these bicycles are more for riding around town than for highways. Jokin, too, hadn't eaten or had breakfast that morning or eaten dinner the night before. Sure, but it isn't the same; he isn't as big, doesn't have the same appetite Joxe Mari does. They made a pact. Because of course they couldn't be arguing out on the highway and they couldn't waste time with a three-course dinner and turn up late for their appointment in Oyarzun. They would stop to eat on the road. Okay. They went into a bar in Rentería and calmed their hunger at the bar with some sandwiches.

"We could have taken a bus in Donostia and saved ourselves the trouble of all this pedaling and sweating."

"What we have to do is save money. We can't just spend it all on the first day."

The man they met with in Oyarzun, fortyish, was fully informed; but you could see he was suspicious. An unwelcoming face on him.

Later on, alone, just the two of them:

"Maybe he doesn't like being called Txapas."

"He can go screw himself."

He greeted them, drily, in Basque. He stared at them without blinking, asked yes-or-no questions, it being understood that we're not here to make small talk. Little by little his brow softened, and eventually he brought them to a cellar where they could spend the night. A strong smell of carpenter's glue. No bed, no mattress. Not even a stinking sink. And when Jokin made even a slight complaint, the guy said that if they didn't like it, they could leave. Alone: this is the struggle. What were they expecting? Luxury, comforts? Joxe Mari emptied his bladder in a corner. Then they spread some cardboard boxes on the floor. A night in the ruined house at the quarry and now this. Two days in a row without supper. Fatigue helped them sleep. They didn't sleep much, but something is better than nothing. Early in the morning, on a whim, Joxe Mari decided to poke around. Going out a low door at the end of the hall, he walked into a garden that flanked the house. Nothing much, a garden wall, grass, and four plum trees. The plums were unripe, but some were turning yellow. Joxe Mari nibbled at ten or twelve where they were least sour. A short time later, Txapas appeared. In cutting, authoritarian fashion he said:

"We're leaving."

Explanations? Zero. So what? We didn't ask for any, either. And the bikes? They stayed in the cellar. Who knows if twenty-odd years later they might still be there, rusty, with flat tires. Txapas used a van to transport them to a solitary spot from which, about half a mile away, you could see the parking lot of the Mamut superstore. And there was morning mist down below, but you could already see above that the sky was clear and that it was going to be a sunny day. The van stopped where a dirt road began.

"This is where you get out."

To each one he gave a copy of the newspaper *Egin* and a pack of Ducados.

"You wait here alongside those trees."

He told them to carry the newspapers and cigarettes so they were clearly visible. He reminded them of the password and wished them luck. And as soon as the two friends got out he left.

Joxe Mari:

"One of us could run over to Mamut and buy food and water. I'm as thirsty as a camel."

"Don't screw around. Suppose the person who's supposed to pick us up comes along and only finds one. Hold out a little longer."

A smile came over Joxe Mari's face as he lay stretched out in the bed in his cell. What a pair of naive fools. At least they had cigarettes. Jokin began to look through *Egin*. Joxe Mari, and this is why he smiles after so many years, walked down a small gully behind them.

"I'll be right back."

"Where are you going?"

He didn't answer. He disappeared in the thicket. And for a few minutes he was hidden. He wiped himself with a couple of pages from *Egin*, not the front page, which was supposed to identify them, and rejoined Jokin near the trees.

"What's up?"

"Nothing."

Minutes later, a car stopped opposite them.

"At what time does the crane pass by?"

"We have to sweep the snow away from the door."

Curt greetings. This guy too wasn't much of a talker, but much more sociable than Txapas. Sitting next to him, the only one who made small talk was Jokin. Joxe Mari, alone in the backseat, suddenly whispered to himself:

"The goddamned plums."

Jokin stared at him without understanding. Now, in the cell, contemplating the bit of blue sky through the window, Joxe Mari finds the memory amusing.

57

In the Reserves

Within his memory, he sees himself looking out another window. Not this one in his cell but the one in a country house in Brittany. Despite all the years that have gone by, boy, it's imprinted in his olfactory memory, alive, exactly as it was, the smell of the wood. A dry smell, perhaps centuries old, that wafted from the beams and the tilted floor made of boards. Jokin and I played, each with a ten-franc coin. They made it roll down the inclined floor. The winner was the one who got the coin closer to the wall, without touching it. Jokin won almost every time because his hand is smaller and nimbler. Admit it. Yes, but it's that my hand was used to the ball in handball, not that shitty little coin that slipped between my fingers. And, of course, it either didn't go far enough or it hit the baseboard.

The two neophyte militants killed time as best they could.

"What does that mean?"

"New."

"You're a clever little fellow. My brother, Gorka, he really knows odd words."

The slow, maddening time in the reserves in the Brittany house. In which house? In all of them. In the first, where they put the two friends up, in the last he shared with Jokin, and in the last where he lived with a new comrade before being integrated into a *talde*. He closes his eyes and evokes the greenness of the country, the interminable rain, the boredom. The daily program of activities: waiting. And then that absence of mountains which for a Basque, no way around it, is deadly. It gnaws away at their joy, it depresses them.

Jokin's departure was a blow to Joxe Mari. They were company for each other, they played, they chatted. And suddenly, separation. Forever?

"I'm sure we'll see each other again."

"In a few years, we'll be historical leaders. You and I in charge of the whole deal. And while the others are breaking their backs and risking their hides, we'll be cozy in Iparralde, deciding the missions and giving orders."

Now the real struggle began, at least for Jokin. At night, the bastard couldn't contain his joy (or his nervousness) about getting out of that isolation in Brittany. And he never stopped talking. It was as if he were on drugs. Joxe Mari, twelve midnight, one a.m., the room filled with cigarette smoke: all that chatter was starting to bust his balls. It's that he never stopped: plans, expectations, memories, anecdotes about their town.

"Remember that time . . . ?"

And he stopped busting them when, and now he was really being an asshole, he said, stay calm, you'll see that five or six years from now they'll transfer you, too.

In reality (he thinks it now, stretched out on the bed in his cell), nothing turned out as they'd imagined. While they were together they used humor to put up with the long hours of inactivity. Jokin, one day while they were strolling in the countryside:

"How the hell are we going to liberate Euskal Herria if we ourselves aren't free, when we have to wait for orders to take a walk and they tell us where we're supposed to go?"

"Don't be a whiner. As soon as they give us guns you'll see if we do any liberating or not."

"We have to make the people from home proud of us."

"For sure. We have to make the town look good."

Before getting into the car, Jokin, how happy he is, looked toward the window, up above, to make a final farewell gesture to Joxe Mari. His fist raised. Midmorning and again rain. Joxe Mari jokingly responded by giving him the finger. He was left alone, more alone than ever before. He saw Jokin stick out his tongue. Does he think he's going to a party or what? And that image, Jokin with his tongue out, is the last he has of his friend.

The car pulled away bouncing along the dirt road. The owner's tractor made the biggest ruts. And it went on raining on the grass and the row of apple trees bordering the road, and also on those other trees, oaks or whatever they were, that blocked the spire of the church there in the town, and closer, it rained on the cows of the house owner, a Breton with a red nose who had shouting matches every night with his wife and with whom they could only communicate by signs.

Months back, in Hendaya, they'd been given the usual welcome. For third-rate recruits, as Jokin said. For rubes, according to Joxe Mari. No brass band to welcome them, no members of the leadership doing the honors.

"Do you two speak French?"

"Not a word."

The man in charge of the welcome reception got right to the point. Look, this, that, and the other thing is what you've got waiting for you. The guy seemed tired. I don't know why, because of the circles under his eyes. There are no real safe places around here. You must be absolutely underground, take great care, discipline and sacrifice. All of it expressed in short sentences as if he wanted to get done as quickly as he could. He added that thing about we're like the cherries in the basket. You grab one and five or six come out attached to it. And that's what we have to avoid at all cost, okay? We can't allow some to fall because of the sloppiness of others.

"The conditions are hard, we've got no reason to pull a fast one on you. This isn't a game."

He provided them with temporary lodging (and clothes and a radio and other tools) in a poultry farm near Ascain. The owner, Bernard by name, an angry Basque-French citizen. He was cold, grim, stretching his neck as if to say: are these really the ones? He seemed to be expecting other guests. More experienced guests? Of higher rank in the organization? And then in the entry to the interior patio, he gave a few shouts to the welcome guy in his own language. Jokin and Joxe Mari couldn't figure out what the fight was about. That the farmer didn't look happy about the presence of the two recruits was obvious. They discovered that he spoke a Basque dialect that with a little effort they could more or less understand. In the following days, there were conversations among them. They became friends. They offered to help on the farm. The guy was a sports fan, including handball. The result: after the second day, his features softened. His wife's, too. One morning there were guffaws in the house. And yes, after three days of keeping out of sight, so as not to be completely idle, they helped a little, to clean up, to bring things in and take things out, all without leaving the farm so no outsider would see them.

One morning of sun and birds, a Renault 5 pulled in to take them away. An important meeting. That's all they said. And as soon as they left they had to put on blindfolds. Over an hour of curves. And finally, the unmistakable sound of gravel under the tires. They were not to peek. And Joxe Mari, now inside the house, could see looking underneath the blindfold reddish tiles and stairs.

"Now you can take off the blindfold."

When the moment for shaking hands came, Santi smiled at them. *Kaixo,* he said; a timid, bland *kaixo* from the two friends. And from the first moment, the interview flowed along well because Santi had friends in the town. That was how the conversation began. And then about the festivals and then about the dancing in the plaza. Santi had information about both of them. What he said left Jokin in open-mouthed wonder.

"So you're the son of the butcher."

He asked them why they escaped. They answered. Also why they wanted to join the organization.

Joxe Mari:

"Burning buses and mailboxes seemed like small stuff to us. We want to take the definitive step."

And they did take it. They'd already taken it. For five days they were locked in a room not much larger than this cell. Three paces wide and five paces long. Maybe a bit longer, but don't think it was much more. He remembers there was a window too high up to look out of. And in any case, it was blocked by a curtain made of thick cloth, dark blue, which practically blocked out all the light. They could hear noises outside: voices and children laughing, the clanking of a tractor or, if it wasn't that, some other farm machine, and a bell that sounded the hours sometimes far off, sometimes close, depending on how the wind was blowing. From time to time a rooster crowed.

Weapons training? Interesting. The theoretical part not so interesting. At least they were amused. The lessons were delivered by an instructor wearing a balaclava. The two first days he came dressed in Bermuda shorts and sandals. He knew a ton about explosives, but when it came to taking apart and assembling the submachine gun he was a blockhead. Next to him, keeping a close eye on things, was the logistics officer, who used an alias Jokin secretly altered to Belarri, because he had a nice-sized pair of ears. Joxe Mari found it impossible to talk to him without staring at his ears. On the day of submachine-gun training, he had to intervene because the guy with the balaclava got all tangled up.

The best part, despite their different talents, was target practice. I remember when we used a 7.65 pistol. *Bam, bam.* Belarri was dumbfounded.

"Shit, guys, where did you learn to shoot like that?"

They also fired a Browning, a Sten, and a Firebird, this last with a silencer. *Swish, swish,* a real pleasure. Belarri, mute with shock, especially with Jokin, who never missed. Joxe Mari thinks that because of Jokin's reputation as a marksman he was the first to be placed in a *talde* where a vacancy had urgently to be filled. Separation was a hard blow.

To lighten up his loneliness he could meet with Koldo, who was living nearby at the time. He didn't like doing it. He and Jokin found him one afternoon by surprise in a bar in Brest. And yes, they did speak, but the words, the tone, the gestures were not as they were in the time they all shared an apartment in the village.

"Listen, you'll have to forgive me. I thought I wouldn't get out of there alive."

"Relax. Soon we'll give them some of their own medicine."

They cracked jokes, agreed to see each other the next day; but they never did. They didn't trust him.

58

A Walk in the Park

This is going to be a walk in the park."

"I'll go in the hardware and you guys wait outside. It's time I made my debut."

They said he might be a drug dealer. The organization confirmed it in a communiqué published some days later in *Egin*. A rapid, easy *ekintza*, nothing spectacular, but good for testing his nerve. That's what Patxo said—to calm him down?—and it was true. Joxe Mari remembered it often because it was his first operation that included a killing. His baptism, with someone else's blood. He'd have to think hard to recall other actions. He's forgotten lots of details about the early ones. They were simple little jobs: a couple of explosions, an attack. The episode in the bar on the other hand was alive in his memory. Not because of the guy. To him it didn't matter who the victim was. You order me to execute so-and-so and I execute him no matter what. His mission wasn't to think or feel but to carry out orders. That's what people who criticize you don't understand. Especially newspaper reporters, sticky flies who wait for the right moment to ask if you're sorry. It's something else altogether when you ask yourself that same question in your cell. He has periods, days, of depression. More and more. Hell, I've been locked up for a long, long time.

He was given the information and a photo. With a nose like that and a beard like that there was no possibility of error. The guy, between thirty and thirty-five, ran a small pub. Sometimes he worked as bartender, sometimes a woman tended bar. The woman was irrelevant. The place was on a street that was practically empty.

Security? None. And there were no problems about making a get-away. Patxo was right calling this a walk in the park.

Sometimes they drew lots to see who would do this and who would do that. Not this time. Joxe Mari insisted he and no one else would do it. Ready to argue the point, Txopo suggested they play rock scissors paper.

"No, the hell with that."

"Okay, okay."

He would walk into the bar, Patxo would wait outside covering the getaway, and Txopo, who was the best driver of the three, would be sitting at the wheel of the car. Again, a walk in the park. They slept on mats on the floor of the place where they stayed. And Joxe Mari, right now in the present, has no memory of having had any dreams that night related to the next day's *ekintza*. They had a TV, they ate what they found in the refrigerator, they watched a movie. That's it.

In the morning, it wasn't as if he was nervous, at least not so nervous he couldn't feign calm with his comrades around, and that's what they were, comrades, not friends. Suddenly there rose up in him again the tension he used to feel hours before an important match back in the days when he played on the handball team. In times like those, he spoke little and did not like to be spoken to, more than anything so he wouldn't lose concentration, so he wouldn't relax too much.

"Let's go."

Off they went. Problems, contretemps, unforeseen events? Nothing. His comrades knew Joxe Mari to be a joker, talkative. Along the way:

"Are you mad about something?"

"How about you stop breaking my balls?"

They went on in silence. The street was empty, few cars, on the outer fringe of the downtown area. They easily found a parking space. The person in question arrived one or two minutes later than the time determined as his regular routine in their scouting report. The beard, the nose: that was the man. He raised the sliding gate without looking around. That guy doesn't realize he's only got a minute to live. And he walked into the bar.

Truth be told: sitting in the front passenger seat, Joxe Mari's heart was pounding. On the way, he pretended to rest his hands on his knees. But he wasn't resting them. He was clutching his legs to control his tremor. He knows there is a before and an after when it comes to your first assassination, though these things, he thinks, depend on the individual. I mean, for example, you blow up a television transmission tower or a bank branch office and of course you cause damage, but damage can be repaired. A life can't. Now he thinks it over objectively. In those days, something else concerned him. What? That his nerves would put him at risk. He was afraid of looking soft, uncertain in the presence of his comrades, or that the *ekintza* might fall apart because of him.

Better not to think too much. He got out of the car decisively, convinced he left the tremor and the palpitations behind him. He didn't close the door completely. And Patxo, who was in the backseat, did the same. Did they speak to each other, look at each other? What for? They had it all planned, and the intense sunlight soon struck their faces.

Joxe Mari saw balconies with clothing hung out to dry. This is not a neighborhood where rich people live. How odd, no? To think something like that in such a moment, with the weight of the Browning under his jacket. One side of the street faced the mountain. There below, the expressway. An ugly place. Farther on, a group of children were playing, scattered over a lot with debris and bushes on its edges. What does "farther on" mean? Between 350 and 500 feet. They were too far away and having too much fun to notice the two young men heading, one behind the other, toward the bar. Joxe Mari's heart wasn't pounding as hard. The same thing happened when he played handball. As soon as the referee blew his whistle to start the match, he calmed down but without losing tension.

As he walked along the sidewalk he stopped hearing Patxo's footsteps behind him. He passed an entryway with its glass door and number. What number? How am I going to remember that after all these years? On the other hand, he does remember that to enter the bar you had to go up two stairs. Or was it three? The metal gate wasn't all the way up, just enough that he wouldn't have to duck his head. And immediately he noticed the smell of old cigarette smoke, of a dump with bad ventilation. It took his eyes a few seconds to get used to the half-light. And he was disconcerted when he didn't find the victim inside the bar. The place wasn't much bigger than this cell, though it was longer, with a door opened in the rear where the nose and beard suddenly appeared.

"Do you mind waiting a bit? We aren't quite open yet."

The guy wore a chain around his neck. The silvery links reflected the weak light coming from the single burning bulb. The links ran down his slightly hairy chest and disappeared under his shirt, so Joxe Mari couldn't know what kind of medal he was wearing. He fixed his gaze on the space just below his throat, the length of two chain links. He brought the muzzle of the Browning to that spot and fired. He had enough time to see the sudden, bloody wound before the man collapsed to one side and, as he violently fell, knocked over a barstool.

He was still moving there on the floor. As he tried to get up, he choked:

"Don't shoot. Just take the money."

To Joxe Mari the fact that the victim didn't die instantly was an outrage, especially because he'd taken him for a common thief. The plaintive tone, the painful attempts to stand up. Joxe Mari was convinced that the guy was trying to evoke his sympathy. You can't fool me. He saw the rows of bottles, the rail where people rest their feet. And he remembered his instructor's maxim: we don't assassinate, we execute. Be very careful about finishing the job. He took a step forward and without losing his calm, destroyed the man's head.

Silence finally returned. Two steps away, wide open, the cash register. I could have taken advantage of the situation. Who would find out? He took nothing. Not even water from the faucet. And that is proof (he told himself as he exited the bar) of the justice of our struggle.

59

A THREAD OF GLASS

A reckless cabbie. Or is it normal to drive like this through the streets of Rome? He honked his horn and scattered a group of tourists clustered around their guide in the middle of the street, contemplating a historical building. And then, what a labyrinth of narrow streets, how many curves! Rolling down his window the cabbie waved his arm to greet a natty waiter trying to attract patrons by standing at the entrance to the terrace (awning and large potted plants) of a restaurant. They passed stretches of cobbled street. And in the backseat, between bounces, clutching each other's hand, Aránzazu and Xabier exchanged glances every other second as if saying: what have we gotten ourselves into? Do we laugh or do we scream for help?

They got out at the entrance to the hotel Albergo del Senato. There they were, right next to the Pantheon, with its granite columns and all those people taking photos; nearby, an open carriage for tourists with its bored horse and its romantically drowsing driver, and at the center of the plaza, the fountain surrounded just then by teenagers—high-school students?—all with yellow kerchiefs around their necks, caps the same color, and backpacks.

Aránzazu paid the fare. They shared their money, and she was pulling out banknotes. A million lire. The cabbie, making gestures like a squirrel and speaking like one, too, drove off, *buona giornata*, as quickly as he'd driven them. And before entering the hotel, carrying their luggage, deeply breathing in the warm afternoon air, Aránzazu said to Xabier in a low voice:

"I swear to God, for a while I thought the driver was kidnapping us."

Xabier, how different he was then, at least in his moments of leisure: ironic, witty, sarcastic (not so much in the hospital). His response:

"You don't have to imagine it. He really did. The ransom was the fare."

From the fourth-floor window, did they see the Piazza della Rotonda? Are you kidding? They were given a room that looked nothing like the one in the pamphlet the travel agent showed them. Spacious? Yes. Clean? Also yes. But the window opened onto a dark interior patio. Facing them, a blackish brick wall with big windows cut into it. A poetic detail, according to Aránzazu: a cat curled up on a ledge. And further up, near the eaves, a heroic bush that clung to life by sinking its roots into a crack in the wall.

"No complaints?"

"No, I like the cat."

"Interior patios bring certain advantages. I'll bet that at night the people with rooms overlooking the plaza can't sleep a wink because of the noise."

"The poor things. They've been swindled. Even though I don't know them I'm sorry for them."

"Remember the meaning of our trip."

"I wasn't thinking about anything else. How good you smell!"

And he began undressing her right there at the window, and she, completely deferential after making sure no one could see them from the patio, beautiful, joyful lips, let him and even spread her legs and raised her arms and struck poses that facilitated the smooth removal of her clothes.

She'd begged him: let's have no misunderstandings, he should express his desires without holding anything back, physical desires or any other kind, and she would do the same with hers. Companions, friends, lovers, fused identities. Three days in Rome would allow them to plumb the depths of their relationship. Xabier quickly took off his clothes. He penetrated her, the two of them chest against chest. She guessed his intention and rested one foot on the edge of a chair and, wide open, their coupling was consummated without either using hands. Entangled, without shifting their bodies, they simultaneously turned their eyes toward the patio. The wall, the cat, the bush. Still, united, without embracing, she with her hands together on the back of his neck, his even with her kidneys. A pleasurable habit they had. The sensation of being two in one without one possessing the other. She, whispering, as if afraid of annoying:

"Do you want more?"

At night, he said. They remained immobile, silent, one minute, two, both immersed in their fantasies and thoughts, until his member, softening little by little, escaped its warm refuge.

"Shall we eat?"

They went out. Where? They strolled about for a while. This way, that way, and without planning it they ended up at Piazza Navona. The fountain with those statues that to Aránzazu seemed monstrous, the splendid spring sunlight, a row of nuns that emerged in Indian file from that church, and right in front of them the Spanish bookstore, to which they decided to return after satisfying their hunger but not later than tomorrow.

Leaving the plaza at an angle, heading toward the river, they stopped at a restaurant. We're going in here, whether it's good or bad, expensive or cheap, because by then hunger was tyrannizing their bodies. Salad, gnocchi, and for him fish, which wasn't bad but was nothing to write home about.

"No complaints, okay? Just look at what luck we've had with the weather."

"This *orata*, don't you think they caught it in the fountain? I'm saying it because it tastes like the feet of a statue."

"Xabier, please, they'll hear you."

"They're Italians. They don't understand us."

"They understand every word. If you want to criticize, do it in Basque."

And they made a toast with *vino rosso della casa*, accomplices in laughter, in mischievous glances, in happiness. He told her in Basque, how good you smell. She reminded him that they swore they would visit Rome to enjoy themselves. They'd agreed to all that days before setting out. Aránzazu imagined a thread of glass they were holding up, he at one end, she at the other. Three days in Rome with a thread that could snap at any moment. That was their fear. And Xabier, joking:

"To our honeymoon."

"Calm down, my friend. Not so fast."

She'd only gotten her divorce a little more than two months ago. Ugh, it was hard going, trying to talk about her previous marriage. By the same token, it was hard (impossible?) for her to erase eight years of painful memories. Her ophthalmologist ex-husband and Xabier saw each other in the hallways, in the elevator, in the hospital parking lot. Also in the Anoeta Stadium since both were members of the Real Sociedad, with seats no more than thirty feet apart. Xabier tried, with the appropriate dissimulation, to avoid him. And? It's the one thing that annoyed him. The ex, once the divorce was finalized, found out about his relationship with Aránzazu and, in the hospital cafeteria, told him to take care of her, not to leave her alone, and he added that she was an adorable but fragile woman.

"Take very good care of her."

Where does he get off butting in that way? And that's exactly what's happening, I mean you don't want problems, especially in the workplace, so he opts for diplomacy and silence. All in all: nothing. He made a vague gesture of agreement with his head turned toward the waitress, could you get me the check? He didn't finish his latte and was going to say goodbye, and had parted his lips to say it, but the other was faster:

"I wish the two of you all the happiness in the world. Really. But it won't be easy. I know from experience."

That afternoon, he told Aránzazu what happened and she burst into tears.

"You probably think I'm exaggerating."

That was the first time he saw her cry. Pretty, discreet, immersed in elegant sadness. A sensitive woman, thirty-seven years old, three years older than he. He was fascinated watching her moist eyes. He embraced her, consoling, delighting in her fragrant warmth, he touched his cheek on her black hair and kissed her lips. There was a charm in that way of not ruining her eye shadow with the corner of a tissue; also, perhaps, a touch of anxious coquetry and a great fear. Let's see if I'm going to be the one who exaggerates. The part about fear was real. It was there inside her like an opaque pain. The fear of being incapable of a real love, and this was her last attempt. She told him so one Saturday afternoon while they were passing time before a comedy at the Teatro Principal.

"You, definitively, are the last. I don't have the slightest doubt about it. If our relationship doesn't work, this unfortunate lady will never again fall in love, absolutely never."

It was during that conversation that the idea of the trip came to Aránzazu.

"Let's go far away from here for a few days, far away from our work and all the people we know. Three or four days where we're together twenty-four hours a day. By the end, we'll know how far we're willing to go, if we can put up with each other, if we want to create a relationship beyond sex. What do you think? But we have to split the expenses fifty-fifty."

Then they entered the theater. When they left, as they passed through the door, she said that thing about the thread of glass, revealing her fear. At the age of thirty-seven she felt like a wilting flower. What did she have to offer? Love, of course. That for sure. But if Xabier had other priorities (having children, for example), she thought it would be hard for him to be happy with her. That fear soured her days, accompanied her to Rome, surfaced again down there. Where? In that walkway along the Tiber. The two of them had taken a seat on a projection from the wall that was like a bench. They'd just eaten. The sun was shining on them. And the calm, turbid river flowed along. Suddenly, a stone he found on the ground gave him an unfortunate, puerile idea.

"If I manage to throw it to the other shore it means nothing and no one will ever separate us."

"Don't do it, please. It's better not to tempt fate."

"You think I can't do it?"

"I think you can, but the river is wide."

"Let's see, let's see."

He took off his sports jacket. That chest, those shoulders are wide, but he's not young anymore. Doesn't he realize that? He made a short run, this man who normally was so judicious, such a doctor, such a rational man, and threw the rock hard, with masculine desires to impress a woman. The stone flew at great speed through the clear air of the early afternoon. The two of them watched it, barely a black speck that went off, began to fall, plop into the water.

"Well, it was only a game."

From there they went on to the Sistine Chapel.

60

Doctors with Doctors

Txato was leaving the table to have a siesta. He pointed out that they'd just met the woman, that it was too soon to judge her; but Bittori, severe, cutting, still wearing her apron, insisted: male doctors with female doctors, male nurses with female nurses. Then came her disdainful lip and the satirical wag of her neck:

"The cute little couple. For God's sake, she's three years older than he is. Does this innocent need a second mother or what?"

"Come on now."

"Well, am I right or not?"

"And if our son hears you talking like that you'll know if you're right or not."

"I'm talking to you. There's no reason for Xabier to hear anything."

They'd left a few minutes earlier, holding hands. At their age! The cute, happy little couple. People in town must be laughing their heads off. Sunday and clouds. The Real team was playing at five. At the end of the match, she'd pick him up, reel him in, and keep pulling the line until she lands the fish and stuffs him into the creel.

Bittori opened the balcony door wide.

"You can't breathe in here. Don't tell me she isn't over the top. Even the consommé tasted like perfume."

"Well, I didn't notice. Now, you're not going to tell me she isn't good-looking."

"What do you know about it? Go on, get to bed and dream about trucks."

The four of them could just as well have gone to a restaurant.

Txato had suggested it immediately. And the fact is he didn't want to meddle in anyone's business. Xabier made the same suggestion a little later over the telephone, encouraged by Aránzazu, who wanted to present herself "on neutral territory." Both father and son were willing to pay the bill, but Bittori said absolutely not. Her motive? In her opinion, in restaurants everyone behaves artificially and it was easier to get to know people at home.

Txato:

"You'd rather spend the whole morning cooking?"

"So what? When you brought me to your village to meet your family, your mother made the food. Chickpea soup and fried chicken. I still remember. And when we were done, I helped her clean up. On the other hand, this grande dame didn't even offer to lend a hand. Very elegant, that one, and nicely made up and all, but she could certainly see that I was taking away the plates and she didn't lift a finger. Nice manners!"

They were expected at half past one. A quarter hour earlier, Bittori had set Txato to keep an eye out, without their seeing you, understood?, next to the balcony door with strict instructions. One, he shouldn't even think of touching the curtains, which are freshly washed; two, he was to warn her as soon as he saw them coming down the street, since for nothing in this world did she want to receive that woman wearing an apron.

" 'That woman'? Her name is Aránzazu."

"I couldn't care less what her name is."

Besides, she wanted to look her over before the introductions. Oh yes, three: he should not sample anything on the table—asparagus in mayonnaise, Jabugo ham, cod croquettes, barnacles, shrimp.

"I know exactly how many and how much there is."

Txato doing sentinel duty, God give me patience, watched over the street, which was practically deserted because it was Sunday. And at the appointed hour, punctual, holding hands, they entered his visual field, she carrying a bouquet. How tall she is, how good-looking, how elegant. Impressed, he enjoyed a few moments of pleasure contemplating the woman before he warned Bittori, who came in from the kitchen taking nervous steps and loosening her apron as fast as she could.

"The shoes don't go with the dress."

"To me she looks like a monument of a woman."

"Don't touch the curtains, please."

"She's a knockout! She's almost as tall as our son."

"That black hair is not natural. And that brooch on her lapel, from here, looks like a stain. I'd say the lady doesn't have much taste."

After the couple said their farewells, didn't Txato, who had eaten and drunk enough for three, have his siesta? He tried. Bittori, busy in the kitchen, could not calm down. She, the mother in monologue, the mother in pain, had a heart-to-heart talk with the soapsuds. Her son with that woman, a mere auxiliary nurse. She emitted adverse opinions toward an audience composed of filthy dishes. To the scouring pad she said this, to the faucet she said something else. She received no answers, and did not find the understanding she desired. At all costs, she needed the proximity of human ears. At home, in those moments, she found no other ears but those of Txato. As a result, regretting the effect on her husband's digestion and repose, she entered—is that entering?—okay, she burst into the room. She came in from the kitchen talking to herself, drying her hands on her apron. Never quiet, she sat on the edge of the bed. She shook her husband.

"How is it possible you can sleep so calmly?"

Goodbye, siesta. His tongue thick, he muttered, what's wrong, what's going on? Bittori didn't answer. She didn't even seem interested in conversing. She didn't want someone to talk to her. All she wanted was ears.

"I don't see how Xabier can be happy with that woman. She may have all the virtues you like. But I, for my part, don't see them anywhere. To me she looks like a total lunatic. She didn't even taste the seafood. Or the ham. I spent the whole morning roasting a suckling pig, which I went all the way to Pamplona to buy, and it turns out she's a vegetarian. Come on!"

One action perpetrated by the guest did not escape Bittori's attention. Which? Thinking no one was watching, she brought those brightly painted lips of hers to Xabier's ear into which she whispered a request—an order? And the innocent, a man who obeys a subordinate, letting a few seconds pass to pretend the request was coming from him, said:

"*Ama*, would you mind removing the piggy's head?"

All eyes focused on the platter holding the golden-brown, juicy, pacific little animal at the center of the table. Half a suckling pig specially ordered from a butcher in Pamplona. The money it had cost Bittori, to say nothing of the two-way trip on the bus! And all to provide the guest with a first-rate product.

Before she bought suckling pigs from Josetxo. She bought everything from him. She relied on him, was friendly with him. Now they don't even say good morning to each other.

"Well?"

"It's just that Aránzazu isn't used to it."

He defended her, of course. And she'll take us for primitive carnivores. Bittori could only feel Xabier's attempted mediation as a knife in the back.

"Can you imagine our son living with a person like that? My God! In this house, all our lives we've been eating meat and fish. And besides all these herbivores are full of manias. What a way she has of talking! Playing the part of the professor, explaining everything all the time. A mere auxiliary nurse! I don't like her. She's got the dumb doctor's number all right. He may know a lot about surgery, but about living with a woman he knows nothing. She took one look and said: I'll take this one. A divorcée as clever as a hungry rat. A secondhand woman, who's had more experiences than she's had hot meals. She eats like a bird. The cake, not one bite. She'd like to, but this morning she had her daily dose of carbohydrates. As pretentious as they get! Did you see the look on her face when I said I got up at seven this morning to bake it? She doesn't have the slightest interest in us. She's got eyes on the prize, catch the surgeon who owns his own house and earns a good salary. Did you see the look on her face when I asked if she wanted to bring home a slice of cake in the Tupperware? No thank you, don't bother. I felt like slamming it in her face."

"Just tell me when the sermon is over. I'm still interested in getting some sleep."

"And all that stuff about Rome, to me it stinks to high heaven! I don't believe they're sharing the expenses fifty-fifty. I know Xabier. I'd bet anything he's paid for the lot."

Many years later, in a visit to the cemetery, sitting on the edge of the grave as she sat on the edge of the bed that distant day, Bittori was still mulling over the matter.

"Of course, I'd like to see Xabier with a wife. But properly married and not with the first woman to sweet-talk him and smile at him like that nurse he brought to dinner one Sunday, remember her? I forget her name. What a bitch! As soon as I saw her I figured out her intentions. You know very well I've got a good eye for things like that. And of course, if it's all going to make our son unhappy, I'd rather he stayed a bachelor."

61

A Pleasing Smallness

Her face distorted, her footsteps energetic. As soon as he saw her walking toward him in the corridor, he supposed she was coming to scream at him. The newly widowed woman who came into what until yesterday was her husband's bedroom. She asked a nurse about it, and she, perhaps without the appropriate consideration, gave her the news.

Now she's coming to blame someone. Xabier believes it's usually women who can't accept the natural fact of death. They look for someone to blame—a murderer? And there he is, a white hospital coat, available for insults, reproaches, accusations: the doctor on duty.

Under the same circumstances, husbands are usually more easily managed. Generally, they collapse into themselves. The women (the younger women maybe not) explode, pouring out unrestrained emotions. This, at least, is his experience after two decades in the profession. Every so often, a lady just loses it in his presence. An elderly lady of limited culture but with a great capacity for verbal eruptions. Xabier has put up with similar predicaments. He endures them with equanimity.

This octogenarian has gone too far. Between screams and sobs, she's managed to offend, to cause an internal agony. Convinced that the doctor—because he's evil? because he's lazy?—didn't do all he could to save the patient, she said to him, in familiar language, out of her head, howling that:

"If it had been your father instead of my husband, I'm sure you wouldn't have let him die."

She threatens him with a lawsuit. And he, paralyzed. The allusion to his father, might it have been because of the deceased's age? She's waving her arms in the air. She opens her mouth to exaggerated size. She's missing a few molars. And he, impassive, while she recounts that in a hospital in Logroño they cured her of a perforation of her . . . She searches for the correct term, doesn't find it, and concludes, brusquely, with a vulgar synonym: guts.

Without moving a single facial muscle, Xabier stares into the depth of those weeping, ridiculous, furious eyes. A moment later, with the lady a bit calmer, Xabier asks her with cold respect:

"Do you know my father?"

"No. And I don't have to. But for sure if your father was the sick one you'd have worked harder."

That was all he wanted to find out. If she knew him, if she knows what happened. Xabier has not the slightest interest in continuing to listen to the old lady. He doesn't even offer his sympathy. He politely asks her to excuse him, but he has to take care of other patients. After a while, his spirits at low ebb, he's seated at the desk in his office. He pours cognac into a plastic cup. He downs it in one gulp. He fills the glass again, never taking his eyes off his father's photo. His severe eyebrows, the ears that, fortunately, neither he nor his sister inherited. In Xabier's ears the screeching voice of the lady in the hallway still echoes. You wouldn't have let him die. *Aita*, did I let you die? In any case, he didn't stop it from happening. You didn't stop it from happening, Xabier. Who says that? His father's serious eyes say it. And ever since, you haven't dared, it shamed you, you considered yourself unworthy to tear chunks of happiness from life.

After the second drink, he looked up at the spiderweb, looking for good moments of the past, which he did have, of course he had them, and not only in childhood, when it's easier to harbor illusions. Now, on the other hand, he's experiencing something like a repulsion for happiness.

How many times has he been tempted to ask the cleaning women please not to clear away that web! Just one blow would deprive him of so many memories. It would deprive him, without going any farther, of this one he's having now, after the third shot of cognac, which restores to him the image of Aránzazu. When, where? If he put his mind to it he could date it precisely. Everything that has happened in his life has taken place at a determined temporal distance from the death of his father. He got his degree seven years before, he attended that cardiovascular- surgery congress in Munich nine years after. In the same way historical facts are dated in relation to the birth of Jesus Christ. And Aránzazu is prior to the zero point and also a little, very little, after, barely a few hours after.

He remembers the place and the time. The Gaviria café, on the Avenida, at nightfall. It's summer. A year and a few months before. But neither he nor she could know what would happen in that instant. Since all the outdoor seats were taken, they decided to sit inside.

He swallows another cognac, which will later oblige him to take a taxi home. He can't explain why such an apparently trivial episode should come to mind; but you can't ask a cobweb to choose its victim. It grabs, if in fact it does grab, what lands on it, even if, as in the case of this memory, a pleasing smallness, a game played by incipient lovers.

He, the doctor still doing his residency, is seated here; she, the auxiliary nurse, is at the opposite end of the table. It isn't their first date. They've slept together twice. The last time, last night, but what does that mean? He stares at her, scrutinizing; he can't stop himself. Aránzazu has for a while been relating, with visible intensity, an episode from her private life. What's she saying? Something about when she was married. He's barely listening. Fascinated, he observes her lips and for a moment he doesn't care that she notices. Those lips when Aránzazu speaks and when she takes an elegant drag on her cigarette. Cool, feminine lips, nicely shaped, that move naturally and when she pronounces the letter *u* suggest a kiss that vanishes into the air. Enchanting lips over which he would pass his tongue slowly right now. Those lips in Aránzazu's attractive face are tormenting him. And I, who work with bodies, who must make an effort not to see in them only organs and blood vessels and muscular tissue and bones, find myself carried away by an irresistible erotic impulse.

"What are you looking at?"

"I imagine you've been told quite often that you're very pretty."

"In other words, you're not listening to me."

"That would be impossible."

"I'm not the woman I once was. The years have gone by."

"Nature outdid herself in your case."

"Come on, Xabier, you're going to make me blush."

Then he placed his right hand flat on the table, palm upward like a beggar asking for money. Chimpanzees also hold their open hand out to their fellows to ask reconciliation, I don't know, as a hospitable, peaceful sign (I read it somewhere). And Aránzazu responded, placing her much smaller hand on Xabier's, palm against palm.

The spiderweb, up there, held that concise, distant memory. Touch told him that in Aránzazu's hand there was a deep concentration of humanity. A warm, smooth hand. The hand of a woman who has suffered disillusion and, certainly, suffering; who has worked a lot, a hand that has taken things away, carried things, lifted things, and which is, was, a marvelous instrument of pleasure.

He is seeing her with her delicate skin, her slender, confident fingers, the nails red. Suddenly he felt in his hand the entire person her touch announced with an enormous flood of tenderness. Dear God, this woman is in love right down to her marrow.

62

HOUSE SEARCH

The four of them were asleep when the raid began. There were at least six of them, some wearing ski masks, screaming when it seemed unnecessary. There were even more in the entryway. Others cordoned off the street. A squad of the Guardia Civil. *Bam, bam,* open up! Miren, in bed, to Joxian:

"Who should answer the door?"

"Go see who it is."

"Who do you think it is? The police of course."

First they rang the buzzer. Then they pounded on the door. By then the whole neighborhood must have been awake. Miren, with the night-table lamp on, quickly slid her feet into her slippers and pulled her bathrobe over her nightgown. To Joxian she said that:

"This must be about Joxe Mari."

No sooner had she cracked open the door than they pushed it open. She saw the barrel of a gun. She saw two black boots on the doormat. Come on, get out of the way. They'd come to search. And the *txakurras* scattered themselves over the house so quickly that she wasn't sure how many had entered.

They gathered the four of them in the dining room. Gorka in underpants and barefoot. They'd given Arantxa enough time to slip something on, but she, too, had nothing on her feet. And Joxian, in pajamas with a large urine stain on his pajama bottoms.

The search warrant? It didn't occur to them to ask to see it. What could they know? They also knew nothing about Joxe Mari, all except Gorka, as they found out later, but the boy hadn't wanted to tell them anything. In any case, the police did have a search warrant. The one holding it was the same man who said that sooner or later they'd catch the terrorist and then they'd teach him right from wrong. Then he tossed the warrant to the floor, so you can blow your nose with it, and then asked which was Joxe Mari's room.

"My son doesn't live here."

"Your son's official residence is this house and we know you have weapons."

"Well, he doesn't live here."

Tell us which room is his or we'll turn this place upside down. Then to Gorka, who are you, how old are you? And Miren thinks that if the boy were two years older, they'd have taken him away. Gorka identified himself. Still very young. Self-conscious, he asked if he could get dressed.

"Nobody leaves this room."

Shortly after, another *txakurra* ordered the four of them out on the landing, just as they were, saying be very careful about opening a drawer or touching anything. And he shoved Gorka either for no reason whatsoever or because he wasn't moving quickly enough.

Soon after the four left the apartment, the court clerk, with a sleepy face, appeared and greeted them as if they were lifelong friends. Two armed Guardia Civiles guarded them, one on the stairway leading to the second floor, the other up against the street door.

Miren's face was tense, hard, expressing rage. She offered Gorka her bathrobe, you're going to be cold; but the boy, gloomy and silent, didn't accept.

Every so often the lights would go out. The guard standing at the street door was right next to the switch and he triggered it from time to time. The neighbors' peephole was covered with tape. An X. I don't know if despite that the neighbors saw or not, but at a given moment, one of them, he or she, silently opened the door a little, enough to reach out a hand and toss two blankets onto the floor of the landing.

Joxian was shivering. Gorka was shivering. Father and son distributed the blankets. Arantxa said she didn't need to cover up. Don't bother asking Miren: anger warmed her. From inside the apartment came disturbing noises from time to time. Miren muttered:

"They're going to wreck the apartment."

Arantxa asked the guards if we can sit down and one of them, shrugging his shoulders, answered that he didn't give a shit if you sit or don't sit. So, the girl sat on the stairway to the next floor; Gorka, wrapped in the neighbors' blanket, soon joined her. Joxian, after a long while, sat on the floor. He constantly checked his watch, worried because at six he had to go to work. Only Miren remained standing, stiff, dignified, resentful.

At a certain moment, they began to hear voices in the street. Young people from the village who had jumped out of bed and clustered on street corners in the darkness were shouting slogans in chorus: police, murderers; *txakurrak kanpora* and the usual.

The search went on for almost four hours. They even brought a dog into the apartment; in Miren's opinion, so it could drool all over our things and, in case you didn't notice, to piss and shit. The way they left the flat was as if a hurricane had ripped through it. What for, when Joxe Mari had left practically nothing in his old room? The one who suffered most was Gorka. They took away his school portfolio, a notebook with manuscript poems, an album of photos and similar objects. Arantxa lost a dozen videos.

The day dawned gray. Joxian rode his bicycle to the foundry. He skipped breakfast and having a good wash, but even so he was going to be late. Arantxa had time to put her room back together before going to work. She was complaining that they'd poured out a bottle of perfume, a gift from Guillermo. One of the drawers on the dresser had lost a pull. Gorka's room looked the worst. Jesus, Mary, and Joseph! His mother said, go on, get to the *ikastola*, that she would take care of cleaning up.

Over the course of the morning she put things into plastic bags to throw them into the garbage. Things, some new, that she found tossed on the floor. Socks, underwear; clothing, and objects she imagined touched by the hands of the Guardia Civil or the snout of the dog. And even though they were her things and those of her husband and children, she felt nauseated touching them. She picked them up with two forks, there was no other way. And the most valuable things she tossed into the washing machine or, if they weren't clothing, set them to soak in the kitchen sink. Breathing the air in her own house made her nauseous. She opened the windows. She used bleach to wash the floor, passed wet rags over the furniture, disinfected door knockers. After a while she cleaned again what she'd already cleaned because she had the feeling that there remained signs, smells, who knows what, of the filthy souls of the *txakurras*.

Toward ten in the morning she knocked at the door of the neighbors. The spy hole was still blocked by two strips of tape. Who is it?

"It's me."

They opened the door. And Miren, thankful, returned their blankets. They asked her in. She accepted. She said she didn't want to be alone in her raped house.

"Oh my dear, what things you say."

The neighbors told their side of the story. The noise, the voices, the fright. They couldn't sleep the whole night. They made coffee for Miren. They got out a box of cookies. She, too, told her version of what happened. How awful the business about Joxe Mari was! They knew nothing about him except that he wasn't in town. At eleven she said she had to go and she left. Hoping to speak with Josetxo or Juani to ask them if their place had been searched, she left the house, leaving the windows wide open. If a robber comes in, let him rob.

63

POLITICAL MATERIAL

She caught Juani at a bad moment, all by herself in the butcher shop.

"Where's Josetxo?" she asked over several heads.

"At the doctor's."

"If you like, I can come back later."

"No, wait."

After a while, the two women could talk for a minute alone.

"Do you know anything?"

"Nothing."

"Last night they destroyed our flat."

"No one in town talks about anything else. They're coming to our place today."

"Maybe."

"What were they looking for?"

"Joxe Mari's things. They call him a terrorist. They thought they'd find weapons. Since there's nothing, they took the first things that came to hand."

"Josetxo is nervous. He thinks our sons have entered the armed struggle. We're not going to see those two for a long time."

"What strange ideas your husband has."

"Patxi was here yesterday. He told us that if we have any of Jokin's papers we should throw them out right away. He couldn't be clearer. Okay, now I have to leave you."

"He didn't say where those two have gone?"

"I asked him of course. He wasn't very talkative. The only thing he wanted was for us to throw out the papers as soon as possible."

"Damn, he sure didn't come to our house to give us a heads-up."

And then, walking along, she remembered, connected, put two and two together, suspected. Okay! The previous afternoon she'd surprised Gorka standing—with his shoes on!—on top of a chair, pulling Joxe Mari's posters off the wall. On the floor were two plastic bags filled with newspapers and magazines. She'd once asked him why don't take that junk off the wall now that your brother isn't living with us. He: no way, *ama*, if he finds out he'll give me a beating.

"Hey, what are you doing standing on that chair?"

"Nothing. I'm going to change the look of the room a little."

"And you couldn't put some newspaper down?"

Heading home, Miren went along talking to herself on the street. When people said hello, she answered without turning her face. If the *txakurras* saw the posters, we'd have been in for it. They'd have taken us all in handcuffs to the station. One thought intrigued her. Gorka did in our house what Patxi asked Juani and Josetxo to do immediately in theirs. What a coincidence, no? This will have to be explained.

As soon as he walked through the door, she interrogated him without giving him a chance to take off his shoes. He should explain why he'd pulled down Joxe Mari's posters. Because he wants to put up different posters in their place.

"And where are those other posters. All I see are bare walls."

"For heaven's sake, *ama*, I was thinking I'd collect them one at a time."

"What did you do with your brother's posters?"

"I threw them out."

"They weren't yours."

"They were dirty and old."

"And some magazines and papers Joxe Mari kept in the dresser?"

"I need space, and he's not around."

She looked him in the eye from close up. One second, two, and at the third, *smack,* she gave him a slap.

"That for not telling me the truth."

Doing what Jokin and his brother asked him to do, Gorka went down to the town and in the Arrano told Patxi what he had to tell him. And Patxi said shit, double shit, triple shit, and without skipping a beat went into action, did things, organized things. Finally, after sending the boy on his way, since he was supposed to be collecting the first of the bicycles for Jokin and his brother, come back here, he called him back. It was then he asked if there was still any of Joxe Mari's material in the house of his *aitas*. Material?

"Political material, you know what I mean."

It took him a few seconds to figure out the idea. Okay: posters, propaganda, *Zutabe*. Yes, there is, quite a bit. He should destroy it instantly.

"As soon as you can, get me?"

He didn't explain why he should carry out that cleanup and it didn't occur to Gorka to ask for an explanation. He understood, of course, the essence of the message: that he was to hurry.

To his mother:

"Now you know."

"Why didn't you tell me when I asked?"

"What's the difference? Aren't you happy the *txakurras* found nothing?"

"And since you've been such a busy boy, do you know where your brother is?"

"I'm clueless."

"Are you sure?"

"I swear, *ama*. But you can probably figure out where."

"Where, in that case?"

"You know better than I do. The only thing I'd like is for all of you to leave me in peace."

He ran out of the room. Tall, skinny, more round-shouldered with every day that passed. He locked his door and didn't come out. Miren: the beets are getting cold, that she's had a busy morning, too busy for him to make problems for her. She grew more and more impatient, raising her voice, she told him this and threatened him with that. Then the noise of a capitulating key. Gorka took his place at the kitchen table. He began to eat, looking into his plate. His eyes were irritated, as if he'd been crying, his face covered with pimples.

He ate this, he ate that. With good appetite, that's for sure. And from time to time Miren turned her eyes toward him. To see if he was eating, or if he was crying? Finally, she passed him the fruit bowl without saying a word. And when she took away the plate of chicken bones, she touched his hand. Gorka instantly jerked his away, intent on avoiding a possible caress.

He got up from the table. Before he could escape from the kitchen, Miren asked him if he'd liked his dinner. Gorka shrugged his shoulders and she didn't pursue the matter.

64

WHERE IS MY SON?

The four of them ate their usual supper in the kitchen at the usual time. This woman has fish mania. Fried, in sauce, doesn't matter: fish on Monday, on Tuesday, and so on and so on until death frees us of suppers. And yes, they like it, some of them more, others less; but, in Joxian's opinion, we might have something different every once in a while.

"On Sunday, we had croquettes."

"Sure, cod croquettes, screw that."

Miren, who ignored these complaints, first prepared escarole with chopped garlic, oil, and vinegar. Then she brought out the leftover noodle soup from the previous evening, and last but not least placed on the center of the table protected by its oilcloth covering a platter of breaded anchovies. For the women, tap water. The men usually shared a pitcher of wine and soda water, more of the latter than the former.

Arantxa, sarcastic:

"Let's hope the cops don't pay us another visit tonight."

Miren seemed to shudder:

"Listen here, that's enough of that, we had a bad enough time without anyone having to remind us of it."

"Maybe they'll come back to return my videotapes and give me money to buy a new bottle of perfume."

"Enough out of you."

"I'm going to sleep with my clothes on just in case."

Her mother ordered her to shut up. Joxian intervened on behalf of his daughter.

"Soon we won't be able to say anything in this house."

Say anything? With the children present? With Arantxa being a comedian? Miren, tempted to reveal during dinner a private chat she had during the afternoon, decided to deal with the issue alone with Joxian when they were in bed. In bed, without preambles:

"I talked to Patxi."

"Which Patxi?"

"The one who runs the tavern. He knows a ton of things."

Midway through the afternoon, Miren went into the Arrano. How many people were there—four or five boys? No more. The music so loud that even the deaf could hear it. I don't know why the neighbors don't protest. Or maybe they do, but only among themselves because you're better off being on the boys' good side. And it seems as if Patxi, thirty-plus years of age, earring in one ear, was waiting for her. How so? As soon as he saw her take one step into the tavern, he signaled her to follow him into the storage room.

Joxian shook his head.

"I don't know who the hell ordered you to get mixed up in something that doesn't concern you."

"Me? For the sake of my son I'll get mixed up in whatever I have to. Want me to tell you or not?"

In the storage room it smelled of sour wine and moldy humidity. The stone walls and the rafters were still there from when it was a stable. Miren remembered. So many years ago. She was a little girl and her family often sent her to buy milk fresh from the cow there.

Patxi closed the door. Before Miren said a word, he asked her to remain calm. She answered that she *was* calm. Was she? Of course not.

"Do you know where Joxe Mari's gone? Tell me right now."

"Come now, Miren, calm down."

"Damn it, I already said I'm calm. I'm my son's mother. It's only normal that I'd want to know where he's gone to."

"He's underground."

"Fine. And where is that? He doesn't have to move. I'll go to him."

Impossible. It wasn't the way it used to be, when family members would visit the south of France on weekends and bring money, clothes, and cigarettes to the refugees. The blame belongs to the

Antiterrorist Liberation Groups: the militants had no choice but to take precautions.

Joxian:

"In other words, we can't visit him."

"Isn't that what I just said?"

"In that case, Josetxo is right. We won't be seeing those two for a thousand years or so."

"Patxi says there are two possibilities. Our son will either go to Mexico or some other country like that or join the organization."

"I'd rather he go far away."

"What you'd rather is of no interest to anyone."

"It's of interest to me. I know what I'm saying."

"What you know wouldn't fill a shot glass."

She didn't tell him—why bother?—that there came a moment when Patxi rested his hands on Miren's shoulders. To her it seemed a gesture not so much of affection but of recognition, of homage, as if saying to her: you have good reason to be proud of your son. And with his hands here, on her shoulders, he told her, calming her, explaining things to her, that there existed internal channels for the distribution of mail among militants and family members.

"Ah, so he can write us?"

"And you can write to him."

"Can I send him packages? His birthday is coming up soon and I wouldn't like it if he didn't get a little present."

In bed, Joxian instantly turned over to stare at her.

"Did you really say that? Do you think Joxe Mari has gone off to the colonies?"

"Where do you get off saying things like that? He's my son. I gave birth to him. Did you? You didn't even find out about it until the next day."

"Okay, enough with the sermon, all you do is bust my balls with the story of how you gave birth to him."

"Me in pain and you in the bar, and you don't like me to remind you of it. So he's my son and I don't want winter to come and him being cold or that his birthday comes and he gets sad because he doesn't have a present."

Patxi took his hands off Miren's shoulders. He told her to forget about packages at least for the time being; but that she should go home in peace because the organization never leaves a man behind. He repeated what he said about pride, adding that if there were many men like Joxe Mari in Euskal Herria we would have been free years ago. Before they left the storage room, he assured her that the moment there appeared any communication (letter, note, whatever) he would personally deliver it to her house. He pointed to the door in front of them. He told her that:

"When we're outside of here we won't be speaking again."

And then, in the tavern, right in front of five or six boys, he kissed her goodbye.

To Joxian:

"Well, now I've given you all the information,"

"What information did you give me? We still don't know where he is or what he's doing. Of course, you don't need much imagination to figure that out. No one joins ETA to be a gardener."

"We don't know if he joined ETA. He might well be on his way to Mexico. But if he did join, it's to free Euskal Herria."

"It's to kill."

"If I find out about anything I won't tell you."

"I didn't bring up my son so he could kill people."

"Brought up? Who did you bring up? I never saw you do anything with your children, ever. You spend half your life in the bar and half your life on your bicycle."

"And every day I have a nice vacation at the foundry, screw that."

Their eyes met for an instant. Disdainful, distant? In any case, devoid of cordiality. Then Miren turned off the light and giving an energetic twist rolled over on her side, her back to her husband. He in the darkness said that:

"If I were twenty years younger, I'd take off tomorrow to look for him, beat the shit out of him, and bring him home."

Miren did not reply.

65

BLESSING

They were still speaking. They were still sharing secrets and snacking together on Saturday afternoons in San Sebastián. And they could easily have brought along other women from the village. Juani, who was a great friend, or even Manoli, whom they saw less, but no. In their Saturday ritual there was no space for anyone else, not even for their husbands. Are you kidding? Let them go play cards or ride their bikes and leave us in peace. They also went to mass together and sat next to each other.

Miren dunked her churro in the hot chocolate. She said, chewing, as she wiped the tips of her fingers with the paper napkin, that ever since the night of the search she hasn't been comfortable in her own house.

"Why is that?"

"I don't know how to explain it to you. It's as if they'd dirtied it. It's an invisible filth that you know is there. No matter how often I wipe it down, it's still there and it makes me so sick I can't stand it. And whenever I see a Guardia Civil car on the street, it makes my stomach turn."

"I understand you perfectly."

"Something has changed at home. We're not the way we were before Joxe Mari took off for France. Gorka doesn't speak. I don't know what's wrong with him. Are you traumatized? I ask him. He doesn't answer. Arantxa laughs at me, at her father, at the people in our town, at everything. I think that boy from Rentería has made her dumber than she already was. And Joxian and me, what can

I say? For a long time now, we just don't get along. One argument after another."

"The business with Joxe Mari must have affected him."

"Affected? It's broken him. I couldn't begin to tell you. Before, I never saw him cry, not even at funerals. Now, when you least expect it, there he is with red eyes and pouting. He runs to the bathroom so no one will see him."

"What about you, how are you bearing up?"

"Well, I'll always back my son no matter what. I don't give a damn what people say. Of course I'd rather he were nearby, working and starting a family, but since it's not that way, you have to play the hand you're dealt. To tell the truth, and I'm only telling you, okay?, it's Joxian's fault that I feel so uncertain. She looked around at the nearby tables to make sure no one was listening and, bringing her mouth to Bittori's ear, whispered: he says that if Joxe Mari takes up arms he won't look at him again ever. His hope is that he goes to Mexico or some place like that as a refugee. But if he doesn't go, then what? I was thinking about talking to Don Serapio."

"To the priest? What can a guy like that tell you?"

"He might give me some advice, who knows. Juani made confession with him and felt relieved."

"Then talk to him. Except for the time you'll spend, you've got nothing to lose."

On Sunday, the two friends, arm in arm, went to high mass. Again and again, Miren looked toward the statue of Saint Ignatius of Loyola and with a trembling lip she whispered to him. What? That he watch over her son, that he take care of him now that she couldn't. It's impossible, she said to herself, that such a generous, noble boy join a criminal organization, as the Spanish newspapers call it. He's got such a big heart. He's always doing for others, on the handball team, at work, everywhere, how can he not do for his country? You were Basque, too, right, Ignatius?"

Bittori:

"What did you say?"

"Nothing. I was praying."

They took communion. They walked forward, then back, one before the other, along the center aisle, heads down, hands together.

Almost the devotion of nuns. More precisely, of almost nuns. Remember? They were so close to joining a convent. And after so many years they agreed, half joking, half serious, on the same idea: every time one of them had an argument with her husband, she repented for having chosen, what dopes we were, matrimony over nuns' habits.

"The only consolation, the children, Sister Bittori."

"There's no going back, Sister Miren."

Before opening her mouth and extending her tongue to receive the consecrated host, Miren whispered to Don Serapio that I'll pass by after, okay? And the priest, discreet, slow-moving, nodded.

Once mass was over, the congregation made for the doors. Don Serapio blew out the candles on the altar; preceded by the altar boy, who opened the door for him, he entered the sacristy. And that was the moment Miren was waiting for to go and speak to him.

"Will you come?"

"It's better you go alone. This is very intimate. I'll wait for you in the plaza and if there's anything, you can tell me."

Don Serapio was taking off the chasuble when Miren entered the sacristy. As soon as he saw her, his brow covered with perspiration, he ordered the altar boy to leave. Held back by some obligation or other, the adolescent did not immediately obey.

"Hey, didn't I tell you to take off?"

The altar boy then dashed out of the sacristy, leaving the door open. Can you believe it? The grumbling priest, striding decisively, shuts it. As soon as he was alone with the woman, he offered her a chair with sweetened gestures. And as he sat down, he asked if she was visiting him about the same matter as Juani, Josetxo's wife. Miren nodded.

He took her hand, on top of the table, between his pale hands, not made for hard work like Joxian's, which are rough and look like burned stone. Why is he taking my hand? And patting the back of hers he said:

"Remove all doubts and remorse from your mind. This struggle of ours, mine in my parish, yours in your house, working for your family, and Joxe Mari's struggle, wherever he is, is the just struggle of a people in their legitimate wish to decide their own fate. It is the struggle of David against Goliath, a struggle I've talked about often during mass. It isn't an individual, egocentric struggle but, above all, a collective sacrifice, and Joxe Mari, like Jokin and so many others, has joined it, with all the consequences. Do you understand?"

Miren nodded affirmatively. Don Serapio, understanding, tender, patted the back of her hand twice. And then he went on:

"Has God shown that he doesn't want Basques in his presence? God wants his good Basques at his side in the same way he wants— take note of this—good Spaniards and Frenchmen and Poles. And he made us Basques the way we are, tenacious in our purposes, hardworking, and firm in the idea of a sovereign nation. For that reason, I would go so far as to assert that on us has fallen the Christian mission of defending our identity, therefore our culture, and above all our language. If our language disappears, tell me, Miren, tell me frankly, who will pray to God in Basque, who will sing to Him in Basque? Shall I answer? No one. Do you think that Goliath, wearing the Guardia Civil three-cornered hat, with his barracks-basement torturers, is going to move a finger in favor of our identity? They searched your house the other day, in the middle of the night. Didn't you feel humiliated?"

"Oh, Don Serapio, don't remind me of it, it makes me gasp for air."

"See? The same humiliation that you and your family had to endure is suffered daily by thousands of people in Euskal Herria. And the very same ones who mistreat us are the ones who then talk about democracy. *Their* democracy, theirs, which oppresses us as a people. Which is why I say to you, completely honestly, that our struggle isn't only just. It's necessary, today more than ever. It's indispensable because it's defensive and has as its objective peace. Haven't you ever heard the words of our bishop? Go home in peace. And if one day in the months that follow or whenever it is you find your son, tell him from me, from his parish priest, that he has my blessing and that I pray a lot for him.

Miren left the sacristy, crossed the church, and went out a side door. What a priest. Listening to him speak, I felt a desire to follow in Joxe Mari's footsteps. For one instant, without stopping, she turned her eyes toward the statue of Saint Ignatius. Maybe you should learn to encourage people.

She walked out into the plaza. The blue Sunday, the pigeons, the children running around in the shade of the linden trees. Bittori? There she was, sitting on a bench. Miren walked straight toward her.

"Let's go. I'll tell you about it along the way."

"You look relaxed."

"The next time Joxian starts in with his sorrows and fears, he's going to hear about it. Now all my ideas are clear."

66

Klaus-Dieter

She met Klaus-Dieter. She fell in love with Klaus-Dieter. That mane of straight blond hair which shook when he danced and also, though less, when he walked. Six feet two, a mountain of handsome boy. And German. With the novel perspective that included: a new nation, another culture, another language, other gestures, other smells, and goodbye, perhaps forever, to all this. Goodbye to my unbearable mother, to my land, which I loved and to which I am today indifferent and which I sometimes hate, and goodbye to everything around me, so boring, so foreseeable. Goodbye or, if not goodbye, from here to old age in a straight line.

The boy was part of the group of young Germans who studied for half a year in the liberal arts program. What did they study? No one knows for sure. Something related to language, or maybe just language. Some mornings she could see them, nine or ten, boys and girls, in the university cafeteria, at first all together, clustered, smiling, a bit on the dumb side, not really noisy considering how many there were. Then, as it happened every year around this time, the usual thing occurred. Little by little they began mixing in with the native student population. Nothing bizarre: friendships formed, romances, which generally lasted until the day the foreign member of the couple had to go home.

Nerea saw him a couple of times. He attracted her because the boy was, quite frankly, really something; but what does that mean? So many men attracted her, including some professors. They'd never run into each other at any party, at any bar; there was no opportunity, no flirting: she'd never spoken to him. Did he speak Spanish?

At least he was studying Spanish, no? And besides, talking, at times, and depending on the circumstances, is superfluous. As to meeting him, she met him later.

Meanwhile, her *aita* was murdered, and she, did she cut all her ties, go out very little, isolate herself? None of that, with one exception: when conversation with classmates turned to politics, she lost interest, looked away, went to the bathroom. She felt a kind of sexual pressure which she hadn't felt before her father died, at least not with the same intensity. She tried, unsuccessfully, to find a reason for her constant physical desire. Because pleasure, real pleasure, she only felt a tiny bit. I've never been one for easy orgasms. She used sex to relax, that was all there was to it. And also (before and during, but more before than during) her self-esteem went up. There were days when she practically had none. Especially in class, when she realized that even if she paid close attention she didn't understand her professors' explanations. Then she would take an anguished look around, toward her classmates who were taking notes, who raised their hands to participate in discussions, even to argue with the instructor, and it seemed to her that all of them were brighter and better prepared than she was, and that a brilliant future awaited them, while hers would be domestic, monotonous, the future of someone no one finds interesting, no one likes, a person who experiences a vivid rejection looking in the mirror.

She often went out looking for men. She wouldn't accept just anyone. She sought athletic, neat boys. And charming, agreeable, extroverted, she always got her man. All she had to do was put on a jolly expression a few yards away and the fly would come to the spiderweb. Sometimes the dry, cold *cierzo* would be blowing through the streets of Zaragoza or it would be pouring rain or she was simply too lazy to change her clothes, and then she took the easy way out: she could call José Carlos from a nearby telephone booth. She would say: come over. And the boy would come to the apartment, satisfy her, and leave.

It wasn't until March that the affair with Klaus-Dieter began, at a moment when he only had a few weeks left before going back to his homeland. There was no other reason for all the haste and for the misunderstanding, because it was a whopper of a misunderstanding. She still smiles when she thinks of it. It was beautiful while it lasted and besides you cannot deny that, without knowing it, he helped you to finish your academic work. How could that be? To keep up with him, she hit the books hard, passed all her exams, freed herself from the old promise she'd made years back to her deceased father that she would get her degree. A degree, by the way, that mattered absolutely nothing to her.

The party took place one Friday in the Colegio Mayor Pedro Cerbuna, a university residence and cultural center. Depressed, she was tempted to stay home. With little hope that he'd answer, she telephoned José Carlos. A roommate answered. No, he wasn't there, he'd gone home and wouldn't be back until Sunday. And Nerea imagined him back on Sunday afternoon with the usual package of sausages (breakfast, spicy chorizo, et cetera) and before coming back, on Saturday, I suppose also on Sunday, strolling with his official girlfriend along the riverbank, holding hands, because she won't go any farther, which didn't bother him in the slightest because for sex he had Nerea, who had to listen—her legs spread, in her narrow and creaking rented bed—to her friend's village anecdotes.

She was just about to hang up:

"Do you know if anything interesting's going on in the city tonight?"

The boy mentioned a party or concert, he wasn't sure which, in Pedro Cerbuna. And he added, even though Nerea hadn't asked for his opinion, that it was a preppy party. Nerea went on to ask her roommates if they felt like going with her. They declined. What to do? She went into her room ready to spend the final hours of the day reading a novel; but she put herself in a good mood with the bit of cocaine she had left and at about nine she set out on the hunt.

There he was, taller than everyone around him, dancing away with that cute blond shaking of his hair. Shirtless, his face red from jumping around so much, awkward. Twenty, twenty-two, twenty-four years old? One thing for sure, the boy was enjoying himself. He was swaying back and forth and shaking violently, for sure not the way they danced in his country. But here, aside from a few school-mates, who knows him?

Suddenly their eyes met above a few heads, and that was enough for Nerea. She wouldn't know how to express what she felt. She thinks of clichés: interior earthquake, magic moment, Cupid's arrow. And the boy must have noticed her fascination because he stood there staring at her with an expression of shock on his face and even reduced the intensity of his dancing. He smiled at her with beautiful teeth.

Out on the street, she was devouring him with kisses. Nerea, what are you doing, Nerea, what's wrong with you? She had to hang on to his neck because he was about six inches taller than she was and pull his head down to reach his mouth with her own avid, impatient mouth. And she was clinging, the huntress caught, to his body, her sex moist, on the verge of screaming. What can he think of me?

He lived quite far away, in a flat he shared with two other German students, out toward San José. Nerea didn't care about the distance. She would have followed him to the ends of the earth. He spoke with a marked accent. He called her "Neguea." She would have eaten him alive. The accent made him even more attractive. He made grammatical mistakes that delighted Nerea. And she, who'd never spoken a word of German, pronounced his name, and probably pronounced it badly or with her own marked accent, as she deduced from Klaus-Dieter's laughter, the bastard, and from the obvious pleasure he got making her repeat it again and again.

By then it was after two in the morning. They were walking along, the air cool, the moon there above the rooftops, on streets with barely any traffic, the entire night for them alone. They were as free as could be. They paused from time to time to tangle their tongues, to slowly caress their faces, to frenetically touch each other's body hidden behind a tree, in the darkness of some entryway. She, in love like a fifteen-year-old in love with a rock star; he, more restrained, but in no way standoffish. Perhaps he was timid. And at the end of the long road, a bed.

67

Three Weeks of Love

They lived together for three weeks. They divided their time between his flat and hers. The advantage of Nerea's place? It was
close to the university. Its principal inconvenience? The bed was
narrow and, for him, too short. Klaus-Dieter's apartment was the
opposite. It was far from the university, but there they had a double
bed where, along with being able to roll around as much as they
liked, they could sleep comfortably.

What a great three weeks! Even today, two decades later, Nerea
would still remember the nights and the days, with their mornings
and evenings. She even thought of a title: *Anthology of Happiness*.
She doesn't think she could compile enough autobiographi-
cal material for a big book or a long movie. She would include
episodes from her childhood, a few memorable trips, bits of joy
here and there, and of course the three weeks she spent in Zaragoza
with her German boy. She never again loved anyone with the same
passion, never again gave herself so completely. Not even to Quique, but what more could that conceited jerk expect? Aren't you
exaggerating?

It was a shame she'd met Klaus-Dieter too late, when he only had
a short time left in his half year in Zaragoza before returning to the
University of Göttingen, where he was studying. Since the two of
them were aware of that situation, they fell in love quickly. But wait:
not in a compulsive way (okay, on some nights it was compulsive).
They loved each other without stopping, which is not the same
thing. Nerea did everything possible to be near her blond boy at
all hours of the day and night. She stopped going to her classes and

instead went to his or waited for him outside, sitting on a bench in the corridor smoking. They ate together, they slept together, and from time to time they even showered together

Some mornings, when she woke up before Klaus-Dieter, Nerea would remain still for a long time in wonderment. His charming features, his well-formed body. She would bring a hand close to his mouth; she loved to feel the slow exhalations of air on her palm. Or, carefully so she wouldn't awaken him, she would playfully roll a lock of his hair around her finger. And she even cut off a lock near the back of his neck with stealthy scissors. A beautiful little sheaf about two or two and a half inches long. Why did she do it? To possess something of him she could look at and touch when he'd gone back to his country.

During the luminous beginnings of day, Nerea liked to caress Klaus-Dieter's face with a nipple. His lips asleep, his eyelids shut, his cheek still unshaven, with tiny blond hairs that pleasantly scratched her most sensitive part. And she awakened him softly. He, knowing the game, would smile without opening his eyes. I'll bet no woman in your cold land has ever loved you like that. Sometimes Nerea said it aloud; but he, what was he going to say when he didn't understand even half the words?

Then Nerea went on caressing him with her warm breasts all the way down along his body. And she paused at his stomach and the inner face of his thighs lightly covered by down, and she kissed and licked his sex, and the morning light came through the window, and that was a daily delight which would not last long, but was marvelous while it lasted.

Willing to please her German boy, she became fond of tea, she who had been such a coffee addict before. And we're not talking about the typical teabag dunked without charm or mystery in a cup of water. Klaus-Dieter brought the tea with him from Germany in a metal box. And the cloth strainer, black from use. In the kitchen, a fascinated Nerea observed the simple ritual, taking careful note of the various steps, the proper quantity of tea, the exact amount of time the strainer remained submerged in the hot water in the teapot. And no sugar or milk was allowed. He usually took the first swallow with his eyes shut, pushing his lips forward as a precaution against scalding himself, and she, always at his side, silently watched him as if witnessing a sacred ceremony.

And the fact is that communication was not really easy between them. Klaus-Dieter spoke Spanish poorly. Nerea did her best in her rusty English. Their ignorance of each other's language kept them from conducting conversations of any depth. Even so, they understood each other simply because of the total commitment they brought to the matter, whether they used signs mixed with individual words and brief phrases, or by using the dictionary. His Spanish improved quite a lot because he practiced it with her. And she, who didn't touch a single book in any of her courses during those three weeks of love, began her first German lessons with the help of a manual she found in a bookstore in Plaza San Francisco. Not only Klaus-Dieter but his roommates Wolfgang and Marcel collapsed in laughter every time Nerea pronounced some German word. To enhance the fun, the little bastards would point to one obscenity or another in the dictionary so she could read it aloud.

Klaus-Dieter was a vegetarian. Nerea wouldn't eat meat when she was with him. He also didn't eat fish or seafood, though he did make an exception for grilled shrimp. He simply adored them. "In Germany little this," he would say. On some afternoons, they would walk to El Tubo and stuff themselves with shrimp and langoustines, which for Klaus-Dieter were both the same: small shrimp and big shrimp. He didn't smoke. That was more problematic for Nerea. Fearful of annoying him, she would smoke in the bathrooms of bars. And on other occasions, as when she waited in the hall at school for him to come out of class, she would chain-smoke.

One day, in bed, Klaus-Dieter, very serious, revealed he was a believer.

"I believe on God."

"In God."

"I believe in God. Do you?"

"I don't know."

He was a member of the Evangelical Lutheran Church. And Nerea, who was seriously considering living with him in Germany, was willing to change her religion just to please him.

He got the idea of her visiting him in Göttingen—without fail.
He insisted:

"Will you come me to visit?"

She promised she would. Because, of course, I'm not letting this
one get away. Where would I find another one like this? And she
promised again in the El Portillo train station, as they, totally infatu-
ated with each other on the platform, used up their final moments
of tenderness. Wolfgang had to yank his friend's arm to get him into
the car. A few seconds later, the train pulled out.

Standing at the window, she watched him disappear. Goodbye,
blond mane. Goodbye, charming smile. She loved him so much;
but so, so much. Other cars followed with other heads at windows
and other hands waving goodbye. In barely a minute, the platform
was empty of people. Nerea stood there alone, her eyes fixed on the
landscape of poles, cables, and rails along which she'd lost sight
of the train. Sad? Yes, but not weepy, since they'd agreed to meet
in Göttingen at the end of summer, when a new semester would
begin for Klaus-Dieter. He promised to write her as soon as he got
to Germany. Will he write me or not? If he keeps his word it means
there's love; if he doesn't, it means I've been nothing more than a
simple instrument for achieving orgasms.

Every morning, Nerea would go downstairs to the entryway to
peer into the mailbox. Also in the evening, even though the mailman usually came between eleven and one and came only once.
After a week, she noted the first cracks in her hopes. Then the cracks
turned into gaping crevices. The tears she didn't weep at the station,
she weeps now all alone. And, accepting reality, she closes the German manual she'd kept open on her desk and puts it, the lock of
blond hair between its pages, into a drawer in the cupboard.

Days later the letter came, the first of a few they exchanged. This
time the tears were tears of joy. That letter was spattered with errors,
one more adorable than the other, with a heart-shaped sticker next
to his signature to dissipate her doubts. She was sure the future was
waiting for her in Germany. Not wasting a second, she went to the
university. She asked different classmates if she could photocopy
their notes. Now she missed no classes, now she went to no parties,
did not go out at night. Now she spent her time in the library or in

her room studying in a way she had never studied before. Her plan: get her degree in the summer, pack her bag, and goodbye.

Just before taking her exams, she ran into José Carlos one morning on the campus. Hey, it's been a long time since she called him, had she been sick, wouldn't you like me to pass by your place one of these days? She looked at him as if he weren't there. With contempt? More with indifference. She said no and went her way.

68

GRADUATION

Nerea passed her examinations and got her bachelor's degree. Two months of intensive study enabled her to put together an acceptable quantity of knowledge. On Saturday afternoons, as a reward for her dedication during the week, she would see a movie at the Palafox Theater. The film didn't really matter. Sometimes she watched the same one she'd seen the week before simply because it had left her with a pleasant memory.

She chose the Palafox because El Tubo was near and she liked fulfilling a ritual. When she left the theater, she went into a bar and enjoyed a plate of grilled shrimp, immersed in memories of her German boy. What can he be doing at this moment? Might he remember me? The shrimp and perhaps a yogurt later on, in her flat, was all she had for dinner. At night, back in her room, she was still hard at work on the books and the law notes until at about midnight, sometimes before, her head informed her: girl, enough for today. She lost ten pounds in two months.

She turned out for her examinations supplied with more than knowledge. Some wisdom she carried in crib sheets hidden in her sleeves. More than anything out of insecurity. Like a lifejacket, she said to herself, in case she found herself shipwrecked in the unfathomable depths of ignorance. In fact, she never used the notes except to copy four bits of trivia for the philosophy of law examination.

Any As? Not a one. She didn't need them. It wasn't that she had the feeling of having reached a goal but rather that she'd shed a heavy load. Are you sure? Very sure. The morning the last of her grades was announced, she stood at the exit to the school, on the entrance steps. and chose one cloud among the many—which? that one way over there—and she whispered to it:

"*Aita*, now you see I've done what you asked me to do. Now I'm free to decide my future on my own."

There was no obstacle to her projected trip to Germany. Walking along the street, she laughed to herself. I'm going nuts, just like *ama*. Months ago, she learned from Xabier that her mother had taken to walking up to Polloe to chat with Txato's grave. When he told her, Xabier was visibly moved. He was afraid his mother was getting depressed, but the depression was all his. He was afraid she'd never recover from that blow, but it was he who never recovered. Nerea treated it as trivial. She said, to remove all drama from their dialogue, that if you had to pay to get into the cemetery, their mother wouldn't go. Xabier did not find the joke funny.

Leaving University City, Nerea thought she would find a telephone booth and give her mother the good news. Should I call or not? Some considerations fed her doubts. She saw a booth and passed by. On Fernando el Católico, after more than a few hesitations, she made up her mind. Because, of course, how am I going to hide the fact that I've finished my studies from my mother? She inserted the coins, dialed the first three numbers, and hung up. Why? I know her. She's going to say something that will sour my day of triumph.

For two weeks, she hid the news. I'll call her tomorrow. But tomorrow would come, and Nerea would put off making the call until the next day. This she did again and again. To buy time, to be at peace. Her mother had moved to San Sebastián. How about living with her? A nightmare. How about returning to the village? Even worse. The last time she was there, friends and acquaintances from old times cut her cold. She made some calculations, spoke with her roommates, and decided. To do what? To stay in Zaragoza for the summer. They warned her:

"Zaragoza in summertime is an oven."

She didn't care. It was also the place where Klaus-Dieter sent letters to her. Of course she could send her blond boy her address in San Sebastián. Could she? Which address? The only one she had was her mother's. So forget that. She could just imagine the scene. Nerea, a letter from Germany came for you. Who's writing to you?

Have you got a boyfriend? And let's not forget that she could just as easily open the envelope, under the pretext that she hadn't seen to whom the letter was addressed. She could do that.

Her roommates: one, like Nerea, canceled her rent contract at the end of July; the other, who still had a year of studies left, was hoping to stay in the apartment. What she'd do, she said, is advertise for two new roommates as soon as vacation was over. Nerea asked if she'd let her keep her room during August and September. And so that her friend wouldn't have to pay the whole rent during that time, she offered to pay her share directly to her instead of paying the house owner. The roommate was delighted to accept.

Zaragoza in August: 100, 104, 111 degrees. Sun, deserted streets. Those days dragged on eternally. She dedicated herself to reading novels, to taking walks at sunset, when the heat began to let up, and to learning German. A difficult language. She couldn't get it through her head that at this point in history, people in bakeries, hospitals, talking from window to window, could express themselves in declensions, in the style of the ancient Romans. She searched the yellow pages for a language school where she could sign up for an intensive course. In August? They didn't even answer the phone.

Days of stagnation, of boredom. Even so, better to spend them in this torrid solitude, in twilight strolls, and, from time to time, in the pool at the Zaragoza Hípica with a fascinating book than to dedicate them morning to night to the infinite supply of maternal reproaches. Over the telephone, the few times she called her: why was she still in Zaragoza since she had her degree? Well, you see . . . And she just told her any old lie. That would be followed immediately by saying she couldn't really hear, how hard it is to hear, I can't hear a word you're saying, or that she'd run out of change for the telephone. From Germany and Klaus-Dieter, not a single word.

For Nerea, the worst part of that season of solitude and suffocating heat was the absence of mail. Already in July, Klaus-Dieter's letters were coming less frequently. In August, not a one arrived. Nerea knew why, which took nothing away from her feeling disillusioned every time she peered into the mailbox and found it, as she did yesterday and the day before yesterday, empty. What was going on? Nothing, Klaus-Dieter had taken a trip to Edinburgh, where he'd be staying for a month. During that period, she sent a dozen letters filled with German expressions to his Göttingen address. Some of those expressions she copied out of the manual; others, less conventional, she composed helter-skelter with the precarious aid of the dictionary. At the beginning of September, she received, hallelujah, an answer. He'd returned from his trip, missed her, *I missing you*, and reminded her that she promised to visit him in October.

Her father brought her to Zaragoza. Xabier brought her back.

"*Ama* asked me to do it. And since I don't have to work today, here I am."

The reason for driving to her? To transport her abundant belongings. It took them a long time to pack them into the car. Just the books filled two large boxes. Xabier folded down the rear seats to make the trunk space larger. He filled it to the brim.

"Where can we eat?"

Before starting out, brother and sister went to a nearby restaurant. They chewed, drank, spoke.

"*Ama* was worried because you didn't come home."

"But I told her I had things to take care of before I left Zaragoza."

"That's what I thought. University things?"

"Romantic things."

The succinct expression, uttered in a juvenile, challenging tone, did not upset Xabier, who went on cutting up his veal cutlet as if nothing had happened. Sometimes, distracted, he glanced over at the other people eating at nearby tables. His sister's confessions didn't seem to arouse his curiosity or make any impression on him at all until he heard the word. Which word? Which do you think? "Germany." The fork poised in the air with a piece of meat speared on it: Xabier fixed his eyes on Nerea. Was it shock? In any case it was alarm.

"What are you planning to do?"

"On the ninth, I'm taking the train there. I'm buying a one-way ticket."

"Does *ama* know about it?"

"For now, only you know."

The conversation frayed. The remarks made by each speaker flowed along separated by islands of silence. And the discontinuous, slow-moving verbal river was ideal for carrying evasions, circumlocutions, trivia. Xabier did not finish his meal and asked for the check.

"Or did you want dessert?"

"What?"

"If you have dessert, we can stay a bit longer. I don't want to hurry you."

"No, no. Do you mind if I have a cigarette before we get going?"

Twenty minutes later they'd left behind, according to Nerea, what could be considered the last building in Zaragoza. Xabier drove and she, assuming a theatrical, celebratory pose and a tone of false nostalgia, improvised a brief farewell speech. She waxed satirical, lowering her voice. That she was finishing a stage in her life, that she would take with her a fine memory of the city but that she did not intend to return until three thousand years had passed.

Xabier waited a long time before breaking his silence.

"I see *ama* as being very alone, and I'm afraid that she's going to lose all sense of reality. I try to spend as much time as I can with her, but my work absorbs me. She has the illusion that you are practicing law. Didn't I tell you?"

"I hate the law."

"Okay, well, I don't go to the hospital just for fun. We've all got to make a living, don't you think?"

"Yes, but not by doing any old thing and for me being a lawyer is worse than any old thing. To tell the truth, I see my future far away from here. I met someone. I'm going to give it a try."

"You seem very happy."

"Does that bother you?"

"Not at all. All I ask is that you avoid the subject when *ama* is around. You can imagine that in our family not everyone has a reason to be happy."

"Brother, I know that hole. And I'm not going to fall into it. May I ask you a question? Just out of curiosity. You don't have to answer if you don't want to." Without taking his eyes off the road, Xabier nodded. "Ever since *aita* died . . ."

"He didn't die, he was murdered."

"The result is the same."

"For me there is an essential difference."

"Fine. Ever since he was murdered—it will be a year ago soon—have you laughed even once? I don't know, in a spontaneous way, at some silly thing someone at the hospital said, maybe seeing a movie. Have you ever forgotten everything just for a moment and given out even a tiny giggle?"

"It's possible. I don't remember."

"Or have you disallowed yourself any happiness?"

"I don't know what happiness is. I suppose it's a subject you know all about. You seem to have become an expert. I limit myself to breathing, to doing my job, and to looking after *ama*. That gives me more than enough to do."

"You talk about *ama* all the time."

"I think she's in a bad way, in the hole you mentioned. It worries me."

"You're a good son. I on the other hand don't seem to worry. Is that what you're suggesting? That everything just slips off me? That I only worry about my own things?"

"No one is making demands on you or accusing you of anything. You can be calm on that score. *Aita*'s business has been sold off. Economically speaking we're not in bad shape. You're young, take advantage of it while you can."

They agreed to change the subject. They had just entered Navarra. Sun, plains, dry landscapes. Suddenly Nerea:

"Have you heard anything about Aránzazu?"

"I haven't heard anything about her for a long time. The last thing I was told is that she'd gone to Ghana as an aid worker, but don't hold me to that because I'm not really sure. Why do you ask?"

"No reason. I liked her."

At that point they stopped talking. Later, when they'd left Tudela behind, Nerea turned on the radio.

69

THE BREAK

The graffiti against Txato ruined Joxian's appetite. And deprived him of his best friend. If this happens in a city, it's okay, but in a small town where we all know one another, you can't keep up a relationship with someone who's been marked. That Sunday he was thinking about all those things along the road from Zumaya to his house. He'd set out with Txato, he was returning without him. Who's going to be my *mus* partner now? After lunch, which didn't appeal to him, which he couldn't finish, he walked out of the bar with the others; but on the first hill, he pretended his strength was fading and fell behind. Then, before reaching Guetaria, he decided to get off his bike, sit down on a boulder, face the sea, and gather his thoughts. The sea is huge. The sea is like God, who is both near and distant, which reminds us just how small we are, damn it to hell, and could, if it wanted, destroy us. It was harder than ever for him to reach the village. In Orio he was on the verge of taking the bus. What about the bike? He could leave it locked up somewhere. And if someone robs it? That's right, because around here there are lots of outsiders. Dispirited, he went on pedaling, paying no attention to the traffic, absorbed in somber cogitation.

When he walked into the apartment, Miren, from the kitchen, wearing her apron, looked him in the eye. Not severe, not frowning: questioning. He expected a row because he was late. She said nothing more than:

"Go on, take a shower."

And that almost sounded like the tenderness of past times. She didn't even speak to him in the hard tones she'd used on other occasions or as when she softly tells him something normal and ordinary, but because of her voice and the expression on her face he realizes the lightning will strike any time now.

"I'm not hungry."

"Well, sit down and watch how I eat."

And they spoke, seriously, gulping their soup, chewing little lamb chops, the two of them seated at the table without the company of their children.

"You do know, right?"

"First the Joxe Mari business and now this."

"It's not the same."

"Disgrace on top of disgrace."

"She called. Must have been at around ten. I hung up on her."

"And just yesterday the two of you were in the café."

"Yesterday was yesterday, today is another day. Our friendship is over. Get used to it."

"So many years. Aren't you sorry about it?"

"What makes me sorry is Euskal Herria, the fact that they don't let her be free."

"I'm not going to get used to it. Txato is my friend."

"He was. And be very careful about being seen with him. The best thing would be for them to get out. With all the money they have, what would it matter to them to buy a house somewhere else? What they want to do is provoke."

"They won't go. Txato is stubborn."

"The struggle forgives no one. They'll leave or they'll be thrown out. Let them choose."

Just before ten in the morning, the phone rang. Miren hadn't the slightest doubt: it's she. An hour and a half earlier she received another call that got her out of bed. Juani: did she know, that she wasn't surprised, that for a long time now.

And she concluded:

"They got rich by exploiting the working class and now the bill has come due. I'm not the only one saying it. The townspeople are saying it. I'm telling you because we all know that you and she are good friends."

Miren, her freshly washed hair still not dry, went out to the street with a handkerchief on her head and wearing slippers. She didn't have to go far. There were graffiti on the walls of the church: Txato stool pigeon, oppressor, *alde hemendik, Herriak ez du barkatuko*. All in that style. It wasn't one tag or two; there were twelve, fifteen, twenty, and they went on down the street and up the street. Many hands had been busy. This is a big, well-planned thing. She had a presentiment: is she calling me to find out if I know and to ask me to go with her and talk and that we save the day for her? They're always taking advantage of others.

And in fact, Bittori did call. The church bells had yet to ring out ten. Miren, who was in the bathroom putting rollers in her hair, ran to the telephone intent on breaking off the relationship.

"Hello."

"Miren, it's me. Did you . . . ?"

As soon as she recognized the voice, she hung up. What nerve. My son risking his life for Euskal Herria and this scum never stops exploiting the people. Well, they know how to dish it out, now they can learn to take it. And muttering to herself she went back to the bathroom to finish putting in the rollers.

Days went by without Miren seeing her. How many? A good number, at least two weeks. Doesn't she ever leave the house? She saw him once, at a distance, when he was in his car leaving the street where his garage is.

About her she only knew what Juani told her. What was that? Well, that she had the nerve to come into the shop. She waited her turn, ordered. Juani told her, we're out of that. She ordered something else, I don't remember what, and Juani again told her they were out of it. Then, tensing up and putting on ladylike airs, she said fine, cut me a quarter pound of this York ham and she pointed her finger at it and Juani gave her a look that would have put a hole through the wall and said for you we are out of everything.

Miren saw her one morning in the street. Just a bit, two seconds. Miren had run into the priest by chance. Did she have any news about Joxe Mari. We're still waiting. A lie. As of today, Patxi had passed on two letters, but that's something that we should keep to ourselves.

They were talking. Don Serapio full of questions as usual. And just then Miren saw her over the priest's shoulder. She was coming toward them with that old, worn-out handbag she would use on

Saturdays in San Sebastián and she had shadows under her eyes.
With all the money they make and she uses a handbag a beggar
would throw away. She's a miser. Miren quickly moved to Don Serapio's side so she could turn her back to Bittori. Miren and the priest
were standing in the center of the sidewalk. The other woman,
tough crap, had to step into the street to go her way. She said no
hellos, and no hellos were said to her. She didn't look at them, and
they didn't look at her. And immediately, Miren changed position
so she was face-to-face with the priest again.

Don Serapio after a few seconds:

"You don't speak to each other?"

"Me talk to her? Are you joking?"

"For their own good, they should leave town."

"Go tell them, because it seems to me they can't take a hint."

On the other hand, Joxian did speak once, in secret, to Txato.
He waited for him near the garage. When? One night after dinner,
using the pretext that he was taking out the garbage, he went out
to meet him. It was weighing on his conscience and he had to clear
it. He'd tried before, unsuccessfully, by raising his eyebrows at Txato
as he passed him on the street. And finally, he decided to carry the
garbage bag down to the street, a chore that usually fell to Gorka.

But Txato came home from work at different times every day. He
was taking precautions. And it was only in that dark street where
Txato had his garage that Joxian wanted to meet him. Finally, one
night he was able to speak to him.

"It's me."

"What do you want?"

Joxian's hands were shaking, his voice was tremulous and he
couldn't stop looking up and down the street, as if he was afraid
someone might see him talking to Txato.

"Nothing. Just to say I'm sorry, that I can't say hello to you
because it would cause me problems. But that if I do see you on the
street, I want you to know that I'm saying hello with my thoughts."

"Has anyone ever told you that you're a coward?"

"I tell myself that all the time. But it doesn't change anything.
Can I give you a hug? No one can see us here."

"Leave it for when you have the courage to do it in the light of
day."

"If I could help you, I swear . . ."

"Don't worry. I'll get along with your mental hellos."

Txato strolled off calmly, his shadow under the faint light of the street lamp. Joxian waited for his old friend to turn the corner and start walking home. He would never see Txato that close again. Txato was walking with one hand in his trouser pocket. It wasn't long before he passed the exact spot where, one rainy afternoon that was getting nearer and nearer, an ETA militant would take his life.

Homelands and Follies

It was written in newspapers that a shepherd found him. The shepherd was leading his sheep through some arid fields in the province of Burgos, and there was the corpse, disfigured and half eaten by wild animals.

The shepherd declared to the Guardia Civil that next to the dead man there was a pistol. The minister of the interior considered that such a circumstance was sufficient to confirm the hypothesis that it was suicide. The kind of weapon strongly suggested the dead man was connected to ETA.

In one of the deceased's pockets, the Guardia Civil found an identification card with a false name. That night, television news showed the photograph. In the village, everyone recognized it.

In private, Patxi told Juani and Josetxo that for a good while the organization had lost track of Jokin.

"You should be prepared for the worst."

The coffin arrived wrapped in an *ikurriña*. Rain and umbrellas. Police murderers! hundreds screamed in the street. Jokin's funeral was a massive event, fists held high, the crowd promised him revenge, and they buried him. And during the summer, a huge picture of him presided over the saint's day festival from the balcony of the town hall.

His parents were devastated. The butcher shop closed for several days. But while Juani recovered little by little, locking her grief within, finding consolation in prayer, Josetxo fell into a deep depression. Well, that's what people said. Which people? The neighbors. And Juani as well. During those days, she visited Miren's house a couple of times to unburden herself. She talked about Josetxo's interminable silences and the long hours her husband spent in bed during the day, that there was no way to get him up and around.

The two women agreed that Joxian should have a talk with him, keep him company, and maybe, who knows, lift his spirits man-to-man. Joxian, when he got home that night:

"You sent me once and it was horrible."

He grumbled, swore, cursed. Troublemakers, busybodies, meddlers. And Miren, impassive, went on dipping fish in batter with the window open. She let him talk the way you let a clock wind down.

Later on, in bed:

"Listen here, if you don't want to go, don't go. Tomorrow I'll tell Juani you refuse to do it, and that's that."

"You keep your mouth shut, you've been a big enough pain in the ass for one day."

And once again he mumbled to himself along the way. He feared that Josetxo was going to cry his eyes out the way he did the first time, and how am I going to deal with that. It was almost closing time. There were no customers in the butcher shop. The smell of meat, of suet. And Josetxo behind the counter, wearing his white apron spattered with blood, burst into tears, violently shaking his shoulders, with deep, guttural hiccups. Huge, muscular, he threw himself on Joxian, who patted his powerful back, trying to buck him up in his own way:

"Motherfucker, Josetxo, motherfucker."

He couldn't think of anything else to say. He tried to find words but only found curses and blasphemies. And he wasn't even sure he was expressing them properly. Besides, Josetxo was a good guy, but a real friend? No. Txato was a friend. Him for sure, even if they didn't speak to each other anymore. He wasn't very sure of the butcher, who never went in for playing cards in the bar or bicycling.

Josetxo decided to lock up a little earlier than usual. He asked Joxian to pull down the metal shutter because he didn't want anyone passing by to see him in that condition. Then, with his hands on his hips, gazing languidly at the ceiling, he calmed down little by little. He put one of his enormous hands on Joxian's shoulder, as if to say that beginning now I can converse.

"I kind of figured you'd be coming."

"It was my wife and yours who thought up the idea. Now I'm here with you again, and I don't know what to say."

"Finally, someone who doesn't lie. Thank you for that."

He offered Joxian a seat in the back room. He offered a drink (it'll have to be alcohol free) he kept in the refrigerator. He offered food. Without formalities: if he wanted a bite, he should just look in the display case.

"Take whatever you like. I have no bread."

Joxian refused everything except the offer of a chair.

"Don't even think about consoling me. If you've got a brain in your head, run to find your son. In France, wherever. You grab him, you slap him across the face, and you bring him home or turn him over to the cops. Pray they arrest him as quickly as they can. They'll jail him, but at least you won't lose him the way I lost mine."

Sitting in the chair, Joxian remained silent but with an expression appropriate to the moment on his face.

"They didn't even let me take charge of the funeral. They seized my son and used him to put on a patriotic show. For them his death was a great opportunity. To use him for political purposes, see? The way they use everyone. A bunch of jackasses is what they are. Naive. And the same goes for Joxe Mari. They get them all charged up, they give them a gun, and off we go to kill people. In my house we never talked about politics. I have no interest in politics. Are you interested in politics?"

"Not in the slightest."

"Their heads get crammed with bad ideas, and since they're young, they fall into the trap. Then they think they're heroes because they're carrying a pistol. And they don't realize that they get back nothing at all, because at the end there's no reward except for jail or the grave, they've abandoned their work, their families, their friends. They've given up everything just to do what a couple of users order them to do. And to destroy the lives of other people, leaving behind widows and orphans on every corner."

"Now don't you go around saying things like that."

"I'll say whatever the fuck I want."

"They'll make your life miserable."

"I had a son and I lost him. What does life matter to me?"

"Just look at Txato. No one talks to him anymore."

"You should talk to him, you're his friend."

"They'd do the same to me they're doing to him."

"A country of lying cowards! Look here, Joxian, listen to me. Stop this nonsense and go find Joxe Mari."

"That's not as easy as you think."

"If I knew where Jokin was I'd have turned him over to the police. I'd still have a son even if he was in jail. And it wouldn't matter if he stopped talking to me. You can get out of jail. You can't get out of a grave."

After almost an hour of talk, Joxian left the butcher shop downcast. He'd planned to play cards at the Pagoeta. How could I concentrate on the cards after everything that guy said? He went straight home with the package of cold cuts and sausage Josetxo had given him.

Miren, surprised:

"You're back this soon? Were you able to lift his spirits?"

"Not even one inch, but he did lower mine. Never ask me to see him again."

71

TWISTED DAUGHTER

It was January. A Tuesday morning. A gray, rainy workday. For an event as important as this, which will remain in memory forever, you have to find a spring or summer weekend, for God's sake!, with a blue sky, nice temperature, and all the relatives dressed up nicely, all clustered together in front of the photographer at the entrance to the church. Of course, what low-class people. Arantxa had called. When? At just after eleven. Miren answered. She didn't congratulate her. Dry, serious, she said you don't treat your mother like that. And the mother had no interest in the details of the matter, no interest in anything. She said goodbye, hung up, and refused to cry. Me? Let her live her life.

After two, Joxian came home from the foundry.

"Bad news."

"They arrested him?"

"She got married."

"Who?"

"Your daughter."

"That's bad news?"

"Are you dumb or what? She married the guy from Salamanca in a civil ceremony. And now think a minute and figure it out. Without the blessing of God, without telling us, with no banquet. What are they, Gypsies?"

Suddenly Joxian's eyes widened. Owl eyes set in fatigued features: from six a.m. on, standing at the furnace. He disagreed. First, in his opinion, the news of his daughter's wedding was great, and it should be celebrated, what the hell. Second, how long have they

been living together? She didn't know. Two, three years? Anyway,
quite a while, which had been a point of contention for Miren. So
it was high time they formalized their relationship. And for Joxian,
the fact that his daughter was marrying the man she loved didn't
seem any reason for disgust, just the opposite. And the boy, our
son-in-law, is not from Salamanca. He was born in Rentería. And
even if he had been born in Salamanca, who cares?

"As far as I'm concerned, he might as well be Chinese, black, or
a Gypsy. He's the one my daughter chose. That's it."

"You're stupid, you've always been stupid, and you'll die stupid.
You don't know what you're talking about. Did a roof tile fall and
hit you on the head? Go on, since you think you're so smart, go tell
Don Serapio that your daughter got married outside the church to
a man who doesn't speak Basque."

"To a proper, hardworking man who respects and loves her."

That was too much for Miren: she tore off her apron and threw
it against the chair back. She shouted, biting the words, as she ran
out of the kitchen so she could lock herself in the bathroom:

"Oh, Jesus, how alone I am, how alone!"

Other days passed by, other rains fell. In February, the two families agreed to meet in a restaurant. Miren, sarcastic, celebration in
the intimacy of the family, as if it were a funeral. A total of seven
at table: the married couple, their parents, and Gorka, who, contradicting his mother, refused to wear a suit and tie because after
dinner he planned to get together with his friends and didn't want
them to make fun of him. Miren insisted, inflexible, making it an
obligation. Arantxa and Guillermo agreed with the boy, who turned
up for the meal in a sweatshirt and sneakers, and was the first to
leave.

The other men dressed according to tradition and their wives'
wishes. The suits were too wide here, sagging and ballooned out
there. The three of them looked like proletarians on a special day
of elegance, disguised by their respective wives, all of whom took
charge, stand still, don't move, of tying the knot in their ties.

The women looked better. With more taste and more style. All
three with hairdresser hairdos. Arantxa wore the dark-green dress
she'd worn the morning of the wedding, a fabric rose the same color
pinned to her hair; Miren, a navy-blue number she'd bought in a

San Sebastián shop; and Angelita, her fat stuffed into a combination of blouse and skirt, the blouse white, the skirt beige, which gave Miren an opportunity to criticize her that night in bed.

Joxian, his face toward the wall, tried in vain to silence her verbal eruption. The day had been long, and he needed rest. Miren, her back against the headboard, paid no attention. She asked:

"What did you think of all that?"

"It was fine. The meat a little tough."

Why did you say anything? Don't you see that makes the conversation go on? He was sorry, not about his answer, but for having said anything. But it was too late.

"Tough? Stiff as a board. And the consommé, nothing special. We've eaten in better and cheaper places. But of course when you do things improperly, that's what happens."

"In case you didn't know, tomorrow I have to go to work."

"Arantxa and her mother-in-law seem to get on well. Did you see how she helped her unfold the napkin? And then, how she cleaned that spot of mayonnaise off her mustache? Because if that's not a mustache, I'm a bishop. The tenderness Arantxa never gave to her mother, she gives now to that fat lady from Salamanca."

"Okay, okay. Don't start."

"Anyone could see you were having a good time with your son-in-law. What were you two laughing at?"

"You've got it in for him, too? The guy is a sweetheart, couldn't be more affectionate. What worries me is that he'll be henpecked by our daughter."

"It looked like you two were having a private talk."

"We both like sports."

"And your little sentimental performance? Where do you get off bawling like that in front of everybody? When you feel like that, you should step outside or go to the bathroom, and not make a spectacle of yourself. I've never been so ashamed in all my life."

"I already told you I couldn't stop myself."

"What you couldn't stop doing was guzzling champagne. I'm not blind. Right away I saw you scratch your side."

"Don't confuse one thing with another. I remembered our son. The family celebrating and him God knows where."

"You made us look ridiculous. The last straw would have been if you started talking about Joxe Mari in front of them. I'd have broken a plate over your head, I swear."

"Fine. May I go to sleep now?"

Miren turned off the lamp on her side. Joxian had turned his off a long while before. Did they keep silent? He did. In the darkness, Miren, without changing position in bed, went on pouring out comments, criticisms, reproaches.

"I see them as being out of place. They're friendly, polite, whatever you like, but you can see they're not from here. That way of speaking, those gestures. I actually think they chew differently. Start getting ready to have a grandchild whose last name is Hernández. Just thinking about it gives me liver pains. That's what makes me want to cry and not Joxe Mari, who's out defending the cause of Euskal Herria. I don't know, Joxian, I don't know. What did we do wrong? Do you know? How did we produce such a twisted daughter? Joxian, are you asleep?"

72

A SACRED MISSION

It was in San Sebastián that the names of those who'd won the literary prizes for young people were announced. These were annual competitions held by the Provincial Savings Bank in Guipúzcoa. Miren only half understood the information she heard over the telephone, so that at dinnertime, when Gorka came home, the only thing she could tell him was that:

"A gentleman called asking for you. He says you've won something in the savings bank."

Until the next morning, Gorka, about to turn eighteen, could not confirm the news he was hoping for. He'd won the first prize in the category Poetry in Basque with a poem titled "Mendiko ahotsa." His first success.

No one, not even his best friends, knew he'd entered a literary contest. It wasn't the first time. If I win, terrific; if I don't, who's going to find out? But in fact, the whole town found out, because on the afternoon when he was handed the prize a journalist interviewed him, and the young author's photo appeared the next day in the culture section of *El Diario Vasco*. The other newspapers in the area also published the story, but without photos or interviews. Each winner was given ten thousand pesetas.

"Ten thousand? Son of a bitch!" Joxian gave his son a large smack of joy on his back. And he looked at him with a big, approving smile on his face, his lower lip hanging open in pride. "What are you waiting for? Get to your room and write. You can get rich."

Miren:

"What do you intend to do with the money?"

"I don't have the money yet."

"When you do."

"I need clothes and shoes."

The one who was happiest about that modest triumph was Joxian. In the Pagoeta he happily put up with his friends' benevolent jokes. That since he was a blockhead, where had this brilliant boy sprung from? Genes, he said. They countered:

"Must be your wife's genes."

And he defended himself with good humor:

"That woman's genes? Don't think so."

He had to promise his card-playing friends that even if he won the match, he'd pay for the jug of wine out of his own pocket. And he also treated some others scattered around the bar.

The next day the owner of the foundry came to the furnace to congratulate him. Joxian, overwhelmed by his own modesty, hastily took off his soot-blackened glove to shake that white, powerful hand connected to a wrist adorned with a famous brand of watch. Which brand? Who knows?

To Gorka in the kitchen:

"To buy a gadget like that I'd have to work a lot of days and you'd have to win a lot of prizes."

Silently, Miren felt pride. A pride of absorption, which passed from outside to inside, like a sponge filling up. And except for sporadically stretching her neck, she barely revealed the satisfaction she felt.

"Are you happy, *ama?*"

"Of course I am."

During the days that followed, whenever Gorka walked in, Miren immediately transmitted the congratulations from this one and that one. Her pupils dilated in a kind of euphoria, she enumerated the people she'd met in the street who asked her to congratulate: who? The writer? No, the guy who'd won ten thousand pesetas, the one who'd appeared in the papers, photo and all, which was what really dazzled people. And all of that produced in Miren an intense, silent contraction of pleasure, as if her bones, viscera, organs, muscles, and even her veins and arteries had compressed into a central point in her body, which caused her a pleasure that contained more than a little compensation:

"It's about time people envy us."

Arantxa, over the telephone, told her brother to be careful. Of course she was happy. Very happy. Bravo, champ, she said to dissipate any doubts. And that she'd always believed in him. She didn't forget to transmit congratulations from Guille, who also sent along a big hug. Then she said something about him not exposing himself too much.

"You understand me."

Gorka didn't understand. She realized he was confused, because after a few seconds of silence, she added that:

"The best thing would be for you to write your things and not let anyone take advantage of your talent."

"Until now everyone has been very friendly with me."

"That's fine. Did anyone in the town take any interest in your prize-winning poem? Did anyone read it?"

"Not a soul."

"Now do you understand me?"

"I think I'm beginning to understand."

Gorka recalled his sister's warning a few days later, as he was walking to the church, where Don Serapio was waiting for him. That morning Miren had run into the priest, who said he wanted to talk to Gorka and personally congratulate him.

"If you go over at five, you'll find him in the sacristy."

"What does he want to tell me?"

"What do you think? He wants to congratulate you."

"All this is a little exaggerated. I've only written one poem."

"In this town there aren't many people who can win a poetry prize. So go see the priest at five and let yourself be loved, okay? But make sure you shower before you go."

He went unwillingly, overwhelmed with timidity. He'd never before been alone with the priest. He scratched his nose every two seconds to protect himself from Don Serapio's halitosis. The priest, as he spoke, tapped the tips of his fingers together. On his face there frequently appeared a grimace of pained tenderness. He expressed himself calmly in a proper, seminary Basque, scattered with old-fashioned idiomatic expressions.

"Ours has been a hardworking, adventurous people of brave and pious men. We've shaped wood, stone, iron, and we've sailed all the seas; but unfortunately, over all those centuries, we Basques haven't paid enough attention to letters. What can I tell you that you don't already know? You, as I understand it, are a great reader and, as we've just seen, a poet."

Inhibited, Gorka nodded. Directly ahead of him, a wall mirror next to the hanger where the priest hung his chasubles reflected his skinny image, his slightly (quite) squashed nose. The priest went on:

"God has given you talent and vocation, and I, my son, in his name ask you to be disciplined and to place your abilities at the service of our people. This is a task that falls very specially to you young people who are now beginning to write. You have energy, health, and a long future before you. Who better than you to shape a literature that will become the central column in the protection of our language? Do you understand what I'm saying?"

"Of course."

"Our language, the soul of all Basques, must find a support in its own literature. Novels, theater, poetry. All of it. It isn't enough that children go to the *ikastola*, that their parents speak and sing to them in Basque. Writers who will raise the language to its maximum splendor are needed now more than ever. A Shakespeare, a Cervantes, in Basque, that would be marvelous indeed. Can you just imagine?"

Gorka watched himself in the mirror, nodding affirmatively.

"Oh, this enthusiasm of mine! What I wanted to do was to tell you to go on educating yourself and writing so that our people will construct a culture that will also be the product of their own hands. When you write, it is Euskal Herria that writes from within you. We know of course that this is a huge responsibility, perhaps too huge for a man who is still young and inexperienced like you. But it is a beautiful mission, believe me, a very beautiful mission, and one that in these moments of our history, I say without fear of exaggeration, is a sacred mission. You have a blessing, Gorka. If you're constrained by some necessity, no matter what it is, don't hesitate to visit me. I'll lend you a hand whenever necessary so you can dedicate yourself to the noble office of writer."

After half an hour Gorka left the sacristy completely dumbfounded. The priest bade him farewell with an embrace. That unexpected impact of their chests impressed the boy. A physical closeness for which he was unprepared. Does he take me for one of the chosen? As he walked down the street, a hollow formed within him, like an existential gas, the result of his astonishment. How odd: Don Serapio never once mentioned Joxe Mari. How odd: he didn't reproach him, which he thought the priest certainly would: I don't see you very often at mass. And he remembered, how could he not remember?, what Arantxa recently said to him over the telephone. The priest hadn't shown the slightest interest in his poem.

As soon as he entered the apartment, his mother asked him:

"What did Don Serapio want from you?"

"What was he going to want? He congratulated me."

"Just what I thought."

Days later, who speaks to Gorka about the literary prize? No one. Not even his mother, who had congratulated him at home. So, tranquility. Finally. Or that's what he thought. And thank heaven for that, because he was fed up with congratulations and jokes, and pats on the back, some sincere, the rest not. And above all, he was fed up with his own poem which, when he reread it alone in his room, suddenly seemed so weak that he couldn't look at it without being ashamed.

In sum, people stopped bothering him and on Saturday night he walked into the Arrano Taberna. Just being inside the place bothered him more and more, seeing the photo of his brother, having people ask about him. And the smoke, and the noise, and the stink, and the badly washed glasses, sometimes with traces of lipstick on them. But your friends drag you along and you go. If you don't, someone notices. And if someone notices, that's bad.

Just then he approached the bar. His group had ordered a fresh round of calimocho. This time it was Gorka's turn to fetch the glasses. Patxi, on the other side of the bar, his features tense, fixed a hard stare on him. He leaned over:

"You're making a big mistake and I don't like it."

Gorka's eyebrows flew up. For two or three seconds his face was paralyzed with a grimace of shock. And he was afraid to look into the bartender's severe eyes.

"What's the problem?"

"Let this be the last time you speak to a fascist newspaper and that you accept money from a banking entity that exploits workers. We can't undo the first part. I hope it won't be repeated. The second can be fixed. Know what this is?"—he placed before the boy's horrified face the bank set aside for prisoners. "Ten thousand pesetas will fit nicely in here."

73

IF YOU'RE HERE, YOU'RE IN

Her workday at the shoe store over, Arantxa walked out to the street, and there, waiting for her in the first shadows of nightfall and looking like a sad dog, was her brother Gorka. What's up? He needed a favor. If he could stay in her apartment for a few days. Why? Life in town was becoming very difficult for him.

"And the *aitas*, what do they have to say?"

"I wanted to talk to you first."

She reminded him:

"We only have one bed. Ours."

It didn't matter to him if he had to sleep on top of a blanket on the floor and use towels for a pillow. Arantxa, gesticulating, asked him to calm down. They had a sofa, but it might be too short.

"You never stop growing."

She asked him if he was running away from the police. Answer: no. Are you sure? I'm sure. Arantxa gave a sigh of relief. Your friends, then?

"My friends and someone else."

Brother and sister agreed to take the bus to Rentería and that Gorka would explain with Guillermo present what was going on in the town.

"Because if you're going to spend a few days with us, Guille has a right to know the reason, don't you think?"

"Of course."

Scene: Guillermo and Arantxa on the sofa before dinner. Gorka facing them sitting on a chair brought in from the kitchen because the young married couple, though they worked and worked, still hadn't saved enough to finish furnishing their place. Gorka told in greater detail what he'd already told his sister while they were on the bus. In the presence of his brother-in-law, he began with the conclusion:

"I either leave town or follow in Joxe Mari's footsteps. There's no alternative. The pressure is on. I seem soft to them. They say books are eating my mind and they laugh at me. They've started calling me *Kartujo*. And the worst thing is they are making me do things I don't agree with. Right now, there's no friend I can talk to the way I'm talking to you. I practically don't speak out of fear I'll say the wrong thing. And last night was too much. I'm very tired. I haven't slept for a minute. I was on the point of hiding out in the hills, but then I thought of you two."

"Tell Guille what you told me on the bus."

Yesterday, in a corner of the Arrano, Peio whispered to Gorka and another friend that he had four Molotov cocktails in a hiding place. Guille: who was Peio?

"One of the guys I hang around with. He gets more and more radical every day."

Arantxa added details:

"His father was the biggest drunk in town. Every day you'd see him staggering up the street. He died."

Apparently, Patxi allowed Peio to take a few empty bottles. The boy got the gasoline on his own. He bought it? Are you kidding? He uses a rubber hose to drain it out of the gas tanks of cars and trucks. It's very easy. He made the cocktails. He added motor oil so the fire, as he put it, would be stickier. He was practicing alone in the quarry. He had four left over.

"He's really fascinated by weapons and the struggle, and one of these days he'll join ETA."

Peio proposed an *ekintza* when it got dark. He couldn't think of an objective. Did anyone have any ideas? First, they talked about the town hall. The door still had the burn marks from the last time.

"What abut the *batzoki*?"

Juancar:

"Don't you dare. My *aita*'s probably in there playing *mus*."

Gorka kept quiet. He was drinking his calimocho in silence and furtively glancing at the clock, waiting for the opportune moment to say goodbye. This was getting really bad. He saw his two friends were committed, their eyes glittering from the alcohol they'd consumed. Peio was saying that it was too bad there hadn't been a row that afternoon with the cops so they could roast two or three. Now they were talking about setting fire to the car of some enemy of Euskal Herria. By then, after all that talking and gesticulating, the entire tavern was aware of what they were openly planning in the corner. That was when Patxi came over to order them to take a walk. Because of course in the Arrano he doesn't want problems. For compromising matters, there is a back room. And in the same moment, as if in passing, he insinuated, telling them without telling them that there was this guy who owned trucks.

"At first I didn't understand because I was more concerned with getting away than with anything else. Peio and Juancar understood immediately that Patxi was referring to Txato."

Guille: who was Txato?

Arantxa:

"I've talked about him a couple of times. The man with the shipping company. A man who doesn't roll over because of threats from ETA. It seems he doesn't pay the revolutionary tax or he's late in paying or he doesn't pay enough, I don't know. There are so many rumors! The fact is that they've set up a persecution campaign to throw a scare into him and all the people in the town are against him. A good man. For my father a brother, and for me almost an uncle. Now we don't speak to him or his family even though they never did anything to us. This is a crazy country."

And Gorka, cornered by his friends between the table and the wall, defended himself. He couldn't, seriously, he couldn't, he had to go. They insisted. All they'd need was an hour. Not even. The plan was simple: toss the four Molotov cocktails, come back to town, and you off to your fucking books. From the bar, Patxi saw them, apprentice *gudari*, arguing and waving their arms. Again he went to their corner, this time with the excuse of picking up their glasses.

"Mind telling me what the hell's going on?"

"This guy, *Kartujo*, says he isn't coming."

"He's a coward."

"Can you believe he's Joxe Mari's brother?"

Gorka kept silent, and Patxi turned to him, serious, calm:

"Look, son, when you're in a group and you know the plan of action, you stick with it to the end and you don't squeal. If you didn't want to take part, you should have left sooner. No one's forcing you. But if you're here, you're in. And now get out of here, the three of you. You can pay for your drinks tomorrow. Or they'll be on the house. According to how you do."

Gorka was now marked a squealer. From there to informant there was about an inch. That broke down his resistance. And he was suddenly so eaten up by shame that he felt as if he'd walked down the street naked, his tall, bony body where everyone could see it. A ball of disgust formed in his throat. He felt himself to be chickenhearted, a plucked chicken, and nothing worried him more than the fear the others would see his sadness. The others, what did they do? As they walked they repeated Patxi's argument in a tone of recrimination until Gorka finally said, okay, enough, let's go. And off they went, jolly, slightly drunk, shouting *gora ETA, amnistia osoa,* and other slogans, to get the cocktails Peio had hidden.

With the bottles in a bag, they walked toward the river. It was dark then, but with a purple border of sky above the mountains. They agreed that each one would throw one cocktail, but that Peio, who had made them, would get to throw two. When they were near their objective, Juancar hissed to be quiet. They confirmed that the entry gate was locked. Too high to jump over it. Besides, there was barbed wire on top. Bad luck: there were only two trucks. One next to the warehouse door.

"Damn, how far away it is."

It would be impossible to hit it with a bottle thrown from outside. The other was parked with its front bumper against the wall. Difficulties? At least three. First, the chain-link fence made it necessary to toss the bottles straight up, as if they were mortar projectiles. That means you can't aim properly. The second difficulty was the impenetrable thicket of blackberry bushes growing in front of the wall, which would keep them from getting close to the target. And the third difficulty? They were surrounded by trees, so the whole place was dark, so dark they couldn't even see where they were walking.

There was no light in the office.

"Great. We're alone."

Peio, impatient, threw the first cocktail. He threw it as high as he could so it wouldn't hit the fence. With no accuracy. The bottle burst on the asphalt. The advantage was that now the flames enabled them to see the truck better.

"They told me it was my turn. I could see I wasn't going to hit the truck. They couldn't hold it against me since Peio had also failed. And suddenly, as we were lighting the rag, we heard a voice shouting: bastards, bastards. And not only that. *Bam!* A shot. I swear. And there was Txato coming toward us, running along the esplanade. *Bam!* Another shot. I don't know if he was really trying to shoot us, but it was clear he had a gun.

" 'Shit, this guy's going to kill us. Let's take off.' And we didn't have hoods or anything else to cover our faces. Anyway, I think it was too dark for him to recognize us. Instead of chasing after us, Txato went to put out the fire. I think that if he wanted to he could have killed the three of us. I couldn't sleep and today I've spent hours going from one place to another. I'd be grateful if you'd let me stay here a few days. Then I'll figure a way to leave town. If I stay there, I'll end up just like Joxe Mari."

Arantxa stood up.

"That's enough. I'll make supper. Meanwhile, you call home and tell the *aitas* what the situation is."

"I can't tell them about what happened yesterday."

"Make something up."

"What?"

"Guille, what would you say in his place?"

"Me. I don't know. That someone wants to beat me up or something like that."

74

Personal Liberation Movement

For a while, Gorka found refuge in solitude. He slowly distanced himself from his friends. And he never went into the Arrano Taberna. He studied, read, wrote poems and stories. These he immediately destroyed, convinced they were worthless. He didn't get depressed. I'm learning. Meanwhile, he nourished the vague hope he would someday get a job, but where? In the foundry, as his father suggested several times? Joxian offered to speak with the people in the office. That's not happening. Twenty-one years old and still living with his family. His father was frantic, thinking him an oddball; his mother scolded him constantly. To wake him up, she said, certain that he'd turned out lazy.

From time to time, Gorka went to book presentations, lectures, and round tables in San Sebastián. He would hang around other writers and actually met a few. He stopped borrowing books from the town library. More than anything else it was to avoid running into people he knew in the street or in the reading room. Instead he became a regular in the municipal library in the Parte Vieja neighborhood of San Sebastián, where he would spend entire afternoons bent over books, encyclopedias, newspapers.

But he knew he couldn't disconnect himself from the town as long as he lived with his parents. Festivals, public events, telephone calls from friends drew him away from what he loved. He trained himself in the art of ducking out, becoming a master of dissimulation. When it came to the demonstrations he simply had to attend, he figured out a way to stand in strategic places. First at the side of his friends, later a few steps away from them, and once he was aware his presence had been noticed, he'd stop to talk with anyone, if possible with older people; he would linger on the sly, and when the opportune moment came he'd disappear.

He often would leave the town for days at a time. Which is how he arranged things with Arantxa. He moved into her apartment and in that way progressively detached himself from his group. And he was no parasite. He lent a hand to his sister and brother-in-law in everything he could. While they were at work he cleaned their house. He helped them wallpaper the living room. Alone, he painted the kitchen ceiling. And in the spirit of exchanging one favor for another, he tried to teach his brother-in-law some basic elements of Basque. They had to give it up because it was impossible. Guille had absolutely no talent for languages.

Luck ran into Gorka one day and favored him. How so? Well, the boy found a job or the job found him and outside the town as well; not well paid, not a bit, but to his taste: employee in a San Sebastián bookstore. The owners met him, he came to a book presentation, they asked him. Listen, how would you like et cetera. He didn't hesitate. It was success in what he mentally called his Personal Liberation Movement, the objective of which was limited to a single point: achieve independence. It isn't only that he'd earn a tiny salary; it's that his job allowed him to lose sight of the town every day without his having to give explanations to anyone, because everyone knew where he was going every morning he got on the bus.

While he worked in the bookshop he published book reviews in Basque, published a few literary works in magazines, and also, though only sporadically, articles on cultural matters in the newspaper *Egin*. Publishing in *Egin* gave him a free pass in his hometown. No one reproached him, no one was suspicious of him. Was it true they barely ever saw him? Sure, but he published in *Egin*.

One afternoon he saw Patxi on the street. From one sidewalk to the other:

"Your article yesterday was very good. I didn't understand a thing, but I liked it. Keep up the good work."

Basque became his main source of income. Lucrative? For the time being, he was surviving. He did everything. He wrote jacket copy, pamphlets, did short translations. A publisher accepted a thin book for children. At the last minute, without consulting him, they changed the title. They called it *Piraten itsasontzi urdina*. Gorka wasn't horrified, but he did prefer his own title. That interference in his writing troubled him.

Arantxa told him not to take it to heart and encouraged him to dedicate the bulk of his creative efforts to children's literature.

"As long as you write for kids, they'll leave you alone. But you'll be sorry, my boy, the minute you get involved with national issues. In any case, if you must write for adults, set your stories far from Euskadi. In Africa or America, the way others do it."

Good luck took a liking to him and granted him, under more-than-favorable conditions, his wish to abandon his native town forever. What happened? One afternoon he met Ramuntxo. In fact, Gorka hadn't planned to attend the opening of a Basque painting exhibit at the Altxerri Gallery, but he missed his bus. It was raining, the gallery was nearby. So, to pass the time, he walked into the show as if an invisible string were pulling him in. And there was Ramuntxo with a canapé of shrimp, hard-boiled egg, and mayonnaise in his hand. They chatted. Ramuntxo, who was eleven years older, was astonished at how well Gorka spoke Basque. They got along well. And from the gallery, to speak more calmly, they went to the bar on the ground floor. They became even friendlier, until finally, at about ten at night, Ramuntxo offered to drive Gorka to his town. Gorka, delighted, not only because of the favor but because for the first time in a long while he found that somewhere in the world there existed a person other than his sister with whom he could talk without restraining his frankness.

Two months later, he moved in with Ramuntxo in Bilbao. The initial idea was that he would work for him as a secretary and also that he would edit texts broadcast on the radio. Ramuntxo, divorced, father of a daughter, Amaia, he loved madly, brought Gorka to live with him in his flat on Licenciado Poza Street. He gave him a bedroom and an office, and he paid him quite a bit more than the owners of the San Sebastián bookstore.

He forbade him to write a single line for *Egin*.

"Don't fall into that trap. You listen to me."

Gorka composed some texts that were so beautiful, so profound, and so well written that after a while Ramuntxo decided to bring him into the radio station. He had no problem getting his young friend accepted by the staff. And for Gorka that was like ascending to heaven.

It was not a station with wide broadcast range. Approximately 80 percent of the programming was in Basque. And some announcers mangled the grammar. All the better for Gorka, who read marvelously well, expressed himself fluidly, and had an enormous control over the language. He also had a good voice, so in a short while he went from being an assistant editor, in charge of the record collection, responsible for making coffee, and messenger boy to speaking at the microphone, first along with Ramuntxo and later alone.

He liked huge amounts of work, to the point that he stayed at the station after his workday finished. He sat next to the sound technician so he could learn how to work the control panel. He also kept an eye out in case some writer, artist, or singer came to the city. He would then run to find them and record interviews. He did the same later with athletes and anyone who was famous and who would bother to answer his questions.

Ramuntxo saw how enthusiastic he was and got him a half-hour program dedicated to Basque literature broadcast every day at ten p.m. except Saturdays and Sundays. Gorka was a happy man.

75

A Porcelain Vase

Aránzazu, wearing sunglasses, made herself comfortable on the forward deck and Xabier rowed. On the stern, the name of the boat *Lorea Bi*. Before, there had been a *Lorea Bat*. It belonged to Aránzazu's brother and he gave them the key. When she was still a girl, she liked to go for a spin around the bay on the *Lorea Bat*, which was heavier and harder to manage than this current boat. On board, girlfriends from high school, the occasional boyfriend, rarely herself alone. The *Lorea Bi* has an outboard motor, but Xabier has decided to use the oars. After all, we don't have to empty Aránzazu's brother's gas tank just so we can enjoy an afternoon.

"What? It's four drops of gas!"

"A little exercise will do me good. I recommend it to my patients and it turns out I'm the one who leads the sedentary life I reproach them for."

A perfect day. A blue afternoon at the end of spring. The water in the port tranquil, with fish that turn from side to side, lighting up the depths with flashes of silver. Sitting above, along the edge of the narrow entry to the harbor, six or seven fishermen with poles are lined up, most of them boys. Because it was low tide, a wide swath of wall covered with algae was visible. And Xabier, pessimistic, suspicious:

"All we need is for one of those fools to hook us."

They went out into the bay. In the open space, the *Lorea Bi* began to rock. The formidable volume of the water was obvious, the power of the waves a warning. What do they say? What they always say:

that the water lives and you are tiny animals on a floating shell. Heavy seas? Of course not, but if you're not used to the sea, the constant rocking is intimidating, and the breeze can get impetuous. Aggressive, it wraps itself around you, whipping, because it knows you have no defense. Aránzazu, her hair a mess—how pretty she is—had to tie it back in a bun.

She was afraid of something else.

"I'd like to open a hole in your forehead so I could take a peek from time to time at your brain and find out what you're thinking and feeling. When I was a little girl, my girlfriends and I made time capsules. Each one dug a little hole in the ground and tossed in daisies, clover leaves, some little piece of jewelry, a lock of hair; we would seal them with a piece of glass and the next day come back to see what was there. Well, I'd do the same thing with your forehead to see what's going on inside you."

"Don't restrain yourself on my account. When I'm asleep you can perform that trepanation and I'm sure I wouldn't even notice. You know how soundly I sleep."

Xabier keeps up a slow rowing rhythm. I don't want to get blisters on my hands. A slight but continuous push is all you need for the *Lorea Bi*, which is light (plastic reinforced with fiberglass), to slide over the surface of the water. Where are they going? Nowhere in particular. To be alone with the city right in front of them. The farther out into the bay they go, the fewer the noises that reach them, and even those are muffled.

Aránzazu, staggering and now without her sunglasses, has moved to the forward seat so she can look Xabier in the eye when she speaks to him. And to steady herself when she goes from one end of the boat to the other, she leans on his shoulders for a moment. Those hands are warm, soft, there is velvet, velvet in love, in those hands. And then Aránzazu took off her shoes, which are more like slippers, her blue blouse, her jeans, and, wanting sun, sits there in a bikini. Her feet, the nails with dark red polish, are small and still girlish.

"I don't know what I can do, *maitia*, to get on your mother's good side. And it isn't as though I'm not trying. But I swear I'm running out of options. What should I do?"

"My mother's mental world is very small. Don't worry. One of these days she'll discover how marvelous you are and you'll be friends."

"I doubt it. She can't forgive me, a simple auxiliary nurse, for having stolen her son."

"She said that to you?"

"I see it, Xabier. I've got eyes."

"The most beautiful eyes I've ever seen in my life."

Another compliment? Deserved, of course. She was pretty, with a touch of maturity: just my type. Neither too old nor too young. A ripe woman, with her first wrinkles at the edges of her eyelids, which made her even more attractive, while there is still no resignation, but health, a good supply of hope, joy, despite the divorce that left her disoriented, with psychological tears, until Xabier turned up.

Her lips, full, perhaps the best feature of her charming face. And when she opened them, her fresh, white, marvelous teeth appeared. How much I remember of her!

When they were between the island and Mount Urgull, no boats nearby, gently rocked by the waves, Aránzazu asked him to put suntan cream on her back. I see bodies every day, but this is the body I love. He loved her. He loved her a great deal. And she:

"For a while now I've been having the same dream again and again. Should I tell it to you?"

"Go ahead."

"I'm walking through a forest or up a mountain with horrible cliffs. I'm carrying a porcelain vase in my arms. I can't describe it. Someone whispers in my ear that it's valuable. It would be a terrible thing if it were to break."

"I can guess the ending. The vase falls out of your hand and smashes with a hellish crash."

"I must have dreamed that episode more than five nights over the past few weeks. It makes me think I'm obsessing. The vase, other times a bottle, always breaks. In the dream I felt like crying, but I'm ashamed. People point fingers at me and instead of helping they criticize me. I don't know where to hide. Then I start running like a madwoman and suddenly I realize that I'm holding a vase or a bottle or some other fragile object that's going to break and which, in fact, does break."

"You should write, you've got ideas."

Once he'd covered her back with cream, Xabier lifted the top of her bikini, more than anything so he could touch her breasts, caress them with the excuse of putting suntan cream on them. Did she ask him to? No, but Aránzazu denies him nothing related to her body. If he's touching, let him touch. If he's sucking, let him suck. If he's entering, let him enter. She told him even before those happy days they spent in Rome. Don't hide your desires from me, use me for your pleasure when you want and as you want in exchange for sincere affection. She's happy with that. If he understands her. Of course.

Her breasts are rather small, sag a bit, but are extremely sensitive. So that if he massages, squeezes, kisses delicately, with minute tenderness, it isn't infrequent that she has a flash of pleasure and wants more.

She asks him, her eyes closed, concentrating on the agreeable sensations, if in the hospital he gets erotically aroused when he's treating beautiful women.

"In the operating room never. During consultations I won't say it doesn't happen. It can happen that a whiff of perfume makes me forget for an instant that I'm a repairman for bodies. I think it happens to everyone. Not to you?"

"Not much."

"I've treated authentic beauties, but how can you become fascinated knowing that inside those bodies a tumor is growing or that the kidneys have stopped working?"

They agree on a route as they leave the bay. Where to? There, behind the island, where they'll be completely alone. Xabier starts rowing again.

"Now that I'm thinking about it, I can't remember having an erection during working hours."

As he maneuvers the oars, he evokes expressions of pain, bleeding wounds, sicknesses. He evokes naked bodies, yes, naked, even young and well-formed bodies, but full of suffering and anguish, bristling with tubes, unconscious, sentenced most certainly to death today, tomorrow, within three weeks, and he is not there to get erections. Not at all. Not even to allow himself to be swept away by compassion.

The *Lorea Bi* slides swiftly ahead. There are whitecaps on the sea. The blades of the oars softly enter the water, which gets darker, deeper, and more agitated. No one. Not even a sail, not even the outline of a ship from here until the far horizon. And Aránzazu lit a cigarette and stretched out in the sun, her back resting on a towel she'd spread over the platform at the prow, her feet on the seat. Xabier contemplates her foreshortened body. How is it possible to be so beautiful? The svelte, smooth, well-shaped legs that trotted through life until they reached me. The knees, the thighs with a few touches of cellulite, thighs that carry Aránzazu along the street of bitterness. She is pretentious. She said she wasn't, that it was a matter of pride. And he fixed his eyes on the lower half of her bikini, on the cloth behind which on other occasions there was the hint of her sex in soft relief, but not that afternoon.

"Who was the first?"

"One of my brother's friends, in my parents' house. I was fifteen."

"A precocious child."

"On the one hand, I was dying of curiosity. On the other, I saw clearly that if I didn't let him the guy was going to rape me. I haven't the slightest doubt about it. There was no one in the house. My brother hadn't come home yet. So I pretended that I wanted to, and by pretending to be docile, the thing barely lasted a couple of minutes."

"You're not going to tell me you weren't traumatized for life."

"I wasn't. And it didn't hurt much."

An hour and a half later, they began their return. The tide was turning. Expending the same energy they used to row out, they moved twice as quickly. At times Xabier managed to synchronize his rowing with the push of the waves. Then the *Lorea Bi* shot ahead. In no time at all it entered the bay.

The sun was going down. The seascape, in those sunset distances, copied the intense yellow of the sky. There was a chill in the air and Aránzazu was already putting her clothes back on. They made plans: they would have brochettes in the Parte Vieja and then go home, since the next day both were on morning duty.

Nearing the Aquarium, they heard the first clap of thunder. Immediately after, the second. They sound like firecrackers, but the locals know: it's the police firing rubber bullets at demonstrators.

"There's a row on the Bulevar."

"Future terrorists in training. An hour of ruckus, they'll set fire to something, and then a bar crawl in the Parte Vieja."

Xabier, rowing, went off on a rant and Aránzazu was surprised by the vehemence of his words. So what? It's that:

"I've never heard you talk like that. You seem to be someone else."

"I'm thinking about my father and it's hard for me to control myself."

"They're still after him?"

"They never stop. The other day some boys tried to set fire to a truck. He was on guard. They couldn't do it. I felt chills when he confessed he was on the verge of making a mistake, according to him the worst mistake a man can make."

"You're scaring me. What mistake?"

"I didn't ask. I saw in his face that he didn't want to go into the subject any deeper. But I have my suspicions. Actually, I'm pretty sure."

"It didn't enter his mind to resort to violence?"

"I think he keeps a gun at the office and that he felt a strong temptation to use it to defend himself."

They were getting closer to the port. In the background, above the houses, a column of black smoke was rising.

"A mistake of that kind can bring about reprisals. Violent people love it when all of us take part in their game. That way they'll have proof about the war that only exists in their minds. I don't want to hurt you, *maitia*, but that's what I think."

"No, that's just what my father thinks. Cool as can be, he says they're going to kill me someday. I repeat that he should come and live in the apartment you and I helped him buy in San Sebastián. He says he'll make a decision soon. He pretends to be strong, but I know from my mother that some nights he cries in bed."

"How can they hurt your father, a good, *euskaldun* Basque?"

"All that and owner of a business. All this madness about the armed struggle has to be financed. Don't forget that. On the streets of the town there are still graffiti against him. Think the neighbors give any thought to erasing them? The more I think about it, the more enraged I get."

"I see you suffer, *maitia*, and it breaks my heart. Shall we leave the brochettes for another day?"

"Probably all for the best. I've suddenly lost my appetite."

76

Go On, Cry in Peace

No one told him. He didn't know. I'm the son. He wasn't sure from whom. Nor was it necessary. They must have noticed by the expression on his face. Aside from the fact that a surgical gown, it goes without saying, inspires an instinctive respect. They let him through. The gray afternoon, his heart pounding, in the last second he noticed the bloodstain. It's that you couldn't see it clearly on the wet ground. He almost stepped in it. It happened here. He didn't know. No one told him. In his mind, the red traces took on the form of footprints along the short path to his parents' house. Or now only his mother's house?

If Txato had really died, wouldn't he be stretched out on the ground, covered by a sheet, waiting for the inspecting officer to order the removal of the body? And there were no ambulances in sight next to the *Ertzaintza* patrol cars. Therefore, they've taken him away. Therefore, while there's space for medical intervention, there's a thread of hope.

Two *ertzainas* emerged from the apartment chatting informally. One burst out laughing. When they met the surgical gown on the stairs they fell silent. A hasty salute. Xabier supposed they would have expressed their sympathy just in case. Are you a relative of the deceased, the victim, the murdered man, the executed man; in sum, of the dead man? They were very sorry, very sorry for your loss. But instead of expressing any sympathy they went on walking down the stairs. A bit later, when Xabier was pushing the door the *ertzainas* had left ajar, he heard them resume the babble of trivialities.

He entered. He entered taking cautious steps, like someone try-

ing not to interrupt a sleeper's rest. The familiar smell, the vestibule in half-light. He hadn't visited the house for months. Why?
Because he was avoiding the town. Simple as that. He felt he was
being watched, watched with evil intentions, and twice already it
happened that as he walked along the street people he'd known all
his life did not respond to his greeting. So for some time, when he
wanted to see his parents, he preferred they come to San Sebastián.

On the wall peg hung Txato's old sheepskin jacket, the one he'd
had for so many years. And Xabier couldn't help stretching out a
hand to touch it. I don't know why I touched it. Just a few seconds,
as if he were trying to prove to himself that some vestige of its
owner's life remained in the jacket.

He walked toward the only place in the flat where there was
light, and indeed, there in the living room was his mother. Heart-
broken, teary-eyed, sobbing? In those moments, Bittori was observing the street from between the blinds. And when she heard her son
arriving, she brusquely turned toward him, and in her features there
was angry serenity, haughty fortitude, a kind of dignified tension
that erased any hint of grief from her features.

"I don't want you to give me an injection."

She could calm down on her own. Not him; emotionally
wrenched, he threw himself into his mother's arms.

"Go on, cry in peace if that helps you. No one's going to see me
shed a single tear. That's a pleasure I'm not going to give them."

But Xabier couldn't control himself, bent over his mother, envel-
oping her in a grief-stricken embrace. He was broken in sorrow:
his mother in old slippers, the felt of one spattered with blood;
his mother pretending to be strong, his gray-haired mother, his
wretched mother, and to one side of them, on the table, the reading
glasses Txato used at home, the ballpoint pen, the newspaper open
to the crossword puzzle. And during that attack of weeping I hear
her ask me if I want her to make something to eat. Has she been so
affected that she's lost all notion of reality? Was she denying what
happened?

Just the opposite, Bittori hadn't the slightest doubt that:

"He's dead. Get used to the idea."

"Who told you?"

"I just know it. When I saw him he was still breathing, but it was almost over. I can tell you for certain he won't come back from this. I think his head was blown open. Txato's gone, you'll see."

"I suppose they took him to the hospital."

"They did, but it's useless. You'll see."

Poor Nerea when she finds out. We have to get word to her as soon as we can. Xabier, calmer now, looked in the drawer his mother was pointing to for the slip of paper with the telephone number on it. They answered the telephone immediately. Not even two rings. The usual voices and noises of a bar in the background. He left the message without going into detail. He only made clear who he was and formulated the request. Which was? That they tell his sister to call her family as soon as she could. He emphasized that it was urgent. To be sure, he repeated Nerea's address. The man at the bar told him he didn't have to, that he remembered the girl.

"Are you sure that *aita* was alive when they put him in the ambulance?"

"I didn't leave his side for a second. His eyelids were fluttering, and I didn't stop talking to him because I thought: if I don't talk to him, I'll lose him. But he couldn't answer me. He was bleeding to death. Look, when I got home I had to change clothes."

"I wish you'd tell me if he was conscious or not."

"Listen, you're going to make me faint. His eyelids moved. A little."

"Was it you who called the police and the ambulance?"

"I didn't call anyone. They suddenly appeared with the sirens going full blast. Some neighbor must have made the call. I was screaming my head off. They probably heard me in the next town."

After his siesta, Txato had coffee; actually some cold remnants at the bottom of the pot. Bittori, who heard him grunt, offered to make a fresh pot, but Txato, either because he saw her dozing on the sofa, her arms crossed in the position a napping person falls into, or because as usual he was in a hurry, refused her offer.

"I'll make do with what there is."

He left the house. At what time? A little before four. And she was pained now for not accompanying him to the vestibule to give Txato a kiss that might have been the last of his life. God forbid. She would have preferred using her energy in a tenderer farewell, after so many years being married to him and two children, instead of wasting it on a stupid conversation about hot or cold coffee.

"If you were to ask me, I'd say I only remember the noises. First, the sound of the door when he left for work, then his footsteps on the stairs, the nothing, me on the sofa with my eyes closed, thinking: let's see if I can get a half-hour snooze. And suddenly the shots. Don't ask me how many. But that it was shots I didn't doubt, not for a second. Then I ran to the balcony. I saw Txato down on the sidewalk and no one else. I didn't see who shot or even if it was just one person. Well, I didn't stand there staring but instead ran down to the street and when I saw all the blood I started screaming like a madwoman. Do you think anyone came to help? Because I tried to lift your father. I said to myself: I've got to get this man on his feet. He's heavy. So I started talking to him. Look, I was so frantic that I said: I love you. We never said that to each other. Not even before we were married. We just couldn't say it. We showed it without words. But I just had to talk and talk or he's going to slip away. And at least, look, if he dies, he'll at least know I loved him. No one helped me. The street, empty. The windows, closed. And it was pouring. I'm telling you, no one. Someone who saw everything through a crack must have called the police and the ambulance. Otherwise I can't explain how they got here so quickly. In ten minutes the *Ertzaintza* was already here. And a little after that, the ambulance."

The telephone rang. Nerea? Bittori signaled to her son—run, run—to answer the phone. Xabier, standing next to it, only had to twist around and stretch out his arm.

"Hello?"

"*Gora ETA!*"

He hung up.

"Obviously that wasn't your sister."

"There are people who only want to hurt us. Probably better we don't answer the phone."

"But what if Nerea calls?"

Besides, Bittori was waiting for the hospital to call. Xabier:

"Don't worry. I'll deal with that."

He dialed a number. He said hello, spoke, asked. And whoever it was he was talking to gave him another number he wrote down in a notebook. He then dialed that number. His mother behind him on the sofa. And he with his back toward her, as if blocking her out.

"I'm sorry, Xabier. There was nothing to be done."

He said thank you. Thank you for what? For nothing. It was a way to fake calm. And he hung up. His mother was behind him. It was difficult to turn around. He avoided looking straight at her. He searched for words: they just informed me that, you have to know that. But instead of saying any of that he said he was going to the hospital to find out and that he would call from there to keep her abreast of the situation. He asked her:

"If you hear them insulting you, hang up the phone right away. Promise?"

77

Evil Plans

Two days after the funeral, Txato was buried in the Polloe cemetery. Few people stood at the graveside. No absence weighed as heavily on Bittori as that of Nerea. Nerea was embittering her mourning; she wouldn't forgive her. Xabier, understanding, reasonable, conciliating, mediated between mother and daughter. It was useless. He couldn't console the one or persuade the other. It seemed to him his mother's rage grew deeper and deeper. He called the bar in Zaragoza again and again trying to contact his sister and convince her to come home as soon as possible. That first thing would be unpleasant, because he knew he was becoming a nuisance to the owner of the bar. The second thing, simply, didn't work, since Nerea had decided she would not face the fact of her father's death. So that's it? In a final blast of spite, his mother told Xabier that it was all the same to her, that Nerea should go about her life as she intended to go about hers, and that:

"Know something? I don't believe in God."

The morning of the burial was gray. At least it wasn't raining, and no wind was blowing. Because up there, where can you take cover? Crosses, headstones, paths. Below, the tile roofs of the city wrapped in autumnal mist. People say it's a pretty cemetery. Some consolation! A few people gathered at the vault and when the capstone was pulled aside, the coffin of Grandfather Martín became visible. Relatives from Azpeitia came, people you only see at weddings and burials. Bittori's sister came even though she understood nothing, because the poor thing was out of touch with reality. A half-dozen neighbors came, lowering their voices as they expressed their sympathy. Along with them, two employees from Txato's business. It's understandable. Far away from the town, no one can see them, no one's going to criticize them. Bittori, her eyes sunken, calm, thanked each one for attending.

On the afternoon of the funeral, the Azpeitia people asked about Nerea.

"She wasn't able to come. You know, she's studying in Zaragoza."

Xabier, son and bodyguard, never left Bittori's side. He was next to her when the first goodbyes began, when he noticed the woman wearing dark glasses, standing about twenty paces from the rest, as if she were visiting another grave. It's she. Who? Who else? Aránzazu. After what happened between them, Xabier did not expect to see her again. Perhaps in passing from time to time, hi, hi, in the parking lot or in the hospital cafeteria.

To his mother:

"I'll wait for you at the gate."

"Where are you going?"

He didn't answer. He didn't have to. Bittori had just recognized the nurse. But didn't he say he'd cut off their relationship?

As he approached Aránzazu, prettier than ever, Xabier noticed the silence that formed behind him. Serious, professional, he shook her hand. He wasn't going to kiss her with all those people there, was he?

They started to walk toward the gate, always keeping a foot or so between each other, making a slight detour from the others.

"I kept apart from the others so I wouldn't cause any bother."

"You know you don't bother anyone."

"I liked your father. From the first day we met he was friendly toward me. I can't say the same about your mother."

"Forget that. I'm begging you, please."

"I came to say goodbye to your father and to protest against terrorism. If this were a decent country, the cemetery would be overflowing with people."

"What can you do?"

"At the same time, it's an opportunity to say goodbye to you as well, forever."

"You're leaving?"

Listen, Xabier, what does it matter to you? It's true, I don't know why I asked. In reality, everything was talked out between the two of them, talked out by both, broken by him, in a corner of the café in the London Hotel. And she, who was a good-hearted person, you can't deny that, made the noble gesture of attending Txato's burial; at the same time, the burial of a love in which she'd invested many hopes, much of herself, all of her energy. That love, which was so fragile, and you smashed it, yes, you, lies buried in your father's grave. Two evenings before, when the inevitable tears began to cede their place to resignation, Aránzazu had said:

"The person who killed your father broke what joined us together."

She didn't seem resentful. Even though she wasn't lacking reasons for being resentful. Xabier, you rat, how could you treat her that way? What? Don't play dumb. At first she didn't understand. Just after Txato's death she thought Xabier was blinded by rage and sorrow. And, open and good, she was ready to provide him with tenderness, to relieve a part of his sufferings; for her part, she would take them onto her own back. She promised him love, faithful company, more than ever in the tragic hour, and with tear-blurred eyes she told him:

"I'll make you happy, *maitia*, I swear."

"But I mustn't be happy."

"Who's stopping you?"

"I'm stopping myself. At this moment I can't think of a more monstrous crime than the egoistic pretension of being happy."

"I feel empty."

She confessed, as if talking to herself, her bad luck with men; she said goodbye, left the hotel, and now she was in the cemetery, wearing sunglasses on a gray day.

"If you don't mind, a friend of mine will pass by your flat to pick up my things. She'll bring along the things you left in mine."

"As you wish. Believe me—"

She interrupted him.

"What I believe doesn't matter. I've found a new horizon when I least expected to. I followed an acquaintance's suggestion and sent in an application to Doctors Without Borders. It's still early for a response, but I was told by telephone they urgently need nurses and that with my CV they'd accept me with no problems. So I'm leaving the hospital, leaving this city, and soon I'll be enrolled in a preparatory course. And the fact is that the other night, after we said goodbye, I was walking along Paseo Nuevo with evil plans."

"Don't be silly."

"There was no one around. It was dark. It would have been easy. A delightful setting for a romantic suicide. It was really tempting. And then I thought: let's see, Aránzazu, there are so many people suffering in the world, experiencing hunger, epidemics, wars. Why don't you do something for others? Something that might help those most in need and give a positive meaning to your life. That's the decision I made."

"I think it's a great decision."

In a bit, they reached the cemetery gate.

"Maybe you should embark on a similar adventure."

"I'll think about it."

They parted with a formal handshake. She, having barely taken a few steps, turned her smiling face toward him:

"Thanks for the good moments."

"Thank you."

"You shouldn't have thrown that stone in Rome."

Standing next to the gate, Xabier watched her walk away. Aránzazu's final smile left him feeling bittersweet. A scene of tears, shouts, accusations: that would have been much easier to digest. Her way of walking, her slim figure, her upright shoulders. He almost called her. More: he felt a strong temptation to run after her.

But then his mother was next to him, taking hold of his arm.

"Didn't you say you'd broken up with her?"

"She came to say goodbye. She's going far away."

"All to the good. That one wasn't for you. I realized that the same day you introduced her."

78

THE SHORT COURSE

That he was going to spend a long time being held in reserve he knew already. He'd talked it over with Jokin. Being together made the gray rains of Brittany, the interminable waiting, the boredom more bearable, and as long as they were discreet, they wouldn't lack amusement. They were well aware that more than one militant had simply blown off all discipline. They hadn't. Well, a little, just as long as they didn't get a reputation as rebels.

Sometimes they rode through the countryside on bicycles that belonged to the house owner. They stole fruit, hunted frogs, carved figures in wood with a knife, and once they went to the festival held in a nearby town where they drank a kind of cider, to give it some sort of name, which according to Joxe Mari tasted like *pixa*.

But Jokin was made part of an operating group. Joxe Mari was left alone later with Patxo, who was a nice guy but wasn't Jokin. Joxe Mari did not really trust him. Why? I don't know. There was always some distance. Something you noticed in how you treated each other. You get along fine, okay. But it's as if there was a tiny noise in the motor. Something wasn't quite right.

After a time, the French gendarmes, together with elements of the Judicial Police, men from the French border patrol, and secret agents from the Renseignements Généraux captured Santi Potros in a house in Anglet. Everyone was supposed to be careful, and guess what? The cops found a leather attaché case. Inside, solid gold: a ledger with the names of more than four hundred active ETA militants, their aliases, their home addresses, their telephone numbers, the kind of car they were using, and even its registration. They fell in the following weeks.

Patxo thought that if he and Joxe Mari had been called up, they would have been captured, too. He also thought that:

"The organization will have to find replacements. You'll see that one of these days now, they'll be telling us: okay, boys, get a move on."

But it didn't happen that way. Their inactivity went on for several more months. During that time, Joxe Mari received a letter from his parents sent through the organization's internal communication system. It contained an article from *Egin* with all the details about the "strange" death of Jokin. It shook Joxe Mari to the core. He couldn't remember ever crying that much, not even as a child. And to keep Patxo from seeing him, he pretended to be sick and didn't eat for two days, keeping to his bed the whole time.

"Do you see the armed struggle clearly?"

Patxo didn't hesitate:

"I got into this fully aware of the consequences."

"Didn't you say that your old man has to be pushed around in a wheelchair?"

"I did. What about it?"

"Maybe you should be helping him."

"My sisters take care of that."

He just couldn't feel himself getting any closer to that boy. And besides, Joxe Mari thought it was strange to be stuck with someone who didn't come from the same town. Patxo grew up in Lasarte. He had no Basque names in his family and didn't even speak Basque. Why did this guy join the struggle? What is he, a donkey who paints stripes on himself to look like a zebra? And he suspected he was a Guardia Civil mole. In any case, he preferred not to talk to him about personal matters.

Years later, he told his mother during one of her visits to the prison that during those days when he found out about Jokin he was on the verge of asking to be allowed to leave.

"A fine time to have ideas like that. We've got Koldo right here in town, all nice and cozy with his Mexican wife and children."

Joxe Mari had practically made up his mind. In fact, he thought he'd tell Patxo the next time he saw him, but then Patxo brought in a sealed note informing them they would soon undertake an intensive course so they could be incorporated into the struggle as soon as possible.

Patxo saw things clearly:

"Comrade, there's no going back. The game begins now."

"If that means getting out of here, I'm up for anything."

It was raining when they boarded the train. It didn't stop raining during the whole trip. Then a transfer to another city, then a transfer to another city. In the mid-afternoon they reached Bordeaux, where it was still raining as hard as it had during the morning.

In a bar at the station they met the man in charge of picking them up. The guy was a speed demon, and I had to swallow the glass of wine I'd just been served in one gulp. In the car, he ordered them to put on a blindfold and to slide down in the seat. Joxe Mari knew the drill from when he and Jokin had gone to the interview with Santi Potros. After an hour or so of riding, they entered a house where music was playing. Only then could they take off the blindfold.

For eight days, they were locked in a room with no windows, three steps wide and five steps long. Too small for two, which forced them into a physical closeness that drove Joxe Mari crazy. With Jokin he'd have shared even his underwear. He just didn't have the same confidence with this guy. He suffered most at night. Dear old Patxo must have had a deviated septum. The fact is that when he fell asleep he made an unbelievably annoying noise. Not that he snored. The one who snored was Joxe Mari. Patxo made a noise like a whistling growl. And it continued until dawn.

They could only leave the room to go to the bathroom on the lower floor. They were to see and remember as little as possible. Often there was music playing full blast inside the house. In that way, the one set of occupants had no idea what the others were doing. A *talde*, the instructor told them, works as an isolated unit so that if you're captured they can't get information out of you that might compromise the general functioning of the organization, understand? Both men nodded affirmatively.

During the morning, the theoretical classes bored Joxe Mari

to death. He would take stealthy peeks at his watch and mentally count the minutes left until lunch. Study was never his thing. Even as a boy in the *ikastola*, he had to make enormous efforts to concentrate. The same occurred during the militancy classes; but during the afternoon they went on to practical matters, using weapons, and then a lively enthusiasm took hold of him and he quickly felt the way he did in the old days, when he would dash up to the quarry with his friends to experiment with Molotov cocktails, bombs, and rockets. That was for him: the action, the movement, not the incredibly boring sermons on the theory of explosives, which filled him with crushing fatigue.

He and Patxo practiced assembling and disassembling weapons. They learned to prepare booby traps and car bombs. What else? They set up timing mechanisms. Then they'd explode the blasting cap in a steel barrel filled with sand. They learned everything there was to know about hiding places and mailboxes and how to pick car locks. The instructor insisted on teaching them safety measures and then it was be very careful and watch out et cetera. He explained how they were to behave in case they were arrested. Firing practice was limited to one afternoon and only with a pistol because the French police were always watching. It wasn't as easy as it was years back when they took target practice in the neighboring woods. A shame as far as Joxe Mari was concerned. He liked nothing more than target practice.

He kissed the butt of the Browning.

"I like this more than screwing."

He made them laugh. The jerks: did they think he was joking? The instructor:

"Buddy, the one doesn't exclude the other."

At night, the last he'd be locked up in that house, Joxe Mari couldn't sleep. His worries, the echo of the recent shots, Patxo's whistling breathing. So he started talking to himself. In a low voice? No chance: in a normal voice, as if he were talking to someone. Just after two in the morning. He already saw himself aiming his weapon and not exactly at paper targets. Patxo woke up. In the darkness:

"What are you talking about over there?"

"Who holds the record for executions in ETA?"

"Who the hell knows? De Juana or someone in the Madrid group."

"Do you know if he's taken out more than fifty?"

"Why in hell would you ask me? Look what time it is. In a couple of hours we've got to get going."

For several minutes they stopped talking in the dark. And Patxo went back to making the breathing noise that got on Joxe Mari's nerves. Suddenly:

"The death of Jokin is going to cost the state a lot of blood. I'm going to mow down so many that someday I'll be in the record books as ETA's bloodiest militant."

"Jesus, man, enough is enough."

"My friend is not worth less than a hundred dead. I'll keep count. Every time I knock one off I'll mark a check in a notebook."

"That means you're turning the armed struggle into a personal matter."

"And who cares what you think, jerkoff. You'd be better off learning to breathe when you sleep."

79

THE TOUCH OF THE JELLYFISH

Perhaps it was cooler than Joxe Mari had thought it would be before they set out, but he didn't notice until he and Patxo, hunched over in the backseat, their faces close to their knees so they wouldn't see, wouldn't know, arrived at the house where the boss or one of the bosses was waiting. The fact is that when their guide told them he had to bring them to an interview with some higher-ups, Patxo and he thought they'd be introduced to Ternera. But the man who was in that house in Bordeaux, or in the neighborhood of Bordeaux, or who the hell knows where, was Pakito.

So, that business about it's being cool, what's it all about? Well, when he was standing opposite the boss, who had a dead smile on his face and eyes like those of a fish beginning to rot, Joxe Mari was hit by a blast of cold air that made him think: damn, I should have put on my sweater. It's the same as when you're in the supermarket: you go into the frozen-food section and a sudden lowering of the temperature catches you by surprise. The window was closed, giving Joxe Mari the feeling that the cold emanated from that man, who, despite the fact that he was a boss, received them with obvious timidity.

Or maybe all that was nothing more than his imagination, aroused by the fascination the novice feels in the presence of a veteran in the armed struggle. He was supposed to have killed Moreno Bergareche—Pertur—and to have ordered the execution of Yoyes and Ordizia, and to have blown up a barracks in Zaragoza when there were children inside. He shook Patxo's hand. He patted me on the back, leaving me with the feeling I'd been touched by a jellyfish.

It was the blessing, the definitive entry into ETA. And the immobile smile and the turbid fish eyes were still there.

He offered them a seat on the sofa.

"You're the one who played handball?"

Very clever. I thought: he's been supplied with facts so he pretends to know everything. But apparently, and according to what others said who also spoke with him, it was nothing more than a desire to be friendly. In fact, he said he sincerely hoped they'd be comfortable being part of an operational *talde*.

A detail-obsessed man, a calculating man, he showed them a map of the province of Guipúzcoa. On the paper, he traced a circle with his index finger.

"This is your zone. Here you two can do whatever you like. Police, the Guardia Civil, *ertzainas,* whatever crosses your path. We have to hit hard until the state sits down to negotiate with us."

The first thing Joxe Mari saw was that his village was within the circle Pakito drew, which to him seemed neither good nor bad. The major geographical reference was the Oria river. That's what they'd be called: the Oria cell, made up of three men. The third, Txopo, was waiting for them in a rented flat.

"You don't have to do anything in Donostia. Stay out. There are others in place there. But within this zone"—again he pointed to the map—"you're the proprietors. There you can do all the damage you like."

He then gave them Brownings along with clips and bullets. Also phony documents, a plastic bag filled with money, and finally another, larger bag, with explosives, fuses, and various components for making bombs.

"You yourselves will identify the objectives in your zone, okay? And make things happen. Don't hold back."

A problem with the *mugalaris*, what problem? no idea, kept the two freshly minted militants in the house of a French couple, a place so lost in the solitary wilderness you could only reach it by driving off the highway between Urrugne and Ascain. Six days of waiting they spent taking walks through the woods. No one told them they couldn't go on hikes. One afternoon they tried out the pistols. Which meant in fact they were following the advice they'd received in the instruction course, since, according to the instructor, it's important to make sure the arms are in working order before going into action. So they went up a dirt road to a secluded place surrounded by trees, and took turns: while one stood guard the other amused himself taking a few shots.

One night they had a disagreeable surprise. By then Joxe Mari, it had to happen, was more or less used to his companion's whistling breathing. Even so, sometimes he just couldn't stand it and felt like walking over and smashing his nose with his fist.

Unable to fall asleep, he turned on the light. It was the middle of the night. Then he saw them. They were coming out from under a picture hung on the wall above the bed. What? Bugs. Bugs with crawling in several directions, neither quickly nor slowly. He smashed one, one larger than the others, at random. And when he lifted his finger he saw the bloodstain on the wall. Bedbugs. He woke up Patxo and the two of them were killing bedbugs for an hour.

"The Oria cell in action."

"Look, Patxo, if what you're looking for is an alias, I've got a good one for you: Jerkoff."

Joxe Mari realized something: all those nights of troubled sleep were making him bitter. He got mad over any triviality. He became argumentative, impatient, a faultfinder. He had an argument in Basque, since he spoke not a syllable of French, with the lady of the house about the food. Shouting, aggressive, he called it garbage. Scanty, tasteless, and badly prepared. And in the afternoon, when he came home from work, the husband threatened to throw him out of the house.

Early in the evening, locked in his room with Patxo, he nostalgically evoked his mother's cooking:

"I never met anyone who can cook like her. I can imagine her right now frying fish at home. We always had fish for dinner. The smell reaches me even here. Can't you smell it? Crusted red mullet and fried garlic?"

And he stretched his neck and sniffed the air in the room as if those maternal mullets were floating under his nose.

"You're not going to get all sentimental on me now, are you?"

"Not sentimental, not mental. Ever since we walked into this house I've been hungry. I'd eat a steak this big with peppers and French fries."

They didn't even have a TV. So after smashing four or five bedbugs they put out the light earlier than usual. And as soon as Patxo began to annoy him with his respiratory whistle, Joxe Mari, as stealthily as he could, dragged his mattress out into the hall. He slept like a log the whole night, and he really needed it. Early the next morning he walked out into the countryside, gathered a bouquet of wildflowers, and at breakfast time, joking, smiling, presented them to the lady of the house. That ingratiating act enabled him to get on her good side.

That same day, toward afternoon, a blackish-purple Renault van came to pick up the two militants. They went toward Ibardin. The weather? Cloudy but dry, with some breaks in the clouds where you could spot the first stars. As night was falling, they got out of the van in a wooded place. Out of the thicket came two young shadows. They wasted no time in conversations and, slipping on our packs, which weighed a ton, they started up the mountain with us behind. In a short time they were enveloped in such a dense darkness you couldn't see your hand in front of your face. I have no idea how those *mugalaris* knew where to go; they must have known the route by heart. Later the moon came up. Now they could recognize forms, shapes, masses, and see one another.

The four of them walked in silence for almost an hour until they came to the top of a hill. From there they could make out the silhouette of Mount Larrún and the glowing points of light in Ventas de Ibardin. Just then, the group stopped and one of the *mugularis*, after listening carefully, bleated an imitation of a goat. He was answered by another similar bleat not far away. It was the signal for changing the *mugalaris*. That's how Joxe Mari and Patxo understood that they'd crossed the border. And they immediately began the descent to Vera de Bidasoa.

When they were behind the cemetery chapel, they were told to stay put. They waited with their packs almost half an hour until they were signaled to walk down to the highway. The mist rising from the river erased the houses. And the truth is we were cold. It was getting light when they got into a car. Along the road to Irún they stopped several times, waiting while one of them who was up ahead on a motorcycle came back to confirm that the road was free of cops. The trip ended at the first hour of morning on Avenida Zarauz in San Sebastián. In a bus shelter they met up with Txopo, whom they didn't know.

80

THE ORIA CELL

Stretched out on the bed in his cell, Joxe Mari remembered. What? That he turned twenty-one that year and was the youngest of the three. Not that there was a great age difference. Txopo, at twenty-four, was the oldest.

"Why did they nickname you Txopo?"

"Kid stuff."

When he was a little boy he would play soccer in a grassy playground near his house. A clothesline stretched between two metal rods was the goal. They couldn't have a real match because there weren't enough kids or space. So they played three against three, four against four, but no more than that, and he was the only goalkeeper. He blocked shots by both teams and liked to broadcast the games.

"What do you mean?"

He would give each player the name of a soccer star and from the goal he would comment on the critical moments in the game as if he were a radio announcer. And since he often referred to himself as Txopo, in memory of Iribar, his idol at the time, he adopted the nickname forever.

Patxo, also a soccer player, rooted for Real Sociedad. "Are you fucking kidding me, you were for Athletic?"

"I admit it proudly."

"Well, we're off to a good start. But listen, why didn't you volunteer for the Vizcaya cell?"

"Because no one told me I'd end up working with a guy like you."

And Joxe Mari, to reconcile them, joined in:

"Okay, boys, that's enough. There are other sports, you know."

"Is that right, what are they?"

"Handball."

Just to get his goat, they retorted:

"Come on, that's no sport."

"Well, what is it, then?"

"Handball has the same relationship to soccer that ping-pong has to tennis."

"Or like a hand job to a fuck."

And they laughed, *ha ha ha ha,* the bastards, while he stood there glaring at them, not moving an eyelash.

Txopo took on chores appropriate for a support militant. Behind his back, so he wouldn't risk enraging him, Patxo called him our messenger boy or simply the messenger. Everything he knew about fighting, about militancy, about weapons—which was considerable—he'd learned on his own without passing through the recruitment channels in France. He didn't lack astuteness or organizational skills, and he had experience. Before joining with Joxe Mari and Patxo he'd never directly participated in an *ekintza,* but from the shadows he had helped some of Donostia's satellite cells solve logistical issues. That's what he did best.

"Someday I'll be running ETA."

I see him as a spider, always calm, hidden, waiting for his prey. He wasn't one for demonstrations and much less for run-ins with the cops. His strategy, in his own words, was to keep calm, learn, and call as little attention as possible to himself. Patxo didn't understand:

"At your age, how can you be so old?"

"When your brain grows a little, you'll understand."

Txopo had no police record. He'd never been arrested. He was committed to the cause, with an ideological preparation that Patxo and Joxe Mari, more men of action, lacked. He was also more highly educated than they were. He'd done a year of geography and history at the Mundaiz campus of the University of Deusto. When it came time to take the exams at the end of the term, he didn't show up. He let some time pass and enrolled again. He was from a well-to-do family.

Joxe Mari liked him from the start. The reason? Txopo was an ace when it came to practical matters. He made difficult things easy for you, he solved problems, he was cautious and provident. And he knew how to cook.

He'd rented the apartment on Avenida Zarauz, a fourth-floor with elevator, about a month earlier. He paid punctually and with under-the-table cash, with no other contract than a verbal agreement with the house owner. Was there a garage? Yes, but since it was shared with others and raised the rent, he turned it down. He moved into the apartment to await the arrival of his comrades, letting it be known to everyone he ran into coming and going that he was a student. To promote that image he came in and went out every day carrying an attaché case and the odd book.

One advantage of the apartment: nearby there were bus stops so they could travel to the interior of the province and also get to the center of the city. Txopo said that:

"It's better to live where you don't do things. You can strike and withdraw to lead a normal life like anyone else. And here in Donostia, in a neighborhood like this, it's much easier to pass unnoticed. Three new guys in a town where everybody knows everybody else, where at the most there are no more than four bars, that catches people's eye."

"Jesus, Txopo, how'd you get so smart?"

Days before our arrival, the guy had been inspecting the zone. The fact is he was as hardworking as an ant, as calculating as a spider, which, before it does anything else, makes its web. He went, he came, he looked for. Walking along the Igara highway he'd found a stupendous spot to dig a weapons cache. It wasn't far. On foot, fifteen minutes. The three of them went there one Sunday, walking with about a hundred paces between them. When they reached an abandoned homestead, its roof collapsed, they left the highway to walk up a steep hill, heading toward the hermitage of Ángel de la Guarda. Soon they found themselves in a stand of pines. Until that point, they'd walked along a path covered with brambles and nettles, a sign that no one had passed through there in a long while. Patxo and Joxe Mari approved of the spot.

Without places to hide weapons we can't do anything. In that matter the three of us were in agreement. Just before, they'd sent a first report to the higher-ups. They enumerated details relevant to free movement, they described the zone, they asked for a car and supplies. As far as they themselves were concerned, they were ready. It didn't matter to Patxo that they were storing weapons and explosives in the flat. Txopo was totally opposed. He explained. And Joxe Mari, the leader of the cell, had the last word. He sided with Txopo, always making an exception for weapons they'd need for immediate self-defense.

"If we hide our supplies, they can be used by other comrades in case the *txakurras* grab us. We've got to set up the caches quickly."

First step: buy two plastic drums. That's easy. But how to transport them without raising suspicion? They needed a car. Patxo:

"Okay, we'll steal one."

Txopo became exasperated:

"You've seen too many movies."

He said he'd take care of things. How did he do it? No idea. He got two plastic drums, blue and with screw caps, that could hold about sixty gallons. He borrowed a van. From whom? No idea. He refused to answer. Since we insisted, he said that it was from a cousin, a plumber, but God knows. And he hid the two drums in that ruined homestead along the road to Igara. Inside the drums, also brand-new, the shovels for digging holes. The guy forgot nothing.

"Shit, Txopo, I don't know why we bother to come along when the two of us are just extras."

"You do things right or you don't do them at all."

Txopo was damn good. Txopo was worth a lot. There have been bosses in ETA who weren't worth even half of him.

Early one morning they went to the pine stand. Calmly, listening to the birds sing, they buried the drums, one here, one a bit farther up. Then they covered over the sites with pine needles. When they finished, you couldn't tell anyone had been digging.

Stretched out in the bed in his cell, Joxe Mari remembered.

81

ONLY THE SAD DOCTOR
WENT TO SEE HER OFF

At midmorning, October 9, Nerea boarded the train to Paris. There, in the afternoon, before continuing her journey on the night train, she would have a few hours to stroll around the neighborhood of the Gare du Nord, providing she could leave her bags in a secure place.

More or less at the same time in the morning, Bittori, who did not want to accompany her daughter to the station, me? that's your business, went up to the cemetery. Just for once and without setting a precedent, she hiked up the entire Eguía hill on foot. She needed cool air and physical exercise to release her anger, which was burning in her stomach. Until the last moment, she was certain that Nerea would come into her room and say: *ama*, you're right, I'm staying here. Are you really staying? Yes, it was a crazy idea, I don't know what I was thinking. She didn't come in. So she, who had been awake in bed for over an hour, her ear tuned to Nerea's preparations, did not see her off.

Because of her haste, her rage, she'd left the square of plastic at home. Doesn't matter. The stone, a sunny morning, was dry and the dust I can shed with a few shakes of my skirt.

"She's gone. Yes, Txato. Your darling daughter, the light of your life, remember? Well, she's left us, apparently forever. She's got an attachment in Germany. Don't think she was very communicative. Xabier told me all about it. If he didn't, I'd never find out. That she was taking a trip, that's what she told me, but I believed, I thought, you understand me. She's not coming back. She doesn't give a damn about us. She told me her lover boy's name, but do you think I can remember a name as weird as that? All that money spent on her studies. And now she throws her future into the garbage and what's she going to do there when she doesn't know the language? Press some German's shirts for him? I don't know who he is, never even saw a photo of him. And you down there on your back unable to read the riot act to that slut. Her egoism is beyond anything. She could have been a lawyer, sure. Open her own office, live comfortably, and be the pride of her deceased father. But no. You'll see how she burns through the money you left her in no time."

The one who did turn up by surprise at the station was Xabier.

"Since I don't know when we're going to see you again, I didn't want you to go without a farewell hug."

"Don't you have to work?"

"I made a deal with a colleague."

They made some incidental conversation, praised the sunny morning, hid their feelings. But suddenly, she: that she would have preferred that he hadn't revealed to *ama* the reason for her trip, that she was going to explain things to her from Germany by telephone or in a long letter. Sooner or later, *ama* would have found out. Her reaction? Well, for certain it would have been the same either way, but at least mother and daughter would have spared themselves the disagreeable argument they'd had the night before.

Xabier, disagreeing, acting like a professor both in tone and in gestures:

"No, look, if that's the case you should have hidden your plan from me. I don't intend to keep secrets from *ama* no matter what the subject happens to be. It isn't a matter of her finding out or not. I simply can't conceive of any other relationship with her except one that's clean and sincere."

"You made me the one who gets all the blame. Don't think I'm enthusiastic about this trip, though I do hope things get better the closer I get to my destination. Last night's argument was pretty strong. You see she didn't come to say goodbye. She didn't say goodbye at the house, either. Maybe if you'd kept your mouth shut and let me handle things my way we wouldn't have ended up like this."

"The tactic didn't work. Is that what you mean?"

"What I mean is that you don't have to be my tutor. I'm a big girl now. I'm not being spiteful, you can be sure of that. I know where

I'm going and I know why I'm going. Look around. Do you see a single one of my girlfriends here to say goodbye? I don't have any friends of either sex on this planet. What am I doing in a place like this? Rotting away on my own? Should I be living with *ama*, eating roast chicken with her and you every Sunday, the three of us pouring out a few tears for dessert?"

"You're being unfair and spiteful, even if you deny it."

"You'd like me not to make this trip, right?"

"Not at all. I came to wish you all the best."

"Thanks. But if you'd like to know something, brother, I'd be in a better mood if you could be a bit more joyful."

"The joy I leave to you."

"And that, wasn't that said with spite?"

"We're at the end of the line here. The fact is you're doing the right thing by going. Anyway, what are you leaving behind? A broken family, a murdered father."

"What I'm leaving behind are you and *ama*. Not *aita*. I've got *aita* here inside."

And she energetically, vehemently brought her hand to her heart.

"Well said, sister. I'm not going make a big deal about our sorrows. All that I ask is that from time to time you call *ama*. Say a couple of pleasant things to her, send her the odd letter, okay? Maybe a package of things made where you are. So she feels loved, get me? It'll cost you nothing."

They kept talking until the train pulled in. When do you arrive? Will someone be there to meet you? Will you send us your address? Those things and then a show of goodwill: if you need anything, if you have to do some paperwork, don't hesitate to.

"And what did you say his name was?"

"Klaus-Dieter."

Xabier nodded affirmatively, repeated the name to himself. Was he giving her some kind of approval? And he again asked Nerea not to forget *ama*. Because *ama* and besides *ama*, and on and on with *ama*.

As she was about to board the train, he affectionately kissed his sister on both cheeks. And he helped her lift the heavy suitcase. Then, brusquely, he turned around and headed toward the exit before the train started to move. Nerea suspected: he doesn't want me to see him get upset.

Her brother, Dr. Sad: a tall man, thinner every day, gray (since when?) around the temples, who walked staring at the ground. So he doesn't have to say hello if he happens to meet someone he knows? There's a lot of loneliness in those shoulders marching away. Would he turn to wave goodbye to his sister? He didn't.

And Nerea went on observing him through the window of her car. I'll leave without crying. It sounded like the words from some song. Poor Xabier, working hard his whole life to raise himself to a good social position, to please his mom and dad. There he goes, dodging bodies, the guy who never broke a plate, the guy who doesn't know how to buy his clothes on his own, with his navy-blue sweater on his shoulders, the sleeves tied over his chest, and his checked shirt with no one to press it. Now in a few seconds he'd be entering the station. Not even then did he turn around.

Seconds later, the doors closed. The train pulled out. Going slowly, it entered the Gros neighborhood. There, from a few windows facing the tracks, was clothing hung out to dry. For a long while Nerea remained standing, enjoying her intense feeling of farewell. The port of Pasajes, Mount Jaizquíbel, the vacant lots in Rentería: she thought she was seeing it all for the last time and it didn't matter to her. I'll leave without shedding a tear. Finally, just before the border, she sat down. Her passport! With her heart pounding, she searched her bag for it. There it was. God, what a fright.

82

HE'S MY BOYFRIEND

Dead tired, Nerea got out of the train at the Göttingen station at the end of the afternoon on October 10. How it was raining! You just can't describe it. Beyond the roof covering the platform floated a fog right at ground level. As they burst, the raindrops turned into vapor. Or at least that's how it looked. And in the distance, above the rooftops and the trees, a radiant clarity was opening a path through the storm clouds. The entire afternoon was all strange light and a noise of violent rain.

People? Few. And her blond boy wasn't there. Maybe inside the station itself, keeping out of the bad weather? No. Or outside in the square? No again. No doubt he just left, fed up with waiting. She should have arrived hours ago, but there was a railroad workers' strike in Belgium, bad luck, which forced the night train to make a huge detour, and of course Nerea missed her next connection. Now she was alone in the Göttingen station with a heavy suitcase and the fatigue of more than twenty-four continuous hours of travel. She gave a satisfied look around. Soon all this will be familiar to me.

She knew Klaus-Dieter's address by heart. During the trip she'd practiced the pronunciation of the street and the house number. She knew how to count to one hundred in German. More: during the trip she'd studied vocabulary. Two hundred and fifty-five words she selected. Words she imagined common. In sum, names for this, for that, and some thirty adjectives, numerous verbs. And today, during the morning and early in the afternoon, she reviewed the list several times. Who knows, maybe German will someday be my principal language. Mine and the language of my three half-blond children, two girls and one boy. She had foreseen everything and she was smiling: each one with one hazel eye and one blue. Oh yes, the boy would be named after his deceased grandfather.

She had the address written on a piece of paper: Kreuzbergring 21. Before he left for Edinburgh, Klaus-Dieter explained in a letter filled with charming errors that the street was behind the university, about a fifteen-minute walk from the station. Where is the university? No idea. The rain wouldn't let up. Nerea felt unable to pronounce the word Kreuzbergring in a comprehensible way. And even supposing she did say it more or less properly, how was she going to understand the explanations that would follow? So instead of asking for help from a local, she got into a taxi and showed the driver the slip of paper.

She almost fell asleep in the cab. Wishing to gather impressions of her new world, she stared through the window at details of the city as if she were looking through a cellophane veil of fatigue. This was only normal: the whole night, she'd barely slept because of the *click-clack* of the train. An entire night of nods, heat, the not-desired company of five unfamiliar, breathing, barefoot bodies in their respective bunks, she resting, thank heaven, on the highest, and an old man right below Nerea, wearing an undershirt, who after half an hour was snoring like a worn-out cowbell.

The taxi ride took less than five minutes. Nerea couldn't manage German marks, so she wouldn't have to count her money, she paid with a one-hundred-mark bill and thinks, she's not sure, she gave a tip that was too large. Otherwise, the effusive helpfulness of the cabbie, who carried her suitcase up to the entryway, and filled her ears with words that were no doubt friendly but which she didn't understand.

Nerea paused at a row of not especially clean mailboxes. There it was: Klaus-Dieter Kirsten, written with a felt marker on a slip of paper, next to two other names. And she imagined the hand of the German mailman as he placed those letters of hers overflowing with tenderness, nostalgia, and loneliness in the mailbox, letters written during the torrid Zaragoza summer. She took her perfume out of her bag and dabbed herself twice, clutching her suitcase in two hands as she climbed creaking wooden stairs, one flight, two, three. On the landing, near the door, was a piece of furniture attached to the wall, a kind of backless dresser with five shelves packed with shoes. Nerea rapidly smoothed her hair before ringing the buzzer, already prepared for the embrace, the kiss on her mouth.

Shortly after, some footsteps came across the wooden floor. The door opened. A girl with short blond hair stared, first at Nerea's eyes, then at her suitcase, and then again at her eyes. The girl, chubby, thin lips, made not the slightest attempt to converse with her or to invite her in. Putting on her best smile, Nerea asked:

"Klaus-Dieter?"

The girl repeated, corrected?, aloud the name, with her face turned toward the interior of the apartment. And without waiting for the person she called to appear began to scold in her language. Nerea didn't understand a single word but it was as if she understood. The expression tending toward rage, the voice loud: that's universal. Klaus-Dieter immediately appeared at the door. Timid, ashamed, serious, he stuttered out a hello devoid of charm, empty of affection, and formally extended his hand toward Nerea without stepping out to the landing to hug her, without inviting her in. He was wearing enormous, worn-out indoor clogs. And his wool jacket with elbow patches was unlikely to make a princess fall in love.

For the first and only time, the girl spoke to Nerea. In English.

"He's my boyfriend. And who are you?"

By then Nerea had understood the meaning of the situation. She first answered the girl in English, carefully pronouncing her words, without losing her calm:

"I thought he was my boyfriend."

Without waiting for an answer, she turned to him, looking him straight in the eye:

"Do I have to sleep in the street?"

It was obvious that the girl was driven wild by the attempt of a strange woman to communicate with her partner in a language incomprehensible to her. Now she was shouting more loudly and pointing a threatening finger at Klaus-Dieter as she slapped his arm. She went back into the flat howling. Klaus-Dieter was now alone with Nerea. Not even then did he have the decency to step out onto the landing. In his poor Spanish he said:

"I sorry for problem. You wait here please. I call Wolfgang, okay? He big apartment for you sleep."

As he slowly closed the door, he nervously repeated in defective Spanish, faintheartedly, his face close to the diminishing open space, that he would call his friend Wolfgang. Nerea remained on the landing for about a minute. Do I laugh, do I start crying? What the hell do I do? Through the partition, she could hear the groans of the girl. You keep him, sweetie. He's my gift to you.

She went down to the street with her heavy suitcase. Had everything been, from the very beginning, a misunderstanding? Perhaps he didn't know how to express himself, perhaps I misunderstood. But why, how, and the letters, and his insisting I visit him, and the address, and my arrival date, and. The guy, is he simply a jerkoff? In other words, did I fall in love with a jerkoff? I got on the wrong side of my own mother because of a jerkoff? Isn't it that the jerkoff here is me? And now what do I do, so tired I'm falling down, in a foreign country?

It was still raining, though not as hard, and the clear area from before had become larger and was almost over the city. Night had yet to fall, but it would come soon. She asked in English where the city center was. She started walking in the direction pointed out to her. As she crossed what seemed to be a university campus, she would have sworn that a boy walking in the opposite direction who passed about thirty feet away from her was Wolfgang. She wasn't sure and didn't bother to find out. These boys were one thing in Zaragoza and something else here.

Her eyes were shutting from sleep, she was thirsty, her legs hurt. She wasn't thinking about anything. Not thinking about anything? I swear, in those moments nothing at all mattered to me. On the other hand, she studied the facades in search of the saving word. Which word? What else? Hotel. On one of the many streets she found one. Expensive, dear, clean, filthy? She was unconcerned. As soon as she got into the room, she emptied a bottle of mineral water. That was her dinner. It wasn't even nine o'clock when she went to bed. She instantly fell asleep.

83

A Bit of Bad Luck

At eight in the morning, after an invigorating shower, Nerea went downstairs to have breakfast. As she filled her plate, she thankfully remembered *aita*. The fact is that without you I couldn't allow myself these luxuries. Yesterday's disappointment left her with no sorrow whatsoever. How strange, no? Shouldn't she be in a state of despair? To what do we owe this sensation of relief? She figured it out: the boy she was attached to in Zaragoza was not the one she saw yesterday in the clogs and wool jacket. The accent of the other Klaus-Dieter when he spoke Spanish seemed delightful; the accent of yesterday's idiot, even if it was the same, was disgusting. What about those three half-blond children? Actually, my dear, they're no problem, because other, different ones will be born in their place. We come into this world like people who've won the lottery. John Doe, congratulations, it's your turn to be born; you get a body, a place is found for you in a uterus, and finally a person we usually refer to as mother gives birth to you. She took two croissants. Careful, Nerea, happiness is fattening. The tray holding jars of marmalade and honey of various sorts looked excellent.

In a good mood, rested (she'd slept eleven and a half hours straight through), clean, breakfasted. And now, what? She opened the curtains, looked through the window of her room: clouds but no rain, low buildings, a garbage truck, two workers wearing safety vests working in a ditch. This looks like a small town to me. The possibility of running into Klaus-Dieter and his chubby girlfriend (your vegetarian lover betrayed you: he ate shrimp and langoustines) or any of the other German students from Zaragoza was sufficient argument against exploring Göttingen. Go home? A nice humiliation that would be! You're back so soon? Yes, it's that.

Before departing, she lightened her luggage. Out with the CDs, books, Pilar sweets, the box of Frutas de Aragón, the four little bottles of beer like the ones she and he drank in the Zaragoza bars, and other gifts for the love of her life. Out as well with the thick Spanish-German dictionary, the grammar book, the exercise manual with answers at the end, and other things that, in truth, only had meaning in case of a prolonged stay in Germany. The hotel staff will be overjoyed when they see that Santa Claus's niece has spent the night in this room. And the lock of blond hair, the relic of an amorous passion, venerated even yesterday, today hated as a repellent excrescence (Nerea, don't be mean!), she flushed down the toilet.

The receptionist gave her a map of Göttingen so she reached the nearby station easily. Her intention: get on the first train that would take her to an interesting city, so she could experience new places; in sum, so she could wander around Europe before going home and getting her law degree, find a job, get pregnant, let's see.

At one in the afternoon she was in Frankfurt. She booked into a downtown hotel, less expensive than yesterday's; ate a dish of *penne all'arrabiata* in an Italian restaurant—it tasted wonderful; went shopping, strolled about in no particular direction. In a two-story bookshop she sat down to leaf through an atlas. With the book open on her lap she studied possible routes. To Munich first, that for sure. There she would decide whether to go to Austria or to Switzerland, or to head for Freiburg and the Black Forest. If I go to Switzerland and the mood takes me I'll go on to Italy.

Later on she called her mother from the hotel room. She would have told her that she'd gone from being a lovebird to being a tourist; but Bittori was uncommunicative, so dry and brusque that Nerea lost her desire to bring her up to date on her adventures, and after reciting to her mother a few ambiguous remarks about weather and food, she said goodbye. She didn't even tell her where she was calling from. And Bittori never asked. She didn't even ask how everything had gone or even if the trip had been okay. She asked nothing.

The sun came up on October 12. A clear day and a pleasant temperature were an invitation to stroll around Frankfurt. And with that idea, her camera, and a map of the city Nerea left the hotel at midmorning. The next day she would begin a new phase, so that in each city on her program she would spend two nights and one full day, unless the place dazzled her and she extended her visit. She would decide en route. After all, she was doing her own thing, just as I intend to do until the day I die. And insofar as the expenses are concerned, she took them as a reward for getting her degree. Since my mother did not see fit to reward my efforts, I'll give myself this trip, and let them try to take it away from me.

Calm, taking photos, she looked for the river and accidentally found the house where Goethe was born. She read the prospectus the hotel staff had given her: reconstructed after the war. She didn't go in. Why, when it wasn't the real thing? Even so, standing opposite the famous facade she lusted after culture and history. And to balance the day, she divided it into an instructive morning, lunch in a place frequented by locals, and an afternoon of fun and shopping.

Having made her decision, she turned left at a corner, spotted the tower and reddish walls of Saint Peter's Church, and went there. She entered the church, which didn't seem particularly great to her, and as she left, instead of walking directly to the river, she followed the street ahead of her because she decided to visit at all costs the modern-art museum. She saw art, or what's called art today; she walked all the way around the cathedral with the idea of photographing it from different angles, bought sunglasses, and then, her feet tired, in need of food and drink, reached the river and walked over a bridge that passed through a narrow, tree-covered island, to the opposite side.

That bridge took her to the Sachsenhausen neighborhood. The people at the hotel reception desk had recommended it to her. And on the margin of a city map she'd jotted down the name and address of a restaurant. There she ate in a place with long wooden tables she shared with others. Roasted ribs and French fries accompanied by a tangy sauce that later had her belching. She satisfied her thirst with local cider, sweeter and less turbid than the cider served in her hometown bars. There was one thing she didn't like. What? Well, that she attracted masculine stares, the stares of young men sitting at her table who tried to catch her eye, who smiled at her and raised their mug and glasses and tried several times to engage her in conversation. She paid them no more attention than that required by elementary norms of courtesy. I'm sorry, dear friends, but I've used up my quota of Germans for this lifetime.

She had her coffee elsewhere. Where? Sitting on the deck of the boat she took for a tour of the Main. The autumn sun paused pleasantly on her face and she, out of pure delight, simply had to nap, her arms crossed, paying no attention to the explanations in English and German coming from the loudspeakers, though from time to time she did peer at the rows of buildings on either side of the river. At times, she felt the gentle passing of a breeze over her face. It was a kind of cool caress that deepened her sense of well-being. No one spoke to her except, briefly, the woman who served her coffee and a complimentary cookie. She was alone with herself, without thinking, without suffering, without remembering, free. A moment of perfection. She opened her eyes: the blue sky stretched over the city. She closed her eyes: she again felt herself lulled by the hum of the engine.

And later, once again on land, everything twisted. Not immediately: Nerea had time to look into shop windows, go into stores, try on clothing. But at five fifteen in the afternoon, a bit of bad luck induced her to take this street rather than that other street, and she ran into the scene. About a hundred yards ahead she saw people clustered; a bit beyond them, above the line of heads, a streetcar was stopped, also two ambulances were stopped. And Nerea, overwhelmed by curiosity, a fateful decision, went with her shopping bag in hand to see. Several policemen kept passersby from getting too close to the accident. Nerea managed to find her way to the edge of the sidewalk. Her heart gave such a strong leap that for a moment she thought she was going to faint. She immediately walked away, but it was too late because she'd already seen what she should not have seen, the physical image of death, the dead body inert, covered by a blanket that left the feet exposed, resting next to the stopped streetcar, next to the emergency people who were doing nothing because there was nothing to do.

The map of Frankfurt, without which she could not find her hotel, was trembling in her hands. *Aita, aita,* she was saying. And some people turned to look at that girl with a foreign aspect who was walking quickly, crying and hiccuping. At the reception desk, she could not keep her voice from breaking when she asked to be awakened at five a.m. A taxi brought her early to the airport.

84

BASQUE MURDERERS

It was Xabier's idea that the three of them should go to Zaragoza. He made such a convincing argument that he and his parents left early so they could make the best use of the day. He drove. A Sunday at the end of January of that fateful year, but at the time they had no idea of what was to come. The reason, excuse actually, for the excursion: Real Sociedad was playing in the Romareda at five against Real Zaragoza. Xabier told his father that Aránzazu's work schedule had been changed. There was nothing to be done. She couldn't go with him. He didn't like traveling alone, and it was a pity to waste the two tickets for which he'd paid good money. Txato, before answering, looked toward the window. He briefly contemplated the only thing visible: clouds. And he said he'd be delighted to see a Real match, even if they were a bunch of slackers.

Bittori did not look in any direction; with no hesitation she joined the other two. Soccer? It didn't matter to her. She hadn't seen Nerea since the end of the year. In passing, this controlling mother, this curious mother, wanted to take a look at Nerea's new apartment. She knew the old one, over in Torrero, which was quite far from the university. That one looked fine to her. Clean and all that. But she hadn't examined the present flat. We'll see, we'll see.

On the way, father and son agreed to meet with Nerea somewhere other than her apartment. If they didn't, according to Xabier:

"She's going to think, and rightly, that we're going to be doing a white-glove inspection of the furniture."

"Listen here, cleanliness hurts no one."

Txato kept silent.

"*Ama*, she lives with two roommates. We can't burst into her flat like an inspection team."

"I never said anything about that."

"And suppose she has a personal guest?"

"She's known since Thursday we're coming to see her."

"Maybe I'm not being clear. When I said 'personal guest,' I meant an intimate guest."

"That's her problem."

And the fact is that come what may Bittori had to go up to Nerea's apartment. Why? Because she was bringing her a jar of cuttlefish in its ink she'd made herself, preserved tomatoes, fava beans (at two hundred and eighty for two pounds, they should play music), Tolosa beans, and other things she enumerated, she by herself in the backseat, counting off with the tip of her index finger each thing on the fingers of her other hand.

"You two will understand that I'm not traipsing around Zaragoza loaded down with food."

Txato interrupted:

"If only you'd told me before, we could have come by truck. Do you think your daughter is going hungry or what?"

"You keep quiet."

"Why should I keep quiet?"

"Because you're not a mother and because I'm telling you to."

They stopped at the Valtierra service station at Bittori's request. And while she went to relieve herself of her urgent problem, father and son got out of the car to stretch their legs. One, without enthusiasm, suggested they go into the café. The other was for losing as little time as possible, so they stayed where they were. Txato, still a smoker at that time, lit a cigarette.

"On Friday, they stuck chicken guts in our mailbox. It was an awful mess. And I'd better not mention the stink. *Ama* told me not to tell you anything. So you wouldn't worry."

"If I could I'd make you leave the village today when we get back from Zaragoza."

"But you can't. We cleaned out the mailbox. They can't make me give in. It's people from the village. Who else? Kids. But one thing, if I catch one of them he'll be in big trouble. You know what my lawyer's like."

Xabier took a look around.

"Why don't you bring the business here. Look at these fields. How peaceful. You'd have the highway right at hand. You'd be in Euskadi in the twinkling of an eye. How about it?"

Txato imitated his son's exploratory gaze.

"A bit dry, all this."

"But here you can breathe."

"There's air in the village, too. And employees and mechanics and truck drivers, don't forget that. Around here I know no one."

"I'm not going to be a pain every time we're together. I'm only saying that if anything serious happens to you or to *ama* I'd never be able to forgive myself."

"Come on now, don't be such a worrier. How right your mother was. I don't know why I told you anything."

At ten they were in the outskirts of Zaragoza. The weather turning cold (fifty degrees according to an outdoor thermometer), but dry. On López Allué Street they couldn't find a parking space so they double-parked. And finally, despite all they said, the three of them went into Nerea's apartment. She herself insisted they come up.

Going up the stairs with her daughter, Bittori made a little joke.

"I'm warning you. These two are here to see if you've got everything clean."

Once inside, Txato:

"And your roommates?"

"They aren't here. Some weekends they go home to their parents."

The whole family. The last time the four of them were together, when was it? New Year's Eve. And when would they be together again?

Never, but they don't know that. Bittori would remind Txato of that fact sitting at his graveside.

"It was the last time the four of us were together, remember." She imagined the dead man under the slab contradicting her: "Of course I'm sure. The next summer, Nerea was with us for only a little more than a week. And at that time, Xabier went on vacation with that nurse who was trying to snare him. Do I have a good memory or what?"

Txato made a gesture typical of him. Bittori interpreted it as a way of marking his territory. Just like a dog who leaves his mark with urine wherever he goes. Except that Txato did it with money. And even though he tried to cover it up, she, who sees even where she doesn't see, and if she doesn't see smells it, caught him red-handed hiding two five-thousand-peseta notes in Nerea's desk, under a book, all the while thinking no one was watching him.

"You were a splendid man, husband. Especially with your daughter, your favorite, who came to neither your funeral service nor your burial."

Nerea showed them the flat. Here's this, here's that. Also, though they didn't go in, her roommates' rooms. They, a benevolent inspection team, followed her around the apartment making approving gestures and comments. And Txato, who seemed moved to see his daughter in a flat, a city, a setting unknown to him, said the same thing on three occasions:

"If you need anything, all you have to do is ask."

The third time, Bittori cut him off:

"You're turning into a parrot."

The four went out. Nerea led them, hanging on to her father's arm. And they made their way slowly, chatting all the while, along several avenues—along Gran Vía, down the full length of Paseo de la Independencia, which at those hours was practically empty, and the Tubo, where the scent of fried food hung in the air. Txato, even though it wasn't yet noon, was already asking where there was a good restaurant. The four entered the Basilica of Our Lady of the Pillar. Bittori kneeled to make a few prayers to the Virgin. She was still practicing her faith. The others waited outside for the woman who'd once wanted to be a nun, Sister Bittori. They laughed, accomplices in the joke, now that she couldn't hear them. And in the plaza there were people wearing Real Sociedad insignias. Some, seeing Xabier's white-and-blue scarf, waved hello.

Txato:

"Who are they?"

"No idea."

The food? Good. The only one who complained was Bittori when she saw the check, convinced that:

"Because of our accents they saw we were from somewhere else and they said to themselves: we'll make them pay more."

The other members of the family disagreed, unanimous in the opinion that if we compare this to San Sebastián, we paid an acceptable price. On the street, Nerea confirmed that Zaragoza (rents, food, entertainment) was a city where you could live well on less money than in other places.

Bittori wouldn't relent:

"Well, it still seems to me that they pulled a fast one on us."

In the Plaza de España, Txato and Xabier took a cab to the soccer stadium. The women first made their way to an ice cream parlor on Paseo de la Independencia, then, walking back to the apartment where Bittori, just let me do this, insisted on cleaning the windows. And once she got started she went on to the bathroom and the kitchen furniture. And this despite the fact that in her opinion, which she expressed repeatedly, the flat was clean.

"The problem is that I just can't sit still."

Father and son meanwhile took their places, standing in a curve in the stadium, mixed in with the Donostia fans. The players had yet to take the field, but the insults began to rain down on them: ETA criminals, shitty Basques, Basque murderers, and more in that line. They answered by singing and by waving *ikurriñas* along with white-and-blue banners, and they said to one another:

"Pay no attention. We're here to cheer on the team."

Txato was upset:

"I didn't expect this."

"It's okay, *aita*. There are stadiums where it's much worse than this. You just have to get used to it and turn a deaf ear."

"They're close to us. From where they are they could pelt us with rocks."

"Calm down. All this is part of a ritual. And since we're going to win, we'll get even watching the smoke pour out of their ears."

Zaragoza won 2–1, thanks to a penalty kick made by their goalkeeper. With ten minutes left to play, the score stood at 0–0. The win soothed the spirits of the local fans, who now limited themselves to giving the finger to the white-and-blue aficionados. Outside the stadium, the sky dark now, Xabier stuffed his scarf into a coat pocket.

"I'd rather not look for trouble, see? We've got to watch out."

It took them a good while to find a cab. Finally, they got one that took them to López Allué. They said goodbye to Nerea. Kisses and hugs at the entryway. And Txato on the verge of tears:

"Daughter, if you need anything, all you have to do is ask."

They went to the car. The two side mirrors were broken, and there were dents—from kicks?—on the chassis. Well, at least they could go home. Xabier, en route:

"Don't think I hadn't considered this."

"Considered what?"

"That it was risky leaving a car with San Sebastián plates parked on the street all day."

The windshield wipers were also broken. They discovered that later on in the Imácoan service area, where Bittori asked to stop because she urgently needed to go to the restroom.

Txato, having lit a cigarette, to Xabier:

"Don't worry about the repairs. I'll take care of it."

"You're not going to take care of anything."

"I'll pay."

"You're not going to pay."

They went on like that until Bittori came back to the car.

85

THE APARTMENT

Txato delegated the purchase of the apartment in San Sebastián to Xabier, who in turn passed it off to Aránzazu after she said to him:

"Just leave this to me, *maitia*. I'll talk to my brother. He knows all about this stuff."

What Txato didn't want was a palace that would cost millions.

"I've never lived in luxury and I don't need it now."

"You weren't thinking of sticking *ama* in some dump, were you?"

"*Ama*, outside of the village, isn't going to be comfortable anywhere."

"I suggest you think of the apartment purchase as an investment."

Txato did not have a clear idea about moving to San Sebastián, at least not in the near future. Xabier insisted: the move was urgent. And Nerea, too, as soon as she learned about the graffiti on the village walls. Those two have come to an agreement behind my back. Txato gave in or pretended to give in to avoid any confrontations with his children. He let time pass, he simply did nothing, although, yes, he did go along with the purchase of a flat in San Sebastián, but he said they'd only leave the village if things got really bad.

"Well, they are bad."

"Worse, then."

And he added that you don't abandon ship just because there's a storm. Only when it's sinking. And just suppose that they make your life impossible? Well, in that case Txato and Bittori would move to San Sebastián, where he would figure out (calmly?), we'll see, the way to move the business to La Rioja or any other place near Euskadi so he wouldn't be too far away from the majority of his clients.

"And your sister would be able to use the new apartment because she's going to have to live somewhere when she gets her degree."

Aránzazu's brother in short order told Txato about two purchase possibilities. Both were privately owned flats the price of which could be negotiated with the owners. The brother expressed himself well, had a good appearance (although too much hair gel), and concluded:

"Two bargains, believe me."

If Txato didn't buy them, he would. According to Aránzazu, that's how her brother made a living—selling dear what he bought cheap. And then, using his earnings, he would spend three or four months in a row traveling abroad.

Txato thought the idea of not working all year round from Monday to Sunday was strange. Xabier signaled to him not to make any comments about that. Txato changed the subject.

"Okay, okay, we'll have to take a look at them."

He suspected Bittori would reject both apartments, but he brought her along so she could give her opinion. She thought the one in the Gros neighborhood, spacious, with views onto Paseo de la Zurriola, was cold, too exposed to the humidity of the sea. And besides, a sixth-floor. No way. The other, on Urbieta Street, made a negative impression on her because the parquet was worn, the ceilings were too high, the noise—just by chance there was drilling on an upper floor, from which she deduced that the partitions were not thick enough. And there was street noise.

"I can smell exhaust fumes from here."

Txato knew it all along: God himself couldn't figure that woman out. At home, she went on and on about the need to leave the village, to bring the trucks to some peaceful place and lose sight of all these evil and envious people surrounding us here, and no sooner did he initiate some plan so they could move away, Bittori smashed it to bits.

Some time later, Aránzazu brought news of a new apartment for sale. She quoted her brother's words. That it would be crazy not to take advantage of a bargain like this. More bargains. This time father and son agreed to leave Bittori out of the purchase process. They walked up a piece of the Aldapeta hill.

"Just wait, you'll see that *ama* will have all kinds of objections to this climb."

They examined the flat. A fourth-floor with elevator; the property of three heirs who did not get along with one another and who were in a hurry to translate into cash the inheritance they were now selling cheap. And Aránzazu's brother, representing Txato, bought it for a considerable sum; nevertheless, a much lower price than the one the three owners could have asked if they'd been smarter.

Bittori wasn't present for the handing-over of the keys. But finally it was impossible to hide the purchase from her any longer. Aránzazu picked her up in her car and as they waited for her to arrive, a beautiful afternoon, nice temperature, Txato and Xabier went out onto the balcony. The island of Santa Clara was visible. Urgull was visible, as was the peak of Igueldo along with a stretch of sea under the yellow afternoon sky.

"This is pretty. *Ama* will like it."

"I don't think you know her. Even if you were to give her the Alhambra in Granada, she'd rather stay in the village."

Father and son rested their elbows on the railing. In front of them was a horse chestnut tree that needed only a yard more of growth to reach the fourth floor. They looked at the nearby buildings, the parked cars, the deserted street. A calm place, a well-to-do neighborhood.

"Do you change the route you take to work?"

"Sometimes, if I remember."

"You promised you would."

"Those people, if they want to get you, they'll get you. I can go this way today, that way tomorrow. But sooner or later you're going to pass the spot where they're waiting for you."

"What worries me is that you're so calm."

"Do you want me to be nervous?"

"Not nervous. Alert."

"Look, Xabier, the bastards who telephone to insult me and threaten me—the ones who paint the graffiti—those I don't worry about. They don't scare me. They're just jerks from the village. What do they want? For me to be scared at home or for me to move somewhere else. I'm not afraid of them. *Ama* thinks they're trying to make life impossible for us because we're not poor anymore. They knew us in tougher times, when we were like them, poor bastards. Now they see we have a son who's a doctor, a daughter who's at university, they see me with my trucks, and they can't stand it, so by one means or another they try to make my life bitter. They think that all I have I've robbed. So, having worked the way I've worked has screwed us."

"These people are bad: all the more reason to take precautions."

"Bah, let them come. I'll invite them to dinner, see? And since they've been busting my balls, this year I'll skip my contribution to the festival. They're going to learn who Txato is. I'm more of a Basque than all of them put together. And they know it. Until I was five, I didn't speak a word of Spanish. A blast of machine-gun fire destroyed my father's leg (may he rest in peace) while he defended Euskadi at the Elgueta front. Even when he was old, he gritted his teeth every time the pain came back. What is it, does it hurt? we would ask him. Fuck Franco and his whore mother is what he'd answer. And they had him in jail for three years, that they didn't execute him was a miracle."

"*Aita*, what are you trying to tell me with all this? Do you think ETA cares about what happened to your father?"

"What the hell, don't they say they're defending the Basque people? Well, if I'm not the Basque people, then who is?"

"*Aita*, please! You have to understand that ETA is, how should I put it?, an action mechanism."

"If you want me not to understand you, just keep talking that way."

"ETA has to keep acting without interruption. They have no other choice. A long time ago they became automatons. If they aren't causing damage, they don't exist, they have no other purpose. This Mafia style of theirs has nothing to do with the will of the individuals in ETA. Not even the chiefs can stop it. Sure, they make decisions, but that's mere appearances. There's no way they can stop making decisions, because the terror machine, once it gains speed, can't be stopped. Understand?"

"Nothing."

"All you have to do is read the newspapers."

"I think you worry too much."

"They killed Yoyes in cold blood and he was one of their leaders. They don't have any pity for their own and you want them to pity you because your father fought fifty years ago in a battalion of *gudaris*? Come on. What worries me is how naive you are."

"My boy, I haven't studied like you. Everything you're saying sounds like philosophy to me. I can't understand how a bunch of guys who claim to be defending Basques can kill *euskaldunes*. They want to build Euskadi, so they kill Basques? It's different when they kill Guardia Civil officers or people from outside. That's bad, but within the logic of the terrorist, it makes sense."

"There is no such logic. It's nothing more than delirium and more likely nowadays a business."

"We've got to let things cool down. Time will go by, they'll forget me. You'll see. They can screw themselves. Look, the only thing that annoys me is that I can't ride my bike on Sundays. But aside from that, they don't even mess up my hair."

Aránzazu's car slowly came up the hill. The first to get out was Bittori. She looked up, a petulant expression on her face. She spotted her husband and her son out on the balcony. She didn't wait until she got to the flat. From the street, not worrying that she could be heard from other buildings:

"I know you bought it without asking me."

Txato, in a low voice, to Xabier:

"This is the one who scares me. How mean she can be!"

86

He Had Other Plans

He heard the rain from bed. It seemed to whisper: Txato, Txato, wake up, get out of bed, time to get wet. Perhaps to postpone the moment when he'd have to expose himself to the bleak weather, or because the washed-out light filtering through the curtain made him lazy and made his eyelids heavy or because his appointment with a client from Beasáin had been canceled, he didn't have anything much to do at the office that afternoon, he extended his siesta beyond his usual time. What does that mean? That he slept over an hour without dreams or worries while other times twenty or thirty minutes of sleep was more than enough.

Sitting on the edge of the bed, he felt an almost irresistible desire to light a cigarette, but he didn't. An addiction he'd overcome, though from time to time the temptation would come back. One hundred and fourteen days ago he smoked his last cigarette. He kept count and every day a balloon of pride expanded around it. There were a few cases of lung and esophagus cancer in his family. Also in Bittori's family and in the village as well. He didn't want to run the same risk. He had other plans.

He put on his shoes. What am I going to do? A superfluous question to ask this man who would live in his office if he weren't married. Besides, you've got to keep an eye on things. You can't trust the employees or leave them alone. And if the phone rings, what then? Suddenly he was in a hurry. A hurry? Remorse for having put—for just over an hour—bed before work. And he smoothed out the bedspread as best he could so that at night Bittori wouldn't be complaining.

In the living room, the newspaper, open to the crossword puzzle, along with his reading glasses was still on the table. If he'd slept less, he could have tried to finish it. The fucking Philippine island four letters long, which he's run into before, and he never remembers its name. A common fruit in the valleys of the Pyrenees. No idea. And sitting on the sofa with her arms crossed, Bittori tiredly opened her eyes as she heard him coming. What time was it?

"Just coming on four."

"Get stuck in the sheets or what?"

Disappointment in the kitchen: there was no coffee, only some cold dregs in the pot left over from breakfast. Txato grumbled to himself. Bittori, who sleeps without sleeping, who never completely slept even at night, heard him.

"I'll make you a fresh pot."

He knows he wanted it the usual way, already prepared so he wouldn't have to wait and he could dash out to work. Not without a touch of spite, he lied and claimed he was in a hurry.

"I'll make do with what there is."

So he drank that black liquid directly from the pot. Bittori was still stupefied with sleep on the sofa. The bitterness of the disgusting mud made Txato grimace. Finally, after muttering a curse, he went to the doorway. He didn't go over to Bittori and she didn't come over to him. He said goodbye, not dryly but baldly.

"See you at dinner."

Bittori nodded her head affirmatively, as if to say: I'm responding to your words, but I'm really fast asleep, I don't feel like talking so make do with this nod. And she closed her eyes again.

On the stairway, Txato turned on the light. The afternoon's dark gray got into everything, chewed away colors, made shadows thicker. And when he got to the entryway, he peered into the mailbox. He wasn't looking for mail. The mailman had already come by in the morning. Sometimes filth or papers with insults and threats written on them were stuffed into the mailbox; although for two months now they'd left him in peace on that score. On the other hand, just days before, his name inside a target appeared on the wall of the music kiosk. A neighbor woman told Bittori in whispers. Know what? If she hadn't told her, they wouldn't have found out because for a long time now neither of them has gone to the plaza. It was, well, it was an attack. But it's one thing for them to annoy and offend you and another that the people of the village (okay, some of them) demand your death.

He left the entryway but didn't go all the way out. He'd taken a step outside the house. He immediately stepped back. Rain and gray. There was no traffic: well, yes, just then a van was driving off at the bottom of the hill. No one was walking on the street despite the hour, but you wouldn't believe how it was pouring. Standing in the doorway, he was tempted to go back for his umbrella. Bah, she'd be sleeping and anyway there's only a short distance between here and the garage. Txato tried to gather strength to start running. However, before he did he took a confirming look at the clouds without the slightest hope the rain would stop.

There was the banner above the street, stretched between his balcony and the street lamp opposite. PRESOAK KALERA, AMNISTIA OSOA. From time to time they hang one up, not always with politi-cal content. Some are related to the village festivals. A few years ago, they asked him, he consented, unwillingly; but listen, it's not a good idea to have bad relations with the people in the village, especially the boys. So every so often they come with a ladder and tie the end of a banner to his railing. And why his balcony and not the one just up the street or the other down the street? Because of the fucking streetlight, which had to be right opposite.

One day when they'd filled his mailbox with filth he charged up the stairs in a rage. Bittori, seeing him in a fit, cursing his head off, with a knife in his hand, asked him where are you going.

"To cut the strings on the banner."

She stopped him cold.

"You're not cutting anything."

"Out of the way, Bittori, I'm pissed off here."

"Well, just calm down. I don't want more problems than we already have."

Bittori wouldn't step aside, and Txato, though cursing and swear-ing, throwing his beret against the wall, had to accept the fact that once in a while they tie a banner to the railing on your balcony.

Just as he did as child, he counted:

"*Bat, bi, hiru.*"

And he headed for the garage. Running? Only the first three

steps. Then he slowed down. Actually he was neither walking nor running, the one so he wouldn't spend more time exposed to the rain, the other so he wouldn't slip on the wet pavement. What he did was adopt a trot appropriate to a barrel-assed man of a certain age. After all, he had spare clothes at the office.

And how it rained. Damn. As if the clouds had been waiting to empty themselves all at the same time on top of him. In the gutter a stream had formed. It still hadn't struck four and it seemed night had fallen on the village. And at this time of day it's still early to be turning on the public lights.

An agile, blurred figure emerged from between two cars parked next to the opposite sidewalk. His hood kept Txato from seeing his eyes. He was coming toward him, but not directly. Who was he? An individual a bit over twenty, some village boy who was protecting himself from the pouring rain by lowering his face. Jumping, he reached the sidewalk behind Txato. Txato kept going and only had a little way to go to reach the corner.

Then, behind his back, very close to him, a shot rang out.

And then another.

And another.

And another.

87

Mushrooms and Nettles

For a long time, disturbing rumors about the financial state of the factory had been circulating. They talked about, they said that. And Guillermo began to sleep little and badly for fear of losing his job. His son, Endika, was two and a half at the time. And the girl had yet to be born but was on the way. He and Arantxa, comfortable in their simple, lower-middle-class life with hopes for prospering in the future, were happy or that's what they believed/said. Which, in the opinion of both, is the same thing, but all of it would come tumbling down if they lose their economic footing.

In bed, late at night:

"Without my salary from the paper mill, tell me how we're going to make do."

"Maybe you'll be lucky and they'll fire other people."

"Who?"

"Lower your voice, you're going to wake up the baby."

"Of all the people in the office who would they have a greater reason to fire if not me?"

"The older ones, so they can keep the younger ones. And if they do fire you, you'll find something. Meanwhile we'll make do on my salary. It isn't much, but every little bit helps."

"It isn't enough, Arantxa. I've tallied up our expenses, and it just isn't enough. And soon there will be four mouths to feed in this house."

She'd hidden from him an incident that took place at the shoe store. What incident? That the woman who owned the shop, dryer than dry, had scolded her for not waiting longer to become pregnant again. And then from a fellow worker she learned that the owner had been criticizing her behind her back. She decided not to tell Guillermo so as not to increase his worries.

Guillermo, in a bad mood, anguished, could not drop the subject:

"Forget about vacation, about a new car, about everything."

"Calm down, my friend. You'll see that we'll get ahead if we fight side by side."

"I wanted us to be happy, but it wasn't meant to be. Can we ever be happy in this world? I don't know why we were born."

"Please, Guille. Perfect happiness only happens in the movies. You're asking too much."

"I'm not asking, I'm demanding. I'm a hardworking, serious man. I do what I'm told to do. I do it well. I want my share, my modest share."

A few days later he came home earlier than usual. He dropped his termination notice on the kitchen table and hugged Endika against his chest for a long while. A two-year-old baby and he with no job, with no future prospects: a good-for-nothing.

"Don't say that."

"That's what I am. A superfluous man. The factory keeps on running just fine. The typical poor slob who needs his wife to give him some change so he can have a drink in the bar."

Guillermo: a man adrift. Mornings, he would go out into the hills, he'd return with wild strawberries, nettles, mushrooms. Sitting at the kitchen table he gave lessons: about whether the mushrooms were edible, if you can brew a tea with the leaves. What he was doing was convincing himself he was feeding the family. He'd be out at dawn, transformed into a mountaineer with his boots and his backpack for collecting. And he brought back everything, apples as well, who knows from what orchard, and hazel branches he cut into tiny pieces to build a castle for the child. Other times, weather permitting, he took his rod to fish at the mouth of the port or on the Jaizquíbel rocks. He came home silent, glancing around angrily, fond of strolling around alone, and you couldn't disagree with him because he'd blow up. And when Ainhoa was born, worse still.

The first time he held her in his arms he told her:

"Bad luck, little girl. You were born into a poor family."

Often, he would break his long silences to blurt out remarks like that, always with a hint of resentment in his words. Arantxa kept quiet, long-suffering, resigned, so she wouldn't make things worse. Sometimes she just couldn't take any more. What the hell, I have my feelings, too, you know. And she would express her opinion, trying not to get angry.

"Your pride has taken a hit."

"What would you know about it, dumbass?"

That was the routine. Vulnerable, aggressive, bitter. And no more cutie, sweetheart, darling from before. In bed, she gave in. Because, of course, if you deprive him of that, he'll flip out and beat me up. They had routine sexual encounters, with no pleasure for her, and a rapid release for him. Tenderness: zero. But not the opposite, either, not at all. Their sex was more or less a formality that produced a sad slapping of stomachs.

A few days after he lost his job, Guillermo was already depressed and was already talking that nonsense about jumping in front of a train. And later, he started making predictions in the presence of his children, who were still so young, predictions about a bleak future in an affected tone that the children couldn't understand and weren't spoken so they would understand. He'd suddenly bend over Ainhoa's crib, and paint, in a speech meant for adults, an atrocious panorama of privations. And he did the same with Endika. He'd suddenly lift him in his arms and say something negative, ill-omened, sorrowful.

He lent even less of a hand with the household chores than he did when he worked at the paper factory. Why? Because he felt it was humiliating for him to vacuum the floor, wash dishes or windows.

"I wasn't born to be a housewife."

"Really, and I was?"

It was in situations like that when Guillermo would seriously blurt out that stuff about throwing himself onto the train tracks or swallowing a bottle of bleach. Arantxa would fume, her teeth clenched, her eyes moist, but she could also see her children, so tender, so fragile, and she chose to hold it all in. Depending on the day of the week, she would unburden herself with a workmate. She would tell her this, that, disconnected details, but not everything, not the most intimate things, since they were not linked by a close friendship. Girlfriends, real girlfriends, she had none. The couple had distanced themselves from their hometown friends. In Rentería, Arantxa only got together from time to time with neighbors and, more frequently, with people close to Guillermo. Also, she'd rather lose an eye than tell anything to her mother. Miren knew that her son-in-law was unemployed. It never occurred to her to ask if they needed any help.

The people Arantxa did open her heart to were Angelita and Rafael. She even revealed to them that their son threatened to throw himself in front of a train and drink bleach. This is what they said. Rafael: don't worry; Angelita: you keep calm. And they helped with unlimited generosity. For a year, Rafael paid their monthly mortgage bill; every week Angelita went to the supermarket with Arantxa and paid for everything (the shopping cart piled high) with her credit card. And Guillermo? He knew nothing about it. He made do with walking in the hills picking mushrooms and talking to himself.

Until, ten months after he'd lost his job, when something unexpected happened. On one of any number of afternoons, as he pushed Ainhoa's pram across the Plaza de los Fueros, Guillermo ran into his friend Manolo Zamarreño. Manolo saw him, waved to him to stop, and came over smiling, carrying a message of hope and something else. What? A telephone number written on a slip of paper. He was to call immediately, today if possible, because there was a job open in the offices of the Mamut superstore and they were urgently looking for a replacement.

"Call. Maybe you'll be lucky, but hurry up."

And thus it was that Guillermo abandoned the nettles and mushrooms in favor of numbers. He earned less than he did in the paper factory, but he was earning something. In a matter of days, his good humor returned along with a desire to live. He became affable, chatty, generous, and asked Arantxa to forgive him for the bad months he'd put her through, but that she should please understand that during the whole time he'd been suffering overwhelming anguish.

"Two children, unable to feed them, you understand."

When he got his first paycheck, he treated her to dinner in a restaurant. And the next day, home from work, he brought her a rose. Arantxa put it in a vase with water without making much of a fuss because Ainhoa, as usual, was crying in her room. And the next morning, as she was leaving the house, Arantxa threw the flower into the garbage.

88

BLOODY BREAD

It was Thursday, June 25. Guillermo and Arantxa had managed to schedule a week of vacation at the same time. They couldn't always manage it, but this time they did. By then, both of them working, they could allow themselves a few modest indulgences. And since the children were a little older (Endika was six, the girl about to turn four), they could travel with them without the inconveniences and limitations of traveling with babies.

Yesterday the four of them went to the Biarritz beach; today they were going to have dinner at the house of *amona* Miren, and tomorrow, well, we'll see. They had a secondhand car. Not great but good enough for their needs.

That Thursday's problem: they had no bread for their midday meal. That problem is easy to solve. Guillermo—if only all our disasters were like that—offered to step down to the bakery immediately and buy half a baguette. Jovial, he asked, with the front door open: who wanted to go with him. To separate the children, who never stopped fighting, Arantxa said:

"Take Endika, he's driving me crazy."

And Guillermo (let's go, champ) brought him along.

A Thursday they'd never forget, a Thursday that could have cost the lives of father and son. They wouldn't have been the first and they wouldn't have been the last. Holding hands, they passed next to the black scooter holding hidden explosives. Guillermo, I swear to God, recalled it. Arantxa:

"Are you sure?"

He was absolutely certain, because it annoyed him to see the moped parked on the sidewalk and he made a comment about it to his son, something like: that's something you shouldn't do, that's bad, or anyway something like that.

A few yards beyond, at the door of the bakery, he ran into Manolo Zamarreño, who was coming out with a baguette. It was five, maybe ten minutes after eleven. And Manolo, as he exchanged a few commonplaces with Guillermo, messed up Endika's hair as a kind of caress.

On the street, right next to them, his escort was waiting.

Escort? Yes. His friend José Luis was murdered in a bar in Irún, and he took over as legal counsel to the People's Party in the Rentería Town Council. Guillermo, at home, when he found out:

"You've got to have guts to take on a job like that."

"Guille, if I were the kind of woman who goes to mass, I'd be praying for him. May the Almighty protect him. And if he's removed, I hope you won't think to take his place, okay?"

"Me? Are you nuts? I want to live."

Manolo had only had the position for a few days and, to begin, they burned his cars. They insulted him, they put up degrading posters, they painted his name inside a target. But he wouldn't back down. He declared to the press: "I was born here and I'm staying right here." And indeed, he did stay a week, another, not many, until his fatal moment that Thursday in June when he stopped off to buy his daily loaf of bread and stopped to chat for a few seconds with Guillermo.

One was entering the bakery, the other leaving. After the brief conversation, Manolo made his way along the sidewalk with his guard behind him. Guillermo was waiting his turn at the counter. Suddenly there was an awful roar. Endika fell to the floor. The noise of broken windows. And Guille quickly put him back on his feet. Then, paternal, nervous, falsely calm, he said:

"Don't cry, don't move from this spot, I'll be right back."

And he went out.

The scooter exploded right in front of a doorway marked number 7. Manolo? He didn't see him. He did see his escort, sitting on the ground, his back resting against a car, his face blackened. Vehicles damaged. A momentary, thick, smoky silence. And then the first voices, a woman's screams, people (neighbors) who gathered to stare.

And Manolo?

There he was. Where? Between two cars, stretched out on his own blood, lots of blood. He was black from the explosion, which seemed to have caught him full on. Almost naked, wearing only his underwear and shoes. On his wrist, a watch. And the bread he just bought split in half.

With the child in his arms, don't look, don't look, Guillermo had no choice but to pass close to the place with the wreckage and the dead man and the escort sitting on the ground before the police came and the street was cordoned off.

"Did you look? Tell me the truth."

"No, *aita*."

"Swear?"

"I didn't see anything."

On the street, he met Arantxa, who was running toward him as fast as she could, her eyes alarmed.

"Are the two of you all right? What happened?"

"Manolo."

"What?"

"Manolo."

He opened his mouth and all he could say was that: Manolo.

"Manolo Zamarreño?"

He nodded, the boy still in his arms. There was no need to explain. Arantxa, in a stupor, slapped her palm against her forehead. And they didn't say another word. They hastily went up to the flat, where she in a fit of panic had left the iron on and the baby alone. The first siren soon began to howl, getting closer and closer, already in the neighborhood.

Just then, the telephone rang. Angelita. What happened? What an explosion. Arantxa, with the children standing there, told her without telling, said it without saying it, but telling her she wasn't alone and her mother-in-law, fully understanding the situation, assured her she understood.

Guillermo installed his grief and indignation in the kitchen like someone driving a post into the ground, sitting at the table, his head

in his hands. The rest of the family went into the children's room.
They followed their mother in intimidated silence. Their father was
wailing. Arantxa brought the transistor radio with her. With her ear
pressed to it, the volume turned down, she heard a confirmation: a
bomb attack in the Capuchinos neighborhood, one dead.

She arranged Ainhoa's hair. She rearranged it. She did it all over
again. There were still two hours left before they would go to her
parents' house for dinner, but she needed any task to fill in the time
and to recover her calm and to give herself over to the relief, the
enormous relief, *mmm*, to be with her children, to touch them, to
feel them, to know they were safe and sound.

Endika, sitting still at her side, grabbed on to the waistband
of her skirt the same way you hold on to the rail in the bus. His
mother walked a few feet to get some hairpins out of a dresser
drawer and the boy followed her silently. When she came back it
was the same, without releasing his hold on her skirt.

Through the partially open door came Guillermo's diminishing
sobs, deeper now, not as high-pitched as before, barely audible, broken. At the beginning, Arantxa, to protect her children, was tempted
to close the door. She instantly changed her mind. Let them hear,
let them learn, let them know what kind of country they're growing up in.

In the kitchen, Guillermo was talking now, ranting about politics. He disparaged nationalism, which poisons consciences, he was
saying, which put so many young Basques on the path of crime. And
he distributed guilt: to the *lehendakari* with their forked tongues,
to the hypocritical bishop, to the *abertzales* up to their ears in the
blood of others, and to all those evil, spying neighbors who tell
ETA at what time the victim passes through this and other places.
Resentful, he mocked them:

"Well, here you have a Spaniard you can knock off without any
problem when he goes to buy bread. He's a father with a family?
Well, he should have thought of that before he became a legal counselor. Yes, but he's in a pro-Spanish party that oppresses us and
besides we've got a conflict here."

Jesus, Mary, and Joseph, is that guy going on like that with the
window open? Arantxa decided to find out.

"People will hear you."

"Let them hear me."

The kitchen window was closed.

"You don't live alone, you know."

"A ferocious hatred has taken hold of me. It's as if the nettles were pricking me inside my body. Arantxa, honey, tell me something that will end this hatred that's tearing me apart. Hating is the last thing I want in life."

"Let it all out, protest, go ahead, but don't shout. Outside the house, not a word. Okay? Don't make trouble for me. We'll go to the funeral, we'll express our sympathy. We don't have to sacrifice our manners."

"In the condition I'm in, I can't go to your parents' house, understand? You go with the kids."

"Of course you're not coming. All we need is for you to mention my brother and start arguing with my mother who's such a fanatic nowadays."

"Her poor boy in jail, a first-class killer."

"Okay, enough. You promised we'd never bring up that subject in front of my parents. The children have a right to visit their grandparents."

At about one thirty, Arantxa left the house with the children in their Sunday best, clean, fresh smelling. Ainhoa went over to give her father a kiss. Endika, behind her with a fearful voice:

"Are you sad, *aita*?"

"Very sad."

"Because of what happened to Manolo?"

"So you did look."

"But only with one eye."

He hugged the boy, hugged Arantxa, walked them to the door, watched them go down the first flight of stairs, and when they turned around to say goodbye he blew them a kiss.

89

The Air in the Dining Room

If Miren only knew. If she only knew what? That when she wasn't there her grandchildren sometimes called her the bad *amona*. All of Arantxa's efforts to make them change their opinion were useless. She realized: they'll probably be quiet to please me, but I can't keep them from feeling what they feel.

Even little Ainhoa, about to turn four, sensed a hint of rejection in *amona* Miren, which in the case of Endika, depending on the situation, was open hostility.

Exactly the opposite was true for Angelita and Rafael. In part because they spent more time with the children and saw them every day. They had more options to offer them amusement and affection. They were mild mannered by nature, generous, funny, and devoid of Miren's harshness and severity. In truth, Miren didn't behave that way because of bad faith but because that was her nature. She had always been that way, harsh in temperament, impatient with her own children, her husband, in reality with the whole world.

As far as *aitona* Joxian was concerned, well, to put it bluntly, the man mattered little. Okay, nothing. As a general rule, Ainhoa and Endika saw him once or twice a month; but when they saw him he would sit in his chair, motionless, dull, silent, without the energy to suggest activities, and often it was as if he really weren't there.

Once already, Endika asked his mother why *aitona* Joxian spoke so little.

"Maybe he doesn't have anything to say."

"*Aita* says it's because *osaba* Joxe Mari is in jail."

"Maybe."

The Thursday of the Rentería attack, when Arantxa got to her parents' house with the children, *aitona* Joxian still hadn't returned from the Pagoeta, which explained why Miren was sulking.

She opened the door. Joy? Not a jot. Actually, just the opposite, that unwelcoming, annoyed glitter in her eyes.

"I thought it might be your father. He still hasn't come home from the bar. I'll have a little talk with him about that."

Then she turned to her grandchildren with curt tenderness, her worn-out slippers, her apron spattered with blots of moisture. And doesn't it occur to her to fix herself up, put on a good face, say something to the kids to make them laugh and make them feel welcome, have a little present for them, a surprise?

She doesn't lean over far enough for the children to kiss her without some difficulty. And she reproaches Endika because he came in without saying hello.

"Cat got your tongue or something?"

She asks the girl who combed her hair so badly, and to Arantxa:

"Isn't your husband coming?"

"He didn't feel well."

She doesn't bother to ask if he's ill, if he's hurt himself, nothing. Why is that? She just can't bring herself to do it. If you were to dig around in her intimate thoughts, she'd defend herself, saying that all her life she's done nothing but work. There was the proof: the table set, the whole house saturated with the delicious smell of food, the heat of the oven. Once again, she'd worked like mad. The whole morning. Even in the afternoon, when she made the béchamel sauce for the croquettes. She was certainly worn out, convinced that no one ever thanks her, no matter what she prepares.

And her obsession with Basque. That vindictive, demanding attitude, testing the grandchildren every time they visited. She asked them questions to make them speak the language of the homeland, and they spoke it naturally, easily, though with the limitations that went along with their age. And it wasn't unusual that if Guillermo was there, the children would pass into Spanish without realizing it.

Miren would stop them, cutting, rigorous:

"We speak Basque here."

Which was a form of pretending Guillermo wasn't really there. Often she spoke to him through Arantxa.

"Ask your husband if he wants more chickpeas."

And Arantxa, what else?, would turn to Guillermo and translate the question. Guillermo never lost his sense of humor.

"Tell her to supply me with eighteen units."

Joxian walked in scratching his ribs, a sign he'd been drinking. Miren doesn't care if he drinks a lot or a little. All she needs is to see him make that unconscious scratch even once to become furious. She held back because her daughter and her grandchildren were present. Even so, in the dining room, Arantxa could hear her mother scold him in a low voice as he took off his shoes. Because he was late? But it was 2:25 and they agreed they'd start eating at 2:30. Or might it be because she hoped he'd arrive earlier to lend a hand? But when has this man ever lent a hand in this house?

The air in the dining room, above the table covered with appetizers, how much work!, seemed stretched tight. There was a tension there like some elastic substance that could snap at any moment. The children, who in their way also must have noticed the disturbing phenomenon, were politely silent, expectant, holding in— mother's orders—their demand for the croquettes set out in perfect order on a porcelain platter.

Wearing slippers, doing his best to cover up the fact that he'd just been reprimanded, *aitona* walked into the dining room. Before, when he entered the house, he'd said a short hello, given a bland kiss. And as soon as he started to take his usual seat, with his back to the balcony door, Miren asked him if he'd washed his hands. With his grandchildren and daughter present, he didn't argue but went like a little lamb to the bathroom to wash his hands and keep peace during the festivities.

With all five seated at the table, they chewed and drank, Joxian, like the others, drank water, since you've had more than enough wine this morning. And in the air, between the heads bent over the plates, that airy-human tension persisted, perceptible even to the children, who on other occasions had shown themselves to be lively but who now were strangely silent. But the story of the day was in the air and everyone knows it and no one mentions it, why ruin a family gathering? They don't see one another that frequently. Anyway, within an hour or an hour and a half we'll be gone.

It was easy to see that the matter he'd heard about in the Pagoeta was burning inside Joxian. In a free moment, when Miren carried the dirty plates to the kitchen and was getting clean saucers out of the cabinet, he asked Arantxa, in a low voice, who the dead man was. She answered in a similar whisper:

"A friend of Guille's."

"Are you serious?"

"The man who helped him find work."

"You've got to be kidding."

Miren, loaded down with plates, back in the dining room:

"What are you talking about?"

"Nothing at all."

Nothing at all? The tension in the air increased. One more tug and it splits. But suddenly there was custard, celebrated with joy by the children, and an opportune action by Joxian, who gave a fifty-cent piece to each grandchild. Peace and dessert. Then he almost ruined everything. How? He grabbed the remote control without thinking. He had already pointed it at the television set and was just about to turn it on. The result would have been, Rentería, bomb, a death in the Capuchinos neighborhood. Arantxa managed to stop him in time by means of a discreet kick under the table. It's possible Miren detected it. Or had she suspected already that there had been a secret communication between father and daughter?

When she was alone washing dishes in the kitchen, at a random moment she called Endika, six years old, into the kitchen using some meaningless pretext and then the air exploded. Miren managed to wheedle out of the child the reason his *aita* hadn't come to dinner. And the boy, who had not been taught how to dodge the astuteness of his *amona*, told her the truth. From his child's point of view, but the truth. Among the other things he said were:

"Some bad men killed a friend of my *aita*."

"He's been crying all morning."

"What kind of a man cries all morning?"

The question upset Endika, who back in the dining room told his mother. Joxian reacted reflexively. He tried to hold his daughter back, grabbing her by the wrist, but his aged, arthritic hand lacked the necessary agility. Arantxa got up from the table with an energetic, angry impulse, went straight to the kitchen in the same humor, and there took place what could not be stopped from taking place.

"Listen here, what did you say to the boy?"

"And you two, what did you say to him about bad men?"

Those contorted faces, those angry stares, those words that fly like bullets.

Arantxa, aggressive, challenging, started speaking in Spanish.

"It's only by a miracle that I didn't lose a son and that I'm not a widow. Both of them passed by a bomb half a minute before the explosion."

"Here we aren't fighting against innocent people."

"Oh, and are you fighting? Should I congratulate you for what happened this morning?"

"That counselor, that friend of your husband, was in the PP."

"Are you insane? Above all else he was a good person and a father with children and a man with the right to defend his ideas."

"He was an oppressor. And let me remind you that you have a brother rotting away in a Spanish prison thanks to good people like that."

"That son you're so proud of: they proved he committed bloody crimes. That's why he's in jail, because he's a terrorist. Let me repeat that: because he's a terrorist, not because he speaks Basque, which is what you told Endika once. You're a liar, worse than a liar."

"How dare you speak that way about my son, a *gudari* who's risked his life for Euskal Herria?"

"Well, why don't you go to the houses of your son's victims and explain that to them. I'd like to see you look them in the eye."

"Those are your husband's friends. Let him go."

"Why do you never call Guillermo by his name? Does the word burn your mouth? I suppose that for you he's an oppressor."

"He's not much of a Basque."

"He was born here, before I was."

"Hernández Carrizo and he doesn't speak Basque. If he's a Basque . . ."

At that point, Arantxa decided the conversation was over. She passed by Joxian, who had been observing the argument from the doorway, gloomy, unable to intervene.

"Out of the way, *aita*. I don't know how you've been able to stand her all these years."

"Daughter, don't go."

Arantxa called the children, picked up their shoes so they could put them on out on the landing or even on the street, it's all the same to me, and without saying a word or saying goodbye, she kicked them out of the flat. Miren maintained a resentful, hard, stony silence in the kitchen, and Joxian, staggering with sorrow, tried to stop his daughter and his grandchildren.

"Don't leave, please."

It was useless. Five years passed before Arantxa spoke to her mother again.

90

FRIGHT

At that time, helmets weren't popular. Are you kidding? Maybe some jerk who wanted to look like a professional rider would wear a little one, but that's about it. They wore caps, sunglasses, and bicycling gear because that way no one would recognize them. One afternoon, Joxe Mari rode through the village checking each side of every street out of the corner of his eye. Patxo, the previous afternoon, had challenged him:

"Got the balls?"

"Well, there's not much to brag about. My village is filled with people riding bikes. No one would stop to look."

And that's how it was. No one on the street seemed to realize that the powerfully built bicyclist wearing a cap and dark glasses was Joxe Mari. He rode along the street that borders the plaza, passed right in front of the Pagoeta, went down to the river. From the opposite bank, he saw his father (his beret, the checked shirt, his back bent, how old he looks) busy in the garden. Patxo asked him what he was looking at.

"Nothing. I wanted to say goodbye to my village."

Unless it was raining, the two of them preferred bicycles to cars or public buses for reconnoitering throughout the province in search of objectives, their principal, not to say their only, business at that time. The bikes enabled them to go to the same place separately but without losing sight of each other. And they set a signal so that the one who rode ahead could warn the one behind about any danger. Distance: not less than fifty, not more than one hundred yards. And when they entered a town they never went into the same bar. At the end of their excursions, first one, then the other would bring up his bike in the elevator. Raised on the rear wheel they fit. In the flat, they met with Txopo, who, free of duties, imitated or tried to imitate the normal life of a student.

In the weapons courses, they'd been taught to be extremely careful. A light on in a room at any hour of the day meant that one of them was in the flat and that there were no problems. All the lights out and a coin in the mailbox, left there by the last one out: flat empty. If the coin wasn't there: careful, don't go up. The same if a towel was hung halfway out of a window or there was light in all the rooms or the doormat wasn't in the agreed-upon place. One time, Patxo forgot to follow the rules. If Txopo hadn't stepped in, Joxe Mari would have punched him.

They were on the move, a workday, cold, gray, but without rain or wind, through the Andoáin, Villabona, and Asteasu zone. More than anything so they wouldn't be inactive and because after a bleak week of winter, the weather finally invited them to take a ride on their bicycles. They could do nothing else but pedal here, there, because their communication link had given them a note from the bosses ordering them to do nothing until they received new orders. This led them to conclude that Donostia was preparing some huge *ekintza* and that they shouldn't interfere or that the organization had come to some kind of secret agreement with the government.

Joxe Mari was depressed.

"We're a second-class *talde*."

And Patxo tried to raise morale.

"Don't worry. When the opportunity arises, we'll strike a spectacular blow and they'll start respecting us."

"Sure, as long as the state doesn't drop its drawers. Because if the armed struggle ends all of a sudden, tell me what we will have contributed."

"Don't be so pessimistic. I think it will go on for a few more years."

In Recalde, near the funeral parlor, almost at the end of the day's excursion, Joxe Mari stopped as he'd done on other occasions to give his comrade a few minutes' lead, and then he started out and

when he arrived, what the hell is that guy doing standing there?,
he was surprised to see Patxo outside the entryway. Upstairs, the
lights were out.

They gathered at the building's corner.

"The coin isn't there."

"Let's get out of here."

Not losing any time, they went toward the El Antiguo neighborhood. They didn't stop until reaching a short time later Benta
Berri Plaza. There: what do we do now? They decided, first, to
calm down, then make a plan. It was now completely dark. It was
nine p.m. Fewer and fewer vehicles passed through the zone. They
hadn't noticed the cold while they were pedaling, but now it was
settling in their bones. And Joxe Mari, whose big body was beginning to note the lack of dinner, swallowed down the last bit of
the chocolate he usually carried on those excursions, along with
bananas and apples.

One thing was clear: at night, in bicycling gear on the street, they
would attract too much attention.

"Dressed like this, where are we going to go?"

"And with this cold closing in and these light clothes we're going
to freeze if we stay outdoors."

"Son of a bitch."

"I think we should go back and take a look. It could be that
Txopo forgot to leave the coin in the mailbox. It happened to me
once."

"If he was careless, I'll bust his ass."

"Let's go."

The apartment windows were still dark. On the deserted streets,
there were no suspicious movements, though who the hell knew
if there were *txakurras* hiding in some parked car or behind the
curtains of some nearby apartment. They left the bicycles leaning
against the post of a traffic light. They were breathing out a dense
mist. Patxo was shivering and didn't hide his fear of getting sick.
Joxe Mari tried to keep warm jumping up and down and doing
gymnastic exercises. He grumbled constantly. Lots of curses, lots of
swearing, but he couldn't break out of his indecision.

Patxo, practically frozen, his nose red, had an idea:

"It's enough if one of us goes up. If they're waiting for us, they'll grab him, and the other can escape."

"You're an asshole. If they grab you it's just as if they grabbed me and vice versa. Just from the beating the cops will give you in the cell, you'll be singing the Our Father in Latin, Russian, and in a ton of languages you don't even know."

The freeze was settling in, the clothing inappropriate for the time and place, the hunger, cold, and fatigue, it all pushed them to make the decision they finally made. They went up to the flat separately, one in the elevator, another up the stairs. The doormat? In its place. A good sign. But careful, the door wasn't locked. So what? They'd already put a key in the lock. Patxo, who was first in, turned on the vestibule light. Silence. They'd released the safety on their Brownings, because without hardware they go nowhere. For that reason they wore fanny packs whenever they went out on their bicycles.

They found Txopo, what did they do to you? on the floor in his room, his cheek resting on a puddle of vomit, conscious and doubled up.

"If I move, it's worse."

Suspicious, naive, it took them a few seconds to understand that their comrade's problem was some physical breakdown. Until he said, where the hell were you, you bastards? they kept aiming their pistols at the walls, the ceiling, the dresser, at Txopo himself. Why hadn't he turned on the light? Idiots, because he couldn't move. Couldn't they see that for themselves? A terrible pain hit him the moment he came into the building. Suddenly, in the elevator. Using his last bit of strength, he managed to enter the apartment. Where did it hurt? Here. And here was a thigh, but also his back and then one side of his stomach. So, what do we do? He threatened to shout for help if they didn't get him any. They tried to get him up. Impossible: it hurt even more. And the vomit and the stink.

"We've got to clean this up."

"You clean it up."

Joxe Mari signaled to Patxo to follow him into the kitchen. They whispered with the door closed.

"We can't let the emergency medical people in here. Too risky."

"Sure, but we have to do something right away, because if this guy drops dead we'll have an even bigger problem."

Txopo's moans from the floor of his room drove Joxe Mari mad. He cut off the talk, now authoritarian, the boss, resolute:

"Change clothes or put on a jacket, get the car, and wait outside the entryway."

"Are you nuts? We've got the boxes holding the weapons in the trunk."

The look in Joxe Mari's eyes eliminated argument, that gaze is like a blowtorch. Patxo: if this ends badly it won't be his fault. He got dressed quickly, grumbling the whole time. As he left the flat he muttered something or other about responsibility. And Joxe Mari looked into Txopo's room to say: be cool, don't worry, hang in there, and things like that. Then he rapidly changed clothes.

From the kitchen window, he saw the Seat 127 supplied to them by the car-theft cell driving up along the street. The trunk filled with boxes. Shit: on the one hand, they send you weapons and material for making bombs, on the other they tell you nothing. They had planned to use the cover of darkness to put all of it in sport bags, carefully bring it up to the apartment, examine it, and decide what they should hide in the cache and what not to hide.

There was no time to lose. Joxe Mari tugged Txopo's feet to get his face out of the puddle of vomit. Disgusting. My *ama*, she's great in situations like this. He used a towel to clean him up a bit. He went out to the stairway and pressed the elevator button. The neighbors? In their flats. He saw little of them. He could hear a television set somewhere. Casually, he picked up his comrade as if he were a sack. Looking through the peephole he confirmed that no one had come up in the elevator. Then he went out with Txopo over his shoulder, went down to the entryway, and as soon as Patxo signaled that the street was deserted he quickly loaded his suffering, groaning comrade in the rear seat. He sat up front and gave the order to get moving.

"Where to?"

"Just go straight. I'll tell you."

They left Txopo in an ambiguous position—sitting? doubled up?—on a bench in the Ondarreta gardens, near the highway that goes up to Igueldo. Patxo was worried about his comrade.

"He's going to freeze to death."

Joxe Mari said nothing until they crossed Matía Street, when a public telephone caught his eye.

"Stop. I'll get out here. You go back to the flat."

First of all, he entered a nearby bar. And while he drank a beer, he looked through the telephone book. Later, using the pay phone, he called the Red Cross Hospital, whose facade was visible on the other side of the street. Not giving much of an explanation he said:

"Listen, there's a boy here in great pain."

He said where, and when he was sure they'd understood him, he hung up. Barely a minute later, an ambulance passed by, heading, he supposed, to the place he described.

Two days went by, two long days without any news of Txopo. Suddenly, the door buzzer rang. They jumped up. Could it be him? From the intercom, they heard: open up. They learn that the same night he went into the hospital he managed to pass the kidney stone that was torturing him out in his urine. Just to be sure, they kept him in the hospital for twenty-four hours under observation. He asked his comrades to forgive him for being a nuisance and thanked them for their help. What about celebrating? How? He offered to cook a grand meal for them. Squid in its own ink, hake, whatever they wished. Joxe Mari:

"You remind me of my *amatxo,* because she always makes fish for supper."

Txopo told them he'd buy the ingredients and take care of everything. All they needed were their appetites. Okay, kid. He went right into his room. On the floor, still: the filthy towel and the now dry puddle of vomit.

91

THE LIST

Through the usual channels, they received the list of names and addresses. Businessmen from their zone, restaurant owners, shop owners, people with property who hadn't settled accounts with the organization. A total of nine. The note had no instructions attached to it, nor were any necessary. One name caught Patxo's eye.

"Here's one from your village."

"We call him Txato. He's got a trucking company alongside the river, just above my father's garden. I didn't know he was one of the ones who doesn't pay. Son of a bitch!"

Txopo's suggestion: since the objective is known and easily found, why not begin with him? It would be a matter of finding out what his haunts were, what time he's there, if he's accompanied, and all that.

Patxo saw an opportunity to make a joke.

"Maybe Joxe Mari doesn't like the idea. Since the guy's a neighbor in his village, maybe the thing changes a little."

"What changes? Are you retarded or what? It doesn't matter to me where the enemy's from. Even if he were a family member. If we have to eliminate him, we eliminate him. We don't discuss orders or disagree with them."

They agreed that he wouldn't take part in the spying since that would put both his security and the cell's at risk. But he did go to the village with his comrades the first night, in the Seat 127. Without getting out of the car, he explained things to them. This is the business. He lives here, on the second floor. There where it says Arrano Taberna, you'll have to ask for Patxi. And then he limited himself to supervising the actions of the *talde* from the San Sebastián flat. So there would be no doubts:

"When we're done, if we decide to strike, I'll be there."

With his habitual caution, Patxi, who never took part in actions, who was never arrested, even though he was the boss of the *abertzale* gang in the town, found them a place to stay through a third party. Then he informed them he was no longer involved in the matter and asked them not to come into the Arrano. Joxe Mari, understanding:

"He's right. Everybody there knows everybody else. Two outsiders would attract a lot of attention. Let's just have one of us stay, that's enough."

Patxo set up shop in the village for a week. It was Txopo's job to travel each day from one flat to the other with information, messages, notes, but he always slept in the San Sebastián apartment, where he also wrote up the reports, for which Joxe Mari was profoundly thankful since he just couldn't deal with words.

Seven days were enough for Patxo to gather enough information. More than enough, he said. And he brought his comrades up to date on his investigation.

"It turns out that the guy who lent me the room works in the objective's company."

"What's his name?"

"Andoni."

"I know him. He's a troublemaker from the LAB union."

"With his help I've accumulated a ton of details related to the capitalist's life. Andoni by the way can't stand him."

Joxe Mari, disagreeing, reminding them of the rules:

"It seems to me that the armed struggle is not a matter of standing or not standing someone. It isn't our job to knock off people we don't like. If that were the case, I'd have to put four bullets into Andoni. Why? Because he's a bad animal. It's family inheritance. In the Franco days, his uncle Sotero would hang a Spanish flag on his balcony and now he's in Herri Batasuna. I just don't trust guys like that, what can I say? As a person, I like Txato more, but it's obvious I have to act against him because the liberation of Euskal Herria demands it."

"Okay, okay, don't get so pissed off and let Patxo make his report."

"Which I was about to do. The capitalist changes his route a lot but he doesn't have many options to chose from. He drives. Andoni, who told me lots of things about him, confirmed that he has no fixed work schedule. You can see he's the boss; he comes and goes whenever he feels like it. But remember this: the first thing he does when he leaves the entryway to his house is to walk to a garage that is not on the same street as his house but on the next one, around the corner."

"Now tell me something I don't know. As a kid, I was in that garage any number of times."

"In those forty or fifty yards between the entryway and the garage it would be easy to grab him, whether he was coming or going. Especially between the garage and the corner, which seems to me a terrific spot for an *ekintza*. The street is narrow, quite dark, and almost no one, not people or cars, passes through. Kidnapping him would be nothing."

"Sure, but we don't have the infrastructure. Where would we put him? And besides we couldn't do that without consulting the higher-ups. So forget the kidnapping. Txato would recognize me with his eyes closed, just from my voice. Forget about that idea."

"I didn't say we should kidnap him, just that it would be easy to do it."

"Okay, explain yourself better."

"He never goes to bars. Andoni had already given me that detail. Before he did go. Now he doesn't because the *abertzale* gang in the village has scared the shit out of him. And he gets up and out early in the fucking morning. Between one and one thirty he usually goes home to eat. In the time I was in town there was only one time when he didn't show up. Andoni says that depending on which day of the week it is he sometimes eats in the office. He goes back to work at about half past three, give or take a minute. On Monday, he went back at a quarter to four. As always, he walks to the garage and picks up his car, a red Renault 21. Carrying out an *ekintza* at the end of the day would be, I think, complicated. The day before yesterday it was already eleven and the guy still hadn't turned up. I took off."

"Escort?"

"Nothing. I tell you this objective is ripe for the picking."

Joxe Mari didn't see the matter quite as clearly, he shook his head, doubted: first we should, we'd have to. His comrades had no difficulty whatsoever in demolishing each one of his objections. That the business was a piece of cake: a minimum of logistical effort, victim with no escape route, a village where even the street-lights are *abertzales*. An easy place to get away from. Who could ask for anything more? No problem. He went on bringing up this and that, with his scruples and his what-ifs. They: Patxi had prepared the situation with a campaign of graffiti and persecution, and that:

"At this very moment, not a soul would lift a finger to help the businessman."

"Shit, what I don't want is for Patxi, Andoni, and the others to think that they're the godfathers of the *ekintza*. We're not their hunt-ing dogs. Who can guarantee that afterward they don't go around town saying this, that, and the other thing, and what if there's a mole among them? They've given us their help. Fine. But the when, the where, and the how, we'll decide here among ourselves."

"Okay, if that's the problem, we can just let some time pass before we strike."

"That's what I was talking about, that the way you described it the thing was way too hurried. And the fewer people involved, the better."

That's exactly what they did. Through the end of spring, the whole summer, and part of autumn, they were busy with other names on the list. One of them was the owner of a metalworking shop in Lasarte. As soon as they saw that the objective, a fat man about sixty years old, usually parked his car in a vacant lot near the shop, they thought: why don't we use a car bomb? More than anything to experiment, because they hadn't built a single bomb since taking the weapons course. It was high time they made their first. So, the next day, Joxe Mari visited the site and in the twinkling of an eye placed the bomb in the car's undercarriage. From there, he and Patxo went to spend the afternoon in a nearby cider bar and calmly wait for the explosion. They bet drinks:

"If the bomb goes off before eight, I win."

Their explosion made no roar, so nobody won the bet. After nightfall, they left the cider bar. What a strange thing. Maybe the shop owner walked home or biked, or someone picked him up, or who the hell knows. When they got to the flat they asked Txopo.

He didn't have the faintest idea. They turned on the TV, then the radio, and finally the citizens band radio to pick up police communications. Nothing. The next day they expected the news from one moment to the next. All in vain. They let another twenty-four hours go by before approaching the place. This time they went by bicycle. The fat man's car wasn't in the lot. Maybe on the other side of the shop or behind it? No. Conclusion: the bomb hadn't gone off.

Joxe Mari, in a bad mood, recalling the words the instructor always repeated:

"It's not the bomb that failed but us."

And together they reviewed the steps they'd taken in preparing the bomb. In the course, they made a point of saying they had to test things. They had. What the hell could have happened?

Patxo:

"Know what I think? I think the fat guy smelled something fishy and called the *txakurras*."

"I don't think so. If the TEDAX had intervened, the action would have reached the newspapers. I think the bomb fell off the car and is in some ditch somewhere."

To purge any self-doubts, they agreed to blow up the fat man's shop. Not even the foundation would survive, God damn it. And Joxe Mari and Patxo went over one morning to study the place and see where they should place the bomb so it would cause the most damage possible. But instead of the metalworking shop they found an empty building. Not even the sign over the entrance was left. They realized the owner must have freaked out and closed the business or moved it to a safer location. The bomb they'd built, with fifteen pounds of ammonal and a timer, they used for someone else on the list, the owner of a bar. The media highlighted the magnitude of the destruction. No regrets about the wounded.

92

The Child She Loved Most

He was told he had a visitor. There they were once again: his mother's eyes behind the glass. In them, there is an initial uncertainty, an expectant tremor until they see him arrive, big, apparently healthy but without hair. Then they soften; they become clear, caring, maternal; she seems to retain a touch of youth despite features more and more marked by the ravages of age.

Aita rarely comes to the prison, once or twice a year. She attributes it to how tiring the long bus trip is and to the fact that your father is no longer the man he once was, and she launches into an attack against the state (Miren never says "Spain") for its policy of scattering prisoners far and wide. But Joxe Mari knows that his mother would rather Joxian not come. He gets overcome with emotion. Every time he comes he starts crying; his son, so many years, I'll die without seeing him free. And she thinks all that hurts Joxe Mari's morale.

Besides, they usually fight during the trip. Over nothing. Even before they start, at home, she criticizes the way he shaved or she tells him he's got hairs growing out of his ears; then, on the bus, she warns him, scolds him, reproaches him right in front of other prisoners' families. That's her way of grinding down his pride, and he gets mad, madder, and finally counterattacks awkwardly, livid, weak. It's the same on the trip home. So it's better he stay behind.

Joxe Mari expected the usual: complaints about how uncomfortable the trip was, the inhumanity of scattering prisoners all over Spain, the heat of Andalucía. Why do they have to punish the family members of the prisoners? And also, the usual gossip about the village, the recent deaths, Arantxa's slow rehabilitation.

But today was different. Anyway, careful with what we say, they feel they're being watched. They speak in Basque, but the guards probably secretly record their conversation and have a translator. So they don't go near politically delicate subjects or, if they absolutely have to, they speak in whispers with circumlocutions and shared expressions, and half-words. After so many years, they've become experts in that kind of communication. They understand each other, get along well, need only an exchange of glances to fathom each other's thoughts. And she, so sparing all her life in expressing her emotions, once told him point-blank, with the glass between them, that he was the child she loved most.

And what was today's news? Suddenly, ten minutes into their conversation, Miren starts speaking mysteriously, she mumbles, she says. What? That there's a problem keeping her from sleeping at night. And seeing her expression of worry, Joxe Mari understood this was one of those matters it was better not to speak openly about in the meeting room. *Aita?* Arantxa? Miren shakes her head. The crazy woman? She nods affirmatively. Again? She nods again while she brings her hand to the glass and shows him the words written in tiny letters on her palm: "She wants to know if it was you who shot her husband."

"Tell her to go to hell."

"She won't give up."

"Why do you let her get near you?"

"She didn't speak to me. I'd like to see her try! But, *aita*, you know how he is. He lets her and she checks to see when she can catch him in the garden. And then Arantxa writes things to her on her iPad whenever they meet. And I tell Celeste: when you see that lady, get away from her. But, my boy, no one listens to me."

She covers up by bringing up an unimportant matter. If the food has been all right lately.

"They always use too much salt."

Meanwhile, Miren showed her son the palm of her other hand. "What should we tell her?"

"Because if we don't say anything, she's going to drive us crazy. I already told you I can't sleep."

"Aren't there a couple of boys in the village who can put a scare into her? In my day, things like that never happened."

"The village is not what it used to be. Now you don't see graffiti or posters the way you did before. The whole thing's a little dead."

"Shit, there's got to be someone. Speak with you-know-who."

"Since he closed down the tavern we hardly ever see him. It seems no one wants to know anything. Now all the talk is about the peace process and that we have to ask the victims for forgiveness. Forgiveness my ass. Aren't we the victims? There are fewer and fewer of us, we've been abandoned. And if you open your mouth, they ask us to apologize for terrorism."

In his bed, Joxe Mari stared at the piece of sky outlined by the square of the window. Blue afternoon sky, crossed by the stream of white smoke from a plane. I can feel myself sinking. His stomach was burning. They say they put drugs in the food to keep the prisoners calm. And in his case, a guy famous as an ETA hard man, they probably give him a double dose. Could it be that or something even worse? A horrible future: to die of cancer here, without ever returning to the village. He's thought about it often. There have been cases.

Instead of the blue sky what he saw now through the window was his mother's hands and what he'd been able to read on them. Don't come to me with mournful widows. If they want to rewind their story, they should go to the archives. What's done is done. So the armed struggle is over? Perfect. *Gora ETA* for all time to come, and eyes on the future.

Suddenly, against his will, it began to rain hard. Where? In memory. He was sinking slowly but surely. The hard man, the first to begin hunger strikes and the last to end them, the one who took the podium in assemblies to mock prisoners who swallowed the hook of being reintegrated into society.

But a man can be like a ship with a steel hull. The years pass, and cracks begin to appear. Through them leak the waters of nostalgia contaminated by loneliness, and the water of awareness that he's made mistakes and the water of not being able to correct the mistakes, and the water that corrodes so much, the water of repentance you feel but about which you do not speak out of fear, out of shame, out of not wanting to look bad in front of comrades. And so the man, a ship with cracks, can sink at any moment.

From the cell window, one can only see gray. It hasn't stopped raining since the previous afternoon. One advantage is that bad weather takes people off the street. No one feels like stopping to talk, everyone's in a hurry to get to wherever they have to go. A short distance from the corner was the telephone booth. Really, it was as if someone had put it there deliberately to make the *ekintza* easier. How so? Well, on the one hand, when you're inside you don't get soaked; on the other the booth was a hideout and at the same time an unbeatable observation post. And if some local came by? He could pretend he was talking on the phone. Also, the slightly fogged glass helped. And with my hood up, perfect. A townsperson would have to stick his head into the booth to see he was the man inside.

He saw the red Renault 21 appear at the corner. His heart skipped a beat. Nerves? Yes, a bit; but not the way it was at the beginning, when his legs would shake. After so many attacks, he learned to keep calm. He'd talked about it with Patxo who, he said, felt the same thing every time the moment to act approached.

"It's normal. We aren't psychopaths."

An instinctive impulse led him to feel the shape of the Browning in the pocket of his sweatshirt. Above all, no failures. He could make out Txato's blurred profile in the car. Those big ears have maybe three or four minutes of life left. A calming detail: the objective was alone. Patxo, in all the days he'd spent checking things over in the village, never saw him leave or come back accompanied.

After Txato had probably turned the corner, Joxe Mari, his eyes fixed on the second hand of his watch, waited until half a minute had passed before he left the phone booth. It was a bit of extra time alive he conceded to Txato, so he could open the garage door without being alarmed or suspicious. It seemed the second hand was moving more slowly than usual. Come on, come on. He got to the corner in time to see Txato go back to the car and go into the garage. The plan: when he came out, Joxe Mari would go toward him and execute him. One shot he thought would not be enough. Better to be sure in case the victim recognizes him and survives. Then, without delay, but also not in a wild run that might possibly catch the eyes of neighbors, he would make his way to the place where Patxo was waiting with the car.

Txato took a while to come out to the street. What was he waiting for? Did he think maybe it might stop raining? Joxe Mari was getting soaked. He hugged the wall at the corner of the building to keep as much out of the rain as he could. He knew there was no back door to the garage, so sooner or later Txato had to come out to the street to walk home. And he did come out, without an umbrella. There he was, filling his lungs with the last oxygen he'd ever breathe, ten steps away. Looking at him in profile, as he turned the key in the lock, you could see a slight tremor in his lips like someone talking to himself or singing softly. As soon as he started to walk he saw me. The Browning in my hand inside my pocket and Txato, what's he doing?, what the hell is he doing?, comes over to this side of the street and walks straight toward me. That scene was not part of the script.

"Joxe Mari of all people. You're back? I'm happy."

Those eyes, those enormous ears, that friendly expression. His father's friend who bought him ice cream when he was a boy. The church bell rang one o'clock. That familiar, metallic, peremptory sound to him was the same as the word *"no."* Don't do it. Don't kill him. The two of them stood speechless face to face. And it was clear that Txato expected an answer to his friendly words. I'm a member of ETA and I've come to execute you. But he didn't say that. He couldn't say it. The bell had rung out a "no" from on high. It's that it was Txato, what the hell. His eyes, his ears, his smile. And Joxe Mari turned and went away, not running, no, but at a quick pace.

He got into the car, slammed the door.

"It wasn't possible. There was a neighbor between us. Get going, let's eat."

"Did he see you?"

"I don't think so."

"We can try again when he goes to work. What do you think?"

"I don't know."

"A lot of days have gone by and we haven't struck."

"Right, but next time you get in the phone booth and I'll wait in the car. I got wet enough today."

"Okay by me."

Miren was signaled that her time was ending, ma'am. And she did not bother to look at the officer who spoke to her. She got out of her chair, began to say goodbye to her son.

"Well, then, *maitia*, courage, right? I'll be back in a month or less if your sister doesn't have a relapse."

"Don't talk to the crazy woman, *ama*. Promise me. Not a word. If she wants to find out she can consult the documents in the national court."

"She's made it her business to barge into our lives. She's a sticky one."

"Pay no attention. She'll unstick."

93

THE LAND OF THE SILENT

It happens that Ramuntxo heard the news at home on the radio while Gorka, who hadn't the slightest idea of what happened, was at the radio station, busy recording first an interview with a publisher and then another with a Bilbao bookseller.

Midafternoon of a typical workday. Two workmates were talking in the office next door. One of them, just arrived from the street, said, among other things: it won't stop raining, there was an attack, when does Ramuntxo get in? Gorka gave those words not the slightest importance.

So what if it was raining when his workday wouldn't end for several hours? As far as the attack, he was so used to ETA's committing violent acts that one more would hardly surprise him. Over the years, he'd developed a crust of conformity. Am I the only one? It isn't that the murders they committed left him indifferent but that they'd become a routine that numbed his organs to indignation and sorrow. So unless the attack had increased the number of victims, like the one at the Barcelona Hipercor, which really did embitter his day, or that among the dead there might be children, he limited himself to being informed about what happened and kept his opinions to himself.

It was just the opposite of how he felt whenever he heard about the arrest of a cell: his heart would beat faster and he would run to see if his brother was among the prisoners. Gorka wanted him removed from the armed struggle. He'd told Ramuntxo (and no one else) on several occasions.

"The day they capture him I'll be happy. For his sake, but also for the sake of my family. He's destroyed my parents' lives."

A little before seven, Ramuntxo reached the station. The shoulders of his raincoat were splattered with moist spots.

"Did you hear about the attack this afternoon?"

"I know nothing about it."

"A businessman from your village was shot to death."

"What's his name?"

"I don't remember the name, but if you like, we can find out right away."

"No, forget about it, leave it."

Which was the same as his saying: I'll find out on my own, when no one's near me checking my reaction. And even though, no matter how hard he reviewed names and faces, he had no idea who the victim might be, he still sensed that when he did learn his identity, he was going to suffer a disagreeable, sad? surprise.

He thought about factory and shop owners, about businessmen, about people in the village who might have a business. He recalled a few, without exception declared nationalists, aside from being *euskaldunes*, people ETA might pressure a bit, as they'd done so many times, especially to get cash out of them, but without taking their lives, since in that case the organization would have to deal with the PNV. So since he couldn't figure it out on his own, and since his curiosity was aroused more than it would normally be, at a certain moment, without saying goodbye to his workmates, he went down to the corner bar.

Txato. On the bar was the cup with the decaf coffee he'd just been served. He didn't taste it. Txato. His picture in black-and-white on the TV screen. What a shock. Txato. Back at the station, in the elevator, he felt a painful sensation of sadness in his throat when he remembered that Txato was the man who taught him to ride a bicycle when he was little. His father helped, too, but the one who really gave him good advice and explained the right way to pedal without falling was Txato. And he ran alongside me in the parking lot of his business, holding on to and then letting go of the seat of Xabier's bike, always ready to grab me whenever I leaned over too far to one side. He promised him that if he learned to ride he'd give him a bike and he did, the first bike I ever had, and now he's dead, murdered."

Ramuntxo saw him walk in and instantly read in his face where he was coming from and what he'd found out.

"So you knew him."

"They must have done it by mistake. The must have gone looking for someone else and killed someone they shouldn't have."

"He must have been one of the people who refused to pay the revolutionary tax."

"He and my father were *mus* partners, lifelong friends, although my sister told me over the phone that something happened between them recently and they weren't speaking."

"Well, somehow he got involved politically."

"I don't think so. He was apolitical and a good man, too. He created jobs for others, took an active part in village life, and was of course *euskaldun*."

"Good or not, he must have done something. ETA doesn't kill people for no reason. And I'm not defending the armed struggle. Don't misunderstand me."

"I just don't know. I haven't been over there in a long time and for sure I'm ignorant about a few things."

"Would you like to go this weekend and take Amaia with us?"

"No, better not."

Later on, Ramuntxo went into the studio to do his program about current music in Euskal Herria. Gorka used that opportunity to call home using the radio-station phone.

"*Ama*'s not home. She went to the plaza for a demonstration to ask for amnesty."

"Just a few hours after someone from the village was killed?"

"I said to her you've got a screw loose. And the way it's pouring. But she's got *abertzale* fever. No one can stop her."

Joxian sounded drained, fearful, vacillating. He said he didn't want to go out of the house. So he wouldn't hear the details of what happened? It's that the rain never lets up. And his rheumatism. And perhaps, finally, sincere:

"Besides, I just don't want to see anybody."

Their conversation, already disjointed, entered into stagnant silence, which Gorka broke after a few seconds:

"Where was he killed?"

He mentioned no names. Neither the father nor the son even spoke the name or nickname of the victim.

"Just by his house. You could see they were waiting for him."

"So you two were no longer together."

"How do you know that?"

"*Aita*, every once in a while I talk with one of my friends from the village."

"And with Arantxa?"

"With her, too."

Joxian thought about his deceased friend. Despite everything. Here in my heart. They didn't speak, one because of what people would say, the other because of Miren, who couldn't stand him. Don't even think of hanging around with that guy, she would say to him. Don't you realize someone could see you? It has to be about Joxe Mari, for sure. It's driven her crazy. Or about the death of the butcher's son, too. That death brought a lot of resentment to the village. Around here no one believes he took his own life. And as far as Joxian is concerned, he would express his sympathy to Bittori, because that's what proper people do after so many years of friendship, but he just can't do it. Joxian did not feel strong enough to leave the house. And going in secret, how else?, and looking her in the eye. Aside from what the poor woman must be suffering and that he recognizes that he doesn't know how to handle things like this. Since he couldn't go, maybe Gorka could write her from Bilbao, a postcard with a black border.

"You sign 'Gorka and family.'"

"Why don't you do it? You wouldn't have to look her in the eye. You could sign 'Joxian and family,' that would work."

"Son, is it asking too much for you to write a couple of lines? How often do I ask you for favors?"

"Okay, I'll look into it."

That night, Gorka was giving Ramuntxo a massage on a folding table they'd bought for that purpose. They covered it with towels so they wouldn't dirty it since they usually covered each other with oil.

As he rubbed Ramuntxo's back, Gorka recited all the details related to his conversation with Joxian.

"Are you going to write the widow?"

"Of course not. If there's no way out, I'll tell my *aita* that I did. How's he going to find out otherwise? Why do I act this way?"

"Out of cowardice."

"Exactly. Because I'm just as big a coward as he and so many others are these days. In my village people are probably saying in low voices so no one hears them that this is savagery, useless bloodshed, you don't build a nation that way. But no one will lift a finger. By now they've already hosed down the street so there won't be a trace of the crime. And tomorrow there will be whispering in the air, but deep down it will be business as usual. People will turn out for the next demonstration in favor of ETA, knowing that they'd better be seen with the rest of the herd. That's the price you pay to live in peace in the land of the silent."

"Okay, but don't get all bent out of shape about this."

"You're right. What right do I have to reproach anyone? I'm just like them. Can you imagine us on the radio tomorrow condemning today's murder? Before noon, we'd have our funding cut or they'd fire us outright. It's the same with books. If you step over the line, you become a pariah, even an enemy. If you write in Spanish, then you do have possibilities. They publish you in Madrid or Barcelona and maybe if you're lucky and talented you get ahead. It's not that way for those of us who write in Basque. They'd close all doors to you, invite you to nothing, you cease to exist. I see clearly that I'll spend my life writing for children even though I'm fed up with witches, dragons, and pirates."

"What about that novel you were planning?"

"The notes are there. I'll probably write it. If I do, I'll have half the story take place in Canada and the other half on some remote island."

"My boy, this just isn't your day. Finish the massage and let's go to bed."

94

AMAIA

Ramuntxo had custody of Amaia every other weekend. Taking care of his daughter, whom he adored, meant forty-eight hours of fear, insecurity, stress, and disappointments. He was convinced: he was no good as a father, that he did everything wrong. And the little girl, well, she didn't contribute even an ounce of goodwill to ease the difficulties. Gorka had no doubts: that little animal had some kind of personality disorder. As soon as he heard her arrive he was on guard. Let's see what she breaks this time.

After the divorce, the mother had gone with the girl to live in Vitoria, which forced Ramuntxo, every other weekend, to make two car trips, first on Friday afternoon when he drove to pick his daughter up, and then on Sunday when he brought her back, almost always angry with himself. The pattern, with few exceptions, invariably repeated itself. On Friday, he traveled full of expectations that the child later destroyed. Ramuntxo was extremely permissive, spoiled her, and obeyed all her caprices without Amaia's paying him back with even an expression of happiness, not to say enthusiasm. How can such a young child contain so much coldness? The only answer Ramuntxo could come up with was that the mother spoke ill of him at all times.

When Gorka met her, Amaia was eight. Even then she was an inexplicable being, with only one expression on her face: dead serious. At any moment, she would play some mischievous prank on you, give you a nasty answer with a kind of calm malice, find the exact spot that would drive you insane. Out of nowhere she would do or say something appropriate for a mentally challenged child; a minute later she would show signs of a superior intelligence. Time did not make things better. The older she got, the more complicated she became, more unforeseeable, and, above all, more difficult to satisfy. A kind of blackmail in Gorka's opinion.

Ramuntxo:

"Don't say things like that, you'll depress me."

She was pretty. A little doll with curls, the blackest of eyes, and long, fine lips that gave her charming face a prematurely adult look. There were days when she spoke little. Hours in silence, absorbed, indolent. On other days, it took patience and effort to make her shut up. If you spoke to her in Basque she would answer in Spanish; if you continued the conversation in Spanish, she'd switch to Basque. At dinnertime you just never knew what would happen. One day she'd devour two helpings of spaghetti with tomato sauce and cheese; on the next visit she'd reject what she seemed to have liked so much the previous weekend. And it was that way with everything: with games, with the places where father and daughter went to have fun, with the stories Ramuntxo told her at night in bed before turning out the light. Today yes, tomorrow no, and vice versa. And sometimes she'd burst into tears for no apparent reason. It was then Ramuntxo would panic. What do I do? What do I do? Even his eyes would fill with tears. Crushed and sad, he would confess to Gorka that he just didn't know how to manage the child and that if things go on like this, I'll lose her.

"Did you ever try to shake her up with a good slap?"

"No, and I'll never try that. She'd tell her mother and then I'll be left with a court order forbidding me to see my daughter."

"Well, maybe, in her way, Amaia is asking you to do it. *Aita*, give me a slap, get me out of this labyrinth."

"It's easy to see you aren't a father. That's the dumbest thing I've ever heard you say."

The arrival of the girl at the flat every two weeks also had direct consequences for Gorka. What? Well, to begin with, he had to sleep in his office on a thin, fold-up mattress. As long as the child was around there would be no massages, no intimacy for the two inhabitants of the apartment. Ramuntxo did not have a second bed except the one used by his daughter. Gorka tried to stay out of the house as much as possible. He often spent the entire day at the station, reading books, writing stories and poems, and taking care of the next week's work; or he would go on a movie binge in different theaters; or, weather permitting, he'd hike along the bank of the estuary all the way to Erandio or even farther, to Algorta. He'd come back by bus. He even visited his sister in Rentería, without telling his parents. He barely ever went to the village. Only when it was impossible not to go. At Christmas and other holidays. To avoid the rainstorm of maternal reproaches. So he wouldn't run into anyone on the street.

"*Kaixo, Kartujo.* It's been a while."

He would rather put up with the girl's outbursts, even though he suffered for Ramuntxo. A typical bit of mischief: there they were at home, calm, cool, and collected, the girl seated in front of the TV, and suddenly they'd be startled by the noise of a glass or pottery object smashing. The two adults instantly investigated. A picture all too familiar to them materialized: Amaia, her face expressionless and the floor around her covered with shards. Ramuntxo wouldn't dare reprimand her in case she told her *ama.* He would explain, implore, dismiss the event as unimportant, pick up the scattered pieces or discreetly ask Gorka to clear them away while he diverted the child's attention elsewhere. The same thing happened when she destroyed Gorka's alarm clock. Ramuntxo immediately bought him a new one, pretending nothing had happened.

Neither man thought Amaia threw things on the floor out of malice. But neither thought they fell by accident. And of course trying to find any sign of intention in her face was useless.

One time, Gorka caught her scratching the back of her hand with a fork, drawing blood. Also, she was in the habit of lining up objects anywhere: on the rug, on the table, in the bathtub. Rows of carrots she'd taken out of the refrigerator, circles of teaspoons, towers of books, of compact discs, of anything.

That child is not normal, that child's got a screw loose. Of course, you couldn't say that to Ramuntxo because he'd fall into a pit of anguish.

And then, one Saturday, Gorka came back from the village, where he'd gone that afternoon. There was no avoiding things. Arantxa had called him at the station.

"I imagine you've heard."

"Yes. And let me tell you something: I'm happy."

"They're probably beating him to a pulp."

"Well, I wasn't talking about that."

"I agree that it's for his own good that he be taken out of circulation. But you've got to visit the *aitas*. We can't abandon them now. I'm going to see them in the afternoon, when I get out of work."

The Guardia Civil had arrested Joxe Mari. And with him the other two members of the Oria cell. That was the lead story in the day's news programs. Gorka had, for special situations, prerecorded material, so he got permission to leave the station. But with the promise that he'd be back by the next afternoon. And he went by bus, kept his parents company, slept in the bed of his adolescence, and Saturday morning, aren't you going to stay for the demonstration? I can't, but it's for your brother, he went back to Bilbao. When he arrived, he found Ramuntxo out of control.

"Amaia."

"What happened to her?"

"She isn't here, she ran away. I went out for a minute to get bread and when I got back I found the door open and her gone."

While Gorka, to console him, gave Ramuntxo a hug, Ramuntxo let his imagination run wild. The girl, a runaway, could have fallen into the hands of sex traffickers. Then he painted a truculent picture of organ sales and sexual exploitation. He imagined himself stripped of his right to be with his daughter or even with a long jail sentence.

"Did you go looking for her?"

"I asked around in stores and bars. No one's seen her. What should I do? Call the *Ertzaintza*? But if I do call, the word will get to the press, my ex will find out, the story will explode out of all proportion."

"I think we should take a look around. You on one side of the street, me on the other."

They didn't go far. A neighbor they ran into on the way out of the building told them the girl had been seen on the roof terrace of the building. And sure enough, there she was, happy as could be, inside a square she'd made by lining up photos from her father's album. Relieved, Ramuntxo picked her up. Not a word of recrimination. Gorka picked up the photos. And back in the flat, Amaia, eleven years old at the time, said with her habitual seriousness that she wanted to go home to her mother.

95

Jug Wine

Joxe mari askatu. That was the first thing that caught Gorka's attention as he got out of the bus. A huge banner spread across two facades. And then at regular intervals, posters with his brother's photo and the same demand for his freedom. That's how you manipulate a man and fabricate a hero. If the people around here only knew the repugnance all this makes me feel. He walked quickly, impelled by the hope that no one would stop him before he got to his parents' house.

A small group did stop him at the entrance to a bar. He put up with all of it right there on the sidewalk, stoic, a weak smile, slow eyelids, five or six embraces, some moist with sweat.

"We're with you all the way."

"If you need anything, you can count on us."

Aside from saying a plain thank you, he didn't know what else to say. Maybe they thought he was depressed because Joxe Mari'd been arrested. They offered him drinks. Come on, come on. He showed them the most mournful face in his repertoire of phony expressions, as he claimed, not exactly with regret, that he'd just arrived and had to see his parents as soon as possible. His well-modulated Basque impressed them and he knew it. Perhaps under other circumstances they might have dragged him willingly or not to the bar. This time, understanding, they did not insist. And Gorka could move on, his back hot from being patted.

The entryway with its usual smell and darkness. And suddenly, at the foot of the three steps up, a figure, who?, with bad breath embraced him. Don Serapio had just left his parents' flat.

"You've come to be with your family in these difficult moments? I think that's a good thing, my boy. I see you've become a grown man and a judicious one as well. I see your *ama* as strong. A woman of iron, eh? It's your *aita* who worries me more."

After a few seconds, Gorka's eyes got used to the dim light. Then he had no difficulty making out the priest's mellifluous grimace, the watery shine of his eyes. He seemed shorter than he did in the past. Could he be shrinking?

"Poor Joxian. May God have mercy on him. I don't know how he'll deal with this situation. I learned from your mother that he spent all day in his garden. He didn't even come home to eat."

"I guess I'll have to go get him."

"Go on, my boy, go on. I pray a lot for all of you and for Joxe Mari. I pray to God to ask that he be treated in a humane way. Don't lose courage. Be strong. Your parents need you. How are things in Bilbao?"

"Good."

The priest gave him a farewell pat on the arm, near his shoulder, which to Gorka seemed the sort of gesture people make when someone dies. And dressed all in black, but without his cassock, he adjusted his beret and walked out to the street.

He could hear voices inside the flat. The calm voices of women. His mother's, for sure. The other? He recognized it. He put an ear to the door. It isn't Arantxa's voice—she said she would come after work. Is it Juani's voice? He pressed his ear harder and yes, inside was the butcher's wife. In the half-darkness he glanced at his watch. It still wasn't too late. What should I do? Standing on the landing, he imagined his entrance into the family apartment, how *ama* would receive him with reproaches about how he hasn't visited in such a long time or even called on the phone, all that in front of the mother of the guy who killed himself. Or was he murdered? To himself he said, me in there now, no way, not even if I were nuts. He poked his head out of the entryway to make sure the priest was gone, which he was. He made his way to the garden.

He found his father in the shed, barefoot, drunk.

"So you came?"

"Here I am."

He'd made a shaky table putting a board on top of a rabbit cage, and in the same way, a chair, using another cage. And on top of the table a glass and an old jug of wine covered with dust and spiderwebs.

"I'm not going home until I drink all of it."

Joxian did not seem surprised by his son's arrival. When he saw him, he turned off the transistor radio. The smell inside the shed was powerful. Of humidity, of rotten vegetation, of strong wine. The rabbits, calm. Some made a nervous, chewing motion. Thick veins ran along the backs of Joxian's hands. Swollen, calloused hands, where already symptoms of arthritis were visible.

"Do we know anything about my brother?"

"Your brother is a murderer. That's all we know. Think that doesn't mean much? Now he'll get the punishment he deserves and more, because the bastards from the court are dying to make an example of the jerks with guns. *Ama's* right. I've been a soft father. All of this might have been fixed with a few timely beatings. What do you think?"

"In this country, we fix too many things with beatings. That's our style. So we know nothing?"

"Until they finish beating the shit out of him, we're not going to know anything."

Joxian's drunkenness wasn't that of the penniless alcoholic. He'd been a moderate but tireless drinker from early on. Every once in a while, he'd have an extra glass. But today's drunkenness, what should we call it? A wish to dull reality, an attempt at rebellion, a punishment for not having been a good father? Considering how much he'd drunk he was articulate. He was not having difficulty thinking. He wasn't scratching his side. He would fix his eyes on a spot, keep it there a long while, and suddenly drink, not tasting the wine, sometimes shaking his head reproachfully. Gorka, standing at the entrance. watched him with heart bursting with compassion, also with a touch of disgust. Today, this man would drink an ocean of wine. His feet, purplish, swollen, deformed.

"Listen here, you aren't involved in things with that gang, are you?"

"No, *aita*. I work at the radio station, they pay me, I don't hurt anyone."

"Be very careful about following in your brother's footsteps, okay? You see where they lead. God, what a stretch in jail he's going to get. There's a lot of blood in all this. Did you hear all the things they're accusing him of? I don't think I'll live to see him out of jail. Just add twenty, thirty years to how old I am now. Man! By then I'll be under the earth."

And to cut off the sob that was rising in his throat, he quickly took another swallow of wine. Father and son remained there for a long while in silence, without looking at each other. Suddenly:

"Did you see *ama*?"

"I came straight here."

"How did you know I was in the garden?"

"The priest told me."

"The priest? Don't mention his name. The old crow. He's one of the worst, let me tell you. He tells the boys tales, puts ideas in their heads, and gets them all worked up. And when what happens happens, he steps back, delivers a sermon, and administers communion with the face of a little saint. You can't say that to *ama* because she'll get like a wild bull. But are you dumb or what? I tell her. Don't you see that the priest opens the basement of the church so the boys can store banners and posters and cans of paint down there? She says none of that matters. Joxe Mari, as far as I know, was not born with a pistol. The priest, his friends, whatever, led him down the bad path. And since he's got very little here—he pointed a finger at the center of his forehead—he went for it."

Then he invited his son to have a drink. Gorka was tempted to accept just to empty the jug sooner. But he didn't see any other glass on the improvised table except the one his father was using, so he declined the offer.

"There's something I want you to know, *aita*."

"I was told Joxe Mari was in the village when Txato was killed. I can't get that out of my mind."

"It has to do with my intimate life."

"A big coincidence, don't you think? What the hell was that dumbass doing here on the day my best friend was killed? If it turns out it was his cell, I'll never forgive him."

"In Bilbao, I live with a man." Busy lighting another cigarette, Joxian wasn't listening. "We live together. His name is Ramón. I call him Ramuntxo."

"For sure, the first time I see him, wherever it is, I'm going to ask him eye to eye. And it won't do him any good to lie to me, his father, because I'll read the truth in his eyes."

Gorka decided to cease his barely initiated confession. How could he not realize that this wasn't the right moment, that his father was not in the best condition to pay attention and understand? The place was good. He'd dreamed about the scene at different times. He saw himself, as he was now, alone with Joxian in the garden shed and he told him the secret behind his mother's back. From his father he could expect an expression of understanding. In the worst case, Joxian would simply accept things. Condemnation? None. This man either blesses or keeps quiet. And for sure he'd keep the secret just as Arantxa was keeping it. Suddenly, with night falling, there she was in the garden.

"The stink in this pigsty won't let me breathe. *Aita*, you're drunk on your ass." To her brother: "And what are you doing here? *Ama's* practically foaming at the mouth thinking you're still in Bilbao. She sent me to ask if she has to make dinner or what. She bought enough sardines for a regiment."

Gorka helped his father stand up while Arantxa, still speaking, looked for his shoes among the rabbit cages.

"Sure you can walk?"

"Fuck yes."

"What do you think about the *gudari*?"

"Now at least we'll know where he is."

"That's exactly what I said to Guille. But *ama's* in a highly revolutionary state. I'm not surprised you hid from her. Juani choruses everything she says and no one can stand them. A great team."

96

NEREA AND SOLITUDE

It was Bittori who telephoned the lawyers in San Sebastián. Could they take her daughter on, so she could learn the ropes? They took her on without a contract, with a salary more symbolic than anything else, and all because one of the lawyers owed favors to Txato, may he rest in peace, or perhaps out of pity because of what happened to him. Lots of busywork, supreme boredom, dry, arrogant bosses, scanty salary. That's how Nerea, after a few months, described the first job she ever had to her mother. The maternal response:

"It's better than nothing. Everybody begins on the bottom."

Bittori's dream: just as Xabier had become a prestigious surgeon, her daughter should become a lawyer or a judge. The same dream, of course, that the deceased Txato would have wanted to see come true.

One year and three months after joining the lawyers, Nerea gave it up. She announced that she was quitting and then, of course, they offered her improvements in her work conditions and a contract and a permanent position. I'm sorry, but it's too late. She said goodbye, and Bittori had to give up her dream forever.

During that entire period, Nerea secretly perused job offers, and once she passed the necessary test, she landed a job in the Tax Office on Oquendo Street. Later they transferred her to the offices for the Errotaburu neighborhood. She wasn't motivated by economic necessity. Her father had solved those problems for her. Even though he had only a little secondary school education, he had a talent for dealing with bureaucratic and administrative matters.

Besides, Xabier gave her the advice of a judicious brother about her inheritance. Nerea saved, bought stock, invested; she was well-off. But of course we have to fill our lives with reasons, have an order and a direction, provide each new day with a really stimulating reason to jump out of bed, if not with illusions, at least with energy, and keep pure inactivity from paralyzing you right down to your thoughts.

"My dear daughter, what a philosopher you've become."

She bought a three-room apartment in the Amara neighborhood for cash. She made alterations and furnished it. Her mother: why was she spending when the two of them would fit perfectly in her place?

"What strange ideas you have, *ama*. We'd never stop fighting."

Days came and went, the twentieth century was ending and she met men. Actually, they met her. Meaning that smiling seducers surrounded her, flattered her, pretended they were running into her by chance. Even one of the lawyers from her old office, this one is hard to believe, married with three children, made advances. She'd figured out his game days earlier and quickly quashed his lascivious assault. Destroying families did not fit into her plans.

She made female friendships. At the gym, at work. But with no one from her village. That was missing. And if someone asked where are you from, she would say she was a native of San Sebastián. She joined a little group of women, one of whom was a thirty-one-year-old widow. From time to time, during Saturday dinners, on the beach, in cafés, the women chatted about the sorrow caused by the death of a loved one and about how hard it was to get over the disaster. Nerea listened without saying anything because she had no intention of revealing that she was the daughter of a murdered man.

Aside from sporadic sexual adventure, from time to time she did try love, as she understood it.

"How do you understand it?"

She confessed to her girlfriends her hope to live for many years with someone, to have children, though no more than two. Everything quite calm, clean, and bourgeois, after an old-fashioned wedding.

"Your father leading you down the aisle."

"That can't happen. My father died two and a half years ago of cancer. He smoked a lot."

Once she turned thirty, Nerea decided she'd had enough of flirtation. Adventures? No thanks. She'd already had enough. And she told the circle of smiling faces the story of the blond heartthrob she followed like a fool all the way to Germany and the monumental shock she'd suffered there. Even though her friends knew the adventure right down to its minor details, they never tired of hearing about it, and Nerea had to tell it again very often. Why? Because it was a sure source of amusing comments and giggles. On the other hand, she never mentioned the Frankfurt pedestrian run over by the streetcar.

Her increasingly infrequent attempts to achieve lasting love, canasta, carpet, and slippers, led every time to unhappy endings. Disillusioned and fed up with men, she would say to herself: girl, you're never going to fall in love ever again. But the weeks went by, the months, and when she least expected it, she again experienced, where?, above, below, between her legs, a tickle of excitement and enthusiasm. It was like relapsing into an addiction she thought she'd overcome. A name, a face, a new tone of voice burst into her life; they aroused a sticky sensation of loneliness that at all hours she felt clinging to her body. It all filled her with euphoria, with agreeable nervousness, until, when time had passed, for one reason or another the mirage evaporated and once again she confirmed that this fascinating being whose nearness made her pulse rise was nothing but a projection of her desires and that in reality the guy was insufferably vulgar and egoistic.

The longed-for exception: Eneko, eight years older than she. They knew each other from the Tánger bar, where Nerea routinely had her midday cocktail during the period when she was working in the Oquendo Street offices. The two of them were often in the bar at the same time since he worked nearby, in a real-estate office in Guipúzcoa Plaza. An exchange of glances, greetings, more glances, and finally Eneko gathered up enough courage to approach her. Hi, I'm so-and-so, I work nearby, what would you think about our getting to know each other? That simple. A simple, direct man without pretentions. One of those men as yet not burned by matrimonial acid, who turn up for a date with a rose or a gift book. Defects?

None that at first sight she couldn't forgive: not much taste in clothing, slightly overweight, fond of soccer.

Nerea got used to his company, to the slightly paternal touch of this man, older than Xabier, who transmitted tranquility and, something few could do, could make her laugh. Eneko, a sofa man: soft, fluffy, perfect for peace of mind. On rainy days, he covered her with his umbrella while he got wet. That kind of small thing meant a great deal to Nerea. And after a few months she was wrestling with the idea of suggesting something more than going out together because the man frankly seemed right to her. The question posed by her girlfriends: if there was love. Of course, but there was friendship, too, which was not the same thing. Nerea said it was friendship that held a couple's relationship together when love lost energy and heat.

Despite all that, a black, bottomless crevice separated them. It accompanied them at all times during the almost ten months they were living so closely together, and they didn't see it. In fact, Eneko never saw it. So, if he's still alive, what became of him? Maybe he goes on wondering what could have gone wrong. And it was the fact that just as she never spoke about what happened to her father, he never spoke about what happened to a brother who was serving a sentence for crimes related to terrorism in the Badajoz prison. Love, friendship, laughter, the sofa man, the rose or the gift book, all of it was swallowed in a matter of seconds by that deep crevice.

This is how it happened. Evening was coming on one January Monday in 1995. Nerea and Eneko agreed to take their usual walk through the Parte Vieja, nibble a couple of brochettes they'd wash down with wine, and ultimately go to his flat or hers or each one to his own because tomorrow, *maitia*, is a workday. From bar to bar, sharing an umbrella, they made their way along 31 de Agosto Street. Nerea was laughing at some jokes Eneko was telling. When they got to the La Cepa bar, her laughter suddenly stopped. She heard on radio news that five or six hours earlier an ETA gunman had murdered the deputy mayor in there while he was eating with some comrades from his political party.

"Isn't this where Gregorio Ordóñez was killed?"

"I won't be shedding any tears for him. Thanks to guys like that my brother is in jail."

"A brother in jail?"

"In Badajoz. Haven't I ever told you? He'll be in for some time."

"Why is he locked up?"

"What else could it be? Fighting for what he loves."

They reached the church of Santa María. Eneko went back to his jokes, but there was no more laughter on his girlfriend's lips. Nerea wasn't even listening. She detached herself from his arm using the excuse that she had to dig something out of her bag. What do I do? Start running? Her features, pure rigidity, a phony smile, were a mask of serenity. Inside, such anxiety had been unleashed that she couldn't stop herself from releasing a not inconsiderable amount of urine. The road to the Bulevar became eternal. He went on talking, jovial, chatty; she kept silent. At the bus stop, in a mix of repugnance and terror she said goodbye after allowing herself to be kissed on the cheek. Even though there were empty seats next to the windows facing the sidewalk where he was waiting to wave to her as he usually did, Nerea sat on the other side. On her way back to Amara, the way to justify breaking things off with him occurred to her. She called him as soon as she got home. That there was another man in her life. An infallible lie in such cases. She said it and without waiting for his reaction hung up. She could have told him the truth, but then she would have had to mention her father. She'd rather die.

She told her girlfriends four vague reasons about the end of the relationship. They weren't all that interested. The clique dissolved in the years that followed, although once in a while they got together for dinner. The usual thing happened: some found partners, the widow remarried, another got a job in Barcelona. Things like that. And Nerea? Well, there she was, stuck to her loneliness. She compensated herself with trips to the ends of the earth: to Alaska, to New Zealand, to South Africa. Also by filling her free time with activities: she took courses at a language school to perfect her English, she went to the gym more often, she took a cooking course. Sometimes, yes, she would go out with some friend who was separated or about to separate who would spend hours telling her about her family problems and marital problems and ask her for advice, asking someone who had no experience whatsoever as a mother or wife.

And that was that, time went by and she turned thirty-six. Thirty-six! How quickly time passes. But I'm not going to get bitter. And since it was festival time in San Sebastián, she went with a girl-friend to the flag raising in Plaza de la Constitución. They danced, they drank, and they went on drinking, and at a certain moment, very late at night, Nerea found herself in a taxi with a man who had perfect teeth, who smelled marvelous, who played with her breasts, and don't ask me any more about it because I don't remember. I do have some blurry memories. I know from the sound of water that he showered at about sunrise. Then he came and undressed her. Nerea facedown on a strange bed, so drunk she was about to pass out. She deduced that the man had penetrated her since during the morning hours she found dried sperm on her thighs. He was waiting for her in the living room, luxuriously decorated. He was very handsome, wearing a navy-blue silk dressing gown at a table set for breakfast, with flowers, and candles and a ton of delicious things to drink and eat. Whatever I tell you is nothing compared to what was there. It was then, when she sat down opposite him, that Nerea learned his name: Enrique.

"Though my friends call me Quique."

97

The Parade of Murderers

Hours after meeting him, Bittori judged him with no compassion whatsoever: totally conceited. The vainest man on the face of the earth. A man who wears out mirrors, fumigated with perfume, a man who only speaks so he can hear himself talk. And with biting irony, she asked Nerea if this gentleman went to bed wearing a suit and tie. Nerea warned her to start getting used to him because he'd entered her life to stay.

"You're not going to tell me you don't think he's handsome."

"He's too handsome."

"And elegant."

"Much too. Let's see how you figure out keeping other women from stealing him. You'll have to keep an eye on him twenty-four hours a day."

Bittori was unaware that Quique and Nerea had resolved that issue beforehand. The agreement cost her sleepless nights and tears; but in the meantime, she made her calculations, balanced advantages against inconveniences and ultimately, advised by a girlfriend, decided to pay back his egoism with her own. To hell with it. And she gave in. From the first instant, she noticed a kind of interior widening of her person. What? How? Let's say I felt liberated. Another consequence: between the two of them a complicity was born that through all these years has provided a solid foundation for their relationship, despite repeated and practically regular breaks.

By way of explanation, Nerea gave a girlfriend an example:

"I doubt there exists in the world a couple who has separated more times than we have. Once, at his place, I told him that I was breaking up with him forever, that this was the definitive separation. But it was raining and I'd been at the hairdresser just a few hours before and I had no umbrella. So I decided to stay and together we spent one of the most tender and most romantic nights I can remember."

At no time did Quique make up stories. He turned up late for a date with a fresh scratch on his chin. He excused himself, explicit and unperturbed:

"Honey, sorry I'm late. I was with some chick and the thing took longer than I thought it would."

In Nerea's head, like a luminous explosion, a single word lit up: "separation." And after the pyrotechnic explosion a weeping willow of sparks flowered and on each spark she could read: it's over. This guy not only cheats on me but actually rubs his insolence in my face. They'd barely been going out a few months. And now this. Nerea was in love from head to foot and back again and would have sworn that Quique, courteous, tender, a handsome bastard, loved her, too. In her embarrassment, she looked all around as if she were looking for the hidden camera that would confirm the joke.

"What's the matter?"

He seemed sincerely surprised. Nerea, my dear dope, do I have to explain it to you? He did:

"Honey, other men are tennis fanatics or they collect stamps and coins. Me, what can I say?, I like sex. I need the sensation of possessing feminine bodies. Hundreds, thousands, as many as I can for as long as I can. This is a sport I'm quite good at, see? It has nothing to do with our relationship, which is simply marvelous. I love you to death. You're my Nerea, my one and only. You mustn't doubt that ever. On the other hand, the women who supply me with orgasms, the ones I go to bed with without knowing even what their names are or where they live, mean nothing to me from the point of view of my feelings. I'll say it again: NOTHING. They're an instrument of pleasure. That's all. You see I'm not keeping any secrets. Don't you go to the gym? Well, I do the same thing, except that instead of getting on a treadmill, I exercise with an attractive body. I'd be really sorry if you didn't accept me as I am."

"And would you accept my doing the same with masculine bodies?"

"Wait a minute. When did I ever tell you not to do this or not to do that?"

"Okay. Give me some time. I'll have to think it through."

She got up. They were on the terrace of the Caravanserai, a blue afternoon with children and pigeons, and Nerea, serious, walked around the cathedral, upset, asking herself: God, what the hell am I doing? Why don't I just tell him to go to hell? Okay, if I do tell him to go to hell, how do I get him back right away? And she imagined scenes, one more humiliating than the next, more shameful, all of them the opposite of what she understood as a couple's relationship, I don't know, a normal relationship, reasonable, with canasta and slippers. Each one there for the other, fidelity, things like that. Of course, here I am thirty-six years old, not about to let the last train pull out on me, especially a train as well put together as this one.

She set up an urgent meeting with a girlfriend she could trust. Sunken eyes after a sleepless night. On the table, café con leche and croissants. After listening to the details of the matter, the friend asked Nerea with no preambles whatsoever if she loved Quique.

"Well, I'm afraid I can't say I don't. If I didn't I would already have ditched him. The problem is that I don't want to share him. I want him all to myself."

"And what do you give him in exchange? You're thirty-five."

"Thirty-six."

"Look here, Nerea my dear, it doesn't seem to me you're in as difficult a situation as the one you described to me last night on the phone. If you really love him you don't have many options. Either an immediate break, where you lose everything and go back to being alone with your thirty-seven years—"

"Thirty-six."

"—or you play your cards cleverly and tolerate his fondness for orgasms. It hurts, I know, but the important thing is winning the game."

"What if he falls in love with another woman?"

"What I think is that the risk is greater with men who are unsatisfied and repressed."

"What if he gets an infection? Like AIDS, for instance, and he gives it to me?"

"I see. Call him and tell him it's all over."

"Are you nuts?"

"Then you have to accept him as he is."

"It's going to cost me."

"It will cost you, but you can do it."

"He's a pig."

"He's *your* pig, Nerea. Be kind to him."

She didn't want to meet him in any of their usual spots. Why? So as not to exaggerate her submissiveness. Quique, tender over the phone, asked no questions, accepted. Hidden behind the kiosk on the Bulevar, Nerea saw him arrive punctually and perfectly dressed and take a table at the Barandiarán café. Meanwhile, she sat on a public bench where Quique couldn't see her, and for twenty minutes she amused herself watching the crowd. Let him wait. Before going over to him, she touched up the shadows under her eyes looking into a compact mirror and put on her wrists a few drops of an expensive perfume she'd just bought.

Because you know I'm not going to let this conceited fop beat me out in elegance or aroma. She walked through the mob with the exaggerated movements of a model, click-click-clicking her high heels, her hair loose, knowing she was being watched by various men and also by Quique, who from the terrace saw her walking straight toward him. Halfway there, her lips disobeyed her. That smile, Nerea, don't deny it, was a dead giveaway. Just one? It was *the* giveaway. And Quique stood up to receive her all kisses, elegant, helping to seat her like a well-mannered gentleman.

Nerea got straight to the point.

"Never ever before my eyes."

She said nothing else. Quique made a slight gesture of approval, made sure the waiter was taking care of them, removed from an inside pocket of his blazer a small leather box. He handed it to Nerea in silence. Inside, a chain holding a gingko leaf—all in gold. Without making a fuss, Nerea judged it pretty. After which, Quique brought his mouth close and she kissed him.

They chatted. He sipped his whiskey on the rocks and from time to time raised the glass to look through the liquid; she, since she had an English class in about an hour, just had tonic. Just then, they saw emerge from Calle Mayor, just a few yards from where they were sitting, the usual parade of families of imprisoned ETA members. Men and women marched forward at a snail's pace, divided into two parallel files, some talking among themselves, others silent. Each of them carried a long pole. On it, a poster. The poster was the photo of a captured ETA militant with his name below. The photos, all of young people, were the sons, brothers, or husbands of those carrying the poles. And pedestrians made way to let them pass.

Walking through the Parte Vieja, Nerea had come upon processions like that on myriad occasions, often as she suddenly turned a corner. Neither up close nor from a distance did she pay them any attention. As if they didn't exist. She turned her back to them and good riddance. She spotted Miren in the row nearest the terrace, grim and stiff, carrying her son's photograph. Nerea had seen her other times.

Quique:

"There goes the parade of murderers."

"Speak more softly. I don't want problems."

Then he bent forward to whisper into Nerea's ear:

"There goes the parade of murderers." And straightening up and in his normal tone of voice: "Is that better? I have the same opinion no matter whether my tone is loud or low."

Now it was Nerea who leaned her mouth toward him and he who brought his to hers to complete the kiss.

98

WHITE-DRESS WEDDING

They set the date for the wedding. A few days later, a woman stopped Nerea on a street in the Amara neighborhood.

"I'm going to kill myself and it's your fault."

The woman, apparently, had been waiting for her. Nerea didn't know her and didn't ask her name. She tried to get past her, but the woman (about thirty, attractive) wouldn't let her go.

"You'll never make him as happy as I can."

Nerea began to understand. There was despair in that face staring at her closely with challenging, fierce, irritated eyes suggesting she'd recently been crying. The woman went on, not aggressive, not insulting, but with a raised index finger of warning and clear signs of suffering nervous distress.

"Don't fool yourself. Do you think that at your age you're going to give him satisfaction?"

Nerea, hold it all in. Nerea, hold it all in. Nerea did not hold it all in.

"Why don't you kill yourself once and fucking for all and leave me in peace?"

The woman, obviously, was not expecting such a reaction. She stood there dumbfounded, hypnotized, rooted to the spot. And Nerea took advantage of her shock to leave her behind and continue on, *click, click*. She never saw her again. Could she have killed herself as she said or promised? Did she promise? Don't be perverse, my dear.

She was tempted to tell Quique about the incident, but why bother. She supposed the woman was one of the many who'd spread her legs for him. Poor thing. Perhaps one who wasn't happy to work for the firm SOINC (Suppliers of Orgasms Incorporated) and wanted to fight me for the throne.

She asked Xabier for advice. Either community property or separation of property. Which did he think better. With no hesitation, he chose the second. And he added that he wasn't saying it out of hostility toward Quique.

"After all, his economic situation is solid. But, considering what might happen in the future, it would be better if you had the final say about your estate yourself."

And that's what she did at the office of the notary, and Quique made no objection. They married, he an atheist, she with religious doubts, in the Cathedral of the Good Shepherd. Bittori said she would only come to the cathedral if the bishop did not perform the service. She said that gentleman only took mercy on murderers, that they should please never mention his name in her presence because it turned her stomach, and that it was principally because of him she'd lost her faith. Quique's parents, from Tudela in Navarra, had kept theirs. And more for them than anything else and, in passing, to give the event some class, they had a church wedding, both of them wearing white.

For several months, the smiles of the newlyweds (with Miramar Palace in the background) decorated the window of a photographer's shop located in one of the porticos in Guipúzcoa Plaza.

The banquet, held at a restaurant in Ulía with a view of the sea, went on until late in the afternoon. Bittori, about to say goodbye, a bit drunk?, said something that intrigued Nerea.

"I wish you great happiness, because you're really going to need it."

Nerea repeated what she'd said to Xabier a little later in a private moment.

"Please pay no attention whatsoever. *Ama* has the story she has. And on special days like today it's possible she's hounded by memories."

That was a Saturday. On Monday, the newlyweds took a train to Madrid. They walked around, they visited, they made love abundantly, since he was pressured by the illusion, the haste?, of being a father as soon as possible, which for him meant entering the hotel room and getting right down to business without even pulling back the bedspread. On such occasions, the grief-stricken face of the woman who'd told her on the street that she'd never give her husband satisfaction came into her mind. Accommodating, submissive, she carried out Quique's instructions: get into this position, turn over, come closer. Barely had they caught their breath and he was reviewing names for the baby, which upset Nerea because that brings, as she said, bad luck.

In Madrid, they boarded a flight to Prague. They'd planned to spend the rest of their honeymoon there. It was Nerea's idea. One of her girlfriends told her the city was marvelous. There's this, and there's that; there's the so-and-so bridge, and the who-knows-what cathedral. Prague? Okay, we're going to Prague. Whatever you say, darling. Half owner of a business that produced and distributed liquor, Quique thought the trip would offer him a stupendous opportunity for an on-site examination of the possibilities for doing business in the Czech Republic, a nation in which at the time he had no clients. And with the intention of trying his luck he packed his bags with a mass of prospectuses with information in English about his products along with a cardboard box containing about twenty tiny bottles of different liquors. He said that:

"In Germany and Austria every year they buy a ton of sloe gin from us. I don't see why the Czechs wouldn't like what their neighbors like."

"And what are you going to do with those prospectuses? Hand them out in the Prague supermarkets?"

"You leave that to me, because I'm a good hand at these things."

In Prague, as in Madrid, they strolled around taking photos, visited with great interest, coupled with procreative ends. But there was a glitch in the form of an unexpected episode that still comes up when they recall their Prague honeymoon. And it was that, two days into their visit, they agreed to walk to the Malá Strana neighborhood, have lunch there, and see and photograph any historical places or curious details in the cityscape they might find along the way. The sunny weather favored the plan. Also an easy-to-use map the hotel people had given them.

Along cobblestone streets they went down to the Charles V Bridge. And pronouncing admiring phrases they crossed the small tunnel that separates the two towers at the entrance. Nerea, wearing sunglasses, wanted to be photographed at the foot of one of the statues. She left her bag at the rail as she fixed her hair and then that boy of fourteen, fifteen, or at the most sixteen popped up, grabbed the bag by the straps, and, seen and not seen, started running. Nerea noticed instantly. She shouted the word "bag" toward Quique, toward the stone figures, and toward all of Europe, and had time enough to mention the contents: her passport, the visa. All of which spurred her husband into action.

Quique took off after the thief. That was the first time in her life Nerea'd ever seen him run. And did he run quickly! Also, the circumstances were in his favor. Because just as the boy had to dodge slow, almost stationary tourists, those same tourists got out of the way for Quique. The thief ran right into an Asian man. By then he saw himself caught and who knows if beaten to a pulp by that speedy foreigner and had no better idea than to toss the bag into the river with the likely hope that it would create a dilemma for his pursuer.

There was no dilemma. Instantly abandoning the chase, Quique ran to the railing. Nerea, about thirty yards away, saw him take off his shoes at top speed and put something in his shoe. His Patek Philippe? What else? The Vltava, where it passes through Prague, is wide. Now we're going to have trouble. And she was tempted to shout to him, for God's sake, so he wouldn't jump; but he did jump, feet first, and she ran over to grab his shoes and the luxury watch.

There below was Quique, wearing his 120-euro white shirt in the muddy water, showing Nerea the recovered bag, as he swam calmly, happily, manly toward the nearby shore. A group of Asians applauded from the bridge. And Nerea, with Quique's shoes in her hand and the Patek Philippe in a safe place, felt like a piece of overripe fruit about to burst from love. They met at the shore. Despite the wet, she threw herself into Quique's arms. And numerous cameras scattered around them recorded the embrace. The sopping-wet husband and the happy bride made their way back to the hotel. As they crossed the bridge hand in hand, Nerea recalled the SOINC who'd accosted her weeks before in the street.

99

THE FOURTH MEMBER

Long years in prison weigh on you. They weigh heavily. Arguments with comrades tire you out, demoralize you; the same with run-ins with jailers and the hunger strikes. Solitude, which on one hand can be a refuge, can also eat away at you. Stretched out on his bed, Joxe Mari feels insecure. For certain it was a mistake to answer the letter from Txato's wife. God help me if *ama* ever finds out. I don't even want to think about it. But this is exactly what he hasn't been able to stop doing for a long time now, and since he wrote to Bittori, with even greater intensity: going round and round with his doubts, emptying the sack of memory at his feet; in a word, brainwashing himself. Here in prison thinking too much weakens you. It puts you face-to-face with the bitter truth. Here's your life, son, tossed aside like a pile of trash inside the four walls of a cell.

Caught up in rumination, he looks down at the floor, and what does he see? What do you think he sees? The floor here, which immediately turns into the floor in that flat on Avenida Zarauz one August Saturday so many years ago now, the city in festival mode. It was time for a general cleanup. Before the three of them took turns at the chore. That system caused problems. Is it my turn? Is it your turn? Always the same thing. All the work landed on the sucker whose turn it was. And mind you, they limited themselves to the absolutely essential, wipe this down with a rag, the vacuum cleaner a bit over there, just so they wouldn't be up to their necks in filth. It was Joxe Mari who decreed: guys, on Saturdays, we all do a cleanup. And the three of them set up a barracks-like plan. Okay, you do the bathroom, you the living room, I'll take care of the kitchen. *Bim, bam, boom*, all done in an hour.

They had the radio on. As usual. You've got to keep the radio on. Just in case something happens. They find out whether there was a police raid yesterday, if there was an *ekintza* and where, if one of the *taldes* had fallen. It seems that the more secret some information should be, the faster the media made it public. And of course, that can suit those in the struggle to a T. How so? To take precautions and clear out in time if things went wrong. You never know.

Since approximately three in the afternoon, they knew that something big had taken place in the Morlans neighborhood. A radio announcer said that Morlans was cordoned off. The press was not allowed to enter. Who kept them out? The Guardia Civil. Shots were heard in the distance, many shots, and at least one explosion. The details were vague and scarce, but enough to reveal that the cops were carrying out a large-scale operation in San Sebastián.

Right from the start, Joxe Mari sensed trouble:

"Txopo, drop whatever you're doing and keep an eye on the street."

At around six, they got their first confirmation. The *txakurras* went up against the Donosti cell. There was talk of three dead in a Morlans apartment. The announcer added that there had been arrests in other places, though he did not say which places.

Joxe Mari to Txopo, who was still standing at the window:

"Anything?"

"Nothing."

But he was suspicious. When you least expect it, those bastards come and break down the door. To Patxo:

"I think you and I should take off and that Txopo should stay behind."

"What do we have to do with the Donosti cell? We don't know them at all and we're not their support *talde*."

"All our intelligence-gathering work may well have helped them. And we share the same link with the higher-ups, who the hell knows. Let's go, even if it's only for one night. Txopo will tell us tomorrow if there were any odd movements on the street."

Until then there had been three of them; now there were four.

The incessant suspicion of being watched. One more member. And a very influential one. They talked it over in the dark on a side of Mount Igueldo where they spent the night in sleeping bags. Patxo wasn't entirely convinced.

"Okay, how do you explain that they haven't come for us yet?"

"Because they hope they can pull one thread and get the whole skein."

"Is it possible you're getting a little paranoid?"

"The other day I rode up in the elevator with a neighbor. Hi, hi. It's the second time I'm seeing the guy in a short time. I don't know how you feel but things like that don't seem coincidences to me. And look at what happened today in Morlans. At some moment or other, the *txakurras* picked up somebody's trail. So they said: look, if we follow this bird sooner or later we'll find the flock. That's how this war works, Patxo. Don't try to make it more complicated."

"If it was that easy, they'd have finished off ETA already."

"Not even God can beat ETA. We lose militants, of course. But for each one who falls, two or three enter. We've got gunpowder for a good while."

An explosion goes off in the distance.

"What was that?"

And soon after, the night, toward the city, lit up in luminous cascades, in huge clover leaves of multicolored sparks. It was the fireworks for Grand Week over the bay. Joxe Mari and Patxo sat down to look at them from the edge of the thicket, and, forgetting their recent conversation, gave opinions about each pyrotechnical display.

"Look at that, will you."

"Damn, how pretty it is."

Once the show was over, they went back to the darkness of the trees and fell asleep in their sleeping bags in a summer night on the mountain.

There was a cricket concert. Patxo was cursing:

"All those people down there, sons of bitches, having a party, lining up to buy ice cream, and us up here breaking our asses for their freedom. Sometimes I feel like grabbing my automatic and, *bang, bang*, giving them a bit of what they deserve."

"Calm down, when we've got the whip, they'll dance."

At seven the next morning they turned up for their meeting with Txopo behind the law school.

"Well?"

"Nothing."

But Joxe Mari, bags under his eyes, hair messed up, was still suspicious. He ordered Txopo to find a temporary place for them to stay. Until then, they would sleep outdoors in the sleeping bags. Patxo expressed his opposition. Then Joxe Mari turned the suggestion into an order, and there will be no more discussion. He sealed his authority with a pair of obscenities. It wasn't easy to argue with Joxe Mari. He had strong, muscular arms and he was alarmed.

On Monday, Txopo told them they could stay in the apartment of a fellow student and his girlfriend, but that the couple had conditions. What were they? That they not go outside so no one would see them coming and going since the flat was in a seven-story building at the entrance to Añorga. There was a lot of neighborhood traffic, so they were to leave at the latest on Friday. To Joxe Mari that seemed a reasonable period of time. He showed his usual concern with food matters. Txopo: food wasn't a problem, all their hosts had to do was buy two loaves of bread instead of one.

"Okay."

In the afternoon they boarded the Lasarte bus. They got off at the Añorga stop, where the lady of the house was waiting for them. She led them to the apartment, which was in a building near the railroad tracks. She was pudgy, friendly, chatty, with the bangs typical of a woman on the *abertzale* left. Their host was rather silent, sour, and under his nose was a curved scar of the kind left after a harelip operation. By mutual agreement they decided to hide their real names, which in our case made sense since they didn't know us, while we could ask Txopo what their names were or look downstairs at the mailbox, but it was fine. It was a matter of adding a touch of adventure to routine.

As they ate dinner, they had a few laughs choosing nicknames. When they didn't forget them, they confused them, creating ridiculous scenes. So the couple took on the names Queen and Jack, while Joxe Mari and Patxo became Bread and Chocolate. This was her idea, but it was merely a simple pastime on that first day and was totally useless, because going forward when they spoke to one another they never used the agreed-on names or simply said: listen, you; unless, in the case of Patxo, who every other time he spoke called Joxe Mari by his name, just as Joxe Mari did to him.

Jack sulked from the start. Joxe Mari noticed that there's something wrong with this guy. And Patxo, at night, the two of them whispering to each other from bed to bed, also thought this guy doesn't like having us in his house. She on the other hand, talkative and a good cook, always created a happy mood. Let's just see if this isn't the problem:

"Jealousy?"

"For sure."

"Well, I don't see any reason for it."

And Joxe Mari, on his prison bed, his eyes fixed on the ceiling, even though his morale is way down, can't keep from smiling. Jack wasn't dumb; but of course, since during the summer season he worked renting umbrellas at the Ondarreta beach, he had no choice but to say goodbye in the morning and spend the whole day away from home. And on Tuesday, the Queen, big bosoms, walked into the bathroom scantily clad, pretending she hadn't realized Patxo was showering even though she could hear the water splashing on the floor. Once inside (oh dear, sorry), Patxo figured out her intention and, what else would he do?, invited her into the shower stall. And within range of Joxe Mari's hearing—he was in the living room reading the newspaper—they reached the stage of squeals and panting.

That night:

"You screwed her, didn't you?"

"Get ready, because tomorrow I'm sure it'll be your turn."

But Joxe Mari, as soon as he saw her coming, was ready to reject her. The thing is that this kind of situation always makes me feel awkward. I'm useless. And that prudish Josune never taught me. Besides, as he said alone to Patxo, he had his doubts about Jack. Mad with jealousy, he was more than capable of turning them in. The thought disturbed Joxe Mari mightily, annoyed as he was by the constant lascivious insinuations of the little fatty. Damn it, she's in heat. So on Thursday, without even having breakfast, they thanked their hosts for their hospitality and, with a half-hour interval between them, went back to the flat on Avenida Zarauz. Txopo assured them that during all those days he'd been keeping watch on the street and that he'd seen nothing suspicious.

100

THE FALL

They embarked on a rapid series of *ekintzas*, and if they didn't commit more it's because supplies were slow in getting to them. They complained: what's going on? Their connection, in a bad mood, told them they weren't the only ones. An ammonal bomb that they'd placed on the route of a convoy of the Guardia Civil failed to explode, and look, if it had gone off, it would be raining cops, and they'd have gained a lot of points within the organization.

They blew up a car dealership belonging to someone about whom they said this that and the other thing. Could it be true? Who cares? They blew it up. The building had to be evacuated. A bank robbery helped them improve their finances, which had really become a problem. They were living with less money than was proper. And they had already planned right down to the last detail the execution of a retired policeman when they found out that the entire leadership of ETA had been captured in a villa, house, chalet, or whatever it was outside of Bidart.

Total confusion. Even worse: the feeling they were orphans. What should they do? Joxe Mari, concerned, pessimistic, remembered that when they arrested Potros they found a long list of militants. I wonder if when those useless bastards were arrested the cops found the whole layout of the organization. Patxo spoke up:

"I'm not going back to the mountains."

They decided to wait to see what happened and suspend activities until the situation was cleared up. The three of them spent the entire day outside the flat. As a precaution and at the insistence of Joxe Mari, who saw plainclothes agents hidden in the clouds. They acquired fishing equipment. In good or bad weather, they made their way to the Tximistarri rocks. All except Txopo, who preferred movies and libraries to waiting for hours for the cork to sink. Before leaving, they put tiny pieces of thread and adhesive tape between the door and the frame. And under the doormat, a thin, curved piece of glass taken from a wineglass: if someone stepped on it, it would break. At nightfall, the first to return would check the door and the mat. If everything was as they left it, he would go in and turn on the signal light.

Months of uncertainty. When the hell are they going to reestablish command? They were without any connections. They received no weapons. Txopo had to turn to his parents for help paying the rent. Meanwhile the Spanish state relaxed and celebrated the Universal Exposition in Seville and the Olympic Games in Barcelona. One morning, Joxe Mari said fuck it, I'm going to take a chance. So he hopped aboard the Topo train at the Amara station and got out in Hendaya. After three days in France, he came back to the flat, starving, filthy, demoralized.

"ETA will never again be what it was. The hit we took in March was too hard."

"Who are the new bosses?"

"There are a few of them. They don't make things any clearer. They don't know whether they're coming or going."

Despite everything, he didn't come back empty-handed. He'd set up a meeting in a bar in the Gros neighborhood with a militant who could put him in touch, let's see if I've understood him, with one of the new chiefs or with someone close to him or something like that. Joxe Mari was dubious. He ordered Patxo an hour before the meeting to go have a drink.

"What?"

"Nothing."

Then he went and gave the guy a letter Txopo typed out in which the three of them asked to be transferred to Iparralde and to be in the reserves for a time. They justified their requests: we're not functioning properly, we need to be brought up to date in things like preparing bombs, we're ignorant of strategy. They had to wait several weeks for an answer. Request approved. And they assigned them a team of *mugalaris*. Txopo followed them a few months later.

Patxo was given a job on a poultry farm, the property of a French couple with nationalist convictions. With the owners and their children and with the help of a manual he started learning Basque. Didn't he already speak it? No, actually, except for the twenty or so words you pick up automatically, which was the reason his comrades always scolded him severely. If you don't speak Basque, you're not Basque, they would say, even if you're in ETA. He would always protest that he was dedicated to the cause of independence. They told him to go to hell.

And as for Joxe Mari: he expressed having the greatest interest in increasing his knowledge of explosives. The failed attack on the Guardia Civil convoy was a thorn in his memory. And Txopo? Txopo finally went through the arms course. So when they all went back to the struggle, the three of them were convinced they formed a more competent, stronger, deadlier *talde* than before.

Five months later they were arrested. And still, after so many years, Joxe Mari asks himself what went wrong, who went wrong? Was the organization chock-full of moles, as people said? Did the three members of the *talde* lower their guard? I didn't, but Patxo? There's no other explanation. What at first was mere suspicion soon became a certainty. They were caught just a few days before they were to make a spectacular attack, when they had everything ready: the time, the place, the car bomb. And Joxe Mari had not the slightest doubt that someone squealed. During the trial in the National Court, whenever he happened to be with Patxo in the holding tank, he wouldn't deign to speak to him. He didn't even honor him with a glance. As if he didn't exist.

It took him a long time to change his opinion, though even now he's still convinced it was Patxo's fault they were caught. I recognize that it didn't make sense for him to collaborate with the *txakurrada* just so he could serve a long sentence in jail, where he is still. So he didn't betray us, not at all; but he was imprudent.

One night they saw he was melancholy, down.

"What's wrong with you?"

"My father is dying. I don't think he'll last much longer."

Red lights flashed inside Joxe Mari's head:

"How did you find out?"

Understanding that he'd already said too much, Patxo had no

choice but to confess he'd secretly visited his family. When? Actually, several times. A serious lapse in discipline. His comrades demanded details. He gave them, each one worse than the other. His father, skeletal, pale, suffering terrible pains. His father who no longer recognized anyone. His father who.

"Okay, enough."

It hadn't even been a month since they'd changed apartments for security reasons. And now this. Joxe Mari could not get to sleep that night. He got out of bed several times. From the dark room, he spied on the deserted street, the burning street lamps, the parked cars. Five, ten minutes, and he went back to bed. In the morning, he spoke alone to Txopo.

"I've got a bad feeling. What do you think?"

"It may well be that no one saw him and that you're worrying over nothing."

"It's certain that our names are on some piece of paper intercepted by the police. Or maybe some prisoner has named us while they were beating the shit out of him. So, all they have to do is put a plainclothes *txakurra* near our *aitas'* houses. They get one and they get us all. Should we get the hell out?"

"Again? Wait a few days. Let's carry out this *ekintza* and then we'll change our place of residence."

He let himself be convinced, he who was so careful, so suspicious. Maybe he sensed he was tired. Tired of what? Of all the coming and going, of watching out, of spending his life in a constant state of nervousness and tension, and of this fucking underground life that eats away at you little by little. He could have defended himself because between the explosion at the door and the instant when the first *txakurra* charged into his room shouting at the top of his lungs he had time to grab his pistol. But screw it. I'm still young and someday they'll let me out. It was 1:25 a.m. In the first moment, I felt relief. Probably because I was deluded and hadn't the slightest idea about what was waiting for me.

101

"Txoria txori"

As soon as he feels, senses, smells the dust of sorrow floating up from the floor, he starts whistling his favorite song. He doesn't have to think about it. It comes on its own. He's deeply grateful for that song. His mind works that way. Sometimes, when he walks to the dining room or in the patio or after saying goodbye to his mother in the visitors room, he seeks its tranquility: *Hegoak ebaki banizkio*, whispering it so low that it's as if he were merely thinking it, always imitating the voice of Mikel Laboa. He's promised himself: the day he's set free, as soon as he gets to the village, he'll go up to the mountain to sing "Txoria txori" with no other witnesses than the grass and the trees.

As they were leading him out of the flat, his eye happened to land on Laboa's CD. He hadn't listened to it for a long time. There it was, on the table, and there it remained. For Joxe Mari, it was the last image of the world that had been his until then, the world he was leaving behind forever.

The search went on for several hours. The police kept them apart, each one in a different room, their hands behind their backs in cuffs. Weapons? Yes indeed, there were a few. The rest of their supplies were in the cache; but the *txakurras* would find all that out later. In the presence of the court clerk they questioned him. And this, what is it? And where do you have? And where are you storing? They put them in different vehicles. Joxe Mari was the last one they brought to the street.

"Let's go, tough guy."

It was getting light. The coolness of the morning, the chirping

birds, neighbors looking out of windows. And as he entered the
van, a punch from a Guardia Civil who thought Joxe Mari was
staring at him brusquely tore him out of his dazed drowsiness. He
wasn't to look at him. And next to him, another Guardia Civil said
in mock calm:

"You fucked up, *gudari*."

They forced him to keep his head between his legs, the way
it was when he went for his interview with Pakito. And in that
position, the song came into his mind for the first time, *Hegoak
ebaki banizkio / nerea izango zen*. They traveled at high speed. For a
moment, he felt safe within the song. It was going to be his refuge,
his deep lair. I hide there and make them think they've got me.

Destination point: the Intxaurrondo barracks. After taking his
fingerprints and his mug shots, they stripped him, and one guard
said we're going to treat you okay here, but you have to deserve it.
We don't give gifts. They removed the earring from his ear. No fag-
gots allowed. And they covered his head in a balaclava. They must
have put it on backwards because he saw nothing. They locked him
up in a cell. No insults, no shoving, no beating. The hours went by.
He heard footsteps and muffled voices. Suddenly some screams of
pain, moaning. Patxo? Joxe Mari, still handcuffed, tried to fight the
cold remembering the song.

At some moment in the morning they took him for interrogation. He should be smart, his buddies confessed and left him
holding the bag. Coward, traitor, incompetent, they'd called him
everything.

"Nice friends you've got, they blame you for being caught by us."

The *txakurras* riddled him with questions whose answers they
knew only too well. Trivial questions: what was his name, what
were his comrades' names, how old was he, where was the cell's
apartment. And the questions, questions, questions were repeated
so quickly that Joxe Mari couldn't finish answering them. Sometimes one voice in front of him and one behind or at the side would
ask two different questions at the same time. And even though he
saw no one, he realized because of the various voices, the footsteps,
and other noises that he was surrounded by a large number of
the Guardia Civil. Suddenly six, seven, eight continuous punches
rained down on him. Someone was shouting near his ear. He only

understood isolated words: "patience," "you deny," "getting tired,"
"collaborate." All shouted. And threats. And more punches. And
insults. He fell off the chair, did they knock him down? They beat
him while he was flat on the floor, fucking murderer, myriad kicks
all over his body. With his hands behind his back he couldn't defend
himself.

They sat him back on the chair. Someone spoke in a low voice.
What did he say? No idea. Whispers. Now came other questions.
And he realized that in the brief time it took him to answer they
weren't beating him, so he tried to lengthen his answers by adding
details, most of them superfluous. And it was clear they'd squeezed
a shitload of information out of Txopo and Patxo. Which was why
the questions now referred to minute matters from the daily life
of the three militants and to concrete aspects of attacks, of supply
deliveries, about all of which the *txakurras* knew everything.

They wanted names. The slightest hesitation was matched with
a punch. And then there was that Guardia Civil, at some distance,
who suggested putting a bullet in the back of the ETA man's fucking
neck and throwing him into the sea. Joxe Mari's face was burning
under the balaclava. And the song? It didn't come to him, he didn't
remember it, he couldn't think. After two, three hours of beatings
they still hadn't asked about the cache sites. Maybe it was a trap
built into the interrogation. He decided to tell where they were.
Maybe that way they'll stop beating me. He said: the weapons are
in such-and-such a place. Is that right? So why didn't he say so
before? And how could they know he wasn't lying? They took off
the balaclava. And at the same time a hand brutally pulled his hair
to lower his head: they forbade him to look at their faces. They
brought over a map of the province. They even gave him water.
Lukewarm but water nevertheless. And in an instant, he was pointing to a place. He noticed that the site of the cache was marked with
an X. So, they knew. They didn't even bring him there. For sure,
they'd already gone with one of his comrades or with both and dug
up the containers.

After night had fallen, they pushed him into a vehicle, with three
txakurras who went on asking him questions, more than anything
to humiliate him. What did he think of the Spanish flag. If he had
a girlfriend and how many times had he screwed her. That sort of

thing. And except for a few punches at the start of the trip, they didn't beat him during the whole ride to Madrid. Since last night's dinner he hadn't eaten a thing. But hunger wasn't his principal problem. Sleep was worse. And as soon as his eyes closed and his head sagged under the weight of fatigue, they yanked hard at his hair.

"Wake up, *gudari*."

Then they started talking among themselves about their own lives. They left him in peace, though they still kept watch in case his eyes closed. They did close. It was impossible for them not to close. The *txakurras* shook him violently, they pulled his hair. Finally, they let him sleep for a while. Suddenly the song came to me. *Ez zuen aldegingo*. Or maybe he just dreamed it. Nothing, a few seconds, words without images. And that did me a lot of good.

When they woke him up, still at night, the vehicle was crossing the streets of Madrid at top speed. The final destination? The general headquarters of the Guardia Civil, on Guzmán el Bueno Street. He doesn't know what's waiting for him. How the hell would I know? I thought that at Intxaurrondo they'd given the standard beating. In the parking lot, they made him stand for a while, his face to the wall. They know his comrades have also just arrived and this was so they wouldn't see one another. A brick building. Offices and holding areas. They brought him to an underground cell. They warned him: help us out, don't look at anyone's face or talk to any other prisoners in case you pass any.

And an infernal circle begins for Joxe Mari: it begins at the cell, moves to the interrogation room, then to the medical examiner, then back to the cell, and then starts over. Four days incommunicado including the Intxaurrondo barracks time. He should collaborate, not put up a fight, he shouldn't be too smart for his own good, he should collaborate, collaborate, the fun is over. They put a mask on his face. Then a balaclava, then another, three in all. He sweats, trembles. These guys also want names. Had he been with so-and-so, if he knew this guy. They accused him of attacks. He denied it and they instantly smacked him several times in the head with clubs or sticks covered with something, I don't know what, foam rubber or insulating tape. More questions, more punches. So he wouldn't have any illusions, they made him hold a pistol and a clip, still with his hands behind his back. He was to hold tight so his fingerprints would be sharp. Congratulations, ETA man. You just became the murderer of someone or other.

"This is what we call reliable evidence."

And suddenly, come on, do ten deep knee bends. Questions about his private life, his parents, his friends, the village bars, the *ikastola*, the *abertzale* people in town. More knee bends and the elevator. He doesn't understand. They'll teach him. They put him opposite the wall and there he has to hunker down, get up, hunker down again, and go on like that, covered with sweat, for a long time.

They put a plastic bag over his head. The lack of air made him panic. He fought out of pure anguish. He was so strong it took several agents to subdue him. Two, three sitting on him while another tightened the bag around his neck. Death was inside the bag. There comes a point after which you fall onto the other side. Then there is no oxygen to bring you back to life, and they have to get rid of your body. Your open mouth tries at all costs to breathe in a bit of air, no matter how little. But all that comes in is the plastic. They know the critical point. Joxe Mari feels his lungs are about to explode. On the verge of passing out, they allow him a gulp of air before bringing him once again to the edge of suffocation. They do that eight, nine times. And finally, yes, he lost consciousness.

He told the medical examiner they'd tortured him. And the doctor in a bored voice told him that he could only include wounds in the report and nothing about subjective opinions or value judgments. Any broken bones? Any hemorrhaging? Nothing? In any case, he should speak to the judge, though it won't do you much good. Joxe Mari, his face swollen, but without visible wounds, did not make a point of it. And after, whenever he visited the infirmary, he limited himself to finding out the date, the time, and to drink water.

The second, or was it the third night?, they subjected him to electric charges. Naked, wearing the balaclava, flat on his back on the rough floor, they applied the electrodes to his legs, his testicles, behind his ears. He folds up, throws up, screams. Sometimes his body experiences a violent shudder, when they make the electrodes spark close by to scare him. And more questions and more punches, truncheon smacks on the forehead and on the back and on the shoulders. They want to know when he joined ETA, who recruited him, what his training was like, who does the teaching, who gives the orders. And punches and electrodes. They brought him to the doctor, his body spotted with reddish stains, small burns, and a few bleeding wounds. The doctor put some ointment on them. He said it was six p.m.

A day later, the program changed. They got him out of the underground cell. And one of the agents who accompanied him to the office warned him along the way:

"Be very careful not to say anything different from what you've told us, because if you do we'll bring you downstairs again and you won't come out alive."

Upstairs, charm, manners, and the presence of a legal-aid lawyer. The questions don't differ from those asked in the basement interrogations, but when asked calmly and not shouted they had a conversational air. He followed instructions. It didn't matter as long as he avoided the savagery of the interrogations. And he signed the papers disdainfully, without looking at them.

There was no more mistreatment. In the morning, they made him bathe. As he got dressed, a *txakurra* in a good mood spoke to him. Did he think that at his age it was worthwhile to join ETA just so he could spend years in jail, throw away his youth, and make his parents suffer, instead of enjoying life, starting a family, and things like that. He offered him a cigarette.

"I don't smoke."

During the morning, the same officer led him to the office of the National Court. Joxe Mari had a ball of hatred in his chest. A hard, hot ball. I never felt that, even during the *ekintzas*. He rejected the lawyer assigned to him. He demanded someone of his own ideological persuasion, someone experienced in defending ETA prisoners. After a long discussion, they called in a woman lawyer, the questioning began. As soon as he heard the first question, Joxe Mari said he'd been tortured. The judge rolled his eyes.

"Here we go again."

The judge, in a bad mood, looking over some papers, suggested he present his charges in court. He added that this was neither the moment nor the place to do so. And Joxe Mari knew he was powerless and the ball of hatred never stopped growing inside his body, and when all was said and done, it was all the same to him.

He denied the accusations and, to end that circus once and for all, said he was ready to answer questions, which he did, dry and sharp, in a marked Basque accent.

After he'd made his statement, they brought him to the cells. There they left him alone for a long time to wait for the van that would carry him to jail. It smelled of moisture, of old air. And on the wall, surprise, there were phrases in Basque and the ETA anagram, and the outline of Euskal Herria with the motto *Gora Euskadi askatuta* inside it. A pity he didn't have a ballpoint pen. A kind of euphoria came over him, perhaps because he didn't feel he was alone even if he was alone, I understand what I'm saying. And he began to sing, first in whispers, then in a normal voice: *Hegoak ebaki banizkio*.

102

THE FIRST LETTER

Dear Joxe Mari." Dear? Are you crazy? She scribbled out the word as soon as she saw it written. Opposite Bittori, on the wall, hung Txato's photo. You, stay calm, I'm only trying things out here. The sheet of paper was profaned by that insincere, formulaic greeting. Bittori grabbed another from the pile resting on one side of the table. She wrote leaning forward awkwardly so that she could withstand the pain in her stomach, a pain that hadn't let up since the last hour of the afternoon. Ikatza was dozing lightly a short distance away on one of the sofa cushions. From time to time she opened her eyes. From time to time she licked a paw. And more than half an hour had passed since midnight.

"Hi, Joxe Mari." Utterly corny. "*Kaixo*, Joxe Mari." She grimaced. That expression meant pretending there was an intimacy they didn't have. Finally, she simply wrote his name followed by a colon. She was tempted—punctiliousness?—to call herself the Madwoman, which is how his family refers to me. She found that out from Arantxa, whom she often met on the street, always in the company of that caregiver with the face of an Indian from the Andes who wheels her around. "My parents call you the Madwoman, but pay no attention to them." Bittori thought that if she revealed that confidence she might cause a rift between brother and sister. So she didn't reveal it. Instead she wrote: I'm Bittori, you probably remember me, it's not my intention to annoy you, believe me I'm free of hatred, et cetera. She reread the first paragraph with disgust, but what else can I do? Just keep going, and if there's a problem, you can correct it.

On a separate sheet, she'd listed the subjects she wanted to bring up in the letter. Not many. And it wasn't her intention to go on too long. Why go to all that trouble when he might not answer me? Even so, those few issues had kept her tense and brooding, insecure and sleepless, for several days. She got right to the point. It wasn't rancor that moved her. Her reason for writing him? To learn the details of how her husband died. Especially, who fired the shots. More: that she was willing to forgive, but under one condition. Which was? That he ask her for forgiveness. She added that this wasn't a demand but a plea. All that: didn't it mean she was lowering herself excessively? It didn't matter. She wrote that because of her illness she only had a short time left. She instantly erased the sentence. Just then another stab of pain came over her. Ikatza must have noticed, because she woke up alarmed.

"I've reached an age when I don't think I have much life left in me." She reread. Yes, those words sounded more discreet. The truth seemed too strong. If I say it outright, he'll think I'm lying. Even worse: that I'm trying to make him feel sorry. Only she knew the truth. Not even her children, though she thought it unlikely Xabier didn't suspect something. If he didn't, why would he insist she visit the oncologist? Blaming old age was less melodramatic. For sure, when he reads that part, he'll think about his mother, as aged as Bittori. That will soften him. And of course, she would be very grateful if, before they buried her, he told her the circumstances of Txato's death. She needed to know, that was all.

She came to the delicate matter of telling him why should we fool ourselves, because Txato, the day he was killed, when he got home at lunchtime, told her he'd seen Joxe Mari and that he'd stopped for a moment to talk to him. And even though she hadn't attended the trial at the National Court, because no one bothered to tell her about it, she found out from his sentence that it had been proven that Joxe Mari was implicated in the murder. She erased. In the death of her husband. "I'm asking you, from the bottom of my heart, to tell me your version of the events." If he didn't like the idea of writing, she was willing to visit the prison to speak directly to him and that way there will be no paper trail if that's the problem. Her only desire, she repeated, was to learn the truth before she died and to forgive. She erased. And that he ask her forgiveness and that she forgive instantly and have that peace and then I can die.

Two o'clock. Bittori reread the letter scattered over with crossed-out words. I'll make a clean copy in the morning. Just then her first wave of nausea rolled over her. Oh God. Immediately, a second wave. When the third hit, she vomited onto the table, she couldn't help it, and of course onto the letter and a little on the pile of paper. When she leaned back from the table, she fell or let herself fall, she doesn't really know. She does remember that the stab of pain inside her stomach was so intense it forced her to go into a fetal position on the carpet. Despite all that, she was still not ready to believe in God the way others do when they find themselves facing the great blackness. What for? If I die, I die. She made an effort to drag herself to the telephone, just over there, nine feet away, on top of the bureau, but nevertheless so far away. Far away? Unreachable. I'm not getting over this one. I'm here, and I'm staying here. My children. Before she lost consciousness, the last thing she saw was Ikatza, who had come over to rub against her face. The cat caressed her forehead with her black fur and her smooth tail. Ikatza, silent, Ikatza, black, Ikatza pretty. You might be the last thing I see in this life.

She woke up at about ten, the living room brimful of morning light. Pain? Not a trace. Mysteries of the body. She cleaned house slowly, dividing the work into short segments. What we don't want is. And she opened doors and windows to air the place. She telephoned Xabier, and mother and son spoke for five minutes about trivia. She then called Nerea, and mother and daughter spoke for half an hour about trivia. At midday, she ate nothing. She didn't dare. She picked at some Swiss chard, a tiny bit of potato, both left over from the previous evening, more than anything because she hated to throw food away, but it was useless. Why is that? She was afraid to send solid food to her painful guts. And finally, to trick her hunger, she made herself a big cup of chamomile tea.

Should she travel to the village before five? It didn't make much sense. Joxian was a man who slept his siesta, so as a general rule he gets to the garden at about midafternoon. The first time, Bittori waited for him to arrive hidden among the trees on the other side of the river. Then she realized she could also observe him from the bridge, though only through a clear space in the hazelnut bushes. If she stayed on the bridge near the bus stop, she'd save herself a long walk. The only thing she wanted in this case was to see him arrive.

To avoid her completely, Joxian hid in the shed, but this man doesn't fool me. Besides, I'm not about to shout to him. Are you kidding?

For a moment, she considered the possibility that Joxian might reject her letter. Would he dare? He is a bit cowardly after all. He was even when young. She took the envelope out of her bag. She should just put it there. Where? On top of a rabbit cage. As if it made him sick to his stomach to touch it.

"I'll give the letter to Miren and say it's from you, okay? But after that it's out of my hands. She's the one who visits."

"You don't go to see your son?"

"Me? Very little."

The first few times she went to see him at the garden, Joxian was standoffish, brusque. Bittori didn't know whether it was out of timidity or anger. Because this man is not the kind who bears a grudge. He's not a hating guy. What do I have to lose? And by always being friendly with him, even if the poor man felt so uncomfortable, she gradually wore down his harshness.

Joxian, red-faced (from wine?), jutted his chin toward the letter:

"This is going to be trouble for me."

"Well, I'd give it to your wife, but something tells me she doesn't want to see my face, though I have no idea what I did to her."

"There's no way to know if she'll bring it to my son."

"Why? It's written with good intentions."

"Damn it, you're stirring up things that shouldn't be stirred."

Did he give the letter to Miren? How can I be sure: he went two days in a row without visiting the garden, at least at his usual time. Also, since it was raining there was no need to water the plants. But what about the rabbits? He'd have to feed them, wouldn't he? Bittori concluded that to avoid her Joxian came down to the garden at the last hour of afternoon or when night had already fallen, or early in the morning.

On the third day, Bittori walked through the village with little hope of finding Joxian. After going here and there, she went into the Pagoeta to have a decaf coffee. By then, her almost daily presence in the streets of the village had stopped being noticed by anyone. In the bar, no one spoke to her, but by the same token they didn't glare at her. She paid, and as she left, a few people coming in greeted her with a slight nod of the head.

She decided, it wasn't raining, to cross the plaza toward her house and then to make a small detour so she could pass by Joxian's place. A few steps later she spotted the wheelchair and the small woman with Indian features sitting next to it at the rail. Without hesitating, she made her way toward them through the shadows cast by the linden trees. And Arantxa's face lit up with joy, as it did whenever she saw her. With a brusque gesture of her good hand she demanded her iPad. The caregiver handed it to her. Bittori leaned over to kiss Arantxa, who responded with her usual mute delight. And, as if possessed by haste, she nervously started pressing the keys with one finger. It was clear she urgently wanted to communicate something. Bittori read: "My mother tore up your letter."

"She tore it up?"

Arantxa nods. She writes again: "Don't give her any more letters. She won't bring them. She's bad."

Her thin, pale finger scrambles among the rows of letters. The caregiver remains silent, her eyes fixed on the screen. Bittori reads: "If you want to write to the terrorist in my family there is a solution."

"What solution?"

Just write directly to him at the prison. At the prison? Arantxa answers with two decisive nods. She tries to articulate words. She makes some high-pitched, incomprehensible sounds. Sometimes she is able to phonate a bit; but today, what's wrong? No matter how hard she tries, she can't do it, she falls into despair, she gets blocked up. Then she writes: "He's in Puerto de Santa María I, module 3. You just put his name on the envelope and it will definitely get to him."

"Do you think he'll read the letter?"

Arantxa gestures with her hand, as if expressing doubt. The other, spastic hand, she keeps pressed to her stomach.

103

The Second Letter

And now with not the slightest trace of joy or any other recognizable feeling on her face, her features frozen, she saw Bittori walk toward the far end of the plaza. She's a good woman. There were a few pigeons pecking around on the ground mixed in with some hopping sparrows, and on the side street, in front of the houses was the man delivering propane gas, filthy, powerful, raising the hundredth tank of the day to his shoulder.

Celeste waited until Bittori disappeared to say:

"Miren will be furious if she finds out we stopped to talk with that lady."

Arantxa's paralyzed neck wouldn't allow her to turn her head around to confront her caregiver, standing behind the wheelchair, face-to-face. So she wrote with a furious finger on the iPad keyboard: "Are you going to tell her?"

"Of course not, Arantxa. What do you take me for? But look around at all the people who may be keeping an eye on us."

She didn't want to create a lie by asking Bittori about the content of the letter. Why, when she already knew. Did she read it? Of course. And she kept it, oily stains and all, in a drawer.

Three nights before they were getting ready to eat dinner, and I think the entire province of Guipúzcoa reeked of my mother's fish and fried garlic. Arantxa in her wheelchair next to the table. The window wide open. Out the window flow smells and smoke. And suddenly the familiar sound of the key in the lock. Joxian walked in scratching his side, his beret a bit fallen toward his neck. In a plastic bag, he carried lettuce, beans, and other greens he grows in the garden, and he put it all down there, next to the urn of the Virgin that goes from house to house and which it was their turn that day to take care of. And with his free hand, because the other never stopped scratching his ribs as if he were playing a harp, he pulled the white envelope out of the inside pocket of his sheepskin jacket.

"It was given to me so you could bring it to Joxe Mari."

Miren, clenching her teeth, fury in her eyes, sought confirmation:

"Who gave it to you?"

"Who else? The Madwoman."

"You talked to her?"

"What can I do when she walks into the garden? Hit her with a stick?"

"Give it here."

She snatched the letter. She tore it in half. She brought the halves together, then with a haughty expression on her face, tore the halves. She tore it all again. And then she threw the shreds into the garbage pail she kept in a cabinet with a door below the sink.

"Dinnertime."

Did they argue? No. The only thing was that he wasn't to go down to the garden for a few days. And what about the rabbits? Did he have to let them die of hunger?

"You can go early to feed them."

"She'll probably climb over the wall and stick letters in the cracks in the door."

"Don't bring them here. Better to burn them."

The next day he got up almost as early as he did during his time at the foundry so he could take care of his animals as soon as possible. It was then he surprised Arantxa in the kitchen, and what are you doing here? As if she didn't see him. Sitting in the wheelchair opposite the sink, Arantxa had the garbage can on her lap. With a finger, she asked her father to be quiet. This took place at the time when, leaning on a cane and on the furniture, on anything handy, she, with her will of iron, was able to get up on her own and take short, hesitant, trembling steps despite her paralyzed foot. She'd already fallen down twice but without serious consequences. Finally, with the fingers of her good hand covered with grease, she extracted the final piece of the letter from the stinking can.

Joxian, in whispers:

"If *ama* finds out, she'll raise the roof."

Arantxa: shrugs her shoulders, a blasé shake of her head, as if saying who cares?, I'm not afraid of her. She cleaned up the torn letter on her mother's apron, hung behind the door. She moved away awkwardly in her wheelchair. Her father tried to help her. She, surly, rejecting, wordlessly informed him she needed no help. But he, as usual, was overcome with compassion. How was his daughter going to move the wheelchair with only one hand? Actually, just as she did a short time before, only in the opposite direction.

"Go on, go on."

And trying not to make noise so that Miren, still asleep, wouldn't hear them, he quickly wheeled her to her room.

Alone, on the side of the bed where there are no safety bars, having smoothed out the sheets as best she could, she reconstructed the letter. "Joxe Mari: it's Bittori writing to you. You're probably surprised that." So by midmorning, when she ran into Bittori, Arantxa was aware of the letter's contents. She hesitated between putting the papers back into the garbage and keeping them, but keeping them for what purpose. Well, she'd see. And for now, she hid them in a dresser drawer.

At one, Celeste brought her back to the house. Father, mother, and daughter ate, their eyes fixed on the TV, *Wheel of Fortune*. But Joxian, wrapped up in himself, sleepy, is not interested in the program. And besides, the cheers of the youthful audience drive him mad.

"Couldn't we lower the volume a bit?"

After lunch, while passing the time waiting for the ambulance that takes her to afternoon physical therapy, Arantxa wrote to her brother on her iPad. She told, she explained, she announced that Bittori, Txato's wife, would write him in prison "and I'd like you to answer her, this is your sister asking you, your sister who doesn't forget you, *ama* needn't know." In that severe but affectionate tone. She finished: "She's a good woman. *Muxu bat.*" It's bad luck that a left-handed woman can't use her left hand. She worked like mad, not accepting her limitations, with more rage than skill, to copy the text onto a sheet of paper, foreseeing that, of course, the attempt would be a failure. Did she fail? Completely.

She hadn't planned to see her children until Saturday, and today was Thursday. What to do? Who could transcribe the letter and immediately mail it? A delicate matter: whoever does it will read the letter. She discarded her father. Celeste? I won't see her until tomorrow. Besides, I don't trust her. It isn't that she'd be carrying tales to Miren, not at all. But for sure she tells her family things about her everyday experiences with the incapacitated woman (or paralyzed woman, I have no idea what word those people would use) and who's to know if they don't go around gossiping.

An hour of physical therapy. When she arrived, she said hello in a way that everyone present would understand:

"Hi."

As a result, surrounded by white gowns, she was praised and congratulated. It's important to raise the patient's morale. It's the norm there, even though Arantxa is extremely annoyed when people speak to her as if she were a child and treat her the way they treat children and old people. I'm not retarded.

The rehabilitation plan: exercises intended to reduce the hypertonia in her left hand and arm. Then they'd work with her lower extremities. The therapist asked her if the tingle had recurred. No, it hadn't. A good sign. Progress is slow, slow, but there *is* progress. And at the end of the hour they'll try to stand her up and have her hold herself in place, and walk a few yards, of course with support.

There was too much hustle and bustle in the room, a constant coming and going of therapists, patients, and those accompanying them. And voices. Arantxa did not have her iPad at hand. So there was no possibility of asking anyone to do her that favor, but later on there was, when she was alone with the speech therapist and she could explain her request. She:

"Is the letter very long?"

Not at all. Fourteen lines. The best thing would be for Arantxa to send it as an e-mail right then and there, and she at night, as soon as she got home, would write it out and slip it into a mailbox near her street. She promised. Did she keep her promise? Arantxa had her doubts. But after a month, she got a postcard inside an envelope, why didn't her mother read it?, from Joxe Mari. It contained jokes and affectionate remarks, and a postscript that said: "She wrote." He didn't say who and didn't have to. "And I answered her."

104

The Third Letter
and the Fourth

A letter from his sister, what a surprise, arrived. Open, of course. Joxe Mari is closely monitored. His time out in the courtyard is limited, approximately every two weeks they move him to another cell, they read his mail, they photocopy it and archive the copies.

The first time his sister has written to him in more than fifteen years. He doesn't count the Christmas cards with formulaic messages that inevitably ended "and a prosperous"—was she teasing him?—"New Year from this family that doesn't forget you."

Once, at the beginning, she added a few lines of encouragement to a letter from his parents but that was that. Arantxa, the Spaniard in the family, but he loves her just the same. As far as I'm concerned, she could be wrapped in the Spanish flag. I wouldn't allow it for any other relative, even my little brother. He the very least. Arantxa is my sister, hell. She married that asshole who left her. That's her punishment for being a Spaniard.

Suddenly Joxe Mari remembers his mother saying, super serious in one of those phone calls he has a right to, that his sister had a very bad accident in Mallorca. What was my sister doing in Mallorca? On vacation with Ainhoa. And then Miren of course doesn't have the slightest delicacy.

"I spoke with a doctor down there. Insofar as I understood, she's going to be stupid forever."

It wasn't her handwriting. Of course, someone had written for her because she can't. And she announced a letter that would likely arrive soon. From whom? From Bittori, Txato's wife. Just what the doctor ordered. And that he should please not talk about this with *ama*. Joxe Mari's initial joy faded. What is all this? He knew from his mother, she told him just recently in the visitors' room, that the woman is ripe for internment in the Mondragón madhouse and that:

"She's gotten into her head to hound us. She won't leave *aita* in peace. Ever since the armed struggle ended, the enemies of Euskal Herria have become emboldened. They seem to think they're the only ones who've suffered. It's obvious that what they're looking for is revenge. They want to harass us so that we give up our dignity and ask their forgiveness. Me? Ask for forgiveness? Never."

Two days later he was handed the letter announced by his sister. His first impulse? To rip it up right there in front of the guard. It was then he understood why Arantxa, doubtless in a big hurry, had written to him. To restrain him. To rein in his instincts. If she hadn't written, the Madwoman's letter would have gone right down the toilet. But as soon as he was alone, he read it.

This is a trap to undermine my morale. As if I wasn't already down from being in a Spanish extermination prison. The humble tone, the fear of annoying, the ridiculous request. But who the hell does this old lady think she is? And I'm supposed to pass information about an *ekintza* to her? So the prison cops can get it, too? So she can show it to some super-fascist journalist?

He ripped up the letter. "She's a good woman." Not a chance in the world. But it was useless for him to get rid of the snips of paper as quickly as he could because now he knew the contents of the letter. "I'm Bittori. You may remember . . ." Even after a week had gone by, the carefully written lines persisted in appearing in his memory. He even invented a voice for them. The voice of Txato's wife as he remembered it. He heard it all the time. In the dining room, in the recreation patio, at night in bed while he waited for sleep to overcome him. A ghost that chased after him. He often dreamed of old times. Now even more. And he saw himself as he was then, standing outside the entrance to the Pagoeta, slurping an orange or lemon ice Txato bought for his children and for him and his brother and sister, all children, the street sunlit and people in their Sunday best. And the church bells. And the smell that flowed out of the bar, grilled shrimp, cigar and cigarette smoke.

He let some time pass, but finally he got fed up with all those imaginary ices and with smelling grilled shrimp down there in the uncontrollable depth of his mind. And he told himself: answer her with any dumb thing to get her back. Make her understand you aren't going to play her game. And that's what he did. In an instant, he wrote her: hostile, militant, rejecting. Nothing, four lines. That he wasn't sorry, that all he wanted was an independent Euskal Herria, socialist and *euskaldun*; that he was still in ETA, and that this was the last time he'd answer a letter. He then sent a postcard to his sister and handed over the two envelopes so the cops could check them before sending them on or, if they liked, wipe their asses with them or, if they liked, eat them with tomatoes.

He went on resisting. Other ETA prisoners, more and more, were quitting the organization, and that hurts. Pakito himself, if you can fucking believe it. The guy who'd given him his first pistol, the guy who said: kill everything you can. Pakito, who when the rest of us were going through our thousandth hunger strike secretly ate in his cell. And Potros and Arróspide and Josu de Mondragón and Idoia López. Were they expelled? Not a one. Why expel anyone? That would be like throwing you over the side of a beached ship. And about a year ago, and not for the first time, they'd asked Joxe Mari if he'd sign that letter where the forty-five signatories of this letter reject violence and ask forgiveness of the victims. Like children sorry they'd done a bit of mischief. Repentant, at this stage in the game and, above all, for what purpose? Really repentant? What they really want is to go home. Traitors. Softies. Egoists. To sacrifice yourself for this. For nothing. For absolutely nothing. He'd been thinking about it for a long while. In reality for years, and every time he sees his aged, decrepit mother in the meeting room, or when he found out about his sister, or when he thinks about his niece and nephew and realizes he doesn't know them and can't play with them, or when he finds out his *aita*'s become a slob rotting from sadness. Was it his fault? Probably. And the Spanish state stronger than ever. The emboldened enemy wants to settle accounts with us. The organization abandons the struggle and leaves us prisoners tossed aside like useless rags. He got a sudden flash of rage and disgust, a punch on the wall, so hard he skinned his knuckles, and he was crying a long while in the loneliness of his cell, first in silence, with his hands pressed to the wall, as if he were being searched; later, without changing position, when he again remembered the orange and lemon ices of his childhood, with sobs that could be heard outside, but he didn't care. He didn't care about anything.

The next morning, he sat down to write on a piece of lined notebook paper.

> *Bittori:*
>
> *Forget the letter I sent the other day. I was angry when I wrote it. It happens from time to time. Now I'm calm. I'll be brief. I did not shoot your husband. It doesn't matter who did it because your husband was an ETA objective. We can't turn back the clock. I'd rather it never happened. Asking forgiveness is difficult. I'm not mature enough to take a step like that. The truth is I didn't join ETA to be a bad guy. I was defending a few ideas. My problem is I loved my people too much. Am I supposed to repent that? That's all I have to say. I'm asking you to write no more letters. I'm also asking you to stay away from my family. I only wish you the best.*

He wrote a stark goodbye: *agur*. And now, what next? He didn't like the idea that some functionary would read the letter. Not because it contained compromising or relevant information, which it did not. It was something else. It was too intimate a letter. Here, even if I don't go into details, it's as if I were stripping naked.

He'd heard talk about the services of Pecas, an ordinary prisoner, second grade, drug addict, smashed-flat nose. A guy who when he talks with his marked Andalusian accent you see his tongue because he's missing teeth, both above and below. He did favors for cash. Joxe Mari approached him in the recreation patio.

"Pecas, when do you go out on leave?"

"Saturday."

"Want to earn five euros?"

"Depends. What's the job?"

"Drop a letter in a mailbox."

"That costs ten."

"Okay."

105

RECONCILIATION

So Miren and Arantxa went five years without speaking. They didn't call, they didn't send Christmas cards, they didn't wish each other a happy birthday. Nothing. And during all that time, Miren never saw her grandchildren and wasn't invited to either first communion. Invited? She never even received the usual commemorative cards. And in all those years she never saw her son-in-law, either, though that mattered little to her because she felt no love for him.

Hardheaded, mother and daughter, like fence posts, was what Joxian said. Like fence posts? Just his way of expressing himself. But he, yes, he would from time to time take the bus to San Sebastián and another from there to Rentería, to visit Arantxa and Guillermo. He would bring them greens and fruit from his garden, and once in a while a rabbit (at first alive, later skinned and ready for the pot, because the children, after playing with the animal, were horrified at the idea it would have to be killed). He'd spend the afternoon with his grandchildren, buy them trinkets, give them some money when he left. In sum, even if he was dull, silent, with no spark, he played the part of grandfather with great goodwill.

To keep the peace at home he would visit his daughter behind Miren's back. That he was going down to the garden and wouldn't be back until dinner. By the third or fourth time, Miren liberated him from his childish lies.

"Do you really think I don't know where you go?"

How did she find out? No idea. From then on, Joxian didn't bother with lies. If he was going to the garden, he would say clearly that he was going to the garden. And if he was going to see his family in Rentería, then he'd only say he was going out.

Back home, Miren simply asked:

"Well?"

"They're fine."

And that was all, unless Joxian, melancholy, prolonged the brief dialogue and asked if she might think of visiting her grandchildren someday.

"Me? They know where I live."

What Joxian didn't tell Miren was that Arantxa and Guillermo were at each other's throats. Sometimes, when he got to their flat, standing outside the door, he would hear them screaming at each other. And the children there, witnessing their parents' continual fights. Joxian would walk into the apartment with his sheaf of leeks or his bag of apples and find his daughter in tears, his grandchildren terrified, and Guillermo, looking like a madman, would stomp out of the flat without saying hello and slam the door behind him.

Arantxa, in a low voice, would tell her father that:

"I put up with it for the sake of the children."

For a long time Arantxa denied her body to Guillermo. Actually, she wouldn't even allow him to pat her on the shoulder as he passed by. And since the apartment was small, after the night when she decided she'd never again have sexual relations with her husband, they still went on sharing a bed, but not for long, ten or twelve days back-to-back until Arantxa bought herself a thin mattress that folded into three parts and from then on, she spread it on the floor and slept in her daughter's room.

Their last sexual encounter, she remembers, what a repulsive thing. Like two insects. Not a single loving word, not one damn kiss at the end. They'd had an argument during dinner about something or other, because they no longer argued about specific things but about everything and nothing, especially about nothing. And he, in bed, was suddenly in the mood. And go ahead, put it in. He finished immediately. She told herself: this is the last time. I'm not this guy's property. And she hated his smell, which before she liked so much. His nasal tone of voice, his explanatory chatter, his know-it-all ways all became unbearable to her.

Guillermo, arrogant, offensive:

"I'm going to the whorehouse."

"I see. So until now I've been your whore and free into the bargain."

Arantxa had a desire that grew stronger every day, a desire she couldn't satisfy. Why? Because she didn't earn enough in the shoe store.

What help could she expect from her mother when they weren't even speaking? From her father, yes, some help: lettuce, hazelnuts, and from time to time a few awkward words of consolation. From her in-laws, who were good people, the same: favors and cordiality for which she was thankful, that made life more bearable, but which did not supply her with the economic relief she longed for.

She knew she was trapped. It wasn't that Guillermo was earning much more; but, of course, with the two salaries the family could get along without hardships. On her way to work, on her way home, in the house, and, really, everywhere at all times, she was making calculations, always with the idea of separating from her husband. The mortgage, food, clothes, school costs. Expenses with even more expenses attached; expenses that she couldn't pay with her modest saleswoman's salary. Then she forgot the bills. She'd say to herself: I'll just leave, I'll find something, I'll remake my life. And then Endika would come into the kitchen with some request and a little later Ainhoa would appear needing something, and Arantxa would again understand she was trapped at the bottom of a well from which she could never escape.

What mattered least to her is that Guillermo (she stopped calling him Guille, he doesn't deserve it) goes out with other women. Some nights he didn't come home. Arantxa never called him to account. Jealousy? To the contrary, she was wishing he'd get involved with one of them, ask for a divorce, and disappear from her life.

One weekend he went to Jaca with his sweetheart. Arantxa found out from Endika:

"*Aita* went to Jaca with a girl."

"How do you know that?"

"Because I asked him if he'd take me and he said he can't because he's going with a girl."

"That must mean he's got a steady girlfriend."

"Of course."

At least he didn't hold back money to support the family. At home he never lifted a finger. No cleaning, no cooking. He never did. His mother did. Angelita, less and less able to move around because of her rheumatism and her bad hip, frequently came to the flat. She ironed, washed windows, made food for the children. And she could also count on Rafael to drive his grandchildren to one place or another and then pick them up. So on that side of things, Arantxa had no complaints. Her principal problem was her economic dependency. If I had a larger income, I'd already be divorced. But the apartment, but the children. Subjugation, chains, uncertainty. Fear? Possibly. And when she was alone she consoled herself thinking up plans for when her children were adults and lived away from home.

One Friday in May, Guillermo and Arantxa got tangled up in one of the bitterest arguments she can remember. A dispute that didn't escalate even farther because in a flash of panicked rage, Arantxa grabbed her purse and without changing out of her slippers dashed out of the house. That day ETA assassinated two national policemen in Sangüesa by putting a bomb under their car.

A few days earlier it was the fifth anniversary of the attack that ended the life of Manolo Zamarreño. Guillermo was still affected. In fact, he never again bought bread in the neighborhood bakery. One night he went out with a can of paint to cover over graffiti, ETA HERRIA ZUREKIN, which appeared that afternoon next to the entryway. And Arantxa tried to dissuade him, look, you're only going to get into trouble, but he went downstairs, I don't give a shit, and the next morning there was a huge white stain on the wall.

And it's my opinion that it was because of his sorrow and his painful memories and the rage that burned inside Guillermo that he lost control of himself. For the first time in ages, husband and wife agreed to do something as a family outside the house. And with their children they went to mass, with the idea of honoring the assassinated friend. Days later, *bam*, bomb and two men lose their lives in a similar way and at a time similar to when Manolo was killed. Who were the victims? Two policemen who'd come to Sangüesa with their mobile office to expedite making identification cards. And Guillermo's blood was boiling. That had to be the cause. Arantxa can't think of any other explanation. Husband and wife hadn't seen each other all day. She came home from work at nightfall. At the first sign of discord, because of something of no importance whatsoever, Guillermo exploded. What wild eyes, what bitterness, how he bellowed. Two men with children, he was saying. Two poor men murdered because they were wearing uniforms.

"Murdered by men like your brother."

My brother? They never spoke about him. Why does he bring him up when he knows it can hurt me? And then he adds he hopes he rots in jail. Who? Joxe Mari? Arantxa asked that he forget about her brother. He thought she was defending him, that she was defending that fucking murderer. Endika, sitting there, doing his homework, and Ainhoa in her room, doubtless listening to everything. Listening to their father shouting at the top of his lungs, in a harsh monologue, disrespectfully cursing, damning the moment when he agreed to give his children Basque names. Why did he? To make their *abertzale* grandmother happy, a woman they no longer spoke to.

"My children are Spanish, and I'm a Spaniard."

"Someone might hear you."

"Let them hear me. Or is it that you can't be a Spaniard in Spain?"

Arantxa ripped off her apron. She threw it on the floor. She uttered an ugly expression. She admits it. She felt offended. Because of being Basque? No, because to me being Basque or Spanish or any other damn thing means nothing. But she wouldn't allow him to insult her brother. So she said what she said, and he, who was a pain in the ass and a know-it-all, and a miserable jerk, but not violent, at least not until that day, raised his hand. To slap her? Why else? It was then, face-to-face with the monster that she'd rejected, that she recoiled in fright. She looked around. If she sees a knife or a kitchen spoon, scissors, something she can use to defend herself, it's certain she'd grab it. What she did grab was her bag hanging on a peg in the vestibule, and she left the house with a drumroll of palpitations in her breast. She was still in her slippers. And her bag, well, she took her bag because it occurred to her just then that she had her wallet in it. When she closed the door she heard behind her that Guillermo was calling her a nationalist. Something that, in his mouth, was an insult.

Her first thought? To spend the night with her in-laws. They lived nearby, at hand, but along the way she became doubtful. It's that she saw herself, horror of horrors, explaining things to them, revealing for their consideration the truth of her turbulent marriage. And, careful now, because she couldn't overlook the possibility that they might side with their son (an only child, family prince) or that they might ask her, especially Angelita, to be a submissive wife, a submissive daughter-in-law. So she counted her money in the light of a shop window and yes, she had enough for the bus.

An hour later, Miren opened the door. She didn't seem surprised, as if she'd been expecting her. She looked down at Arantxa's slippers. She said nothing. And right then and there, after five years, mother and daughter kissed each other, neither cold nor cordial.

"Going to have dinner?"

"What are you having?"

"Ratatouille and cod."

"Well, if you'll allow me to join you . . ."

"Girl, what silly things you say. How could I not allow you?"

The three of them ate in the kitchen. Arantxa never told her parents about the fight she'd had with Guillermo, and they never asked her why she was paying them this unexpected visit. They stuck their respective forks into slices of tomato with chopped garlic in oil laid out on a platter. Joxian, looking down, was smiling.

Miren:

"Mind telling me why you're laughing?"

Arantxa stepped in with a plausible answer from her father:

"Let him laugh. At least there's one person in the family who laughs."

106

CAPTIVITY SYNDROME

And then, as she found out much later, without her knowing it a priest had given her the last rites in the hospital. Her greatest fear, that she'd be declared dead. Suppose a novice doctor came into the room (or an experienced doctor but not friendly toward Basques), a nurse who was too young, maybe unhappy with her salary, which would cause her to work unwillingly, and seeing her still, any one of them might say without trying to get better proof: this woman isn't alive anymore, have her taken to the morgue, a new patient needs her bed.

Arantxa, a statue, could only blink. She could make no other movement. So when someone entered her room she never stopped blinking. They realize I'm not dead. She saw, heard, thought, but she could neither move nor speak. And she understood in her anguish everything being said around her. Tubes and catheters came out of her; she was surrounded by wires, machines, and she was living, if you can call that life, with the aid of a respirator.

A captive in an inert body. A mind captured in a suit of armor made of flesh. That's what she'd become. With sorrow she remembered her children and thought about her job, thought about what she'd say to the owner, can you imagine anything as stupid, when she got back, if she ever got back. What bad luck. At the age of forty-four. She had a thought that came to her often: perhaps it would have been better to die. At least the dead don't, that is we don't, make so much trouble for everyone.

Her mother suddenly appeared in her visual field.

"*Kaixo, maitia*. Since the doctor says you understand, I'll tell you, just in case that's true. Guillermo came to take Ainhoa home. He got to Palma yesterday. Now he pretends to be nice, but he doesn't fool me. We spoke awhile, and I'll tell you about it. He's come to say goodbye. Try to understand me. To say goodbye forever because you, of course, in the state you're in, don't interest him. Since you can't iron his shirts anymore . . . Anyway, I'd better keep my mouth shut. *Maitia*, blink your eyes twice so I know you understood me."

Half an hour later, Guillermo came in.

"Can you hear me?"

Arantxa couldn't fend off his kiss on her forehead. She didn't even see Guillermo's face. What expressions would he be making? Outside her visual range, he didn't have to put on fake expressions of sorrow. If it weren't for his voice, she would have no idea who was speaking to her. Why is he whispering? Does he think he's in a morgue and that you have to show proper respect for the dead?

"You don't have to worry about Ainhoa, okay? I'll take charge of her. I'm really sorry about what happened. Your mother told me you understand everything said to you."

Guillermo brought his face forward so she finally could see it. An experiment? He withdrew it little by little and, yes, Arantxa could follow the motion a bit, not much, with her eyes. As soon as she figured out he was testing her, she shut her eyes. As if she were sleeping. Guillermo couldn't guess that she was begging him from the depth of her silence not do any more talking, that he should go take care of his children and leave her in peace. But let's see: didn't he realize that his presence in that room made the tragedy of her disability all the more apparent and painful? What a pain this man is. It's impossible to express in words how much she dislikes him.

"I don't want to leave without thanking you."

That's all I need to hear.

"For many things you know about. For the years we've had together. For the children you gave me."

That I gave you? Brother, what a scene. Is he drunk?

"And the good times. I confess I'm responsible for the bad times. Seriously. I accept my guilt and I sincerely ask your forgiveness."

To Arantxa it seemed as if Guillermo was reciting words he'd memorized or that he was reading from a paper, like a cheat sheet passed to him in school. Unable to turn her head, she couldn't see for herself. And he just kept on going:

"I imagine your mother told you I came to say goodbye. That's true. Just as I said it to her yesterday, I say it to you now. My decision has nothing to do with what happened to you. Remember, we talked about this a long time ago."

A sport of nature. Because just as we have eyelids so we can stop seeing when we want to stop seeing, we could have sound blocks in our auditory canal. We could close them and then we wouldn't have to hear what we don't want to hear.

"This is the best thing for all of us, also for the children. In only one more year Endika will be an adult. Ainhoa needs a few more. Soon they will follow their own roads through life and won't need us or at least not as much as they did when they were small. What sense does it make for you and me to grow old together when we'd never stop arguing and making the years we have left bitter? I'm going to move in with a person you already know about. Frankly, I think I've fulfilled my obligations as a father. I'll go on fulfilling them, so don't worry about that. I love my children with all my heart. I have the right to a bit of happiness."

Won't he shut up? Arantxa kept her eyes shut. The only thing that interested her: that Guillermo not simply abandon the children. The rest didn't concern her. But her children. Oh dear, her children. And if that other woman doesn't treat them well?

"Of course, you'll get the portion of our property you're entitled to. Half of the apartment and things like that. I don't wish any more misfortune for you than you have already had. And if it should happen that at a certain moment you need my help, you can count on me. I'm very sorry for what's happened."

Suddenly, another voice. Where? Nearby. A harsh, strong, angry voice. A nurse? No, her mother. What's she saying? That we don't need your compassion. In other words, she's been spying. She reproached Guillermo for wearing black clothing:

"Are you wearing mourning before time, or what?"

Arantxa couldn't see either one. Guillermo silent, is he still there? He wasn't defending himself. And her mother never stopped criticizing him for this, that, and the other thing—his outfit, how long it took him to get to Mallorca, and that he's left it to her to carry the load. But, *ama*! Then Miren ventured into delicate territory: money, tenderness, how bad a husband he was. They could have stepped outside to argue, but they didn't. The nurses, why do they allow this noise? Or out on the street. But maybe Miren was trying to teach her daughter a lesson. This is how you should deal with egoists and swine.

After hearing all that, you knew Guillermo wouldn't be able to hold back anymore: he counterattacked. It seems he was leaving the room, because his voice now came from farther away. He spoke calmly, politely, professionally. And he concluded saying that his definitive separation from Arantxa:

"Has nothing to do with what happened. The two of us had already settled this. Our children know about it and accept it. So there's nothing here about me escaping or of foisting the load on you. You might show a little respect. If not for me, at least for your daughter, whom I'd never call a load. You, however, call her just that. Take this to cover any expenses my daughter may have incurred."

And he left. Miren went on grumbling. She put a hand with two fifty-euro bills into her daughter's visual field. She shook them.

"He threw this money at me. He's got no manners at all."

That man is not a miser. As a husband, a disaster; but as a father, Arantxa had no complaints. And she was sure that no matter what happened he'd never abandon his children. Besides, why would anyone have to carry a load? That's right, a load. I'd have done the same thing if he'd gotten a stroke.

What really pained Arantxa is that after everything that happened and despite the fact she felt almost no affection for him, he left the ICU without giving her a kiss, the last kiss, and all because of the inopportune presence of her mother.

Her mother. There she was, still grumbling. And Arantxa, her eyes closed, thought about how useful it would be if we could close our ears when we wanted.

107

Meetings in the Plaza

On the opposite side of the jai alai court, on one of the corners of the plaza, just above the public lavatories, there is a small open space bounded by a rail. For a long while now, Arantxa waited for Bittori there every morning or the other way around, because sometimes it was Bittori who got there first and was waiting seated on the bench. The fact is they didn't have to plan their meetings.

The townspeople knew all about those morning meetings between Bittori and Arantxa. People whispered that since the paralytic can't put up a fight or run away, the other takes advantage.

"But does anyone know what she says to her?"

"Bah, what does it matter? Since poor Arantxa doesn't even understand . . ."

At first the meetings were brief. What does "brief" mean? Well, a few minutes: a hello kiss, a brief conversation with the help of the iPad, a kiss goodbye. In the bars, at the doors to shops, in the walkway, or at the bus stop, people commented that this is odd, because if Arantxa doesn't want to see that lady why does she let herself be wheeled to the same spot every morning?

"Or does the Indian woman make her go?"

"I doubt that."

The meetings got longer and longer. There were happy faces and harmony between the two women with the silent complement of Celeste standing behind the wheelchair. All that was obvious even at a distance. People came to Joxian with all kinds of stories, and Miren filled her husband's ears with complaints and protests, but none of it mattered to him. Nothing? He would answer with a frown:

"So my daughter has some happiness, what am I supposed to do, take it away from her? Hell, so they see each other and talk. What harm do they do?"

Miren was consumed with rage.

"You're a dumbbell."

And off she goes, with the window wide open so the entire world can hear her, saying she'd been betrayed; abandoned by everyone. Sometimes she got an attack of fury, tore off her apron, and took off, slamming the door behind her, marching energetically to the butcher shop, to pour out her woes to Juani, who advises her to do one thing one day and the opposite thing the next, always with sad brows because of her son who took his own life or was murdered and because of her husband who died of a cancer as large as his sorrow. All so people can say that it's the others who supply the victims and that they don't.

On one item, the two women did agree:

"Without ETA it's like walking around naked. No one defends us."

Miren's attempts to keep her daughter from seeing the Madwoman failed. If she screamed, too bad. If she threatened, too bad. If she played the role of the aggrieved party, sorrowful, hurt, mournful, the same. Everything she said irritated her daughter. Arantxa would answer back with hard words on the screen of her iPad, tense up, refuse to eat, throw her plate off the table, spit into the food.

"My God what a temper you've got and how much work you make for me."

Severe, intimidating, Miren tried to influence Celeste, who had to be something of an accomplice, because without her help, how the hell could my daughter get to that woman on her own? Standing in the kitchen, Arantxa in her wheelchair about to go out for a walk, Miren would say to Celeste, hold on, come here, we've got to talk. And the polite caregiver, the harmless little thing, the sweet Andean who was efficiency personified, who expressed herself better than an archbishop despite her meager schooling, partially rebelled.

"Mrs. Miren, if my services don't please you you'll have to do without them. I feel love for Arantxa and feel I'm responsible for her well-being. It destroys my soul when Arantxa gets angry and feels sad."

Miren, sullen and bossy, fired her. She'd find another servant soon enough. Did she say "servant"? She said it, humiliating the woman who did so much for her daughter. Celeste, on the outside at least, did not change expression. She leaned her small body over to give Arantxa a farewell kiss. Arantxa brusquely pulled back her face, not much, the little her neck allowed. And stretching out her good arm she threw everything on the table to the floor: the fruit bowl, the salt shaker, a box of eggs, the magazine *Pronto*. She didn't throw more because there was no more. Pears, bananas, grapes, and apples rolled across the floor; four or five eggs split wide open, and others merely cracked; the salt spread violently all over among shards of glass and the magazine cover with the photo of a bull-fighter and a famous bride. Arantxa opened her mouth with its twisted lips and didn't speak. She shook her head, turning bright red. Though she had no voice, it was just as if she were shouting. That silence of hers reverberated, earsplitting. And despite the fact that her ability to gesture was limited, it was impossible to overlook her anguish, the paralyzed rage of her grimace.

Miren exhaled powerfully. And it was as if with that mouthful of air all the anger that filled her lungs left her. Even so, she gave an astonished look at the ceiling as if to postpone her awkwardness for a second. Then to Celeste, with phony brusqueness:

"Listen, girl, excuse me for what I said. All of you are making me dizzy."

And Celeste, rehired, stooped to pick up the scattered fruit and clean the smashed eggs off the floor. But Miren stopped her, saying:

"Okay, okay, it's better you take this one out, I'll take care of the rest."

Did she take her out? Without losing a second. Did she bring her to the plaza? By the shortest route, except at the end. Why so? Because there's no ramp, they have to make a detour to go up the hill close to the houses. Once above, it's easy to push the chair over the asphalt.

Bittori was waiting for them in the usual place. Seeing them, she waved something in the air to say hello, a sheet of paper, a piece of paper? At a distance it looked like a handkerchief, but it wasn't. Arantxa offered her cheek, and Bittori kissed it, praising her healthy appearance and her good color this morning, at the same time she ran her hand, all tenderness, over Arantxa's short hair.

"I started to think you weren't coming."

"We had some fun at home because of a surprise."

Arantxa, furrowing her brow, wrote on the iPad: "Tell her the truth." Then Celeste set aside her well-mannered discretion:

"Miren reprimanded me and fired me, but later she rehired me. How bad I felt. She doesn't like it that you and Arantxa see each other."

Arantxa agreed, nodding her head at each word her caregiver spoke, as if saying: exactly, that's how it happened. And Bittori's piece of paper, unfolded, was a lined notebook sheet that contained Joxe Mari's second letter. This one wasn't like the first, harsh, the letter of a combative militant, who was angry and bad and stubborn and.

Arantxa stretched out her hand, the only one she could, with obvious impatience and a desire to read her brother's letter. And she did read, shaking her head. Out of disgust? More likely in a friendly reproach, with the kind of disagreement that exists between brother and sister, as if to say, this fool is on the right path, but he's still got a long way to go. She handed the sheet back to Bittori. With a calm finger, she wrote on her iPad: "He's scared to death, but don't worry. I'll make him ask you to forgive him."

"He tells me not to write him again. What would you do?"

And Arantxa, joyful, answered: "The fish has taken the hook. All we have to do is pull him out of the water."

Bittori, since she's not good at understanding metaphors, asked for a clarification. "You write him. I'll write him, too." And right away, she wanted Bittori to push her around the church. To Celeste: "You wait here." Bittori, astonished and perhaps fearful. The meaning of that little journey was not lost on her. A provocation. More: a challenge. When her mother finds out, and she will find out, because in this town everything is known, she's going to hit the ceiling!

Bittori pushed the wheelchair under the roof of branches created by the lime trees in the plaza, and she went toward the jai alai court, years back covered with graffiti in favor of ETA and symbols of the *abertzale* left, a pure green since the attacks had ceased and the Town Council ordered the walls painted, because you have to turn the page and look toward the future and there should no longer be winners and losers. They slowly went around the church, very slowly, not so much to show themselves to the people, few in any case because it was early, but mostly because Bittori's pain was coming back. She could barely stand it because it was intensifying and soon she had to give up and turn Arantxa back over to Celeste.

She said goodbye to them, lost sight of them, and went down the stairs holding on to the banister and went on no more than thirty or forty yards. She had to sit down on the ground, then collapse onto the dusty paving stones, and while she was being taken care of, by whom?, by some passersby, she recognized Miren's irate voice a few steps away.

"Leave my daughter in peace."

She did not repeat it. She added nothing. And Bittori, minutes later, when she'd recovered, wasn't sure if she'd really heard those words or if she'd imagined them.

108

MEDICAL REPORT

Nerea telephoned her brother to tell him his name was in the newspaper.

"In which newspaper?"

"In *Egin*. They name you as the doctor who took care of the ETA man brought in the other day. They say, according to your statements, there had to be torture."

"I gave no interviews to anyone, much less to that filthy rag."

My statements? What's this got to do with me? He couldn't manage to think clearly. It was nine a.m. He'd gone to bed late. At what time? He didn't remember. Between three and four in the morning. And only then because he ran out of cognac, because if he hadn't he would have been sitting in front of the computer until dawn. Dryness in his mouth and the hint of a headache. Sleep? That would come in the afternoon at the hospital.

He went out to find the newspaper. He had yet to eat breakfast. Actually it was Nerea's call that got him out of bed. He usually bought the paper at a book-and-stationery store near his apartment. Not every day but often. *El Diario Vasco*, sometimes the Spanish newspaper *El País*. And when something big happened, both.

He's known the bookseller for several years. And now he was embarrassed to ask for *Egin*. It was the bookseller himself, a lifelong socialist, who always called the *abertzale* newspaper a rag. And Xabier adopted the expression.

A few yards from the bookstore he stopped. I'm not going in there. And since it was a warm morning, with a south wind and a brilliant sky, he walked to a kiosk on the Avenida. After he read the article, he tossed the newspaper into the trash and went into a café nearby to have breakfast.

It was a lie that he'd made any kind of statement.

The terrorist, twenty-three years old, walked into the hospital on his own two feet on the previous Monday, surrounded by the Guardia Civil. He was complaining of sharp pains in his side. He bent over as he walked, made suffering faces, had trouble breathing. A captain signaled to Xabier his intention to speak to him privately.

"Look, Doctor, pay no attention to anything this character says. He's a murderer. He resisted arrest and there was nothing to be done except capture him by force. You can't show them any consideration. You know how dangerous these guys are."

He alleged that the terrorist was armed at the time of his arrest and that these people have instructions from their organization to say they've been tortured. And Xabier? He said nothing. If this officer only knew whose son I am. He looked him straight in the eye until the officer finished saying all that. Then, with composure?, actually with self-possession, he turned and entered the room where the patient was waiting for him.

"Doctor, they tortured me. It really hurts right here. I think I've got something broken."

If this boy knew what others of his kind did to my father. It was a mental burst of fire. Because, after all, I'm not made of ice. And Nerea, on the phone, said she understood him, that she doesn't know what she would have done in his place, perhaps the same.

A patient. That's what Xabier saw in that boy. A body in need of medical assistance. What this face, this chest, these extremities have done is none of my business. For now. When he's finished his work, or within a few hours, or tomorrow, then, sure, it will interest me. More: it will deprive me of sleep.

The door remained open, the voices and footsteps of the Guardia Civil officers could be heard. He asked the closest if the door could be closed. From the hallway, they answered no. Not in an impolite way. The white lab coat inspired respect, this we know.

"Understand, it's for safety's sake."

As soon as he saw the patient naked from the waist up, Xabier banished any trace of personal thought. Two female nurses helped the bruised man remove his clothes. He couldn't do it alone. All they left him with were his underpants. The ETA man, the terrorist, the in-all-likelihood murderer. Now he thinks it over. In those moments, as he said to Nerea on the phone, he thought of nothing but doing his job properly.

"Damn, brother, what integrity you've got."

"Don't believe it. I just do what I'm supposed to do. That's what they pay me for."

The hematoma on his eye told Xabier what kind of lesions he was going to find. He confirmed his suspicions, after the patient was undressed, finally with his underpants removed as well, about the contusions all over his body. And on the left side an enormous bruise that ran from his shoulder blade to his hip, which even to the naked eye suggested there was a serious internal wound. Its origin? It was not his business to find out, though you'd have to be blind not to guess the cause of those abrasions and cuts on his knees and ankles. Xabier ordered that the patient be admitted as soon as possible to the intensive care unit. The captain:

"Are you sure?"

What did he think? That we'd put on a few bandages and give him back?

"He's got subcutaneous lesions. Probably broken ribs and a punctured lung. The relevant tests will have to be made, but I can tell you that the patient's condition is serious."

"As you well know, the patient is a terrorist and under arrest. He will be under heavy guard. That will apply to those who enter the room where he's placed."

What do I care? But of course, he didn't argue. Showing the palms of his hands as if to prove his innocence:

"I'm just doing my job."

"So are we, God damn it."

That challenging, thuggish, barracks style of speech accompanied by a penetrating stare intimidated Xabier. He wanted no more conversation. He was already thinking of taking an antidepressant as soon as he was alone. He reflexively checked the time on his watch. It was like raising an imaginary wall between himself and the Guardia Civil officer. And suddenly he remembered his mother.

Why? If it weren't for her, I'd be practicing medicine many miles from here, maybe even on a different continent, in those remote lands where Aránzazu went. But I can't leave *ama* alone.

He was fully aware that an investigation ordered by the Police Court of San Sebastián was under way because of the forensic physician's report. After gathering up the facts derived from his general examination of the patient, Xabier composed his own report: multiple contusions, fracture of the ninth left-side rib, pulmonary contusion, pneumothorax on the left side, periocular hematoma, left eye, with hemorrhage, subcutaneous emphysema from the cervical region to the pelvis; hematomas, abrasions, cuts on both legs. He set it all down in short, cold sentences. He added that the patient had been brought to the hospital by agents of the Guardia Civil in order that his wounds be examined after arrest. And that the undersigned declares as the origin of his wounds punches and kicks to the head, the thorax, the abdomen, and lower extremities. Once he finished, without rereading (not his usual style) the text, he included the date and signed it.

Three days later, the patient left intensive care. Xabier was informed that a gentleman wanted to speak to him. He did not want to receive him in his office. It's harder there to get rid of pests. Besides, he's got the photo of his father on his desk and he doesn't like outsiders to see it. There might be the smell of cognac in the air. So he went out into the hall.

It was a man in his thirties, red-faced, thick, corpulent, and I'd bet diabetic. The brother of the ETA man, who came to thank him. Xabier: you're welcome. And as he did with the Guardia Civil captain, he told this man that he'd only done his job.

Immediately, it was clear that this big guy hadn't turned up in the hospital merely to express his gratitude. He was trying to see if the doctor would confirm that his brother had been tortured.

"What is your opinion?"

All Xabier did was repeat in a rather more colloquial idiom the content of the medical report, which was what appeared the next day in *Egin* as a statement by him to the newspaper.

Nerea on the telephone:

"You should have told him that ETA murdered our father. I'd like to see his face then."

"I was tired. It didn't occur to me to say it."

"God knows if he really was the ETA man's brother."

"I had the same suspicion from the start. Don't say anything to *ama*, okay?"

"The thought would never enter my mind. Are you crazy?"

109

If the Wind Hits
the Burning Coal

They talked it over once, sitting at the table, after Txato had been dead for a few years. Should we go to meetings of terrorism victims? Never. Brother and sister and mother agreed on that point:

Bittori:

"I'm not going to put my sorrow on display in some shop window. You two can do what you like."

It was Nerea who invented the image of the burning coal we carry within us.

"And each one of us is going to have to find their own way to extinguish it little by little."

Ama added that if the wind blows on the coal the flame grows. The fact is that the three of them, without confessing it to one another, felt the effects of the fire they held inside themselves whenever there was a terrorist episode. It wasn't one of the subjects that habitually came up in their conversations. They allowed ETA crimes to go by without commenting on them, as if they'd agreed in a tacit accord to keep silent. They often talked about Txato, but only rarely about the fact that he was murdered. They preferred to chat, joking, smiling, about his obstinacy and his jug-handle ears, his good heart. And from time to time Bittori would ask her children not to forget him. None of them had any intention of living the rest of their lives being mainly victims and nothing more than victims. During the morning: victims; during the afternoon: victims; and during the night: victims.

Xabier:

"At the same time, you can't deny that we are victims."

Bittori put the serving spoon in the soup bowl.

"True, but let's eat before the soup gets cold."

And the years went by along with the rains, the bombs, and the shots. A new century arrived and, some time later, one morning in November Xabier found out from the newspaper that in San Sebastián they would be celebrating Remembrance Days for Victims of Terrorism and Terrorist Violence, organized by the Victims of Terrorism in Basque Country Collective. And he wasn't going to go because he never goes to those sorts of events, convinced that he'd leave depressed about them and then wander in the darkness of his mental labyrinths.

But by chance, he found the name of the judge who'd presided in his father's case on the list of participants scheduled for that day and he thought it over and became curious and it occurred to him he could attend the talk as an anonymous spectator. After all, no one knows me, many years have gone by, and I can sit far away from the speakers' table.

An hour before the start of the program, Xabier was still vacillating: fear, doubts, a touch of anxiety he tried to treat with a pill. He left his house not knowing for certain which way he'd go. The sky, already black, the streets packed with vehicles, he started walking with no plan other than to let his feet choose the route. The route he took after a detour that was hardly short ended at the main entrance to the María Cristina Hotel, in one of whose meeting rooms on the street level the judge, a writer, and other participants would speak one after another in a few minutes. My feet decided for me, and Xabier, his heart pounding, downed a double cognac and then another at the Tánger Bar nearby. Why? To calm his nerves. To gather courage. Would someone recognize me? He bided his time and walked into the room when the program had already begun and the public's attention was fixed on the speakers.

He sat near one of the doors in the next-to-last row among people he didn't know. Before him, rows of backs and necks, and quite a few empty chairs. Forty, fifty people? No more than that. Opposite the rear wall, the table with speakers and microphones. The judge wasn't there. Someone finished speaking, turned the program over to the writer, there was tepid, polite applause. And he said that:

"There are books that grow inside you over the years waiting for the right moment to be written. Mine, which I've come to talk to you about, is one of them. The initial idea . . ."

With all appropriate discretion, Xabier, in the rear, tried to identify the people present. It wasn't easy since they all had their backs to him. Not forgetting the fact that he personally knew no victims of ETA or their families. He did, true enough, know about some, the ones everyone knows about from having seen them on television or their photos in newspapers.

"And this project to compose, by means of a fiction, a testimony to the atrocities committed by the terrorists arises in my case from two motives. On the one hand, the empathy I have for the victims of terrorism. On the other, my total rejection of violence and any aggression committed against the rule of law."

The writer then asks himself why he didn't join ETA when he was young. An astonished silence spreads throughout the audience, which is holding its breath.

"After all, I, too, was a Basque teenager, exposed like so many other boys of my time to propaganda that favored terrorism and the doctrines on which that terrorism is founded. I've thought it all over many times and I think I've found the answer."

There in front, in the first row, reserved for speakers, was the judge waiting for his turn to speak. The judge is famous. His head is bald, burnished, so he's easily recognizable. Besides, at that time he appeared frequently in the media about some trial I don't remember. As far as Xabier knew, the judge was no longer attached to the National Court.

"So I wrote against the suffering inflicted by some men on others, trying to show what that suffering consisted of and, it goes without saying, who generated it, and what physical and psychic consequences it leaves in survivors."

And in the third or fourth row, in a moment in which the person he was observing turned his head a bit, Xabier made out a familiar profile.

"Therefore, I wrote against crimes perpetrated under the guise of politics, in the name of a homeland where a handful of armed people, with the shameful support of one sector of society, decides who belongs to that homeland and who should either leave it or die. I wrote without hatred against the language of hatred and against forgetting and the oblivion cooked up by those who try to concoct a history at the service of their projects and totalitarian beliefs."

He wasn't sure. A woman wearing a beige wool beret, sitting right behind the person in question, kept Xabier from getting a clear view, yes, sure, she's so well-known, the sister of Gregorio Ordóñez. What's her name? María Ordóñez, Ester Ordóñez, Maite Ordóñez. He couldn't recall her real name. Suddenly: Consuelo Ordóñez. Damn, that was a hard one.

"But I also wrote out of the desire to offer something positive to my fellow man, in favor of literature and art, which means in favor of the good and noble that human beings hold within them. And in favor of the dignity of ETA's victims in their individual humanity, not as mere numbers in statistics where each one's name is lost, along with their faces and their identities."

Which is exactly what my mother doesn't want: that her suffering and the suffering of her children become material for a writer so he can compose a book or a director so he can make a movie, and that they be applauded after, and win prizes, while we go along bearing the burden of our tragedy.

"I tried to avoid the two capital dangers in this kind of writing: sentimentality, on the one hand; and on the other, sanctimony, being didactic. That's why, in my opinion, we have interviews and newspaper articles as well as forums like this one."

In the second row, near the aisle, reddish hair, Xabier recognized Cristina Cuesta, whose father, like his, had been murdered. It was she all right, no doubt about it. And on her left, Caty Romero, the widow of a sergeant in the San Sebastián Municipal Police, who apparently, I don't know where I read it, was dedicated to cleansing the police of agents who collaborated with ETA or supplied them with information and, of course, the terrorists put an end to that with two bullets.

"I tried to answer concrete questions. How does a person live intimately the disaster of having lost a father, a husband, a brother in an attack? How does a widow, an orphan, a person who's been mutilated face life after a crime?"

The writer spoke calmly. Xabier thinks his intentions are good, but he does not believe anything will substantially change because someone's written a book. It seems to him that, until now, Basque writers have paid little attention to the victims of terrorism. The victimizers are far more interesting—their crises of conscience, their sentimental backstories, and things like that. Besides, ETA terrorism is useless if you want to attack the right. The civil war is much better for that.

"... trying to paint a representative panorama of a society subjected to terror. Perhaps I'm exaggerating, but I firmly believe that the literary defeat of ETA is under way."

At that moment, the woman sitting right behind Consuelo Ordóñez, the one with the beige beret, turns her head slightly to one side, for barely a fraction of a second, but enough for Xabier's heart to take a leap when he recognized those features so familiar to him. What is my sister doing here, the one who said she wouldn't attend a meeting of terrorism victims even if they paid her? The same thing he was doing. He realized how absurd the question was, a question to which he dedicated not even half an instant of reflection, since he was concerned with other, more pressing thoughts. What thoughts? Well, for instance, how to find a way for Nerea not to see him. He calculated the number of steps, not more than three, that separated him from the door. He didn't hesitate. Taking advantage of the fact that the applause for the writer would conceal the noise of his movements, he stood up, went out into the corridor, and started walking rapidly, almost running, toward the door.

110

CONVERSATION IN THE AFTERNOON

They hadn't seen each other in a long time. How long? It doesn't matter. Two, three weeks. Meanwhile, there was news about Bittori. Not good news; one fact, especially, was extremely worrisome. Xabier and Nerea agreed that the telephone was not the best medium for a long discussion about serious matters related to their mother. What should we do? Don't you think? They agreed to meet as soon as possible, somewhere in the heart of the city. A cold afternoon, but sunny. Nerea suggested walking along Paseo Nuevo and conversing near the wide, blue sea. Free of obligations, Xabier had no problem accepting his sister's suggestion.

Along the way, people, children, a row of vendors selling artisanal objects. It was almost impossible to walk because of the crowds. Up ahead, municipal workers using high-pressure hoses were scouring away ETA graffiti on a lateral wall of the La Brecha fish market. To avoid being splashed, brother and sister hugged the opposite facade.

"Some day not too far from now few people will remember what happened."

"Don't get worked up, Xabier. That's the way life works. Ultimately, oblivion always wins."

"But we don't have to be its accomplices."

"And we aren't. Our memories can't be erased with high-pressure hoses. You'll see, though, that we the victims will be accused of refusing to look toward the future. They'll say we're seeking revenge. People are already saying just that."

"We bother them."

"You can't imagine how much."

When they reached the San Telmo Museum, they got to the point. Xabier asked Nerea to tell him about the cat. What was that all about? What was that?

"Ikatza is dead and *ama* doesn't know it. Something tells me it's better she not find out."

"How did you find out?"

"Yesterday I went to her place. Quique drove me to San Bartolomé Street. He's always in a hurry, and he never stopped complaining that he had an important meeting with a client, that it was my fault he was going to be late, so I said: stop here, I'll walk up the hill. I didn't have good vibrations, understand? I call *ama* and she doesn't answer the phone. I call again, and again no answer. That for two days. So, it seemed better just to go take a look."

"She spends the day in the village."

"Sometimes she goes up to the cemetery. She hasn't lost that fixation with *aita*'s grave. But I was surprised that she didn't answer at the time she usually has supper."

Nerea had gone up part of the Aldapeta hill. On the asphalt, she saw a mass of reddish flesh and black hair. Cars were rolling over it. The bus ran over it. And she stopped on the sidewalk for an instant, enough time to recognize the collar. She visited her mother, and after an hour, when she was about to say goodbye, she asked out of the blue about the cat.

"Where is she, I don't see her."

"She's off doing her business. Any time now, she'll turn up on the balcony with a bird in her mouth."

Covering her mouth and nose with her hand, Nerea separated the dead animal from the asphalt. When no cars were coming, using a branch from a bush, she pushed the pieces of flesh and hair to the curb on the other side of the street, where there is no sidewalk, certain that her mother wouldn't be able to see it. Finally, using the same branch to hook it first, she tossed the sticky collar over a wall.

She told the story to her brother with an expression of repugnance.

"You did a good thing hiding it from *ama*."

"I was gagging as I walked down to San Bartolomé. So I went into the first bar I saw to have a drink. I'm not the kind who drinks at the wrong time of day, but I needed to get rid of the nausea I felt on my tongue."

They walked from one side to the other, breathing in the morning breeze; a long, misty line of coast stretching into the distance; and below the walkway, the succession of waves that smash and foam against the breakwater. Nerea to her brother: he should tell what he'd brought up on the telephone in greater detail.

"Remember Ramón Leal?"

"The ambulance driver? Sure."

"A week ago he came to my office because he'd been told, because someone had said. What? That our sainted mother had been seen pushing Arantxa's wheelchair around the village square. That is, with Arantxa in the chair. Just imagine the scene: the two of them alone strolling in broad daylight where it's impossible they wouldn't be seen. Why? And whose idea was it? And how is it that there wasn't a third person with them, the caregiver who comes every day to look after Arantxa? You can imagine the gossip running wild among the neighbors."

"All that is a bit odd. It's been so many years that our families haven't spoken to each other. I haven't seen Arantxa since my student days. Even so, I still think of her as a friend. She was the only one of all of them who behaved like a human being with us. Did you ask *ama* about it?"

"I think *ama* is suffering some kind of mental disturbance. I didn't want to make things worse. But you should have seen the shock on Ramón's face."

"What can Arantxa's *aitas* be thinking?"

"Joxian, I imagine, is still a simple soul who takes things as they come. But his wife?"

"Miren must have taken it like a kick in the teeth."

"I also learned from Ramón that after her stroll with Arantxa, *ama* fainted on the street and people had to help her. I decided to step in, so I called you."

The setting sun traced a fringe of nervous mirrors over the surface of the water. Boats? None. A ferry returning, near the entrance to the bay, that's it. Xabier and Nerea leaned on the railing. Xabier covered his incipient baldness with a brimmed cap; she, who until a few years ago wore wool berets, was bareheaded. Behind them, Oteiza's sculpture passed its boring hours, rusty, waiting for the next storm. A few steps away from them, a fisherman using a rod stared hard at the bobbing of his white cork in the undulating waters.

"I made her come with me in the car. Where are we going? You'll soon see. I arranged several appointments for her with Arruabarrena. She promises to go, but she never does and she lets time go by and I suspected from her blood analysis that something wasn't right in our mother's body. Arruabarrena examined her. He did all sorts of tests. The day before yesterday he called me. I was to see him as soon as I could. The instant I saw his face, I knew he was going to give me the worst possible news."

"He confirmed it was cancer?"

"Uterine cancer. Very advanced. If it had been detected earlier, it could have been operated on with some guarantee of a cure, but she didn't take care of it, I wasn't attentive enough, and now she has other organs affected, including the liver. Anyway, I'll spare you the clinical details. They're no fun, that I can assure you."

"How much time does she have left?"

"At the most, Arruabarrena gives her two or three months, but she could just as easily die tonight. With surgery and invasive treatment her life might be extended to the end of the year. It isn't worthwhile."

"Was she informed?"

"Arruabarrena still hasn't talked to her. He asked me if I thought it would be better if I communicate the diagnosis to *ama*, after all, I'm the patient's son aside from being a doctor. I think he's right. I think I'm largely responsible for not having seen the problem when we still had time to deal with it."

"This is not the time for recrimination. I think *ama* knows more about how sick she is than she lets on."

"In the car, she complained she didn't need to go to the doctor, that all her life she had bad periods and stomach cramps."

Brother and sister started walking again. They walked down the Aquarium steps and reached the port. The first lights were being turned on in the city.

"In any case, Arruabarrena and I came up with a palliative treatment. We'll do everything possible so *ama* doesn't suffer."

Nerea rested a hand on Xabier's shoulder. They walked along like that for a while, not speaking, not looking at each other, until Nerea broke the silence. What did he intend to do when *ama* was no longer with us?

"You know I only live in this city for her sake. It's a promise I made to *aita* the day he was buried. I said to him: don't worry, I'll take care of her, she won't be left alone. You see that after all I wasn't up to the job. My plan is to make sure I fulfill her old desire to share a grave with *aita* in the village cemetery and then leave. Where? No idea. Far away, that's for sure. Where I can be useful to people in need. What about you?"

"I'm staying here."

They detoured around the streets in the Parte Vieja—too crowded. Their conversation began again at the bar of a café on Bulevar. As night fell, they said goodbye, serious, calm, with gentle brushing of cheeks. He went here; she went there. By then the sky was completely dark, and the bearable chill of the afternoon was being replaced by the harsher cold of the night. As he walked along Elcano Street, Xabier felt his sense of smell caressed by the warm aroma of roasted chestnuts. The chestnut vendor's stand was at the corner of Guipúzcoa. A dozen chestnuts cost two and a half euros. As he was paying, the carillon at the Town Council building rang out eight o'clock. And Xabier, the pleasing warmth of the paper packet of chestnuts in the palm of his hand, sat down on a bench in the plaza, under the waning moon visible through the naked branches of a tree. He easily peeled the first chestnut. Very good. Just right, neither hard nor burnt. And the pleasurable warmth that extended inside his mouth thickened the mist of his breath. The second chestnut, also very good. Too good. He stood up. He emptied the almost full packet in a trash bin, so that the chestnuts fell one by one onto the garbage inside. Then he started walking toward Avenida, blending in with the crowd.

111

A Night in Calamocha

As a general rule, Miren went to visit Joxe Mari on the bus belonging to the Women in Favor of Amnesty. Joxian accompanied her from time to time. At the beginning. Then, as the years passed, more and more sporadically.

One winter Saturday, a long time ago, they had an accident a few miles from Calamocha. After that, Joxian had no desire to travel. That wasn't the only reason. The other, the principal reason, was Miren. She's so bossy, they argued, you can't talk about her son. Joxe Mari is like her leg at about the groin. Don't touch it because right away she jumps, what a woman.

The day of the Calamocha business they'd left in the morning for a family face-to-face in the Picassent prison, but they hadn't gone by bus but rather in Alfonso and Catalina's car, because at that time their son was in the same prison.

You wouldn't say the two couples were linked by close friendship. Miren criticized them behind their backs, principally because they didn't speak Basque. Joxian doesn't care what language they speak. In any case, he didn't think much of them. Why? He would shrug his shoulders: no idea.

But after all, Alfonso and Catalina were from their village, though they'd come in the sixties from somewhere or other. As far as Miren was concerned they had nothing Basque at all, not even the air they breathed. Especially the woman, you could tell from her accent where she came from. They'd produced a son, an ETA militant who at the time was in jail with Joxe Mari. And it seemed the two boys got along well.

Don Serapio stopped Miren one day in the street. What a busy-body. The priest was chatting with Catalina under the town hall portico. The priest stops to talk to everyone. He governs souls and bodies. Or he tries to. Because if you go to mass, there's no one there, except on certain days. He saw Miren, who had stopped to buy cheese from a street vendor, and he called to her: *kaixo*, Miren, and she couldn't pretend to be deaf because he was about eight steps away. So she forgot about buying cheese and went over to him. It turns out that Catalina, standing there, and her husband were thinking about going to see their son the same day that she and Joxian were going, something the priest was fully aware of.

Joxian, at midday:

"That's what you get for blabbing."

"He's my confessor."

"Go to some other village to confess."

Net result: that in the presence of Don Serapio, Miren and Catalina agreed, there was no way out, to travel, the four of them, to Picassent in Alfonso's car. Well, it almost happened that the priest would have to officiate at a funeral mass for all four of them.

The accident happened on the return trip. Days later, a note about it appeared in *Egin* after Alfonso telephoned a newspaperman from Teruel. On the way out, Joxian sat in the front passenger seat next to Alfonso, driver and pain in the ass. Probably for that reason he can't stand him. A know-it-all. Never shuts up. About soccer, cars, food, mushrooms: he knows all about everything. And at one point in the trip he put on a zarzuela cassette. Miren, under her breath, when they separated inside the prison:

"It's in the blood. The only thing they forgot to do was shout long live Spain."

On the return, when he was about to get into the car, Joxian found that Catalina was sitting up front. He had no choice but to sit in back alongside Miren. They'd barely gotten under way when she pinched him on the thigh so he wouldn't tell something about Joxe Mari which he'd already begun to reveal.

Two days later, at home:

"You should thank Saint Ignatius that Catalina stole your seat."

"My guardian angel is smarter than hers."

Alfonso, his hands on the wheel, took charge of the conversation. He was praising his son, who works out a lot in jail and began studying English. Unfortunately, they have to talk to him in only one ear because on the other he can barely hear a word. And he accelerates, passes a truck, and explains:

"It's because of the beatings they gave him when he was arrested."

Miren would butt in from time to time.

"And didn't you lodge a complaint?"

"Why bother, when they pay no attention? Our sons are in the clutches of the state."

"Well, they beat my Joxe Mari, too. A bunch of them. One at a time they wouldn't dare because he's so big."

Joxian, lost in thought, sad as always when he leaves Joxe Mari behind (okay, son, stay well), was staring at the landscape, out of touch with the conversation. Out of touch up to a point. They'd been driving a good while and now it was his turn to covertly nudge Miren so she'd stop talking. They were passing through Teruel as afternoon was coming to an end. Lonely fields, with patches of snow; a row of mountains in the distance about to fade into darkness, and outside the car a bitter cold. Suddenly, Catalina made a naive slip of the tongue. Maybe she assumed an intimacy where there is none. Or it might simply be she didn't know to what extremes Miren could go in her patriotic-political fever.

The ETA prisoners in the Picassent prison had received word they were to go on a hunger strike. The lawyer arrives and says: strike. And Joxe Mari, who in this as in so many other matters was overly strict, was keeping an eye on his comrades. A hard man. Which made Miren feel proud, saying later in the village that Joxe Mari's made of steel, that no one can make him bow.

To which Catalina replied that they'd been allowed to bring into the meeting room a bag of madeleines she'd baked herself, that depending on whether the prison guards liked you or not they could either let you bring in food or not, since once they didn't and this time they did.

"He ate every one of them right there."

Miren leaped:

"Well, of course they let you bring in food. They know the prisoners are on strike and this is how they break it, so they aren't united."

"For heaven's sake, no one knows about it."

"Well, I know. Being on strike means everyone or no one."

And she said nothing more because of Joxian's surreptitious nudge. In the car, an uncomfortable silence ensued, and Alfonso used it as an opportunity to slip in a zarzuela cassette, not the same one he'd played in the morning, but much the same, much the same, and they still had many miles of Spanish music ahead.

Nowadays castor oil
is not too hard to take.
Why so?
You just take a tiny pill
And the effect is just the same.

Suddenly it happened. How? Miren doesn't remember. Joxian, lost in his sorrows and thoughts, was dozing off with his arms crossed. He barely noticed. A curse from Alfonso followed by a screech from Catalina woke him up. What's going on? The car had gone headfirst into a ditch on the side of the road. Miren was the first to get out. The door on Joxian's side wouldn't open. The two in front, silent. And the zarzuela singers as well.

Miren, outside, grabs Joxian.

"Come on, get out."

And she extracts him by pulling on his arm, and in a matter of seconds they feel the bite of the cold. Joxian asked Miren if she was hurt.

"No. We've got to get them out."

Alone, way out in the country. A wasteland at nightfall. And the sky cloudless, dotted with the first stars, announced that it was going to freeze up. They ran to help Alfonso. There were no problems, but the door was jammed. So Joxian yanked him out of his seat by tugging under his arms. They couldn't see his face, all covered with blood. Joxian tried to sit him on the rocky ground, but it wasn't necessary. His wounds weren't serious. Or at least that's what he was saying. A cut on the forehead and another on his scalp, which turned his gray hair red. Nothing more. But he panicked about his wife, still in the car, calm, quiet, with her head fallen over one shoulder. On the other side of the car, Miren vainly tried to open the door.

"Get over here, you two. See if you can do it."

Joxian, a furnace operator in a foundry, calloused hands, power-ful arms, ran over and tugged on the door handle, one foot against a protruding piece of the dented chassis for leverage, his teeth clenched, until he yanked the door open and there was Catalina, not bloody or anything, how great that woman smelled, but saying in agonized-plaintive whispers:

"My legs, my legs."

Meanwhile, Miren, standing in the middle of the highway, stopped a white van going in the opposite direction. The driver offered to get the hurt woman to Teruel and carefully helped to lay her down in a space in his load, just enough room for her and for Alfonso, who'd rolled his sweater around his head like a turban to stop the bleeding. The van vanished in the darkness. Miren and Joxian got their things and those of Alfonso and Catalina out of the trunk in case thieves came by.

"Did you see Catalina's legs?"

"Both of them broken. You don't have to be a doctor to know that."

"She can pray they set them properly and that they heal."

The inhospitable place was absolutely silent. They quickly put on more clothing. How cold it is, and what do we do now? They had no idea where they were. Between Teruel and Zaragoza, that for sure. There were no houses, no lights, and no traffic signs. Not even a refuge in that desert, I don't know, a shepherd's cabin, a thicket where we can get some protection.

Miren:

"Are you sure you aren't hurt? Tell me the truth."

"I'm fine, damn it."

"You're covered with blood."

"It must be Alfonso's."

"Put something around your neck, you're going to get a chill. That's what happens when you lose heat."

"Don't get all wound up. We'll have to make a report to the Guar-dia Civil."

"I'd rather die than talk to Joxe Mari's torturers."

"So, what do we do?"

"Think."

Miren thought she remembered their passing near a village a while ago, but she wasn't sure. In a daze, Joxian neither knew nor remembered. The best thing would be to stop a car. They saw one coming with its lights on. They didn't wave. They were certain that the driver would realize what their situation was when he saw the crashed car. It didn't stop.

"How do you expect them to stop if you don't wave?"

"Well, if you're so smart, why don't you wave?"

"Okay, let's not argue."

The next one, after a few minutes passed, did stop. Were they hurt?

They said no, trembling with cold. The driver said he was going to Calamocha, nearby, his village, and if they wanted he could drive them. He did. He introduced himself as Pascual. Fifty or so years old, a potbelly, a bit of a blabbermouth: before the third curve in the road he'd already revealed his cardiac arrhythmia and his diabetes.

"Is this still the province of Teruel?"

"Yes, ma'am."

"Well, we won't be getting home today."

"It would be difficult. The last bus for Zaragoza already left."

Miren explained where they were going and with whom they'd been traveling and what had happened.

"So all of you were on vacation?"

"That's right. In Benidorm."

The man saw the bloodstains on Joxian. It was impossible not to see them. And he again asked if you aren't hurt. Joxian explained that the blood wasn't his. This Pascual, in his marked Aragonese accent, made a suggestion when the first houses in Calamocha came into sight:

"Why don't you come home with me? My children are in Zaragoza, the eldest working in a bank and two studying at the university, and my girl in Paris, married to a French musician, a really nice guy. Polite, calm. Of course he doesn't speak a word of Spanish, but we understand each other well enough. As you'll see, there's room, I assure you, for an army. You can rest, wash off the blood, and tomorrow, as calm as you please, I'll drive you to the train station in Zaragoza, where I have to go anyway. I'm a widower and as I said I live in a big, empty house."

He made them a succulent dinner, offered them a bedroom with a beamed ceiling, and a bed with cold, heavy sheets, and bright and early, after breakfast, kind and jovial, drove them to Zaragoza. Miren and Joxian wanted to pay him. No, not a chance. They insisted, awkward, timid. Pascual answered back, patting his belly with both hands, that the famous stubbornness of the Aragonese was nothing compared to theirs. Along the way, he praised the Basques. Noble, hardworking people. The bad part has to do with ETA attacks. They said goodbye outside the Portillo station. It was Sunday and a north wind was killing. The next day, in the afternoon, Miren went to the San Sebastián post office. She'd rather die than go to the village post office. What business is it of anyone around here that I'm contacting a gentleman in the province of Teruel? In the box, a couple of pounds of Tolosa beans, a jar of pickles wrapped in padded plastic, an Idiazábal cheese in a vacuum pack, and no more because nothing else would fit in the box.

Joxian joked:

"You beat the Aragonese guy from Calamocha in stubbornness."

"I'm not stubborn. I'm thankful."

"I hope this doesn't mean you're turning Spanish."

"Get out of my sight, you jerk, you stupid jerk."

112

WITH THE GRANDSON

Things look awful, Joxian. Awful? More than awful. A son in jail I may never see free again, because for sure I'll die before it happens; another in Bilbao, who never calls, never writes, never visits, Miren suspects because he's ashamed of his family; and the daughter, who hasn't spoken to her mother for more than a year and who doesn't get along with her husband. Joxian mulled over his tribulations on the Rentería bus and what bad luck we have. Couldn't we be just a little bit more normal? And suddenly, seeing the looks on the faces of the other passengers, he realized he must have been talking out loud to himself. I'm losing it, the way geezers do. Which is what I am. He was sitting in a seat reserved for senior citizens and pregnant women.

He got out at his usual stop. This was during the time when he would visit his grandchildren behind Miren's back. When he left the house, he'd say he was going to the garden. And he really did go there; he'd gather up some greens or fruit, and would sometimes add a rabbit which he would kill and skin on the spot, since he couldn't do it in front of the children, and then he'd take the bus at the industrial polygon stop.

He was about to press the door buzzer, in his plastic bag three or four leeks, escarole, and a handful of hazelnuts, when he suddenly longed to return home. Guillermo shouting, Arantxa shouting, little Ainhoa bawling: a madhouse. He rang the buzzer. The sound of the buzzer silenced everyone instantly except for the girl, who went on crying her eyes out. Even so, ten or twelve seconds passed before the door opened. A burst of pungent smells: food, bodies, closed space. Guillermo, dry, in a huff, said hello and made for the street.

What a bad scene. Everywhere, disorder and filth. The furious, tearful stare of Arantxa, surrounded by a ring of sunken eyes, profoundly depressed Joxian. Ainhoa, five years old, stops sobbing when she sees *aitona* and runs to see the potential gifts hidden in the bag. Spurred on by the same curiosity, Endika, seven years old, also runs over quickly, pushes his sister, who defends herself by pushing back, and finally both children express a shared disappointment when they see the greens and nuts. Arantxa:

"Would the two of you like to go outside with *aitona*?"

Both in one voice:

"No."

"Why not? He always buys you trinkets."

The boy reinforces his no with a shake of his head.

"Well, *ama*, I just get bored."

Joxian can't think of anything to say. He doesn't know how to trick them, he doesn't promise them anything. He seems tired, apathetic, and he ends up looking toward Arantxa to ask her with not a trace of vigor in his voice how she's doing.

"You can see for yourself. Terrible, with a ton of work to do, the house, the kids, and a husband who treats me worse than a dishrag. I don't even have time to be unhappy."

"Do you remember Catalina?"

"Which Catalina?"

"Alfonso's."

"The one who was left lame after the accident she had with you and *ama*? I read the obituary note in the paper."

"She was sickly for a long time. Tomorrow's the funeral."

"What became of her son?"

"He's still there. In Badajoz, I think. He had a lot of blood on his hands."

"More than my brother?"

"Much more."

Endika interrupts their conversation.

"*Ama*, I'm hungry."

"Get a yogurt from the refrigerator."

"There's none left."

Arantxa sweet-talked the boy with maternal fussing to go out with *aitona* to have a snack somewhere. To her father: please do me the favor of taking him out. And Ainhoa? She flatly refused to go with them, unmoved by the sweetness of her mother's words: jelly bun, cake, cream. Her lower lip, offended, fell. And she didn't say why she didn't want to go and she didn't go.

"That's that, *aita*, go out with the boy."

"Would you like me to bring you something, *maitia?*"

The girl answered no with two disgusted shakes of her childish head.

Grandfather and grandson left the apartment. At the entryway, Endika did not allow his hand to be held. He thought he was much too old to be walked along that way. They walked into the neighborhood bakery, where the boy ordered two doughnuts, one sugar coated, the other chocolate coated. And while Joxian counted out his money, the boy, hungry, gluttonous, took the first bites. By the time they were back on the street, he'd eaten both.

"The bomb went off here. I was with *aita* inside the bakery."

"What bomb?"

"The bomb that broke my bedroom windows. A man who was a friend of my *aita* died and his name was Manolo. He was lying right there, *aitona*, where that black car is. I saw him."

"Why did you look?"

"I didn't look."

"So how could you see?"

"Well, I looked a little bit with this eye."

"Would you like to go to the swings?"

"Okay."

This wasn't the first time the boy brought up the bomb. He couldn't forget the explosion. It's also true that as he grows up, he takes an interest in the matters of his elders, asks questions.

In the playground, grandfather and grandson sit down on a bench. The shouts of children. Here and there, mothers and fathers with baby carriages. Out of nowhere, Endika:

"*Aita* says some bad men planted the bomb."

"That sounds right. Should we get something to drink?'

"When the Guardia Civil catches them, they'll put them in jail the way they did with *osaba* Joxe Mari."

"Did your *aita* tell you that, too?"

"No, it was Grandma Angelita who said that."

Joxian was tempted to agree with boy. So that he wouldn't go around saying that. So that it would all be over as soon as possible. And because every mention of his son was like getting hit with a bat.

"Would you show me *osaba*'s photo?"

He hadn't asked that in a long time.

"Why do you want to see it?"

"Come on, *aitona,* show it to me."

Joxian got the faded, wrinkled photo out of his wallet. It showed Joxe Mari at the age of eighteen, smiling, long-haired, with a beard. He was just short of becoming a professional handball player.

"He's got an earring."

"Will you wear one, too, when you're older?"

"No, because they stick a needle in your ear and it does a ton of damage. Is it true *osaba* Joxe Mari's in jail for being a super-bad guy?"

"Is that what Grandma Angelita says?"

"No, that's what my *aita* says."

"Well, I suppose he must have done something. I don't think he's in jail for wearing an earring."

A short while later, Joxian went back with the boy to the apartment. He gave a hundred-peseta coin to each grandchild; to his daughter a five-thousand-peseta banknote to help out with the household expenses, as he said, and he left. On the bus back to San Sebastián, the same thing happened to him as happened on the trip out. What? He suddenly noticed that people were staring at him. He must have been talking to himself.

113

Uphill Finish

He said to himself: if it rains, I won't go. It was nine in the morning. He looked out the window. It was raining; he went. I'll put on my parka, my waterproof trousers, and that's it. Miren, as he was getting ready to leave:

"Who in the world would go out on his bicycle with this weather? You think you're still twenty?"

Arantxa, in her wheelchair, gave her father a thumbs-up sign, though it wasn't clear whether as a joke or as a sign of approval.

"Even your daughter's laughing at you."

Whatever doubts he had had nothing to do with his health or his strength. Let's see, how many times had he done all the course stages set by the cyclotourism club on rainy days? Rain, sun, or wind, now he only signs up for the short runs, of thirty or forty miles at the most. You know how it is, age, aches and pains, with the passage of time the hills seem steeper. About three years ago, he pedaled one Sunday with his friends all the way to Ondárroa. A beating. On the way back, his chest throbbed with palpitations. Careful, Joxian, be very careful. He had to stop to rest several times. He got home late to dinner. A row.

His doubts centered on the bicycle. It gets wet, it gets covered with mud, it can break, and it isn't (carbon fiber frame, Campagnolo groupset) just any bike. It cost him a ton of cash, he improved it little by little, substituting some elements for others that were better and more expensive. So, before setting out, he went into the Pagoeta to have a coffee to get in the proper mood and see if the rain let up, still not totally convinced he should get out on the highway.

Lo and behold, it stops raining. And not only that, but there are breaks in the clouds, and, before he got to San Sebastián, at about Martutene, the sun came out. Joxian was wearing his club uniform: green-and-white top and black shorts, along with his own personal helmet and gloves. I don't know if in a place as serious . . . More than anything it was so Miren wouldn't get suspicious and bombard him with questions and sermons.

He went up the hill in the Eguía neighborhood without difficulty, though slowly. And at the last steep point, he saw noisy children off to his right, divided up into teams in a schoolyard; and to the left a flower shop he entered when it occurred to him to buy a simple, cheap bouquet, because I don't like fancy things. All he had to do was dismount, what a pain, he realized he'd left his bike lock home.

He parked the bike so he could keep an eye on it from inside the flower shop. He told them what he wanted and what it was for with one eye here and the other there. All in all, he wasn't in the shop for more than two minutes. They showed him one bouquet, small, with different sorts of flowers. He didn't want to see any others. That one was fine. He paid and left and was waiting outside the cemetery for about twenty minutes with his helmet on since he didn't want to let go of either the bicycle or the bouquet.

To one side of the fence, on the wall, next to the black plaque listing the visiting schedule there was another, smaller one that said neither dogs nor bicyclists were allowed entry. Damn it to hell. And now what do I do? Meanwhile, a bus stopped down below. Bittori, black overcoat, got out. And taking a look at the plaque, she told Joxian not to worry because:

"What they don't allow is people riding their bicycles around the graves. Walking them is fine."

"Are you sure?"

"Come along, Joxian, I know what I'm talking about."

They entered the cemetery, empty at that early hour of the morning on a workday, with the exception farther up, of whom?, of two maintenance employees preceded by a noisy vehicle. So how could a bicycle matter, when it makes no noise and gives off no smoke?

As they moved up the gentle slope, amid graves and trees (pines, cypresses) they could see other solitary visitors scattered in the thick grayness of marble and cement. Joxian and his bicycle occupied half of the wide path. Bittori acted as guide one or two steps in front. But at times she looked back, and he saw her smile. Why is this woman smiling in a place where happiness is so inappropriate? She's nuts and no one can tell me otherwise.

"I didn't know if you would come."

"Here I am."

"You're a man of your word."

"My daughter and you got me into this. I kept my promise. Let's hope you keep yours and that you don't tell Miren all about it."

"You can rest assured on that account. Arantxa isn't wrong to say you've got a good heart. All anyone has to do is see the bouquet you've brought. Txato will love it."

Joxian could only muster harsh cordiality, but Bittori's wild remarks disarmed him.

"Okay, okay."

"And he'll be envious when he sees you dressed in the club uniform."

"Don't say things like that."

"No, I just thought you did it as a way of paying your respects."

They arrived. In the distance, on the ocean side a splotch of threatening rain was lurking; but above Polloe the sun was still shining. On the asphalt path the dry stains got bigger. Joxian stared ahead, serious, inhibited?, at the headstone with its simple cross and the four names lined up in a vertical row. He didn't know who the dead were, though judging by the death dates (there was one from 1963) and the shared last name, except in one case, he concluded that they must be old relatives. On the lower part was the name of his friend. Not his nickname.

"Here he is. He's been waiting for many years to be moved to the village cemetery. We haven't done it yet to avoid happening to him what happened to Gregorio Ordóñez, who's buried farther down. If you want, I'll show you later. There was a time when they painted offensive graffiti on his tombstone. You must have read about it in the papers. The *abertzales* show no mercy, not even to the dead."

Joxian, looking down, keeps silent. Is he meditating, praying? Suddenly he fixed his eyes on his friend's name, on the date of his death. His death on the corner. The corner between the house and the garage where he kept his car and his bicycle. And after the date, Txato's age on the rainy afternoon of the shots.

Bittori never stopped talking.

"I told you yesterday that your son has sent me letters. Listen, it made me really happy when he told me he wasn't the one who did the shooting."

Joxian does not open his mouth. Out of that man wafted a timid, pensive silence; a silence that moved from outside to within him, from then to now, in contrast to Bittori's insistence, which ruined the intimacy of the moment.

"Aren't you going to say to him what you said to me in the garden? I thought that was why you came."

Now, at last, he moves. How? He turns his face to Bittori. Stupefied; his glassy eyes, where a kind of faded supplication condenses: a leave-me-in-peace, a why-don't-you-respect.

"Would you leave me alone, please? A minute."

He saw her slowly walk away along the road the two of them had climbed a bit before. Until he was certain Bittori was at a distance from which it would be impossible for her to study his features, hear his whispers, he did not look back at the grave.

She stopped about thirty steps away, between two large mausoleums. Standing still on the road, her hand on her visor to protect her eyes from the sun's rays, she observed Joxian standing before her husband's grave, the strange and slightly comic figure of the poor man in the row of slates and headstones and crosses with his brightly colored bicycling gear and his bicycle, which he pampers in the same way Txato pampered his.

And she saw him place the bouquet on the stones. Where could he have gotten it? Could he have brought it from the village? I don't think he would have risked having his wife find out. Joxian, his helmet in his hands, made the sign of the cross. And if he said something, she couldn't hear it; but just the mere fact that he came to the cemetery as he'd promised the previous afternoon in the shed in the garden gave Bittori a profound satisfaction.

Then, abruptly, Joxian began walking toward her, pushing the bicycle with both hands. He'd finished, how quickly, the visit to the man who was his friend, his best friend. Joxian reached Bittori. Without stopping, in a hasty voice, with phony naturalness:

"Well, I'm off."

"It did me a world of good that you came."

Joxian didn't respond to that. Why this sudden haste? Why this brusque way of taking off? Bittori soon got her answer. Joxian managed to take four steps when his first sob came. He walked more quickly. He was going toward the exit with his bicycle, his face lowered, and a visible tremor in his shoulders.

114

A PANE OF GLASS BETWEEN

Just before Joxe Mari was transferred from the Picassent prison to the Albolote penitentiary—because of a serious incident involving a prison guard—he finally received a visit from his brother.

He would complain to his mother. What's going on with Gorka, why doesn't he come, I'd really like to see him. Miren would say he didn't visit them, either, and look how close he is, and that neither she nor Joxian knows what's going on with that boy, who seems to be hiding from us.

Miren tried to convince him on one of the rare times they spoke over the telephone. How did she try? Well, in her usual way, by picking a fight accompanied by a hailstorm of reproaches, and of course she made things worse. Months went by before they heard anything about him.

Arantxa interceded during one of Gorka's secret visits to her Rentería apartment. She had met with Joxe Mari on one occasion. No more, because Guillermo absolutely forbade it, just as he'd forbidden Arantxa to bring their children to meet their terrorist uncle, that's all I need.

Arantxa's request, reasonable, from sister to brother, devoid of acrimony, moderate as a plea, did not convince Gorka.

"We'll see."

When he says we'll see he really means no. Nevertheless, his sister's words left him uncertain. More than that: possessed by an uncomfortable inner whisper. Remorse? Probably. So to purge himself of this annoyance he explained the situation to Ramuntxo, and what would you do, and he decided for him. Meaning, that he should set up a visit to his brother as soon as possible. Which is what Gorka did, but not really desiring it, and the next month, the three of them went to Picassent: Ramuntxo at the wheel, Amaia at his side, bribed with a paternal promise that they'd go shopping in Valencia, and in the backseat, Gorka, alone, depressed, regretting after the first mile he'd ever embarked on this trip.

"How would you describe your relationship with your brother?"

"I'd say nonexistent."

"Are you afraid of him?"

"Are you trying to interview me?"

"I'm interested for your sake. Are you afraid of him or not?"

"Before I was. Now I don't know. I haven't seen him in a long time."

"You don't like us to talk about these things?"

"They pain me and you know it. Which is why I don't understand why you want to sour the day for me."

"I'm sorry. End of interview. Dear public, a few words from our sponsor and we'll be right back with other subjects."

Gorka said goodbye to Ramuntxo and Amaia in the prison parking lot. Tall, ungainly, joyless, he entered the building. As if he were a steer at the gates to the slaughterhouse. After passing through the standard security check, he was assigned a visiting room. A narrow box, an uncomfortable hard-plastic chair, suffocating heat, a lot of filth, especially on the glass, and on the left and on the right all those people talking at the top of their lungs, mouths close to the microphones, God knows what bacteria bred there.

He saw his brother before his brother saw him. He was struck by his loss of mass and especially of hair. He couldn't keep from staring at his brother's hands, the hands of a handball player who was powerful, strong, the brother he admired and feared so much as a child, hands later transformed into instruments for taking the lives of human beings, how many?, only he could know, and for a moment he felt a slight chill and a poignant, sad happiness for not being his brother or being where he was.

Joxe Mari must have noticed something on his brother's face before he sat down, something that wiped out the smile on his own face. For a few seconds, they stared at each other, serious, scrutinizing, separated by the pane of glass. And it was Joxe Mari who spoke first.

"As you see, I can't give you a hug."

"Don't worry."

"I was dying to see you, brother."

"Well, here I am."

"I feel you're cold. Aren't you happy to see me?"

"Of course I'm happy, but I'd have preferred seeing you somewhere else."

"Of course, asshole, me too."

He might have spared Gorka the asshole part. That was aimed at the old Gorka, the skinny, withdrawn teenager. Talking down, the voice of the bully. Gorka didn't like it and he pulled back, openly distancing himself from the microphone, which was like telling his brother in so many words: cut it out, I'm not your subordinate in the cell. And there was nothing at all in Joxe Mari that didn't produce an intimate, living repulsion in him. Aside from the fact that the place stank. Don't they ever ventilate it? Pity? None. His eyes, perhaps the part of him that's changed least in all these years, were the eyes that had looked at his victims before he executed them. And his bald forehead was that of a murderer, above the eyebrows of a murderer, the nose of a murderer, the mouth (teeth in bad shape) of a murderer. I'm thinking these things, but it wouldn't be right to say them and I wouldn't dare.

They exchanged superficial details of their respective private lives. Two strangers pretending to have intimacy. It was useless to try to converse as they did when they shared a bedroom in their parents' house. Gorka protected himself, making up questions so he wouldn't have to talk about himself. The forty minutes he'd spend in that rattrap would seem like eternity.

There's no doubt that Joxe Mari is also beginning to feel disgusted. How so? It's that no affection, or understanding was coming from the other side of the glass. Much less a smile. What's going on? He was trying to read in the depths of his brother's eyes and what he saw in them he did not like. He was not fond of sentimentality. He suddenly hardened his expression.

"In your heart you condemn my militancy, right? And you have contempt for it."

Gorka wasn't expecting that. He was on guard.

"Why do you say that?"

"It's easy to see that the *aitas* pressured you to visit me. You can't fool me."

"I came on my own."

"Don't misunderstand me. I'm not keeping you here, especially if you plan to make my situation worse. Or do you think I don't get it?"

"I didn't make such a long trip to make anything worse. And I didn't come here to play the part of your little brother. And of course I don't approve of the things you did that got you here. I never did."

"So you're the kind who thinks I deserve to be here?"

"That's a question you'd have to ask your victims."

"I've taken a lot of hits since I was arrested. None hurt me as much as what you're saying. My own brother, Jesus!"

"It's because I'm your brother that I'm telling you what I think. Would you rather I lie, that I congratulate you for the pain you've caused to God knows how many families? And what for?"

"To save my people."

"By spilling the blood of others? That's beautiful."

"By spilling the blood of our oppressors who smash us every day and don't let us be free."

"That also goes for the children you've killed?"

"If it weren't for this glass, I'd explain it to you in a way you'd really understand."

"You're threatening me?"

"Looks like it."

"If you like, you can shoot me. You've killed others for less in the name of a people you never consulted about it."

"Let's just forget about it. I can see we're not going to understand each other."

"You started it."

"Some of us heard the call of the homeland. Others dedicate themselves to leading a comfortable life and having a good time. I suppose it's always been like that. Some sacrifice themselves, others take advantage."

"Who has a comfortable life?"

"Well, not me, that's for sure."

"I do radio programs in Basque, I write books in Basque, I help our culture. That's my way of contributing something to our people, but something constructive, without leaving a ton of orphans and widows in my wake."

"You're a great talker. You can see you work in radio. And things are going fine for you, right?"

"I'm not complaining."

"I was told you're living with a man. And you condemn what I've done. You were always a little odd, but I never imagined you'd go that far."

Gorka, mute, his features paralyzed, his face burning with sudden anger. And his brother with a sarcastic, scolding expression on his face:

"*Ama* thinks you're ashamed of us. I can tell you that I'm the one who's ashamed of having a faggot for a brother who doesn't give a shit if he drags our name through the mud. That's why you never go to the village, right?"

"Who told you I live with a man?"

"What difference does it make? Or do you think that just because I'm in a Spanish extermination prison information doesn't get to me?"

"I live with someone who loves me and whom I love. I imagine that for you it's as if I were talking in Chinese. What can a gangster understand about love?"

Gorka said that last bit as he stood up, angrily shoving the chair. He brought his mouth one last time to the microphone, but he thought better of it and swallowed the words that rose in his throat. He turned on his heel, and as he was about to leave that hot and filthy and fetid shithole of a room, he heard behind him Joxe Mari's words, begging him with a novel, in him never-seen-before humility, to come back, don't go off now, because we have to have a t—"

On the trip back to Bilbao, a long trip, a red-and-yellow summer afternoon, Amaia asleep on her seat, Ramuntxo asked him how the meeting had gone and if he was thinking of coming back another time.

"We'll see."

That was all he said. Then he fell asleep or pretended he was sleeping.

115

MASSAGE SESSION

Ramuntxo agreed to stretch out on the massage table as Gorka insisted he do; but that wasn't going to change anything because massage or no massage he was certain he was going to kill himself. What was the problem? Well, his ex, that scheming slut, that snake whose principal obsession in life was injecting him with her mortal venom, had finally done it.

It had been four weeks since Ramuntxo had driven to Vitoria to pick up Amaia. The child was sixteen at the time. Gorka: not a good age to be spending a weekend in her father's company, no matter how many gifts he buys her, no matter how many of her whims he satisfies. The girl had gotten fat. But more than obesity, it was acne, bad luck that, that made her ugly. Her character had soured. She practiced an aggressive variation on unhappiness.

Gorka tried to stay on the sidelines; but from time to time the pity Ramuntxo inspired in him made it impossible and he stepped in.

"Don't you realize she tyrannizes you?"

"Of course I realize it. What do you want me to do?"

Every other weekend, Ramuntxo drove his daughter to Bilbao and brought her back on Sunday afternoon. At the usual hour, he rang the buzzer. No one buzzed him in. He passed the time in a nearby bar. He went back. More buzzer pushing. From the street, there was no light visible in the flat. And he didn't find the scheming slut's car in the neighborhood. He took advantage when a neighbor left the entryway to go in and go up to his ex's apartment. The doormat, how odd, wasn't there. Ramuntxo rang her bell, pounded on the door. *Bam, bam, bam,* nothing. It wasn't the first time something like this took place. Nerves, curses, insults against the evil female who's spent years sabotaging the father-daughter relationship.

Ultimately, what else could he do? Ramuntxo drove back to Bilbao alone, in a rage, ranting, sad. And what the hell was he going to do with the ticket he'd bought for the movie? As had happened before, mother and daughter had taken a weekend trip (they love Madrid) and had forgotten to tell Ramuntxo. Or rather, they never intended to tell him so they could make him suffer.

For Gorka, relief. A peaceful weekend. The girl was one headache after another. As long as he can, Gorka avoids her—spending more time at the station, taking long walks, or meeting up with someone or having lunch with someone else. The idea was to spend the least amount of time at home as possible.

Before, he made use of the days Ramuntxo spent with his daughter to visit Arantxa and play uncle for a few hours. A few times he even slept over, stretched out uncomfortably on the living room sofa; but that, too, ended. It's been ages since he's seen his niece and nephew despite the fact that his sister apologized for speaking out of turn. It was she (who else could it have been?), as Gorka suspected, who told Joxe Mari that he was living with a man in Bilbao. Nice way to keep a secret! Gorka felt betrayed by the only member of his family in whom he could confide, the one he really loved. He did not hurl recriminations at his sister for her indiscretion. He said goodbye to her with his usual minimum of expressions and words, but ever since he's neither gone to Rentería nor called.

Ramuntxo's opinion was:

"Your problem is that you don't know how to forgive."

"A bigger problem for me is when people don't respect me."

A few more days went by with no news of Ramuntxo's daughter. For him: bad omens. He decided to visit Vitoria during the week.

"Will you go with me?"

"I have to record an interview."

"Please."

They left at two one afternoon. And the story of the buzzer, the windows with no light, repeated itself, along with the car belonging to that scheming slut, that snake, that was absent from any local street. Her name was still in the slot on the mailbox. Inside there were no letters or advertising brochures packed in as usually happens when the person in question is away for a while. What if she made a deal with someone to empty the mailbox at regular intervals? Nervousness, suspicion, fears that led to hypotheses that were weirder and weirder. Gorka suggested they go up to the ex's apartment and ask the next-door neighbor.

"Moving men came and took away everything. Furniture, the refrigerator, mattresses."

"When?"

"A couple of weeks ago."

"And since then you haven't seen either my daughter or her mother?"

"Remember, it's August. They may be on vacation like most of the people around here."

Who takes the furniture out to the country, the refrigerator or the mattresses to the beach? A last hope: find confirmation by calling the school. Vain hope, since at that time all the teachers were spending their time relaxing in some tourist spot. On the way back to Bilbao, Ramuntxo brought up the possibility of a lawsuit. Gorka dissuaded him. He should wait a bit, that, given who those two were, they probably decided on the spur of the moment to accept an offer from some travel agency. In any case, the whole thing seemed a spontaneous decision.

"And why wouldn't they tell me?"

"Because they probably thought you'd be opposed to the idea. Tell the truth, you *would* be opposed, right?"

"On the days when it's my turn to be with Amaia, I would."

"See?"

"What about the furniture?"

"That I can't explain, but for sure there is some explanation. Maybe they moved to another apartment in Vitoria. You won't deny that the city has better neighborhoods than the one they've lived in until now."

The letter came in September. It was Gorka who just before noon picked up the letters in the mailbox. As soon as he saw the United States stamp he conceived a fateful suspicion. On the back of the envelope was the name of the sender, Amaia, and nothing else. No last name, no address. And since those were difficult days at work and an anguished silence constantly floated through the house, Gorka decided to hide the letter from Ramuntxo. He was even tempted to destroy it to spare him the emotional turbulence he knew it would cause. He held on to it for a week. Finally, he handed it over, pretending he'd just found it in the mailbox.

After reading it, Ramuntxo ran straight to the bathroom to vomit and to make pitiful sounds that were like howls of anguish mixed in with hiccups. The wrinkled sheet of paper was tossed onto the rug. Gorka read:

Aita:
     Ama *got a job in the United States and now we're going to live here forever.* Please *don't come looking for us. If I make some money, I'll come to see you when I'm older.*

Ondo pasa,
Amaia

The girl made trouble even at a distance. And what a lack of affection from a daughter who said one day—and I heard her:

"*Aita*, leave me in peace, you're a poor slob."

That, of course, you can't mention to Ramuntxo because he'd die of pain. Gorka suggested he think things through under the shower. Then he gives him a massage of the kind he liked, you know, with a happy ending, though the man, the poor slob, showed himself open to anything but pleasure. Gorka insisted until Ramuntxo gave in, saying it was all the same to him because in any case he was thinking of killing himself.

"Today. I don't know how. I'll think of a way. But don't worry, because I'll commit suicide far from home so the police don't come around to bother you."

In the shower, he launched into a monologue; a tragic figure. Gorka meanwhile reread the letter. Cold rose from that sheet of paper. The fact that there were no spelling errors made him suspicious. Considering how terrible a student Amaia was, barely passing, having to repeat her last year, might the mother have taken a hand here? He sniffed, first the envelope and then the letter.

Ramuntxo came out of the bathroom half-dry. His obvious sorrow and his nakedness, a little twisted as well as hairy and pale, made him look like an old, sickly child. He dropped facedown on the massage bed and tried to start crying again, but it was clear he was out of tears. So he started in again with the story about how he was going to kill himself today far away from home. Meanwhile, Gorka massaged his neck, his shoulders, his back with loving, oily hands.

"Suing would be useless. I'm sure the penal code doesn't cover this case as a kidnapping. Her mother can allege she lives in another country for work reasons and that she's never stopped me from seeing my daughter. All I have to do is take a plane every two weeks."

"As far as I can see, where they're living is unclear."

"Don't think about it anymore. That filthy fox has taken off with Amaia as far as she could. Don't you see that it bothered the hell out of her that I got along with my daughter?"

"What if the letter was a trick?"

"Damn it all, Gorka, don't start in with your writer's fantasies. This isn't a novel. This is pure reality."

Gorka asked him to turn over. He massaged his chest, his stomach; he paused at the penis until he provoked an erection; he continued along the thighs. He said that:

"In a novel, I would make the divorcée pretend to move to the United States with her daughter. A girlfriend or someone at work who was traveling there could offer to mail the previously written letter from Chicago or San Francisco. The mother and the daughter would move to Madrid, for example, since both Amaia and your ex love the capital so much. And for the father I can think of a happy ending after he's survived this particular mental torture by resorting to psychiatric treatment and whatever else is necessary. But not suicide. That would be too simple. Maybe the protagonist could go to the U.S. and while there looking for his daughter meet a woman, Samantha, a seductive blonde with a turbulent past involving drugs and prostitution."

"What are you waiting for? Start writing."

And he continued with the massage and with words of affection and consolation that he prolonged after Ramuntxo's rapid, meager ejaculation.

116

ARAB SALON

They celebrated it, intimate, in love, in the restaurant of the Gran Hotel Domine, the two of them face-to-face, at a table along the huge window that faced the gray, sparkling curves of the Guggenheim. It was July, the temperature agreeable and the sky blue: a perfect day. Ramuntxo was euphorically tipsy.

What were they celebrating? Well, the previous evening the Congress of Deputies had approved the law making same-sex marriage possible, the work of the Spanish Socialist Workers' Party, a party that inspired in Ramuntxo an old and insuperable aversion, though going forward he'll have to think it over and it's possible in the next elections, not that it would be a precedent but merely to show his gratitude, he might give it his vote.

Gorka on the other hand systematically refuses to participate in any kind of election. He isn't thankful, doesn't support, doesn't punish. Everything that emits an odor of parties and politics inspires in him rejection? Actually indifference. Serious, he raised his glass to complete the toast made by Ramuntxo, who'd been extremely talkative all morning. He said this, happy with wine:

"Someday I'll ask you to marry me."

"You've been drinking, obviously."

"I'm serious, *bibotza*. For the moment, it's too soon. First we'll have to see how this new law works itself out."

"It looks as if you've held on to at least a pinch of sanity. Don't waste it."

"Of course, we have to be prudent. This society, which until recently recited the rosary every afternoon, do you really think it's ready for a change of that caliber? Well, as Luis Cernuda puts it, my "boy who arose when the light fell along Conquero hill," I look at you, I look at you more, I don't stop looking at you, and do you know what I think?"

"Come on, poet, let's have it."

"I would swear you don't completely discard the idea of matrimony."

"Well, handsome, you'd have to deserve matrimony."

"As would you, who do you think you are?"

Mayor Azkuna married them five and a half years later in the Arab Salon of the town hall. He officiated behind a splendid display of white roses, the first ravages of the sickness that would kill him visible on his face. He made a speech, occasionally moving, occasionally amusing, dotted with literary quotations and pleasant anecdotes, some related to his old friendship with Ramuntxo, whom he always referred to as Ramón. Among the guests, there was no lack of laughter or, at the end, moist eyes. The happy couple wore ties for the occasion, both in light gray suits. As someone said: twins. And the kiss was a mere peck. Gorka's fault: he was frozen by timidity. It was so much the case that Azkuna, from his podium, with folksy eloquence, demanded a second kiss, but now a real kiss. The wedding company responded to the mayor's demand with a joyful chorus, and then the newlyweds, joined in an embrace, obeyed the demand of all present (about twenty friends and workmates) and kissed with such wild passion that it provoked a salvo of applause and whistles.

Congratulations, hugs, words of encouragement, and the usual joking friend who hoped they'd be rewarded with many children. That they married with love, anyone could see. But if any of the witnesses thinks that the outlandish event in the Arab Salon was the fruit of a spontaneous decision; that is, a caprice, then they are mistaken. Ramuntxo and Gorka married, like so many other couples, for practical reasons. Also, perhaps especially, because of Ramuntxo's fears, since a year before he'd had a kidney removed.

A tumor was discovered. For now, everything is going well. He's escaped dialysis, but he has serious doubts. So do the doctors. Metastasis? Until now, they've found nothing. Alone in the hospital room, the two of them decided to formalize their relationship.

Gorka, who was opposed because after all why do it, was convinced by his companion's arguments: inheritance, property, beginning with the apartment, which we are going to co-own as soon as I'm released, if I'm released, and for example, my pension, you have to think about the pension you'll receive when I'm no longer around. Back at home, Ramuntxo quickly made a will favoring Gorka. And out of him he got the promise that he'd look after Amaia's economic needs in case that.

It had been more than ten years since Ramuntxo had any news about his daughter. The important dates, her birthday, Christmas would roll around.

"Think she remembers me?"

Nothing, no letters, not even a postcard. And Ramuntxo suffered. Often, alone or with Gorka's help, he tried to find some trace of Amaia on the Internet. Then he extended his searches to social media. And, just in case, he included the mother in the investigations. On some list, on some membership or participant roster, on the bottom of some photo, I don't know, somewhere, the name of one or the other has to appear. Or might they have changed identity?

He didn't let Amaia's birthday or Christmas pass without buying the girl, by now a woman, the appropriate present. He piled up the packages with their colored ribbons and congratulatory cards inside the armoire, and they took up more and more space, and when Gorka asked him, why are you doing this, why are you tormenting yourself, he would answer that:

"My heart tells me she'll come back. I want her to know that I've never stopped thinking about her for a second in my life. Promise me that if I die you'll give her the presents."

For Gorka, the marriage plans crashed into an obstacle impossible to avoid: his parents. Not because they might disapprove of his decision, something he had few doubts about, but for the shame they'd suffer (or which he imagined they would suffer) as soon as news of his wedding made the rounds of the village.

He talked with his mother once in a blue moon. With greater frequency during the months that followed his sister's stroke. They talked about specific subjects: Arantxa, the weather, food, gossip. Almost nothing about Joxe Mari and never anything about Gorka's personal life. At most he would tell a few trivial things about his work as an announcer. Joxian, allergic to the telephone, rarely picked it up. He limited himself to having Miren send his regards and to ask when he might visit them.

Fear of horrifying his parents and that they would make a disagreeable scene kept Gorka from consenting to marriage. But wait, how can I put this, Ramuntxo didn't demand it, either. It was a romantic, beautiful possibility but in no way an urgent need. Then Ramuntxo got sick. He was on the verge of dying, as the two of them were told later. Then the situation changed. And accepting his cowardice, which he's never denied, Gorka wanted to get married without his family's knowing about it. Ramuntxo was opposed to that.

"No way. If you don't want to, don't invite them. My mother wouldn't be coming, but she's gaga and doesn't recognize herself in the mirror. But you at least have to give the news to your *aitas*."

"You know I wouldn't dare."

"Listen to me. Don't ever think you can build your life on lies and silence. That's the worst thing, let me assure you of that."

"In any case, I'll write them a letter, okay? If I tried the telephone, my knees would be knocking from fear."

And he did write them a note, which despite its brevity tied him up for an entire afternoon. Ramuntxo read it at dinnertime and approved it after suggesting a few changes. A week before the wedding, Gorka finally gathered up the courage to mail it. They didn't answer. So he assumed his parents had repudiated him and that they would be huddling in horror or shame, not daring to appear on the street.

Just married, Gorka and Ramuntxo happily walked hand-in-hand down the town hall stairs. There the usual shower of rice awaited them. And from one car or another came some festive honking. The guests shouted: kiss, kiss, raising a hubbub that drew the attention of passersby. There were more hugs and congratulations. Gorka's hair captured numerous grains of rice. It was pointed out to him and he tried to shake them out with his hand. Suddenly, when he just happened to turn his head toward the sea, he saw them. Who? Who else? His family on the sidewalk opposite; the three of them grouped apart and seemingly fearful of getting involved, his mother in charge of the wheelchair, his father wearing a beret with his sweater over his shoulders.

Ramuntxo saw his strange reaction, the change of expression that announced something disturbing was happening to his husband.

"What's wrong?"

"They're here."

And they went to meet them. Ramuntxo, jovial; Gorka, timorous, serious, inhibited.

"So you came?"

Miren, in a singsong voice, energetically bobbing her head:

"How could we not come to our son's wedding? Is this my son-in-law?"

Transformed into a little lady, stretching her neck, she offered a cheek. And in no time flat, she asked Ramuntxo a question in Basque, no doubt to make sure he spoke it, I know her well. Ramuntxo answered in a way that made everyone laugh, except Gorka, of course, who still had a funereal face. Why? He couldn't help feeling sorry for his father with his empty smile. Teary-eyed, standing next to the railing, not knowing what to do, what to say, he looked as if he'd suddenly been transported to another planet.

Miren stepped in quickly with a reprimand:

"Listen here, Joxian, no tears, okay?"

In her wheelchair, Arantxa was a silent fountain of joy. She waved her good hand around, shouted in silence, laughed out loud with her eyes. Ramuntxo leaned over to plant a kiss of overflowing cordiality on her forehead. Then he gave Joxian, who only reached the height of Ramuntxo's tie, a bear hug, patting him on the back. And the elegant son-in-law had, finally, the fortunate, the lucky, the astute idea to declare how happy he was to have such a pretty mother-in-law. Miren, inflated with satisfaction:

"I came all the way to Bilbao to stand by my son. I even bought new shoes."

And everyone stared at her feet.

Taxis arrived. Miren, as soon as she got out, grabbed Gorka by the arm and holding on tight walked into the restaurant. Are you saying that the family came to the wedding banquet? What a dumb question. Of course they came.

The newlyweds sat next to each other. On Ramuntxo's right

there was an empty chair, for his daughter. He explained everything to the guests during his brief greeting speech. And to Gorka's left sat Miren, who at a certain moment slipped her son under the table an envelope with a thousand euros in it, our wedding present. Any less, she said, would be paltry. And she whispered in his ear:

"Joxe Mari asked me to congratulate you."

117

THE INVISIBLE SON

Quique, dressed to the nines. Suit, tie, and the dissonant element, name-brand sneakers, because that's the way he is. And Nerea, whose hem was about four inches above her knees. Pink lips, eye shadow, fishnet stockings, and high heels. Let them stare. Since they met at the end of the last century, they've happily shared those moments of moving freely, exhibiting themselves, provocative, wealthy. Together they formed juxtaposed centers of perfume that emanate outwards.

They caught—hi, we're so-and-so—a table between two of the wooden columns supporting the beams. A good spot, far from the kitchen door and the entrance to the restaurant. What day of the week was it? Saturday, nine thirty p.m. Quique had found out that afternoon that one of the investments he'd made the previous year in preserves, supposedly Lodosa peppers (supposedly?, well they bring them in at a low price from Peru), had folded with large losses all around. He told Nerea protected behind a cynical smile, with perfect teeth. And the Portuetxe grill was booked solid.

Quique, with the menu in his hands, became explicative, narrative:

"This place, when I was a child, was a village. When we were boys, we came here to fish with hazelwood poles and ordinary tackle. Suet, balls of bread. But we didn't fish here because at this point the river flowed white, I mean really white, I swear, the fault of the milk center, so we did our fishing farther up, past the Cilvetis junkyard. We even got trout in those days."

Nerea suggested the appetizers, and Quique, who wasn't listening, agreed to everything without paying attention. When he saw the platter of endive and salmon and *txangurro* on the table, he asked in surprise:

"Did you order this crap?"

And Nerea answered indeed I did, sweetheart, and then he said he'd be happy with scrambled eggs and mushrooms. The bottle of red wine, forty-five euros, he sent back. He sniffed, whirling the wine around in his glass, he sipped with closed eyes before disdainfully rejecting it. Another was brought. He repeated his sniffing and tasting, and finally accepted, in exchange for inflicting a deliberately pedantic and grandiloquent enological lecture on the waitress. He and Nerea clinked their glasses. She:

"I can read your mind. The first wine was fine."

"Of course. Better than this one. But when you're dealing with wait staff, you've got to assume a hierarchical superiority. Now the kitchen staff is probably scared shitless. They'll do their very best. It's only normal. Their lives depend on it. And whatever we order, they'll bring the best they have."

"Or they'll spit on the plate. If I see even a bubble in the sauce I won't taste it."

"What does the endive taste like?"

"Endive. And the mushrooms?"

"Mushrooms."

About to celebrate twelve years of marriage, with myriad breakups followed by passionate reconciliations, they still lived in separate apartments. Your space, my space. Your filth here, mine there. And they talked about it, dipping bread in the sauce, Quique in a jubilant rapture because he'd suddenly confirmed something. What? He realized that for the first six years of their marriage, he'd never stopped begging her to move in with him (one roof, one bed; yes, but only one bathroom), while ever since then, until now, another six years, give or take a month, it's been she who's done the begging and he who's done the refusing.

"You know why I refused. But I don't know why you're refusing."

"I liked your secret. Of course, I had no idea what it was because it was a secret. The idea that you're hiding something important from me about your private life and that I would come and take it away from you and destroy it turns me on. It would be like stealing your undies after raping you. But just look, if you think about it carefully, I'm the one who comes away losing. I get the disillusion of the boy who's smashed his favorite toy. That's why I don't want us to live together. I'd be very sorry to get to know you so well that there would no longer be a margin, no matter how slim, for surprise."

An indiscreet comment by Bittori ruined the secret. And when she noticed that she'd made a huge mistake, she tried naïveté.

"Oh dear, you mean you didn't know?"

A bitter pill for Nerea, sitting next to Quique on the sofa with the expression of a liar caught in the act and Ikatza on her lap. In the version she'd told Quique on previous occasions she said her father had died of lung cancer. And she would add calculated narrative embellishments to make the lie seem even more true to life.

Once the truth was revealed, it was as if Nerea no longer saw the need for separate domiciles. In her place, *my palace* as she called it in English, she maintained a memory museum dedicated to her *aita*, and the last thing she would ever want in her house would be witnesses, questions, hands that touch, snatch, smudge things. An exposition of paternal relics: photos, newspaper articles ("ETA Assassinates Businessman in"), articles of clothing worn by the deceased, objects that belonged to him. For instance? The candle in the shape of a cactus that I gave him when I was a little girl, a fountain pen, cyclotourism and *mus* tournament trophies, his shirt with two bullet holes, objects from his office, a few pairs of his shoes, including the ones he was wearing the afternoon of the attack. In sum, things of great sentimental value for Nerea, who'd been given them, some by her mother, others by Xabier. And his pistol.

It was her brother who had the idea of bringing the shirt to the cleaners. If it had been up to Nerea, she would have kept it with the bloodstains. And after Quique found out how the father-in-law he never met died, the fact is that Nerea no longer felt the need to hide her relics from him any longer, except that now it seemed he didn't want that junk belonging to a terrorism victim anywhere near him. The photos were the limit for him. The rest he thought macabre. Nerea was unwilling to part with any of it. How could she? So they went on living in separate flats, though they got together frequently, almost every day, not always, according to the mood of the day.

As usual, Quique placed his cell phone on the table, next to his plate, and every other minute he looked at it. It may be Saturday, but business never rests. And while he attacked his grilled monkfish with almonds (Nerea, Portuetxe-style codfish), the jingle of Whats-App announced the arrival of a message. Nothing, just some crap from Elizalde, a short video, funny, of a bald soccer player who gets hit in the face with the ball over and over again. They were partners, they are friends, they text each other funny things. Nerea had her own theory.

"That guy's poking around to find out if you're free and the two of you can go out on the prowl tonight."

"If you hadn't had that falling out with Marisa, the four of us would be able to be here having dinner and laughing our heads off."

"I'm still wondering why I didn't scratch her eyes out."

The two women get along well. Friends? Let's not exaggerate. Their relationship reached the level of agreeable conversations, occasional outings to the El Corte Inglés department store in Bilbao, and even the exchange of some intimate secrets, but without going too far. And for good reason, they had different natures, different tastes, and different interests. And then in the café at El Corte Inglés, Marisa, who according to Nerea was perhaps a bit envious, goes and says pretty much out of the blue that:

"It's none of my business, but if I were you I'd keep an eye on your husband. He's quite a skirt chaser."

They returned separately to San Sebastián, Nerea by bus, the other in her car. And that's how things stand today.

"She tried to break up our marriage, and I just can't allow that."

"How's that cod?"

"Okay, but I don't really like it with red wine."

"So let's order white wine."

"Elizalde, doesn't he cheat on that idiot?"

"All the time."

"The standard-model jerk who thinks she knows everything."

The waitress brought the white wine. Did they want to taste it? Quique asked her to leave the bottle on the table. If it was bad, they'd call her over.

"That gold necklace with the ginkgo leaf that I gave you, you don't wear it anymore?"

"I threw it in the Thames the day I went nuts. But don't worry, because I know exactly where it fell and I can get it back anytime."

"I'll give you another. I don't want you to freeze."

She was enraged, howling in the morning solitude of her room, more enraged with herself than with him. It's just that, for openers, she can't stand it when Quique pretends, as they walk down the street, that he's holding the hand of the child they don't have. In London, he repeated that act. No once, but several times. The last time, the one that unleashed her rage, happened when Nerea saw him from the hotel window. Quique was coming to pick her up, dressed up, elegant, and at the moment he crossed the street, he held the little hand of his invisible son. Could he have known she was watching him from a fifth-floor window? I'm getting like my mother, who peeks out the window when we leave. And noting that resemblance infuriated her.

Nerea skipped dessert. He didn't: flan, coffee, and a glass of sloe brandy, which he only ordered after making sure they had the brand he sells.

For several years, Nerea was convinced Quique was sterile. And the fact is that he, depressed, shared that supposition. She convinced him to have his semen analyzed. Why? I don't know, sometimes there's a low sperm count or they don't wag their tails and are useless. The laboratory results showed that Quique's semen is of good quality. So the infertility in that case fell to her, so she defends herself:

"Maybe your aim is off."

Nerea stopped looking for men, breeding bulls who resembled Quique physically. Because, of course, if you have a blond baby or a black one, how can you explain that? She was thinking of imitating a cuckoo and putting someone else's egg in her husband's nest, but couldn't do it. And she had inseminators by the ton at her disposal.

For some time now, he's had this thing about holding the hand of the child he doesn't have, that he'll never have, at least not with me. He knows this morbid game, a way of throwing her infertility in her face?, jangles my nerves. Quique was suffering and she was suffering and she was enraged because he was suffering.

"The check, please."

Nerea was faster when the moment came to hand the waitress her credit card. She added a tip equal to the price of the wine Quique had rejected. Outside the restaurant, they started making out, slobbery kisses, feeling each other up in the semidarkness, under the starry sky.

"Jesus, you're not wearing panties."

"So you won't steal them."

"I adore the scent of your sex. I'd screw you here and now."

"It's not a good spot. The river runs white here."

"That was a long time ago."

"I'd rather we go up beyond that junkyard you talked about."

And instead of going back to town, they took the Igara highway, toward mountainous places, toward higher ground, tree-covered darkness.

118

Unannounced Visit

From her brother, Nerea learned that Bittori and Arantxa met almost every morning in the village square. It was also Xabier who told her on which days and at what time her old friend came to the hospital for physiotherapy. The information included the veiled suggestion that she visit Arantxa. Nerea spontaneously decided she would visit her. But there is one thing, sometimes there's a tiny little woman from Ecuador with her and other times it's her mother.

"What are you saying? That Miren would bite me or something?"

"I'm just telling you in case you don't want to run into her."

How long had it been since they'd seen each other? Mmm, since the days when Nerea was studying law in San Sebastián. Let me think. More than twenty years before she went to study in Zaragoza? Arantxa was already married by then, working as a saleswoman in a shoe store, and living in Rentería with her husband. She lost sight of her, a decade went by, another decade went by, and the third had begun. A long time after the last time they saw each other, when?, no idea, Arantxa had her stroke. About that as well, Nerea had found out from Xabier.

"The truth is that it's upsetting to see her the way she is now."

"Stop protecting me, brother. Can I talk to her?"

"She understands everything. To communicate, she uses an iPad. You ask her something, and she answers in writing. I know she's getting help from a speech therapist, but I don't know if she can articulate comprehensible words."

One Wednesday, Nerea went up to the hospital. Following

Xabier's instructions, she located the person who would get her where she wanted to go. She found Arantxa in her wheelchair, alone in the corridor, passing the time while she waited for someone to bring her to physiotherapy.

I almost fainted from sorrow. Her hair short, lots of gray; one hand clenched, useless, her neck awkward, and her facial features slightly but still visibly deformed. It took Nerea a few seconds to recognize in that broken woman the friend of her adolescence. And her first thought was: shit, what hits we take from life. And her second: I hope she doesn't get angry because I didn't tell her I was coming.

"Arantxa, sweetie, look who's come to see you."

Half a second of shock and doubt as she turned her head. And then, suddenly, her entire face transformed into a grimace of joy. After receiving a ritual kiss, Arantxa stretched out her right hand to touch, hold, what anguish, to try to hug her friend who was already stepping back. And Arantxa tried to speak and simply couldn't, and she put so much effort into expressing herself that for a moment it looked as if she were choking.

"I'll leave you two alone, you probably have a lot to tell each other."

With affectionate, compassionate?, knuckles Nerea caressed her friend's cheek. Arantxa in turn gave her a look of resignation, as if to say: take a good look, this is all there is. Or something like that.

Nerea opted for being loquacious, in order to lower the dramatic temperature of the meeting. That she'd learned from her brother, that she'd found out, that she'd been told. And she concluded, sincerely:

"What shitty luck."

By then Arantxa had taken the iPad out of the space between her body and the side of the wheelchair, sad eyed, nodding. With the device in her lap, she wrote:

"I'm really happy to see you."

"Just what I'm saying. How is it going?"

"Badly."

"That was a stupid question. Sorry."

And seeing that Arantxa was laughing, Nerea imitated her, though her lips were slack.

"I'm divorced."

That pale, thin index finger made agile jumps among the keys. When she finished her sentences, Nerea looked at the screen and read.

"My ex left me. It doesn't matter."

She asked if Arantxa had any children. She knew how many. Xabier had told her, but the fact is Nerea was having trouble adapting to that spoken-written form of conversation, and in the hope of seeming more natural, she asked formal, stupid questions.

Arantxa, ironically imitating the victory sign, raised two fingers.

"What I love most in life. They live with him, but I see them a lot. If they visit, I'll introduce you."

She went on, letter by letter, but quickly, to specify ages, wrote their names, declared her children clever, good-looking, tender.

"They took after me."

"You're proud of them, right?"

She said yes by vigorously nodding her head. And she asked about Nerea's life. Nerea gave her a summary: married, no children, a job in the finance ministry. And as she leaned over to see the screen again, she couldn't avoid a bite of emotion when she read that her friend found her very pretty.

"Don't believe it. The years are piling up for me, too."

"I live with my *aitas*. I see your mother a lot."

"That's right, she told me."

"I'm sorry about her sickness."

Hmm, so she's right up-to-date.

"Xabier and I try to be with her as much as possible. Xabier does more. You know he's been a mama's boy all his life."

"Bittori's great sorrow is that she's going to die without my brother asking all of you for forgiveness."

"True, she's missing that consolation."

"I'm always pressuring Joxe Mari. I never stop."

She nodded, joining and separating the tips of her fingers several times to show she sent him lots of letters or messages or whatever.

"My brother is afraid."

"Afraid?"

"He's afraid that Bittori will go to the newspapers with some statement of his where he asks forgiveness. His comrades might find out."

Coming from way down the hall, there appeared a smile filled with white teeth, an examination robe no less white and clean, and a young face: the chatty physiotherapist, who spoke with sympathy:

"What's this, my beauty, you've got a visitor?"

Arantxa hastily wrote something on the iPad screen. The physiotherapist immediately showed she agreed. She then asked Nerea to wait there without moving, that they would call her. Nerea waited alone in the corridor. What can these women be dreaming up? To judge by their faces, it had to be something amusing. In a bit, they did call her. She walked into the rehabilitation room. They'd prepared a surprise for her. Arantxa standing up, on each side a physiotherapist. Insecure, tense, she managed to take a step without help, no one holding on to her, a short, stumbling step, oh God don't let her fall, two, four in all. And from behind they brought over the wheelchair so she could sit down. Praise, applause from all those present. Nerea too applauded. And then she was on the verge of tears.

She said goodbye to Arantxa a few minutes later, not without promising she'd come again. Nerea walked down the hall, lost in thought, actually in worries. Her mother, of course. And just before she reached the stairs, I'm happy I came, a voice greeted her from nearby, with a hello that was dry, cutting, and to which Nerea responded without taking the time to see who'd greeted her. She turned her head. She saw Miren's back as she made her way toward the corridor. Is that Miren? Of course it was Miren, accompanied by a boy about eight inches taller than she and a very pretty girl with long hair pulled back in a ponytail. Judging by their age, by the fact that they were with Miren, and because it couldn't be any more obvious, she concluded they were Arantxa's children.

119

PATIENCE

That night, Nerea called her brother. She'd promised she would. She told him, without getting tangled up in too many details, how her visit with Arantxa that afternoon had gone. She did not forget to tell him that Miren had said hello to her.

"It can't be. Are you sure?"

"Well, there was no one next to me, so the greeting had to be for me. A rapid hello. She didn't give me enough time even to see her face."

She concluded by bringing up the matter that most concerned her.

"Arantxa knows all about *ama*'s sickness."

"I can't imagine what kind of information she has. I still haven't told *ama* what the diagnosis is."

"*Ama* is no fool. She knows that no one goes to the oncologist to cure a sore throat. For sure she intuits what's wrong with her even if she can't put a name to it."

"I'd appreciate it if you'd pay her a visit and lay the groundwork. Right now, I'm a little down."

"Take it easy. I'll go tomorrow."

"Do me one favor. If she disagrees with you, don't argue with her."

Nerea bought her mother a bouquet—a bad idea, as she soon found out. Passing by a florist on the way to her mother's house, she thought: I'll give her some flowers as a sign of goodwill. Bittori, as soon as she saw them:

"Hey, I'm not dead yet."

Patience. Before she went in, standing on the landing, Nerea asked about the doormat she'd brought from London.

"You've asked me about it before. You might have figured out that I didn't like it."

"You never said anything."

"Dear daughter, there are things you just don't have to say."

Patience, patience. She remembered her brother's request: that she please not argue with her.

"What's going on with your husband? Have you separated again?"

"He's still around."

"That guy's always around somewhere."

"*Ama*, he's got a lot of work. Don't be so nasty."

Bittori put the bouquet in a vase with water. She said they smelled nice and that on Saturday, if you don't mind, I'll bring them to Txato. Nerea complained that it was cold there in the living room. She said it looking at the balcony door, which was wide open.

"It's in case the cat comes home. I'm starting to think something terrible has happened."

"Yesterday I visited Arantxa in the hospital."

"She told me all about it this morning."

"I see. Actually, I came by to tell you, but if you already know everything . . ."

"I know her part. Not yours."

Patience. Sitting down, she here, her mother on the other side of the coffee table, the vase with the flowers between them along with two cups of instant decaf coffee. Nerea explained her reason for going up to the hospital and how her meeting with Arantxa was arranged. And Bittori interrupted her every other second:

"Yes, I know all that. And now you're going to tell me that Arantxa took six steps without anyone's help."

"Four."

"She told me six."

"When I was leaving, I saw her mother. Did Arantxa tell you that, too?"

"No, she didn't."

The late-afternoon coolness, carrying a note of oceanic humidity, flowed through the balcony door. Light? Not much. Sufficient for Bittori. Nerea was uncomfortable because she felt as if she were inside a cave inside a house. If I'd only known, I'd have brought a lantern. And on the wall, the pendulum clock lazily, routinely rang out eight o'clock. The setting was weird, of a sad heaviness and with poor lighting. A characteristic scent covered the knickknacks, the walls, the furniture, not quite repulsive but exactly the opposite of cozy. And it was the same smell that emanated from her mother's clothes and body when she hugged her.

"Did you stop to talk to her?"

"No way. By the time I realized who it was saying hello to me, she'd gone along with her grandchildren."

"Oh, she was with her grandchildren? What are they like?"

"The boy, tall; the girl, good-looking. I only saw them from behind. But Arantxa told me a few things you haven't mentioned to me."

"What things?"

"She was sorry, she said, about your sickness. I was surprised she was better informed than I was about that."

"You may be informed. Because, at least I think so, you talk to your brother from time to time. What Xabier doesn't know is that the other day I called Arruabarrena. The doctor told me that he'd talked it all over with Xabier, who has to give the explanations of what has to be explained. So, that was on Friday a week ago and here I am still waiting. During that time, your brother has called me every day. Think he told me anything about the results of the tests? Not a word. And now you turn up with flowers. You two make a great team!"

"The flowers are a sign of affection. Nothing else."

"If we don't communicate within the family, it's natural that some don't know what's happening to others."

"Well, now you've got a chance to talk with me. And I'd appreciate it if you turned on the lamp. You're sitting right there and I can barely see your face."

"The problem is that if I turn it on, mosquitoes come in."

Patience. Nerea, joking, asked her mother if by any chance she remembered where she'd put her coffee cup. And she pretended to look for it, feeling around on the table. Damn, well, turn on the light, but close the balcony door first. Nerea, delighted. Not wasting a second, she did the first, then the second.

"I've lived this long and maybe I'll live a little more. I know what I have inside my body. I'm not going to subject myself to chemotherapy or any of those other tortures. I want to join my husband, it's about time, and no one's going to stop me. To live one more year? Two? What for? I was killed a long time ago. From that moment on I've been nothing more than a ghost. At most, half a person. And that only because something has to remain where you feel the pain others cause you and because, as well, with two children, you go on as long as you can." Nerea seemed about to say something, but Bittori cut her off. "I'm talking here. You two don't have to worry about your inheritance. It's all arranged. No reason for you to fight. It's fifty-fifty. And now, listen to what I'm going to say. I'm telling you because it isn't possible to talk to your brother about these things. He gets depressed right away."

Nerea stared at her mother's serene face, decisive, lucid. And it was as if she were seeing her for the first time in her life. During other moments, she'd stared at the flowers. They did look like a funeral-parlor decoration.

"This is what I want. You'll bury me with *aita* in Polloe, my coffin on top of his. There is room for one more body. Please, leave my wedding ring on my finger, the same as we did with his when we buried him. And make sure I'm wearing the white shoes I wore on my wedding day. You can find them in the closet in my room. That's a job I can't give to your brother. He doesn't understand and couldn't do it. But you're a woman, there's no need to explain certain things to you. Place two obituary notices in *El Diario Vasco*, one in Spanish the other in Basque. And in both make sure *aita*'s nickname appears. No funeral for me. And now, the most important thing, even though in fact everything is important. If you see that within a year or two or however many it takes, the political situation calms down, that terrorism has ended, you should move the two of us to the village cemetery. That's all I ask of you."

"Have you talked this over, any of it, with Xabier?"

"How the hell can I talk to him if he hasn't come by in ages. And these are things I don't want to talk about on the phone."

"Okay, since we're being sincere, I've found out you're determined to have Miren's son ask your forgiveness and Arantxa is doing everything she can to make him do it. True?"

"Why do you think I'm still alive? I need that forgiveness. I want it and I demand it, and until I get it I have no intention of dying."

"Your pride is really out of this world."

"It isn't pride. As soon as you place the last slab and I'm resting with Txato, I'll tell him: the idiot asked to be forgiven, now we can rest in peace."

120

The Girl from Ondárroa

Conditions in prison didn't break him down. And you can believe they were tough. In some jails they're worse than in others. We'll soon see what the future holds for him. This whole thing is getting harder and harder. Naturally the years are taking their toll; but he doesn't believe it's time that split him like a dry log, though at the same time, we're not going to discount it. It was, principally, something else. What? Joxe Mari attributes the start of his moral collapse to the girl from Ondárroa. He's convinced. Starting with that story, which at the beginning was so beautiful, the termite of sadness got inside him, damn it to hell, you don't notice, but it goes on eating you up, eating you up, and finally the wood's all filled with holes.

He saw his father cry on the other side of the glass in the meeting chamber. The old man filled him with sorrow; but it was a sorrow, how can I put it?, just on the surface, meaning that at the end of the visit the old man carried it away with him, loaded onto his back. By then he had no room left for sorrow. Euskal Herria above all else. The cause he'd sacrificed himself for, his reason for being, his everything. And seeing his father leave, he felt, what?, hell, disappointment. That's the word. The disappointment of having a soft father, of having been engendered by a weak man.

"*Ama*, it's better he doesn't come."

"Don't worry, the next time I'll leave him home."

By himself, Joxe Mari searched within himself for signs of weakness the way you might examine your body looking for who knows what, fleas or lice. He searched for those possible signs with a ferocious desire to exterminate them, I'm damned if I want some psychological nuisance to get me. And if in the courtyard, in the television room or any other place he saw a depressed comrade with moist eyes, he scolded him, demanded discipline, we're still militants. Being weak, seeming weak? He'd rather have an arm cut off.

Not even the hunger strikes wore him down. And you know they're a pain in the ass. But if we've got to go on a hunger strike, we go on a hunger strike. Whether it's to demand the freedom of some organization prisoner afflicted with a serious illness, or to protest penitentiary policy, or because ETA, through its prison network, has given the order, or for whatever reason. And he checked to make sure no comrade visited the prison store too often. Or to make sure no one sent one of the *arruntak* to buy chocolates, potato chips, and things like that. His longest strike lasted forty-one days, in Albolote. I drank tons of water. And he lost twenty pounds, so that when his mother saw him at a visit, she was horrified.

"Hey, you don't have cancer, do you?"

He answered that he was as fit as a fiddle. A lie. He felt dizzy all the time and no strength to do anything. And he didn't tell her that for a few days he'd been peeing red urine. He considered telling the doctor, but he rejected the idea so he wouldn't have to face a bad diagnosis. Then there was an assembly, they all voted in favor of stopping the strike, and after a few days, my *pixa* was normal. Joxe Mari blames the hunger strikes for his habitual constipation and for a hemorrhoid that still makes him go through hell.

The long months of isolation, too, didn't wear him down. Twenty hours a day locked in the cell. During the summer, a heat that kills you. The guards shout orders at the top of their lungs. Visits, reduced to eight, ten minutes. And the pain in the ass of nighttime checks, every two hours or whenever they felt like it. And betweentimes, they'd beat on the cell door so you wouldn't sleep. They would suddenly burst in. Shouts, get undressed, deep knee bends. That was how it went. Along with the usual insults. But no matter what they did they couldn't get me down.

When Miguel Ángel Blanco from the People's Party was executed in 1997, three guards punched him around. Well, actually one guard. The other two held him down. News of the kidnapping reached the prison three days before. As soon they heard about ETA's ultimatum, Joxe Mari whispered to a companion that:

"They're going to blow that boy away."

At the end of the afternoon on July 12, it was revealed that he'd been shot twice in the head. They'd brought him to a hospital in San Sebastián. He hovered between life and death. At about daybreak, the news programs confirmed his death. Attacks that included fatalities created a perceptible tension in the prison. And hard stares. One of the guards:

"Well, are you happy?"

Joxe Mari doesn't recall if he smiled. He might have, but not for the reasons the guard imagined. When night fell, they staged a phony cell check and they went after him. A punch here, a punch there.

"That's payback for your little smile from before, you ETA piece of shit. If you want more, just ask."

Years back, in Picassent, he got into a fight with two ordinary prisoners. It was during supper. Why? A trifle. Actually, if a couple of guys didn't like your face that was enough. And even though he knocked them down, *wham bam*, with no trouble, he couldn't prevent one of them from catching him off guard and cutting open his head with a chair. Blood by the bucket and eight stitches. The warden comes along and just like that solitary. Just one of so many incidents. There are worse cases, sometimes with deaths. Time passed, Joxe Mari was moved to another jail, he began to go bald and one day, looking at himself in the mirror, he realized he didn't have enough hair to cover the scar.

So many things happen. No one outside the prison finds out about them. Besides, no one likes to tell his family, to keep them from worrying. But just the same: Joxe Mari remained firm, hard as stone, a mast standing tall in the storm, because aside from his physical strength, he wasn't lacking resources to help him weather adversities, low moments, and everything else that came along. What resources? Above all else, the group. The group is fundamental, the union of comrades. He told that to his mother:

"They're my family here."

To that was added ideological loyalty. What he wasn't accustomed to do when he was free, he did now. What was that? He took an interest in politics. Before, all the palaver and theoretical crap seemed like detours on the road toward the objective. The armed struggle on the other hand was the shortcut. Now he carefully read articles, pamphlets, and any publication or communiqué that came from the organization. He wasn't simply happy to feed his awareness that he was still involved in the struggle but actually set about gathering arguments to justify that struggle and show clearly that it was just and necessary. Oh, and supported by the majority of Basques. From that conviction, he drew courage. And whenever an opportunity arose (for example, during the weekly meetings when the ETA prisoners decided how they were going to behave inside the prison, in accordance with the slogans they received from outside), he would launch into an argument that was hot and heavy, fanatical.

He was especially comforted when he could speak in Basque with some comrade or with a group. Sometimes they sang songs from the homeland, "Izarren hautsa," something by Lete, by Laboa, by Benito Lertxundi, without raising their voices too high in order not to provoke. Or they told jokes. It was then that Joxe Mari felt transported far away from there, to a place without guards or walls or bars, telling the same jokes, singing the same songs as loudly as they could and drinking cider, calimocho, or beer in the company of his oldtime friends. Closing his eyes, he was able to feel the scent of his village, of the leeks his father would bring from the garden, and another scent, which for him was the greatest, that of freshly cut grass. Already in Albolote and later, with greater intensity, in cellblock 3 of Puerto I, he wrote poems. They gave him a pleasant feeling of intimacy. He never dared to show them to anyone because he knew they weren't worth much. Also out of modesty. When he wrote them, he recalled Gorka, his love of solitude and books. What could his brother be doing just then?

All in all, hate was the most effective antidote Joxe Mari had for the poison of nostalgia, for remorse, and for the feeling of defeat. A profound and slow-burning rage was born within him. Since he couldn't release it, he kept it boiling in his chest. Not when he was carrying weapons did he ever experience anything comparable. In those days, he had other motivations. I don't know, the sense of obligation. So a guy has to be executed? Okay, put two rounds into him, no matter who he is. This hatred now was pure and hard, the result of beatings, humiliations, the certainty that what they were doing to him they were doing to his people. Hatred for Joxe Mari was like a cool drink during the summer heat, like warmth on winter nights. It immunized him from any sentimentality. If he could kill with a look, he wouldn't have hesitated: he would have caused a chain of deaths in each one of the prisons where he was held.

And then along came Aintzane, the girl from Ondárroa, two years younger than Joxe Mari. Her parents ran a restaurant where she also worked. Before meeting her, Joxe Mari had received letters from other Basque girls. In bars of *abertzale* persuasion, the *herriko tabernas* and other places, it was common practice to put up posters with photos of jailed ETA militants. And next to the photos the name of the prisoner and the prison where he was being held. Joxe Mari and his comrades received letters with some frequency from girls who thought they were genuine heroes. Letters overflowing with admiration and sympathy, with the desire to transmit encouragement and help the imprisoned *gudaris* feel less isolated. Letters that over time could arouse amorous expectations.

Joxe Mari and Aintzane were exchanging letters for over a year before their first meeting. At first they wrote in Basque. They switched to Spanish when they realized that increased the surveillance on their correspondence and now the letters were delivered more rapidly to Joxe Mari. One day she visited him in the interview room of Puerto I. She was, well, not fat, but big and powerfully built, pretty, quick to laugh, naturally likable, and very advanced in her thinking. It was her idea to arrange a conjugal visit as soon as Joxe Mari, overcoming his awkward timidity, confessed in the meeting room that he in reality had never until then done that, even though he'd had a girlfriend in his village, but she was a prude.

"She wouldn't let me kiss her on the street."

And for an instant the interview room rang with Aintzane's noisy guffaw.

Joxe Mari let himself be guided. He received tenderness, caresses, loving words whispered into his ear, and he enjoyed it. That was the problem. At night, unable to fall asleep, he suddenly understood, and it was as if the ceiling of the cell had fallen on top of him, that the best things in life were getting away from him. Not that he hadn't thought that before. It's that now for the first time he had the physical sensation that he'd wasted his youth.

A few days later, during a televised soccer match between Real and Athletic, he concentrated not on the ball, not on the way the game developed, but on the people crowding the seats at the Anoeta Stadium, Basques like him waving *ikurriñas*, with banners, some demanding that prisoners be brought to jails in Euskal Herria, and he watched them jumping around, singing, and enjoying themselves. And he also saw some pictures that accompanied the news about the high temperatures in the north of the peninsula, and the La Concha beach appeared filled with people in bathing suits, relaxed Basques, Basques who were perhaps happy, who strolled along the shore, swam, sunned themselves, lovers stretched out on towels, boys in canoes, toddlers digging in the sand with plastic shovels. And suddenly a bitter taste filled his mouth and even went beyond his mouth, to the very center of his convictions and thoughts.

He and Aintzane had another intimate encounter with its flash of rather hasty pleasure. The place, truth be told, with that bed where God knows how many couples had been, didn't exactly invite romantic illusions. Once again alone, Joxe Mari sensed that something inside him was fighting to bring him down, that mast he was began to bend, the entire ship was sinking. Some time later, Aintzane stopped writing. Well, I suppose she found someone else. These things happen. The only thing is that in jail they hurt more.

121

CONVERSATION
IN THE MEETING ROOM

At first, at the very beginning, Miren would visit Joxe Mari two and even three times a month. She would leave home resolute, heroic, fighting. And when the prison came into view, a fury would surge in her. She would complain about the lack of hygiene in the interview chambers; she would question whether the forty minutes allowed for the visit had actually gone by; she would face down the guards on duty, speaking to them in a familiar way, scolding them for the scattering of "Basque prisoners," as if she could blame them just because they were wearing uniforms. Why did they have to make family members travel so far? What difference does it make whether your son is in this jail or in another closer to home? After all, he's behind the same bars that are everywhere. Ma'am, if you wish to lodge a complaint, please see. Languages, accents, wills all collided, and one day, in Picassent, after an arduous trip, with a flat tire, and we almost got killed, they denied her access to the meeting hall. Just like that. Or that's what she said to everyone in the village. Later, she calmed down. She calmed down? Are you kidding? What she did is vent her feelings on the bus, both coming and going. Over time, she learned to hold in her rages. Over time, she learned to swallow her indignation, to accept things.

And before Joxe Mari's first year in jail was over, Miren fell into the routine of visiting him once a month. And she's done that right until now, with few exceptions, as when Arantxa had her stroke. Miren spent three months taking care of her daughter, and during that period could not visit Joxe Mari. What about Joxian? He goes with her, at the most, twice a year. At first more often, but they would fight.

Joxe Mari and Miren would always converse in Basque, deliberately enigmatic if the subject required it, with many things understood but unspoken, in case they were being recorded.

"Josetxo's gone. Funeral's on Monday. You know, for what happened. It was a fast-moving cancer."

"What about the butcher shop?"

"Juani's had to take over. What else could she do? Lots of people buy there. We all help as much as we can."

Joxe Mari was well aware of his mother's efforts to lift his spirits. And her pride when, giving him news of the village, she would list the names of people who'd asked for him and sent regards.

Once when she visited him at holiday time she told him that:

"The guy from the tavern asked me for your photo. Now I know why. You and the others are on the facade of the town hall. This big. And under the photos your names. In between, a banner in favor of amnesty. I pass by every morning and say hello to you. Leaving mass, the first thing I see, right there and huge, is your face. These people stop me, those people stop me. I'm to give you a hug from them. And if you need something, don't hesitate. The shopgirls don't want me to pay. What I say to them is please let me. Finally, after I beg them, they do charge me because they see I don't want to take advantage. But if I ask for four pounds of potatoes, they probably give me eight for the same price. And one even slips a head of lettuce in my bag even though *aita* brings them from his garden. The fish lady is the same. She gave me a bream the other day. Hey, girl, don't be that way, I say to her. Pays me no attention. There was a demonstration outside the town hall. All the boys singing to you. I got goose bumps. And the bands stop outside the house to dedicate a song to each of us. I pray to Saint Ignatius that he protect you. I pray to him often. Take care of him for me, I say. When mass is over I stay in the church alone speaking to him. A little while ago, Don Serapio came over to me. He says he prays for you, too, and he blessed me in your name."

"What's-his-name wrote me. The *abertzale* left in the Town Council wants to see if they'll name a street after Jokin and me."

"Ah, that I didn't know."

"It's a mess, but I don't think it's a good idea. They say it's an apology."

"Bah, what the hell do they know?"

Years and wrinkles. Years and gray hairs and the loss of hair. Miren, one day:

"Are you eating well?"

"I eat what they give me."

"Well, today I think you're a little thin. Do you know about that guy Patxo who was with you?"

"The last thing I heard is that he was in Cáceres II."

"A traitor."

"What do you mean?"

"He signed a letter with some others."

"So that's it. He's one of them?"

"They dropped their drawers. So they can be let out. Juani asked me the other day if you also. 'Are you crazy?' I said. 'My Joxe Mari?' The look I gave her, well, I don't think she'll ask again."

Another time when Miren came she saw he was angry. What was wrong?

"Arantxa told me about Gorka when she called."

"We don't know anything about him. Didn't you know we hardly ever speak?"

"He's a faggot."

"Where'd you hear that?"

He told her. Gorka was living with some guy.

"For the first time in my life I'm happy I'm in jail. If I were out, I don't know what I'd do."

"When *aita* finds out he'll have a fit. Son, everything's turning out bad for us. What bad luck."

"And the people in the village, what will they say? Holy Mother, I'd rather be here than hearing them."

Fists clenched, Joxe Mari vented his rage, against his brother who:

"Even when he was a kid, he was weird in the balls. Now he makes you the mother of a faggot and me the brother of a faggot and drags our name through the gutter. I'm still waiting for him to be kind enough to visit me just one damn time."

Occasional illnesses, some family problem, something unforeseen that comes up, all keep Miren from visiting her son. Only a few times. In such cases, what did she do? Well, she'd make up for it another day and would go two weekends in a single month. Even if she had to crawl, she'd go see her son. And if they send him to the Canary Islands, something nasty guards threatened Joxe Mari with on more than one occasion, I'll learn to swim, just let them try to stop me.

The woman who was never sad, the woman who was always strong and combative, once, only once over so many years, lost her iron self-control. Tears came to her eyes, her voice broke. And Joxe Mari, when he saw her like that, felt a kind of terror and didn't know what to say and he'd never forget the visit that ended up knocking down in him the thing that had begun to fold years before, when that girl from Ondárroa taught him physical love.

It was when Arantxa had her stroke. Miren, serious, hard, had given him painful news over the phone. And three months went by when she didn't come to see me, though she did call him from time to time and regularly sent him money for his expenses at the store.

"For now, she's in a clinic in Cataluña. The townspeople are all supporting us. Whatever I tell you can't really describe it. In the Arrano and in all the bars and stores they set up banks for her. No need to worry on that account."

"What do the doctors say?"

"They try to give us hope; but I read the truth in their eyes. As far as dying, they say she won't die, but she'll never speak or walk or anything. I mean she eats through a tube that goes right into her stomach."

At that point, her voice cracked with sadness. She covered her face with her hands. And on the other side, Joxe Mari places his hands on the glass, not knowing what to say except *ama, ama*, he so huge, so overwhelmed by the situation and at the same time such a helpless child inside his massive body, even though he wasn't by far what he once was. After a few minutes, Miren calmed down, moved on to other subjects, and kept calm until it was time to leave.

The years passed; the visits followed one on another. Miren:

"I gave him your congratulations. He was very happy. And very elegant. In gray, wearing a tie. Maybe next time I'll bring photos. We waited outside the town hall. After a bit, he and his husband came out. Ramuntxo is his name. I've gotten used to calling him his husband. Listen, he's a great guy. He's got a daughter. A very sad story. I'll tell you some other time. On the stairs, a crowd of friends waited for them and then started throwing rice. They saw us on the other side of the street and came right over, and I wasn't sure how Gorka was going to react when he saw us. He didn't invite us. But, what the hell, we went there. *Aita* cursing me for making him leave the village. We thought he was going to yell at Gorka. Me, I'm saying, get along now and shut up. Celeste's husband drove us to Bilbao in his van. The poor guy was left waiting for us out on the street until midnight. If it weren't for him we couldn't have gotten Arantxa into the seat. Because you'd be amazed at how stiff *aita's* become. So all went okay. The dinner, because we stayed to dinner, we had to, was top-notch, with me sitting next to Gorka wearing my new shoes, and everything okay. Son, what can I tell you? That he turned out the way he turned out? Juani says there are worse things. I've talked this over a lot with Saint Ignatius and he says I'm right."

"Do you think my brother is happy?

"I'd say he is."

"Then that's enough. No need to pick it all over."

122

Your Jail Is My Jail

Alone in his cell, Joxe Mari, now forty-three years old—seventeen of which he's spent in prison—abandoned ETA. Just an ordinary day, before going to bed, he glanced over at a photo his sister sent him and said to himself: enough is enough. That simple. No one found out because he told no one. Not even his comrades or his family. No one. And that was half a year before the organization's announcement of the cessation of the armed struggle.

He left ETA and slept soundly. His convictions had weakened a long time ago. Everything influences such decisions: the loneliness of prison; doubts, which are like mosquitoes in summer; certain attacks that, no matter how hard you squeeze them, simply won't fit in the ever-narrowing space of habitual justifications; the comrades he took to be deserters at first and who now he understands and secretly admires.

It's over. In the future, count me out. And he didn't waver, months later, when he saw those three hooded men announce on television that ETA had decided to put an end to the armed struggle. He considered it a matter that didn't concern him.

A comrade, seemingly confused, disconcerted, asked him what his opinion was.

"I don't have an opinion. Why do I have to have one?"

"Jesus, man, you've changed."

In other times, he would have looked for a chance to argue, would have given a long harangue. Nowadays he just said what he had to say; some days not even that. He'd become solitary, thoughtful. He seemed calm, but he was as calm as a fallen tree. His solitude was deliberate, the solitude of a man who grows more fed up with each passing day. And he was as cautious as he was fed up. His meditations, those of a conscience where little by little slogans, arguments, the entire sentimental junkyard which had darkened his intimate truth lost any meaning. And just what was that truth? What else could it be? Well, that he'd done damage, that he'd killed. And what for? The answer filled him with bitterness: for nothing. After all that blood, no socialism, no independence, not one fucking thing. In his heart of hearts he firmly believed he was the victim of a fraud.

I suppose that *ama*, devoted as she is to Saint Ignatius of Loyola, must know that the saint too was a man of arms in his youth. Did he kill? Joxe Mari tried to find out by looking in an encyclopedia they had in the jail. He didn't find the information, but he was certain. He killed, and he's probably in heaven.

In his case, the change was not caused by war wounds or pious books. He thinks there were multiple reasons. And reasons within reasons that led to other reasons and to the current situation, that of a man with no other landscape than the four walls of his cell, overwhelmed by the weight of what he'd done in the name of principles created by others and which he, obedient and naive, bought into.

Year after year, he would cling to hopes (the next elections, the Lizarra pact, negotiation with the Spanish government, the internationalization of the conflict), none of which ever came to fruition. Never. Here the only thing that comes to fruition is that one year ends and another begins. And then without warning, that photograph came, the first he'd ever seen of his sister in her wheelchair: the ax stroke that brought down the tree. Or the ship's mast, who cares?

Arantxa had sent it by ordinary mail. In the letter included with the photo, written as usual by the Ecuadorian caregiver, Joxe Mari read: "I've been asking *ama* to bring you a photo of me. She won't hear of it. She tells me to wait, that lately you've seemed in low spirits. But I really want you to see me as I am now. Where does this having to hide things come from? And since we're on the subject, I've seen a photo of you without hair and with a double chin, you look more and more like *aita*, with the same dumbass face all the men in our family have."

His poor sister. He never stopped loving her, not even when she married that Spanish asshole from Rentería, who ended up leaving her flat. And it gave him a chill just to take the photo out of the envelope. Now he realized something: he hadn't been able to attach what he knew to an image. His sister. The painful, absolutely conclusive reality of her disability and the wheelchair.

When they took the photo, Arantxa looked straight into the camera. Now she was looking right at Joxe Mari from the photo. Her eyes pressed into slits by her smile, her eyes seemed smaller than they were in his memory. Her mouth, isn't it slightly twisted? And that exaggerated way of smiling, you can't fool me, that's the usual thing that happens when you can't control your facial muscles. You could see how she'd aged, in the wrinkles and in all the gray in her hair. It's been cut short, what a shame. Short hair ruined her looks. On her lap, the iPad. One hand useless, closed, a bracelet, like some toy, on that arm. And one of her feet wrapped in a kind of orthopedic sock or ankle support, you can't tell which.

In the same letter, Arantxa wrote: "You've got your jail, I've got mine. My body is a life sentence. One day you'll be released. We don't know when, but you will get out. I'll never get out of mine. There's another difference between us. You're there because of what you did. What did I do to deserve it?" That last sentence, actually the entire passage, hit Joxe Mari hard. That day he skipped going out to the recreation yard. He avoided conversation. He barely ate anything. He didn't visit the library, his favorite refuge recently. Shortly after going to bed, he looked at the photo and decided to abandon ETA without saying a word to anyone, not to his comrades, not to the organization.

And not to his mother.

She was well aware, when she made her next visit to the prison, that Arantxa had sent a photo, so she showed him others. Arantxa in the village square, Arantxa with Celeste, with *aita* at the entrance to the garden, with Gorka and his husband the day of the wedding, in the kitchen, standing up as she took a few tremulous steps during a physiotherapy session. Photos that Joxe Mari commented on with interest, calmly, even making jokes; pictures that didn't affect him as violently as the first did.

His sister continued to write him. She followed no routine. She might send him two letters one week and then let a month pass without writing another. The year ended. During January, Arantxa sent him another photograph. On the back it said: "Here I am with my best friend." There was Bittori, standing behind the wheelchair, not as jolly as Arantxa, but even so, happy. It was hard for Joxe Mari to recognize Txato's wife in that thin, visibly deteriorated woman. How old she looks. She's aged worse than *ama*. There was an explanation for her appearance: "She tells me everything. We see each other practically every day. We're close friends. She knows she only has a little time left. She refuses to get treatment. Why, when she's lost all her illusions? She says she's struggling to stay alive as best she can because she's hoping for a human gesture from you. She wants nothing else. Your broken-down disaster of a sister begs you. Don't disappoint me. Put another way: ask her forgiveness. What would it cost you? It hurts me that you don't do it."

Women: how they know how to tangle us up. In bed, his mind a blank, Joxe Mari was staring at the square of blue sky out the window. For a long time, he didn't move a muscle, listless, his hands joined under his chin. Finally, thoughts came to him. Actually images. Time was a film of his life running backwards. Soon he left the jail and entered another and then another, he was mistreated, later arrested, he went back to the armed struggle, to the rainy afternoon when Txato looked him in the eye, to the pub where he'd shot a man for the first time, to France, to the village, and when he reached the age of nineteen, the speeding mental images suddenly stopped. He then imagined a different destiny, one that culminated in the great dream of his life, to be on the FC Barcelona handball team.

He confirmed it to himself: asking forgiveness takes more courage than firing a weapon, than setting off a bomb. Anyone can do those things. All you have to be is young and credulous, with hot blood. And it isn't only that you need balls to sincerely make up for, even if it's only verbally, the atrocities you've committed. What stopped Joxe Mari was something else. What? How do I know? Come on, confess. Damn, suppose the old woman shows the letter to a newspaperman, then they'll set up the usual circus of the repentant terrorist, people in the village will speak badly of him and yank his photo out of the Arrano Taberna. *Ama* would faint.

123

CLOSED CIRCLE

Cloudy afternoon. Bittori goes out on the balcony to check on the storm, which was rolling in from the sea. Clouds from one side of the horizon to the other. It was raining hard and you're not going up to Polloe by yourself, let me drive you up. That morning, at times, the sun had broken through. Bittori chatted with Arantxa as usual in a corner of the plaza. Just before midday, she got on the bus, and she didn't have enough time to get home before the sky began to pour down so much water you couldn't see. And it hasn't stopped raining since then.

Xabier on the telephone:

"Where do you get off going to the cemetery with the way it's pouring out there?"

"I have important things to tell Txato."

"*Ama*, please forget those games."

He passed by, the shoulders of his raincoat wet, to pick her up at four. Bittori was ready when he arrived. She picked up her umbrella and put the letter in her purse. In this woman's eyes, every once in a while, a flash of happiness lights up. And if not of happiness, of joy. Xabier knows the reason. It's that yesterday, late, the three of them met. Nerea, alarmed, asked what the fuss was all about. And her mother told them, she showed them the letter and read it with badly dissimulated euphoria, while the faces of her children darkened with grief.

"This is what you wanted so much?"

"Exactly this, my girl."

"Well, now you have it. Congratulations."

Now it's time to tell Txato. On the landing, Xabier noticed that his mother was going out in her slippers.

"Good thing you noticed."

From time to time along the way, Xabier took his eyes off the traffic for an instant and turned to look at Bittori. Really admirable, considering how sick she is. And the windshield wipers, *clak, clak*, did their job without resting.

Bittori:

"I see this rain and you can't imagine what it reminds me of."

"That it was raining this way the day *aita* was murdered."

"How did you guess?"

"It's rained just as hard many times since then."

He dropped his mother off by the cemetery entrance. It was an afternoon flood. And Bittori got out slowly, awkwardly, possibly impeded by a stomach pain that she wouldn't bring up. She didn't want him to accompany her. No. Should he wait for her? Okay, if you like, but she wouldn't be more than half an hour. And between the words of the son and the words of the mother resounded a noise of myriad drops smashing with whispered violence against the earth and with a note of lively sparking on Bittori's umbrella. At least it wasn't windy. SOON IT WILL BE SAID OF YOU WHAT IS NOW SAID OF US: THEY DIED! Macabre and trivial. And how people fight against returning to the planet the atoms they've borrowed. Actually, what's rare and exceptional is to be alive. Xabier waited for his mother, wearing ritual black, to enter the cemetery before he found a parking space nearby.

In her purse, Bittori carried the square of plastic and the kerchief, but what for? How can I sit down on those flooded slates?

"Txato, Txatito, can you hear me? It's raining the way it did on the afternoon they murdered you. Today I've got news."

And she told him, standing at the grave site, under her umbrella, that without Arantxa, without her generous mediation, she would not have succeeded in closing the circle. She softened the terrorist, convinced him to take the step he'd taken. How did she do it? Well, because she loves him. He's her brother, that I understand. She doesn't justify his actions. To the contrary, she judges them, severely, without secondary considerations. But he is her brother. She's trying by all means possible to liberate him from himself, to pull him out of his atrocious past. And when she learned of the remorse of the prisoner in his far-off jail, she wrote me on her iPad: "Something's changing in him. He's thinking a lot. Good sign."

But he was frightened.

"I'll bet you can't imagine the idea that came into his head."

To send her a symbolic object instead of an explicit request for forgiveness. That boy must feel very alone; well, he's a full-grown man now who long ago thought nothing and now, apparently, thinks too much. Arantxa interceded with her brother, that Bittori wouldn't like that idea.

"And of course I didn't like it. That was two weeks ago. And forgive me for not being able to come see you. But it's that since all this news came in and my having had some days with pains, I had no way to get up to the cemetery."

Joxe Mari considered, what an idea, sending her an object. What object? No idea. One that could fit inside an envelope. A photo, a drawing. And that he would send the thing to Bittori and that would mean he was asking forgiveness.

"I told Arantxa that I wouldn't go along with that, that I'm in no mood to fool around. And she wrote me on her iPad that if she were in my place she wouldn't go along, either. The problem is that the scaredy cat's afraid that if he sends me a letter asking forgiveness I'm going to run with it to the newspapers. Where does he get these ideas? He must be slightly off his rocker after so many years in jail. It never entered my mind to talk to newspaper people. It's the last thing I'd like, to appear in the newspapers, that they'd come to my house to take photos and ask questions."

So she answered now. Arantxa, a short while later: that if she could give Joxe Mari a guarantee of maximum discretion. She did give him the guarantee, offended that anyone could doubt she would be honorable. And yesterday morning the letter came.

"Shall I read it to you?"

She read (she practically knew it by heart):

Kaixo, *Bittori.*
Following my sister's advice, I'm writing you. I'm a man of few words, so I'll get right to the point.

I'm asking forgiveness from you and your children. I'm very sorry. If I could make time go backwards, I'd do it. I can't. I'm sorry. I can only hope you will forgive me. I'm already suffering my punishment.

All best,
Joxe Mari

The rain fell on the graves and on the asphalt path and the dark trees that flanked the path. Headstones, soaking wet, and a fresh aroma of silence. The dense clouds floated over the city, and beyond, over the mountains and over the distant sea. There was not another human silhouette to be seen in the entire cemetery.

"Fine, don't you think? I had a great need of these words. My manias, Txato. Soon I'll join you. Now I know I'm coming in peace. Meanwhile, warm up the grave for me the way in other times you warmed up the bed. I'll leave you now, because Xabier is waiting for me. The children know that as soon as it's possible they're to bring us both to the village. So you can rest easy. Let's hope it doesn't rain on the day of my burial the way it's raining today. The poor grave-diggers. They'll get soaked. And the flowers, too."

Xabier got out of the car to wave to his mother to tell her where he was, about ninety feet down the hill. It went on raining. Did she want to go anywhere? No, home.

"*Aita* says hello."

"So you spend your time talking to yourself, right?"

"It consoles me. Anyway, there's no one there to hear me. Now, if by any chance you think I'm crazy, you may be mistaken."

"I never said that."

"Before I forget, Txato asks when you're going to get married. He says it's about time."

Silence fell inside the car. Stopped at a red light, the street foggy gray, Xabier turned to look at his mother.

"Actually, I do think you're crazy."

The light turned green, and Bittori burst into laughter.

124

Soaking

A cloudy afternoon. In Miren's house, routine scenes after dinner. She, scouring pad and suds, had finished washing the pots and pans in the sink. She hung her apron on the nail behind the door and poked her head out of the kitchen window to confirm whether it had stopped raining. It was pouring, and in the dining room, she said to her daughter, you won't be able to go out this afternoon.

"It would probably be a good idea to call Celeste so she doesn't make a wasted trip here."

Joxian, sleepy, mute, stayed in the kitchen drying the dishes with a rag. And Arantxa, paying no attention to her mother's words, was writing letters on the screen of her iPad.

"What's that you're writing?"

Arantxa showed her what she'd written: "There is something you have to know, even if it hurts you." Miren, suspicious:

"If it's anything to do with that woman, don't tell me anything. Damn, all that's missing now is for you to invite her here."

The irate finger now wrote more quickly. "In this house, you're the only one who doesn't know."

"Know what? What are you talking about? Can we just skip the theatrics?"

"Joxe Mari has asked her for forgiveness."

"Hey, Joxian, did you know about this?"

From the kitchen:

"About what?"

"Don't play dumb. About Joxe Mari."

"Of course. Arantxa told me before dinner."

"So why the hell didn't you say anything to me?"

"What's the big deal? You're being told right now."

Miren, Miren, this is really something you didn't expect. She spoke, cursed?, under her breath. It couldn't be, she didn't believe it. These fools have misunderstood something.

"I was just with him ten days ago. He said nothing about it."

The church bells rang out three o'clock. Arantxa's nervous finger tripped over the iPad resting on her lap. "He wouldn't dare tell you. He's afraid of you."

Tired of stretching her neck, and expecting new revelations, Miren brought a chair over to the wheelchair. Sitting down, serious: Arantxa should tell her everything. There was no bitterness in her words, not even anger. The sentences followed one after another on the screen, for Miren, more and more wounding as they went on.

"He's asking forgiveness in a letter."

"Bittori read it to me this morning."

"And what if she wrote it herself? Everybody knows she's crazy."

"I know Joxe Mari's handwriting."

"My brother isn't the only member of this family who's asked her for forgiveness."

"Who else?"

"Ask in the kitchen."

"Joxian, get in here. I want you to clear up just what you've been doing behind my back."

Joxian came into the dining room drying his hands on his sweater. Without getting upset, he told all, clearly, and precisely, and then went to have his siesta. Miren, to her daughter:

"Anything else?"

"That's all."

Later, he in bed, the daughter unable to speak, watching the television news, Miren did not have to give them any explanations. Nothing about where are you going, no goodbye, nothing. Without going into the bedroom where, who knows, Joxian might wake up, she left wearing a housedress. As she left, the door made a cautious, pained click instead of the usual angry slam.

Where is she going? It's pouring down rain. Like the afternoon when that man was killed. So let's see why he has to ask forgiveness. Having crossed the street, she snapped her tongue in disgust. She should have brought an umbrella, but I'm not going back now. She felt betrayed, victim of a family plot and, of course, convinced that the rain was falling only on her.

The butcher shop, closed. Normal: it wasn't even four yet. She saw light inside and went in, not for the first time, through the entryway. She understands me. Who else would? The silent half-light smelled of suet, meat, cold cuts. Her neighbors had better be used to it by now. She rang the buzzer, which sounded shrill, cacophonic. What was most certain: the door would open, and Juani would appear with her ears ready to receive her friend's verbal stream, a friend who needs to unburden herself at all costs.

But it didn't open. Instead, through the closed door:

"Who's there?"

"Me."

"Who?"

"Me, Miren."

She should wait a minute. How odd. If you're there, what are you waiting for to open up? As soon as Miren saw Juani's hair let down, she guessed: she isn't alone. She only stayed a bit. She said hello to him, a man who, despite his years, still had a good presence. So these two are involved? And to cover up, she bought a few slices of this and a quarter pound of that.

"Sorry for coming by at this hour, but I'm really busy. I'll pay you tomorrow."

"Don't worry about it, dear."

She went back out to the street, back to the bleak afternoon and the puddles. Before she went into the church, she tossed the plastic bag of cold cuts into a trash basket. Soaked from head to toe, she sat in her usual pew. Votive candles were burning at the altar. How many she'd lit over the course of her life to ask favors from God, thinking about the well-being of the household, seeking divine protection for her children.

The church was empty and Miren sopping wet. If the priest walks in, I'm walking out. She was in no mood to talk to anyone. Only with the statue of the saint from Loyola, up there on its corbel. Well done, Ignatius, well done. A good bit of work you've done for me. After all is said and done, I'm going to be the bad person.

She addressed bitter reproaches to him. Out loud, whispered?

No, as always, in her mind. She cast doubt on the saint's capacity to be our great patron. You're on the wrong road. Come now, why do we have to ask forgiveness? What about the crimes committed by the Antiterrorist Liberation Groups? Has anyone asked forgiveness for them and for the torturing in the barracks and stationhouses, and for the diaspora, and for all the oppression of the Basque people? And if what we did was so bad, why didn't you stop it in time? You let us go on and now it turns out that the sacrifice was for nothing, that thousands of us Basques who love what is ours have been mistaken idiots. Come on, Ignatius, that can't be right. Cure my daughter, get my son out of jail, or I'll never speak to you again. Damn, don't you see that I'm suffering, too?

She got up. On the spot where she'd sat for ten, fifteen minutes there was a stain of moisture. It was cold in the church. And Miren suddenly got a chill. Oh Lord, now I'm going to get sick. She went out to the street and it was raining. Blackish sky, minimal light, and deserted streets. Miren used the trees as umbrellas, but they were practically useless. By chance she looked over at the trash basket. There was the plastic bag with the cold cuts. She picked it up and brought it home, because it's not like we're the kind of people who throw food away.

125

Sunday Morning

It's been many, too many, weeks since she's seen her. The previous afternoon, Bittori made a decision. If she got up in the morning and found the bowls she'd left on the balcony at the end of the afternoon untouched, with water in one and cat food in the other, then she'd resign herself to thinking that Ikatza was gone forever. The consequences? Well, even if her heart was broken, she'd toss not only the bowls but the scratching pole, the kitty litter, the brush, and, in sum, all of the animal's utensils into the garbage. She got up rather earlier than usual. The first thing she did was to walk out on the balcony. Wearing only underclothes, she contemplated the clear sky, a wide stretch of sea, Santa Clara Island, Mount Urgull, knowing she was privileged to be living there, with box-seat views of the bay, even if there is a building that blocks her view of the beach. Then she looked over to the corner and confirmed that the bowls were just as she'd left them the previous evening.

Just before seven in the morning, Miren heard Joxian putting his bicycle in the kitchen. Sunday. His dumbass mania for cleaning it up and oiling it in the house. One day, he asked her, joking?, if she was jealous of the bike. Maybe, because you know, when was the last time he'd caressed her? Jesus, not even when he got her pregnant! He reserves his tenderness for his bicycle, the jug in the bar, and the garden. Miren didn't want to get out of bed so she wouldn't have to share the kitchen with him. She was in no mood for conversation. She'd slept terribly. Why? Because of the music and the firecrackers and the partiers the whole damn night making a racket in the street. Once upon a time, she'd liked the village festivals. Now less and less. *Bam*. She heard the noise of the front door. Joxian had gone out. Where did he say he was going? No idea. Miren waited five minutes, huddled under the sheets, just in case Joxian forgot something and came back. Later, unhurriedly, she got up.

Bittori found some coffee left over from the previous day at the bottom of the pot. She told herself that with some milk and a splash of tap water it would be enough for a cup. Reheated coffee and a few crumbs of stale bread, that was her breakfast. After straightening up the room and fixing herself up, she went to work on Ikatza's things, which she stuffed into a plastic bag. She couldn't carry it all downstairs at once. First she tossed a few things into the bin, then others. And then she went back up to get her purse and a food container. She put a portion of cooked meat and potatoes, peppers and tomato sauce into it: her intention was to have lunch at her house in the village. Walking down the street, she felt a bit odd. Without pain, but fatigued, and constantly out of breath, so before she reached the bus stop, she stopped several times to take a deep breath and gather strength.

Celeste entered the apartment at nine. She's got a key. That way she doesn't have to ring the buzzer. Over the years, she's become like a family member. She arrives, says hello, scatters joy, and immediately sets about her chores as caregiver. The first thing, give Arantxa a shower. Now that she can stand up, even if she has to hold on to the grip with her good hand, it's easier. Miren and Celeste are extremely careful. One holds Arantxa, the other soaps her up and rinses her off. They have experience. The operation doesn't last more than five minutes. And then the two of them dry her. As they were drying her pale, paunchy body, it happened that Arantxa suddenly said: *ama*. Miren instantly turned off the hair dryer. She seemed to hear something. But of course, she couldn't be sure because of the dryer's noise. Arantxa repeated the word. It was and wasn't her voice from old times. Celeste praised her with a jovial waving of arms. Miren remembered that when she was a baby, the first word Arantxa spoke was *ama*, before *aita*.

It was just after ten when Bittori got out of the bus. Music, where?, nearby. And paper garlands hung from facade to facade. Normal, no?, that people should live their lives. First of all, she walked toward her house. More than anything, to get rid of the food container. She ran into the band at the corner, its members gathered in the very place where, on a distant day, her husband was hit with four bullets. *Boom, boom.* Green shirts, white trousers. And the bass drummer, his face bright red with alcoholic happiness, seemed intent on drowning out the notes played by his comrades by pounding out a storm. That went on until the song was over. There was no way to pass through them, so Bittori stepped down onto the street. Out of the blathering group, a jolly voice arose: Hey, Bittori! She waved without stopping. She turned her head for an instant, but she couldn't know who'd shouted to her.

Miren hurried things along. She was expecting Joxe Mari's Sunday call. She likes to be alone when she talks with her son. To Celeste, would you please dry Arantxa off. A blue morning, festival in the streets. Come on, come on, let's have fun. Finally, the phone rang. Five minutes: that's all the time allotted to the prisoner. If only she could telephone, but calls from outside were not allowed. She didn't hide her joy from Joxe Mari: Arantxa said *ama.* You could understand her perfectly, so she's learning to talk. And she got excited, and Joxe Mari, at the other end of the line, did as well, though he was, as always, serious. News? Nothing. Well, one thing. After talking to the doctor, he'd decided to have his hemorrhoid operated on. He can't stand it anymore. And now that the heat has come back down here, his suffering was unspeakable. Miren mentioned the village festival, but didn't want to go into too much detail so her son wouldn't be tormented by melancholy thoughts. Instead, she repeated that Arantxa had said, after her shower, *ama.* And the five minutes were up.

Bittori had no microwave at her village house. She poured the contents of the container into a saucepan as old as the hills, but still useful, and said to herself: I'm going outside, and when I come back, I'll heat up the food. She also decided to buy half a loaf at the bakery.

Meanwhile, Miren, thinking about saving time, spread out the fried ground beef on the platter, poured in the béchamel sauce, and sprinkled bits of cooked cauliflower on top. And when I get back from mass, I'll throw on the grated cheese and turn on the oven. And as for the bicyclist, if he comes home late, he can eat cold food.

Festival, Sunday, nice weather: the plaza was overflowing with people. Children running around, groups talking, and bordering the square, the outdoor tables of the bars packed. The leafy lime trees spread their agreeable shade over the asphalt. And Bittori found Arantxa and her faithful caregiver in their usual corner. She leaned over to kiss her friend. Nearby, the bell in the steeple summoned the faithful to noon mass. Celeste immediately told Bittori that Arantxa had said a word that morning. They both turned toward Arantxa with the clear desire to get her to repeat her feat. Arantxa, not without effort, satisfied them. Bittori, moved, took her by the hand. She told her she'd do it, that she herself wished it with all her heart, and that she should never give up. Arantxa, with her twisted smile, nodded her head several times affirmatively.

For two months, Miren hadn't been at mass seated in her usual place. Angry with the saint from Loyola, she passed along the right flank of the church, but today she's back in her place near the statue. Don Serapio delivered his solemn, tedious, repetitive sermon in an old man's voice. All masses are the same, you can't fool me. In the pews, there were only a few of the faithful. Youth? In front, two girls and that was it. Miren, in her thoughts, gave thanks, but she was severe, almost taking an admonitory tone. It's a good start, Ignatius, but you just have to understand, saying a single word and speaking, I mean really speaking, are two different things, right? We expect something more. And as far as the other one is concerned, fix up his hemorrhoid. That's all I ask, because I can see you don't want to get him out of jail for me. The end of mass interrupted her mental chat.

Bittori said goodbye to Arantxa and Celeste at the corner of the plaza. Miren emerged from the church. The one intended to get to the bakery quickly because they would be closing; the other intended to join up with her daughter, maybe have an aperitif with her and Celeste, and go home after to attend to dinner. The two women spotted each other at a distance of about fifteen feet. At that moment, the sun was shining into Bittori's face; she placed her hand over her eyes like a visor and she must have realized I saw her; well, I'm not changing my route. Miren approached walking with Sunday-slow steps, unconcerned, in the shadow of the lime trees and that woman is looking at me, but she's not too clever if she thinks I'm going to swerve away. They moved forward in a straight line, the one toward the other. And lots of people in the plaza saw

it all. The children didn't. The children went on dashing to and
fro and shouting. Among the adults, a rapid ball of whispers took
shape. Look, look. And what friends they were before.

The encounter took place at the music kiosk. It was a brief
embrace. They looked each other in the eye for an instant before
separating. Did they say anything? Nothing. They said nothing.

GLOSSARY

This glossary contains Basque terms that appear in the novel. Its only purpose is to help readers unfamiliar with the Basque language.

abertzale: a patriot, one who supports an independent Basque homeland

agur: goodbye

aita: father. The final vowel is stressed: *aitá*

aitona: grandfather

alde hemendik: get away, get lost

ama: mother. The final vowel is stressed: *amá*

amatxo: an affectionate, diminutive form of *ama*

amnistia osoa: general amnesty

amona: grandmother

arruntak: a name ETA prisoners use to refer to ordinary prisoners

askatu: to free. Here in its imperative sense: free, set free

aurresku: a Basque dance performed to honor someone

barkatu: the infinitive form of the verb "to forgive" (and its command form): forgive, pardon

bat: one

batzoki: political and social seat of the PNV, the Basque Nationalist Party

belarri: ear

beltza: black; a term applied to the antidisturbance agents of the *Ertzaintza* because of the color of their uniforms

bertsolari: a kind of minstrel who improvises songs in Basque

bi: two

bibotza: an affectionate form of address; heart

bietan jarrai: to follow the two paths: one, the military forces, symbolized by the ax, the other, intelligence or political cunning, symbolized by the serpent

chistulari: the musicians who play the chistu, a small flute, in traditional Basque music

cipayo: an insulting nickname applied to *Ertzaintza* agents

dispersiorik ez: No! to the scattering of ETA prisoners around Spain rather than keeping them in Basque Country

egun on: good day

ekintza: action, attack

ene!: wow!, holy cow!

entzun: verb used in command form: listen here

erribera: riverbank

ertzaina: an agent or officer of the *Ertzaintza*

Ertzaintza: regional police force of Basque Country

ETA: *Euskadi Ta Askatasuna,* Basque Homeland and Liberty

ETA herria zurekin: ETA, the people are with you

euskaldun: a person who knows Basque

Eusko gudariak: Basque soldiers; title of a popular song used as an anthem by the *abertzale* left

faxista: fascist

gora ETA: long live ETA

gora Euskadi askatuta: long live free Basque Country

gudari: combatant, soldier, specifically on who fights for the Basque cause

herriak ez du barkatuko: the people will not forgive

herriko taberna: the social seat of the *abertzale* left; literally "the people's tavern"

hiru: three

iepa: hi

ikastola: school

ikatza: coal

ikurriña: flag; in practice, the Basque flag

Iparralde: the northern zone; a term used to refer to French Basque Country

izarren hautsa: stardust; a song with lyrics by Xabier Lete and music by Mikel Laboa

jarraitxu: a member of *Jarrai*, the socialist and independentist youth organization

kaixo: hi

kanpora: beat it, get lost

kartujo: a Carthusian monk, a recluse

kontuz: be careful, watch out

lehendakari: title given to the president of the Autonomous Government of the País Vasco

lorea: flower

maitia: (pronounced my-*tee*-ah, emphasis on second syllable): dearest, my love

mariskada: an abundant seafood dinner

mendiko ahotsa: the voice of the mountain

mugalari: a person well versed in local terrain who helps others to cross the border between France and Spain

muxu: kiss

neska: girl

ondo pasa: hope things go well for you

ongi etorri: literally, welcome; used as a noun, it means a welcoming homage

osaba: uncle

piraten itsasontzi urdina: the blue pirate ship

pixa: pee, urine

poliki: little by little

polita: feminine adjective: pretty, good-looking

presoak kalera amnistia osoa: prisoners to the street; general amnesty

talde: attack cell

Topo: nickname for the narrow-gauge train linking San Sebastián to Hendaya

txakurra: dog; insulting nickname applied to police officers

txakurrada: dog; used as a collective term for all police officers

txalaparta: a traditional percussion instrument made of planks rhythmically pounded with wooden sticks

txapeo: a prisoner who refuses to go out to the recreation yard and remains in his cell the entire day

txoko: corner

txoria txori: "the bird is a bird" (approximate translation); celebrated song by Mikel Laboa, included on his album *Bat-hiru* (1974), lyrics by Joxean Artze:

> *If I'd clipped its wings*
> *it would have been mine,*
> *it would not have flown away.*
> *If I'd clipped its wings*
> *it would have been mine,*
> *it would not have flown away.*
> *But that way*
> *it would have ceased to be a bird.*
> *And I . . .*
> *I loved the bird.*
> *And I . . .*
> *I loved the bird.*

zure borroka gure eredu: your struggle, our model
Zutabe: the name of ETA's internal news bulletin

A NOTE ON THE TYPE

This book was set in Birka, a typeface designed by Franko Luin (1941–2005) and released by Linotype corporation in 1992. Born in Trieste of Slovene origin, Luin was active as a designer and typographer in Sweden from 1961 until his death. Luin took Garamond as his inspiration for Birka, but the letterforms show an equal debt to Frederic Goudy's Venetian revival fonts of the early twentieth century.

COMPOSED BY NORTH MARKET STREET GRAPHICS
LANCASTER, PENNSYLVANIA

PRINTED AND BOUND BY BERRYVILLE GRAPHICS
BERRYVILLE, VIRGINIA

DESIGNED BY BETTY LEW